THE BEST KNOWN WORKS OF
GUSTAVE FLAUBERT

THE
BEST KNOWN WORKS OF
GUSTAVE FLAUBERT

Three complete, unabridged novels:
Madame Bovary, The Temptation of Saint Anthony,
Salammbô.

THE BOOK LEAGUE OF AMERICA
New York

1941
BLUE RIBBON BOOKS

CL
PRINTED IN THE UNITED STATES OF AMERICA

TO

MARIE-ANTOINE-JULES SENARD,

MEMBER OF THE PARIS BAR
EX-PRESIDENT OF THE NATIONAL ASSEMBLY, AND FORMER
MINISTER OF THE INTERIOR.

DEAR AND ILLUSTRIOUS FRIEND,—

Permit me to inscribe your name at the head of this book, and above its dedication; for it is to you, before all, that I owe its publication. Reading over your magnificent defence, my work has acquired for myself, as it were, an unexpected authority. Accept, then, here, the homage of my gratitude, which, how great soever it is, will never attain the height of your eloquence and your devotion.

GUSTAVE FLAUBERT.

CONTENTS

MADAME BOVARY

PART I

WE WERE IN CLASS when the head-master came in, followed by a "new fellow," not wearing the school uniform, and a school servant carrying a large desk. Those who had been asleep woke up, and every one rose as if just surprised at his work.

The head-master made a sign to us to sit down. Then, turning to the class-master, he said to him in a low voice—

"Monsieur Roger, here is a pupil whom I recommend to your care; he'll be in the second. If his work and conduct are satisfactory, he will go into one of the upper classes, as becomes his age."

The "new fellow," standing in the corner behind the door so that he could hardly be seen, was a country lad of about fifteen, and taller than any of us. His hair was cut square on his forehead like a village chorister's; he looked reliable, but very ill at ease. Although he was not broad-shouldered, his short school jacket of green cloth with black buttons must have been tight about the armholes, and showed at the opening of the cuffs red wrists accustomed to being bare. His legs, in blue stockings, looked out from beneath yellow trousers, drawn tight by braces. He wore stout, ill-cleaned, hob-nailed boots.

We began repeating the lesson. He listened with all his ears, as attentive as if at a sermon, not daring even to cross his legs or lean on his elbow; and when at two o'clock the bell rang, the master was obliged to tell him to fall into line with the rest of us.

When we came back to work, we were in the habit of throwing our caps on the ground so as to have our hands more free; we used from the door to toss them under the form, so that they hit against the wall and made a lot of dust: it was "the thing."

But, whether he had not noticed the trick, or did not dare to attempt it, the "new fellow" was still holding his cap on his knees even after prayers were over. It was one of those head-gears of composite order, in which we can find traces of the bearskin, shako, billycock hat, sealskin cap, and cotton nightcap; one of those poor things, in fine, whose dumb ugliness has depths of expression, like an imbecile's face. Oval, stiffened with whalebone, it began with three round knobs; then came in succession lozenges of velvet and rabbit-skin separated by a red band; after that a sort of bag that ended in a cardboard polygon covered with complicated braiding, from which hung, at the end of a long thin cord, small twisted gold threads in the manner of a tassel. The cap was new; its peak shone.

"Rise," said the master.

He stood up; his cap fell. The whole class began to laugh. He stooped to pick it up. A neighbour knocked it down again with his elbow; he picked it up once more.

"Get rid of your helmet," said the master, who was a bit of a wag.

There was a burst of laughter from the boys, which so thoroughly put the poor lad out of countenance that he did not know whether to keep his cap in his hand, leave it on the ground, or put it on his head. He sat down again and placed it on his knee.

"Rise," repeated the master, "and tell me your name."

The new boy articulated in a stammering voice an unintelligible name.

"Again!"

The same sputtering of syllables was heard, drowned by the tittering of the class.

"Louder!" cried the master; "louder!"

The "new fellow" then took a supreme resolution, opened an inordinately large mouth, and shouted at the top of his voice as if calling some one the word "Charbovari."

A hubbub broke out, rose in *crescendo* with bursts of shrill voices (they yelled, barked, stamped, repeated "Charbovari! Charbovari!"), then died away into single notes, growing quieter only with great difficulty, and now and again suddenly recommencing along the line of a form whence rose here and there, like a damp cracker going off, a stifled bomb.

However, amid a rain of impositions, order was gradually re-established in the class; and the master having succeeded in catching the name of "Charles Bovary," having had it dictated to him, spelt out, and re-read, at once ordered the poor devil to go and sit down on the punishment form at the foot of the master's desk. He got up, but before going hesitated.

"What are you looking for?" asked the master.

"My c-a-p," timidly said the "new fellow," casting troubled looks round him.

"Five hundred verses for all the class!" shouted in a furious voice, stopped, like the *Quos ego*, a fresh outburst. "Silence!" continued the master indignantly, wiping his brow with his handkerchief, which he had just taken from his cap. "As to you, 'new boy,' you will conjugate '*ridiculus sum*' twenty times." Then, in a gentler tone, "come, you'll find your cap again; it hasn't been stolen."

Quiet was restored. Heads bent over desks, and the "new fellow" remained for two hours in an exemplary attitude, although from time to time some paper pellet flipped from the tip of a pen came bang in his face. But he wiped his face with one hand and continued motionless, his eyes lowered.

In the evening, at preparation, he pulled out his pens from his desk, arranged his small belongings, and carefully ruled his paper. We saw him working conscientiously, looking out every word in the dictionary, and taking the greatest pains. Thanks, no doubt, to the willingness he showed, he had not to go down to the class below. But though he knew his rules passably, he had little finish in composition. It was the curé of his village who had taught him his first Latin; his parents, from motives of economy, having sent him to school as late as possible.

His father, Monsieur Charles Denis Bartolomé Bovary, retired assistant-surgeon-major, compromised about 1812 in certain conscription scandals, and forced at this time to leave the service, had taken advantage of his fine figure to get hold of a dowry of sixty thousand francs that offered in the person of a hosier's daughter who had fallen in love with his good looks. A fine man, a great talker, making his spurs ring as he walked, wearing whiskers that ran into his moustache, his fingers always garnished with rings and dressed in loud colours, he had the dash of a military man with the easy go of a commercial traveller. Once married, he lived for three or four years on his wife's fortune, dining well, rising late, smoking long porcelain pipes, not coming in at night till after the theatre, and haunting cafés. The father-in-law died, leaving little; he was indignant at this, "went in for the business," lost some money in it, then retired to the country, where he thought he would make money. But, as he knew no more about farming than calico, as he rode his horses instead of sending them to plough, drank his cider in bottle instead of selling it in cask, ate the finest poultry in his farmyard, and greased his hunting-boots with the fat of his pigs, he was not long in finding out that he would do better to give up all speculation.

For two hundred francs a year he managed to live on the border of the provinces of Caux and Picardy, in a kind of place half farm, half private house; and here, soured, eaten up with regrets, cursing his luck, jealous of every one, he shut himself up at the age of forty-five, sick of men, he said, and determined to live in peace.

His wife had adored him once on a time; she had bored him with a thousand servilities that had only estranged him the more. Lively once, expansive and affectionate, in growing older she had become (after the fashion of wine that, exposed to air, turns to vinegar) ill-tempered, grumbling, irritable. She had suffered so much without complaint at first, when she had seen him going after all the village drabs, and when a score of bad houses sent him back to her at night, weary, stinking drunk. Then her pride revolted. After that she was silent, burying her anger in a dumb stoicism that she maintained till her death. She was constantly going about looking after business matters. She called on the lawyers, the president, remembered when bills fell due, got them renewed, and at home ironed, sewed, washed, looked after the workmen, paid the accounts, while he, troubling himself about nothing, eternally besotted in sleepy sulkiness, whence he only roused himself to say disagreeable things to her, sat smoking by the fire and spitting into the cinders.

When she had a child, it had to be sent out to nurse. When he came home, the lad was spoilt as if he were a prince. His mother stuffed him with jam; his father let him run about barefoot, and, playing the philosopher, even said he might as well go about quite naked like the young of animals. As opposed to the maternal ideas, he had a certain virile idea of childhood on which he sought to mould his son, wishing him to be brought up hardily, like a Spartan, to give him a strong constitution. He sent him to bed without any fire, taught him to drink off large draughts of rum and to jeer at religious processions. But, peaceable by nature, the lad answered only poorly to his notions. His mother always kept him near her; she cut out cardboard for him, told him tales, entertained him with endless monologues full of melancholy gaiety and charming nonsense. In her life's isolation she centred on the child's head all her shattered, broken little vanities. She dreamed of high station; she already saw him, tall, handsome, clever, settled as an engineer or in the law. She taught him to read, and even on an old piano she had taught him two or three little songs. But to all this Monsieur Bovary, caring little for letters, said "It was not worth while. Would they ever have the means to send him to a public school, to buy him a practice, or start him in business? Besides, with cheek a man always gets on in the world." Madame Bovary bit her lips, and the child knocked about the village.

He went after the labourers, drove away with clods of earth the ravens that were flying about. He ate blackberries along the hedges, minded the geese with a long switch, went haymaking during harvest, ran about in the woods, played hopscotch under the church porch on rainy days, and at great fêtes begged the beadle to let him toll the bells, that he might hang all his weight on the long rope and feel himself borne upward by it in its swing. Meanwhile he grew like an oak; he was strong of hand, fresh of colour.

When he was twelve years old his mother had her own way; he began his lessons. The curé took him in hand; but the lessons were so short and irregular that they could not be of much use. They were given at spare moments in the sacristy, standing up, hurriedly, between a baptism and a burial; or else the curé, if he had not to go out, sent for his pupil after the *Angelus*. They went up to his room and settled down; the flies and moths fluttered round the candle. It was close, the child fell asleep, and the good man, beginning to doze with his hands on his stomach, was soon snoring with his mouth wide open. On other occasions, when Monsieur le Curé, on his way back after administering the viaticum to some sick person in the neighbourhood, caught sight of Charles playing about the fields, he called him, lectured him for a quarter of an hour, and took advantage of the occasion to make him conjugate his verb at the foot of a tree. The rain interrupted them or an acquaintance passed. All the same he was always pleased with him, and even said the "young man" had a very good memory.

Charles could not go on like this. Madame Bovary took strong steps. Ashamed, or rather tired out, Monsieur Bovary gave in without a struggle, and they waited one year longer, so that the lad should take his first communion.

Six months more passed, and the year after Charles was finally sent to school at Rouen, whither his father took him towards the end of October, at the time of the St. Romain fair.

It would now be impossible for any of us to remember anything about him. He was a youth of even temperament, who played in playtime, worked in school-hours, was attentive in class, slept well in the dormitory, and ate well in the refectory. He had *in loco parentis* a wholesale ironmonger in the Rue Ganterie, who took him out once a month on Sundays after his shop was shut, sent him for a walk on the quay to look at the boats, and then brought him back to college at seven o'clock before supper. Every Thursday evening he wrote a long letter to his mother with red ink and three wafers; then he went over his history note-books, or read an old volume of "Anarchasis" that was knocking about the study. When he went for walks he talked to the servant, who, like himself, came from the country.

By dint of hard work he kept always about the middle of the class; once even he got a certificate in natural history. But at the end of his third year his parents withdrew him from the school to make him study medicine, convinced that he could even take his degree by himself.

His mother chose a room for him on the fourth floor of a dyer's she knew, overlooking the Eau-de-Robec. She made arrangements for his board, got him furniture, table and two chairs, sent home for an old cherry-tree bedstead, and bought besides a small cast-iron stove with the supply of wood that was to warm the poor child. Then at the end of a week she departed, after a thousand injunctions to be good now that he was going to be left to himself.

The syllabus that he read on the notice-board stunned him: lectures on anatomy, lectures on pathology, lectures on physiology, lectures on pharmacy, lectures on botany and clinical medicine, and therapeutics, without counting hygiene and materia medica—all names of whose entymologies he was ignorant, and that were to him as so many doors to sanctuaries filled with magnificent darkness.

He understood nothing of it all; it was all very well to listen—he did not follow. Still he worked; he had bound note-books, he attended all the courses, never missed a single lecture. He did his little daily task like a mill-horse, who goes round and round with his eyes bandaged, not knowing what work he is doing.

To spare him expense his mother sent him every week by the carrier a piece of veal baked in the oven, with which he lunched when he came back from the hospital, while he sat kicking his feet against the wall. After this he had to run off to lectures, to the operation-room, to the hospital, and return to his home at the other end of the town. In the evening, after the poor dinner of his landlord, he went back to his room and set to work again in his wet clothes, that smoked as he sat in front of the hot stove.

On the fine summer evenings, at the time when the close streets are empty, when the servants are playing shuttlecock at the doors, he opened his window and leaned out. The river, that makes of this quarter of Rouen a wretched little Venice, flowed beneath him, between the bridges and the railings, yellow, violet, or blue. Working men, kneeling on the banks, washed their bare arms in the water. On poles projecting from the attics, skeins of cotton were drying in the air. Opposite, beyond the roofs, spread the pure heaven with the red sun setting. How pleasant it must be at home! How fresh under the beech-tree! And he expanded his nostrils to breathe in the sweet odours of the country which did not reach him.

He grew thin, his figure became taller, his face took a saddened look that made it nearly interesting. Naturally, through indifference, he abandoned all the resolutions he had made. Once he missed a lecture; the next day all

the lectures; and, enjoying his idleness, little by little he gave up work altogether. He got into the habit of going to the public-house, and had a passion
for dominoes. To shut himself up every evening in the dirty public room,
to push about on marble tables the small sheep-bones with black dots,
seemed to him a fine proof of his freedom, which raised him in his own
esteem. It was beginning to see life, the sweetness of stolen pleasures; and
when he entered, he put his hand on the door-handle with a joy almost
sensual. Then many things hidden within him came out; he learnt couplets
by heart and sang them to his boon companions, became enthusiastic about
Béranger, learnt how to make punch, and, finally, how to make love.

Thanks to these preparatory labours, he failed completely in his examination for an ordinary degree. He was expected home the same night to
celebrate his success. He started on foot, stopped at the beginning of the
village, sent for his mother, and told her all. She excused him, threw the
blame of his failure on the injustice of the examiners, encouraged him a
little, and took upon herself to set matters straight. It was only five years
later that Monsieur Bovary knew the truth; it was old then, and he accepted
it. Moreover, he could not believe that a man born of him could be a fool.

So Charles set to work again and crammed for his examination, ceaselessly
learning all the old questions by heart. He passed pretty well. What a happy
day for his mother! They gave a grand dinner.

Where should he go to practise? To Tostes, where there was only one
old doctor. For a long time Madame Bovary had been on the look-out for
his death, and the old fellow had barely been packed off when Charles was
installed, opposite his place, as his successor.

But it was not everything to have brought up a son, to have had him
taught medicine, and discovered Tostes, where he could practise it; he must
have a wife. She found him one—the widow of a bailiff at Dieppe, who was
forty-five and had an income of twelve hundred francs. Though she was
ugly, as dry as a bone, her face with as many pimples as the spring has buds,
Madame Dubuc had no lack of suitors. To attain her ends Madame Bovary
had to oust them all, and she even succeeded in very cleverly baffling the
intrigues of a pork-butcher backed up by the priests.

Charles had seen in marriage the advent of an easier life, thinking he
would be more free to do as he liked with himself and his money. But his
wife was master; he had to say this and not say that in company, to fast
every Friday, dress as she liked, harass at her bidding those patients who did
not pay. She opened his letters, watched his comings and goings, and listened
at the partition-wall when women came to consult him in his surgery.

She must have her chocolate every morning, attentions without end. She
constantly complained of her nerves, her chest, her liver. The noise of
footsteps made her ill; when people left her, solitude became odious to her;
if they came back, it was doubtless to see her die. When Charles returned
in the evening, she stretched forth two long thin arms from beneath the
sheets, put them round his neck, and having made him sit down on the
edge of the bed, began to talk to him of her troubles: he was neglecting

her, he loved another. She had been warned she would be unhappy; and she ended by asking him for a dose of medicine and a little more love.

II

ONE NIGHT towards eleven o'clock they were awakened by the noise of a horse pulling up outside their door. The servant opened the garret-window and parleyed for some time with a man in the street below. He came for the doctor, had a letter for him. Natasie came downstairs shivering and undid the bars and bolts one after the other. The man left his horse, and, following the servant, suddenly came in behind her. He pulled out from his wool cap with grey top-knots a letter wrapped up in a rag and presented it gingerly to Charles, who rested on his elbow on the pillow to read it. Natasie, standing near the bed, held the light. Madame in modesty had turned to the wall and showed only her back.

This letter, sealed with a small seal in blue wax, begged Monsieur Bovary to come immediately to the farm of the Bertaux to set a broken leg. Now from Tostes to the Bertaux was a good eighteen miles across country by way of Longueville and Saint-Victor. It was a dark night; Madame Bovary junior was afraid of accidents for her husband. So it was decided the stable-boy should go on first; Charles would start three hours later when the moon rose. A boy was to be sent to meet him, and show him the way to the farm, and open the gates for him.

Towards four o'clock in the morning, Charles, well wrapped up in his cloak, set out for the Bertaux. Still sleepy from the warmth of his bed, he let himself be lulled by the quiet trot of his horse. When it stopped of its own accord in front of those holes surrounded with thorns that are dug on the margin of furrows, Charles awoke with a start, suddenly remembered the broken leg, and tried to call to mind all the fractures he knew. The rain had stopped, day was breaking, and on the branches of the leafless trees birds roosted motionless, their little feathers bristling in the cold morning wind. The flat country stretched as far as eye could see, and the tufts of trees round the farms at long intervals seemed like dark violet stains on the vast grey surface, that on the horizon faded into the gloom of the sky. Charles from time to time opened his eyes, his mind grew weary, and sleep coming upon him, he soon fell into a doze wherein his recent sensations blending with memories, he became conscious of a double self, at once student and married man, lying in his bed as but now, and crossing the operation theatre as of old. The warm smell of poultices mingled in his brain with the fresh odour of dew; he heard the iron rings rattling along the curtain-rods of the bed and saw his wife sleeping. As he passed Vassonville he came upon a boy sitting on the grass at the edge of a ditch.

"Are you the doctor?" asked the child.

And on Charles's answer he took his wooden shoes in his hands and ran on in front of him.

The general practitioner, riding along, gathered from his guide's talk that Monsieur Rouault must be one of the well-to-do farmers. He had broken his leg the evening before on his way home from a Twelfth-night feast at a neighbour's. His wife had been dead for two years. There was only his daughter, who helped him to keep house, with him.

The ruts were becoming deeper; they were approaching the Bertaux. The little lad, slipping through a hole in the hedge, disappeared; then he came back to the end of a courtyard to open the gate. The horse slipped on the wet grass; Charles had to stoop to pass under the branches. The watchdogs in their kennels barked, dragging at their chains. As he entered the Bertaux the horse took fright and stumbled.

It was a substantial-looking farm. In the stables, over the top of the open doors, one could see great cart-horses quietly feeding from new racks. Right along the outbuildings extended a large dunghill, from which manure liquid oozed, while amidst fowls and turkeys five or six peacocks, a luxury in Chauchois farmyards, were foraging on the top of it. The sheepfold was long, the barn high, with walls smooth as your hand. Under the cart-shed were two large carts and four ploughs, with their whips, shafts and harnesses complete, whose fleeces of blue wool were getting soiled by the fine dust that fell from the granaries. The courtyard sloped upwards, planted with trees set out symmetrically, and the chattering noise of a flock of geese was heard near the pond.

A young woman in a blue merino dress with three flounces came to the threshold of the door to receive Monsieur Bovary, whom she led to the kitchen, where a large fire was blazing. The servants' breakfast was boiling beside it in small pots of all sizes. Some damp clothes were drying inside the chimney-corner. The shovel, tongs, and the nozzle of the bellows, all of colossal size, shone like polished steel, while along the walls hung many pots and pans in which the clear flame of the hearth, mingling with the first rays of the sun coming in through the window, was mirrored fitfully.

Charles went up to the first floor to see the patient. He found him in his bed, sweating under his bed-clothes, having thrown his cotton nightcap right away from him. He was a fat little man of fifty, with white skin and blue eyes, the fore part of his head bald, and he wore earrings. By his side on a chair stood a large decanter of brandy, whence he poured himself out a little from time to time to keep up his spirits; but as soon as he caught sight of the doctor his elation subsided, and instead of swearing, as he had been doing for the last twelve hours, began to groan feebly.

The fracture was a simple one, without any kind of complication. Charles could not have hoped for an easier case. Then calling to mind the devices of his masters at the bedside of patients, he comforted the sufferer with all sorts of kindly remarks, those caresses of the surgeon that are like the oil they put on bistouries. In order to make some splints a bundle of laths was brought up from the carthouse. Charles selected one, cut it into two pieces and planed it with a fragment of window-pane, while the servant tore up sheets to make bandages, and Mademoiselle Emma tried to sew some pads.

As she was a long time before she found her workcase, her father grew impatient; she did not answer, but as she sewed she pricked her fingers, which she then put to her mouth to suck them. Charles was surprised at the whiteness of her nails. They were shiny, delicate at the tips, more polished than the ivory of Dieppe, and almond-shaped. Yet her hand was not beautiful, perhaps not white enough, and a little hard at the knuckles; besides, it was too long, with no soft inflections in the outlines. Her real beauty was in her eyes. Although brown, they seemed black because of the lashes, and her look came at you frankly, with a candid boldness.

The bandaging over, the doctor was invited by Monsieur Rouault himself to "pick a bit" before he left.

Charles went down into the room on the ground-floor. Knives and forks and silver goblets were laid for two on a little table at the foot of a huge bed that had a canopy of printed cotton with figures representing Turks. There was an odour of iris-root and damp sheets that escaped from a large oak chest opposite the window. On the floor in corners were sacks of flour stuck upright in rows. These were the overflow from the neighbouring granary, to which three stone steps led. By way of decoration for the apartment, hanging to a nail in the middle of the wall, whose green paint scaled off from the effects of the saltpetre, was a crayon head of Minerva in a gold frame, underneath which was written in Gothic letters "To dear Papa."

First they spoke of the patient, then of the weather, of the great cold, of the wolves that infested the fields at night. Mademoiselle Rouault did not at all like the country, especially now that she had to look after the farm almost alone. As the room was chilly, she shivered as she ate. This showed something of her full lips, that she had a habit of biting when silent.

Her neck stood out from a white turned-down collar. Her hair, whose two black folds seemed each of a single piece, so smooth were they, was parted in the middle by a delicate line that curved slightly with the curve of the head; and, just showing the tip of the ear, it was joined behind in a thick chignon, with a wavy movement at the temples that the country doctor saw now for the first time in his life. The upper part of her cheek was rose-coloured. She had, like a man, thrust in between two buttons of her bodice a tortoise-shell eyeglass.

When Charles, after bidding farewell to old Rouault, returned to the room before leaving, he found her standing, her forehead against the window, looking into the garden, where the bean props had been knocked down by the wind. She turned round. "Are you looking for anything?" she asked.

"My whip, if you please," he answered.

He began rummaging on the bed, behind the doors, under the chairs. It had fallen to the ground, between the sacks and the wall. Mademoiselle Emma saw it, and bent over the flour sacks. Charles out of politeness made a dash also, and as he stretched out his arm, at the same moment felt his breast brush against the back of the young girl bending beneath him. She drew herself up, scarlet, and looked at him over her shoulder as she handed him his whip.

Instead of returning to the Bertaux in three days as he had promised, he went back the very next day, then regularly twice a week, without counting the visits he paid now and then as if by accident.

Everything, moreover, went well; the patient progressed favourably; and when, at the end of forty-six days, old Rouault was seen trying to walk alone in his "den," Monsieur Bovary began to be looked upon as a man of great capacity. Old Rouault said that he could not have been cured better by the first doctor of Yvetot, or even of Rouen.

As to Charles, he did not stay to ask himself why it was a pleasure to him to go to the Bertaux. Had he done so, he would, no doubt, have attributed his zeal to the importance of the case, or perhaps to the money he hoped to make by it. Was it for this, however, that his visits to the farm formed a delightful exception to the meagre occupations of his life? On these days he rose early, set off at a gallop, urging on his horse, then got down to wipe his boots in the grass and put on black gloves before entering. He liked going into the courtyard, and noticing the gate turn against his shoulder, the cock crow on the wall, the lads run to meet him. He liked the granary and the stables; he liked old Rouault, who pressed his hand and called him his saviour; he liked the small wooden shoes of Mademoiselle Emma on the scoured flags of the kitchen—her high heels made her a little taller; and when she walked in front of him, the wooden soles springing up quickly struck with a sharp sound against the leather of her boots.

She always reconducted him to the first step of the stairs. When his horse had not yet been brought round she stayed there. They had said, "Good-bye"; there was no more talking. The open air wrapped her round, playing with the soft down on the back of her neck, or blew to and fro on her hips her apron-strings, that fluttered like streamers. Once, during a thaw, the bark of the trees in the yard was oozing, the snow on the roofs of the out-buildings was melting; she stood on the threshold, and went to fetch her sunshade and opened it. The sunshade, of silk of the colour of pigeons' breasts, through which the sun shone, lighted up with shifting hues the white skin of her face. She smiled under the tender warmth, and drops of water could be heard falling one by one on the stretched silk.

During the first period of Charles's visits to the Bertaux, Madame Bovary junior never failed to inquire after the invalid, and she had even chosen in the book that she kept on a system of double entry a clean blank page for Monsieur Rouault. But when she heard he had a daughter, she began to make inquiries, and she learnt that Mademoiselle Rouault, brought up at the Ursuline Convent, had received what is called "a good education"; and so knew dancing, geography, drawing, how to embroider and play the piano. That was the last straw.

"So it is for this," she said to herself, "that his face beams when he goes to see her, and that he puts on his new waistcoat at the risk of spoiling it with the rain. Ah! that woman! that woman!"

And she detested her instinctively. At first she solaced herself by allusions that Charles did not understand, then by casual observations that he let pass for fear of a storm, finally by open apostrophes to which he knew not what to answer. "Why did he go back to the Bertaux now that Monsieur Rouault was cured and that these folks hadn't paid yet? Ah! it was because a young lady was there, some one who knew how to talk, to embroider, to be witty. That was what he cared about; he wanted town misses." And she went on:— "The daughter of old Rouault a town miss! Get out! Their grandfather was a shepherd, and they have a cousin who was almost had up at the assizes for a nasty blow in a quarrel. It is not worth while making such a fuss, or showing herself at church on Sundays in a silk gown like a countess. Besides, the poor old chap, if it hadn't been for the colza last year, would have had much ado to pay up his arrears."

For very weariness Charles left off going to the Bertaux. Héloïse made him swear, his hand on the prayer-book, that he would go there no more, after much sobbing and many kisses, in a great outburst of love. He obeyed then, but the strength of his desire protested against the servility of his conduct; and he thought, with a kind of naïve hypocrisy, that this interdict to see her gave him a sort of right to love her. And then the widow was thin; she had long teeth; wore in all weathers a little black shawl, the edge of which hung down between her shoulder-blades; her bony figure was sheathed in her clothes as if they were a scabbard; they were too short, and displayed her ankles with the laces of her large boots crossed over grey stockings.

Charles's mother came to see them from time to time, but after a few days the daughter-in-law seemed to put her own edge on her, and then, like two knives, they sacrificed him with their reflections and observations. It was wrong of him to eat so much. Why did he always offer a glass of something to every one who came? What obstinacy not to wear flannels!

In the spring it came about that a notary at Ingouville, the holder of the widow Dubuc's property, one fine day went off, taking with him all the money in his office. Héloïse, it is true, still possessed, besides a share in a boat valued at six thousand francs, her house in the Rue St. François; and yet, with all this fortune that had been so trumpeted abroad, nothing, excepting perhaps a little furniture and a few clothes, had appeared in the household. The matter had to be gone into. The house at Dieppe was found to be eaten up with mortgages to its foundations; what she had placed with the notary God only knew, and her share in the boat did not exceed one thousand crowns. She had lied, the good lady! In his exasperation, Monsieur Bovary the elder, smashing a chair on the flags, accused his wife of having caused the misfortune of their son by harnessing him to such a harridan, whose harness wasn't worth her hide. They came to Tostes. Explanations followed. There were scenes. Héloïse in tears, throwing her arms about her husband, conjured him to defend her from his parents. Charles tried to speak up for her. They grew angry and left the house.

But "the blow had struck home." A week after, as she was hanging up some washing in her yard, she was seized with a spitting of blood, and the next day, while Charles had his back turned to her drawing the window-curtain, she said, "O God!" gave a sigh and fainted. She was dead! What a surprise!

When all was over at the cemetery Charles went home. He found no one downstairs; he went up to the first floor to their room; saw her dress still hanging at the foot of the alcove; then, leaning against the writing-table, he stayed until the evening, buried in a sorrowful reverie. She had loved him after all.

III

ONE MORNING old Rouault brought Charles the money for setting his leg—seventy-five francs in forty-sou pieces, and a turkey. He had heard of his loss, and consoled him as well as he could.

"I know what it is," said he, clapping him on the shoulder; "I've been through it. When I lost my dear departed, I went into the fields to be quite alone. I fell at the foot of a tree; I cried; I called on God; I talked nonsense to Him. I wanted to be like the moles that I saw on the branches, their insides swarming with worms, dead, and an end of it. And when I thought that there were others at that very moment with their nice little wives holding them in their embrace, I struck great blows on the earth with my stick. I was pretty well mad with not eating; the very idea of going to a café disgusted me—you wouldn't believe it. Well, quite softly, one day following another, a spring on a winter, and an autumn after a summer, this wore away, piece by piece, crumb by crumb; it passed away, it is gone, I should say it has sunk; for something always remains at the bottom, as one would say—a weight here, at one's heart. But since it is the lot of all of us, one must not give way altogether, and, because others have died, want to die too. You must pull yourself together, Monsieur Bovary. It will pass away. Come to see us; my daughter thinks of you now and again, d'ye know, and she says you are forgetting her. Spring will soon be here. We'll have some rabbit-shooting in the warrens to amuse you a bit."

Charles followed his advice. He went back to the Bertaux. He found all as he had left it, that is to say, as it was five months ago. The pear trees were already in blossom, and Farmer Rouault, on his legs again, came and went, making the farm more full of life.

Thinking it his duty to heap the greatest attention upon the doctor because of his sad position, he begged him not to take his hat off, spoke to him in an undertone as if he had been ill, and even pretended to be angry because nothing rather lighter had been prepared for him than for the others, such as a little clotted cream or stewed pears. He told stories. Charles found himself laughing, but the remembrance of his wife suddenly coming back to him depressed him. Coffee was brought in; he thought no more about her.

He thought less of her as he grew accustomed to living alone. The new delight of independence soon made his loneliness bearable. He could now change his meal-times, go in or out without explanation, and when he was very tired stretch himself at full length on his bed. So he nursed and coddled himself and accepted the consolations that were offered him. On the other hand, the death of his wife had not served him ill in his business, since for a month people had been saying, "The poor young man! what a loss!" His name had been talked about, his practice had increased; and, moreover, he could go to the Bertaux just as he liked. He had an aimless hope, and was vaguely happy; he thought himself better looking as he brushed his whiskers before the looking-glass.

One day he got there about three o'clock. Everybody was in the fields. He went into the kitchen, but did not at once catch sight of Emma; the outside shutters were closed. Through the chinks of the wood the sun sent across the flooring long fine rays that were broken at the corners of the furniture and trembled along the ceiling. Some flies on the table were crawling up the glasses that had been used, and buzzing as they drowned themselves in the dregs of the cider. The daylight that came in by the chimney made velvet of the soot at the back of the fireplace, and touched with blue the cold cinders. Between the window and the hearth Emma was sewing; she wore no fichu; he could see small drops of perspiration on her bare shoulders.

After the fashion of country folks she asked him to have something to drink. He said no; she insisted, and at last laughingly offered to have a glass of liqueur with him. So she went to fetch a bottle of curaçoa from the cupboard, reached down two small glasses, filled one to the brim, poured scarcely anything into the other, and, after having clinked glasses, carried hers to her mouth. As it was almost empty she bent back to drink, her head thrown back, her lips pouting, her neck on the strain. She laughed at getting none of it, while with the tip of her tongue passing between her small teeth she licked drop by drop the bottom of her glass.

She sat down again and took up her work, a white cotton stocking she was darning. She worked with her head bent down; she did not speak, nor did Charles. The air coming in under the door blew a little dust over the flags; he watched it drift along, and heard nothing but the throbbing in his head and the faint clucking of a hen that had laid an egg in the yard. Emma from time to time cooled her cheeks with the palms of her hands, and cooled these again on the knobs of the huge fire-dogs.

She complained of suffering since the beginning of the season from giddiness; she asked if sea-baths would do her any good; she began talking of her convent, Charles of his school; words came to them. They went up into her bedroom. She showed him her old music-books, the little prizes she had won, and the oak-leaf crowns, left at the bottom of a cupboard. She spoke to him, too, of her mother, of the country, and even showed him the bed in the garden where, on the first Friday of every month, she gathered flowers to put on her mother's tomb. But the gardener they had understood nothing about it; servants were so careless. She would have

dearly liked, if only for the winter, to live in town, although the length of
the fine days made the country perhaps even more wearisome in the summer. And, according to what she was saying, her voice was clear, sharp, or,
on a sudden all languor, lingered out in modulations that ended almost in
murmurs as she spoke to herself, now joyous, opening big naïve eyes,
then with her eyelids half closed, her look full of boredom, her thoughts
wandering.

Going home at night, Charles went over her words one by one, trying
to recall them, to fill out their sense, that he might piece out the life she
had lived before he knew her. But he never saw her in his thoughts other
than he had seen her the first time, or as he had just left her. Then he asked
himself what would become of her—if she would be married, and to whom?
Alas! old Rouault was rich, and she!—so beautiful! But Emma's face always
rose before his eyes, and a monotone, like the humming of a top, sounded
in his ears, "If you should marry after all! if you should marry!" At night
he could not sleep; his throat was parched; he was athirst. He got up to
drink from the water-bottle and opened the window. The night was covered with stars, a warm wind blowing in the distance; the dogs were barking.
He turned his head towards the Bertaux.

Thinking that, after all, he should lose nothing, Charles promised himself
to ask her in marriage as soon as occasion offered, but each time such occasion did offer the fear of not finding the right words sealed his lips.

Old Rouault would not have been sorry to be rid of his daughter, who was
of no use to him in the house. In his heart he excused her, thinking her too
clever for farming, a calling under the ban of Heaven, since one never saw
a millionaire in it. Far from having made a fortune by it, the good man was
losing every year; for if he was good in bargaining, in which he enjoyed
the dodges of the trade, on the other hand, agriculture properly so called,
and the internal management of the farm, suited him less than most people.
He did not willingly take his hands out of his pockets, and did not spare
expense in all that concerned himself, liking to eat well, to have good fires,
and to sleep well. He liked old cider, underdone legs of mutton, *glorias** well
beaten up. He took his meals in the kitchen alone, opposite the fire, on a
little table brought to him all ready laid as on the stage.

When, therefore, he perceived that Charles's cheeks grew red if near his
daughter, which meant that he would propose for her one of these days,
he chewed the cud of the matter beforehand. He certainly thought him a
little meagre, and not quite the son-in-law he would have liked, but he was
said to be well-conducted, economical, very learned, and no doubt would
not make too many difficulties about the dowry. Now, as old Rouault
would soon be forced to sell twenty-two acres of "his property," as he
owed a good deal to the mason, to the harnessmaker, and as the shaft of the
cider-press wanted renewing, "If he asks for her," he said to himself, "I'll
give her to him."

At Michaelmas Charles went to spend three days at the Bertaux. The
*A mixture of coffee and spirits.—TRANS.

last had passed like the others in procrastinating from hour to hour. Old Rouault was seeing him off: they were walking along the road full of ruts; they were about to part. This was the time. Charles gave himself as far as to the corner of the hedge, and at last, when past it—

"Monsieur Rouault," he murmured, "I should like to say something to you."

They stopped. Charles was silent.

"Well, tell me your story. Don't I know all about it?" said old Rouault, laughing softly.

"Monsieur Rouault—Monsieur Rouault," stammered Charles.

"I ask nothing better," the farmer went on. "Although, no doubt, the little one is of my mind, still we must ask her opinion. So you get off—I'll go back home. If it is 'yes,' you needn't return because of all the people about, and besides it would upset her too much. But so that you mayn't be eating your heart, I'll open wide the outer shutter of the window against the wall; you can see it from the back by leaning over the hedge."

And he went off.

Charles fastened his horse to a tree; he ran into the road and waited. Half-an-hour passed, then he counted nineteen minutes by his watch. Suddenly a noise was heard against the wall; the shutter had been thrown back; the hook was still swinging.

The next day by nine o'clock he was at the farm. Emma blushed as he entered, and gave a little forced laugh to keep herself in countenance. Old Rouault embraced his future son-in-law. The discussion of money matters was put off; moreover, there was plenty of time before them, as the marriage could not decently take place till Charles was out of mourning, that is to say, about the spring of the next year.

The winter passed waiting for this. Mademoiselle Rouault was busy with her trousseau. Part of it was ordered at Rouen, and she made herself chemises and nightcaps after fashion-plates that she borrowed. When Charles visited the farmer, the preparations for the wedding were talked over; they wondered in what room they should have dinner; they dreamed of the number of dishes that would be wanted, and what should be the entrées.

Emma would, on the contrary, have preferred to have a midnight wedding with torches, but old Rouault could not understand such an idea. So there was a wedding at which forty-three persons were present, at which they remained sixteen hours at table, began again the next day, and to some extent on the days following.

IV

THE GUESTS ARRIVED early in carriages, in one-horse chaises, two-wheeled cars, old open gigs, waggonettes with leather hoods, and the young people from the nearer villages in carts, in which they stood up in rows, holding on to the sides so as not to fall, going at a trot and well shaken up. Some came from a distance of thirty miles, from Goderville, from Normanville, and from Cany. All the relatives of both families had been invited, quarrels between friends arranged, acquaintances long since lost sight of written to.

From time to time one heard the crack of a whip behind the hedge; then the gates opened, a chaise entered. Galloping up to the foot of the steps, it stopped short and emptied its load. They got down from all sides, rubbing knees and stretching arms. The ladies, wearing bonnets, had on dresses in the town fashion, gold watch chains, pelerines with the ends tucked into belts, or little coloured fichus fastened down behind with a pin, and that left the back of the neck bare. The lads, dressed like their papas, seemed uncomfortable in their new clothes (many that day handselled their first pair of boots), and by their sides, speaking never a word, wearing the white dress of their first communion lengthened for the occasion, were some big girls of fourteen or sixteen, cousins or elder sisters no doubt, rubicund, bewildered, their hair greasy with rose-pomade, and very much afraid of dirtying their gloves. As there were not enough stable-boys to unharness all the carriages, the gentlemen turned up their sleeves and set about it themselves. According to their different social positions they wore tail-coats, overcoats, shooting-jackets, cutaway-coats: fine tail-coats, redolent of family respectability, that only came out of the wardrobe on state occasions; overcoats with long tails flapping in the wind and round capes and pockets like sacks; shooting-jackets of coarse cloth, generally worn with a cap with a brass-bound peak; very short cutaway-coats with two small buttons in the back, close together like a pair of eyes, and the tails of which seemed cut out of one piece by a carpenter's hatchet. Some, too (but these, you may be sure, would sit at the bottom of the table), wore their best blouses—that is to say, with collars turned down to the shoulders, the back gathered into small plaits and the waist fastened very low down with a worked belt.

And the shirts stood out from the chests like cuirasses! Every one had just had his hair cut; ears stood out from the heads; they had been close-shaved; a few, even, who had had to get up before daybreak, and not been able to see to shave, had diagonal gashes under their noses or cuts the size of a three-franc piece along the jaws, which the fresh air *en route* had enflamed, so that the great white beaming faces were mottled here and there with red dabs.

The mairie was a mile and a half from the farm, and they went thither on foot, returning in the same way after the ceremony in the church. The procession, first united like one long coloured scarf that undulated across the fields, along the narrow path winding amid the green corn, soon lengthened out, and broke up into different groups that loitered to talk. The fiddler walked in front with his violin, gay with ribbons at its pegs. Then came the married pair, the relations, the friends, all following pell-mell; the children stayed behind amusing themselves plucking the bell-flowers from oat-ears, or playing amongst themselves unseen. Emma's dress,

too long, trailed a little on the ground; from time to time she stopped to pull
it up, and then delicately, with her gloved hands, she picked off the coarse
grass and the thistledowns, while Charles, empty handed, waited till she
had finished. Old Rouault, with a new silk hat and the cuffs of his black
coat covering his hands up to the nails, gave his arm to Madame Bovary
senior. As to Monsieur Bovary senior, who, heartily despising all these folk,
had come simply in a frock-coat of military cut with one row of buttons—
he was passing compliments of the bar to a fair young peasant. She bowed,
blushed, and did not know what to say. The other wedding guests talked of
their business or played tricks behind each other's backs, egging one another
on in advance to be jolly. Those who listened could always catch the
squeaking of the fiddler, who went on playing across the fields. When he
saw that the rest were far behind he stopped to take breath, slowly rosined
his bow, so that the strings should sound more shrilly, then set off again,
by turns lowering and raising his neck, the better to mark time for himself.
The noise of the instrument drove away the little birds from afar.

The table was laid under the cart-shed. On it were four sirloins, six
chicken fricassées, stewed veal, three legs of mutton, and in the middle a fine
roast sucking-pig, flanked by four chitterlings with sorrel. At the corners
were decanters of brandy. Sweet bottled-cider frothed round the corks,
and all the glasses had been filled to the brim with wine beforehand. Large
dishes of yellow cream, that trembled with the least shake of the table, had
designed on their smooth surface the initials of the newly wedded pair in
nonpareil arabesques. A confectioner of Yvetot had been intrusted with the
tarts and sweets. As he had only just set up in the place, he had taken a lot
of trouble, and at dessert he himself brought in a set dish that evoked loud
cries of wonderment. To begin with, at its base there was a square of blue
cardboard, representing a temple with porticoes, colonnades, and stucco
statuettes all round, and in the niches constellations of gilt paper stars; then
on the second stage was a dungeon of Savoy cake, surrounded by many
fortifications in candied angelica, almonds, raisins, and quarters of oranges;
and finally, on the upper platform a green field with rocks set in lakes of
jam, nutshell boats, and a small Cupid balancing himself in a chocolate swing
whose two uprights ended in real roses for balls at the top.

Until night they ate. When any of them were too tired of sitting, they
went out for a stroll in the yard, or for a game with corks in the granary,
and then returned to table. Some towards the finish went to sleep and snored.
But with the coffee every one woke up. Then they began songs, showed
off tricks, raised heavy weights, performed feats with their fingers, then
tried lifting carts on their shoulders, made broad jokes, kissed the women.
At night when they left, the horses, stuffed up to the nostrils with oats,
could hardly be got into the shafts; they kicked, reared, the harness broke,
their masters laughed or swore; and all night in the light of the moon
along country roads there were runaway carts at full gallop plunging into
the ditches, jumping over yard after yard of stones, clambering up the hills,
with women leaning out from the tilt to catch hold of the reins.

Those who stayed at the Bertaux spent the night drinking in the kitchen. The children had fallen asleep under the seats.

The bride had begged her father to be spared the usual marriage pleasantries. However, a fishmonger, one of their cousins (who had even brought a pair of soles for his wedding present), began to squirt water from his mouth through the keyhole, when old Rouault came up just in time to stop him, and explain to him that the distinguished position of his son-in-law would not allow of such liberties. The cousin all the same did not give in to these reasons readily. In his heart he accused old Rouault of being proud, and he joined four or five other guests in a corner, who having, through mere chance, been several times running served with the worst helps of meat, also were of opinion they had been badly used, and were whispering about their host, and with covered hints hoping he would ruin himself.

Madame Bovary senior had not opened her mouth all day. She had been consulted neither as to the dress of her daughter-in-law nor as to the arrangement of the feast; she went to bed early. Her husband, instead of following her, sent to Saint-Victor for some cigars, and smoked till daybreak, drinking kirsch-punch, a mixture unknown to the company. This added greatly to the consideration in which he was held.

Charles, who was not of a facetious turn, did not shine at the wedding. He answered feebly to the puns, *doubles entendres*, compliments, and chaff that it was felt a duty to let off at him as soon as the soup appeared.

The next day, on the other hand, he seemed another man. It was he who might rather have been taken for the virgin of the evening before, whilst the bride gave no sign that revealed anything. The shrewdest did not know what to make of it, and they looked at her when she passed near them with an unbounded concentration of mind. But Charles concealed nothing. He called her "my wife," *tutoyéd* her, asked for her of every one, looked for her everywhere, and often he dragged her into the yards, where he could be seen from far between the trees, putting his arm round her waist, and walking half-bending over her, ruffling the chemisette of her bodice with his head.

Two days after the wedding the married pair left. Charles, on account of his patients, could not be away longer. Old Rouault had been driven back in his cart, and himself accompanied them as far as Vassonville. Here he embraced his daughter for the last time, got down, and went his way. When he had gone about a hundred paces he stopped, and as he saw the cart disappearing, its wheels turning in the dust, he gave a deep sigh. Then he remembered his wedding, the old times, the first pregnancy of his wife; he, too, had been very happy the day when he had taken her from her father to his home, and had carried her off on a pillion, trotting through the snow, for it was near Christmas-time, and the country was all white. She held him by one arm, her basket hanging from the other; the wind blew the long lace of her Cauchois head-dress so that it sometimes flapped across his mouth, and when he turned his head he saw near him, on his shoulder, her little rosy face, smiling silently under the gold bands of her cap. To warm her hands she put them from time to time in his breast. How long ago it all was! Their son would have been thirty by now. Then he looked back and saw nothing on the road. He felt dreary as an empty house; and tender memories mingling with the sad thoughts in his brain, addled by the fumes of the feast, he felt inclined for a moment to take a turn towards the church. As he was afraid, however, that this sight would make him yet more sad, he went right away home.

Monsieur and Madame Charles arrived at Tostes about six o'clock. The neighbours came to the windows to see their doctor's new wife.

The old servant presented herself, curtsied to her, apologised for not having dinner ready, and suggested that madame, in the meantime, should look over her house.

V

THE BRICK FRONT was just in a line with the street, or rather the road. Behind the door hung a cloak with a small collar, a bridle, and a black leather cap, and on the floor, in a corner, were a pair of leggings, still covered with dry mud. On the right was the one apartment, that was both dining and sitting room. A canary-yellow paper, relieved at the top by a garland of pale flowers, was puckered everywhere over the badly-stretched canvas; white calico curtains with a red border hung crossways the length of the window; and on the narrow mantelpiece a clock with a head of Hippocrates shone resplendent between two plate candlesticks under oval shades. On the other side of the passage was Charles's consulting-room, a little room about six paces wide, with a table, three chairs, and an office-chair. Volumes of the "Dictionary of Medical Science," uncut, but the binding rather the worse for the successive sales through which they had gone, occupied almost alone the six shelves of a deal bookcase. The smell of melted butter penetrated through the walls when he saw patients, just as in the kitchen one could hear the people coughing in the consulting-room and recounting their whole histories. Then, opening on the yard, where the stable was, came a large dilapidated room with a stove, now used as a wood-house, cellar, and pantry, full of old rubbish, of empty casks, agricultural implements past service, and a mass of dusty things whose use it was impossible to guess.

The garden, longer than wide, ran between two mud walls with espaliered apricots, to a hawthorn hedge that separated it from the field. In the middle was a slate sundial on a brick pedestal; four flower-beds with eglantines sur- rounded symmetrically the more useful kitchen-garden bed. Right at the bottom, under the spruce bushes, was a curé in plaster reading his breviary.

Emma went upstairs. The first room was not furnished, but in the second, which was their bedroom, was a mahogany bedstead in an alcove with red drapery. A shell-box adorned the chest of drawers, and on the secretary near the window a bouquet of orange blossoms tied with white satin ribbons stood in a bottle. It was a bride's bouquet; it was the other one's. She looked at it. Charles noticed it; he took it and carried it up to the attic, while Emma seated in an armchair (they were putting her things down around her) thought of her bridal flowers packed up in a bandbox, and wondered, dreaming, what would be done with them if she were to die.

During the first days she occupied herself in thinking about changes in the house. She took the shades off the candlesticks, had new wall-paper put up, the staircase repainted, and seats made in the garden round the sundial; she even inquired how she could get a basin with a jet fountain and fishes. Finally her husband, knowing that she liked to drive out, picked up a second-hand dog-cart, which, with new lamps and a splashboard in striped leather, looked almost like a tilbury.

He was happy then, and without a care in the world. A meal together, a walk in the evening on the highroad, a gesture of her hands over her hair, the sight of her straw hat hanging from the window-fastener, and many another thing in which Charles had never dreamed of pleasure, now made up the endless round of his happiness. In bed, in the morning, by her side, on the pillow, he watched the sunlight sinking into the down on her fair cheek, half hidden by the lappets of her nightcap. Seen thus closely, her eyes looked to him enlarged, especially when, on waking up, she opened and shut them rapidly many times. Black in the shade, dark blue in broad daylight, they had, as it were, depths of different colours, that, darker in the centre, grew paler towards the surface of the eye. His own eyes lost themselves in these depths; he saw himself in miniature down to the shoulders, with his handkerchief round his head and the top of his shirt open. He rose. She came to the window to see him off, and stayed leaning on the sill between two pots of geranium, clad in her dressing-gown hanging loosely about her. Charles, in the street, buckled his spurs, his foot on the mounting stone, while she talked to him from above, picking with her mouth some scrap of flower or leaf that she blew out at him. Then this, eddying, floating, described semicircles in the air like a bird, and was caught before it reached the ground in the ill-groomed mane of the old white mare standing motionless at the door. Charles from horseback threw her a kiss; she answered with a nod; she shut the window, and he set off. And then along the highroad, spreading out its long ribbon of dust, along the deep lanes that the trees bent over as in arbours, along paths where the corn reached to the knees, with the sun on his back and the morning air in his nostrils, his heart full of the joys of the past night, his mind at rest, his flesh at ease, he went on, re-chewing his happiness, like those who after dinner taste again the truffles which they are digesting.

Until now what good had he had of his life? His time at school, when he remained shut up within the high walls, alone, in the midst of companions richer than he or cleverer at their work, who laughed at his accent, who jeered at his clothes, and whose mothers came to the school with cakes in their muffs? Later on, when he studied medicine, and never had his purse full enough to treat some little work-girl who would have become his mistress? Afterwards, he had lived fourteen months with the widow, whose feet in bed were cold as icicles. But now he had for life this beautiful woman whom he adored. For him the universe did not extend beyond the circumference of her petticoat, and he reproached himself with not loving her. He wanted to see her again; he turned back quickly, ran up the stairs with a beating heart. Emma, in her room, was dressing; he came up on tiptoe, kissed her back; she gave a cry.

He could not keep from constantly touching her comb, her rings, her fichu; sometimes he gave her great sounding kisses with all his mouth on her cheeks, or else little kisses in a row all along her bare arm from the tip of her fingers up to her shoulder, and she put him away half-smiling, half-vexed, as you do a child who hangs about you.

Before marriage she thought herself in love; but the happiness that should have followed this love not having come, she must, she thought, have been mistaken. And Emma tried to find out what one meant exactly in life by the words *felicity, passion, rapture,* that had seemed to her so beautiful in books.

VI

SHE HAD READ "Paul and Virginia," and she had dreamed of the little bamboo-house, the nigger Domingo, the dog Fidèle, but above all of the sweet friendship of some dear little brother, who seeks red fruit for you on trees taller than steeples, or who runs barefoot over the sand, bringing you a bird's nest.

When she was thirteen, her father himself took her to town to place her in the convent. They stopped at an inn in the St. Gervais quarter, where, at their supper, they used painted plates that set forth the story of Mademoiselle de la Vallière. The explanatory legends, chipped here and there by the scratching of knives, all glorified religion, the tenderness of the heart, and the pomps of court.

Far from being bored at first at the convent, she took pleasure in the society of the good sisters, who, to amuse her, took her to the chapel, which one entered from the refectory by a long corridor. She played very little during recreation hours, knew her catechism well, and it was she who always answered Monsieur le Vicaire's difficult questions. Living thus, without ever leaving the warm atmosphere of the class-rooms, and amid these pale-faced women wearing rosaries with brass crosses, she was softly lulled by the mystic languor exhaled in the perfumes of the altar, the freshness of the holy water, and the lights of the tapers. Instead of attending to mass, she looked at the pious vignettes with their azure borders in her book, and she loved the sick lamb, the sacred heart pierced with sharp arrows, or the poor Jesus sinking beneath the cross he carries. She tried, by way of mortification, to eat nothing a whole day. She puzzled her head to find some vow to fulfil.

When she went to confession, she invented little sins in order that she might stay there longer, kneeling in the shadow, her hands joined, her face against the grating beneath the whispering of the priest. The comparisons of betrothed, husband, celestial lover, and eternal marriage, that recur in sermons, stirred within her soul depths of unexpected sweetness.

In the evening, before prayers, there was some religious reading in the study. On week-nights it was some abstract of sacred history or the Lectures of the Abbé Frayssinous, and on Sundays passages from the "Génie du Christianisme," as a recreation. How she listened at first to the sonorous lamentations of its romantic melancholies re-echoing through the world and eternity! If her childhood had been spent in the shop-parlour of some business quarter, she might perhaps have opened her heart to those lyrical invasions of Nature, which usually come to us only through translation in books. But she knew the country too well; she knew the lowing of cattle, the milking, the ploughs. Accustomed to calm aspects of life, she turned, on the contrary, to those of excitement. She loved the sea only for the sake of its storms, and the green fields only when broken up by ruins. She wanted to get some personal profit out of things, and she rejected as useless all that did not contribute to the immediate desires of her heart, being of a temperament more sentimental than artistic, looking for emotions, not landscapes.

At the convent there was an old maid who came for a week each month to mend the linen. Patronised by the clergy, because she belonged to an ancient family of noblemen ruined by the Revolution, she dined in the refectory at the table of the good sisters, and after the meal had a bit of chat with them before going back to her work. The girls often slipped out from the study to go and see her. She knew by heart the love-songs of the last century, and sang them in a low voice as she stitched away. She told stories, gave them news, went errands in the town, and on the sly lent the big girls some novel, that she always carried in the pockets of her apron, and of which the good lady herself swallowed long chapters in the intervals of her work. They were all love, lovers, sweethearts, persecuted ladies fainting in lonely pavilions, postilions killed at every stage, horses ridden to death on every page, sombre forests, heart-aches, vows, sobs, tears and kisses, little skiffs by moonlight, nightingales in shady groves, "gentlemen" brave as lions, gentle as lambs, virtuous as no one ever was, always well dressed, and weeping like fountains. For six months, then, Emma, at fifteen years of age, made her hands dirty with books from old lending libraries. With Walter Scott, later on, she fell in love with historical events, dreamed of old chests, guard-rooms and minstrels. She would have liked to live in some old manor-house, like those long-waisted chatelaines who, in the shade of pointed arches, spent their days leaning on the stone, chin in hand, watching a cavalier with white plume galloping on his black horse from the distant fields. At this time she had a cult for Mary Stuart and enthusiastic veneration for illustrious or unhappy women. Joan of Arc, Héloïse, Agnès Sorel, the beautiful Ferronière, and Clémence Isaure stood out to her like comets in the dark immensity of heaven, where also were seen, lost in shadow, and all unconnected, St. Louis with his oak, the dying Bayard, some cruelties of

Louis XI, a little of St. Bartholomew's, the plume of the Béarnais, and always the remembrance of the plates painted in honour of Louis XIV.

In the music-class, in the ballads she sang, there was nothing but little angels with golden wings, madonnas, lagunes, gondoliers;—mild compositions that allowed her to catch a glimpse athwart the obscurity of style and the weakness of the music of the attractive phantasmagoria of sentimental realities. Some of her companions brought "keepsakes" given them as new year's gifts to the convent. These had to be hidden; it was quite an undertaking; they were read in the dormitory. Delicately handling the beautiful satin bindings, Emma looked with dazzled eyes at the names of the unknown authors, who had signed their verses for the most part as counts or viscounts.

She trembled as she blew back the tissue paper over the engraving and saw it folded in two and fall gently against the page. Here behind the balustrade of a balcony was a young man in a short cloak, holding in his arms a young girl in a white dress wearing an alms-bag at her belt; or there were nameless portraits of English ladies with fair curls, who looked at you from under their round straw hats with their large clear eyes. Some there were lounging in their carriages, gliding through parks, a greyhound bounding along in front of the equipage, driven at a trot by two small postilions in white breeches. Others, dreaming on sofas with an open letter, gazed at the moon through a slightly open window half draped by a black curtain. The naïve ones, a tear on their cheeks, were kissing doves through the bars of a Gothic cage, or, smiling, their heads on one side, were plucking the leaves of a marguerite with their taper fingers, that curved at the tips like peaked shoes. And you, too, were there, Sultans with long pipes reclining beneath arbours in the arms of Bayadères; Djiaours, Turkish sabres, Greek caps; and you especially, pale landscapes of dithyrambic lands, that often show us at once palm-trees and firs, tigers on the right, a lion to the left, Tartar minarets on the horizon; the whole framed by a very neat virgin forest, and with a great perpendicular sunbeam trembling in the water, where, standing out in relief like white excoriations on a steel-grey ground, swans are swimming about.

And the shade of the argand lamp fastened to the wall above Emma's head lighted up all these pictures of the world, that passed before her one by one in the silence of the dormitory, and to the distant noise of some belated carriage rolling over the Boulevards.

When her mother died she cried much the first few days. She had a funeral picture made with the hair of the deceased, and, in a letter sent to the Bertaux full of sad reflections on life, she asked to be buried later on in the same grave. The goodman thought she must be ill, and came to see her. Emma was secretly pleased that she had reached at a first attempt the rare ideal of pale lives, never attained by mediocre hearts. She let herself glide along with Lamartine meanderings, listened to harps on lakes, to all the songs of dying swans, to the falling of the leaves, the pure virgins ascending to heaven, and the voice of the Eternal discoursing down the valleys. She wearied of it, would not confess it, continued from habit, and at last was surprised to feel herself soothed, and with no more sadness at heart than wrinkles on her brow.

The good nuns, who had been so sure of her vocation, perceived with great astonishment that Mademoiselle Rouault seemed to be slipping from them. They had indeed been so lavish to her of prayers, retreats, novenas, and sermons, they had so often preached the respect due to saints and martyrs, and given so much good advice as to the modesty of the body and the salvation of her soul, that she did as tightly reined horses: she pulled up short and the bit slipped from her teeth. This nature, positive in the midst of its enthusiasms, that had loved the church for the sake of the flowers, and music for the words of the songs, and literature for its passional stimulus, rebelled against the mysteries of faith as it grew irritated by discipline, a thing antipathetic to her constitution. When her father took her from school, no one was sorry to see her go. The Lady Superior even thought that she had latterly been somewhat irreverent to the community.

Emma at home once more, first took pleasure in looking after the servants, then grew disgusted with the country and missed her convent. When Charles came to the Bertaux for the first time, she thought herself quite disillusioned, with nothing more to learn, and nothing more to feel.

But the uneasiness of her new position, or perhaps the disturbance caused by the presence of this man, had sufficed to make her believe that she at last felt that wondrous passion which, till then, like a great bird with rose-coloured wings, hung in the splendour of the skies of poesy; and now she could not think that the calm in which she lived was the happiness she had dreamed.

VII

SHE THOUGHT, sometimes, that, after all, this was the happiest time of her life—the honeymoon, as people called it. To taste the full sweetness of it, it would have been necessary doubtless to fly to those lands with sonorous names where the days after marriage are full of laziness most suave. In post-chaises behind blue silken curtains to ride slowly up steep roads, listening to the song of the postilion re-echoed by the mountains, along with the bells of goats and the muffled sound of a waterfall; at sunset on the shores of gulfs to breathe in the perfume of lemon-trees; then in the evening on the villa-terraces above, hand in hand to look at the stars, making plans for the future. It seemed to her that certain places on earth must bring happiness, as a plant peculiar to the soil, and that cannot thrive elsewhere. Why could not she lean over balconies in Swiss châlets, or enshrine her melancholy in a Scotch cottage, with a husband dressed in a black velvet coat with long tails, and thin shoes, a pointed hat and frills?

Perhaps she would have liked to confide all these things to some one. But how tell an undefinable uneasiness, variable as the clouds, unstable as the winds? Words failed her—the opportunity, the courage.

If Charles had but wished it, if he had guessed it, if his look had but once met her thought, it seemed to her that a sudden plenty would have gone out from her heart, as the fruit falls from a tree when shaken by a hand. But as the intimacy of their life became deeper, the greater became the gulf that separated her from him.

Charles's conversation was commonplace as a street pavement, and every one's ideas trooped through it in their everyday garb, without exciting emotion, laughter, or thought. He had never had the curiosity, he said, while he lived at Rouen, to go to the theatre to see the actors from Paris. He could neither swim, nor fence, nor shoot, and one day he could not explain some term of horsemanship to her that she had come across in a novel.

A man, on the contrary, should he not know everything, excel in manifold activities, initiate you into the energies of passion, the refinements of life, all mysteries? But this one taught nothing, knew nothing, wished nothing. He thought her happy; and she resented this easy calm, this serene heaviness, the very happiness she gave him.

Sometimes she would draw; and it was great amusement to Charles to stand there bolt upright and watch her bend over her cardboard, with eyes half-closed the better to see her work, or rolling, between her fingers, little bread-pellets. As to the piano, the more quickly her fingers glided over it the more he wondered. She struck the notes with aplomb, and ran from top to bottom of the keyboard without a break. Thus shaken up, the old instrument, whose strings buzzed, could be heard at the other end of the village when the window was open, and often the bailiff's clerk, passing along the highroad bare-headed and in list slippers, stopped to listen, his sheet of paper in his hand.

Emma, on the other hand, knew how to look after her house. She sent the patients' accounts in well-phrased letters that had no suggestion of a bill. When they had a neighbour to dinner on Sundays, she managed to have some tasty dish—piled up pyramids of green-gages on vine leaves, served up preserves turned out into plates—and even spoke of buying finger-glasses for dessert. From all this much consideration was extended to Bovary.

Charles finished by rising in his own esteem for possessing such a wife. He showed with pride in the sitting-room two small pencil sketches by her that he had had framed in very large frames, and hung up against the wall-paper by long green cords. People returning from mass saw him at his door in his wool-work slippers.

He came home late—at ten o'clock, at midnight sometimes. Then he asked for something to eat, and as the servant had gone to bed, Emma waited on him. He took off his coat to dine more at his ease. He told her, one after the other, the people he had met, the villages where he had been, the prescriptions he had written, and, well pleased with himself, he finished the remainder of the boiled beef and onions, picked pieces off the cheese, munched an apple, emptied his water-bottle, and then went to bed, and lay on his back and snored.

As he had been for a time accustomed to wear nightcaps, his handkerchief

would not keep down over his ears, so that his hair in the morning was all
tumbled pell-mell about his face and whitened with the feathers of the
pillow, whose strings came untied during the night. He always wore thick
boots that had two long creases over the instep running obliquely towards
the ankle, while the rest of the upper continued in a straight line as if
stretched on a wooden foot. He said that "was quite good enough for the
country."

His mother approved of his economy, for she came to see him as formerly when there had been some violent row at her place; and yet Madame
Bovary senior seemed prejudiced against her daughter-in-law. She thought
"her ways too fine for their position"; the wood, the sugar, and the candles
disappeared as "at a grand establishment," and the amount of firing in the
kitchen would have been enough for twenty-five courses. She put her linen
in order for her in the presses, and taught her to keep an eye on the butcher
when he brought the meat. Emma put up with these lessons. Madame Bovary
was lavish of them; and the words "daughter" and "mother" were exchanged
all day long, accompanied by little quiverings of the lips, each one uttering
gentle words in a voice trembling with anger.

In Madame Dubuc's time the old woman felt that she was still the
favourite; but now the love of Charles for Emma seemed to her a desertion
from her tenderness, an encroachment upon what was hers, and she watched
her son's happiness in sad silence, as a ruined man looks through the windows at people dining in his old house. She recalled to him as remembrances
her troubles and her sacrifices, and, comparing these with Emma's negligence, came to the conclusion that it was not reasonable to adore her so
exclusively.

Charles knew not what to answer: he respected his mother, and he loved
his wife infinitely; he considered the judgment of the one infallible, and yet
he thought the conduct of the other irreproachable. When Madame Bovary
had gone, he tried timidly and in the same terms to hazard one or two
of the more anodyne observations he had heard from his mamma. Emma
proved to him with a word that he was mistaken, and sent him off to his
patients.

And yet, in accord with theories she believed right, she wanted to make
herself in love with him. By moonlight in the garden she recited all the
passionate rhymes she knew by heart, and, sighing, sang to him many melancholy adagios; but she found that she was as calm after this as before, and
Charles seemed to be no more amorous and no more moved.

When she had thus for a while struck the flint on her heart without getting a spark, incapable, moreover, of understanding what she did not experience as of believing anything that did not present itself in conventional
forms, she persuaded herself without difficulty that Charles's passion was
nothing very exorbitant. His outbursts became regular; he embraced her
at certain fixed times. It was one habit among other habits, and, like a dessert,
looked forward to after the monotony of dinner.

A gamekeeper, cured by the doctor of inflammation of the lungs, had given madame a little Italian greyhound; she took her out walking, for she went out sometimes in order to be alone for a moment, and not to see before her eyes the eternal garden and the dusty road. She went as far as the beeches of Banneville, near the deserted pavilion which forms an angle of the wall on the side of the country. Amidst the vegetation of the ditch there are long reeds with leaves that cut you.

She began by looking round her to see if nothing had changed since last she had been there. She found again in the same places the foxgloves and wallflowers, the beds of nettles growing round the big stones, and the patches of lichen along the three windows, whose shutters, always closed, were rotting away on their rusty iron bars. Her thoughts, aimless at first, wandered at random, like her greyhound, who ran round and round in the fields, yelping after the yellow butterflies, chasing the shrew-mice, or nibbling the poppies on the edge of a cornfield. Then gradually her ideas took definite shape, and, sitting on the grass that she dug up with little prods of her sunshade, Emma repeated to herself, "Good heavens! why did I marry?"

She asked herself if by some other chance combination it would not have been possible to meet another man; and she tried to imagine what would have been these unrealised events, this different life, this unknown husband. All, surely, could not be like this one. He might have been handsome, witty, distinguished, attractive, such as, no doubt, her old companions of the convent had married. What were they doing now? In town, with the noise of the streets, the buzz of the theatres, and the lights of the ballroom, they were living lives where the heart expands, the senses bourgeon out. But she —her life was cold as a garret whose dormer-window looks on the north, and ennui, the silent spider, was weaving its web in the darkness in every corner of her heart. She recalled the prize-days, when she mounted the platform to receive her little crowns, with her hair in long plaits. In her white frock and open prunella shoes she had a pretty way, and when she went back to her seat, the gentlemen bent over her to congratulate her; the courtyard was full of carriages; farewells were called to her through their windows; the music-master with his violin-case bowed in passing by. How far off all this! How far away!

She called Djali, took her between her knees, and smoothed the long, delicate head, saying, "Come, kiss mistress; you have no troubles."

Then noting the melancholy face of the graceful animal, who yawned slowly, she softened, and comparing her to herself, spoke to her aloud as to somebody in trouble whom one is consoling.

Occasionally there came gusts of wind, breezes from the sea rolling in one sweep over the whole plateau of the Caux country, which brought even to these fields a salt freshness. The rushes, close to the ground, whistled; the branches trembled in a swift rustling, while their summits, ceaselessly swaying, kept up a deep murmur. Emma drew her shawl round her shoulders and rose.

In the avenue a green light dimmed by the leaves lit up the short moss that crackled softly beneath her feet. The sun was setting; the sky showed red between the branches, and the trunks of the trees, uniform, and planted in a straight line, seemed a brown colonnade standing out against a background of gold. A fear took hold of her; she called Djali, and hurriedly returned to Tostes by the highroad, threw herself into an armchair, and for the rest of the evening did not speak.

But towards the end of September something extraordinary fell upon her life; she was invited by the Marquis d'Andervilliers to Vaubyessard.

Secretary of State under the Restoration, the Marquis, anxious to re-enter political life, set about preparing for his candidature to the Chamber of Deputies long beforehand. In the winter he distributed a great deal of wood, and in the Conseil Général always enthusiastically demanded new roads for his arrondissement. During the dog-days he had suffered from an abscess, which Charles had cured as if by miracle by giving a timely little touch with the lancet. The steward sent to Tostes to pay for the operation reported in the evening that he had seen some superb cherries in the doctor's little garden. Now cherry-trees did not thrive at Vaubyessard; the Marquis asked Bovary for some slips; made it his business to thank him personally; saw Emma; thought she had a pretty figure, and that she did not bow like a peasant; so that he did not think he was going beyond the bounds of condescension, nor, on the other hand, making a mistake, in inviting the young couple.

One Wednesday at three o'clock, Monsieur and Madame Bovary, seated in their dog-cart, set out for Vaubyessard, with a great trunk strapped on behind and a bonnet-box in front on the apron. Besides these Charles held a bandbox between his knees.

They arrived at nightfall, just as the lamps in the park were being lit to show the way for the carriages.

VIII

The château, a modern building in Italian style, with two projecting wings and three flights of steps, lay at the foot of an immense green-sward, on which some cows were grazing among groups of large trees set out at regular intervals, while large beds of arbutus, rhododendron, syringas, and guelder roses bulged out their irregular clusters of green along the curve of the gravel path. A river flowed under a bridge; through the mist one could distinguish buildings with thatched roofs scattered over the field bordered by two gently-sloping well-timbered hillocks, and in the background amid the trees rose in two parallel lines the coach-houses and stables, all that was left of the ruined old château.

Charles's dog-cart pulled up before the middle flight of steps; servants appeared; the Marquis came forward, and offering his arm to the doctor's wife, conducted her to the vestibule.

It was paved with marble slabs, was very lofty, and the sound of footsteps and that of voices re-echoed through it as in a church. Opposite rose a straight staircase, and on the left a gallery overlooking the garden led to the billiard-room, through whose door one could hear the click of the ivory balls. As she crossed it to go to the drawing-room, Emma saw standing round the table men with grave faces, their chins resting on high cravats. They all wore orders, and smiled silently as they made their strokes. On the dark wainscoting of the walls large gold frames bore at the bottom names written in black letters. She read: "Jean-Antoine d'Andervilliers d'Yverbon-ville, Count de la Vaubyessard and Baron de la Fresnaye, killed at the battle of Coutras on the 20th of October 1587." And on another: "Jean-Antoine-Henri-Guy d'Andervilliers de la Vaubyessard, Admiral of France and Chevalier of the Order of St. Michael, wounded at the battle of the Hougue-Saint-Vaast on the 29th of May 1692; died at Vaubyessard on the 23rd of January 1693." One could hardly make out those that followed, for the light of the lamps lowered over the green cloth threw a dim shadow round the room. Burnishing the horizontal pictures, it broke up against these in delicate lines where there were cracks in the varnish, and from all these great black squares framed in with gold stood out here and there some lighter portion of the painting—a pale brow, two eyes that looked at you, perukes flowing over and powdering red-coated shoulders, or the buckle of a garter above a well-rounded calf.

The Marquis opened the drawing-room door; one of the ladies (the Marchioness herself) came to meet Emma. She made her sit down by her on an ottoman, and began talking to her as amicably as if she had known her a long time. She was a woman of about forty, with fine shoulders, a hook nose, a drawling voice, and on this evening she wore over her brown hair a simple guipure fichu that fell in a point at the back. A fair young woman was by her side in a high-backed chair, and gentlemen with flowers in their buttonholes were talking to ladies round the fire.

At seven dinner was served. The men, who were in the majority, sat down at the first table in the vestibule; the ladies at the second in the dining-room with the Marquis and Marchioness.

Emma, on entering, felt herself wrapped round by the warm air, a blending of the perfume of flowers and of the fine linen, of the fumes of the viands, and the odour of the truffles. The silver dish-covers reflected the lighted wax candles in the candelabra, the cut crystal covered with light steam reflected from one to the other pale rays; bouquets were placed in a row the whole length of the table; and in the large-bordered plates each napkin, arranged after the fashion of a bishop's mitre, held between its two gaping folds a small oval-shaped roll. The red claws of lobsters hung over the dishes; rich fruit in open baskets was piled up on moss; there were quails in their plumage; smoke was rising; and in silk stockings, knee-breeches, white cravat, and frilled shirt, the steward, grave as a judge, offering ready-carved dishes between the shoulders of the guests, with a touch of the spoon gave you the piece chosen. On the large stove of porcelain inlaid with copper baguettes the statue of a woman, draped to the chin, gazed motionless on the room full of life.

Madame Bovary noticed that many ladies had not put their gloves in their glasses.

But at the upper end of the table, alone amongst all these women, bent over his full plate, and his napkin tied round his neck like a child, an old man sat eating, letting drops of gravy drip from his mouth. His eyes were bloodshot, and he wore a little queue tied with a black ribbon. He was the Marquis's father-in-law, the old Duke de Laverdière, once on a time favourite of the Count d'Artois, in the days of the Vaudreuil hunting-parties at the Marquis de Conflans', and had been, it was said, the lover of Queen Marie Antoinette, between Monsieur de Coigny and Monsieur de Lauzun. He had lived a life of noisy debauch, full of duels, bets, elopements; he had squandered his fortune and frightened all his family. A servant behind his chair named aloud to him in his ear the dishes that he pointed to stammering, and constantly Emma's eyes turned involuntarily to this old man with hanging lips, as to something extraordinary. He had lived at court and slept in the bed of queens!

Iced champagne was poured out. Emma shivered all over as she felt it cold in her mouth. She had never seen pomegranates nor tasted pineapples. The powdered sugar even seemed to her whiter and finer than elsewhere.

The ladies afterwards went to their rooms to prepare for the ball.

Emma made her toilet with the fastidious care of an actress on her début. She did her hair according to the directions of the hairdresser, and put on the barège dress spread out upon the bed. Charles's trousers were tight across the belly.

"My trouser-straps will be rather awkward for dancing," he said.

"Dancing?" repeated Emma.

"Yes!"

"Why, you must be mad! They would make fun of you; keep your place. Besides, it is more becoming for a doctor," she added.

Charles was silent. He walked up and down waiting for Emma to finish dressing.

He saw her from behind in the glass between two lights. Her black eyes seemed blacker than ever. Her hair, undulating towards the ears, shone with a blue lustre; a rose in her chignon trembled on its mobile stalk, with artificial dewdrops on the tip of the leaves. She wore a gown of pale saffron trimmed with three bouquets of pompon roses mixed with green.

Charles came and kissed her on her shoulder.

"Let me alone!" she said; "you are tumbling me."

One could hear the flourish of the violin and the notes of a horn. She went downstairs restraining herself from running.

Dancing had begun. Guests were arriving. There was some crushing. She sat down on a form near the door.

The quadrille over, the floor was occupied by groups of men standing up and talking and servants in livery bearing large trays. Along the line of seated women painted fans were fluttering, bouquets half-hid smiling faces, and gold-stoppered scent-bottles were turned in partly-closed hands, whose white gloves outlined the nails and tightened on the flesh at the wrists. Lace trimmings, diamond brooches, medallion bracelets trembled on bodices, gleamed on breasts, clinked on bare arms. The hair, well smoothed over the temples and knotted at the nape, bore crowns, or bunches, or sprays of myosotis, jasmine, pomegranate blossoms, ears of corn, and corn-flowers. Calmly seated in their places, mothers with forbidding counte-nances were wearing red turbans.

Emma's heart beat rather faster when, her partner holding her by the tips of the fingers, she took her place in a line with the dancers, and waited for the first note to start. But her emotion soon vanished, and, swaying to the rhythm of the orchestra, she glided forward with slight movements of the neck. A smile rose to her lips at certain delicate phrases of the violin, that sometimes played alone while the other instruments were silent; one could hear the clear clink of the louis d'or that were being thrown down upon the card-tables in the next room; then all struck in again, the cornet-a-piston uttered its sonorous note, feet marked time, skirts swelled and rustled, hands touched and parted; the same eyes falling before you met yours again.

A few men (some fifteen or so), of twenty-five to forty, scattered here and there among the dancers or talking at the doorways, distinguished them-selves from the crowd by a certain air of breeding, whatever their differences in age, dress or face.

Their clothes, better made, seemed of finer cloth, and their hair, brought forward in curls towards the temples, glossy with more delicate pomades. They had the complexion of wealth—that clear complexion that is height-ened by the pallor of porcelain, the shimmer of satin, the veneer of old furniture, and that an ordered regimen of exquisite nurture maintains at its best. Their necks moved easily in their low cravats, their long whiskers fell over their turned-down collars, they wiped their lips upon handkerchiefs with embroidered initials that gave forth a subtle perfume. Those who were beginning to grow old had an air of youth, while there was something mature in the faces of the young. In their unconcerned looks was the calm of passions daily satiated, and through all their gentleness of manner pierced that peculiar brutality, the result of a command of half-easy things, in which force is exercised and vanity amused—the management of thoroughbred horses and the society of loose women.

A few steps from Emma a gentleman in a blue coat was talking of Italy with a pale young woman wearing a parure of pearls.

They were praising the breadth of the columns of St. Peter's, Tivoli, Vesuvius, Castellamare, and Cassines, the roses of Genoa, the Coliseum by moonlight. With her other ear Emma was listening to a conversation full of words she did not understand. A circle gathered round a very young man who the week before had beaten "Miss Arabella" and "Romolus," and won two thousand louis jumping a ditch in England. One complained that his racehorses were growing fat; another of the printers' errors that had disfigured the name of his horse.

The atmosphere of the ball was heavy; the lamps were growing dim.

Guests were flocking to the billiard-room. A servant got upon a chair and broke the window-panes. At the crash of the glass Madame Bovary turned her head and saw in the garden the faces of peasants pressed against the window looking in at them. Then the memory of the Bertaux came back to her. She saw the farm again, the muddy pond, her father in a blouse under the apple trees, and she saw herself again as formerly, skimming with her finger the cream off the milk-pans in the dairy. But in the refulgence of the present hour her past life, so distinct until then, faded away completely, and she almost doubted having lived it. She was there; beyond the ball was only shadow overspreading all the rest. She was just eating a maraschino ice that she held with her left hand in a silver-gilt cup, her eyes half-closed, and the spoon between her teeth.

A lady near her dropped her fan. A gentleman was passing.

"Would you be so good," said the lady, "as to pick up my fan that has fallen behind the sofa?"

The gentleman bowed, and as he moved to stretch out his arm, Emma saw the hand of the young woman throw something white, folded in a triangle, into his hat. The gentleman picking up the fan, offered it to the lady respectfully; she thanked him with an inclination of the head, and began smelling her bouquet.

After supper, where were plenty of Spanish and Rhine wines, soups à la bisque and au lait d'amandes, puddings à la Trafalgar, and all sorts of cold meats with jellies that trembled in the dishes, the carriages one after the other began to drive off. Raising the corners of the muslin curtain, one could see the light of their lanterns glimmering through the darkness. The seats began to empty, some card-players were still left; the musicians were cooling the tips of their fingers on their tongues. Charles was half asleep, his back propped against a door.

At three o'clock the cotillion began. Emma did not know how to waltz. Every one was waltzing, Mademoiselle d'Andervilliers herself and the Marquis; only the guests staying at the castle were still there, about a dozen persons.

One of the waltzers, however, who was familiarly called Viscount, and whose low cut waistcoat seemed moulded to his chest, came a second time to ask Madame Bovary to dance, assuring her that he would guide her, and that she would get through it very well.

They began slowly, then went more rapidly. They turned; all around them was turning—the lamps, the furniture, the wainscoting, the floor, like a disc on a pivot. On passing near the doors the bottom of Emma's dress caught against his trousers. Their legs commingled; he looked down at her; she raised her eyes to his. A torpor seized her; she stopped. They started again, and with a more rapid movement; the Viscount, dragging her along, disappeared with her to the end of the gallery, where, panting, she almost fell, and for a moment rested her head upon his breast. And then, still turning, but more slowly, he guided her back to her seat. She leaned back against the wall and covered her eyes with her hands.

When she opened them again, in the middle of the drawing-room three waltzers were kneeling before a lady sitting on a stool. She chose the Viscount, and the violin struck up once more.

Every one looked at them. They passed and repassed, she with rigid body, her chin bent down, and he always in the same pose, his figure curved, his elbow rounded, his chin thrown forward. That woman knew how to waltz! They kept up a long time, and tired out all the others.

Then they talked a few moments longer, and after the good-nights, or rather good-mornings, the guests of the château retired to bed.

Charles dragged himself up by the balusters. His "knees were going up into his body." He had spent five consecutive hours standing bolt upright at the card-tables, watching them play whist, without understanding anything about it, and it was with a deep sigh of relief that he pulled off his boots.

Emma threw a shawl over her shoulders, opened the window, and leant out.

The night was dark; some drops of rain were falling. She breathed in the damp wind that refreshed her eyelids. The music of the ball was still murmuring in her ears, and she tried to keep herself awake in order to prolong the illusion of this luxurious life that she would soon have to give up.

Day began to break. She looked long at the windows of the château, trying to guess which were the rooms of all those she had noticed the evening before. She would fain have known their lives, have penetrated, blended with them. But she was shivering with cold. She undressed, and cowered down between the sheets against Charles, who was asleep.

There were a great many people to luncheon. The repast lasted ten minutes; no liqueurs were served, which astonished the doctor. Next, Mademoiselle d'Andervilliers collected some pieces of roll in a small basket to take them to the swans on the ornamental waters, and they went to walk in the hot-houses, where strange plants, bristling with hairs, rose in pyramids under hanging vases, whence, as from overfilled nests of serpents, fell long green cords interlacing. The orangery, which was at the other end, led by a covered way to the outhouses of the château. The Marquis, to amuse the young woman, took her to see the stables. Above the basket-shaped racks porcelain slabs bore the names of the horses in black letters. Each animal in its stall whisked its tail when any one went near and said "Tchk! tchk!" The boards of the harness-room shone like the flooring of a drawing-room. The carriage harness was piled up in the middle against two twisted columns, and the bits, the whips, the spurs, the curbs, were ranged in a line all along the wall.

Charles, meanwhile, went to ask a groom to put his horse to. The dog-cart was brought to the foot of the steps, and all the parcels being crammed in, the Bovarys paid their respects to the Marquis and Marchioness and set out again for Tostes.

Emma watched the turning wheels in silence. Charles, on the extreme edge of the seat, held the reins with his two arms wide apart, and the little horse ambled along in the shafts that were too big for him. The loose reins hanging over his crupper were wet with foam, and the box fastened on behind the chaise gave great regular bumps against it.

They were on the heights of Thibourville when suddenly some horsemen with cigars between their lips passed laughing. Emma thought she recognised the Viscount, turned back, and caught on the horizon only the movement of the heads rising or falling with the unequal cadence of the trot or gallop.

A mile farther on they had to stop to mend with some string the traces that had broken.

But Charles, giving a last look to the harness, saw something on the ground between his horse's legs, and he picked up a cigar-case with a green silk border and beblazoned in the centre like the door of a carriage.

"There are even two cigars in it," said he; "they'll do for this evening after dinner."

"Why, do you smoke?" she asked.

"Sometimes, when I get a chance."

He put his find in his pocket and whipped up the nag.

When they reached home the dinner was not ready. Madame lost her temper. Natasie answered rudely.

"Leave the room!" said Emma. "You are forgetting yourself. I give you warning."

For dinner there was onion soup and a piece of veal with sorrel. Charles, seated opposite Emma, rubbed his hands gleefully.

"How good it is to be home again!"

Natasie could be heard crying. He was rather fond of the poor girl. She had formerly, during the wearisome time of his widowhood, kept him company many an evening. She had been his first patient, his oldest acquaintance in the place.

"Have you given her warning for good?" he asked at last.

"Yes. Who is to prevent me?" she replied.

Then they warmed themselves in the kitchen while their room was being made ready. Charles began to smoke. He smoked with lips protruding, spitting every moment, recoiling at every puff.

"You'll make yourself ill," she said scornfully.

He put down his cigar and ran to swallow a glass of cold water at the pump. Emma seizing hold of the cigar-case threw it quickly to the back of the cupboard.

The next day was a long one. She walked about her little garden, up and down the same walks, stopping before the beds, before the espalier, before the plaster curate, looking with amazement at all these things of once-on-a-time that she knew so well. How far off the ball seemed already! What was it that thus set so far asunder the morning of the day before yesterday and the evening of to-day? Her journey to Vaubyessard had made a hole in her life, like one of those great crevasses that a storm will sometimes make in one night in mountains. Still she was resigned. She devoutly put away in her drawers her beautiful dress, down to the satin shoes whose soles were yellowed with the slippery wax of the dancing floor. Her heart was like these. In its friction against wealth something had come over it that could not be effaced.

The memory of this ball, then, became an occupation for Emma. Whenever the Wednesday came round she said to herself as she awoke, "Ah! I was there a week—a fortnight—three weeks ago." And little by little the faces grew confused in her remembrance. She forgot the tune of the quadrilles; she no longer saw the liveries and appointments so distinctly; some details escaped her, but the regret remained with her.

IX

OFTEN when Charles was out she took from the cupboard, between the folds of the linen where she had left it, the green silk cigar-case. She looked at it, opened it, and even smelt the odour of the lining—a mixture of verbena and tobacco. Whose was it? The Viscount's? Perhaps it was a present from his mistress. It had been embroidered on some rosewood frame, a pretty little thing, hidden from all eyes, that had occupied many hours, and over which had fallen the soft curls of the pensive worker. A breath of love had passed over the stitches on the canvas; each prick of the needle had fixed there a hope or a memory, and all those interwoven threads of silk were but the continuity of the same silent passion. And then one morning the Viscount had taken it away with him. Of what had they spoken when it lay upon the wide-mantelled chimneys between flower-vases and Pompadour clocks? She was at Tostes; he was at Paris now, far away! What was this Paris like? What a vague name! She repeated it in a low voice, for the mere pleasure of it; it rang in her ears like a great cathedral bell; it shone before her eyes, even on the labels of her pomade-pots.

At night, when the carriers passed under her windows in their carts singing the "Marjolaine," she awoke, and listened to the noise of the iron-bound wheels, which, as they gained the country road, was soon deadened by the soil. "They will be there to-morrow!" she said to herself.

And she followed them in thought up and down the hills, traversing villages, gliding along the highroads by the light of the stars. At the end of some indefinite distance there was always a confused spot, into which her dream died.

She bought a plan of Paris, and with the tip of her finger on the map she walked about the capital. She went up the boulevards, stopping at every turning, between the lines of the streets, in front of the white squares that represented the houses. At last she would close the lids of her weary eyes, and see in the darkness the gas jets flaring in the wind and the steps of carriages lowered with much noise before the peristyles of theatres.

She took in "La Corbeille," a lady's journal, and the "Sylphe des Salons." She devoured, without skipping a word, all the accounts of first nights, races, and soirées, took an interest in the début of a singer, in the opening of a new shop. She knew the latest fashions, the addresses of the best tailors, the days of the Bois and the Opera. In Eugène Sue she studied descriptions of furniture; she read Balzac and George Sand, seeking in them imaginary satisfaction for her own desires. Even at table she had her book by her, and turned over the pages while Charles ate and talked to her. The memory of the Viscount always returned as she read. Between him and the imaginary personages she made comparisons. But the circle of which he was the centre gradually widened round him, and the aureole that he bore, fading from his form, broadened out beyond, lighting up her other dreams.

Paris, more vague than the ocean, glimmered before Emma's eyes in an atmosphere of vermilion. The many lives that stirred amid this tumult were, however, divided into parts, classed as distinct pictures. Emma perceived only two or three that hid from her all the rest, and in themselves represented all humanity. The world of ambassadors moved over polished floors in drawing-rooms lined with mirrors, round oval tables covered with velvet and gold-fringed cloths. There were dresses with trains, deep mysteries, anguish hidden beneath smiles. Then came the society of the duchesses; all were pale; all got up at four o'clock; the women, poor angels, wore English point on their petticoats; and the men, unappreciated geniuses under a frivolous outward seeming, rode horses to death at pleasure parties, spent the summer season at Baden, and towards the forties married heiresses. In the private rooms of restaurants, where one sups after midnight by the light of wax candles, laughed the motley crowd of men of letters and actresses. They were prodigal as kings, full of ideal, ambitious, fantastic frenzy. This was an existence outside that of all others, between heaven and earth, in the midst of storms, having something of the sublime. For the rest of the world it was lost, with no particular place, and as if non-existent. The nearer things were, moreover, the more her thoughts turned away from them. All her immediate surroundings, the wearisome country, the middle-class imbeciles, the mediocrity of existence, seemed to her exceptional, a peculiar chance that had caught hold of her, while beyond stretched as far as eye could see an immense land of joys and passions. She confused in her desire the sensualities of luxury with the delights of the heart, elegance of manners with delicacy of sentiment. Did not love, like Indian plants, need a special soil, a particular temperature? Sighs by moonlight, long embraces, tears flowing over yielded hands, all the fevers of the flesh and the languors of tenderness could not be separated from the balconies of great castles full of indolence, from boudoirs with silken curtains and thick carpets, well-filled flower-stands, a bed on a raised daïs, nor from the flashing of precious stones and the shoulder-knots of liveries.

The lad from the posting-house who came to groom the mare every morning passed through the passage with his heavy wooden shoes; there were holes in his blouse; his feet were bare in list slippers. And this was the groom in knee-breeches with whom she had to be content! His work done, he did not come back again all day, for Charles on his return put up his horse himself, unsaddled him and put on the halter, while the servant-girl brought a bundle of straw and threw it as best she could into the manger.

To replace Natasie (who left Tostes shedding torrents of tears) Emma took into her service a young girl of fourteen, an orphan with a sweet face. She forbade her wearing cotton caps, taught her to address her in the third person, to bring a glass of water on a plate, to knock before coming into a room, to iron, starch, and to dress her,—wanted to make a lady's-maid of her. The new servant obeyed without a murmur, so as not to be sent away; and as madame usually left the key in the sideboard, Félicité every evening took a small supply of sugar that she ate alone in her bed after she had said her prayers.

Sometimes in the afternoon she went to chat with the postilions. Madame was in her room upstairs. She wore an open dressing-gown, that showed between the shawl facings of her bodice a pleated chemisette with three gold buttons. Her belt was a corded girdle with great tassels, and her small garnet-coloured slippers had a large knot of ribbon that fell over her instep. She had bought herself a blotting-book, writing-case, pen-holder, and envelopes, although she had no one to write to; she dusted her what-not, looked at herself in the glass, picked up a book, and then, dreaming, between the lines, let it drop on her knees. She longed to travel or to go back to her convent. She wished at the same time to die and to live in Paris.

Charles in snow and rain trotted across country. He ate omelettes on farmhouse tables, poked his arm into damp beds, received a tepid spurt of blood-lettings in his face, listened to death-rattles, examined basins, turned over a good deal of dirty linen; but every evening he found a blazing fire, his dinner ready, easy-chairs, and a well-dressed woman, charming with an odour of freshness, though no one could say whence the perfume came, or if it were not her skin that made odorous her chemise.

She charmed him by numerous attentions; now it was some new way of arranging paper sconces for the candles, a flounce that she altered on her gown, or an extraordinary name for some very simple dish that the servant had spoilt, but that Charles swallowed with pleasure to the last mouthful. At Rouen she saw some ladies who wore a bunch of charms on their watch-chains; she bought some charms. She wanted for her mantelpiece two large blue glass vases, and some time after an ivory nécessaire with a silver-gilt thimble. The less Charles understood these refinements the more they seduced him. They added something to the pleasure of the senses and to the comfort of his fireside. It was like a golden dust sanding all along the narrow path of his life.

He was well, looked well; his reputation was firmly established. The country-folk loved him because he was not proud. He petted the children, never went to the public-house, and, moreover, his morals inspired confidence. He was specially successful with catarrhs and chest complaints. Being much afraid of killing his patients, Charles, in fact, only prescribed sedatives, from time to time an emetic, a footbath, or leeches. It was not that he was afraid of surgery; he bled people copiously like horses, and for the taking out of teeth he had the "devil's own wrist."

Finally, to keep up with the times, he took in "La Ruche Médicale," a new journal whose prospectus had been sent him. He read it a little after dinner, but in about five minutes, the warmth of the room added to the effect of his dinner sent him to sleep; and he sat there, his chin on his two hands and his hair spreading like a mane to the foot of the lamp. Emma looked at him and shrugged her shoulders. Why, at least, was not her husband one of those men of taciturn passions who work at their books all night, and at last, when about sixty, the age of rheumatism sets in, wear a string of orders on their ill-fitting black coat? She could have wished this name of Bovary, which was hers, had been illustrious, to see it displayed at the booksellers', repeated in the newspapers, known to all France. But Charles had no ambition. An Yvetot doctor whom he had lately met in consultation had somewhat humiliated him at the very bedside of the patient, before the assembled relatives. When, in the evening, Charles told her this anecdote, Emma inveighed loudly against his colleague. Charles was much touched. He kissed her forehead with a tear in his eyes. But she was angered with shame; she felt a wild desire to strike him; she went to open the window in the passage and breathed in the fresh air to calm herself.

"What a man! what a man!" she said in a low voice, biting her lips.

Besides, she was becoming more irritated with him. As he grew older his manner grew heavier; at dessert he cut the corks of the empty bottles, after eating he cleaned his teeth with his tongue; in taking soup he made a gurgling noise with every spoonful; and, as he was getting fatter, the puffed-out cheeks seemed to push the eyes, always small, up to the temples.

Sometimes Emma tucked the red borders of his undervest into his waistcoat, rearranged his cravat, and threw away the dirty gloves he was going to put on; and this was not, as he fancied, for himself; it was for herself, by a diffusion of egotism, of nervous irritation. Sometimes, too, she told him of what she had read, such as a passage in a novel, of a new play, or an anecdote of the "upper ten" that she had seen in a feuilleton; for, after all, Charles was something, an ever-open ear, an ever-ready approbation. She confided many a thing to her greyhound. She would have done so to the logs in the fireplace or to the pendulum of the clock.

At bottom of her heart, however, she was waiting for something to happen. Like shipwrecked sailors, she turned despairing eyes upon the solitude of her life, seeking afar off some white sail in the mists of the horizon. She did not know what this chance would be, what wind would bring it her, towards what shore it would drive her, if it would be a shallop or a three-decker, laden with anguish or full of bliss to the portholes. But each morning, as she awoke, she hoped it would come that day; she listened to every sound, sprang up with a start, wondered that it did not come; then at sunset, always more saddened, she longed for the morrow.

Spring came round. With the first warm weather, when the pear-trees began to blossom, she suffered from dyspnœa.

From the beginning of July she counted how many weeks there were to October, thinking that perhaps the Marquis d'Andervilliers would give another ball at Vaubyessard. But all September passed without letters or visits.

After the ennui of this disappointment her heart once more remained empty, and then the same series of days recommenced. So now they would thus follow one another, always the same, immovable, and bringing nothing. Other lives, however flat, had at least the chance of some event. One adventure sometimes brought with it infinite consequences and the scene changed. But nothing happened to her; God had willed it so! The future was a dark corridor, with its door at the end shut fast.

She gave up music. What was the good of playing? Who would hear her? Since she could never, in a velvet gown with short sleeves, striking with her light fingers the ivory keys of an Erard at a concert, feel the murmur of ecstasy envelop her like a breeze, it was not worth while boring herself with practising. Her drawing cardboard and her embroidery she left in the cupboard. What was the good? What was the good? Sewing irritated her. "I have read everything," she said to herself. And she sat there making the tongs red-hot, or looked at the rain falling.

How sad she was on Sundays when vespers sounded! She listened with dull attention to each stroke of the cracked bell. A cat slowly walking over some roof put up his back in the pale rays of the sun. The wind on the highroad blew up clouds of dust. Afar off a dog sometimes howled; and the bell, keeping time, continued its monotonous ringing that died away over the fields.

But the people came out from church. The women in waxed clogs, the peasants in new blouses, the little bareheaded children skipping along in front of them, all were going home. And till nightfall, five or six men, always the same, stayed playing at corks in front of the large door of the inn.

The winter was severe. The windows every morning were covered with rime, and the light shining through them, dim as through ground-glass, sometimes did not change the whole day long. At four o'clock the lamp had to be lighted.

On fine days she went down into the garden. The dew had left on the cabbages a silver lace with long transparent threads spreading from one to the other. No birds were to be heard; everything seemed asleep, the espalier covered with straw, and the vine, like a great sick serpent under the coping of the wall, along which, on drawing near, one saw the many-footed wood-lice crawling. Under the spruce by the hedgerow, the curé in the three-cornered hat reading his breviary had lost his right foot, and the very plaster, scaling off with the frost, had left white scabs on his face.

Then she went up again, shut her door, put on coals, and fainting with the heat of the hearth, felt her boredom weigh more heavily than ever. She would have liked to go down and talk to the servant, but a sense of shame restrained her.

Every day at the same time the schoolmaster in a black skull-cap opened the shutters of his house, and the rural policeman, wearing his sabre over his blouse, passed by. Night and morning the post-horses, three by three, crossed the street to water at the pond. From time to time the bell of a public-house door rang, and when it was windy one could hear the little brass basins that served as signs for the hairdresser's shop creaking on their two rods. This shop had as decoration an old engraving of a fashion-plate stuck against a window-pane and the wax bust of a woman with yellow hair. He, too, the hairdresser, lamented his wasted calling, his hopeless future, and dreaming of some shop in a big town—at Rouen, for example, overlooking the harbour, near the theatre—he walked up and down all day from the mairie to the church, sombre and waiting for customers. When Madame Bovary looked up, she always saw him there, like a sentinel on duty, with his skull-cap over his ears and his vest of lasting.

Sometimes in the afternoon outside the window of her room, the head of a man appeared, a swarthy head with black whiskers, smiling slowly, with a broad, gentle smile that showed his white teeth. A waltz immediately began, and on the organ, in a little drawing-room, dancers the size of a finger, women in pink turbans, Tyrolians in jackets, monkeys in frock-coats, gentlemen in knee-breeches, turned and turned between the sofas, the consoles, multiplied in the bits of looking-glass held together at their corners by a piece of gold paper. The man turned his handle, looking to the right and left, and up at the windows. Now and again, while he shot out a long squirt of brown saliva against the milestone, with his knee he raised his instrument, whose hard straps tired his shoulder; and now, doleful and drawling, or gay and hurried, the music escaped from the box, droning through a curtain of pink taffeta under a brass claw in arabesque. They were airs played in other places at the theatres, sung in drawing-rooms, danced to at night under lighted lustres, echoes of the world that reached even to Emma. Endless sarabands ran through her head, and, like an Indian dancing-girl on the flowers of a carpet, her thoughts leapt with the notes, swung from dream to dream, from sadness to sadness. When the man had caught some coppers in his cap, he drew down an old cover of blue cloth, hitched his organ on to his back, and went off with a heavy tread. She watched him going.

But it was above all the meal-times that were unbearable to her, in this small room on the ground-floor, with its smoking stove, its creaking door, the walls that sweated, the damp flags; all the bitterness in life seemed served up on her plate, and with the smoke of the boiled beef there rose from her secret soul whiffs of sickliness. Charles was a slow eater; she played with a few nuts, or, leaning on her elbow, amused herself with drawing lines along the oilcloth table-cover with the point of her knife.

She now let everything in her household take care of itself, and Madame Bovary senior, when she came to spend part of Lent at Tostes, was much surprised at the change. She who was formerly so careful, so dainty, now passed whole days without dressing, wore grey cotton stockings, and burnt tallow candles. She kept saying they must be economical since they were not rich, adding that she was very contented, very happy, that Tostes pleased her very much, with other speeches that closed the mouth of her mother-in-law. Besides, Emma no longer seemed inclined to follow her advice; once even, Madame Bovary having thought fit to maintain that mistresses ought to keep an eye on the religion of their servants, she had answered with so angry a look and so cold a smile that the good woman did not try it on again.

Emma was growing difficile, capricious. She ordered dishes for herself, then she did not touch them; one day drank only pure milk, and the next cups of tea by the dozen. Often she persisted in not going out, then, stifling, threw open the windows and put on light dresses. After she had well scolded her servant she gave her presents or sent her out to see neighbours, just as she sometimes threw beggars all the silver in her purse, although she was by no means tender-hearted or easily accessible to the feelings of others, like most country-bred people, who always retain in their souls something of the horny hardness of the paternal hands.

Towards the end of February old Rouault, in memory of his cure, himself brought his son-in-law a superb turkey, and stayed three days at Tostes. Charles being with his patients, Emma kept him company. He smoked in the room, spat on the fire-dogs, talked farming, calves, cows, poultry, and municipal council, so that when he left she closed the door on him with a feeling of satisfaction that surprised even herself. Moreover she no longer concealed her contempt for anything or anybody, and at times she set herself to express singular opinions, finding fault with that which others approved, and approving things perverse and immoral, all of which made her husband open his eyes widely.

Would this misery last for ever? Would she never issue from it? Yet she was as good as all the women who were living happily. She had seen duchesses at Vaubyessard with clumsier waists and commoner ways, and she execrated the injustice of God. She leant her head against the walls to weep; she envied lives of stir; longed for masked balls, for violent pleasures, with all the wildness, that she did not know, but that these must surely yield.

She grew pale and suffered from palpitations of the heart. Charles prescribed valerian and camphor baths. Everything that was tried only seemed to irritate her the more.

On certain days she chattered with feverish rapidity, and this overexcitement was suddenly followed by a state of torpor, in which she remained without speaking, without moving. What then revived her was pouring a bottle of eau-de-cologne over her arms.

As she was constantly complaining about Tostes, Charles fancied that her illness was no doubt due to some local cause, and fixing on this idea, began to think seriously of setting up elsewhere.

From that moment she drank vinegar, contracted a sharp little cough, and completely lost her appetite.

It cost Charles much to give up Tostes after living there four years and "when he was beginning to get on there." Yet if it must be! He took her to Rouen to see his old master. It was a nervous complaint; change of air was needed.

After looking about him on this side and on that, Charles learnt that in the Neufchâtel arrondissement there was a considerable market-town called Yonville-l'Abbaye, whose doctor, a Polish refugee, had decamped a week before. Then he wrote to the chemist of the place to ask the number of the population, the distance from the nearest doctor, what his predecessor had made a year, and so forth; and the answer being satisfactory, he made up his mind to move towards the spring, if Emma's health did not improve.

One day when, in view of her departure, she was tidying a drawer, something pricked her finger. It was a wire of her wedding-bouquet. The orange blossoms were yellow with dust and the silver-bordered satin ribbons frayed at the edges. She threw it into the fire. It flared up more quickly than dry straw. Then it was like a red bush in the cinders, slowly devoured. She watched it burn. The little pasteboard berries burst, the wire twisted, the gold lace melted; and the shrivelled paper corollas, fluttering like black butterflies at the back of the stove, at last flew up the chimney.

When they left Tostes in the month of March, Madame Bovary was pregnant.

PART II

YONVILLE-L'ABBAYE (so called from an old Capuchin abbey of which not even the ruins remain) is a market-town twenty-four miles from Rouen, between the Abbeville and Beauvais roads, at the foot of a valley watered by the Rieule, a little river that runs into the Andelle after turning three water-mills near its mouth, where there are a few trout that the lads amuse themselves by fishing for on Sundays.

We leave the highroad at La Boissière and keep straight on to the top of the Leux hill, whence the valley is seen. The river that runs through it makes of it, as it were, two regions with distinct physiognomies,—all on the left is pasture land, all on the right arable. The meadow stretches under a bulge of low hills to join at the back with the pasture land of the Bray country, while on the eastern side, the plain, gently rising, broadens out, showing as far as eye can follow its blond cornfields. The water, flowing by the grass, divides with a white line the colour of the roads and of the plains, and the country is like a great unfolded mantle with a green velvet cape bordered with a fringe of silver.

Before us, on the verge of the horizon, lie the oaks of the forest of Argueil, with the steeps of the Saint-Jean hills scarred from top to bottom with red irregular lines; they are rain-tracks, and these brick-tones standing out in narrow streaks against the grey colour of the mountain are due to the quantity of iron springs that flow beyond in the neighbouring country.

Here we are on the confines of Normandy, Picardy, and the Ile-de-France, a bastard land, whose language is without accent as its landscape is without character. It is there that they make the worst Neufchâtel cheeses of all the arrondissement; and, on the other hand, farming is costly because so much manure is needed to enrich this friable soil full of sand and flints.

Up to 1835 there was no practicable road for getting to Yonville, but about this time a cross-road was made which joins that of Abbeville to that of Amiens, and is occasionally used by the Rouen waggoners on their way to Flanders. Yonville-l'Abbaye has remained stationary in spite of its "new outlet." Instead of improving the soil, they persist in keeping up the pasture lands, however depreciated they may be in value, and the lazy borough, growing away from the plain, has naturally spread riverwards. It is seen from afar sprawling along the banks like a cowherd taking a siesta by the water-side.

At the foot of the hill beyond the bridge begins a roadway, planted with young aspens that leads in a straight line to the first houses in the place. These, fenced in by hedges, are in the middle of courtyards full of straggling buildings, wine-presses, cart-sheds, and distilleries scattered under thick trees, with ladders, poles, or scythes hung on to the branches. The thatched roofs, like fur-caps drawn over eyes, reach down over about a third of the low windows, whose coarse convex glasses have knots in the middle like the bottoms of bottles. Against the plaster wall diagonally crossed by black joists, a meagre pear tree sometimes leans, and the ground-floors have at their door a small swing-gate, to keep out the chicks that come pilfering crumbs of bread steeped in cider on the threshold. But the court-yards grow narrower, the houses closer together, and the fences disappear; a bundle of ferns swings under a window from the end of a broomstick; there is a blacksmith's forge and then a wheelwright's, with two or three new carts outside that partly block up the way. Then across an open space appears a white house beyond a grass mound ornamented by a Cupid, his finger on his lips; two brass vases are at each end of a flight of steps; scutcheons* blaze upon the door. It is the notary's house, and the finest in the place.

The church is on the other side of the street, twenty paces farther down, at the entrance of the square. The little cemetery that surrounds it, closed in by a wall breast-high, is so full of graves that the old stones, level with the ground, form a continuous pavement, on which the grass of itself has marked out regular green squares. The church was rebuilt during the last years of the reign of Charles X. The wooden roof is beginning to rot from the top, and here and there has black hollows in its blue colour. Over the door, where the organ should be, is a loft for the men, with a spiral staircase that reverberates under their wooden shoes.

The daylight coming through the plain glass windows falls obliquely upon the pews ranged along the walls, which are adorned here and there with a straw mat bearing beneath it the words in large letters, "Mr. So-and-

*The *panonceaux* that have to be hung over the doors of notaries.—Trans.

so's pew." Farther on, at a spot where the building narrows, the confessional forms a pendant to a statuette of the Virgin, clothed in a satin robe, coifed with a tulle veil sprinkled with silver stars, and with red cheeks, like an idol of the Sandwich Islands; and, finally, a copy of the "Holy Family, presented by the Minister of the Interior," overlooking the high altar, between four candlesticks, closes in the perspective. The choir stalls, of deal wood, have been left unpainted.

The market, that is to say, a tiled roof supported by some twenty posts, occupies of itself about half the public square of Yonville. The town hall, constructed "from the designs of a Paris architect," is a sort of Greek temple that forms the corner next to the chemist's shop. On the ground-floor are three Ionic columns and on the first floor a semicircular gallery, while the dome that crowns it is occupied by a Gallic cock, resting one foot upon the "Charte" and holding in the other the scales of Justice.

But that which most attracts the eye is opposite the "Lion d'Or" inn, the chemist's shop of Monsieur Homais. In the evening especially its argand lamp is lit up and the red and green jars that embellish his shop-front throw far across the street their two streams of colour; then across them as if in Bengal lights is seen the shadow of the chemist leaning over his desk. His house from top to bottom is placarded with inscriptions written in large hand, round hand, printed hand: "Vichy, Seltzer, Barège waters, blood purifiers, Raspail patent medicine, Arabian racahout, Darcet lozenges, Regnault paste, trusses, baths, hygienic chocolate," &c. And the signboard, which takes up all the breadth of the shop, bears in gold letters, "Homais, Chemist." Then at the back of the shop, behind the great scales fixed to the counter, the word "Laboratory" appears on a scroll above a glass door, which about half-way up once more repeats "Homais" in gold letters on a black ground.

Beyond this there is nothing to see at Yonville. The street (the only one) a gunshot in length and flanked by a few shops on either side stops short at the turn of the highroad. If it is left on the right hand and the foot of the Saint-Jean hills followed the cemetery is soon reached.

At the time of the cholera, in order to enlarge this, a piece of wall was pulled down, and three acres of land by its side purchased; but all the new portion is almost tenantless; the tombs, as heretofore, continue to crowd together towards the gate. The keeper, who is at once gravedigger and church beadle (thus making a double profit out of the parish corpses), has taken advantage of the unused plot of ground to plant potatoes there. From year to year, however, his small field grows smaller, and when there is an epidemic, he does not know whether to rejoice at the deaths or regret the burials.

"You live on the dead, Lestiboudois!" the curé at last said to him one day. This grim remark made him reflect; it checked him for some time; but to this day he carries on the cultivation of his little tubers, and even maintains stoutly that they grow naturally.

Since the events about to be narrated, nothing in fact has changed at

Yonville. The tin tricolour flag still swings at the top of the church-steeple; the two chintz streamers still flutter in the wind from the linendraper's; the chemist's fœtuses, like lumps of white amadou, rot more and more in their turbid alcohol, and above the big door of the inn the old golden lion, faded by rain, still shows passers-by its poodle mane.

On the evening when the Bovarys were to arrive at Yonville, Widow Lefrançois, the landlady of this inn, was so very busy that she sweated great drops as she moved her saucepans. To-morrow was market-day. The meat had to be cut beforehand, the fowls drawn, the soup and coffee made. Moreover, she had the boarders' meal to see to, and that of the doctor, his wife, and their servant; the billiard-room was echoing with bursts of laughter; three millers in the small parlour were calling for brandy; the wood was blazing, the brazen pan was hissing, and on the long kitchen-table, amid the quarters of raw mutton, rose piles of plates that rattled with the shaking of the block on which spinach was being chopped. From the poultry-yard was heard the screaming of the fowls whom the servant was chasing in order to wring their necks.

A man slightly marked with smallpox, in green leather slippers, and wearing a velvet cap with a gold tassel, was warming his back at the chimney. His face expressed nothing but self-satisfaction, and he appeared to take life as calmly as the goldfinch suspended over his head in its wicker cage: this was the chemist.

"Artémise!" shouted the landlady, "chop some wood, fill the water bottles, bring some brandy, look sharp! If only I knew what dessert to offer the guests you are expecting! Good heavens! Those furniture-movers are beginning their racket in the billiard-room again; and their van has been left before the front door! The 'Hirondelle' might run into it when it draws up. Call Polyte and tell him to put it up. Only to think, Monsieur Homais, that since morning they have had about fifteen games, and drunk eight jars of cider! Why, they'll tear my cloth for me," she went on, looking at them from a distance, her strainer in her hand.

"That wouldn't be much of a loss," replied Monsieur Homais. "You would buy another."

"Another billiard-table!" exclaimed the widow.

"Since that one is coming to pieces, Madame Lefrançois. I tell you again you are doing yourself harm, much harm! And besides, players now want narrow pockets and heavy cues. Hazards aren't played now; everything is changed! One must keep pace with the times! Just look at Tellier!"

The hostess reddened with vexation. The chemist went on—

"You may say what you like; his table is better than yours; and if one were to think, for example, of getting up a patriotic pool for Poland or the sufferers from the Lyons floods——"

"It isn't beggars like him that'll frighten us," interrupted the landlady, shrugging her fat shoulders. "Come, come, Monsieur Homais; as long as the 'Lion d'Or' exists people will come to it. We've feathered our nest; while one of these days you'll find the 'Café Français' closed with a big placard on the shutters. Change my billiard-table!" she went on, speaking to herself, "the table that comes in so handy for folding the washing, and on which, in the hunting season, I have slept six visitors! But that dawdler, Hivert, doesn't come!"

"Are you waiting for him for your gentlemen's dinner?"

"Wait for him! And what about Monsieur Binet? As the clock strikes six you'll see him come in, for he hasn't his equal under the sun for punctuality. He must always have his seat in the small parlour. He'd rather die than dine anywhere else. And so squeamish as he is, and so particular about the cider! Not like Monsieur Léon; he sometimes comes at seven, or even half-past, and he doesn't so much as look at what he eats. Such a nice young man! Never speaks a rough word!"

"Well, you see, there's a great difference between an educated man and an old carabineer who is now a tax-collector."

Six o'clock struck. Binet came in.

He wore a blue frock-coat falling in a straight line round his thin body, and his leather cap, with its lappets knotted over the top of his head with string, showed under the turned-up peak a bald forehead, flattened by the constant wearing of a helmet. He wore a black waistcoat, a hair collar, grey trousers, and, all the year round, well-blacked boots, that had two parallel swellings due to the sticking out of his big-toes. Not a hair stood out from the regular line of fair whiskers, which, encircling his jaws, framed, after the fashion of a garden border, his long, wan face, whose eyes were small and the nose hooked. Clever at all games of cards, a good hunter, and writing a fine hand, he had at home a lathe, and amused himself by turning napkin-rings, with which he filled up his house, with the jealousy of an artist and the egotism of a bourgeois.

He went to the small parlour, but the three millers had to be got out first, and during the whole time necessary for laying the cloth, Binet remained silent in his place near the stove. Then he shut the door and took off his cap in his usual way.

"It isn't with saying civil things that he'll wear out his tongue," said the chemist, as soon as he was alone with the landlady.

"He never talks more," she replied. "Last week two travellers in the cloth line were here—such clever chaps, who told such jokes in the evening, that I fairly cried with laughing; and he stood there like a dab fish and never said a word."

"Yes," observed the chemist; "no imagination, no sallies, nothing that makes the society-man."

"Yet they say he has parts," objected the landlady.

"Parts!" replied Monsieur Homais; "he, parts! In his own line it is possible," he added in a calmer tone. And he went on—

"Ah! that a merchant, who has large connections, a juris-consult, a doctor, a chemist, should be thus absent-minded, that they should become whimsical or even peevish, I can understand; such cases are cited in history. But at least it is because they are thinking of something. Myself, for example, how often has it happened to me to look on the bureau for my pen to write a label, and to find after all, that I had put it behind my ear?"

Madame Lefrançois just then went to the door to see if the "Hirondelle" were not coming. She started. A man dressed in black suddenly came into the kitchen. By the last gleam of the twilight one could see that his face was rubicund and his form athletic.

"What can I do for you, Monsieur le Curé?" asked the landlady, as she reached down from the chimney one of the copper candlesticks placed with their candles in a row. "Will you take something? A thimbleful of *Cassis?* A glass of wine?"

The priest declined very politely. He had come for his umbrella, that he had forgotten the other day at the Ernemont convent, and after asking Madame Lefrançois to have it sent to him at the presbytery in the evening, he left for the church, from which the Angelus was ringing.

When the chemist no longer heard the noise of his boots along the square, he thought the priest's behaviour just now very unbecoming. This refusal to take any refreshment seemed to him the most odious hypocrisy; all priests tippled on the sly, and were trying to bring back the days of the tithe.

The landlady took up the defence of her curé.

"Besides, he could double up four men like you over his knee. Last year he helped our people to bring in the straw; he carried as many as six trusses at once, he is so strong."

"Bravo!" said the chemist. "Now just send your daughters to confess to fellows with such a temperament! I, if I were the Government, I'd have the priests bled once a month. Yes, Madame Lefrançois, every month—a good phlebotomy, in the interests of the police and morals."

"Be quiet, Monsieur Homais. You are an infidel; you've no religion."

The chemist answered: "I have a religion, my religion, and I even have more than all these others with their mummeries and their juggling. I adore God, on the contrary. I believe in the Supreme Being, in a Creator, whatever he may be. I care little who has placed us here below to fulfil our duties as citizens and fathers of families; but I don't need to go to church to kiss silver plates, and fatten, out of my pocket, a lot of good-for-nothings who live better than we do. For one can know him as well in a wood, in a field, or even contemplating the eternal vault like the ancients. My God! mine is the God of Socrates, of Franklin, of Voltaire, and of Béranger! I am for the profession of faith of the 'Savoyard Vicar,' and the immortal principles of '89! And I can't admit of an old boy of a God who takes walks in his garden with a cane in his hand, who lodges his friends in the belly of whales, dies uttering a cry, and rises again at the end of three days; things absurd in themselves, and completely opposed, moreover, to all physical laws, which proves to us, by the way, that priests have always wallowed in turpid ignorance, in which they would fain engulf the people with them."

He ceased looking round for an audience, for in his bubbling over the chemist had for a moment fancied himself in the midst of the town council. But the landlady no longer heeded him; she was listening to a distant rolling. One could distinguish the noise of a carriage mingled with the clattering of loose horseshoes that beat against the ground, and at last the "Hirondelle" stopped at the door.

It was a yellow box on two large wheels, that, reaching to the tilt, prevented travellers from seeing the road and dirtied their shoulders. The small panes of the narrow windows rattled in their sashes when the coach was closed, and retained here and there patches of mud amid the old layers of dust, that not even storms of rain had altogether washed away. It was drawn by three horses, the first a leader, and when it came down-hill its bottom jolted against the ground.

Some of the inhabitants of Yonville came out into the square; they all spoke at once, asking for news, for explanations, for hampers. Hivert did not know whom to answer. It was he who did the errands of the place in town. He went to the shops and brought back rolls of leather for the shoemaker, old iron for the farrier, a barrel of herrings for his mistress, caps from the milliner's, locks from the hairdresser's, and all along the road on his return journey he distributed his parcels, which he threw, standing upright on his seat and shouting at the top of his voice, over the enclosures of the yards.

An accident had delayed him. Madame Bovary's greyhound had run across the field. They had whistled for him a quarter of an hour; Hivert had even gone back a mile and a half expecting every moment to catch sight of her; but it had been necessary to go on. Emma had wept, grown angry; she had accused Charles of this misfortune. Monsieur Lheureux, a draper, who happened to be in the coach with her, had tried to console her by a number of examples of lost dogs recognising their masters at the end of long years. One, he said, had been told of, who had come back to Paris from Constantinople. Another had gone one hundred and fifty miles in a straight line, and swum four rivers; and his own father had possessed a poodle, which, after twelve years of absence, had all of a sudden jumped on his back in the street as he was going to dine in town.

II

EMMA GOT OUT FIRST, then Félicité, Monsieur Lheureux, and a nurse, and they had to wake up Charles in his corner, where he had slept soundly since night set in.

Homais introduced himself; he offered his homages to madame and his respects to monsieur; said he was charmed to have been able to render them some slight service, and added with a cordial air that he had ventured to invite himself, his wife being away.

When Madame Bovary was in the kitchen she went up to the chimney. With the tips of her fingers she caught her dress at the knee, and having thus pulled it up to her ankle, held out her foot in its black boot to the fire above the revolving leg of mutton. The flame lit up the whole of her, penetrating with a crude light the woof of her gown, the fine pores of her fair skin, and even her eyelids, which she blinked now and again. A great red glow passed over her with the blowing of the wind through the half-open door. On the other side of the chimney a young man with fair hair watched her silently.

As he was a good deal bored at Yonville, where he was a clerk at the notary's, Monsieur Guillaumin, Monsieur Léon Dupuis (it was he who was the second *habitué* of the "Lion d'Or") frequently put back his dinner-hour in the hope that some traveller might come to the inn, with whom he could chat in the evening. On the days when his work was done early, he had, for want of something else to do, to come punctually, and endure from soup to cheese a *tête-à-tête* with Binet. It was therefore with delight that he accepted the landlady's suggestion that he should dine in company with the newcomers, and they passed into the large parlour where Madame Lefrançois, for the purpose of showing off, had had the table laid for four.

Homais asked to be allowed to keep on his skull-cap, for fear of coryza; then, turning to his neighbour—

"Madame is no doubt a little fatigued; one gets jolted so abominably in our 'Hirondelle.' "

"That is true," replied Emma; "but moving about always amuses me. I like change of place."

"It is so tedious," sighed the clerk, "to be always riveted to the same places."

"If you were like me," said Charles, "constantly obliged to be in the saddle——"

"But," Léon went on, addressing himself to Madame Bovary, "nothing, it seems to me, is more pleasant—when one can," he added.

"Moreover," said the druggist, "the practice of medicine is not very hard work in our part of the world, for the state of our roads allows us the use of gigs, and generally, as the farmers are well off, they pay pretty well. We have, medically speaking, besides the ordinary cases of enteritis, bronchitis, bilious affections, and so on, now and then a few intermittent fevers at harvest-time; but on the whole, little of a serious nature, nothing special to note, unless it be a great deal of scrofula, due, no doubt, to the deplorable hygienic conditions of our peasant dwellings. Ah! you will find many prejudices to combat, Monsieur Bovary, much obstinacy of routine, with which all the efforts of your science will daily come into collision; for people still have recourse to novenas, to relics, to the priest, rather than come straight to the doctor or the chemist. The climate, however, is not, truth to tell, bad, and we even have a few nonagenarians in our parish. The thermometer (I have made some observations) falls in winter to 4 degrees, and in the hottest season rises to 25 or 35 degrees Centigrade at the outside, which gives us 24 degrees Réaumur as the maximum, or otherwise 54 degrees Fahrenheit (English scale), not more. And, as a matter of fact, we are sheltered from the north winds by the forest of Argueil on the one side, from the west winds by the Saint-Jean range on the other; and this heat, moreover, which, on account of the aqueous vapours given off by the river and the considerable number of cattle in the fields, which, as you know, exhale much ammonia, that is to say, nitrogen, hydrogen, and oxygen (no, nitrogen and hydrogen alone), and which sucking up into itself the humus from the ground, mixing together all those different emanations, unites them into a stack, so to say, and combining with the electricity diffused through the atmosphere, when there is any, might in the long-run, as in tropical countries, engender insalubrious miasmata,—this heat, I say, finds itself perfectly tempered on the side whence it comes, or rather whence it should come—that is to say, the southern side—by the southeastern winds, which, having cooled themselves passing over the Seine, reach us sometimes all at once like breezes from Russia."

"At any rate, you have some walks in the neighbourhood?" continued Madame Bovary, speaking to the young man.

"Oh, very few," he answered. "There is a place they call La Pâture, on the top of the hill, on the edge of the forest. Sometimes, on Sundays, I go and stay there with a book, watching the sunset."

"I think there is nothing so admirable as sunsets," she resumed; "but especially by the side of the sea."

"Oh, I adore the sea!" said Monsieur Léon.

"And then, does it not seem to you," continued Madame Bovary, "that the mind travels more freely on this limitless expanse, the contemplation of which elevates the soul, gives ideas of the infinite, the ideal?"

"It is the same with mountainous landscapes," continued Léon. "A cousin of mine who travelled in Switzerland last year told me that one could not picture to oneself the poetry of the lakes, the charm of the waterfalls, the gigantic effect of the glaciers. One sees pines of incredible size across torrents, cottages suspended over precipices, and, a thousand feet below one, whole valleys when the clouds open. Such spectacles must stir to enthusiasm, incline to prayer, to ecstasy; and I no longer marvel at that celebrated musician who, the better to inspire his imagination, was in the habit of playing the piano before some imposing site."

"You play?" she asked.

"No, but I am very fond of music," he replied.

"Ah! don't you listen to him, Madame Bovary," interrupted Homais, bending over his plate. "That's sheer modesty. Why, my dear fellow, the other day in your room you were singing 'L'Ange Gardien' ravishingly. I heard you from the laboratory. You gave it like an actor."

Léon, in fact, lodged at the chemist's, where he had a small room on the second floor, overlooking the Place. He blushed at the compliment of his landlord, who had already turned to the doctor, and was enumerating to him, one after the other, all the principal inhabitants of Yonville. He was telling anecdotes, giving information; the fortune of the notary was not known exactly, and "there was the Tuvache household," who made a good deal of show.

Emma continued, "And what music do you prefer?"

"Oh, German music; that which makes you dream."

"Have you been to the opera?"

"Not yet; but I shall go next year, when I am living at Paris to finish reading for the bar."

"As I had the honour of putting it to your husband," said the chemist, "with regard to this poor Yanoda who has run away, you will find yourself, thanks to his extravagance, in the possession of one of the most comfortable houses of Yonville. Its greatest convenience for a doctor is a door giving on the Walk, where one can go in and out unseen. Moreover, it contains everything that is agreeable in a household—a laundry, kitchen with offices, sitting-room, fruit-room, and so on. He was a gay dog, who didn't care what he spent. At the end of the garden, by the side of the water, he had an arbour built just for the purpose of drinking beer in summer; and if madame is fond of gardening she will be able——"

"My wife doesn't care about it," said Charles; "although she has been advised to take exercise, she prefers always sitting in her room reading."

"Like me," replied Léon. "And indeed, what is better than to sit by one's fireside in the evening with a book, while the wind beats against the window and the lamp is burning?"

"What, indeed?" she said, fixing her large black eyes wide open upon him.

"One thinks of nothing," he continued; "the hours slip by. Motionless we traverse countries we fancy we see, and your thought, blending with the fiction, playing with the details, follows the outline of the adventures. It mingles with the characters, and it seems as if it were yourself palpitating beneath their costumes."

"That is true! that is true!" she said.

"Has it ever happened to you," Léon went on, "to come across some vague idea of one's own in a book, some dim image that comes back to you from afar, and as the completest expression of your own slightest sentiment?"

"I have experienced it," she replied.

"That is why," he said, "I especially love the poets. I think verse more tender than prose, and that it moves far more easily to tears."

"Still in the long-run it is tiring," continued Emma. "Now I, on the contrary, adore stories that rush breathlessly along, that frighten one. I detest commonplace heroes and moderate sentiments, such as there are in nature."

"In fact," observed the clerk, "these works, not touching the heart, miss, it seems to me, the true end of art. It is so sweet, amid all the disenchantments of life, to be able to dwell in thought upon noble characters, pure affections, and pictures of happiness. For myself, living here far from the world, this is my one distraction; but Yonville affords so few resources."

"Like Tostes, no doubt," replied Emma; "and so I always subscribed to a lending library."

"If madame will do me the honour of making use of it," said the chemist, who had just caught the last words, "I have at her disposal a library composed of the best authors, Voltaire, Rousseau, Delille, Walter Scott, the 'Echo des Feuilletons'; and in addition I receive various periodicals, among them the 'Fanal de Rouen' daily, having the advantage to be its correspondent for the districts of Buchy, Forges, Neufchâtel, Yonville, and vicinity."

For two hours and a half they had been at table; for the servant Artémise, carelessly dragging her old list slippers over the flags, brought one plate after the other, forgot everything, and constantly left the door of the billiard-room half open, so that it beat against the wall with its hooks.

Unconsciously, Léon, while talking, had placed his foot on one of the bars of the chair on which Madame Bovary was sitting. She wore a small blue silk necktie, that kept up like a ruff a gauffered cambric collar, and with the movements of her head the lower part of her face gently sunk into the linen or came out from it. Thus side by side, while Charles and the chemist chatted, they entered into one of those vague conversations where the hazard of all that is said brings you back to the fixed centre of a common sympathy. The Paris theatres, titles of novels, new quadrilles, and the world they did not know; Tostes, where she had lived, and Yonville, where they were; they examined all, talked of everything till the end of dinner.

When coffee was served Félicité went away to get ready the room in the new house, and the guests soon raised the siege. Madame Lefrançois was asleep near the cinders, while the stable-boy, lantern in hand, was waiting to show Monsieur and Madame Bovary the way home. Bits of straw stuck in his red hair, and he limped with his left leg. When he had taken in his other hand the curé's umbrella, they started.

The town was asleep; the pillars of the market threw great shadows; the earth was all grey as on a summer's night. But as the doctor's house was only some fifty paces from the inn, they had to say good-night almost immediately, and the company dispersed.

As soon as she entered the passage, Emma felt the cold of the plaster fall about her shoulders like damp linen. The walls were new and the wooden stairs creaked. In their bedroom, on the first floor, a whitish light passed through the curtainless windows. She could catch glimpses of tree-tops, and beyond, the fields, half-drowned in the fog that lay reeking in the moonlight along the course of the river. In the middle of the room, pell-mell, were scattered drawers, bottles, curtain-rods, gilt poles, with mattresses on the chairs and basins on the ground,—the two men who had brought the furniture had left everything about carelessly.

This was the fourth time that she had slept in a strange place. The first was the day of her going to the convent; the second, of her arrival at Tostes; the third, at Vaubyessard; and this was the fourth. And each one had marked, as it were, the inauguration of a new phase in her life. She did not believe that things could present themselves in the same way in different places, and since the portion of her life lived had been bad, no doubt that which remained to be lived would be better.

III

The next day, as she was getting up, she saw the clerk on the Place. She had on a dressing-gown. He looked up and bowed. She nodded quickly and reclosed the window.

Léon waited all day for six o'clock in the evening to come, but on going to the inn, he found no one but Monsieur Binet, already at table. The dinner of the evening before had been a considerable event for him; he had never till then talked for two hours consecutively to a "lady." How then had he been able to explain, and in such language, the number of things that he could not have said so well before? He was usually shy, and maintained that reserve which partakes at once of modesty and dissimulation. At Yonville he was considered "well-bred." He listened to the arguments of the older people, and did not seem hot about politics—a remarkable thing for a young man. Then he had some accomplishments; he painted in water-colours, could read the key of G, and readily talked literature after dinner when he did not play cards. Monsieur Homais respected him for his education; Madame Homais liked him for his good-nature, for he often took the little Homais into the garden—little brats who were always dirty, very much spoilt, and somewhat lymphatic, like their mother. Besides the servant to look after them, they had Justin, the chemist's apprentice, a second cousin of Monsieur Homais, who had been taken into the house from charity, and who was useful at the same time as a servant.

The druggist proved the best of neighbours. He gave Madame Bovary information as to the tradespeople, sent expressly for his own cider merchant, tasted the drink himself, and saw that the casks were properly placed in the cellar; he explained how to set about getting in a supply of butter cheap, and made an arrangement with Lestiboudois, the sacristan, who, besides his sacerdotal and funereal functions, looked after the principal gardens at Yonville by the hour or the year, according to the taste of the customers.

The need of looking after others was not the only thing that urged the chemist to such obsequious cordiality; there was a plan underneath it all.

He had infringed the law of the 19th Ventôse, year xi., article 1, which forbade all persons not having a diploma to practise medicine; so that, after certain anonymous denunciations, Homais had been summoned to Rouen to see the procurer of the king in his own private room; the magistrate receiving him standing up, ermine on shoulder and cap on head. It was in the morning, before the court opened. In the corridors one heard the heavy boots of the gendarmes walking past, and like a far-off noise great locks that were shut. The druggist's ears tingled as if he were about to have an apoplectic stroke; he saw the depths of dungeons, his family in tears, his shop sold, all the jars dispersed; and he was obliged to enter a café and take a glass of rum and seltzer to recover his spirits.

Little by little the memory of this reprimand grew fainter, and he continued, as heretofore, to give anodyne consultations in his back-parlour. But the mayor resented it, his colleagues were jealous, everything was to be feared; gaining over Monsieur Bovary by his attentions was to earn his gratitude, and prevent his speaking out later on, should he notice anything. So every morning Homais brought him "the paper," and often in the afternoon left his shop for a few moments to have a chat with the Doctor.

Charles was dull: patients did not come. He remained seated for hours without speaking, went into his consulting-room to sleep, or watched his wife sewing. Then for diversion he employed himself at home as a workman; he even tried to do up the attic with some paint which had been left behind by the painters. But money matters worried him. He had spent so much for repairs at Tostes, for madame's toilette, and for the moving, that the whole dowry, over three thousand crowns, had slipped away in two years. Then how many things had been spoilt or lost during their carriage from Tostes to Yonville, without counting the plaster curé, who, falling out of the coach at an over-severe jolt, had been dashed into a thousand fragments on the pavement of Quincampoix!

A pleasanter trouble came to distract him, namely, the pregnancy of his wife. As the time of her confinement approached he cherished her the more. It was another bond of the flesh establishing itself, and, as it were, a continued sentiment of a more complex union. When from afar he saw her languid walk, and her figure without stays turning softly on her hips; when opposite one another he looked at her at his ease, while she took tired poses in her armchair, then his happiness knew no bounds; he got up, embraced her, passed his hands over her face, called her little mamma, wanted to make her dance, and, half-laughing, half-crying, uttered all kinds of caressing pleasantries that came into his head. The idea of having begotten a child delighted him. Now he wanted nothing. He knew human life from end to end, and he sat down to it with serenity.

Emma at first felt a great astonishment; then was anxious to be delivered that she might know what it was to be a mother. But not being able to spend as much as she would have liked, to have a swing-bassinette with rose silk curtains, and embroidered caps, in a fit of bitterness she gave up looking after the trousseau, and ordered the whole of it from a village needlewoman, without choosing or discussing anything. Thus she did not amuse herself with those preparations that stimulate the tenderness of mothers, and so her affection was from the very outset, perhaps, to some extent attenuated.

As Charles, however, spoke of the boy at every meal, she soon began to think of him more consecutively.

She hoped for a son; he would be strong and dark; she would call him George; and this idea of having a male child was like an expected revenge for all her impotence in the past. A man, at least, is free; he may travel over passions and over countries, overcome obstacles, taste of the most far-away pleasures. But a woman is always hampered. At once inert and flexible, she has against her the weakness of the flesh and legal dependence. Her will, like the veil of her bonnet, held by a string, flutters in every wind; there is always some desire that draws her, some conventionality that restrains.

She was confined on a Sunday at about six o'clock, as the sun was rising.

"It is a girl!" said Charles.

She turned her head away and fainted.

Madame Homais, as well as Madame Lefrançois of the Lion d'Or, almost immediately came running in to embrace her. The chemist, as a man of discretion, only offered a few provisional felicitations through the half-opened door. He wished to see the child, and thought it well made.

Whilst she was getting well she occupied herself much in seeking a name for her daughter. First she went over all those that have Italian endings, such as Clara, Louisa, Amanda, Atala; she liked Galsuinde pretty well, and Yseult or Léocadie still better. Charles wanted the child to be called after her mother; Emma opposed this. They ran over the calendar from end to end, and then consulted outsiders.

"Monsieur Léon," said the chemist, "with whom I was talking about it the other day, wonders you do not choose Madeleine. It is very much in fashion just now."

But Madame Bovary senior cried out loudly against this name of a sinner. As to Monsieur Homais, he had a preference for all those that recalled some great man, an illustrious fact, or a generous idea, and it was on this system that he had baptized his four children. Thus Napoléon represented glory and Franklin liberty; Irma was perhaps a concession to romanticism, but Athalie was a homage to the greatest masterpiece of the French stage. For his philosophical convictions did not interfere with his artistic tastes; in him the thinker did not stifle the man of sentiment; he could make distinctions, make allowances for imagination, and fanaticism. In this tragedy, for example, he found fault with the ideas, but admired the style; he detested the conception, but applauded all the details, and loathed the characters while he grew enthusiastic over their dialogue. When he read the fine passages he was transported, but when he thought that mummers would get something out of them for their show, he was disconsolate; and in this confusion of sentiments in which he was involved he would have liked at once to crown Racine with both his hands and discuss with him for a good quarter of an hour.

At last Emma remembered that at the château of Vaubyessard she had heard the Marchioness call a young lady Berthe; from that moment this name was chosen; and as old Rouault could not come, Monsieur Homais was requested to stand godfather. His gifts were all products from his establishment, to wit: six boxes of jujubes, a whole jar of racahout, three cakes of marshmallow paste, and six sticks of sugar-candy into the bargain that he had come across in a cupboard. On the evening of the ceremony there was a grand dinner; the curé was present; there was much excitement.

Monsieur Homais towards liqueur-time began singing "Le Dieu des bonnes gens." Monsieur Léon sang a barcarolle, and Madame Bovary senior who was godmother, a romance of the time of the Empire; finally, Monsieur Bovary senior insisted on having the child brought down, and began baptizing it with a glass of champagne that he poured over its head. This mockery of the first of the sacraments made the Abbé Bournisien angry; old Bovary replied by a quotation from "La Guerre des Dieux"; the curé wanted to leave; the ladies implored, Homais interfered; and they succeeded in making the priest sit down again, and he quietly went on with the half-finished coffee in his saucer.

Monsieur Bovary senior stayed at Yonville a month dazzling the natives by a superb policeman's cap with silver tassels that he wore in the morning when he smoked his pipe in the square. Being also in the habit of drinking a good deal of brandy, he often sent the servant to the "Lion d'Or" to buy him a bottle, which was put down to his son's account, and to perfume his handkerchiefs he used up his daughter-in-law's whole supply of eau-de-cologne.

The latter did not at all dislike his company. He had knocked about the world, he talked about Berlin, Vienna, and Strasbourg, of his soldier times, of the mistresses he had had, the grand luncheons of which he had partaken; then he was amiable, and sometimes even, either on the stairs or in the garden, would seize hold of her waist, crying, "Charles, look out for yourself."

Then Madame Bovary senior became alarmed for her son's happiness, and fearing that her husband might in the long-run have an immoral influence upon the ideas of the young woman, took care to hurry their departure. Perhaps she had more serious reasons for uneasiness. Monsieur Bovary was not the man to respect anything.

One day Emma was suddenly seized with the desire to see her little girl, who had been put to nurse with the carpenter's wife, and without looking at the almanac to see whether the six weeks of the Virgin were yet passed, she set out for the Rollets' house, situated at the extreme end of the village, between the highroad and the fields.

It was midday, the shutters of the houses were closed and the slate roofs that glittered beneath the fierce light of the blue sky seemed to strike sparks from the crest of their gables. A heavy wind was blowing; Emma felt weak as she walked; the stones of the pavement hurt her; she was doubtful whether she would not go home again, or go in somewhere to rest.

At this moment Monsieur Léon came out from a neighbouring door with a bundle of papers under his arm. He came to greet her, and stood in the shade in front of Lheureux's shop under the projecting grey awning.

Madame Bovary said she was going to see her baby, but that she was beginning to grow tired.

"If——" said Léon, not daring to go on.

"Have you any business to attend to?" she asked.

And on the clerk's answer, she begged him to accompany her. That same evening this was known in Yonville, and Madame Tuvache, the mayor's wife, declared in the presence of her servant that "Madame Bovary was compromising herself."

To get to the nurse's it was necessary to turn to the left on leaving the street, as if making for the cemetery, and to follow between little houses and yards a small path bordered with privet hedges. They were in bloom, and so were the speedwells, eglantines, thistles, and the sweetbriar that sprang up from the thickets. Through openings in the hedges one could see into the huts, some pigs on a dung-heap, or tethered cows rubbing their horns against the trunk of trees. The two, side by side, walked slowly, she leaning upon him, and he restraining his pace, which he regulated by hers; in front of them a swarm of midges fluttered, buzzing in the warm air.

They recognised the house by an old walnut-tree which shaded it. Low and covered with brown tiles, there hung outside it, beneath the dormer-window of the garret, a string of onions. Faggots upright against a thorn fence surrounded a bed of lettuces, a few square feet of lavender, and sweet peas strung on sticks. Dirty water was running here and there on the grass, and all round were several indefinite rags, knitted stockings, a red calico jacket, and a large sheet of coarse linen spread over the hedge. At the noise of the gate the nurse appeared with a baby she was suckling on one arm. With her other hand she was pulling along a poor puny little fellow, his face covered with scrofula, the son of a Rouen hosier, whom his parents, too taken up with their business, left in the country.

"Go in," she said; "your little one is there asleep."

The room on the ground-floor, the only one in the dwelling, had at its farther end, against the wall, a large bed without curtains, while a kneading-trough took up the side by the window, one pane of which was mended with a piece of blue paper. In the corner behind the door, shining hob-nailed shoes stood in a row under the slab of the washstand, near a bottle of oil with a feather stuck in its mouth; a *Matthieu Laensberg* lay on the dusty mantelpiece amid gunflints, candle-ends, and bits of amadou. Finally, the last luxury in the apartment was a "Fame" blowing her trumpets, a picture cut out, no doubt, from some perfumer's prospectus and nailed to the wall with six wooden shoe-pegs.

Emma's child was asleep in a wicker-cradle. She took it up in the wrapping that enveloped it and began singing softly as she rocked herself to and fro.

Léon walked up and down the room; it seemed strange to him to see this beautiful woman in her nankeen dress in the midst of all this poverty. Madame Bovary reddened; he turned away, thinking perhaps there had been an impertinent look in his eyes. Then she put back the little girl, who had just been sick over her collar. The nurse at once came to dry her, protesting that it wouldn't show.

"She gives me other doses," she said: "I am always a-washing of her. If you would have the goodness to order Camus, the grocer, to let me have a little soap; it would really be more convenient for you, as I needn't trouble you then."

"Very well! very well!" said Emma. "Good morning, Madame Rollet," and she went out, wiping her shoes at the door.

The good woman accompanied her to the end of the garden, talking all the time of the trouble she had getting up of nights.

"I'm that worn out sometimes as I drop asleep on my chair. I'm sure you might at least give me just a pound of ground coffee; that'd last me a month, and I'd take it of a morning with some milk."

After having submitted to her thanks, Madame Bovary left. She had gone a little way down the path when, at the sound of wooden shoes, she turned round. It was the nurse.

"What is it?"

Then the peasant woman, taking her aside behind an elm tree, began talking to her of her husband, who with his trade and six francs a year that the captain——

"Oh, be quick!" said Emma.

"Well," the nurse went on, heaving sighs between each word, "I'm afraid he'll be put out seeing me have coffee alone, you know men——"

"But you are to have some," Emma repeated; "I will give you some. You bother me!"

"Oh, dear! my poor, dear lady! you see, in consequence of his wounds he has terrible cramps in the chest. He even says that cider weakens him."

"Do make haste, Mère Rollet!"

"Well," the latter continued making a curtsey, "if it weren't asking too much," and she curtsied once more, "if you would"—and her eyes begged—"a jar of brandy," she said at last, "and I'd rub your little one's feet with it; they're as tender as one's tongue."

Once rid of the nurse, Emma again took Monsieur Léon's arm. She walked fast for some time, then more slowly, and looking straight in front of her, her eyes rested on the shoulder of the young man, whose frock-coat had a black-velvet collar. His brown hair fell over it, straight and carefully arranged. She noticed his nails, which were longer than one wore them at Yonville. It was one of the clerk's chief occupations to trim them, and for this purpose he kept a special knife in his writing-desk.

They returned to Yonville by the water-side. In the warm season the banks, wider than at other times, showed to their foot the garden walls whence a few steps led to the river. It flowed noiselessly, swift, and cold to the eyes; long, thin grasses huddled together in it as the current drove them, and spread themselves upon the limpid water like streaming hair; sometimes at the top of the reeds or on the leaf of a water-lily an insect with fine legs crawled or rested. The sun pierced with a ray the small blue bubbles of the waves that, breaking, followed each other; branchless old willows mirrored their grey backs in the water; beyond, all around, the meadows seemed empty. It was the dinner-hour at the farms, and the young woman and her companion heard nothing as they walked but the fall of their steps on the earth of the path, the words they spoke, and the sound of Emma's dress rustling round her.

The walls of the gardens with pieces of bottle on their coping were hot as the glass windows of a conservatory. Wallflowers had sprung up between the bricks, and with the tip of her open sunshade Madame Bovary, as she passed, made some of their faded flowers crumble into a yellow dust, or a spray of overhanging honeysuckle and clematis caught in its fringe and dangled for a moment over the silk.

They were talking of a troupe of Spanish dancers who were expected shortly at the Rouen theatre.

"Are you going?" she asked.

"If I can," he answered.

Had they nothing else to say to one another? Yet their eyes were full of more serious speech, and while they forced themselves to find trivial phrases, they felt the same languor stealing over them both. It was the whisper of the soul, deep, continuous, dominating that of their voices. Surprised with wonder at this strange sweetness, they did not think of speaking of the sensation or of seeking its cause. Coming joys, like tropical shores, throw over the immensity before them their inborn softness, and odorous wind, and we are lulled by this intoxication without a thought of the horizon that we do not even know.

In one place the ground had been trodden down by the cattle; they had to step on large green stones put here and there in the mud. She often stopped a moment to look where to place her foot, and tottering on the stone that shook, her arms outspread, her form bent forward with a look of indecision, she would laugh, afraid of falling into the puddles of water.

When they arrived in front of her garden, Madame Bovary opened the little gate, ran up the steps and disappeared.

Léon returned to his office. His chief was away; he just glanced at the briefs, then cut himself a pen, and at last took up his hat and went out.

He went to La Pâture at the top of the Argueil hills at the beginning of the forest; he threw himself upon the ground under the pines and watched the sky through his fingers.

"How bored I am!" he said to himself, "how bored I am!"

He thought he was to be pitied for living in this village, with Homais for a friend and Monsieur Guillaumin for master. The latter, entirely absorbed by his business, wearing gold-rimmed spectacles and red whiskers over a white cravat, understood nothing of mental refinements, although he affected a stiff English manner, which in the beginning had impressed the clerk.

As to the chemist's spouse, she was the best wife in Normandy, gentle as a sheep, loving her children, her father, her mother, her cousins, weeping for others' woes, letting everything go in her household, and detesting corsets; but so slow of movement, such a bore to listen to, so common in appearance, and of such restricted conversation, that although she was thirty, he only twenty, although they slept in rooms next each other and he spoke to her daily, he never thought that she might be a woman for another, or that she possessed anything else of her sex than the gown.

And what else was there? Binet, a few shopkeepers, two or three publicans, the curé, and, finally Monsieur Tuvache, the mayor, with his two sons, rich, crabbed, obtuse persons, who farmed their own lands, and had feasts among themselves, bigoted to boot, and quite unbearable companions.

But from the general background of all these human faces Emma's stood out isolated and yet farthest off; for between her and him he seemed to see a vague abyss.

In the beginning he had called on her several times along with the druggist. Charles had not appeared particularly anxious to see him again, and Léon did not know what to do between his fear of being indiscreet and the desire for an intimacy that seemed almost impossible.

IV

WHEN the first cold days set in Emma left her bed-room for the sitting-room, a long apartment with a low ceiling, in which there was on the mantelpiece a large bunch of coral spread out against the looking-glass. Seated in her armchair near the window, she could see the villagers pass along the pavement.

Twice a day Léon went from his office to the "Lion d'Or." Emma could hear him coming from afar; she leant forward listening, and the young man glided past the curtain, always dressed in the same way, and without turning his head. But in the twilight, when, her chin resting on her left hand, she let the embroidery she had begun fall on her knees, she often shuddered at the apparition of this shadow suddenly gliding past. She would get up and order the table to be laid.

Monsieur Homais called at dinner-time. Skull-cap in hand, he came in on tiptoe, in order to disturb no one, always repeating the same phrase, "Good evening, everybody." Then when he had taken his seat at table between the pair, he asked the doctor about his patients, and the latter consulted him as to the probability of their payment. Next they talked of "what was in the paper." Homais by this hour knew it almost by heart, and he repeated it from end to end, with the reflections of the penny-a-liners, and all the stories of individual catastrophes that had occurred in France or abroad. But the subject becoming exhausted, he was not slow in throwing out some remarks on the dishes before him. Sometimes even, half-rising, he delicately pointed out to madame the tenderest morsel, or turning to the servant, gave her some advice on the manipulation of stews and the hygiene of seasoning. He talked aroma, osmazome, juices, and gelatine in a bewildering manner. Moreover, Homais, with his head fuller of recipes than his shop of jars, excelled in making all kinds of preserves, vinegars, and sweet liqueurs; he knew also all the latest inventions in economic stoves, together with the art of preserving cheeses and of curing sick wines.

At eight o'clock Justin came to fetch him to shut up the shop. Then Monsieur Homais gave him a sly look, especially if Félicité was there, for he had noticed that his apprentice was fond of the doctor's house.

"The young dog," he said, "is beginning to have ideas, and the devil take me if I don't believe he's in love with your servant!"

But a more serious fault with which he reproached Justin was his constantly listening to conversation. On Sunday, for example, one could not get him out of the drawing-room, whither Madame Homais had called him to fetch the children, who were falling asleep in the armchairs, and dragging down with their backs calico chair-covers that were too large.

Not many people came to these soirées at the chemist's, his scandal-mongering and political opinions having successfully alienated various respectable persons from him. The clerk never failed to be there. As soon as he heard the bell he ran to meet Madame Bovary, took her shawl, and put away under the shop-counter the thick list shoes that she wore over her boots when there was snow.

First they played some hands at trente-et-un; next Monsieur Homais played écarté with Emma; Léon behind her gave her advice. Standing up with his hands on the back of her chair, he saw the teeth of her comb that bit into her chignon. With every movement that she made to throw her cards the right side of her dress was drawn up. From her turned-up hair a dark colour fell over her back, and growing gradually paler, lost itself little by little in the shade. Then her dress fell on both sides of her chair, puffing out full of folds, and reached the ground. When Léon occasionally felt the sole of his boot resting on it, he drew back as if he had trodden upon some one.

When the game of cards was over, the druggist and the Doctor played dominoes, and Emma, changing her place, leant her elbow on the table, turning over the leaves of "L'Illustration." She had brought her ladies' journal with her. Léon sat down near her; they looked at the engravings together, and waited for one another at the bottom of the pages. She often begged him to read her the verses; Léon declaimed them in a languid voice, to which he carefully gave a dying fall in the love passages. But the noise of the dominoes annoyed him. Monsieur Homais was strong at the game; he could beat Charles and give him a double-six. Then the three hundred finished, they both stretched themselves out in front of the fire, and were soon asleep. The fire was dying out in the cinders; the teapot was empty, Léon was still reading. Emma listened to him, mechanically turning round the lampshade, on the gauze of which were painted clowns in carriages, and tight-rope dancers with their balancing-poles. Léon stopped, pointing with a gesture to his sleeping audience; then they talked in low tones, and their conversation seemed the more sweet to them because it was unheard.

Thus a kind of bond was established between them, a constant commerce of books and of romances. Monsieur Bovary, little given to jealousy, did not trouble himself about it.

On his birthday he received a beautiful phrenological head, all marked with figures to the thorax and painted blue. This was an attention of the clerk's. He showed him many others, even to doing errands for him at Rouen; and the book of a novelist having made the mania for cactuses fashionable, Léon bought some for Madame Bovary, bringing them back on his knees in the "Hirondelle," pricking his fingers with their hard hairs.

She had a board with a balustrade fixed against her window to hold the pots. The clerk, too, had his small hanging garden; they saw each other tending their flowers at their windows.

Of the windows of the village there was one yet more often occupied; for on Sundays from morning to night, and every morning when the weather was bright, one could see at the dormer-window of a garret the profile of Monsieur Binet bending over his lathe, whose monotonous humming could be heard at the "Lion d'Or."

One evening on coming home Léon found in his room a rug in velvet and wool with leaves on a pale ground. He called Madame Homais, Monsieur Homais, Justin, the children, the cook; he spoke of it to his chief; every one wanted to see this rug. Why did the doctor's wife give the clerk presents? It looked queer. They decided that she must be his lover.

He made this seem likely, so ceaselessly did he talk of her charms and of her wit; so much so, that Binet once roughly answered him—

"What does it matter to me since I'm not in her set?"

He tortured himself to find out how he could make his declaration to her, and always halting between the fear of displeasing her and the shame of being such a coward, he wept with discouragement and desire. Then he took energetic resolutions, wrote letters that he tore up, put it off to times that he again deferred. Often he set out with the determination to dare all; but this resolution soon deserted him in Emma's presence, and when Charles, dropping in, invited him to jump into his chaise to go with him to see some patient in the neighbourhood, he at once accepted, bowed to madame, and went out. Her husband, was he not something belonging to her?

As to Emma, she did not ask herself whether she loved. Love, she thought, must come suddenly, with great outbursts and lightnings,—a hurricane of the skies, which falls upon life, revolutionises it, roots up the will like a leaf, and sweeps the whole heart into the abyss. She did not know that on the terrace of houses it makes lakes when the pipes are choked, and she would thus have remained in her security when she suddenly discovered a rent in the wall of it.

V

It was a sunday in February, an afternoon when the snow was falling.

They had all, Monsieur and Madame Bovary, Homais, and Monsieur Léon, gone to see a yarn-mill that was being built in the valley a mile and a half from Yonville. The druggist had taken Napoléon and Athalie to give them some exercise, and Justin accompanied them, carrying the umbrellas on his shoulder.

Nothing, however, could be less curious than this curiosity. A great piece of waste ground, on which pell-mell, amid a mass of sand and stones, were a few brake-wheels, already rusty, surrounded by a quadrangular building pierced by a number of little windows. The building was unfinished; the sky could be seen through the joists of the roofing. Attached to the stop-plank of the gable a bunch of straw mixed with corn-ears fluttered its tricoloured ribbons in the wind.

Homais was talking. He explained to the company the future importance of this establishment, computed the strength of the floorings, the thickness of the walls, and regretted extremely not having a yard-stick such as Monsieur Binet possessed for his own special use.

Emma, who had taken his arm, bent lightly against his shoulder, and she looked at the sun's disc shedding afar through the mist his pale splendour. She turned. Charles was there. His cap was drawn down over his eyebrows, and his two thick lips were trembling, which added a look of stupidity to his face; his very back, his calm back, was irritating to behold, and she saw written upon his coat all the platitude of the bearer.

While she was considering him thus, tasting in her irritation a sort of depraved pleasure, Léon made a step forward. The cold that made him pale seemed to add a more gentle languor to his face; between his cravat and his neck the somewhat loose collar of his shirt showed the skin; the lobe of his ear looked out from beneath a lock of hair, and his large blue eyes, raised to the clouds, seemed to Emma more limpid and more beautiful than those mountain-lakes where the heavens are mirrored.

"Wretched boy!" suddenly cried the chemist.

And he ran to his son, who had just precipitated himself into a heap of lime in order to whiten his boots. At the reproaches with which he was being overwhelmed Napoléon began to roar, while Justin dried his shoes with a wisp of straw. But a knife was wanted; Charles offered his.

"Ah!" she said to herself, "he carries a knife in his pocket like a peasant."

The hoar-frost was falling, and they turned back to Yonville.

In the evening Madame Bovary did not go to her neighbour's, and when Charles had left and she felt herself alone, the comparison re-began with the clearness of a sensation almost actual, and with that lengthening of perspective which memory gives to things. Looking from her bed at the clean fire that was burning, she still saw, as she had down there, Léon standing up with one hand bending his cane, and with the other holding Athalie, who was quietly sucking a piece of ice. She thought him charming; she could not tear herself away from him; she recalled his other attitudes on other days, the words he had spoken, the sound of his voice, his whole person; and she repeated, pouting out her lips as if for a kiss—

"Yes, charming! charming! Is he not in love?" she asked herself; "but with whom? With me?"

All the proofs arose before her at once; her heart leapt. The flame of the fire threw a joyous light upon the ceiling; she turned on her back, stretching out her arms.

Then began the eternal lamentation: "Oh, if Heaven had but willed it! And why not? What prevented it?"

When Charles came home at midnight, she seemed to have just awakened, and as he made a noise undressing, she complained of a headache, then asked carelessly what had happened that evening.

"Monsieur Léon," he said, "went to his room early."

She could not help smiling, and she fell asleep, her soul filled with a new delight.

The next day, at dusk, she received a visit from Monsieur Lheureux, the draper. He was a man of ability, was this shopkeeper. Born a Gascon but bred a Norman, he grafted upon his southern volubility the cunning of the Cauchois. His fat, flabby, beardless face seemed dyed by a decoction of liquorice, and his white hair made even more vivid the keen brilliance of his small black eyes. No one knew what he had been formerly; a pedlar said some, a banker at Routot according to others. What was certain was, that he made complex calculations in his head that would have frightened Binet himself. Polite to obsequiousness, he always held himself with his back bent in the position of one who bows or who invites.

After leaving at the door his hat surrounded with crape, he put down a green bandbox on the table, and began by complaining to madame, with many civilities, that he should have remained till that day without gaining her confidence. A poor shop like his was not made to attract a "fashionable lady"; he emphasised the words; yet she had only to command, and he would undertake to provide her with anything she might wish, either in haberdashery or linen, millinery or fancy goods, for he went to town regularly four times a month. He was connected with the best houses. You could speak of him at the "Trois Frères," at the "Barbe d'Or," or at the "Grand Sauvage": all these gentlemen knew him as well as the insides of their pockets. To-day, then, he had come to show madame, in passing, various articles he happened to have, thanks to the most rare opportunity. And he pulled out half-a-dozen embroidered collars from the box.

Madame Bovary examined them. "I do not require anything," she said.

Then Monsieur Lheureux delicately exhibited three Algerian scarves, several packets of English needles, a pair of straw slippers, and, finally, four eggcups in cocoa-nut wood, carved in open work by convicts. Then, with both hands on the table, his neck stretched out, his figure bent forward, open-mouthed, he watched Emma's look, who was walking up and down undecided amid these goods. From time to time, as if to remove some dust, he filliped with his nail the silk of the scarves spread out at full length, and they rustled with a little noise, making in the green twilight the gold spangles of their tissue scintillate like little stars.

"How much are they?"

"A mere nothing," he replied, "a mere nothing. But there's no hurry; whenever it's convenient. We are not Jews."

She reflected for a few moments, and ended by again declining Monsieur Lheureux's offer. He replied quite unconcernedly—

"Very well. We shall understand one another by and by. I have always got on with ladies—if I didn't with my own!"

Emma smiled.

"I wanted to tell you," he went on good-naturedly, after his joke, "that it isn't the money I should trouble about. Why, I could give you some, if need be."

She made a gesture of surprise.

"Ah!" said he quickly and in a low voice, "I shouldn't have to go far to find you some, rely on that."

And he began asking after Père Tellier, the proprietor of the "Café Français," whom Monsieur Bovary was then attending.

"What's the matter with Père Tellier? He coughs so that he shakes his whole house, and I'm afraid he'll soon want a deal covering rather than a flannel vest. He was such a rake as a young man! Those sort of people, madame, have not the least regularity; he's burnt up with brandy. Still it's sad, all the same, to see an acquaintance go off."

And while he fastened up his box he discoursed about the doctor's patients.

"It's the weather, no doubt," he said, looking frowningly at the floor, "that causes these illnesses. I, too, don't feel the thing. One of these days I shall even have to consult the doctor for a pain I have in my back. Well, good-bye, Madame Bovary. At your service; your very humble servant." And he closed the door gently.

Emma had her dinner served in her bedroom on a tray by the fireside; she was a long time over it; everything was well with her.

"How good I was!" she said to herself, thinking of the scarves.

She heard some steps on the stairs. It was Léon. She got up and took from the chest of drawers the first pile of dusters to be hemmed. When he came in she seemed very busy.

The conversation languished; Madame Bovary gave it up every few minutes, whilst he himself seemed quite embarrassed. Seated on a low chair near the fire, he turned round in his fingers the ivory thimble-case. She stitched on, or from time to time turned down the hem of the cloth with her nail. She did not speak; he was silent, being as captivated by her silence, as he would have been by her speech.

"Poor fellow!" she thought.

"How have I displeased her?" he asked himself.

At last, however, Léon said that he should have, one of these days, to go to Rouen on some office business.

"Your music subscription is out; am I to renew it?"

"No," she replied.

"Why?"

"Because——"

And pursing her lips she slowly drew a long stitch of grey thread.

This work irritated Léon. It seemed to roughen the ends of her fingers. A gallant phrase came into his head, but he did not risk it.

"Then you are giving it up?" he went on.

"What?" she asked hurriedly. "Music? Ah! yes! Have I not my house to look after, my husband to attend to, a thousand things, in fact, many duties that must be considered first?"

She looked at the clock. Charles was late. Then she affected anxiety. Two or three times she even repeated, "He is so good!"

The clerk was fond of Monsieur Bovary. But this tenderness on his behalf astonished him unpleasantly; nevertheless he took up his praises, which he said every one was singing, especially the chemist.

"Ah! he is a good fellow," continued Emma.

"Certainly," replied the clerk.

And he began talking of Madame Homais, whose very untidy appearance generally made them laugh.

"What does it matter?" interrupted Emma. "A good housewife does not trouble about her appearance."

Then she relapsed into silence.

It was the same on the following days; her talks, her manners, everything changed. She took interest in the housework, went to church regularly, and looked after her servant with more severity.

She took Berthe from nurse. When visitors called, Félicité brought her in, and Madame Bovary undressed her to show off her limbs. She declared she adored children; this was her consolation, her joy, her passion, and she accompanied her caresses with lyrical outbursts which would have reminded any one but the Yonville people of Sachette in "Notre Dame de Paris."

When Charles came home he found his slippers put to warm near the fire. His waistcoat now never wanted lining, nor his shirt buttons, and it was quite a pleasure to see in the cupboard the nightcaps arranged in piles of the same height. She no longer grumbled as formerly at taking a turn in the garden; what she proposed was always done, although she did not understand the wishes to which she submitted without a murmur; and when Léon saw him by his fireside after dinner, his two hands on his stomach, his two feet on the fender, his cheeks red with feeding, his eyes moist with happiness, the child crawling along the carpet, and this woman with the slender waist who came behind his armchair to kiss his forehead:

"What madness!" he said to himself. "And how to reach her!"

And thus she seemed so virtuous and inaccessible to him that he lost all hope, even the faintest. But by this renunciation he placed her on an extraordinary pinnacle. To him she stood outside those fleshly attributes from which he had nothing to obtain, and in his heart she rose ever, and became farther removed from him after the magnificent manner of an apotheosis that is taking wing. It was one of those pure feelings that do not interfere with life, that are cultivated because they are rare, and whose loss would afflict more than their passion rejoices.

Emma grew thinner, her cheeks paler, her face longer. With her black hair, her large eyes, her aquiline nose, her birdlike walk, and always silent now, did she not seem to be passing through life scarcely touching it, and to bear on her brow the vague impress of some divine destiny? She was so sad and so calm, at once so gentle and so reserved, that near her one felt oneself seized by an icy charm, as we shudder in churches at the perfume of the flowers mingling with the cold of the marble. The others even did not escape from this seduction. The chemist said—

"She is a woman of great parts, who wouldn't be misplaced in a sub-prefecture."

The housewives admired her economy, the patients her politeness, the poor her charity.

But she was eaten up with desires, with rage, with hate. That dress with the narrow folds hid a distracted heart, of whose torment those chaste lips said nothing. She was in love with Léon, and sought solitude that she might with the more ease delight in his image. The sight of his form troubled the voluptuousness of this meditation. Emma thrilled at the sound of his step; then in his presence the emotion subsided, and afterwards there remained to her only an immense astonishment that ended in sorrow.

Léon did not know that when he left her in despair she rose after he had gone to see him in the street. She concerned herself about his comings and goings; she watched his face; she invented quite a history to find an excuse for going to his room. The chemist's wife seemed happy to her to sleep under the same roof, and her thoughts constantly centered upon this house, like the "Lion d'Or" pigeons, who came there to dip their red feet and white wings in its gutters. But the more Emma recognised her love, the more she crushed it down, that it might not be evident, that she might make it less. She would have liked Léon to guess it, and she imagined chances, catastrophes that should facilitate this. What restrained her was, no doubt, idleness and fear, and a sense of shame also. She thought she had repulsed him too much, that the time was past, that all was lost. Then, pride, the joy of being able to say to herself, "I am virtuous," and to look at herself in the glass taking resigned poses, consoled her a little for the sacrifice she believed she was making.

Then the lusts of the flesh, the longing for money, and the melancholy of passion all blended themselves into one suffering, and instead of turning her thoughts from it, she clave to it the more, urging herself to pain, and seeking everywhere occasion for it. She was irritated by an ill-served dish or by a half-open door; bewailed the velvets she had not, the happiness she had missed, her too exalted dreams, her narrow home.

What exasperated her was that Charles did not seem to notice her anguish. His conviction that he was making her happy seemed to her an imbecile insult, and his sureness on this point ingratitude. For whose sake, then, was she virtuous? Was it not for him, the obstacle to all felicity, the cause of all misery, and, as it were, the sharp clasp of that complex strap that buckled her in on all sides?

On him alone, then, she concentrated all the various hatreds that resulted from her boredom, and every effort to diminish only augmented it; for this useless trouble was added to the other reasons for despair, and contributed still more to the separation between them. Her own gentleness to herself made her rebel against him. Domestic mediocrity drove her to lewd fancies, marriage tenderness to adulterous desires. She would have liked Charles to beat her, that she might have a better right to hate him, to revenge herself upon him. She was surprised sometimes at the atrocious conjectures that came into her thoughts, and she had to go on smiling, to hear repeated to her at all hours that she was happy, to pretend to be happy, to let it be believed.

Yet she had loathing of this hypocrisy. She was seized with the temptation to flee somewhere with Léon to try a new life; but at once a vague chasm full of darkness opened within her soul.

"Besides, he no longer loves me," she thought. "What is to become of me? What help is to be hoped for, what consolation, what solace?"

She was left broken, breathless, inert, sobbing in a low voice, with flowing tears.

"Why don't you tell master?" the servant asked her when she came in during these crises.

"It is the nerves," said Emma. "Do not speak to him of it; it would worry him."

"Ah! yes," Félicité went on, "you are just like La Guérine, Père Guérin's daughter, the fisherman at Pollet, that I used to know at Dieppe before I came to you. She was so sad, so sad, to see her standing upright on the threshold of her house, she seemed to you like a winding-sheet spread out before the door. Her illness, it appears, was a kind of fog that she had in her head, and the doctors could not do anything, nor the priest either. When she was taken too bad she went off quite alone to the seashore, so that the customs officer, going his rounds, often found her lying flat on her face, crying on the shingle. Then, after her marriage, it went off, they say."

"But with me," replied Emma, "it was after marriage that it began."

VI

ONE EVENING when the window was open, and she, sitting by it, had been watching Lestiboudois, the beadle, trimming the box, she suddenly heard the Angelus ringing.

It was the beginning of April, when the primroses are in bloom, and a warm wind blows over the flower-beds newly turned, and the gardens, like women, seem to be getting ready for the summer fêtes. Through the bars of the arbour and away beyond, the river could be seen in the fields, meandering through the grass in wandering curves. The evening vapours rose between the leafless poplars, touching their outlines with a violet tint, paler and more transparent than a subtle gauze caught athwart their branches. In the distance cattle moved about; neither their steps nor their lowing could be heard; and the bell, still ringing through the air, kept up its peaceful lamentation.

With this repeated tinkling the thoughts of the young woman lost themselves in old memories of her youth and school-days. She remembered the great candlesticks that rose above the vases full of flowers on the altar, and the tabernacle with its small columns. She would have liked to be once more lost in the long line of white veils, marked off here and there by the stiff black hoods of the good sisters bending over their prie-Dieu. At mass on Sundays when she looked up, she saw the gentle face of the Virgin amid the blue smoke of the rising incense. Then she was moved; she felt herself weak and quite deserted, like the down of a bird whirled by the tempest, and it was unconsciously that she went towards the church, inclined to no matter what devotions, so that her soul was absorbed and all existence lost in it.

On the Place she met Lestiboudois on his way back, for, in order not to shorten his day's labour, he preferred interrupting his work, then beginning it again, so that he rang the Angelus to suit his own convenience. Besides, the ringing over a little earlier warned the lads of catechism hour.

Already a few who had arrived were playing marbles on the stones of the cemetery. Others, astride the wall, swung their legs, kicking with their clogs the large nettles growing between the little enclosure and the newest graves. This was the only green spot. All the rest was but stones, always covered with a fine powder, despite the vestry-broom.

The children in list shoes ran about there as if it were an enclosure made for them. The shouts of their voices could be heard through the humming of the bell. This grew less and less with the swinging of the great rope that, hanging from the top of the belfry, dragged its end on the ground. Swallows flitted to and fro uttering little cries, cut the air with the edge of their wings, and swiftly returned to their yellow nests under the tiles of the coping. At the end of the church a lamp was burning, the wick of a nightlight in a glass hung up. Its light from a distance looked like a white stain trembling in the oil. A long ray of the sun fell across the nave and seemed to darken the lower sides and the corners.

"Where is the curé?" asked Madame Bovary of one of the lads, who was amusing himself by shaking a swivel in a hole too large for it.

"He is just coming," he answered.

And in fact the door of the presbytery grated; Abbé Bournisien appeared; the children, pell-mell, fled into the church.

"These young scamps!" murmured the priest, "always the same!" Then, picking up a catechism all in rags that he had struck with his foot. "They respect nothing!" But as soon as he caught sight of Madame Bovary, "Excuse me," he said; "I did not recognise you."

He thrust the catechism into his pocket, and stopped short, balancing the heavy vestry key between his two fingers.

The light of the setting sun that fell full upon his face paled the lasting of his cassock, shiny at the elbows, unravelled at the hem. Grease and tobacco stains followed along his broad chest the lines of the buttons, and grew more numerous the farther they were from his neckcloth, in which the massive folds of his red chin rested; this was dotted with yellow spots, that disappeared beneath the coarse hair of his greyish beard. He had just dined, and was breathing noisily.

"How are you?" he added.

"Not well," replied Emma; "I am ill."

"Well, and so am I," answered the priest. "These first warm days weaken one most remarkably, don't they? But, after all, we are born to suffer, as St. Paul says. But what does Monsieur Bovary think of it?"

"He!" she said with a gesture of contempt.

"What!" replied the good fellow, quite astonished, "doesn't he prescribe something for you?"

"Ah!" said Emma, "it is no earthly remedy I need."

But the curé from time to time looked into the church, where the kneeling boys were shouldering one another, and tumbling over like packs of cards.

"I should like to know——" she went on.

"You look out, Riboudet," cried the priest in an angry voice: "I'll warm your ears, you imp!" Then turning to Emma. "He's Boudet the carpenter's son; his parents are well off, and let him do just as he pleases. Yet he could learn quickly if he would, for he is very sharp. And so sometimes for a joke I call him Riboudet (like the road one takes to go to Maromme); and I even say 'Mon Riboudet.' Ha! ha! 'Mont Riboudet.' The other day I repeated that jest to Monsignor, and he laughed at it; he condescended to laugh at it. And how is Monsieur Bovary?"

She seemed not to hear him. And he went on—

"Always very busy, no doubt; for he and I are certainly the busiest people in the parish. But he is doctor of the body," he added with a thick laugh, "and I of the soul."

She fixed her pleading eyes upon the priest. "Yes," she said, "you solace all sorrows."

"Ah! don't talk to me of it, Madame Bovary. This morning I had to go to Bas-Diauville for a cow that was ill; they thought it was under a spell. All their cows, I don't know how it is—— But pardon me! Longuemarre and Boudet! Bless me! will you leave off?"

And with a bound he ran into the church.

The boys were just then clustering round the large desk, climbing over the precentor's footstool, opening the missal; and others on tiptoe were just about to venture into the confessional. But the priest suddenly distributed a shower of cuffs among them. Seizing them by the collars of their coats, he lifted them from the ground, and deposited them on their knees on the stones of the choir, firmly, as if he meant planting them there.

"Yes," said he, when he returned to Emma, unfolding his large cotton handkerchief, one corner of which he put between his teeth, "farmers are much to be pitied."

"Others, too," she replied.

"Assuredly. Town-labourers, for example."

"It is not they——"

"Pardon! I've there known poor mothers of families, virtuous women, I assure you, real saints, who wanted even bread."

"But those," replied Emma, and the corners of her mouth twitched as she spoke, "those, Monsieur la Curé, who have bread and have no——"

"Fire in the winter," said the priest.

"Oh, what does that matter?"

"What! What does it matter? It seems to me that when one has firing and food—for, after all——"

"My God! my God!" she sighed.

"Do you feel unwell?" he asked approaching her anxiously. "It is indigestion, no doubt? You must get home, Madame Bovary; drink a little tea, that will strengthen you, or else a glass of fresh water with a little moist sugar."

"Why?" And she looked like one awaking from a dream.

"Well, you see, you were putting your hand to your forehead. I thought you felt faint." Then, bethinking himself, "But you were asking me something? What was it? I really don't remember."

"I? Nothing! nothing!" repeated Emma.

And the glance she cast round her slowly fell upon the old man in the cassock. They looked at one another face to face without speaking.

"Then, Madame Bovary," he said at last, "excuse me, but duty first, you know; I must look after my good-for-nothings. The first communion will soon be upon us, and I fear we shall be behind after all. So after Ascension Day I keep them *recta* an extra hour every Wednesday. Poor children! One cannot lead them too soon into the path of the Lord, as, moreover, he has himself recommended us to do by the mouth of his Divine Son. Good health to you, madame; my respects to your husband."

And he went into the church making a genuflexion as soon as he reached the door.

Emma saw him disappear between the double row of forms, walking with heavy tread, his head a little bent over his shoulder, and with his two hands half-open behind him.

Then she turned on her heel all of one piece, like a statue on a pivot, and went homewards. But the loud voice of the priest, the clear voices of the boys still reached her ears, and went on behind her.

"Are you a Christian?"

"Yes, I am a Christian."

"What is a Christian?"

"He who, being baptized—baptized—baptized——"

She went up the steps of the staircase holding on to the banisters, and when she was in her room threw herself into an armchair.

The whitish light of the window-panes fell with soft undulations. The furniture in its place seemed to have become more immobile, and to lose itself in the shadow as in an ocean of darkness. The fire was out, the clock went on ticking, and Emma vaguely marvelled at this calm of all things while within herself was such tumult. But little Berthe was there, between the window and the work-table, tottering on her knitted shoes, and trying to come to her mother to catch hold of the ends of her apron-strings.

"Leave me alone," said the latter, putting her from her with her hand.

The little girl soon came up closer against her knees, and leaning on them with her arms, she looked up with her large blue eyes, while a small thread of pure saliva dribbled from her lips on to the silk apron.

"Leave me alone," repeated the young woman quite irritably.

Her face frightened the child, who began to scream.

"Will you leave me alone?" she said, pushing her with her elbow.

Berthe fell at the foot of the drawers against the brass handle, cutting her cheek, which began to bleed, against it. Madame Bovary sprang to lift her up, broke the bell-rope, called for the servant with all her might, and she was just going to curse herself when Charles appeared. It was the dinner-hour; he had come home.

"Look, dear!" said Emma, in a calm voice, "the little one fell down while she was playing, and has hurt herself."

Charles reassured her; the case was not a serious one, and he went for some sticking plaster.

Madame Bovary did not go downstairs to the dining-room; she wished to remain alone to look after the child. Then watching her sleep, the little anxiety she felt gradually wore off, and she seemed very stupid to herself, and very good to have been so worried just now at so little. Berthe, in fact, no longer sobbed. Her breathing now imperceptibly raised the cotton covering. Big tears lay in the corner of the half-closed eyelids, through whose lashes one could see two pale sunken pupils; the plaster stuck on her cheek drew the skin obliquely.

"It is very strange," thought Emma, "how ugly this child is!"

When at eleven o'clock Charles came back from the chemist's shop, whither he had gone after dinner to return the remainder of the sticking-plaster, he found his wife standing by the cradle.

"I assure you it's nothing," he said, kissing her on the forehead. "Don't worry, my poor darling; you will make yourself ill."

He had stayed a long time at the chemist's. Although he had not seemed much moved, Homais, nevertheless, had exerted himself to buoy him up, to "keep up his spirits." Then they had talked of the various dangers that threaten childhood, of the carelessness of servants. Madame Homais knew something of it, having still upon her chest the marks left by a basin full of soup that a cook had formerly dropped on her pinafore, and her good parents took no end of trouble for her. The knives were not sharpened, nor the floors waxed; there were iron gratings to the windows and strong bars across the fireplace; the little Homais, in spite of their spirit, could not stir without some one watching them; at the slightest cold their father stuffed them with pectorals; and until they were turned four they all, without pity, had to wear wadded head-protectors. This, it is true, was a fancy of Madame Homais'; her husband was inwardly afflicted at it. Fearing the possible consequences of such compression to the intellectual organs, he even went so far as to say to her, "Do you want to make Caribs or Botocudos of them?"

Charles, however, had several times tried to interrupt the conversation. "I should like to speak to you," he had whispered in the clerk's ear, who went upstairs in front of him.

"Can he suspect anything?" Léon asked himself. His heart beat, and he racked his brain with surmises.

At last, Charles, having shut the door, asked him to see himself what would be the price at Rouen of a fine daguerreotype. It was a sentimental surprise he intended for his wife, a delicate attention—his portrait in a frock-coat. But he wanted first to know "how much it would be." The inquiries would not put Monsieur Léon out, since he went to town almost every week.

Why? Monsieur Homais suspected some "young man's affair" at the bottom of it, an intrigue. But he was mistaken. Léon was after no love-making. He was sadder than ever, as Madame Lefrançois saw from the amount of food he left on his plate. To find out more about it she questioned the tax-collector. Binet answered roughly that he "wasn't paid by the police."

All the same, his companion seemed very strange to him, for Léon often threw himself back in his chair, and stretching out his arms, complained vaguely of life.

"It's because you don't take enough recreation," said the collector.

"What recreation?"

"If I were you I'd have a lathe."

"But I don't know how to turn," answered the clerk.

"Ah! that's true," said the other, rubbing his chin with an air of mingled contempt and satisfaction.

Léon was weary of loving without any result; moreover, he was beginning to feel that depression caused by the repetition of the same kind of life, when no interest inspires and no hope sustains it. He was so bored with Yonville and the Yonvillers, that the sight of certain persons, of certain houses, irritated him beyond endurance; and the chemist, good fellow though he was, was becoming absolutely unbearable to him. Yet the prospect of a new condition of life frightened as much as it seduced him.

This apprehension soon changed into impatience, and then Paris from afar sounded its fanfare of masked balls with the laugh of grisettes. As he was to finish reading there, why not set out at once? What prevented him? And he began making home-preparations; he arranged his occupations beforehand. He furnished in his head an apartment. He would lead an artist's life there! He would take lessons on the guitar! He would have a dressing-gown, a Basque cap, blue velvet slippers! He even already was admiring two crossed foils over his chimney-piece, with a death's-head on the guitar above them.

The difficulty was the consent of his mother; nothing, however, seemed more reasonable. Even his employer advised him to go to some other chambers where he could advance more rapidly. Taking a middle course, then, Léon looked for some place as second clerk at Rouen; found none, and at last wrote his mother a long letter full of details, in which he set forth the reasons for going to live at Paris immediately. She consented.

He did not hurry. Every day for a month Hivert carried boxes, valises, parcels for him from Yonville to Rouen and from Rouen to Yonville; and when Léon had packed up his wardrobe, had his three armchairs restuffed, bought a stock of neckties, in a word, had made more preparations than for a voyage round the world, he put it off from week to week, until he received a second letter from his mother urging him to leave, since he wanted to pass his examination before the vacation.

When the moment for the farewells had come, Madame Homais wept, Justin sobbed; Homais, as a man of nerve, concealed his emotion; he wished to carry his friend's overcoat himself as far as the gate of the notary, who was taking Léon to Rouen in his carriage. The latter had just time to bid farewell to Monsieur Bovary.

When he reached the head of the stairs he stopped, he was so out of breath. On his coming in, Madame Bovary rose hurriedly.

"It is I again," said Léon.

"I was sure of it!"

She bit her lips, and a rush of blood flowing under her skin made her red from the roots of her hair to the top of her collar. She remained standing, leaning with her shoulder against the wainscot.

"The doctor is not here?" he went on.

"He is out." She repeated, "He is out."

Then there was silence. They looked one at the other, and their thoughts, confounded in the same agony, clung close together like two throbbing breasts.

"I should like to kiss Berthe," said Léon.

Emma went down a few steps and called Félicité.

He threw one long look around him that took in the walls, the brackets, the fireplace, as if to penetrate everything, carry away everything. But she returned, and the servant brought Berthe, who was swinging a windmill roof downwards at the end of a string. Léon kissed her several times on the neck.

"Good-bye, poor child! good-bye, dear little one! good-bye!"

And he gave her back to her mother.

"Take her away," she said.

They remained alone—Madame Bovary, her back turned, her face pressed against a window-pane; Léon held his cap in his hand, knocking it softly against his thigh.

"It is going to rain," said Emma.

"I have a cloak," he answered.

"Ah!"

She turned round, her chin lowered, her forehead bent forward. The light fell on it as on a piece of marble to the curve of the eyebrows, without one's being able to guess what Emma was seeing in the horizon or what she was thinking within herself.

"Well, good-bye," he sighed.

She raised her head with a quick movement.

"Yes, good-bye—go!"

They advanced towards each other; he held out his hand; she hesitated.

"In English fashion, then," she said, giving her own hand wholly to him, and forcing a laugh.

Léon felt it between his fingers, and the very essence of all his being seemed to pass down into that moist palm. Then he opened his hand; their eyes met again, and he disappeared.

When he reached the market-place, he stopped and hid behind a pillar to look for the last time at this white house with the four green blinds. He thought he saw a shadow behind the window in the room; but the curtain, sliding along the pole as though no one were touching it, slowly opened its long oblique folds, that spread out with a single movement, and thus hung straight and motionless as a plaster wall. Léon set off running.

From afar he saw his employer's gig in the road, and by it a man in a coarse apron holding the horse. Homais and Monsieur Guillaumin were talking. They were waiting for him.

"Embrace me," said the druggist with tears in his eyes. "Here is your coat, my good friend. Mind the cold; take care of yourself; look after yourself."

"Come, Léon, jump in," said the notary.

Homais bent over the splash-board, and in a voice broken by sobs uttered these three sad words—

"A pleasant journey!"

"Good-night," said Monsieur Guillaumin. "Give him his head."

They set out, and Homais went back.

Madame Bovary had opened her window overlooking the garden and watched the clouds. They were gathering round the sunset on the side of Rouen, and swiftly rolled back their black columns, behind which the great rays of the sun looked out like the golden arrows of a suspended trophy, while the rest of the empty heavens was white as porcelain. But a gust of wind bowed the poplars, and suddenly the rain fell; it pattered against the green leaves. Then the sun reappeared, the hens clucked, sparrows shook their wings in the damp thickets, and the pools of water on the gravel as they flowed away carried off the pink flowers of an acacia.

"Ah! how far off he must be already!" she thought.

Monsieur Homais, as usual, came at half-past six during dinner.

"Well," said he, "so we've sent off our young friend!"

"So it seems," replied the doctor. Then turning on his chair, "Any news at home?"

"Nothing much. Only my wife was a little moved this afternoon. You know women—a nothing upsets them, especially my wife. And we should be wrong to object to that, since their nervous organisation is much more malleable than ours."

"Poor Léon!" said Charles. "How will he live at Paris? Will he get used to it?"

Madame Bovary sighed.

"Get along!" said the chemist, smacking his lips. "The outings at restaurants, the masked balls, the champagne—all that'll be jolly enough, I assure you."

"I don't think he'll go wrong," objected Bovary.

"Nor do I," said Monsieur Homais quickly; "although he'll have to do like the rest for fear of passing for a Jesuit. And you don't know what a life those dogs lead in the Latin quarter with actresses. Besides, students are thought a great deal of at Paris. Provided they have a few accomplishments, they are received in the best society; there are even ladies of the Faubourg Saint-Germain who fall in love with them, which subsequently furnishes them opportunities for making very good matches."

"But," said the doctor, "I fear for him that down there——"

"You are right," interrupted the chemist; "that is the reverse of the medal. And one is constantly obliged to keep one's hand in one's pocket there. Thus, we will suppose you are in a public garden. An individual presents himself, well dressed, even wearing an order, and whom one would take for a diplomatist. He approaches you, he insinuates himself; offers you a pinch of snuff, or picks up your hat. Then you become more intimate; he takes you to a café, invites you to his country-house, introduces you, between two drinks, to all sorts of people; and three-fourths of the time it's only to plunder your watch or lead you into some pernicious step."

"That is true," said Charles; "but I was thinking specially of illnesses—of typhoid fever, for example, that attacks students from the provinces."

Emma shuddered.

"Because of the change of regimen," continued the chemist, "and of the perturbation that results therefrom in the whole system. And then the water at Paris, don't you know! The dishes at restaurants, all the spiced food, end by heating the blood, and are not worth, whatever people may say of them, a good soup. For my own part, I have always preferred plain living; it is more healthy. So when I was studying pharmacy at Rouen, I boarded in a boarding-house; I dined with the professors."

And thus he went on, expounding his opinions generally and his personal likings, until Justin came to fetch him for a mulled egg that was wanted.

"Not a moment's peace!" he cried; "always at it! I can't go out for a minute! Like a plough-horse, I have always to be moiling and toiling. What drudgery!" Then, when he was at the door, "By the way, do you know the news?"

"What news?"

"That it is very likely," Homais went on, raising his eyebrows and assuming one of his most serious expressions, "that the agricultural meeting of the Seine-Inférieure will be held this year at Yonville-l'Abbaye. The rumour, at all events, is going the round. This morning the paper alluded to it. It would be of the utmost importance for our district. But we'll talk it over later on. I can see, thank you; Justin has the lantern."

VII

THE NEXT DAY was a dreary one for Emma. Everything seemed to her enveloped in a black atmosphere floating confusedly over the exterior of things, and sorrow was engulfed within her soul with soft shrieks such as the winter wind makes in ruined castles. It was that reverie which we give to things that will not return, the lassitude that seizes you after everything is done; that pain, in fine, that the interruption of every wonted movement, the sudden cessation of any prolonged vibration, brings on.

As on the return from Vaubyessard, when the quadrilles were running in her head, she was full of a gloomy melancholy, of a numb despair. Léon reappeared, taller, handsomer, more charming, more vague. Though separated from her, he had not left her; he was there, and the walls of the house seemed to hold his shadow. She could not detach her eyes from the carpet where he had walked, from those empty chairs where he had sat. The river still flowed on, and slowly drove its ripples along the slippery banks. They had often walked there to the murmur of the waves over the moss-covered pebbles. How bright the sun had been! What happy afternoons they had seen alone in the shade at the end of the garden! He read aloud, bare-headed, sitting on a footstool of dry sticks; the fresh wind of the meadow set trembling the leaves of the book and the nasturtiums of the arbour. Ah! he was gone, the only charm of her life, the only possible hope of joy. Why had she not seized this happiness when it came to her? Why not have kept hold of it with both hands, with both knees, when it was about to flee from her? And she cursed herself for not having loved Léon. She thirsted for his lips. The wish took possession of her to run after and rejoin him, throw herself into his arms and say to him, "It is I; I am yours." But Emma recoiled beforehand at the difficulties of the enterprise, and her desires, increased by regret, became only the more acute.

Henceforth the memory of Léon was the centre of her boredom; it burnt there more brightly than the fire travellers have left on the snow of a Russian steppe. She sprang towards him, she pressed against him, she stirred carefully the dying embers, sought all around her anything that could revive it; and the most distant reminiscences, like the most immediate occasions, what she experienced as well as what she imagined, her voluptuous desires that were unsatisfied, her projects of happiness that crackled in the wind like dead boughs, her sterile virtue, her lost hopes, the domestic *tête-à-tête,*—she gathered it all up, took everything, and made it all serve as fuel for her melancholy.

The flames, however, subsided, either because the supply had exhausted itself, or because it had been piled up too much. Love, little by little, was quelled by absence; regret stifled beneath habit; and this incendiary light that had empurpled her pale sky was overspread and faded by degrees. In the supineness of her conscience she even took her repugnance towards her husband for aspiration towards her lover, the burning of hate for the warmth of tenderness; but as the tempest still raged, and as passion burnt itself down to the very cinders, and no help came, no sun rose, there was night on all sides, and she was lost in the terrible cold that pierced her.

Then the evil days of Tostes began again. She thought herself now far more unhappy; for she had the experience of grief, with the certainty that it would not end.

A woman who had laid on herself such sacrifices could well allow herself certain whims. She bought a Gothic prie-Dieu, and in a month spent fourteen francs on lemons for polishing her nails; she wrote to Rouen for a blue cashmere gown; she chose one of Lheureux's finest scarves, and wore it knotted round her waist over her dressing-gown; and, with closed blinds and a book in her hand, she lay stretched out on a couch in this garb.

She often changed her coiffure; she did her hair *à la Chinoise*, in flowing curls, in plaited coils; she parted it on one side and rolled it under like a man's.

She wanted to learn Italian; she bought dictionaries, a grammar, and a supply of white paper. She tried serious reading, history, and philosophy. Sometimes in the night Charles woke up with a start, thinking he was being called to a patient. "I'm coming," he stammered; and it was the noise of a match Emma had struck to relight the lamp. But her reading fared like her pieces of embroidery, all of which, only just begun, filled her cupboard; she took it up, left it, passed on to other books.

She had attacks in which she could easily have been driven to commit any folly. She maintained one day, in opposition to her husband, that she could drink off a large glass of brandy, and, as Charles was stupid enough to dare her to, she swallowed the brandy to the last drop.

In spite of her vapourish airs (as the housewives of Yonville called them), Emma, all the same, never seemed gay, and usually she had at the corners of her mouth that immobile contraction that puckers the faces of old maids, and those of men whose ambition has failed. She was pale all over, white as a sheet; the skin of her nose was drawn at the nostrils, her eyes looked at you vaguely. After discovering three grey hairs on her temples, she talked much of her old age.

She often fainted. One day she even spat blood, and, as Charles fussed round her showing his anxiety—

"Bah!" she answered, "what does it matter?"

Charles fled to his study and wept there, both his elbows on the table, sitting in an armchair at his bureau under the phrenological head.

Then he wrote to his mother to beg her to come, and they had many long consultations together on the subject of Emma.

What should they decide? What was to be done since she rejected all medical treatment?

"Do you know what your wife wants?" replied Madame Bovary senior. "She wants to be forced to occupy herself with some manual work. If she were obliged, like so many others, to earn her living, she wouldn't have these vapours, that come to her from a lot of ideas she stuffs into her head, and from the idleness in which she lives."

"Yet she is always busy," said Charles.

"Ah! always busy at what? Reading novels, bad books, works against religion, and in which they mock at priests in speeches taken from Voltaire. But all that leads you far astray, my poor child. Any one who has no religion always ends by turning out badly."

So it was decided to stop Emma reading novels. The enterprise did not seem easy. The good lady undertook it. She was, when she passed through Rouen, to go herself to the lending-library and represent that Emma had discontinued her subscriptions. Would they not have a right to apply to the police if the librarian persisted all the same in his poisonous trade?

The farewells of mother and daughter-in-law were cold. During the three weeks that they had been together they had not exchanged half-a-dozen words apart from the inquiries and phrases when they met at table and in the evening before going to bed.

Madame Bovary left on a Wednesday, the market-day at Yonville.

The Place since morning had been blocked by a row of carts, which, on end and their shafts in the air, spread all along the line of houses from the church to the inn. On the other side there were canvas booths, where cotton checks, blankets, and woolen stockings were sold, together with harness for horses, and packets of blue ribbon, whose ends fluttered in the wind. The coarse hardware was spread out on the ground between pyramids of eggs and hampers of cheeses, from which sticky straw stuck out. Near the corn-machines clucking hens passed their necks through the bars of flat cages. The people, crowding in the same place and unwilling to move thence, sometimes threatened to smash the shop-front of the chemist. On Wednesdays his shop was never empty, and the people pushed in less to buy drugs than for consultations, so great was Homais's reputation in the neighbouring villages. His robust aplomb had fascinated the rustics. They considered him a greater doctor than all the doctors.

Emma was leaning out at the window; she was often there. The window in the provinces replaces the theatre and the promenade, and she amused herself with watching the crowd of boors, when she saw a gentleman in a green velvet coat. He had on yellow gloves, although he wore heavy gaiters; he was coming towards the doctor's house, followed by a peasant walking with bent head and quite a thoughtful air.

"Can I see the doctor?" he asked Justin, who was talking on the doorsteps with Félicité, and taking him for a servant of the house. "Tell him that Monsieur Rodolphe Boulanger of La Huchette is here."

It was not from territorial vanity that the new arrival added "of La Huchette" to his name, but to make himself the better known. La Huchette, in fact, was an estate near Yonville, where he had just bought the château and two farms that he cultivated himself, without, however, troubling very much about them. He lived as a bachelor, and was supposed to have "at least fifteen thousand francs a year."

Charles came into the room. Monsieur Boulanger introduced his man, who wanted to be bled because he felt "a tingling all over."

"That'll purge me," he urged as an objection to all reasoning.

So Bovary ordered a bandage and a basin, and asked Justin to hold it. Then addressing the countryman, already pale—

"Don't be afraid, my lad."

"No, no, sir," said the other; "get on."

And with an air of bravado he held out his great arm. At the prick of the lancet the blood spurted out, splashing against the looking-glass.

"Hold the basin nearer," exclaimed Charles.

"Lor!" said the peasant, "one would swear it was a little fountain flowing. How red my blood is! That's a good sign, isn't it?"

"Sometimes," answered the doctor, "one feels nothing at first, and then syncope sets in, and more especially with people of strong constitution like this man."

At these words the rustic let go the lancet-case he was twisting between his fingers. A shudder of his shoulders made the chair-back creak. His hat fell off.

"I thought as much," said Bovary, pressing his finger on the vein.

The basin was beginning to tremble in Justin's hands; his knees shook, he turned pale.

"Emma! Emma!" called Charles.

With one bound she came down the staircase.

"Some vinegar," he cried. "O dear! two at once!"

And in his emotion he could hardly put on the compress.

"It is nothing," said Monsieur Boulanger quietly, taking Justin in his arms. He seated him on the table with his back resting against the wall.

Madame Bovary began taking off his cravat. The strings of his shirt had got into a knot, and she was for some minutes moving her light fingers about the young fellow's neck. Then she poured some vinegar on her cambric handkerchief; she moistened his temples with little dabs, and then blew upon them softly. The ploughman revived, but Justin's syncope still lasted, and his eyeballs disappeared in their pale sclerotic like blue flowers in milk.

"We must hide this from him," said Charles.

Madame Bovary took the basin to put it under the table. With the movement she made in bending down, her dress (it was a summer dress with four flounces, yellow, long in the waist and wide in the skirt) spread out around her on the flags of the room; and as Emma, stooping, staggered a little as she stretched out her arms, the stuff here and there gave with the inflections of her bust. Then she went to fetch a bottle of water, and she was melting some pieces of sugar when the chemist arrived. The servant had been to fetch him in the tumult. Seeing his pupil with his eyes open he drew a long breath; then going round him he looked at him from head to foot.

"Fool!" he said, "really a little fool! A fool in four letters. A phlebotomy's a big affair, isn't it! And a fellow who isn't afraid of anything; a kind of squirrel, just as he is who climbs to vertiginous heights to shake down nuts. Oh, yes! you just talk to me, boast about myself! Here's a fine fitness for practising pharmacy later on; for under serious circumstances you may be called before the tribunals in order to enlighten the minds of the magistrates, and you would have to keep your head then, to reason, show yourself a man, or else pass for an imbecile."

Justin did not answer. The chemist went on—

"Who asked you to come? You are always pestering the doctor and madame. On Wednesday, moreover, your presence is indispensable to me. There are now twenty people in the shop. I left everything because of the interest I take in you. Come, get along! Sharp! Wait for me, and keep an eye on the jars."

When Justin, who was rearranging his dress, had gone, they talked for a little while about fainting-fits. Madame Bovary had never fainted.

"That is extraordinary for a lady," said Monsieur Boulanger; "but some people are very susceptible. Thus in a duel, I have seen a second lose consciousness at the mere sound of the loading of pistols."

"For my part," said the chemist, "the sight of other people's blood doesn't affect me at all, but the mere thought of my own flowing would make me faint if I reflected upon it too much."

Monsieur Boulanger, however, dismissed his servant, advising him to calm himself, since his fancy was over.

"It procured me the advantage of making your acquaintance," he added, and he looked at Emma as he said this. Then he put three francs on the corner of the table, bowed negligently, and went out.

He was soon on the other side of the river (this was his way back to La Huchette), and Emma saw him in the meadow, walking under the poplars, slackening his pace now and then as one who reflects.

"She is very pretty," he said to himself; "she is very pretty, this doctor's wife. Fine teeth, black eyes, a dainty foot, a figure like a Parisienne's. Where the devil does she come from? Wherever did this fat fellow pick her up?"

Monsieur Rodolphe Boulanger was thirty-four; he was of brutal temperament and intelligent perspicacity, having, moreover, had much to do with women, and knowing them well. This one had seemed pretty to him; so he was thinking about her and her husband.

"I think he is very stupid. She is tired of him, no doubt. He has dirty nails, and hasn't shaved for three days. While he is trotting after his patients, she sits there botching socks. And she gets bored! She would like to live in town and dance polkas every evening. Poor little woman! She is gaping after love like a carp after water on a kitchen-table. With three words of gallantry she'd adore one, I'm sure of it. She'd be tender, charming. Yes; but how get rid of her afterwards?"

Then the difficulties of love-making seen in the distance made him by contrast think of his mistress. She was an actress at Rouen, whom he kept; and when he had pondered over this image, with which, even in remembrance, he was satiated—

"Ah! Madame Bovary," he thought, "is much prettier, especially fresher. Virginie is decidedly beginning to grow fat. She is so finikin with her pleasures; and, besides, she has a mania for prawns."

The fields were empty, and around him Rodolphe only heard the regular beating of the grass striking against his boots, with the cry of the grasshopper hidden at a distance among the oats. He again saw Emma in her room, dressed as he had seen her, and he undressed her.

"Oh, I will have her," he cried, striking a blow with his stick at a clod in front of him. And he at once began to consider the political part of the enterprise. He asked himself—

"Where shall we meet? By what means? We shall always be having the brat on our hands, and the servant, the neighbours, the husband, all sorts of worries. Pshaw! one would lose too much time over it."

Then he resumed, "She really has eyes that pierce one's heart like a gimlet. And that pale complexion! I adore pale women!"

When he reached the top of the Argueil hills he had made up his mind. "It's only finding the opportunities. Well, I will call in now and then. I'll send them venison, poultry; I'll have myself bled, if need be. We shall become friends; I'll invite them to my place. By Jove!" added he, "there's the agricultural show coming on. She'll be there. I shall see her. We'll begin boldly, for that's the surest way."

VIII

AT LAST IT CAME, the famous agricultural show. On the morning of the solemnity all the inhabitants at their doors were chatting over the preparations. The pediment of the townhall had been hung with garlands of ivy: a tent had been erected in a meadow for the banquet; and in the middle of the Place, in front of the church, a kind of bombarde was to announce the arrival of the prefect and the names of the successful farmers who had obtained prizes. The National Guard of Buchy (there was none at Yonville) had come to join the corps of firemen, of whom Binet was captain. On that day he wore a collar even higher than usual; and, tightly buttoned in his tunic, his figure was so stiff and motionless that the whole vital portion of his person seemed to have descended into his legs, which rose in a cadence of set steps with a single movement. As there was some rivalry between the tax-collector and the colonel, both, to show off their talents, drilled their men separately. One saw the red epaulettes and the black breastplates pass and repass alternately; there was no end to it, and it constantly began again. There had never been such a display of pomp. Several citizens had washed down their houses the evening before; tricoloured flags hung from half-open windows; all the public houses were full; and in the lovely weather the starched caps, the golden crosses, and the coloured neckerchiefs seemed whiter than snow, shone in the sun, and relieved with their motley colours the sombre monotony of the frock-coats and blue smocks. The neighbouring farmers' wives, when they got off their horses, pulled out a long pin that fastened round them their dresses, turned up for fear of mud; and the husbands, on the contrary, in order to save their hats, kept their handkerchiefs round them, holding one corner between their teeth.

The crowd came into the main street from both ends of the village. People poured in from the lanes, the alleys, the houses; and from time to time one heard knockers banging against doors closing behind women with their gloves, who were going out to see the fête. What was most admired were two long lamp-stands covered with lanterns, that flanked a platform on which the authorities were to sit. Besides this there were against the four columns of the townhall four kinds of poles, each bearing a small standard of greenish cloth, embellished with inscriptions in gold letters. On one was written, "To Commerce"; on the other, "To Agriculture"; on the third, "To Industry"; and on the fourth, "To the Fine Arts."

But the jubilation that brightened all faces seemed to darken that of Madame Lefrançois, the innkeeper. Standing on her kitchen-steps she muttered to herself, "What rubbish! what rubbish! With their canvas booth! Do they think the prefect will be glad to dine down there under a tent like a gipsy? They call all this fussing doing good to the place! Then it wasn't worth while sending to Neufchâtel for the keeper of a cookshop! And for whom? For cowherds! tatterdemalions!"

The druggist was passing. He had on a frock-coat, nankeen trousers, beaver shoes, and, for a wonder, a hat with a low crown.

"Your servant! Excuse me, I am in a hurry." And as the fat widow asked where he was going—

"It seems odd to you, doesn't it, I who am always more cooped up in my laboratory than the man's rat in his cheese."

"What cheese?" asked the landlady.

"Oh, nothing! nothing!" Homais continued. "I merely wished to convey to you, Madame Lefrançois, that I usually live at home like a recluse. To-day, however, considering the circumstances, it is necessary——"

"Oh, you're going down there!" she said contemptuously.

"Yes, I am going," replied the druggist, astonished. "Am I not a member of the consulting commission?"

Mère Lefrançois looked at him for a few moments, and ended by saying with a smile—

"That's another pair of shoes! But what does agriculture matter to you? Do you understand anything about it?"

"Certainly I understand it, since I am a druggist,—that is to say, a chemist.

And the object of chemistry, Madame Lefrançois, being the knowledge of the reciprocal and molecular action of all natural bodies, it follows that agriculture is comprised within its domain. And, in fact, the composition of the manure, the fermentation of liquids, the analyses of gases, and the influence of miasmata, what, I ask you, is all this, if it isn't chemistry, pure and simple?"

The landlady did not answer. Homais went on—

"Do you think that to be an agriculturist it is necessary to have tilled the earth or fattened fowls oneself? It is necessary rather to know the composition of the substances in question—the geological strata, the atmospheric actions, the quality of the soil, the minerals, the waters, the density of the different bodies, their capillarity, and what not. And one must be master of all the principles of hygiene in order to direct, criticise the construction of buildings, the feeding of animals, the diet of domestics. And, moreover, Madame Lefrançois, one must know botany, be able to distinguish between plants, you understand, which are the wholesome and those that are deleterious, which are unproductive and which nutritive, if it is well to pull them up here and re-sow them there, to propagate some, destroy others; in brief, one must keep pace with science by means of pamphlets and public papers, be always on the alert to find out improvements."

The landlady never took her eyes off the "Café Français" and the chemist went on—

"Would to God our agriculturists were chemists, or that at least they would pay more attention to the counsels of science. Thus lately I myself wrote a considerable tract, a memoir of over seventy-two pages, entitled, 'Cider, its Manufacture and its Effects, together with some New Reflections on this Subject,' that I sent to the Agricultural Society of Rouen, and which even procured me the honour of being received among its members—Section, Agriculture; Class, Pomological. Well, if my work had been given to the public——" But the druggist stopped, Madame Lefrançois seemed so preoccupied.

"Just look at them!" she said. "It's past comprehension! Such a cookshop as that!" And with a shrug of the shoulders that stretched out over her breast the stitches of her knitted bodice, she pointed with both hands at her rival's inn, whence songs were heard issuing. "Well, it won't last long," she added. "It'll be over before a week."

Homais drew back with stupefaction. She came down three steps and whispered in his ear—

"What! you didn't know it? There'll be an execution in next week. It's Lheureux who is selling him up; he has killed him with bills."

"What a terrible catastrophe!" cried the druggist, who always found expressions in harmony with all imaginable circumstances.

Then the landlady began telling him this story, that she had heard from Theodore, Monsieur Guillaumin's servant, and although she detested Tellier, she blamed Lheureux. He was "a wheedler, a sneak."

"There!" she said. "Look at him! he is in the market; he is bowing to

Madame Bovary, who's got on a green bonnet. Why, she's taking Monsieur Boulanger's arm."

"Madame Bovary!" exclaimed Homais. "I must go at once and pay her my respects. Perhaps she'll be very glad to have a seat in the enclosure under the peristyle." And, without heeding Madame Lefrançois, who was calling him back to tell him more about it, the druggist walked off rapidly with a smile on his lips, with straight knees, bowing copiously to right and left, and taking up much room with the large tails of his frock-coat that fluttered behind him in the wind.

Rodolphe having caught sight of him from afar, hurried on, but Madame Bovary lost her breath; so he walked more slowly, and, smiling at her, said in a rough tone—

"It's only to get away from that fat fellow, you know, the druggist." She pressed his elbow.

"What's the meaning of that?" he asked himself. And he looked at her out of the corner of his eyes.

Her profile was so calm that one could guess nothing from it. It stood out in the light from the oval of her bonnet, with pale ribbons on it like the leaves of weeds. Her eyes with their long curved lashes looked straight before her, and though wide open, they seemed slightly puckered by the cheek-bones, because of the blood pulsing gently under the delicate skin. A pink line ran along the partition between her nostrils. Her head was bent upon her shoulder, and the pearl tips of her white teeth were seen between her lips.

"Is she making fun of me?" thought Rodolphe.

Emma's gesture, however, had only been meant for a warning; for Monsieur Lheureux was accompanying them, and spoke now and again as if to enter into the conversation.

"What a superb day! Everybody is out! The wind is east!"

And neither Madame Bovary nor Rodolphe answered him, whilst at the slightest movement made by them he drew near, saying, "I beg your pardon!" and raised his hat.

When they reached the farrier's house, instead of following the road up to the fence, Rodolphe suddenly turned down a path, drawing with him Madame Bovary. He called out—

"Good evening, Monsieur Lheureux! See you again presently."

"How you got rid of him!" she said, laughing.

"Why," he went on, "allow oneself to be intruded upon by others? And as to-day I have the happiness of being with you——"

Emma blushed. He did not finish his sentence. Then he talked of the fine weather and of the pleasure of walking on the grass. A few daisies had sprung up again.

"Here are some pretty Easter daisies," he said, "and enough of them to furnish oracles to all the amorous maids in the place." He added, "Shall I pick some? What do you think?"

"Are you in love?" she asked, coughing a little.

"H'm, h'm! who knows?" answered Rodolphe.

The meadow began to fill, and the housewives hustled you with their great umbrellas, their baskets, and their babies. One had often to get out of the way of a long file of country folk, servant-maids with blue stockings, flat shoes, silver rings, and who smelt of milk when one passed close to them. They walked along holding one another by the hand, and thus they spread over the whole field from the row of open trees to the banquet tent. But this was the examination time, and the farmers one after the other entered a kind of enclosure formed by a long cord supported on sticks.

The beasts were there, their noses towards the cord, and making a confused line with their unequal rumps. Drowsy pigs were burrowing in the earth with their snouts, calves were bleating, lambs baaing; the cows, on knees folded in, were stretching their bellies on the grass, slowly chewing the cud, and blinking their heavy eyelids at the gnats that buzzed round them. Ploughmen with bare arms were holding by the halter prancing stallions that neighed with dilated nostrils looking towards the mares. These stood quietly, stretching out their heads and flowing manes, while their foals rested in their shadow, or now and then came and sucked them. And above the long undulation of these crowded animals one saw some white mane rising in the wind like a wave, or some sharp horns sticking out, and the heads of men running about. Apart, outside the enclosure, a hundred paces off, was a large black bull, muzzled, with an iron ring in its nostrils, and who moved no more than if he had been in bronze. A child in rags was holding him by a rope.

Between the two lines the committee-men were walking with heavy steps, examining each animal, then consulting one another in a low voice. One who seemed of more importance now and then took notes in a book as he walked along. This was the president of the jury, Monsieur Derozerays de la Panville. As soon as he recognised Rodolphe he came forward quickly, and smiling amiably, said—

"What! Monsieur Boulanger, you are deserting us?"

Rodolphe protested that he was just coming. But when the president had disappeared——

"*Ma foi!*" said he, "I shall not go. Your company is better than his."

And while poking fun at the show, Rodolphe, to move about more easily, showed the gendarme his blue card, and even stepped now and then in front of some fine beast, which Madame Bovary did not at all admire. He noticed this, and began jeering at the Yonville ladies and their dresses; then he apologised for the negligence of his own. He had that incongruity of common and elegant in which the habitually vulgar think they see the revelation of an eccentric existence, of the perturbations of sentiment, the tyrannies of art, and always a certain contempt for social conventions, that seduces or exasperates them. Thus his cambric shirt with plaited cuffs was blown out by the wind in the opening of his waistcoat of grey ticking, and his broad-striped trousers disclosed at the ankle nankeen boots with patent leather gaiters. These were so polished that they reflected the grass. He trampled on horse's dung with them, one hand in the pocket of his jacket and his straw hat on one side.

"Besides," added he, "when one lives in the country——"

"It's waste of time," said Emma.

"That is true," replied Rodolphe. "To think that not one of these people is capable of understanding even the cut of a coat!"

Then they talked about provincial mediocrity, of the lives it crushed, the illusions lost there.

"And I too," said Rodolphe, "am drifting into depression."

"You!" she said in astonishment; "I thought you very light hearted."

"Ah! yes. I seem so, because in the midst of the world I know how to wear the mask of a scoffer upon my face; and yet, how many a time at the sight of a cemetery by moonlight have I not asked myself whether it were not better to join those sleeping there!"

"Oh! and your friends?" she said. "You do not think of them."

"My friends! What friends? Have I any? Who cares for me?" and he accompanied the last words with a kind of whistling of the lips.

But they were obliged to separate from each other because of a great pile of chairs that a man was carrying behind them. He was so overladen with them that one could only see the tips of his wooden shoes and the ends of his two outstretched arms. It was Lestiboudois, the gravedigger, who was carrying the church chairs about amongst the people. Alive to all that concerned his interests, he had hit upon this means of turning the show to account; and his idea was succeeding, for he no longer knew which way to turn. In fact, the villagers, who were hot, quarrelled for these seats, whose straw smelt of incense, and they leant against the thick backs, stained with the wax of candles, with a certain veneration.

Madame Bovary again took Rodolphe's arm; he went on as if speaking to himself—

"Yes, I have missed so many things. Always alone! Ah! if I had some aim in life, if I had met some love, if I had found some one! Oh, how I would have spent all the energy of which I am capable, surmounted everything, overcome everything!"

"Yet it seems to me," said Emma, "that you are not to be pitied."

"Ah! you think so?" said Rodolphe.

"For, after all," she went on, "you are free——" she hesitated, "rich——"

"Do not mock me," he replied.

And she protested that she was not mocking him, when the report of a cannon resounded. Immediately all began hustling one another pell-mell towards the village.

It was a false alarm. The prefect seemed not to be coming, and the members of the jury felt much embarrassed, not knowing if they ought to begin the meeting or still wait.

At last at the end of the Place a large hired landau appeared, drawn by two thin horses, whom a coachman in a white hat was whipping lustily. Binet had only just time to shout, "Present arms!" and the colonel to imitate him. All ran towards the enclosure; every one pushed forward. A few even forgot their collars; but the equipage of the prefect seemed to antici- pate the crowd, and the two yoked jades, trapesing in their harness, came up at a little trot in front of the peristyle of the townhall at the very moment when the National Guard and firemen deployed, beating drums and mark- ing time.

"Present!" shouted Binet.

"Halt!" shouted the colonel. "Left about, march."

And after presenting arms, during which the clang of the band, letting loose, rang out like a brass kettle rolling downstairs, all the guns were low- ered. Then was seen stepping down from the carriage a gentleman in a short coat with silver braiding, with bald brow, and wearing a tuft of hair at the back of his head, of a sallow complexion and the most benign appearance. His eyes, very large and covered by heavy lids, were half-closed to look at the crowd, while at the same time he raised his sharp nose, and forced a smile upon his sunken mouth. He recognised the mayor by his scarf, and explained to him that the prefect was not able to come. He himself was a councillor at the prefecture; then he added a few apologies. Monsieur Tuvache answered them with compliments; the other confessed himself nervous; and they remained thus, face to face, their foreheads almost touch- ing, with the members of the jury all round, the municipal council, the notable personages, the National Guard and the crowd. The councillor pressing his little cocked hat to his breast repeated his bows, while Tuvache, bent like a bow, also smiled, stammered, tried to say something, protested his devotion to the monarchy and the honour that was being done to Yonville.

Hippolyte, the groom from the inn, took the head of the horses from the coachman, and, limping along with his clubfoot, led them to the door of the "Lion d'Or," where a number of peasants collected to look at the carriage. The drum beat, the howitzer thundered, and the gentlemen one by one mounted the platform, where they sat down in red utrecht velvet arm- chairs that had been lent by Madame Tuvache.

All these people looked alike. Their fair flabby faces, somewhat tanned by the sun, were the colour of sweet cider, and their puffy whiskers emerged from stiff collars, kept up by white cravats with broad bows. All the waist- coats were of velvet, double-breasted; all the watches had, at the end of a long ribbon, an oval cornelian seal; every one rested his two hands on his thighs, carefully stretching the stride of their trousers, whose unsponged glossy cloth shone more brilliantly than the leather of his heavy boots.

The ladies of the company stood at the back under the vestibule between the pillars, while the common herd was opposite, standing up or sitting on chairs. As a matter of fact, Lestiboudois had brought thither all those that he had moved from the field, and he even kept running back every minute to fetch others from the church. He caused such confusion with this piece of business that one had great difficulty in getting to the small steps of the platform.

"I think," said Monsieur Lheureux to the chemist, who was passing to his place, "that they ought to have put up two Venetian masts with something rather severe and rich for ornaments; it would have been a very pretty effect."

"To be sure," replied Homais; "but what can you expect? The mayor took everything on his own shoulders. He hasn't much taste. Poor Tuvache! and he is even completely destitute of what is called the genius of art."

Rodolphe, meanwhile, with Madame Bovary, had gone up to the first floor of the townhall, to the "council-room," and, as it was empty, he declared that they could enjoy the sight there more comfortably. He fetched three stools from the round table under the bust of the monarch, and having carried them to one of the windows, they sat down by each other.

There was commotion on the platform, long whisperings, much parleying. At last the councillor got up. They knew now that his name was Lieuvain, and in the crowd the name was passed from one to the other. After he had collated a few pages, and bent over them to see better, he began—

"Gentlemen! May I be permitted first of all (before addressing you on the object of our meeting to-day, and this sentiment will, I am sure, be shared by you all), may I be permitted, I say, to pay a tribute to the higher administration, to the government, to the monarch, gentlemen, our sovereign, to that beloved king, to whom no branch of public or private prosperity is a matter of indifference, and who directs with a hand at once so firm and wise the chariot of the state amid the incessant perils of a stormy sea, knowing, moreover, how to make peace respected as well as war, industry, commerce, agriculture, and the fine arts."

"I ought," said Rodolphe, "to get back a little further."

"Why?" said Emma.

But at this moment the voice of the councillor rose to an extraordinary pitch. He declaimed—

"This is no longer the time, gentlemen, when civil discord ensanguined our public places, when the landlord, the business-man, the working-man himself, falling asleep at night, lying down to peaceful sleep, trembled lest he should be awakened suddenly by the noise of incendiary tocsins, when the most subversive doctrines audaciously sapped foundations."

"Well, some one down there might see me," Rodolphe resumed, "then I should have to invent excuses for a fortnight; and with my bad reputation——"

"Oh, you are slandering yourself," said Emma.

"No! It is dreadful, I assure you."

"But, gentlemen," continued the councillor, "if, banishing from my memory the remembrance of these sad pictures, I carry my eyes back to the actual situation of our dear country, what do I see there? Everywhere commerce and the arts are flourishing; everywhere new means of communication, like so many new arteries in the body of the state, establish within it new relations. Our great industrial centres have recovered all their activity; religion, more consolidated, smiles in all hearts; our ports are full, confidence is born again, and France breathes once more!"

"Besides," added Rodolphe, "perhaps from the world's point of view they are right."

"How so?" she asked.

"What!" said he. "Do you not know that there are souls constantly tormented? They need by turns to dream and to act, the purest passions and the most turbulent joys, and thus they fling themselves into all sorts of fantasies, or follies."

Then she looked at him as one looks at a traveller who has voyaged over strange lands, and went on—

"We have not even this distraction, we poor women!"

"A sad distraction, for happiness isn't found in it."

"But is it ever found?" she asked.

"Yes; one day it comes," he answered.

"And this is what you have understood," said the councillor. "You, farmers, agricultural labourers! you, pacific pioneers of a work that belongs wholly to civilisation! you, men of progress and morality, you have understood, I say, that political storms are even more redoubtable than atmospheric disturbances!"

"It comes one day," repeated Rodolphe, "one day suddenly, and when one is despairing of it. Then the horizon expands; it is as if a voice cried, 'It is here!' You feel the need of confiding the whole of your life, of giving everything, sacrificing everything to this being. There is no need for explanations; they understand one another. They have seen each other in dreams!" (And he looked at her.) "In fine, here it is, this treasure so sought after, here before you. It glitters, it flashes; yet one still doubts, one does not believe it; one remains dazzled, as if one went out from darkness into light."

And as he ended Rodolphe suited the action to the word. He passed his hand over his face, like a man seized with giddiness. Then he let it fall on Emma's. She took hers away.

"And who would be surprised at it, gentlemen? He only who was so blind, so plunged (I do not fear to say it), so plunged in the prejudices of another age as still to misunderstand the spirit of agricultural populations. Where, indeed, is to be found more patriotism than in the country, greater devotion to the public welfare, more intelligence, in a word? And, gentlemen, I do not mean that superficial intelligence, vain ornament of idle minds, but rather that profound and balanced intelligence that applies itself above all else to useful objects, thus contributing to the good of all, to the common amelioration and to the support of the state, born of respect for law and the practice of duty——"

"Ah! again!" said Rodolphe. "Always 'duty.' I am sick of the word. They are a lot of old blockheads in flannel vests and of old women with foot-warmers and rosaries who constantly drone into our ears 'Duty, duty!' Ah! by Jove! one's duty is to feel what is great, cherish the beautiful, and not accept all the conventions of society with the ignominy that it imposes upon us."

"Yet—yet——" objected Madame Bovary.

"No, no! Why cry out against the passions? Are they not the one beautiful thing on the earth, the source of heroism, of enthusiasm, of poetry, music, the arts, of everything, in a word?"

"But one must," said Emma, "to some extent bow to the opinion of the world and accept its moral code."

"Ah! but there are two," he replied. "The small, the conventional, that of men, that which constantly changes, that brays out so loudly, that makes such a commotion here below, of the earth earthy, like the mass of imbeciles you see down there. But the other, the eternal, that is about us and above, like the landscape that surrounds us, and the blue heavens that give us light."

Monsieur Lieuvain had just wiped his mouth with a pocket-handkerchief. He continued—

"And what should I do here, gentlemen, pointing out to you the uses of agriculture? Who supplies our wants? Who provides our means of subsistence? Is it not the agriculturist? The agriculturist, gentlemen, who, sowing with laborious hand the fertile furrows of the country, brings forth the corn, which, being ground, is made into a powder by means of ingenious machinery, comes out thence under the name of flour, and from there, transported to our cities, is soon delivered at the baker's, who makes it into food for poor and rich alike. Again, is it not the agriculturist who fattens, for our clothes, his abundant flocks in the pastures? For how should we clothe ourselves, how nourish ourselves, without the agriculturist? And, gentlemen, is it even necessary to go so far for examples? Who has not frequently reflected on all the momentous things that we get out of that modest animal, the ornament of poultry-yards, that provides us at once with a soft pillow for our bed, with succulent flesh for our tables, and eggs? But I should never end if I were to enumerate one after the other all the different products which the earth, well cultivated, like a generous mother, lavishes upon her children. Here it is the vine, elsewhere the apple tree for cider, there colza, farther on cheeses and flax. Gentlemen, let us not forget flax, which has made such great strides of late years, and to which I will more particularly call your attention."

He had no need to call it, for all the mouths of the multitude were wide open, as if to drink in his words. Tuvache by his side listened to him with staring eyes. Monsieur Derozerays from time to time softly closed his eye-lids, and farther on the chemist, with his son Napoléon between his knees, put his hand behind his ear in order not to lose a syllable. The chins of the other members of the jury went slowly up and down in their waistcoats in sign of approval. The firemen at the foot of the platform rested on their bayonets; and Binet, motionless, stood with out-turned elbows, the point of his sabre in the air. Perhaps he could hear, but certainly he could see nothing, because of the visor of his helmet, that fell down on his nose. His lieutenant, the youngest son of Monsieur Tuvache, had a bigger one, for his was enormous, and shook on his head, and from it an end of his cotton scarf peeped out. He smiled beneath it with a perfectly infantine sweetness, and his pale little face, whence drops were running, wore an expression of enjoyment and sleepiness.

The square as far as the houses was crowded with people. One saw folk leaning on their elbows at all the windows, others standing at doors, and Justin, in front of the chemist's shop, seemed quite transfixed by the sight of what he was looking at. In spite of the silence Monsieur Lieuvain's voice was lost in the air. It reached you in fragments of phrases, and interrupted here and there by the creaking of chairs in the crowd; then you suddenly heard the long bellowing of an ox, or else the bleating of the lambs, who answered one another at street corners. In fact, the cowherds and shepherds had driven their beasts thus far, and these lowed from time to time, while with their tongues they tore down some scrap of foliage that hung above their mouths.

Rodolphe had drawn nearer to Emma, and said to her in a low voice, speaking rapidly—

"Does not this conspiracy of the world revolt you? Is there a single sentiment it does not condemn? The noblest instincts, the purest sympathies are persecuted, slandered; and if at length two poor souls do meet, all is so organised that they cannot blend together. Yet they will make the attempt; they will flutter their wings; they will call upon each other. Oh! no matter. Sooner or later, in six months, ten years, they will come together, will love; for fate has decreed it, and they are born one for the other."

His arms were folded across his knees, and thus lifting his face towards Emma, close by her, he looked fixedly at her. She noticed in his eyes small golden lines radiating from black pupils; she even smelt the perfume of the pomade that made his hair glossy. Then a faintness came over her; she recalled the Viscount who had waltzed with her at Vaubyessard, and his beard exhaled like this hair an odour of vanilla and citron, and mechanically she half-closed her eyes the better to breathe it in. But in making this movement, as she leant back in her chair, she saw in the distance, right on the line of the horizon, the old diligence the "Hirondelle," that was slowly descending the hill of Leux, dragging after it a long trail of dust. It was in this yellow carriage that Léon had so often come back to her, and by this route down there that he had gone forever. She fancied she saw him opposite at his window; then all grew confused; clouds gathered; it seemed to her that she was again turning in the waltz under the light of the lustres on the arm of the Viscount, and that Léon was not far away, that he was coming; and yet all the time she was conscious of the scent of Rodolphe's head by her side. This sweetness of sensation pierced through her old desires, and these, like grains of sand under a gust of wind, eddied to and fro in the subtle breath of the perfume which suffused her soul. She opened wide her nostrils several times to drink in the freshness of the ivy round the capitals. She took off her gloves, she wiped her hands, then fanned her face with her handkerchief, while athwart the throbbing of her temples she heard the murmur of the crowd and the voice of the councillor intoning his phrases. He said—

"Continue, persevere; listen neither to the suggestions of routine, nor to the over-hasty councils of a rash empiricism. Apply yourselves, above all, to the amelioration of the soil, to good manures, to the development of the equine, bovine, ovine, and porcine races. Let these shows be to you pacific arenas, where the victor in leaving it will hold forth a hand to the vanquished, and will fraternise with him in the hope of better success. And you, aged servants, humble domestics, whose hard labour no Government up to this day has taken into consideration, come hither to receive the reward of your silent virtues, and be assured that the state henceforward has its eye upon you; that it encourages you, protects you; that it will accede to your just demands, and alleviate as much as in it lies the burden of your painful sacrifices."

Monsieur Lieuvain then sat down; Monsieur Derozerays got up, beginning another speech. His was not perhaps so florid as that of the councillor, but it recommended itself by a more direct style, that is to say, by more special knowledge and more elevated considerations. Thus the praise of the Government took up less space in it; religion and agriculture more. He showed in it the relations of these two, and how they had always contributed to civilisation. Rodolphe with Madame Bovary was talking dreams, presentiments, magnetism. Going back to the cradle of society, the orator painted those fierce times when men lived on acorns in the heart of woods. Then they had left off the skins of beasts, had put on cloth, tilled the soil, planted the vine. Was this a good, and in this discovery was there not more of injury than of gain? Monsieur Derozerays set himself this problem. From magnetism little by little Rodolphe had come to affinities, and while the president was citing Cincinnatus and his plough, Diocletian planting his cabbages, and the Emperors of China inaugurating the year by the sowing of seed, the young man was explaining to the young woman that these irresistible attractions find their cause in some previous state of existence.

"Thus we," he said, "why did we come to know one another? What chance willed it? It was because across the infinite, like two streams that flow but to unite, our special bents of mind had driven us towards each other."

And he seized her hand; she did not withdraw it.

"For good farming generally!" cried the president.

"Just now, for example, when I went to your house."

"To Monsieur Bizat of Quincampoix."

"Did I know I should accompany you?"

"Seventy francs."

"A hundred times I wished to go; and I followed you—I remained."

"Manures!"

"And I shall remain to-night, to-morrow, all other days, all my life!"

"To Monsieur Caron of Argueil, a gold medal!"

"For I have never in the society of any other person found so complete a charm."

"To Monsieur Bain of Givry-Saint-Martin."

"And I shall carry away with me the remembrance of you."

"For a merino ram!"

"But you will forget me; I shall pass away like a shadow."

"To Monsieur Belot of Notre-Dame."

"Oh, no! I shall be something in your thought, in your life, shall I not?"

"Porcine race; prizes—equal, to Messrs. Lehérissé and Cullembourg, sixty francs!"

Rodolphe was pressing her hand, and he felt it all warm and quivering like a captive dove that wants to fly away; but, whether she was trying to take it away or whether she was answering his pressure, she made a movement with her fingers. He exclaimed—

"Oh, I thank you! You do not repulse me! You are good! You understand that I am yours! Let me look at you; let me contemplate you!"

A gust of wind that blew in at the window ruffled the cloth on the table, and in the square below all the great caps of the peasant women were uplifted by it like the wings of white butterflies fluttering.

"Use of oil-cakes," continued the president. He was hurrying on: "Flemish manure—flax-growing—drainage—long leases—domestic service."

Rodolphe was no longer speaking. They looked at one another. A supreme desire made their dry lips tremble, and wearily, without an effort, their fingers intertwined.

"Catherine Nicaise Elizabeth Leroux, of Sassetot-la-Guerrière, for fifty-four years of service at the same farm, a silver medal—value, twenty-five francs!"

"Where is Catherine Leroux?" repeated the councillor.

She did not present herself, and one could hear voices whispering—

"Go up!"

"Don't be afraid!"

"Oh, how stupid she is!"

"Well, is she there?" cried Tuvache.

"Yes; here she is."

"Then let her come up!"

Then there came forward on the platform a little old woman with timid bearing, who seemed to shrink within her poor clothes. On her feet she wore heavy wooden clogs, and from her hips hung a large blue apron. Her pale face framed in a borderless cap was more wrinkled than a withered russet apple. And from the sleeves of her red jacket looked out two large hands with knotty joints; the dust of barns, the potash of washing the grease of wools had so encrusted, roughened, hardened these that they seemed dirty, although they had been rinsed in clear water; and by dint of long service they remained half open, as if to bear humble witness for themselves of so much suffering endured. Something of monastic rigidity dignified her face. Nothing of sadness or of emotion weakened that pale look. In her constant living with animals she had caught their dumbness and their calm. It was the first time that she found herself in the midst of so large a company, and inwardly scared by the flags, the drums, the gentlemen in frock-coats, and the order of the councillor, she stood motionless, not knowing whether to advance or run away, nor why the crowd was pushing her and the jury were smiling at her. Thus stood before these radiant bourgeois this half-century of servitude.

"Approach, venerable Catherine Nicaise Elizabeth Leroux!" said the councillor, who had taken the list of prize-winners from the president; and, looking at the piece of paper and the old woman by turns, he repeated in a fatherly tone—

"Approach! approach!"

"Are you deaf?" said Tuvache, fidgeting in his armchair; and he began shouting in her ear, "Fifty-four years of service. A silver medal! Twenty-five francs! For you!"

Then, when she had her medal, she looked at it, and a smile of beatitude spread over her face; and as she walked away they could hear her muttering—

"I'll give it to our curé up home, to say some masses for me!"

"What fanaticism!" exclaimed the chemist, leaning across to the notary.

The meeting was over, the crowd dispersed, and now that the speeches had been read, each one fell back into his place again, and everything into the old grooves; the masters bullied the servants, and these struck the animals, indolent victors, going back to the stalls, a green crown on their horns.

The National Guards, however, had gone up to the first floor of the townhall with buns spitted on their bayonets, and the drummer of the battalion carried a basket with bottles. Madame Bovary took Rodolphe's arm; he saw her home; they separated at her door; then he walked about alone in the meadow while he waited for the time of the banquet.

The feast was long, noisy, ill served; the guests were so crowded that they could hardly move their elbows; and the narrow planks used for forms almost broke down under their weight. They ate hugely. Each one stuffed himself on his own account. Sweat stood on every brow, and a whitish steam, like the vapour of a stream on an autumn morning, floated above the table between the hanging lamps. Rodolphe, leaning against the calico of the tent, was thinking so earnestly of Emma that he heard nothing. Behind him on the grass the servants were piling up the dirty plates, his neighbours were talking; he did not answer them; they filled his glass, and there was silence in his thoughts in spite of the growing noise. He was dreaming of what she had said, of the line of her lips; her face, as in a magic mirror, shone on the plates of the shakos, the folds of her gown fell along the walls, and days of love unrolled to all infinity before him in the vistas of the future.

He saw her again in the evening during the fireworks, but she was with her husband, Madame Homais, and the druggist, who was worrying about the danger of stray rockets, and every moment he left the company to go and give some advice to Binet.

The pyrotechnic pieces sent to Monsieur Tuvache had, through an excess of caution, been shut up in his cellar, and so the damp powder would not light, and the principal set piece, that was to represent a dragon biting his tail, failed completely. Now and then a meagre Roman-candle went off; then the gaping crowd sent up a shout that mingled with the cry of the women, whose waists were being squeezed in the darkness. Emma silently nestled gently against Charles's shoulder; then, raising her chin, she watched the luminous rays of the rockets against the dark sky. Rodolphe gazed at her in the light of the burning lanterns.

They went out one by one. The stars shone out. A few drops of rain began to fall. She knotted her fichu round her bare head.

At this moment the councillor's carriage came out from the inn. His coachman, who was drunk, suddenly dozed off, and one could see from the distance, above the hood, between the two lanterns, the mass of his body, that swayed from right to left with the giving of the traces.

"Truly," said the druggist, "one ought to proceed most rigorously against drunkenness! I should like to see written up weekly at the door of the townhall on a board *ad hoc* the names of all those who during the week got intoxicated on alcohol. Besides, with regard to statistics, one would thus have, as it were, public records that one could refer to in case of need. But excuse me!"

And he once more ran off to the captain. The latter was going back to see his lathe again.

"Perhaps you would not do ill," Homais said to him, "to send one of your men, or to go yourself——"

"Leave me alone!" answered the tax-collector. "It's all right!"

"Do not be uneasy," said the druggist, when he returned to his friends. "Monsieur Binet has assured me that all precautions have been taken. No sparks have fallen; the pumps are full. Let us go to rest."

"*Ma foi!* I want it," said Madame Homais, yawning at large. "But never mind; we've had a beautiful day for our fête."

Rodolphe repeated in a low voice, and with a tender look, "Oh, yes! very beautiful!"

And having bowed to one another, they separated.

Two days later, in the "Fanal de Rouen," there was a long article on the show. Homais had composed it with verve the very next morning.

"Why these festoons, these flowers, these garlands? Whither hurries this crowd like the waves of a furious sea under the torrents of a tropical sun pouring its heat upon our heads?"

Then he spoke of the condition of the peasants. Certainly the Government was doing much, but not enough. "Courage!" he cried to it; "a thousand reforms are indispensable; let us accomplish them!" Then touching on the entry of the councillor, he did not forget "the martial air of our militia," nor "our most merry village maidens," nor the "bald-headed old men like patriarchs who were there, and of whom some, the remnants of our phalanxes, still felt their hearts beat at the manly sound of the drums." He cited himself among the first of the members of the jury, and he even called attention in a note to the fact that Monsieur Homais, chemist, had sent a memoir on cider to the agricultural society. When he came to the distribution of the prizes, he painted the joy of the prize-winners in dithyrambic strophes. "The father embraced the son, the brother the brother, the husband his consort. More than one showed his humble medal with pride; and no doubt when he got home to his good housewife, he hung it up weeping on the modest walls of his cot.

"About six o'clock a banquet prepared in the meadow of Monsieur Liégeard brought together the principal personages of the fête. The greatest cordiality reigned here. Divers toasts were proposed: Monsieur Lieuvain, the King; Monsieur Tuvache, the Prefect; Monsieur Derozerays, Agriculture; Monsieur Homais, Industry and the Fine Arts, those twin sisters; Monsieur Leplichey, Progress. In the evening some brilliant fireworks on a sudden illumined the air. One would have called it a veritable kaleidoscope, a real operatic scene; and for a moment our little locality might have thought itself transported into the midst of a dream of the 'Thousand and One Nights.'

"Let us state that no untoward event disturbed this family meeting." And he added: "Only the absence of the clergy was remarked. No doubt the priests understand progress in another fashion. Just as you please, messieurs the followers of Loyola!"

IX

SIX WEEKS PASSED. Rodolphe did not come again. At last one evening he appeared.

The day after the show he had said to himself—

"We mustn't go back too soon; that would be a mistake." And at the end of a week he had gone off hunting. After the hunting he had thought it was too late, and then he reasoned thus—

"If from the first day she loved me, she must from impatience to see me again love me more. Let's go on with it!"

And he knew that his calculation had been right when, on entering the room, he saw Emma turn pale.

She was alone. The day was drawing in. The small muslin curtain along the windows deepened the twilight, and the gilding of the barometer, on which the rays of the sun fell, shone in the looking-glass between the meshes of the coral.

Rodolphe remained standing, and Emma hardly answered his first conventional phrases.

"I," he said, "have been busy. I have been ill."

"Seriously?" she cried.

"Well," said Rodolphe, sitting down at her side on a footstool, "no; it was because I did not want to come back."

"Why?"

"Can you not guess?"

He looked at her again, but so hard that she lowered her head, blushing. He went on—

"Emma!"

"Sir," she said, drawing back a little.

"Ah! you see," replied he in a melancholy voice, "that I was right not to come back; for this name, this name that fills my whole soul, and that escaped me, you forbid me to use! Madame Bovary! why all the world calls you thus! Besides, it is not your name; it is the name of another!" he repeated, "of another!" And he hid his face in his hands. "Yes, I think of you constantly. The memory of you drives me to despair. Ah! forgive me! I will leave you! Farewell! I will go far away, so far that you will never hear of me again; and yet—to-day—I know not what force impelled me towards you. For one does not struggle against Heaven; one cannot resist the smile of angels; one is carried away by that which is beautiful, charming, adorable."

It was the first time that Emma had heard such words spoken to herself, and her pride, like one who reposes bathed in warmth, expanded softly and fully at this glowing language.

"But if I did not come," he continued, "if I could not see you, at least I have gazed long on all that surrounds you. At night—every night—I arose; I came hither; I watched your house, its glimmering in the moon, the trees in the garden swaying before your window, and the little lamp, a gleam shining through the window-panes in the darkness. Ah! you never knew that there, so near you, so far from you, was a poor wretch!"

She turned towards him with a sob.

"Oh, you are good!" she said.

"No, I love you, that is all! You do not doubt that! Tell me—one word —only one word!"

And Rodolphe imperceptibly glided from the footstool to the ground; but a sound of wooden shoes was heard in the kitchen, and he noticed the door of the room was not closed.

"How kind it would be of you," he went on, rising, "if you would humour a whim of mine." It was to go over her house; he wanted to know it; and Madame Bovary seeing no objection to this, they both rose, when Charles came in.

"Good morning, doctor," Rodolphe said to him.

The doctor, flattered at this unexpected title, launched out into obsequious phrases. Of this the other took advantage to pull himself together a little. "Madame was speaking to me," he then said, "about her health."

Charles interrupted him; he had indeed a thousand anxieties; his wife's palpitations of the heart were beginning again. Then Rodolphe asked if riding would not be good.

"Certainly! excellent! just the thing! There's an idea! You ought to follow it up."

And as she objected that she had no horse, Monsieur Rodolphe offered one. She refused his offer; he did not insist. Then to explain his visit he said that his ploughman, the man of the blood-letting, still suffered from giddiness.

"I'll call round," said Bovary.

"No, no! I'll send him to you; we'll come; that will be more convenient for you."

"Ah! very good! I thank you."

And as soon as they were alone, "Why don't you accept Monsieur Boulanger's kind offer?"

She assumed a sulky air, invented a thousand excuses, and finally declared that perhaps it would look odd.

"Well, what the deuce do I care for that?" said Charles, making a pirouette. "Health before everything! You are wrong."

"And how do you think I can ride when I haven't got a habit?"

"You must order one," he answered.

The riding-habit decided her.

When the habit was ready, Charles wrote to Monsieur Boulanger that his wife was at his command, and that they counted on his good-nature.

The next day at noon Rodolphe appeared at Charles's door with two saddle-horses. One had pink rosettes at his ears and a deerskin side-saddle.

Rodolphe had put on high soft boots, saying to himself that no doubt she had never seen anything like them. In fact, Emma was charmed with his appearance as he stood on the landing in his great velvet coat and white corduroy breeches. She was ready; she was waiting for him.

Justin escaped from the chemist's to see her start, and the chemist also came out. He was giving Monsieur Boulanger a little good advice.

"An accident happens so easily. Be careful! Your horses perhaps are mettlesome."

She heard a noise above her; it was Félicité drumming on the window-panes to amuse little Berthe. The child blew her a kiss; her mother answered with a wave of her whip.

"A pleasant ride!" cried Monsieur Homais. "Prudence! above all, prudence!" And he flourished his newspaper as he saw them disappear.

As soon as he felt the ground, Emma's horse set off at a gallop. Rodolphe galloped by her side. Now and then they exchanged a word. Her figure slightly bent, her hand well up, and her right arm stretched out, she gave herself up to the cadence of the movement that rocked her in her saddle.

At the bottom of the hill Rodolphe gave his horse its head; they started together at a bound, then at the top suddenly the horses stopped, and her large blue veil fell about her.

It was early in October. There was fog over the land. Hazy clouds hovered on the horizon between the outlines of the hills; others, rent asunder, floated up and disappeared. Sometimes through a rift in the clouds, beneath a ray of sunshine, gleamed from afar the roofs of Yonville, with the gardens at the water's edge, the yards, the walls and the church steeple. Emma half closed her eyes to pick out her house, and never had this poor village where she lived appeared so small. From the height on which they were the whole valley seemed an immense pale lake sending off its vapour into the air. Clumps of trees here and there stood out like rocks, and the tall lines of the poplars that rose above the mist were like a beach when stirred by the wind.

By the side, on the turf between the pines, a brown light shimmered in the warm atmosphere. The earth, ruddy like the powder of tobacco, deadened the noise of their steps, and with the edge of their shoes the horses as they walked kicked the fallen fir cones in front of them.

Rodolphe and Emma thus went along the skirt of the wood. She turned away from time to time to avoid his look, and then she saw only the pine trunks in lines, whose monotonous succession made her a little giddy. The horses were panting; the leather of the saddles creaked.

Just as they were entering the forest the sun shone out.

"God protects us!" said Rodolphe.

"Do you think so?" she said.

"Forward! forward!" he continued.

He "tchk'd" with his tongue. The two beasts set off at a trot. Long ferns by the roadside caught in Emma's stirrup. Rodolphe leant forward and removed them as they rode along. At other times, to turn aside the branches, he passed close to her, and Emma felt his knee brushing against her leg. The sky was now blue, the leaves no longer stirred. There were spaces full of heather in flower, and plots of violets alternated with the confused patches of the trees that were grey, fawn, or golden coloured, according to the nature of their leaves. Often in the thicket was heard the fluttering of wings, or else the hoarse, soft cry of the ravens flying off amidst the oaks.

They dismounted. Rodolphe fastened up the horses. She walked on in front on the moss between the paths. But her long habit got in her way, although she held it up by the skirt; and Rodolphe, walking behind her, saw between the black cloth and the black shoe the fineness of her white stocking, that seemed to him as if it were a part of her nakedness.

She stopped. "I am tired," she said.

"Come, try again," he went on. "Courage!"

Then some hundred paces farther on she again stopped, and through her veil, that fell sideways from her man's hat over her hips, her face appeared in a bluish transparency as if she were floating under azure waves.

"But where are we going?"

He did not answer. She was breathing irregularly. Rodolphe looked round him biting his moustache. They came to a larger space where the coppice had been cut. They sat down on the trunk of a fallen tree, and Rodolphe began speaking to her of his love. He did not begin by frightening her with compliments. He was calm, serious, melancholy.

Emma listened to him with bowed head, and stirred the bits of wood on the ground with the tip of her foot.

But at the words, "Are not our destinies now one?——"

"Oh, no!" she replied. "You know that well. It is impossible!"

She rose to go. He seized her by the wrist. She stopped. Then, having gazed at him for a few moments with an amorous and humid look, she said hurriedly—

"Ah! do not speak of it again! Where are the horses? Let us go back."

He made a gesture of anger and annoyance. She repeated—

"Where are the horses? Where are the horses?"

Then smiling a strange smile, his pupil fixed, his teeth set, he advanced with outstretched arms. She recoiled trembling. She stammered—

"Oh, you frighten me! You hurt me! Let me go!"

"If it must be," he went on, his face changing; and he again became respectful, caressing, timid. She gave him her arm. They went back. He said—

"What was the matter with you? Why? I do not understand. You were mistaken, no doubt. In my soul you are as a Madonna on a pedestal, in a place lofty, secure, immaculate. But I want you for my life. I must have your eyes, your voice, your thought! Be my friend, my sister, my angel!"

And he put his arm round her waist. She feebly tried to disengage herself. He supported her thus as they walked along.

But they heard the two horses browsing on the leaves.

"Oh! one moment!" said Rodolphe. "Do not let us go! Stay!"

He drew her farther on to a small pool where duckweeds made a greenness on the water. Faded waterlilies lay motionless between the reeds. At the noise of their steps in the grass, frogs jumped away to hide themselves.

"I am wrong! I am wrong!" she said. "I am mad to listen to you!"

"Why? Emma! Emma!"

"Oh, Rodolphe!" said the young woman slowly, leaning on his shoulder.

The cloth of her habit caught against the velvet of his coat. She threw back her white neck, swelling with a sigh, and faltering, in tears, with a long shudder and hiding her face, she gave herself up to him.

The shades of night were falling; the horizontal sun passing between the branches dazzled the eyes. Here and there around her, in the leaves or on the ground, trembled luminous patches, as if humming-birds flying about had scattered their feathers. Silence was everywhere; something sweet seemed to come forth from the trees; she felt her heart, whose beating had begun again, and the blood coursing through her flesh like a stream of milk. Then far away, beyond the wood, on the other hills, she heard a vague prolonged cry, a voice which lingered, and in silence she heard it mingling like music with the last pulsations of her throbbing nerves. Rodolphe, a cigar between his lips, was mending with his penknife one of the two broken bridles.

They returned to Yonville by the same road. On the mud they saw again the traces of their horses side by side, the same thickets, the same stones in the grass; nothing around them seemed changed; and yet for her something had happened more stupendous than if the mountains had moved in their places. Rodolphe now and again bent forward and took her hand to kiss it.

She was charming on horseback—upright, with her slender waist, her knee bent on the mane of her horse, her face somewhat flushed by the fresh air in the red of the evening.

On entering Yonville she made her horse prance in the road. People looked at her from the windows.

At dinner her husband thought she looked well, but she pretended not to hear him when he inquired about her ride, and she remained sitting there with her elbow at the side of her plate between the two lighted candles.

"Emma!" he said.

"What?"

"Well, I spent the afternoon at Monsieur Alexandre's. He has an old cob, still very fine, only a little broken-kneed, and that could be bought, I am sure, for a hundred crowns." He added, "And thinking it might please you, I have bespoken it—bought it. Have I done right? Do tell me!"

She nodded her head in assent; then a quarter of an hour later—

"Are you going out to-night?" she asked.

"Yes. Why?"

"Oh, nothing, nothing, my dear!"

And as soon as she had got rid of Charles she went and shut herself up in her room.

At first she felt stunned; she saw the trees, the paths, the ditches, Rodolphe, and she again felt the pressure of his arm, while the leaves rustled and the reeds whistled.

But when she saw herself in the glass she wondered at her face. Never had her eyes been so large, so black, of so profound a depth. Something subtle about her being transfigured her. She repeated, "I have a lover! a lover!" delighting at the idea as if a second puberty had come to her. So at last she was to know those joys of love, that fever of happiness of which she had despaired! She was entering upon marvels where all would be passion, ecstasy, delirium. An azure infinity encompassed her, the heights of sentiment sparkled under her thought, and ordinary existence appeared only afar off, down below in the shade, through the interspaces of these heights.

Then she recalled the heroines of the books that she had read, and the lyric legion of these adulterous women began to sing in her memory with the voice of sisters that charmed her. She became herself, as it were, an actual part of these imaginings, and realised the love-dream of her youth as she saw herself in this type of amorous women whom she had so envied.

Besides, Emma felt a satisfaction of revenge. Had she not suffered enough?
But now she triumphed, and the love so long pent up burst forth in full
joyous bubblings. She tasted it without remorse, without anxiety, without
trouble.

The day following passed with a new sweetness. They made vows to one
another. She told him of her sorrows. Rodolphe interrupted her with
kisses; and she, looking at him through half-closed eyes, asked him to call
her again by her name—to say that he loved her. They were in the forest,
as yesterday, in the shed of some wooden-shoe maker. The walls were of
straw, and the roof so low they had to stoop. They were seated side by side
on a bed of dry leaves.

From that day forth they wrote to one another regularly every evening.
Emma placed her letter at the end of the garden, by the river, in a fissure
of the wall. Rodolphe came to fetch it, and put another there, that she
always found fault with as too short.

One morning, when Charles had gone out before daybreak, she was
seized with the fancy to see Rodolphe at once. She would go quickly to
La Huchette, stay there an hour, and be back again at Yonville while every
one was still asleep. This idea made her pant with desire, and she soon found
herself in the middle of the field, walking with rapid steps, without looking
behind her.

Day was just breaking. Emma from afar recognised her lover's house. Its
two dove-tailed weathercocks stood out black against the pale dawn.

Beyond the farmyard there was a detached building that she thought
must be the château. She entered it as if the doors at her approach had
opened wide of their own accord. A large straight staircase led up to the
corridor. Emma raised the latch of a door, and suddenly at the end of the
room she saw a man sleeping. It was Rodolphe. She uttered a cry.

"You here? You here?" he repeated. "How did you manage to come?
Ah! your dress is damp."

This first piece of daring successful, now every time Charles went out
early Emma dressed quickly and slipped on tiptoe down the steps that led
to the water-side.

But when the plank for the cows was taken up, she had to go by the walls
alongside of the river; the bank was slippery; in order not to fall she caught
hold of the tufts of faded wallflowers. Then she went across ploughed fields,
in which she sank, stumbling, and clogging her thin shoes. Her scarf,
knotted round her head, fluttered to the wind in the meadows. She was
afraid of the oxen; she began to run; she arrived out of breath, with rosy
cheeks, and breathing out from her whole person a fresh perfume of sap,
of verdure, of the open air. At this hour Rodolphe still slept. It was like
a spring morning coming into his room.

The yellow curtains along the windows let a heavy, whitish light enter
softly. Emma felt about, opening and closing her eyes, while the drops of
dew hanging from her hair formed, as it were, a topaz aureole around her
face. Rodolphe, laughing, drew her to him and pressed her to his breast.

Then she examined the apartment, opened the drawers of the tables, combed her hair with his comb, and looked at herself in his shaving-glass. Often she even put between her teeth the big pipe that lay on the table by the bed, amongst lemons and pieces of sugar near a bottle of water.

It took them a good quarter of an hour to say good-bye. Then Emma cried. She would have wished never to leave Rodolphe. Something stronger than herself forced her to him; so much so, that one day, seeing her come unexpectedly, he frowned as one put out.

"What is the matter with you?" she said. "Are you ill? Tell me!"

At last he declared with a serious air that her visits were becoming imprudent—that she was compromising herself.

X

GRADUALLY Rodolphe's fears took possession of her. At first, love had intoxicated her, and she had thought of nothing beyond. But now that he was indispensable to her life, she feared to lose anything of this, or even that it should be disturbed. When she came back from his house, she looked all about her, anxiously watching every form that passed in the horizon, and every village window from which she could be seen. She listened for steps, cries, the noise of the ploughs, and she stopped short, white, and trembling more than the aspen leaves swaying overhead.

One morning as she was thus returning, she suddenly thought she saw the long barrel of a carbine that seemed to be aimed at her. It stuck out sideways from the end of a small tub half-buried in the grass on the edge of a ditch. Emma, half-fainting with terror, nevertheless walked on, and a man stepped out of the tub like a Jack-in-the-box. He had gaiters buckled up to the knees, his cap pulled down over his eyes, trembling lips, and a red nose. It was Captain Binet lying in ambush for wild ducks.

"You ought to have called out long ago!" he exclaimed. "When one sees a gun, one should always give warning."

The tax-collector was thus trying to hide the fright he had had, for a prefectorial order having prohibited duck-hunting except in boats, Monsieur Binet, despite his respect for the laws, was infringing them, and so he every moment expected to see the rural guard turn up. But this anxiety whetted his pleasure, and, all alone in his tub, he congratulated himself on his luck and on his 'cuteness.

At sight of Emma he seemed relieved from a great weight, and at once entered upon a conversation.

"It isn't warm; it's nipping."

Emma answered nothing. He went on—

"And you're out so early?"

"Yes," she said stammering; "I am just coming from the nurse where my child is."

"Ah! very good! very good! For myself, I am here, just as you see me,

since break of day; but the weather is so muggy, that unless one had the bird
at the mouth of the gun——"

"Good evening, Monsieur Binet," she interrupted him, turning on her heel.
"Your servant, madame," he replied drily; and he went back into his tub.
Emma regretted having left the tax-collector so abruptly. No doubt he
would form unfavourable conjectures. The story about the nurse was the
worst possible excuse, every one at Yonville knowing that the little Bovary
had been at home with her parents for a year. Besides, no one was living
in this direction; this path led only to La Huchette. Binet, then, would guess
whence she came, and he would not keep silence; he would talk, that was
certain. She remained until evening racking her brain with every conceivable
lying project, and had constantly before her eyes that imbecile with the
game-bag.

Charles after dinner, seeing her gloomy, proposed, by way of distraction,
to take her to the chemist's, and the first person she caught sight of in the
shop was the tax-collector again. He was standing in front of the counter,
lit up by the gleams of the red bottle, and was saying—

"Please give me half an ounce of vitriol."

"Justin," cried the druggist, "bring us the sulphuric acid." Then to Emma,
who was going up to Madame Homais's room, "No, stay here; it isn't worth
while going up; she is just coming down. Warm yourself at the stove in
the meantime. Excuse me. Good-day, Doctor" (for the chemist much enjoyed pronouncing the word "doctor," as if addressing another by it reflected on himself some of the grandeur that he found in it). "Now, take
care not to upset the mortars! You'd better fetch some chairs from the little
room; you know very well that the armchairs are not to be taken out of
the drawing-room."

And to put his armchair back in its place he was darting away from the
counter, when Binet asked him for half an ounce of sugar acid.

"Sugar acid!" said the chemist contemptuously, "don't know it; I'm
ignorant of it! But perhaps you want oxalic acid. It is oxalic acid, isn't it?"

Binet explained that he wanted a corrosive to make himself some copper-
water with which to remove rust from his hunting things.

Emma shuddered. The chemist began saying—

"Indeed the weather is not propitious on account of the damp."

"Nevertheless," replied the tax-collector, with a sly look, "there are people
who like it."

She was stifling.

"And give me——"

"Will he never go?" thought she.

"Half an ounce of resin and turpentine, four ounces of yellow wax, and
three half ounces of animal charcoal, if you please, to clean the varnished
leather of my togs."

The druggist was beginning to cut the wax when Madame Homais appeared, Irma in her arms, Napoléon by her side, and Athalie following. She
sat down on the velvet seat by the window, and the lad squatted down on a

footstool, while his eldest sister hovered round the jujube box near her papa. The latter was filling funnels and corking phials, sticking on labels, making up parcels. Around him all were silent; only from time to time were heard the weights jingling in the balance, and a few low words from the chemist giving directions to his pupil.

"And how's the little woman?" suddenly asked Madame Homais.

"Silence!" exclaimed her husband, who was writing down some figures in his waste-book.

"Why didn't you bring her?" she went on in a low voice.

"Hush! hush!" said Emma, pointing with her finger to the druggist.

But Binet, quite absorbed in looking over his bill, had probably heard nothing. At last he went out. Then Emma, relieved, uttered a deep sigh.

"How hard you are breathing!" said Madame Homais.

"Well, you see, it's rather warm," she replied.

So the next day they talked over how to arrange their rendezvous. Emma wanted to bribe her servant with a present, but it would be better to find some safe house at Yonville. Rodolphe promised to look for one.

All through the winter, three or four times a week, in the dead of night he came to the garden. Emma had on purpose taken away the key of the gate, which Charles thought lost.

To call her, Rodolphe threw a sprinkle of sand at the shutters. She jumped up with a start; but sometimes he had to wait, for Charles had a mania for chatting by the fireside, and he would not stop. She was wild with impatience; if her eyes could have done it, she would have hurled him out at the window. At last she would begin to undress, then take up a book, and go on reading very quietly as if the book amused her. But Charles, who was in bed, called to her to come too.

"Come, now, Emma," he said, "it is time."

"Yes, I am coming," she answered.

Then, as the candles dazzled him, he turned to the wall and fell asleep. She escaped, smiling, palpitating, undressed.

Rodolphe had a large cloak; he wrapped her in it, and putting his arm round her waist, he drew her without a word to the end of the garden.

It was in the arbour, on the same seat of old sticks where formerly Léon had looked at her so amorously on the summer evenings. She never thought of him now.

The stars shone through the leafless jasmine branches. Behind them they heard the river flowing, and now and again on the bank the rustling of the dry reeds. Masses of shadow here and there loomed out in the darkness, and sometimes, vibrating with one movement, they rose up and swayed like immense black waves pressing forward to engulf them. The cold of the nights made them clasp closer; the sighs of their lips seemed to them deeper; their eyes, that they could hardly see, larger; and in the midst of the silence low words were spoken that fell on their souls sonorous, crystalline, and that reverberated in multiplied vibrations.

When the night was rainy, they took refuge in the consulting-room between the cart-shed and the stable. She lighted one of the kitchen candles that she had hidden behind the books. Rodolphe settled down there as if at home. The sight of the library, of the bureau, of the whole apartment, in fine, excited his merriment, and he could not refrain from making jokes about Charles, which rather embarrassed Emma. She would have liked to see him more serious, and even on occasions more dramatic; as, for example, when she thought she heard a noise of approaching steps in the alley.

"Some one is coming!" she said.

He blew out the light.

"Have you your pistols?"

"Why?"

"Why, to defend yourself," replied Emma.

"From your husband? Oh, poor devil!" And Rodolphe finished his sentence with a gesture that said, "I could crush him with a flip of my finger."

She was wonder-stricken at his bravery, although she felt in it a sort of indecency and a naïve coarseness that scandalised her.

Rodolphe reflected a good deal on the affair of the pistols. If she had spoken seriously, it was very ridiculous, he thought, even odious; for he had no reason to hate the good Charles, not being what is called devoured by jealousy; and on this subject Emma had taken a great vow that he did not think in the best of taste.

Besides, she was growing very sentimental. She had insisted on exchanging miniatures; they had cut off handfuls of hair, and now she was asking for a ring—a real wedding-ring, in sign of an eternal union. She often spoke to him of the evening chimes, of the voices of nature. Then she talked to him of her mother—hers! and of his mother—his! Rodolphe had lost his twenty years ago. Emma none the less consoled him with caressing words as one would have done a lost child, and she sometimes even said to him, gazing at the moon—

"I am sure that above there together they approve of our love."

But she was so pretty. He had possessed so few women of such ingenuousness. This love without debauchery was a new experience for him, and, drawing him out of his lazy habits, caressed at once his pride and his sensuality. Emma's enthusiasm, which his bourgeois good sense disdained, seemed to him in his heart of hearts charming, since it was lavished on him. Then, sure of being loved, he no longer kept up appearances, and insensibly he changed his ways.

He had no longer, as formerly, words so gentle that they made her cry, nor passionate caresses that made her mad, so that their great love, which engrossed her life, seemed to lessen beneath her like the water of a stream absorbed into its channel, and she could see the bed of it. She would not believe it; she redoubled in tenderness, and Rodolphe concealed his indifference less and less.

She did not know if she regretted having yielded to him, or whether she did not wish, on the contrary, to enjoy him the more. The humiliation of feeling herself weak was turning to rancour, tempered by their voluptuous pleasures. It was not affection; it was like a continual seduction. He subjugated her; she almost feared him.

Appearances, nevertheless, were calmer than ever, Rodolphe having succeeded in carrying out the adultery after his own fancy; and at the end of six months, when the spring-time came, they were to one another like a married couple, tranquilly keeping up a domestic flame.

It was the time of year when old Rouault sent his turkey in remembrance of the setting of his leg. The present always arrived with a letter. Emma cut the string that tied it to the basket, and read the following lines:—

"MY DEAR CHILDREN,—I hope this will find you in good health, and that it will be as good as the others, for it seems to me a little more tender, if I may venture to say so, and heavier. But next time, for a change, I'll give you a turkey-cock, unless you have a preference for some dabs; and send me back the hamper, if you please, with the two old ones. I have had an accident with my cart-sheds, whose covering flew off one windy night among the trees. The harvest has not been over-good either. Finally, I don't know when I shall come to see you. It is so difficult now to leave the house since I am alone, my poor Emma."

Here there was a break in the lines, as if the old fellow had dropped his pen to dream a little while.

"For myself, I am very well, except for a cold I caught the other day at the fair at Yvetot, where I had gone to hire a shepherd, having turned away mine because he was too dainty. How we are to be pitied with such a lot of thieves! Besides, he was also rude. I heard from a pedlar, who, travelling through your part of the country this winter, had a tooth drawn, that Bovary was as usual working hard. That doesn't surprise me; and he showed me his tooth; we had some coffee together. I asked him if he had seen you, and he said not, but that he had seen two horses in the stables, from which I concluded that business is looking up. So much the better, my dear children, and may God send you every imaginable happiness! It grieves me not yet to have seen my dear little granddaughter, Berthe Bovary. I have planted an Orleans plum tree for her in the garden under your room, and I won't have it touched unless it is to have jam made for her by and by, that I will keep in the cupboard for her when she comes.

"Good-bye, my dear children. I kiss you, my girl, you too, my son-in-law, and the little one on both cheeks. I am, with best compliments, your loving father,

"THEODORE ROUAULT."

She held the coarse paper in her fingers for some minutes. The spelling mistakes were interwoven one with the other, and Emma followed the kindly thought that cackled right through it like a hen half hidden in a hedge of thorns. The writing had been dried with ashes from the hearth, for a little grey powder slipped from the letter on to her dress, and she almost thought she saw her father bending over the hearth to take up the tongs. How long since she had been with him, sitting on the footstool in the chimney-corner, where she used to burn the end of a bit of wood in the great flame of the sea-sedges! She remembered the summer evenings all full of sunshine. The colts neighed when any one passed by, and galloped, galloped. Under her window there was a beehive, and sometimes the bees wheeling round in the light struck against her window like rebounding balls of gold. What happiness there had been at that time, what freedom, what hope! What an abundance of illusions! Nothing was left of them now. She had got rid of them all in her soul's life, in all her successive conditions of life,—maidenhood, her marriage, and her love;—thus constantly losing them all her life through, like a traveller who leaves something of his wealth at every inn along his road.

But what then made her so unhappy? What was the extraordinary catastrophe that had transformed her? And she raised her head, looking round as if to seek the cause of that which made her suffer.

An April ray was dancing on the china of the whatnot; the fire burned; beneath her slippers she felt the softness of the carpet; the day was brighter, the air warm, and she heard her child shouting with laughter.

In fact, the little girl was just then rolling on the lawn in the midst of the grass that was being turned. She was lying flat on her stomach at the top of a rick. The servant was holding her by her skirt. Lestiboudois was raking by her side, and every time he came near she leant forward, beating the air with both her arms.

"Bring her to me," said her mother, rushing to embrace her. "How I love you, my poor child! How I love you!"

Then noticing that the tips of her ears were rather dirty, she rang at once, for warm water, and washed her, changed her linen, her stockings, her shoes, asked a thousand questions about her health, as if on the return from a long journey, and finally, kissing her again and crying a little, she gave her back to the servant, who stood quite thunderstricken at this excess of tenderness.

That evening Rodolphe found her more serious than usual.

"That will pass over," he concluded; "it's a whim."

And he missed three rendezvous running. When he did come, she showed herself cold and almost contemptuous.

"Ah! you're losing your time, my lady!"

And he pretended not to notice her melancholy sighs, nor the handkerchief she took out.

Then Emma repented. She even asked herself why she detested Charles; if it had not been better to have been able to love him? But he gave her no opportunities for such a revival of sentiment, so that she was much embarrassed by her desire for sacrifice, when the druggist came just in time to provide her with an opportunity.

XI

HE HAD RECENTLY READ a eulogy on a new method for curing club-foot, and as he was a partisan of progress, he conceived the patriotic idea that Yonville, in order to keep to the fore, ought to have some operations for strephopody or club-foot.

"For," said he to Emma, "what risk is there? See" (and he enumerated on his fingers the advantages of the attempt), "success, almost certain relief and beautifying of the patient, celebrity acquired by the operator. Why, for example, should not your husband relieve poor Hippolyte of the 'Lion d'Or'? Note that he would not fail to tell about his cure to all the travellers, and then" (Homais lowered his voice and looked round him) "who is to prevent me from sending a short paragraph on the subject to the paper? Eh! goodness me! an article gets about; it is talked of; it ends by making a snowball! And who knows? who knows?"

In fact, Bovary might succeed. Nothing proved to Emma that he was not clever; and what a satisfaction for her to have urged him to a step by which his reputation and fortune would be increased! She only wished to lean on something more solid than love.

Charles, urged by the druggist and by her, allowed himself to be persuaded. He sent to Rouen for Dr. Duval's volume, and every evening, holding his head between both hands, plunged into the reading of it.

While he was studying equinus, varus, and valgus, that is to say, *katastrephopody*, *endostrephopody*, and *exostrephopody* (or better, the various turnings of the foot downwards, inwards, and outwards), with the *hypostrephopody* and *anastrephopody* (otherwise torsion downwards and upwards), Monsieur Homais, with all sorts of arguments, was exhorting the lad at the inn to submit to the operation.

"You will scarcely feel, probably, a slight pain; it is a simple prick, like a little blood-letting, less than the extraction of certain corns."

Hippolyte, reflecting, rolled his stupid eyes.

"However," continued the chemist, "it doesn't concern me. It's for your sake, for pure humanity! I should like to see you, my friend, rid of your hideous caudication, together with that waddling of the lumbar regions which, whatever you say, must considerably interfere with you in the exercise of your calling."

Then Homais represented to him how much jollier and brisker he would feel afterwards, and even gave him to understand that he would be more likely to please the women; and the stable-boy began to smile heavily. Then he attacked him through his vanity:—

"Aren't you a man? Hang it! what would you have done if you had had to go into the army, to go and fight beneath the standard? Ah! Hippolyte!"

And Homais retired, declaring that he could not understand this obstinacy, this blindness in refusing the benefactions of science.

The poor fellow gave way, for it was like a conspiracy. Binet, who never interfered with other people's business, Madame Lefrançois, Artémise, the neighbours, even the mayor, Monsieur Tuvache—every one persuaded him, lectured him, shamed him; but what finally decided him was that it would cost him nothing. Bovary even undertook to provide the machine for the operation. This generosity was an idea of Emma's, and Charles consented to it, thinking in his heart of hearts that his wife was an angel.

So by the advice of the chemist, and after three fresh starts, he had a kind of box made by the carpenter, with the aid of the locksmith, that weighed about eight pounds, and in which iron, wood, sheet-iron, leather, screws, and nuts had not been spared.

But to know which of Hippolyte's tendons to cut, it was necessary first of all to find out what kind of club-foot he had.

He had a foot forming almost a straight line with the leg, which, however, did not prevent it from being turned in, so that it was an equinus together with something of a varus, or else a slight varus with a strong tendency to equinus. But with this equinus, wide in foot like a horse's hoof, with rugose skin, dry tendons, and large toes, on which the black nails looked as if made of iron, the club-foot ran about like a deer from morn till night. He was constantly to be seen on the Place, jumping round the carts, thrusting his limping foot forwards. He seemed even stronger on that leg than the other. By dint of hard service it had acquired, as it were, moral qualities of patience and energy; and when he was given some heavy work, he stood on it in preference to its fellow.

Now, as it was an equinus, it was necessary to cut the tendo Achillis, and, if need were, the anterior tibial muscle could be seen to afterwards for getting rid of the varus; for the doctor did not dare to risk both operations at once; he was even trembling already for fear of injuring some important region that he did not know.

Neither Ambrose Paré, applying for the first time since Celsus, after an interval of fifteen centuries, a ligature to an artery, nor Dupuytren, about to open an abscess in the brain, nor Gensoul when he first took away the superior maxilla, had hearts that trembled, hands that shook, minds so strained as Monsieur Bovary when he approached Hippolyte, his tenotome between his fingers. And as at hospitals, near by on a table lay a heap of lint, with waxed thread, many bandages—a pyramid of bandages—every bandage to be found at the druggist's. It was Monsieur Homais who since morning had been organising all these preparations, as much to dazzle the multitude as to keep up his illusions. Charles pierced the skin; a dry crackling was heard. The tendon was cut, the operation over. Hippolyte could not get over his surprise, but bent over Bovary's hands to cover them with kisses.

"Come, be calm," said the druggist; "later on you will show your gratitude to your benefactor."

And he went down to tell the result to five or six inquirers who were waiting in the yard, and who fancied that Hippolyte would reappear walking properly. Then Charles, having buckled his patient into the machine, went home, where Emma, all anxiety, awaited him at the door. She threw herself on his neck; they sat down to table; he ate much, and at dessert he even wanted to take a cup of coffee, a luxury he only permitted himself on Sundays when there was company.

The evening was charming, full of prattle, of dreams together. They talked about their future fortune, of the improvements to be made in their house; he saw people's estimation of him growing, his comforts increasing, his wife always loving him; and she was happy to refresh herself with a new sentiment, healthier, better, to feel at last some tenderness for this poor fellow who adored her. The thought of Rodolphe for one moment passed through her mind, but her eyes turned again to Charles; she even noticed with surprise that he had not bad teeth.

They were in bed when Monsieur Homais, in spite of a servant, suddenly entered the room, holding in his hand a sheet of paper just written. It was the paragraph he intended for the "Fanal de Rouen." He brought it to them to read.

"Read it yourself," said Bovary.

He read—

" 'Despite the prejudices that still invest a part of the face of Europe like a net, the light nevertheless begins to penetrate our country places. Thus on Tuesday our little town of Yonville found itself the scene of a surgical operation which is at the same time an act of loftiest philanthropy. Monsieur Bovary, one of our most distinguished practitioners——' "

"Oh, that is too much! too much!" said Charles, choking with emotion.

"No, no! not at all! What next!"

" '——Performed an operation on a club-footed man.' I have not used the scientific term, because you know in a newspaper every one would not perhaps understand. The masses must——"

"No doubt," said Bovary; "go on!"

"I proceed," said the chemist. " 'Monsieur Bovary, one of our most distinguished practitioners, performed an operation on a club-footed man called Hippolyte Tautain, stable-man for the last twenty-five years at the hotel of the "Lion d'Or," kept by Widow Lefrançois, at the Place d'Armes. The novelty of the attempt, and the interest incident to the subject, had attracted such a concourse of persons that there was a veritable obstruction on the threshold of the establishment. The operation, moreover, was performed as if by magic, and barely a few drops of blood appeared on the skin, as though to say that the rebellious tendon had at last given way beneath the efforts of art. The patient, strangely enough—we affirm it as an eye-witness—complained of no pain. His condition up to the present time leaves nothing to be desired. Everything tends to show that his convalescence will be brief; and who knows even if at our next village festivity we shall not see our good Hippolyte figuring in the bacchic dance in the midst of a chorus of joyous boon-companions, and thus proving to all eyes by his verve and his capers his complete cure? Honour, then, to the generous savants! Honour to those indefatigable spirits who consecrate their vigils to the amelioration or to the alleviation of their kind! Honour, thrice honour! Is it not time to cry that the blind shall see, the deaf hear, the lame walk? But that which fanaticism formerly promised to its elect, science now accomplishes for all men. We shall keep our readers informed as to the successive phases of this remarkable cure.' "

This did not prevent Mère Lefrançois from coming five days after, scared, and crying out—

"Help! he is dying! I am going crazy!"

Charles rushed to the "Lion d'Or," and the chemist, who caught sight of him passing along the Place hatless, abandoned his shop. He appeared himself breathless, red, anxious, and asking every one who was going up the stairs—

"Why, what's the matter with our interesting strephopode?"

The strephopode was writhing in hideous convulsions, so that the machine in which his leg was enclosed was knocked against the wall enough to break it.

With many precautions, in order not to disturb the position of the limb, the box was removed, and an awful sight presented itself. The outlines of the foot disappeared in such a swelling that the entire skin seemed about to burst, and it was covered with ecchymosis, caused by the famous machine. Hippolyte had already complained of suffering from it. No attention had been paid to him; they had to acknowledge that he had not been altogether wrong, and he was freed for a few hours. But hardly had the œdema gone down to some extent, that the two savants thought fit to put back the limb in the apparatus, strapping it tighter to hasten matters. At last, three days after, Hippolyte being unable to endure it any longer, they once more removed the machine, and were much surprised at the result they saw. The livid tumefaction spread over the leg, with blisters here and there, whence there oozed a black liquid. Matters were taking a serious turn. Hippolyte began to worry himself, and Mère Lefrançois had him installed in the little room near the kitchen, so that he might at least have some distraction.

But the tax-collector, who dined there every day, complained bitterly of such companionship. Then Hippolyte was removed to the billiard-room. He lay there moaning under his heavy coverings, pale, with long beard, sunken eyes, and from time to time turning his perspiring head on the dirty pillow, where the flies alighted. Madame Bovary went to see him. She brought him linen for his poultices; she comforted, and encouraged him. Besides, he did not want for company, especially on market-days, when the peasants were knocking about the billiard-balls round him, fenced with the cues, smoked, drank, sang, and brawled.

"How are you?" they said, clapping him on the shoulder. "Ah! you're not up to much, it seems, but it's your own fault. You should do this! do that!" And then they told him stories of people who had all been cured by other remedies than his. Then by way of consolation they added—

"You give way too much! Get up! You coddle yourself like a king! All the same, old chap, you don't smell nice!"

Gangrene, in fact, was spreading more and more. Bovary himself turned sick at it. He came every hour, every moment. Hippolyte looked at him with eyes full of terror, sobbing—

"When shall I get well? Oh, save me! How unfortunate I am! How unfortunate I am!"

And the doctor left, always recommending him to diet himself.

"Don't listen to him, my lad," said Mère Lefrançois. "Haven't they tortured you enough already? You'll grow still weaker. Here! swallow this."

And she gave him some good beef-tea, a slice of mutton, a piece of bacon, and sometimes small glasses of brandy, that he had not the strength to put to his lips.

Abbé Bournisien, hearing that he was growing worse, asked to see him. He began by pitying his sufferings, declaring at the same time that he ought to rejoice at them since it was the will of the Lord, and take advantage of the occasion to reconcile himself to Heaven.

"For," said the ecclesiastic in a paternal tone, "you rather neglected your duties; you were rarely seen at divine worship. How many years is it since you approached the holy table? I understand that your work, that the whirl of the world may have kept you from care for your salvation. But now is the time to reflect. Yet don't despair. I have known great sinners, who, about to appear before God (you are not yet at this point I know), had implored His mercy, and who certainly died in the best frame of mind. Let us hope that, like them, you will set us a good example. Thus, as a precaution, what is to prevent you from saying morning and evening a 'Hail Mary, full of grace,' and 'Our Father which art in heaven'? Yes, do that, for my sake, to oblige me. That won't cost you anything. Will you promise me?"

The poor devil promised. The curé came back day after day. He chatted with the landlady, and even told anecdotes interspersed with jokes and puns that Hippolyte did not understand. Then, as soon as he could, he fell back upon matters of religion, putting on an appropriate expression of face.

His zeal seemed successful, for the club-foot soon manifested a desire to go on a pilgrimage to Bon-Secours if he were cured; to which Monsieur Bournisien replied that he saw no objection; two precautions were better than one; it was no risk anyhow.

The druggist was indignant at what he called the manœuvres of the priest; they were prejudicial, he said, to Hippolyte's convalescence, and he kept repeating to Madame Lefrançois, "Leave him alone! leave him alone! You perturb his morals with your mysticism."

But the good woman would no longer listen to him; he was the cause of it all. From a spirit of contradiction she hung up near the bedside of the patient a basin filled with holy-water and a branch of box.

Religion, however, seemed no more able to succour him than surgery, and the invincible gangrene still spread from the extremities towards the stomach. It was all very well to vary the potions and change the poultices; the muscles each day rotted more and more; and at last Charles replied by an affirmative nod of the head when Mère Lefrançois asked him if she could not, as a forlorn hope, send for Monsieur Canivet of Neufchâtel who was a celebrity.

A doctor of medicine, fifty years of age, enjoying a good position and self-possessed, Charles's colleague did not refrain from laughing disdainfully when he had uncovered the leg, mortified to the knee. Then having flatly declared that it must be amputated, he went off to the chemist's to rail at the asses who could have reduced a poor man to such a state. Shaking Monsieur Homais by the button of his coat, he shouted out in the shop—

"These are the inventions of Paris! These are the ideas of those gentry of the capital! It is like strabismus, chloroform, lithotrity, a heap of monstrosities that the Government ought to prohibit. But they want to do the clever, and they cram you with remedies without troubling about the consequences. We are not so clever, not we! We are not savants, coxcombs, fops! We are practitioners; we cure people, and we should not dream of operating on any one who is in perfect health. Straighten club-feet! As if one could straighten club-feet! It is as if one wished, for example, to make a hunchback straight!"

Homais suffered as he listened to this discourse, and he concealed his discomfort beneath a courtier's smile; for he needed to humour Monsieur Canivet, whose prescriptions sometimes came as far as Yonville. So he did not take up the defence of Bovary; he did not even make a single remark, and, renouncing his principles, he sacrificed his dignity to the more serious interests of his business.

This amputation of the thigh by Doctor Canivet was a great event in the village. On that day all the inhabitants got up earlier, and the Grand Rue, although full of people, had something lugubrious about it, as if an execution had been expected. At the grocer's they discussed Hippolyte's illness; the shops did no business, and Madame Tuvache, the mayor's wife, did not stir from her window, such was her impatience to see the operator arrive.

He came in his gig, which he drove himself. But the springs of the right side having at length given way beneath the weight of his corpulence, it happened that the carriage as it rolled along leaned over a little, and on the other cushion near him could be seen a large box covered in red sheep-leather, whose three brass clasps shone grandly.

After he had entered like a whirlwind the porch of the "Lion d'Or," the doctor, shouting very loud, ordered them to unharness his horse. Then he went into the stable to see that he was eating his oats all right; for on arriving at a patient's he first of all looked after his mare and his gig. People even said about this—

"Ah! Monsieur Canivet's a character!"

And he was the more esteemed for this imperturbable coolness. The universe to the last man might have died, and he would not have missed the smallest of his habits.

Homais presented himself.

"I count on you," said the doctor. "Are we ready? Come along!"

But the druggist, turning red, confessed that he was too sensitive to assist at such an operation.

"When one is a simple spectator," he said, "the imagination, you know, is impressed. And then I have such a nervous system!"

"Pshaw!" interrupted Canivet; "on the contrary, you seem to me inclined to apoplexy. Besides, that doesn't astonish me, for you chemist fellows are always poking about your kitchens, which must end by spoiling your constitutions. Now just look at me. I get up every day at four o'clock; I shave with cold water (and am never cold). I don't wear flannels, and I never catch cold; my carcass is good enough! I live now in one way, now in another, like a philosopher, taking pot-luck; that is why I am not squeamish like you, and it is as indifferent to me to carve a Christian as the first fowl that turns up. Then, perhaps, you will say, habit! habit!"

Then, without any consideration for Hippolyte, who was sweating with agony between his sheets, these gentlemen entered into a conversation, in which the druggist compared the coolness of a surgeon to that of a general; and this comparison was pleasing to Canivet, who launched out on the exigencies of his art. He looked upon it as a sacred office, although the ordinary practitioners dishonoured it. At last, coming back to the patient, he examined the bandages brought by Homais, the same that had appeared for the club-foot, and asked for some one to hold the limb for him. Lestiboudois was sent for, and Monsieur Canivet having turned up his sleeves, passed into the billiard-room, while the druggist stayed with Artémise and the landlady, both whiter than their aprons, and with ears strained towards the door.

Bovary during this time did not dare to stir from his house.

He kept downstairs in the sitting-room by the side of the fireless chimney, his chin on his breast, his hands clasped, his eyes staring. "What a mishap!" he thought, "what a mishap!" Perhaps, after all, he had made some slip. He thought it over, but could hit upon nothing. But the most famous surgeons also made mistakes; and that is what no one would ever believe! People, on the contrary, would laugh, jeer! It would spread as far as Forges, as Neufchâtel, as Rouen, everywhere! Who could say if his colleagues would not write against him. Polemics would ensue; he would have to answer in the papers. Hippolyte might even prosecute him. He saw himself dishonoured, ruined, lost; and his imagination, assailed by a world of hypotheses, tossed amongst them like an empty cask borne by the sea and floating upon the waves.

Emma, opposite, watched him; she did not share his humiliation; she felt another—that of having supposed such a man was worth anything. As if twenty times already she had not sufficiently perceived his mediocrity.

Charles was walking up and down the room; his boots creaked on the floor.

"Sit down," she said; "you fidget me."

He sat down again.

How was it that she—she, who was so intelligent—could have allowed herself to be deceived again? and through what deplorable madness had she thus ruined her life by continual sacrifices? She recalled all her instincts of luxury, all the privations of her soul, the sordidness of marriage, of the household, her dreams sinking into the mire like wounded swallows; all that she had longed for, all that she had denied herself, all that she might have had! And for what? for what?

In the midst of the silence that hung over the village a heartrending cry rose on the air. Bovary turned white to fainting. She knit her brows with a nervous gesture, then went on. And it was for him, for this creature, for this man, who understood nothing, who felt nothing! For he was there quite quiet, not even suspecting that the ridicule of his name would henceforth sully hers as well as his. She had made efforts to love him, and she had repented with tears for having yielded to another!

"But it was perhaps a valgus!" suddenly exclaimed Bovary, who was meditating.

At the unexpected shock of this phrase falling on her thought like a leaden bullet on a silver plate, Emma, shuddering, raised her head in order to find out what he meant to say; and they looked at the other in silence, almost amazed to see each other, so far sundered were they by their inner thoughts. Charles gazed at her with the dull look of a drunken man, while he listened motionless to the last cries of the sufferer that followed each other in long-drawn modulations, broken by sharp spasms like the far-off howling of some beast being slaughtered. Emma bit her wan lips, and rolling between her fingers a piece of coral that she had broken, fixed on Charles the burning glance of her eyes like two arrows of fire about to dart forth. Everything in him irritated her now; his face, his dress, what he did not say, his whole person, his existence, in fine. She repented of her past virtue as of a crime, and what still remained of it crumbled away beneath the furious blows of her pride. She revelled in all the evil ironies of triumphant adultery. The memory of her lover came back to her with dazzling attractions; she threw her whole soul into it, borne away towards this image with a fresh enthusiasm; and Charles seemed to her as much removed from her life, as absent forever, as impossible and annihilated, as if he had been about to die and were passing under her eyes.

There was a sound of steps on the pavement. Charles looked up, and through the lowered blinds he saw at the corner of the market in the broad sunshine Dr. Canivet, who was wiping his brow with his handkerchief. Homais, behind him, was carrying a large red box in his hand, and both were going towards the chemist's.

Then with a feeling of sudden tenderness and discouragement Charles turned to his wife saying to her—

"Oh, kiss me, my own!"

"Leave me!" she said, red with anger.

"What is the matter?" he asked, stupefied. "Be calm; compose yourself. You know well enough that I love you. Come!"

"Enough!" she cried with a terrible look.

And escaping from the room, Emma closed the door so violently that the barometer fell from the wall and smashed on the floor.

Charles sank back into his armchair overwhelmed, trying to discover what could be wrong with her, fancying some nervous illness, weeping, and vaguely feeling something fatal and incomprehensible whirling round him.

When Rodolphe came to the garden that evening, he found his mistress waiting for him at the foot of the steps on the lowest stair. They threw their arms round one another, and all their rancour melted like snow beneath the warmth of that kiss.

XII

THEY BEGAN TO LOVE one another again. Often, even in the middle of the day, Emma suddenly wrote to him, then from the window made a sign to Justin, who, taking his apron off, quickly ran to La Huchette. Rodolphe would come; she had sent for him to tell him that she was bored, that her husband was odious, her life frightful.

"But what can I do?" he cried one day impatiently.

"Ah! if you would——"

She was sitting on the floor between his knees, her hair loose, her look lost.

"Why, what?" said Rodolphe.

She sighed.

"We would go and live elsewhere—somewhere!"

"You are really mad!" he said, laughing. "How could that be possible?"

She returned to the subject; he pretended not to understand, and turned the conversation.

What he did not understand was all this worry about so simple an affair as love. She had a motive, a reason, and, as it were, a pendant to her affection.

Her tenderness, in fact, grew each day with her repulsion to her husband. The more she gave up herself to the one, the more she loathed the other. Never had Charles seemed to her so disagreeable, to have such stodgy fingers, such vulgar ways, to be so dull as when they found themselves together after her meeting with Rodolphe. Then, while playing the spouse and virtue, she was burning at the thought of that head whose black hair fell in a curl over the sunburnt brow, of that form at once so strong and elegant, of that man, in a word, who had such experience in his reasoning, such passion in his desires. It was for him that she filed her nails with the care of a chaser, and that there was never enough cold-cream for her skin, nor of patchouli for her handkerchiefs. She loaded herself with bracelets, rings, and necklaces. When he was coming she filled the two large blue glass vases with roses, and prepared her room and her person like a courtesan expecting a prince. The servant had to be constantly washing linen, and all day Félicité did not stir from the kitchen, where little Justin, who often kept her company, watched her at work.

Left Bank Books

399 N. Euclid
St. Louis, Mo. 63108
phone: 367-6731

With his elbows on the long board on which she was ironing, he greedily watched all these women's clothes spread out about him, the dimity petticoats, the fichus, the collars, and the drawers with running strings, wide at the hips and growing narrower below.

"What is that for?" asked the young fellow, passing his hand over the crinoline or the hooks and eyes.

"Why, haven't you ever seen anything?" Félicité answered laughing. "As if your mistress, Madame Homais, didn't wear the same."

"Oh, I daresay! Madame Homais!" And he added with a meditative air, "As if she were a lady like madame!"

But Félicité grew impatient of seeing him hanging round her. She was six years older than he, and Théodore, Monsieur Guillaumin's servant, was beginning to pay court to her.

"Let me alone," she said, moving her pot of starch. "You'd better be off and pound almonds; you are always dangling about women. Before you meddle with such things, bad boy, wait till you've got a beard to your chin."

"Oh, don't be cross! I'll go and clean her boots."

And he at once took down from the shelf Emma's boots, all coated with mud, the mud of the rendezvous, that crumbled into powder beneath his fingers, and that he watched as it gently rose in a ray of sunlight.

"How afraid you are of spoiling them!" said the servant, who wasn't so particular when she cleaned them herself, because as soon as the stuff of the boots was no longer fresh madame handed them over to her.

Emma had a number in her cupboard that she squandered one after the other, without Charles allowing himself the slightest observation. So also he disbursed three hundred francs for a wooden leg that she thought proper to make a present of to Hippolyte. Its top was covered with cork, and it had spring joints, a complicated mechanism, covered over by black trousers ending in a patent-leather boot. But Hippolyte, not daring to use such a handsome leg every day, begged Madame Bovary to get him another more convenient one. The doctor, of course, had again to defray the expense of this purchase.

So little by little the stable-man took up his work again. One saw him running about the village as before, and when Charles heard from afar the sharp noise of the wooden leg, he at once went in another direction.

It was Monsieur Lheureux, the shopkeeper, who had undertaken the order; this provided him with an excuse for visiting Emma. He chatted with her about the new goods from Paris, about a thousand feminine trifles, made himself very obliging, and never asked for his money. Emma yielded to this lazy mode of satisfying all her caprices. Thus she wanted to have a very handsome riding-whip that was at an umbrella-maker's at Rouen to give to Rodolphe. The week after Monsieur Lheureux placed it on her table.

But the next day he called on her with a bill for two hundred and seventy francs, not counting the centimes. Emma was much embarrassed; all the drawers of the writing-table were empty; they owed over a fortnight's wages to Lestiboudois, two quarters to the servant, for any quantity of other things, and Bovary was impatiently expecting Monsieur Derozeray's account, which he was in the habit of paying every year about Midsummer.

She succeeded at first in putting off Lheureux. At last he lost patience; he was being sued; his capital was out, and unless he got some in he should be forced to take back all the goods she had received.

"Oh, very well, take them!" said Emma.

"I was only joking," he replied; "the only thing I regret is the whip. My word! I'll ask monsieur to return it to me."

"No, no!" she said.

"Ah! I've got you!" thought Lheureux.

And, certain of his discovery, he went out repeating to himself in an undertone, and with his usual low whistle—

"Good! we shall see! we shall see!"

She was thinking how to get out of this when the servant coming in put on the mantelpiece a small roll of blue paper "from Monsieur Derozeray's." Emma pounced upon and opened it. It contained fifteen napoleons; it was the account. She heard Charles on the stairs; threw the gold to the back of her drawer, and took out the key.

Three days after Lheureux reappeared.

"I have an arrangement to suggest to you," he said. "If, instead of the sum agreed on, you would take——"

"Here it is," she said placing fourteen napoleons in his hand.

The tradesman was dumbfounded. Then, to conceal his disappointment, he was profuse in apologies and proffers of service, all of which Emma declined; then she remained a few moments fingering in the pocket of her apron the two five-franc pieces that he had given her in change. She promised herself she would economise in order to pay back later on. "Pshaw!" she thought, "he won't think about it again."

Besides the riding-whip with its silver-gilt handle, Rodolphe had received a seal with the motto *Amor nel cor;* furthermore, a scarf for a muffler, and, finally, a cigar-case exactly like the Viscount's, that Charles had formerly picked up in the road, and that Emma had kept. These presents, however, humiliated him; he refused several; she insisted, and he ended by obeying, thinking her tyrannical and over-exacting.

Then she had strange ideas.

"When midnight strikes," she said, "you must think of me."

And if he confessed that he had not thought of her, there were floods of reproaches that always ended with the eternal question—

"Do you love me?"

"Why, of course I love you," he answered.

"A great deal?"

"Certainly!"

"You haven't loved any others?"

"Did you think you'd got a virgin?" he exclaimed, laughing.

Emma cried, and he tried to console her, adorning his protestations with puns.

"Oh," she went on, "I love you! I love you so that I could not live without you, do you see? There are times when I long to see you again, when I am torn by all the anger of love. I ask myself, Where is he? Perhaps he is talking to other women. They smile upon him; he approaches. Oh, no; no one else pleases you. There are some more beautiful, but I love you best. I know how to love best. I am your servant, your concubine! You are my king, my idol! You are good, you are beautiful, you are clever, you are strong!"

He had so often heard these things said that they did not strike him as original. Emma was like all his mistresses; and the charm of novelty, gradually falling away like a garment, laid bare the eternal monotony of passion, that has always the same forms and the same language. He did not distinguish, this man of so much experience, the difference of sentiment beneath the sameness of expression. Because lips libertine and venal had murmured such words to him, he believed but little in the candour of hers; exaggerated speeches hiding mediocre affections must be discounted; as if the fulness of the soul did not sometimes overflow in the emptiest metaphors, since no one can ever give the exact measure of his needs, nor of his conceptions, nor of his sorrows; and since human speech is like a cracked tin kettle, on which we hammer out tunes to make bears dance when we long to move the stars.

But with that superior critical judgment that belongs to him who, in no matter what circumstance, holds back, Rodolphe saw other delights to be got out of this love. He thought all modesty in the way. He treated her quite *sans façon*. He made of her something supple and corrupt. Hers was an idiotic sort of attachment, full of admiration for him, of voluptuousness for her, a beatitude that benumbed her; her soul sank into this drunkenness, shrivelled up, drowned in it, like Clarence in his butt of Malmsey.

By the mere effect of her love Madame Bovary's manners changed. Her looks grew bolder, her speech more free; she even committed the impropriety of walking out with Monsieur Rodolphe, a cigarette in her mouth, "as if to defy the people." At last, those who still doubted doubted no longer when one day they saw her getting out of the "Hirondelle," her waist squeezed into a waistcoat like a man; and Madame Bovary senior, who, after a fearful scene with her husband, had taken refuge at her son's, was not the least scandalised of the women-folk. Many other things displeased her. First, Charles had not attended to her advice about the forbidding of novels; then the "ways of the house" annoyed her; she allowed herself to make some remarks, and there were quarrels, especially one on account of Félicité.

Madame Bovary senior, the evening before, passing along the passage, had surprised her in company of a man—a man with a brown collar, about forty years old, who, at the sound of her step, had quickly escaped through the kitchen. Then Emma began to laugh, but the good lady grew angry, declaring that unless morals were to be laughed at one ought to look after those of one's servants.

"Where were you brought up?" asked the daughter-in-law, with so impertinent a look that Madame Bovary asked her if she were not perhaps defending her own case.

"Leave the room!" said the young woman, springing up with a bound.

"Emma! Mamma!" cried Charles, trying to reconcile them.

But both had fled in their exasperation. Emma was stamping her feet as she repeated—

"Oh! what manners! What a peasant!"

He ran to his mother; she was beside herself. She stammered—

"She is an insolent, giddy-headed thing, or perhaps worse!"

And she was for leaving at once if the other did not apologise. So Charles went back again to his wife and implored her to give way; he knelt to her; she ended by saying—

"Very well! I'll go to her."

And in fact she held out her hand to her mother-in-law with the dignity of a marchioness as she said—

"Excuse me, madame."

Then, having gone up again to her room, she threw herself flat on her bed and cried there like a child, her face buried in the pillow.

She and Rodolphe had agreed that in the event of anything extraordinary occurring, she should fasten a small piece of white paper to the blind, so that if by chance he happened to be in Yonville, he could hurry to the lane behind the house. Emma made the signal; she had been waiting three-quarters of an hour when she suddenly caught sight of Rodolphe at the corner of the market. She felt tempted to open the window and call him, but he had already disappeared. She fell back in despair.

Soon, however, it seemed to her that some one was walking on the pavement. It was he, no doubt. She went downstairs, crossed the yard. He was there outside. She threw herself into his arms.

"Do take care!" he said.

"Ah! if you knew!" she replied.

And she began telling him everything, hurriedly, disjointedly, exaggerating the facts, inventing many, and so prodigal of parentheses that he understood nothing of it.

"Come, my poor angel, courage! Be comforted! be patient!"

"But I have been patient; I have suffered for four years. A love like ours ought to show itself in the face of heaven. They torture me! I can bear it no longer! Save me!"

She clung to Rodolphe. Her eyes, full of tears, flashed like flames beneath a wave; her breast heaved; he had never loved her so much, so that he lost his head and said—

"What is it? What do you wish?"

"Take me away," she cried, "carry me off! Oh, I pray you!"

And she threw herself upon his mouth, as if to seize there the unexpected consent if breathed forth in a kiss.

"But——" Rodolphe resumed.

"What?"

"Your little girl!"

She reflected a few moments, then replied—

"We will take her! It can't be helped!"

"What a woman!" he said to himself, watching her as she went. For she had run into the garden. Some one was calling her.

On the following days Madame Bovary senior was much surprised at the change in her daughter-in-law. Emma, in fact, was showing herself more docile, and even carried her deference so far as to ask for a recipe for pickling gherkins.

Was it the better to deceive them both? Or did she wish by a sort of voluptuous stoicism to feel the more profoundly the bitterness of the things she was about to leave?

But she paid no heed to them; on the contrary, she lived as lost in the anticipated delight of her coming happiness. It was an eternal subject for conversation with Rodolphe. She leant on his shoulder murmuring—

"Ah! when we are in the mail-coach! Do you think about it? Can it be? It seems to me that the moment I feel the carriage start, it will be as if we were rising in a balloon, as if we were setting out for the clouds. Do you know that I count the hours. And you?"

Never had Madame Bovary been so beautiful as at this period; she had that indefinable beauty that results from joy, from enthusiasm, from success, and that is only the harmony of temperament with circumstances. Her desires, her sorrows, the experience of pleasure, and her ever-young illusions, that had, as soil and rain and winds and the sun make flowers grow, gradually developed her, and she at length blossomed forth in all the plentitude of her nature. Her eyelids seemed chiselled expressly for her long amorous looks in which the pupil disappeared, while a strong inspiration expanded her delicate nostrils and raised the fleshy corner of her lips, shaded in the light by a little black down. One would have thought that an artist apt in conception had arranged the curls of hair upon her neck; they fell in a thick mass, negligently, and with the changing chances of their adultery, that unbound them every day. Her voice now took more mellow inflections, her figure also; something subtle and penetrating escaped even from the folds of her gown and from the line of her foot. Charles, as when they were first married, thought her delicious and quite irresistible.

When he came home in the middle of the night, he did not dare to wake her. The porcelain night-light threw a round trembling gleam upon the ceiling, and the drawn curtains of the little cot formed as it were a white hut standing out in the shade, and by the bedside Charles looked at them. He seemed to hear the light breathing of his child. She would grow big now; every season would bring rapid progress. He already saw her coming from school as the day drew in, laughing, with ink-stains on her jacket, and carrying her basket on her arm. Then she would have to be sent to a boarding-school; that would cost much; how was it to be done? Then he reflected. He thought of hiring a small farm in the neighbourhood, that he would superintend every morning on his way to his patients. He would save up what he brought in, he would put it in the savings-bank. Then he would buy shares somewhere, no matter where; besides, his practice would increase; he counted upon that, for he wanted Berthe to be well-educated, to be accomplished, to learn to play the piano. Ah! how pretty she would be later on when she was fifteen, when, resembling her mother, she would, like her, wear large straw hats in the summer-time; from a distance they would be taken for two sisters. He pictured her to himself working in the evening by their side beneath the light of the lamp; she would embroider him slippers; she would look after the house; she would fill all the home with her charm and her gaiety. At last, they would think of her marriage; they would find her some good young fellow with a steady business; he would make her happy; this would last for ever.

Emma was not asleep; she pretended to be; and while he dozed off by her side she awakened to other dreams.

To the gallop of four horses she was carried away for a week towards a new land, whence they would return no more. They went on and on, their arms entwined, without a word. Often from the top of a mountain there suddenly glimpsed some splendid city with domes, and bridges, and ships, forests of citron trees, and cathedrals of white marble, on whose pointed steeples were storks' nests. They went at a walking-pace because of the great flag-stones, and on the ground there were bouquets of flowers, offered you by women dressed in red bodices. They heard the chiming of bells, the neighing of mules, together with the murmur of guitars and the noise of fountains, whose rising spray refreshed heaps of fruit arranged like a pyramid at the foot of pale statues that smiled beneath playing waters. And then, one night they came to a fishing village, where brown nets were drying in the wind along the cliffs and in front of the huts. It was there that they would stay; they would live in a low, flat-roofed house, shaded by a palm-tree, in the heart of a gulf, by the sea. They would row in gondolas, swing in hammocks, and their existence would be easy and large as their silk gowns, warm and star-spangled as the nights they would contemplate. However, in the immensity of this future that she conjured up, nothing special stood forth; the days, all magnificent, resembled each other like waves; and it swayed in the horizon, infinite, harmonised, azure, and bathed in sunshine. But the child began to cough in her cot or Bovary snored more loudly, and Emma did not fall asleep till morning, when the dawn whitened the windows, and when little Justin was already in the square taking down the shutters of the chemist's shop.

She had sent for Monsieur Lheureux, and had said to him—

"I want a cloak—a large lined cloak with a deep collar."

"You are going on a journey?" he asked.

"No; but—never mind. I may count on you, may I not, and quickly?"

He bowed.

"Besides, I shall want," she went on, "a trunk—not too heavy—handy."

"Yes, yes, I understand. About three feet by a foot and a half, as they are being made just now."

"And a travelling bag."

"Decidedly," thought Lheureux, "there's a row on here."

"And," said Madame Bovary, taking her watch from her belt, "take this; you can pay yourself out of it."

But the tradesman cried out that she was wrong; they knew one another; did he doubt her? What childishness!

She insisted, however, on his taking at least the chain, and Lheureux had already put it in his pocket and was going, when she called him back.

"You will leave everything at your place. As to the cloak"—she seemed to be reflecting—"do not bring it either; you can give me the maker's address, and tell him to have it ready for me."

It was the next month that they were to run away. She was to leave Yonville as if she was going on some business to Rouen. Rodolphe would have booked the seats, procured the passports, and even have written to Paris in order to have the whole mail-coach reserved for them as far as Marseilles, where they would buy a carriage, and go on thence without stopping to Genoa. She would take care to send her luggage to Lheureux's, whence it would be taken direct to the "Hirondelle," so that no one would have any suspicion. And in all this there never was any allusion to the child. Rodolphe avoided speaking of her; perhaps he no longer thought about it.

He wished to have two more weeks before him to arrange some affairs; then at the end of a week he wanted two more; then he said he was ill; next he went on a journey. The month of August passed, and, after all these delays, they decided that it was to be irrevocably fixed for the 4th September—a Monday.

At length the Saturday before arrived.

Rodolphe came in the evening earlier than usual.

"Everything is ready?" she asked him.

"Yes."

Then they walked round a garden-bed, and went to sit down near the terrace on the kerb-stone of the wall.

"You are sad," said Emma.

"No; why?"

And yet he looked at her strangely in a tender fashion.

"Is it because you are going away?" she went on; "because you are leaving what is dear to you—your life? Ah! I understand. I have nothing in the world! You are all to me; so shall I be to you. I will be your people, your country; I will tend, I will love you!"

"How sweet you are!" he said, seizing her in his arms.

"Really!" she said with a voluptuous laugh. "Do you love me? Swear it then!"

"Do I love you—love you? I adore you, my love!"

The moon, full and purple-coloured, was rising right out of the earth at the end of the meadow. She rose quickly between the branches of the poplars, that hid her here and there like a black curtain pierced with holes. Then she appeared dazzling with whiteness in the empty heavens that she lit up, and now sailing more slowly along, let fall upon the river a great stain that broke up into an infinity of stars; and the silver sheen seemed to writhe through the very depths like a headless serpent covered with luminous scales; it also resembled some monster candelabra all along which sparkled drops of diamonds running together. The soft night was about them; masses of shadow filled the branches. Emma, her eyes half closed, breathed in with deep sighs the fresh wind that was blowing. They did not speak, lost as they were in the rush of their reverie. The tenderness of the old days came back to their hearts, full and silent as the flowing river, with the softness of the perfume of the syringas, and threw across their memories shadows more immense and more sombre than those of the still willows that lengthened out over the grass. Often some night-animal, hedgehog or weasel, setting out on the hunt, disturbed the lovers, or sometimes they heard a ripe peach falling all alone from the espalier.

"Ah! what a lovely night!" said Rodolphe.

"We shall have others," replied Emma; and, as if speaking to herself. "Yet, it will be good to travel. And yet, why should my heart be so heavy? Is it dread of the unknown? The effect of habits left? Or rather——? No; it is the excess of happiness. How weak I am, am I not? Forgive me!"

"There is still time!" he cried. "Reflect! perhaps you may repent!"

"Never!" she cried impetuously. And coming closer to him: "What ill could come to me? There is no desert, no precipice, no ocean I would not traverse with you. The longer we live together the more it will be like an embrace, every day closer, more heart to heart. There will be nothing to trouble us, no cares, no obstacle. We shall be alone, all to ourselves eternally. Oh, speak! Answer me!"

At regular intervals he answered, "Yes—Yes—" She had passed her hands through his hair, and she repeated in a childlike voice, despite the big tears which were falling, "Rodolphe! Rodolphe! Ah! Rodolphe! dear little Rodolphe!"

Midnight struck.

"Midnight!" said she. "Come, it is to-morrow. One day more!"

He rose to go; and as if the movement he made had been the signal for their flight, Emma said, suddenly assuming a gay air—

"You have the passports?"

"Yes."

"You are forgetting nothing?"

"No."

"Are you sure?"

"Certainly."

"It is at the Hôtel de Provence, is it not, that you will wait for me at midday?"

He nodded.

"Till to-morrow then!" said Emma in a last caress; and she watched him go.

He did not turn round. She ran after him, and, leaning over the water's edge between the bulrushes—

"To-morrow!" she cried.

He was already on the other side of the river and walking fast across the meadow.

After a few moments Rodolphe stopped; and when he saw her with her white gown gradually fade away in the shade like a ghost, he was seized with such a beating of the heart that he leant against a tree lest he should fall.

"What an imbecile I am!" he said with a fearful oath. "No matter! She was a pretty mistress!"

And immediately Emma's beauty, with all the pleasures of their love, came back to him. For a moment he softened; then he rebelled against her.

"For, after all," he exclaimed, gesticulating, "I can't exile myself—have a child on my hands."

He was saying these things to give himself firmness.

"And besides, the worry, the expense! Ah! no, no, no! a thousand times no! It would have been too stupid."

XIII

No SOONER was Rodolphe at home than he sat down quickly at his bureau under the stag's head that hung as a trophy on the wall. But when he had the pen between his fingers, he could think of nothing, so that, resting on his elbows, he began to reflect. Emma seemed to him to have receded into a far-off past, as if the resolution he had taken had suddenly placed a distance between them.

To get back something of her, he fetched from the cupboard at the bed-side an old Rheims biscuit-box, in which he usually kept his letters from women, and from it came an odour of dry dust and withered roses. First he saw a handkerchief with pale little spots. It was a handkerchief of hers. Once when they were walking her nose had bled; he had forgotten it. Near it, chipped at all the corners, was a miniature given him by Emma: her toilette seemed to him pretentious, and her languishing look in the worst possible taste. Then, from looking at this image and recalling the memory of its original, Emma's features little by little grew confused in his remembrance, as if the living and the painted face, rubbing one against the other, had effaced each other. Finally, he read some of her letters; they were full of explanations relating to their journey, short, technical, and urgent, like business notes. He wanted to see the long ones again, those of old times. In order to find them at the bottom of the box, Rodolphe disturbed all the others, and mechanically began rummaging amidst this mass of papers and things, finding pell-mell bouquets, garters, a black mask, pins, and hair—

hair! dark and fair, some even, catching in the hinges of the box, broke when it was opened.

Thus dallying with his souvenirs, he examined the writing and the style of the letters, as varied as their orthography. They were tender or jovial, facetious, melancholy; there were some that asked for love, others that asked for money. A word recalled faces to him, certain gestures, the sound of a voice; sometimes, however, he remembered nothing at all.

In fact, these women, rushing at once into his thoughts, cramped each other and lessened, as reduced to a uniform level of love that equalised them all. So taking handfuls of the mixed-up letters, he amused himself for some moments with letting them fall in cascades from his right into his left hand. At last, bored and weary, Rodolphe took back the box to the cupboard, saying to himself, "What a lot of rubbish!" Which summed up his opinion; for pleasures, like schoolboys in a school courtyard, had so trampled upon his heart that no green thing grew there, and that which passed through it, more heedless than children, did not even, like them, leave a name carved upon the wall.

"Come," said he, "let's begin."

He wrote—

"Courage, Emma! courage! I would not bring misery into your life."

"After all, that's true," thought Rodolphe. "I am acting in her interest; I am honest."

"Have you carefully weighed your resolution? Do you know to what an abyss I was dragging you, poor angel? No, you do not, do you? You were coming confident and fearless, believing in happiness in the future. Ah! unhappy that we are—insensate!"

Rodolphe stopped here to think of some good excuse.

"If I told her all my fortune is lost? No! Besides, that would stop nothing. It would all have to be begun over again later on. As if one could make women like that listen to reason!" He reflected, then went on—

"I shall not forget you, oh! believe it; and I shall ever have a profound devotion for you; but some day, sooner or later, this ardour (such is the fate of human things) would have grown less, no doubt. Lassitude would have come to us, and who knows if I should not even have had the atrocious pain of witnessing your remorse, of sharing it myself, since I should have been its cause? The mere idea of the grief that would come to you tortures me, Emma. Forget me! Why did I ever know you? Why were you so beautiful? Is it my fault? O my God! No, no! Accuse only fate."

"That's a word that always tells," he said to himself.

"Ah, if you had been one of those frivolous women that one sees, certainly I might, through egotism, have tried an experiment, in that case without danger for you. But that delicious exaltation, at once your charm and your torment, has prevented you from understanding, adorable woman that you are, the falseness of our future position. Nor had I reflected upon this at first, and I rested in the shade of that ideal happiness as beneath that of the manchineel tree, without foreseeing the consequences."

"Perhaps she'll think I'm giving it up from avarice. Ah, well! so much the worse; it must be stopped!"

"The world is cruel, Emma. Wherever we might have gone, it would have persecuted us. You would have had to put up with indiscreet questions, calumny, contempt, insult perhaps. Insult to you! Oh! And I, who would place you on a throne! I who bear with me your memory as a talisman! For I am going to punish myself by exile for all the ill I have done you. I am going away. Whither I know not. I am mad. Adieu! Be good always. Preserve the memory of the unfortunate who has lost you. Teach my name to your child; let her repeat it in her prayers."

The wicks of the candles flickered. Rodolphe got up to shut the window, and when he had sat down again—

"I think it's all right. Ah! and this for fear she should come and hunt me up."

"I shall be far away when you read these sad lines, for I have wished to flee as quickly as possible to shun the temptation of seeing you again. No weakness! I shall return, and perhaps later on we shall talk together very coldly of our old love. Adieu!"

And there was a last "adieu" divided into two words! "A Dieu!" which he thought in very excellent taste.

"Now how am I to sign?" he said to himself. " 'Yours devotedly?' No! 'Your friend?' Yes, that's it."

                                        "Your friend."

He re-read his letter. He considered it very good.

"Poor little woman!" he thought with emotion. "She'll think me harder than a rock. There ought to have been some tears on this; but I can't cry; it isn't my fault." Then, having emptied some water into a glass, Rodolphe dipped his finger into it, and let a big drop fall on the paper, that made a pale stain on the ink. Then looking for a seal, he came upon the one "Amor nel cor."

"That doesn't at all fit in with the circumstances. Pshaw! never mind!" After which he smoked three pipes and went to bed.

The next day when he was up (at about two o'clock—he had slept late), Rodolphe had a basket of apricots picked. He put his letter at the bottom under some vine leaves, and at once ordered Girard, his ploughman, to take it with care to Madame Bovary. He made use of this means for corresponding with her, sending according to the season fruits or game.

"If she asks after me," he said, "you will tell her that I have gone on a journey. You must give the basket to her herself, into her own hands. Get along and take care!"

Girard put on his new blouse, knotted his handkerchief round the apricots, and, walking with great heavy steps in his thick iron-bound goloshes, made his way to Yonville.

Madame Bovary, when he got to her house, was arranging a bundle of linen on the kitchen-table with Félicité.

"Here," said the ploughboy, "is something for you from master."

She was seized with apprehension, and as she sought in her pocket for some coppers, she looked at the peasant with haggard eyes, while he himself looked at her with amazement, not understanding how such a present could so move any one. At last he went out. Félicité remained. She could bear it no longer; she ran into the sitting-room as if to take the apricots there, overturned the basket, tore away the leaves, found the letter, opened it, and, as if some fearful fire were behind her, Emma flew to her room terrified.

Charles was there; she saw him; he spoke to her; she heard nothing, and she went on quickly up the stairs, breathless, distraught, dumb, and ever holding this horrible piece of paper, that crackled between her fingers like a plate of sheet-iron. On the second floor she stopped before the attic-door, that was closed.

Then she tried to calm herself; she recalled the letter; she must finish it; she did not dare to. And where? How? She would be seen! "Ah, no! here," she thought, "I shall be all right."

Emma pushed open the door and went in.

The slates threw straight down a heavy heat that gripped her temples, stifled her; she dragged herself to the closed garret-window. She drew back the bolt, and the dazzling light burst in with a leap.

Opposite, beyond the roofs, stretched the open country till it was lost to sight. Down below, underneath her, the village square was empty; the stones of the pavement glittered, the weathercocks on the houses were motionless. At the corner of the street, from a lower story, rose a kind of humming with strident modulations. It was Binet turning.

She leant against the embrasure of the window, and re-read the letter with angry sneers. But the more she fixed her attention upon it, the more confused were her ideas. She saw him again, heard him, encircled him with her arms, and the throbs of her heart, that beat against her breast like blows of a sledge-hammer, grew faster and faster, with uneven intervals. She looked about her with the wish that the earth might crumble into pieces. Why not end it all? What restrained her? She was free. She advanced, looked at the paving-stones, saying to herself, "Come! come!"

The luminous ray that came straight up from below drew the weight of her body towards the abyss. It seemed to her that the ground of the oscillating square went up the walls, and that the floor dipped on end like a tossing boat. She was right at the edge, almost hanging, surrounded by vast space. The blue of the heavens suffused her, the air was whirling in her hollow head; she had but to yield, to let herself be taken; and the humming of the lathe never ceased, like an angry voice calling her.

"Emma! Emma!" cried Charles.

She stopped.

"Wherever are you? Come!"

The thought that she had just escaped from death almost made her faint with terror. She closed her eyes; then she shivered at the touch of a hand on her sleeve; it was Félicité.

"Master is waiting for you, madame; the soup is on the table."

And she had to go down to sit at table.

She tried to eat. The food choked her. Then she unfolded her napkin as if to examine the darns, and she really thought of applying herself to this work, counting the threads in the linen. Suddenly the remembrance of the letter returned to her. How had she lost it? Where could she find it? But she felt such weariness of spirit that she could not even invent a pretext for leaving the table. Then she became a coward; she was afraid of Charles; he knew all, that was certain. Indeed he pronounced these words in a strange manner:

"We are not likely to see Monsieur Rodolphe soon again, it seems."

"Who told you?" she said, shuddering.

"Who told me!" he replied, rather astonished at her abrupt tone. "Why, Girard, whom I met just now at the door of the 'Café-Français.' He has gone on a journey, or is to go."

She gave a sob.

"What surprises you in that? He absents himself like that from time to time for a change, and, *ma foi*, I think he's right, when one has a fortune and is a bachelor. Besides, he has jolly times, has our friend. He's a bit of a rake. Monsieur Langlois told me——"

He stopped for propriety's sake because the servant came in. She put back into the basket the apricots scattered on the sideboard. Charles, without noticing his wife's colour, had them brought to him, took one, and bit into it.

"Ah! perfect!" said he; "just taste!"

And he handed her the basket, which she put away from her gently.

"Do just smell! What an odour!" he remarked, passing it under her nose several times.

"I am choking," she cried, leaping up. But by an effort of will the spasm passed; then—

"It is nothing," she said, "it is nothing! It is nervousness. Sit down and go on eating." For she dreaded lest he should begin questioning her, attending to her, that she should not be left alone.

Charles, to obey her, sat down again, and he spat the stones of the apricots into his hands, afterwards putting them on his plate.

Suddenly a blue tilbury passed across the square at a rapid trot. Emma uttered a cry and fell back rigid to the ground.

In fact, Rodolphe, after many reflections, had decided to set out for Rouen. Now, as from La Huchette to Buchy there is no other way than by Yonville, he had to go through the village, and Emma had recognised him by the rays of the lanterns, which like lightning flashed through the twilight.

The chemist, at the tumult which broke out in the house, ran thither. The table with all the plates was upset; sauce, meat, knives, the salt, and cruet-stand were strewn over the room; Charles was calling for help; Berthe, scared, was crying; and Félicité, whose hands trembled, was unlacing her mistress, whose whole body shivered convulsively.

"I'll run to my laboratory for some aromatic vinegar," said the druggist.

Then as she opened her eyes on smelling the bottle—

"I was sure of it," he remarked; "that would wake any dead person for you!"

"Speak to us," said Charles; "collect yourself: it is I—your Charles, who loves you. Do you know me? See! here is your little girl! Oh, kiss her!"

The child stretched out her arms to her mother to cling to her neck. But turning away her head, Emma said in a broken voice—

"No, no! no one!"

She fainted again. They carried her to her bed. She lay there stretched at full length, her lips apart, her eyelids closed, her hands open, motionless, and white as a waxen image. Two streams of tears flowed from her eyes and fell slowly upon the pillow.

Charles, standing up, was at the back of the alcove, and the chemist, near him, maintained that meditative silence that is becoming on the serious occasions of life.

"Do not be uneasy," he said, touching his elbow; "I think the paroxysm is past."

"Yes, she is resting a little now," answered Charles, watching her sleep. "Poor girl! poor girl! She has gone off now!"

Then Homais asked how the accident had come about. Charles answered that she had been taken ill suddenly while she was eating some apricots.

"Extraordinary!" continued the chemist. "But it might be that the apricots had brought on the syncope. Some natures are so sensitive to certain smells; and it would even be a very fine question to study both in its pathological and physiological relation. The priests know the importance of it, they who have introduced aromatics into all their ceremonies. It is to stupefy the senses and to bring on ecstasies,—a thing, moreover, very easy in persons of the weaker sex, who are more delicate than the other. Some are cited who faint at the smell of burnt hartshorn, of new bread——"

"Take care; you'll wake her!" said Bovary in a low voice.

"And not only," the druggist went on, "are human beings subject to such anomalies, but animals also. Thus you are not ignorant of the singularly aphrodisiac effect produced by the *Nepeta cataria*, vulgarly called cat-mint, on the feline race; and, on the other hand, to quote an example whose authenticity I can answer for, Bridaux (one of my old comrades, at present established in the Rue Malpalu) possesses a dog that falls into convulsions as soon as you hold out a snuff-box to him. He often even makes the experiment before his friends at his summer-house at Guillaume Wood. Would any one believe that a simple sternutation could produce such ravages on a quadrupedal organism? It is extremely curious, is it not?"

"Yes," said Charles, who was not listening to him.

"This shows us," went on the other, smiling with benign self-sufficiency, "the innumerable irregularities of the nervous system. With regard to madame, she has always seemed to me, I confess, very susceptible. And so I should by no means recommend to you, my dear friend, any of these so-called remedies that, under the pretence of attacking the symptoms, attack the constitution. No; no useless physicking! Diet, that is all; sedatives, emollients, dulcification. Then, don't you think that perhaps her imagination should be worked upon?"

"In what way? How?" said Bovary.

"Ah! that is it. Such is indeed the question. 'That is the question,' as I lately read in a newspaper."

But Emma, awaking, cried out—

"The letter! the letter!"

They thought she was delirious; and she was by midnight. Brain-fever had set in.

For forty-three days Charles did not leave her. He gave up all his patients; he no longer went to bed; he was constantly feeling her pulse, putting on sinapisms and cold-water compresses. He sent Justin as far as Neufchâtel for ice; the ice melted on the way; he sent him back again. He called Monsieur Canivet into consultation; he sent for Dr. Larivière, his old master, from Rouen; he was in despair. What alarmed him most was Emma's prostration, for she did not speak, did not listen, did not even seem to suffer, as if her body and soul were both resting together after all their troubles.

About the middle of October she could sit up in bed supported by pillows. Charles wept when he saw her eat her first bread-and-jelly. Her strength returned to her; she got up for a few hours of an afternoon, and one day, when she felt better, he tried to take her, leaning on his arm, for a walk round the garden. The sand of the paths was disappearing beneath the dead leaves; she walked slowly, dragging along her slippers, and leaning against Charles's shoulder. She smiled all the time.

They went thus to the bottom of the garden near the terrace. She drew herself up slowly, shading her eyes with her hand to look. She looked far off, as far as she could, but on the horizon were only great bonfires of grass smoking on the hills.

"You will tire yourself, my darling!" said Bovary. And, pushing her gently to make her go into the arbour, "Sit down on this seat; you'll be comfortable."

"Oh! no; not there!" she said in a faltering voice.

She was seized with giddiness, and from that evening her illness recommenced, with a more uncertain character, it is true, and more complex symptoms. Now she suffered in her heart, then in the chest, the head, the limbs; she had vomitings, in which Charles thought he saw the first signs of cancer.

And besides this, the poor fellow was worried about money matters.

XIV

To BEGIN WITH, he did not know how he could pay Monsieur Homais for all the physic supplied by him, and though, as a medical man, he was not obliged to pay for it, he nevertheless blushed a little at such an obligation. Then the expenses of the household, now that the servant was mistress, became terrible. Bills rained in upon the house; the tradesmen grumbled; Monsieur Lheureux especially harassed him. In fact, at the height of Emma's illness, the latter, taking advantage of the circumstances to make his bill larger, had hurriedly brought the cloak, the travelling-bag, two trunks instead of one, and a number of other things. It was very well for Charles to say he did not want them. The tradesman answered arrogantly that these articles had been ordered, and that he would not take them back; besides, it would vex madame in her convalescence; the doctor had better think it over; in short, he was resolved to sue him rather than give up his rights and take back his goods. Charles subsequently ordered them to be sent back to the shop. Félicité forgot; he had other things to attend to; then thought no more about them. Monsieur Lheureux returned to the charge, and, by turns threatening and whining, so managed that Bovary ended by signing a bill at six months. But hardly had he signed this bill than a bold idea occurred to him: it was to borrow a thousand francs from Lheureux. So, with an embarrassed air, he asked if it were possible to get them, adding that it would be for a year, at any interest he wished. Lheureux ran off to his shop, brought back the money, and dictated another bill, by which Bovary undertook to pay to his order on the 1st of September next the sum of one thousand and seventy francs, which, with the hundred and eighty already agreed to, made just twelve hundred and fifty, thus lending at six per cent. in addition to one-fourth for commission; and the things bringing him in a good third at the least, this ought in twelve months to give him a profit of a hundred and thirty francs. He hoped that the business would not stop there; that the bills would not be paid; that they would be renewed; and that his poor little money, having thriven at the doctor's as at a hospital, would come back to him one day considerably more plump, and fat enough to burst his bag.

Everything, moreover, succeeded with him. He was adjudicator for a supply of cider to the hospital at Neufchâtel; Monsieur Guillaumin promised him some shares in the turf-pits of Gaumesnil, and he dreamt of establishing a new diligence service between Argueil and Rouen, which no doubt would not be long in ruining the ramshackle van of the "Lion d'Or," and that, travelling faster, at a cheaper rate, and carrying more luggage, would thus put into his hands the whole commerce of Yonville.

Charles several times asked himself by what means he should next year be able to pay back so much money. He reflected, imagined expedients, such as applying to his father or selling something. But his father would be deaf, and he—he had nothing to sell. Then he foresaw such worries that he quickly dismissed so disagreeable a subject of meditation from his mind. He reproached himself with forgetting Emma, as if, all his thoughts belonging to this woman, it was robbing her of something not to be constantly thinking of her.

The winter was severe, Madame Bovary's convalescence slow. When it was fine they wheeled her armchair to the window that overlooked the square, for she now had an antipathy to the garden, and the blinds on that side were always down. She wished the horse to be sold; what she formerly liked now displeased her. All her ideas seemed to be limited to the care of herself. She stayed in bed taking little meals, rang for the servant to inquire about her gruel or to chat with her. The snow on the market-roof threw a white, still light into the room; then the rain began to fall; and Emma waited daily with a mind full of eagerness for the inevitable return of some trifling events which nevertheless had no relation to her. The most important was the arrival of the "Hirondelle" in the evening. Then the landlady shouted out, and other voices answered, while Hippolyte's lantern, as he fetched the boxes from the boot, was like a star in the darkness. At midday Charles came in; then he went out again; next she took some beef-tea, and towards five o'clock, as the day drew in, the children coming back from school, dragging their wooden shoes along the pavement, knocked the clapper of the shutters with their rulers one after the other.

It was at this hour that Monsieur Bournisien came to see her. He inquired after her health, gave her news, exhorted her to religion in a coaxing little gossip that was not without its charm. The mere thought of his cassock comforted her.

One day, when at the height of her illness, she had thought herself dying, and had asked for the communion; and, while they were making the preparations in her room for the sacrament, while they were turning the night-table covered with syrups into an altar, and while Félicité was strewing dahlia flowers on the floor, Emma felt some power passing over her that freed her from her pains, from all perception, from all feeling. Her body, relieved, no longer thought; another life was beginning; it seemed to her that her being, mounting toward God, would be annihilated in that love like a burning incense that melts into vapour. The bed-clothes were sprinkled with holy water, the priest drew from the holy pyx the white wafer; and it was fainting with a celestial joy that she put out her lips to accept the body of the Saviour presented to her. The curtains of the alcove floated gently round her like clouds, and the rays of the two tapers burning on the night-table seemed to shine like dazzling halos. Then she let her head fall back, fancying she heard in space the music of seraphic harps, and perceived in an azure sky, on a golden throne in the midst of saints holding green palms, God the Father, resplendent with majesty, who with a sign sent to earth angels with wings of fire to carry her away in their arms.

This splendid vision dwelt in her memory as the most beautiful thing that it was possible to dream, so that now she strove to recall her sensation, that still lasted, however, but in a less exclusive fashion and with a deeper sweetness. Her soul, tortured by pride, at length found rest in Christian humility, and, tasting the joy of weakness, she saw within herself the destruction of her will, that must have left a wide entrance for the inroads of heavenly grace. There existed, then, in the place of happiness, still greater joys,—another love beyond all loves, without pause and without end, one that would grow eternally! She saw amid the illusions of her hope a state of purity floating above the earth mingling with heaven, to which she aspired. She wanted to become a saint. She bought chaplets and wore amulets; she wished to have in her room, by the side of her bed, a reliquary set in emeralds that she might kiss it every evening.

The curé marvelled at this humour, although Emma's religion, he thought, might, from its fervour, end by touching on heresy, extravagance. But not being much versed in these matters, as soon as they went beyond a certain limit he wrote to Monsieur Boulard, bookseller to Monsignor, to send him "something good for a lady who was very clever." The bookseller, with as much indifference as if he had been sending off hardware to niggers, packed up, pell-mell, everything that was then the fashion in the pious book trade. There were little manuals in questions and answers, pamphlets of aggressive tone after the manner of Monsieur de Maistre, and certain novels in rose-coloured bindings and with a honied style, manufactured by troubadour seminarists or penitent blue-stockings. There were the "Think of it; the Man of the World at Mary's Feet, by Monsieur de ! ! !, décoré with many Orders"; "The Errors of Voltaire, for the Use of the Young," &c.

Madame Bovary's mind was not yet sufficiently clear to apply herself seriously to anything; moreover, she began this reading in too much hurry. She grew provoked at the doctrines of religion; the arrogance of the polemic writings displeased her by their inveteracy in attacking people she did not know; and the secular stories, relieved with religion, seemed to her written in such ignorance of the world, that they insensibly estranged her from the truths for whose proof she was looking. Nevertheless, she persevered; and when the volume slipped from her hands, she fancied herself seized with the finest Catholic melancholy that an ethereal soul could conceive.

As for the memory of Rodolphe, she had thrust it back to the bottom of her heart, and it remained there more solemn and more motionless than a king's mummy in a catacomb. An exhalation escaped from this embalmed love, that, penetrating through everything, perfumed with tenderness the immaculate atmosphere in which she longed to live. When she knelt on her Gothic prie-Dieu, she addressed to the Lord the same suave words that she had murmured formerly to her lover in the outpourings of adultery. It was to make faith come; but no delights descended from the heavens, and she arose with tired limbs and with a vague feeling of a gigantic dupery.

This searching after faith, she thought, was only one merit the more, and in the pride of her devoutness Emma compared herself to those grand ladies of long ago whose glory she had dreamed of over a portrait of La Vallière, and who, trailing with so much majesty the lace-trimmed trains of their long gowns, retired into solitudes to shed at the feet of Christ all the tears of hearts that life had wounded.

Then she gave herself up to excessive charity. She sewed clothes for the poor, she sent wood to women in childbed; and Charles one day, on coming home, found three good-for-nothings in the kitchen seated at the table eating soup. She had her little girl, whom during her illness her husband had sent back to the nurse, brought home. She wanted to teach her to read; even when Berthe cried, she was not vexed. She had made up her mind to resignation, to universal indulgence. Her language about everything was full of ideal expressions. She said to her child, "Is your stomache-ache better, my angel?"

Madame Bovary senior found nothing to censure except perhaps this mania of knitting jackets for orphans instead of mending her own house-linen; but, harassed with domestic quarrels, the good woman took pleasure in this quiet house, and she even stayed there till after Easter, to escape the sarcasms of old Bovary, who never failed on Good Friday to order chitterlings.

Besides the companionship of her mother-in-law, who strengthened her a little by the rectitude of her judgment and her grave ways, Emma almost every day had other visitors. These were Madame Langlois, Madame Caron, Madame Dubreuil, Madame Tuvache, and regularly from two to five o'clock the excellent Madame Homais, who, for her part, had never believed any of the tittle-tattle about her neighbour. The little Homais also came to see her; Justin accompanied them. He went up with them to her bedroom, and remained standing near the door, motionless and mute. Often even Madame Bovary, taking no heed of him, began her toilette. She began by taking out her comb, shaking her head with a quick movement, and when he for the first time saw all this mass of hair that fell to her knees unrolling in black ringlets, it was to him, poor child! like a sudden entrance into something new and strange, whose splendour terrified him.

Emma, no doubt, did not notice his silent attentions or his timidity. She had no suspicion that the love vanished from her life was there, palpitating by her side, beneath that coarse holland shirt, in that youthful heart open to the emanations of her beauty. Besides, she now enveloped all things with such indifference, she had words so affectionate with looks so haughty, such contradictory ways, that one could no longer distinguish egotism from charity, or corruption from virtue. One evening, for example, she was angry with the servant, who had asked to go out, and stammered as she tried to find some pretext. Then suddenly—

"So you love him?" she said.

And without waiting for any answer from Félicité, who was blushing, she added, "There! run along; enjoy yourself!"

In the beginning of spring she had the garden turned up from end to end, despite Bovary's remonstrances. However, he was glad to see her at last manifest a wish of any kind. As she grew stronger she displayed more wilfulness. First, she found occasion to expel Mère Rollet, the nurse, who during her convalescence had contracted the habit of coming too often to the kitchen with her two nurslings and her boarder, better off for teeth than a cannibal. Then she got rid of the Homais family, successively dismissed all the other visitors, and even frequented church less assiduously, to the great approval of the druggist, who said to her in a friendly way—

"You were going in a bit for the cassock!"

As formerly, Monsieur Bournisien dropped in every day when he came out after catechism class. He preferred staying out of doors to taking the air "in the grove," as he called the arbour. This was the time when Charles came home. They were hot; some sweet cider was brought out, and they drank together to madame's complete restoration.

Binet was there; that is to say, a little lower down against the terrace wall, fishing for crayfish. Bovary invited him to have a drink, and he thoroughly understood the uncorking of the stone bottles.

"You must," he said, throwing a satisfied glance all round him, even to the very extremity of the landscape, "hold the bottle perpendicularly on the table, and after the strings are cut, press up the cork with little thrusts, gently, gently, as indeed they do seltzer-water at restaurants."

But during his demonstration the cider often spurted right into their faces, and then the ecclesiastic, with a thick laugh, never missed this joke—

"Its goodness strikes the eye!"

He was, in fact, a good fellow and one day he was not even scandalised at the chemist, who advised Charles to give madame some distraction by taking her to the theatre at Rouen to hear the illustrious tenor, Lagardy. Homais, surprised at this silence, wanted to know his opinion, and the priest declared that he considered music less dangerous for morals than literature.

But the chemist took up the defence of letters. The theatre, he contended, served for railing at prejudices, and, beneath a mask of pleasure, taught virtue.

"*Castigat ridendo mores*, Monsieur Bournisien! Thus consider the greater part of Voltaire's tragedies; they are cleverly strewn throughout with philosophical reflections, that make them a very school of morals and diplomacy for the people."

"I," said Binet, "once saw a piece called the 'Gamin de Paris,' in which there was the character of an old general that is really hit off to a T. He sets down a young swell who had seduced a working girl, who at the ending——"

"Certainly," continued Homais, "there is bad literature as there is bad pharmacy, but to condemn in a lump the most important of the fine arts seems to me a stupidity, a Gothic idea, worthy of the abominable times that imprisoned Galileo."

"I know very well," objected the curé, "that there are good works, good authors. However, if it were only those persons of different sexes united in a bewitching apartment, decorated rouge, those lights, those effeminate voices, all this must, in the long-run, engender a certain mental libertinage, give rise to immodest thoughts and impure temptations. Such, at any rate, is the opinion of all the Fathers. Finally," he added, suddenly assuming a mystic tone of voice while he rolled a pinch of snuff between his fingers, "if the Church has condemned the theatre, she must be right; we must submit to her decrees."

"Why," asked the druggist, "should she excommunicate actors? For formerly they openly took part in religious ceremonies. Yes, in the middle of the chancel they acted; they performed a kind of farce called 'Mysteries,' which often offended against the laws of decency."

The ecclesiastic contented himself with uttering a groan, and the chemist went on—

"It's like it is in the Bible; there there are, you know, more than one piquant detail, matters really libidinous!"

And on a gesture of irritation from Monsieur Bournisien—

"Ah! you'll admit that it is not a book to place in the hands of a young girl, and I should be sorry if Athalie——"

"But it is the Protestants, and not we," cried the other impatiently, "who recommend the Bible."

"No matter," said Homais. "I am surprised that in our days, in this century of enlightenment, any one should still persist in proscribing an intellectual relaxation that is inoffensive, moralising, and sometimes even hygienic; is it not, doctor?"

"No doubt," replied the doctor carelessly, either because, sharing the same ideas, he wished to offend no one, or else because he had not any ideas.

The conversation seemed at an end when the chemist thought fit to shoot a Parthian arrow.

"I've known priests who put on ordinary clothes to go and see dancers kicking about."

"Come, come!" said the curé.

"Ah! I've known some!" And separating the words of his sentence, Homais repeated, "I—have—known—some!"

"Well, they were wrong," said Bournisien, resigned to anything.

"By Jove! they go in for more than that," exclaimed the druggist.

"Sir!" replied the ecclesiastic, with such angry eyes that the druggist was intimidated by them.

"I only mean to say," he replied in less brutal a tone, "that toleration is the surest way to draw people to religion."

"That is true! that is true!" agreed the good fellow, sitting down again on his chair. But he stayed only a few moments.

Then, as soon as he had gone, Monsieur Homais said to the doctor—

"That's what I call a cock-fight. I beat him, did you see, in a way!— Now take my advice. Take madame to the theatre, if it were only for once in your life, to enrage one of these ravens, hang it! If any one could take my place, I would accompany you myself. Be quick about it. Lagardy is only going to give one performance; he's engaged to go to England at a high salary. From what I hear, he's a regular dog; he's rolling in money; he's taking three mistresses and a cook along with him. All these great artists burn the candle at both ends; they require a dissolute life, that stirs the imagination to some extent. But they die at the hospital, because they haven't the sense when young to lay by. Well, a pleasant dinner! Good-bye till tomorrow."

The idea of the theatre quickly germinated in Bovary's. head, for he at once communicated it to his wife, who at first refused, alleging the fatigue, the worry, the expense; but, for a wonder, Charles did not give in, so sure was he that this recreation would be good for her. He saw nothing to prevent it: his mother had sent them three hundred francs which he had no longer expected; the current debts were not very large, and the falling in of Lheureux's bills was still so far off that there was no need to think about them. Besides, imagining that she was refusing from delicacy, he insisted the more; so that by dint of worrying her she at last made up her mind, and the next day at eight o'clock they set out in the "Hirondelle."

The druggist, whom nothing whatever kept at Yonville, but who thought himself bound not to budge from it, sighed as he saw them go.

"Well, a pleasant journey!" he said to them; "happy mortals that you are!"

Then addressing himself to Emma, who was wearing a blue silk gown with four flounces—

"You are as lovely as a Venus. You'll cut a figure at Rouen."

The diligence stopped at the "Croix-Rouge" in the Place Beauvoisine. It was the inn that is in every provincial faubourg, with large stables and small bedrooms, where one sees in the middle of the court chickens pilfering the oats under the muddy gigs of the commercial travellers;—a good old house, with worm-eaten balconies that creak in the wind on winter nights, always full of people, noise, and feeding, whose black tables are sticky with coffee and brandy, the thick windows made yellow by the flies, the damp napkins stained with cheap wine, and that always smells of the village, like ploughboys dressed in Sunday-clothes, has a café on the street, and towards the countryside a kitchen-garden. Charles at once set out. He muddled up the stage-boxes with the gallery, the pit with the boxes; asked for explanations, did not understand them; was sent from the box-office to the acting-manager; came back to the inn, returned to the theatre, and thus several times traversed the whole length of the town from the theatre to the boulevard.

Madame Bovary bought a bonnet, gloves, and a bouquet. The doctor was much afraid of missing the beginning, and, without having had time to swallow a plate of soup, they presented themselves at the doors of the theatre, which were still closed.

XV

THE CROWD was waiting against the wall, symmetrically enclosed between the balustrades. At the corner of the neighbouring streets huge bills repeated in quaint letters "Lucie de Lammermoor—Lagardy—Opera—" &c. The weather was fine, the people were hot, perspiration trickled amid the curls, and handkerchiefs taken from pockets were mopping red foreheads; and now and then a warm wind that blew from the river gently stirred the border of the tick awnings hanging from the doors of the public-houses. A little lower down, however, one was refreshed by a current of icy air that smelt of tallow, leather, and oil. This was an exhalation from the Rue des Charrettes, full of large black warehouses where they made casks.

For fear of seeming ridiculous, Emma before going in wished to have a little stroll in the harbour, and Bovary prudently kept his tickets in his hand, in the pocket of his trousers, which he pressed against his stomach.

Her heart began to beat as soon as she reached the vestibule. She involuntarily smiled with vanity on seeing the crowd rushing to the right by the other corridor while she went up the staircase to the reserved seats. She was as pleased as a child to push with her finger the large tapestried door. She breathed in with all her might the dusty smell of the lobbies, and when she was seated in her box she bent forward with the air of a duchess.

The theatre was beginning to fill; opera-glasses were taken from their cases, and the subscribers, catching sight of one another, were bowing. They came to seek relaxation in the fine arts after the anxieties of business; but "business" was not forgotten; they still talked cottons, spirits of wine, or indigo. The heads of old men were to be seen, inexpressive and peaceful, with their hair and complexions looking like silver medals tarnished by steam of lead. The young beaux were strutting about in the pit, showing in the opening of their waistcoats their pink or apple-green cravats, and Madame Bovary from above admired them leaning on their canes with golden knobs in the open palm of their yellow gloves.

Now the lights of the orchestra were lit, the lustre, let down from the ceiling, throwing by the glimmering of its facets a sudden gaiety over the theatre; then the musicians came in one after the other; and first there was the protracted hubbub of the basses grumbling, violins squeaking, cornets trumpeting, flutes and flageolets fifing. But three knocks were heard on the stage, a rolling of drums began, the brass instruments played some chords, and the curtain rising, discovered a country-scene.

It was the cross-roads of a wood, with a fountain shaded by an oak to the left. Peasants and lords with plaids on their shoulders were singing a hunting-song together; then a captain suddenly came on, who evoked the spirit of evil by lifting both his arms to heaven. Another appeared; they went away, and the hunters started afresh.

She felt herself transported to the reading of her youth, into the midst of

Walter Scott. She seemed to hear through the mist the sound of the Scotch bagpipes re-echoing over the heather. Then her remembrance of the novel helping her to understand the libretto, she followed the story phrase by phrase, while vague thoughts that came back to her dispersed at once again with the bursts of music. She gave herself up to the lullaby of the melodies, and felt all her being vibrate as if the violin bows were drawn over her nerves. She had not eyes enough to look at the costumes, the scenery, the actors, the painted trees that shook when any one walked, and the velvet caps, cloaks, swords—all those imaginary things that floated amid the harmony as in the atmosphere of another world. But a young woman stepped forward, throwing a purse to a squire in green. She was left alone, and the flute was heard like the murmur of a fountain or the warbling of birds. Lucie attacked her cavatina in G major bravely. She plained of love; she longed for wings. Emma, too, fleeing from life, would have liked to fly away in an embrace. Suddenly Edgar-Lagardy appeared.

He had that splendid pallor that gives something of the majesty of marble to the ardent races of the South. His vigorous form was tightly clad in a brown-coloured doublet; a small chiselled poniard hung against his left thigh, and he cast round laughing looks showing his white teeth. They said that a Polish princess having heard him sing one night on the beach at Biarritz, where he mended boats, had fallen in love with him. She had ruined herself for him. He had deserted her for other women, and this sentimental celebrity did not fail to enhance his artistic reputation. The diplomatic mummer took care always to slip into his advertisements some poetic phrase on the fascination of his person and the susceptibility of his soul. A fine organ, imperturbable coolness, more temperament than intelligence, more power of emphasis than real singing, made up the charm of this admirable charlatan nature, in which there was something of the hairdresser and the toreador.

From the first scene he evoked enthusiasm. He pressed Lucie in his arms, he left her, he came back, he seemed desperate; he had outbursts of rage, then elegiac gurglings of infinite sweetness, and the notes escaped from his bare neck full of sobs and kisses. Emma leant forward to see him, clutching the velvet of the box with her nails. She was filling her heart with these melodious lamentations that were drawn out to the accompaniment of the double-basses, like the cries of the drowning in the tumult of a tempest. She recognised all the intoxication and the anguish that had almost killed her. The voice of the prima donna seemed to her to be but echoes of her conscience, and this illusion that charmed her as some very thing of her own life. But no one on earth had loved her with such love. He had not wept like Edgar that last moonlit night when they said, "To-morrow! to-morrow!" The theatre rang with cheers; they recommenced the entire movement; the lovers spoke of the flowers on their tomb, of vows, exile, fate, hopes; and when they uttered the final adieu, Emma gave a sharp cry that mingled with the vibrations of the last chords.

"But why," asked Bovary, "does that gentleman persecute her?"

"No, no!" she answered; "he is her lover!"

"Yet he vows vengeance on her family, while the other one who came on before said, 'I love Lucie and she loves me!' Besides, he went off with her father arm in arm. For he certainly is her father, isn't he—the ugly little man with a cock's feather in his hat?"

Despite Emma's explanations, as soon as the recitative duet began in which Gilbert lays bare·his abominable machinations to his master Ashton, Charles, seeing the false troth-ring that is to deceive Lucie, thought it was a love-gift sent by Edgar. He confessed, moreover, that he did not understand the story because of the music, which interfered very much with the words.

"What does it matter?" said Emma. "Do be quiet!"

"Yes, but you know," he went on, leaning against her shoulder, "I like to understand things."

"Be quiet! be quiet!" she cried impatiently.

Lucie advanced, half supported by her women, a wreath of orange blossoms in her hair, and paler than the white satin of her gown. Emma dreamed of her marriage day; she saw herself at home again amid the corn in the little path as they walked to the church. Oh, why had not she, like this woman, resisted, implored? She, on the contrary, had been joyous, without seeing the abyss into which she was throwing herself. Ah! if in the freshness of her beauty, before the soiling of marriage and the disillusions of adultery, she could have anchored her life upon some great, strong heart, then virtue, tenderness, voluptuousness, and duty blending, she would never have fallen from so high a happiness. But that happiness, no doubt, was a lie invented for the despair of all desire. She now knew the smallness of the passions that art exaggerated. So, striving to divert her thoughts, Emma determined now to see in this reproduction of her sorrows only a plastic fantasy, well enough to please the eye, and she even smiled internally with disdainful pity when at the back of the stage under the velvet hangings a man appeared in a black cloak.

His large Spanish hat fell at a gesture he made, and immediately the instruments and the singers began the sextet. Edgar, flashing with fury, dominated all the others with his clearer voice; Ashton hurled homicidal provocations at him in deep notes; Lucie uttered her shrill plaint, Arthur at one side, his modulated tones in the middle register, and the bass of the minister pealed forth like an organ, while the voices of the women repeating his words took them up in chorus delightfully. They were all in a row gesticulating, and anger, vengeance, jealousy, terror, and stupefaction breathed forth at once from their half-opened mouths. The outraged lover brandished his naked sword; his guipure·ruffle rose with jerks to the movements of his chest, and he walked from right to left with long strides, clanking against the boards the silver-gilt spurs of his soft boots, widening out at the ankles. He, she thought, must have an inexhaustible love to lavish it upon the crowd with such effusion. All her small fault-findings faded before the poetry of the part that absorbed her; and, drawn towards this man by the illusion of the character, she tried to imagine to herself his life—

that life resonant, extraordinary, splendid, and that might have been hers if fate had willed it. They would have known one another, loved one another. With him, through all the kingdoms of Europe she would have travelled from capital to capital, sharing his fatigues and his pride, picking up the flowers thrown to him, herself embroidering his costumes. Then each evening, at the back of a box, behind the golden trellis-work, she would have drunk in eagerly the expansions of this soul that would have sung for her alone; from the stage, even as he acted, he would have looked at her. But the mad idea seized her that he was looking at her; it was certain. She longed to run to his arms, to take refuge in his strength, as in the incarnation of love itself, and to say to him, to cry out, "Take me away! carry me with you! let us go! Thine, thine! all my ardour and all my dreams!"

The curtain fell.

The smell of the gas mingled with that of the breaths, the waving of the fans, made the air more suffocating. Emma wanted to go out; the crowd filled the corridors, and she fell back in her armchair with palpitations that choked her. Charles, fearing that she would faint, ran to the refreshment-room to get a glass of barley-water.

He had great difficulty in getting back to his seat, for his elbows were jerked at every step because of t.e glass he held in his hands, and he even spilt three-fourths on the shoulders of a Rouen lady in short sleeves, who feeling the cold liquid running down to her loins, uttered cries like a peacock, as if she were being assassinated. Her husband, who was a mill-owner, railed at the clumsy fellow, and while she was with her handkerchief wiping up the stains from her handsome cherry-coloured taffeta gown, he angrily muttered about indemnity, costs, reimbursement. At last Charles reached his wife, saying to her, quite out of breath—

"*Ma foi!* I thought I should have had to stay there. There is such a crowd —*such* a crowd!"

He added—

"Just guess whom I met up there! Monsieur Léon!"

"Léon?"

"Himself! He's coming along to pay his respects." And as he finished these words the ex-clerk of Yonville entered the box.

He held out his hand with the ease of a gentleman; and Madame Bovary extended hers, without doubt obeying the attraction of a stronger will. She had not felt it since that spring evening when the rain fell upon the green leaves, and they had said good-bye standing at the window. But soon recalling herself to the necessities of the situation, with an effort she shook off the torpor of her memories, and began stammering a few hurried words.

"Ah, good-day! What! you here?"

"Silence!" cried a voice from the pit, for the third act was beginning.

"So you are at Rouen?"

"Yes."

"And since when?"

"Turn them out! turn them out!" People were looking at them. They were silent.

But from that moment she listened no more; and the chorus of the guests, the scene between Ashton and his servant, the grand duet in D major, all were for her as far off as if the instruments had grown less sonorous and the characters more remote. She remembered the games of cards at the druggist's, and the walk to the nurse's, the reading in the arbour, the *tête-à-tête* by the fireside—all that poor love, so calm and so protracted, so discreet, so tender, and that she had nevertheless forgotten. And why had he come back? What combination of circumstances had brought him back into her life? He was standing behind her, leaning with his shoulder against the wall of the box; now and again she felt herself shuddering beneath the hot breath from his nostrils falling upon her hair.

"Does this amuse you?" he said, bending over her so closely that the end of his moustache brushed her cheek. She replied carelessly—

"Oh, dear me, no, not much."

Then he proposed that they should leave the theatre and go and take an ice somewhere.

"Oh, not yet; let us stay," said Bovary. "Her hair's undone; this is going to be tragic."

But the mad scene did not at all interest Emma, and the acting of the singer seemed to her exaggerated.

"She screams too loud," said she, turning to Charles, who was listening.

"Yes—perhaps—a little," he replied, undecided between the frankness of his pleasure and his respect for his wife's opinion.

Then with a sigh Léon said—

"The heat is——"

"Unbearable! Yes!"

"Do you feel unwell?" asked Bovary.

"Yes, I am stifling; let us go."

Monsieur Léon put her long lace shawl carefully about her shoulders, and all three went off to sit down in the harbour, in the open air, outside the windows of a café.

First they spoke of her illness, although Emma interrupted Charles from time to time, for fear, she said, of boring Monsieur Léon; and the latter told them that he had come to spend two years at Rouen in a large office, in order to get practice in his profession, which was different in Normandy and Paris. Then he inquired after Berthe, the Homais, Mère Lefrançois, and as they had, in the husband's presence, nothing more to say to one another, the conversation soon came to an end.

People coming out of the theatre passed along the pavement, humming or shouting at the top of their voices, "*O bel ange, ma Lucie!*" Then Léon, playing the dilettante, began to talk music. He had seen Tamburini, Rubini, Persiani, Grisi, and, compared with them, Lagardy, despite his grand outbursts, was nowhere.

"Yet," interrupted Charles, who was slowly sipping his rum-sherbet, "they say that he is quite admirable in the last act. I regret leaving before the end, because it was beginning to amuse me."

"Why," said the clerk, "he will soon give another performance."

But Charles replied that they were going back next day. "Unless," he added, turning to his wife, "you would like to stay alone, pussy?"

And changing his tactics at this unexpected opportunity that presented itself to his hopes, the young man sang the praises of Lagardy in the last number. It was really superb, sublime. Then Charles insisted—

"You would get back on Sunday. Come, make up your mind. You are wrong if you feel that this is doing you the least good."

The tables round them, however, were emptying; a waiter came and stood discreetly near them. Charles, who understood, took out his purse; the clerk held back his arm, and did not forget to leave two more pieces of silver that he made chink on the marble.

"I am really sorry," said Bovary, "about the money which you are——"

The other made a careless gesture full of cordiality, and taking his hat said—

"It is settled, isn't it? To-morrow at six o'clock?"

Charles explained once more that he could not absent himself longer, but that nothing prevented Emma—

"But," she stammered, with a strange smile, "I am not sure——"

"Well, you must think it over. We'll see. Night brings counsel." Then to Léon, who was walking along with them, "Now that you are in our part of the world, I hope you'll come and ask us for some dinner now and then."

The clerk declared he would not fail to do so, being obliged, moreover, to go to Yonville on some business for his office. And they parted before the Saint-Herbland Passage just as the cathedral struck half-past eleven.

PART III

MONSIEUR LÉON, while studying law, had gone pretty often to the dancing-rooms, where he was even a great success among the grisettes, who thought he had a distinguished air. He was the best-mannered of the students; he wore his hair neither too long nor too short, didn't spend all his quarter's money on the first day of the month, and kept on good terms with his professors. As for excesses, he had always abstained from them, as much from cowardice as from refinement.

Often when he stayed in his room to read, or else when sitting of an evening under the lime trees of the Luxembourg, he let his Code fall to the ground, and the memory of Emma came back to him. But gradually this feeling grew weaker, and other desires gathered over it, although it still persisted through them all. For Léon did not lose all hope; there was for him, as it were, a vague promise floating in the future, like a golden fruit suspended from some fantastic tree.

Then, seeing her again after three years of absence, his passion reawakened. He must, he thought, at last make up his mind to possess her. Moreover, his timidity had worn off by contact with his gay companions, and he returned to the provinces despising every one who had not with varnished shoes trodden the asphalte of the boulevards. By the side of a Parisienne in her laces, in the drawing-room of some illustrious physician, a person driving his carriage and wearing many orders, the poor clerk would no doubt have trembled like a child; but here, at Rouen, on the harbour, with the wife of this small doctor he felt at his ease, sure beforehand he would shine. Self-possession depends on its environment. We don't speak on the first floor as on the fourth; and the wealthy woman seems to have, about her, to guard her virtue, all her bank-notes, like a cuirass, in the lining of her corset.

On leaving the Bovarys the night before, Léon had followed them through the streets at a distance; then having seen them stop at the "Croix-Rouge," he turned on his heel, and spent the night meditating a plan.

So the next day about five o'clock he walked into the kitchen of the inn, with a choking sensation in his throat, pale cheeks, and that resolution of cowards that stops at nothing.

"The gentleman isn't in," answered a servant.

This seemed to him a good omen. He went upstairs.

She was not disturbed at his approach; on the contrary, she apologised for having neglected to tell him where they were staying.

"Oh, I divined it!" said Léon.

He pretended he had been guided towards her by chance, by instinct. She began to smile; and at once, to repair his folly, Léon told her that he had spent his morning in looking for her in all the hotels in the town, one after the other.

"So you have made up your mind to stay?" he added.

"Yes," she said, "and I am wrong. One ought not to accustom oneself to impossible pleasures when there are a thousand demands upon one."

"Oh, I can imagine!"

"Ah! no; for you, you are a man!"

But men too had their trials, and the conversation went off into certain philosophical reflections. Emma expatiated much on the misery of earthly affections, and the eternal isolation in which the heart remains entombed.

To show off, or from a naïve imitation of this melancholy which called forth his, the young man declared that he had been awfully bored during the whole course of his studies. The law irritated him, other vocations attracted him, and his mother never ceased worrying him in every one of her letters. As they talked they explained more and more fully the motives of their sadness, working themselves up in their progressive confidence. But they sometimes stopped short of the complete exposition of their thought, and then sought to invent a phrase that might express it all the same. She did not confess her passion for another; he did not say that he had forgotten her.

Perhaps he no longer remembered his suppers with girls after masked balls; and no doubt she did not recollect the rendezvous of old when she ran across the fields in the morning to her lover's house. The noises of the town hardly reached them, and the room seemed small, as if on purpose to hem in their solitude more closely. Emma, in a dimity dressing-gown, leant her head against the back of the old armchair; the yellow wall-paper formed, as it were, a golden background behind her, and her bare head was mirrored in the glass with the white parting in the middle, and the tip of her ears peeping out from the folds of her hair.

"But, pardon me!" she said. "It is wrong of me. I weary you with my eternal complaints."

"No, never, never!"

"If you knew," she went on, raising to the ceiling her beautiful eyes, in which a tear was trembling, "all that I had dreamed!"

"And I! Oh, I too have suffered! Often I went out; I went away. I dragged myself along the quays, seeking distraction amid the din of the crowd without being able to banish the heaviness that weighed upon me. In an engraver's shop on the boulevard there is an Italian print of one of the Muses. She is draped in a tunic, and she is looking at the moon, with forget-me-knots in her flowing hair. Something drove me there continually; I stayed three hours together." Then in a trembling voice, "She resembled you a little."

Madame Bovary turned away her head that he might not see the irrepressible smile she felt rising to her lips.

"Often," he went on, "I wrote you letters that I tore up."

She did not answer. He continued—

"I sometimes fancied that some chance would bring you. I thought I recognised you at street-corners, and I ran after all the carriages through whose windows I saw a shawl fluttering, a veil like yours."

She seemed resolved to let him go on speaking without interruption. Crossing her arms and bending down her face, she looked at the rosettes on her slippers, and at intervals made little movements inside the satin of them with her toes.

At last she sighed.

"But the most wretched thing, is it not—is to drag out, as I do, a useless existence. If our pains were only of some use to some one, we should find consolation in the thought of the sacrifice."

He started off in praise of virtue, duty, and silent immolation, having himself an incredible longing for self-sacrifice that he could not satisfy.

"I should much like," she said, "to be a nurse at a hospital."

"Alas! men have none of these holy missions, and I see nowhere any calling—unless perhaps that of a doctor."

With a slight shrug of her shoulders, Emma interrupted him to speak of her illness, which had almost killed her. What a pity! She should not be suffering now! Léon at once envied the calm of the tomb, and one evening he had even made his will, asking to be buried in that beautiful rug with velvet stripes he had received from her. For this was how they would have wished to be, each setting up an ideal to which they were now adapting their past life. Besides, speech is a rolling-mill that always thins out the sentiment.

But at this invention of the rug she asked, "But why?"

"Why?" He hesitated. "Because I loved you so!" And congratulating himself at having surmounted the difficulty, Léon watched her face out of the corner of his eyes.

It was like the sky when a gust of wind drives the clouds across. The mass of sad thoughts that darkened them seemed to be lifted from her blue eyes; her whole face shone. He waited. At last she replied—

"I always suspected it."

Then they went over all the trifling events of that far-off existence, whose joys and sorrows they had just summed up in one word. They recalled the arbour with clematis, the dresses she had worn, the furniture of her room, the whole of her house.

"And our poor cactuses, where are they?"

"The cold killed them this winter."

"Ah! how I have thought of them, do you know? I often saw them again as of yore, when on the summer mornings the sun beat down upon your blinds, and I saw your two bare arms passing out amongst the flowers."

"Poor friend!" she said, holding out her hand to him.

Léon swiftly pressed his lips to it. Then, when he had taken a deep breath—

"At that time you were to me I know not what incomprehensible force that took captive my life. Once, for instance, I went to see you; but you, no doubt, do not remember it."

"I do," she said; "go on."

"You were downstairs in the anteroom, ready to go out, standing on the last stair; you were wearing a bonnet with small blue flowers; and without any invitation from you, in spite of myself, I went with you. Every moment, however, I grew more and more conscious of my folly, and I went on walking by you, not daring to follow you completely, and unwilling to leave you. When you went into a shop, I waited in the street, and I watched you through the window taking off your gloves and counting the change on the counter. Then you rang at Madame Tuvache's; you were let in, and I stood like an idiot in front of the great heavy door that closed after you."

Madame Bovary, as she listened to him, wondered that she was so old. All these things reappearing before her seemed to widen out her life; it was like some sentimental immensity to which she returned; and from time to time she said in a low voice, her eyes half closed—

"Yes, it is true—true—true!"

They heard eight strike on the different clocks of the Beauvoisine quarter, that is full of schools, churches, and large empty hotels. They no longer spoke, but they felt as they looked upon each other a buzzing in their heads, as if something sonorous had escaped from the fixed eyes of each of them. They were hand in hand now, and the past, the future, reminiscences and dreams, all were confounded in the sweetness of this ecstasy. Night was darkening over the walls, on which still shone, half hidden in the shade, the coarse colours of four bills representing four scenes from the "Tour de Nesle," with a motto in Spanish and French at the bottom. Through the sash-window a patch of dark sky was seen between the pointed roofs.

She rose to light two wax-candles on the drawers, then she sat down again.

"Well!" said Léon.

"Well!" she replied.

He was thinking how to resume the interrupted conversation, when she said to him—

"How is it that no one until now has ever expressed such sentiments to me?"

The clerk said that ideal natures were difficult to understand. He from the first moment had loved her, and he despaired when he thought of the happiness that would have been theirs, if thanks to fortune, meeting her earlier, they had been indissolubly bound to one another.

"I have sometimes thought of it," she went on.

"What a dream!" murmured Léon. And fingering gently the blue binding of her long white sash, he added, "And who prevents us from beginning now?"

"No, my friend," she replied; "I am too old; you are too young. Forget me! Others will love you; you will love them."

"Not as you!" he cried.

"What a child you are! Come, let us be sensible. I wish it."

She showed him the impossibility of their love, and that they must remain, as formerly, on the simple terms of a fraternal friendship.

Was she speaking thus seriously? No doubt Emma did not herself know, quite absorbed as she was by the charm of the seduction, and the necessity of defending herself from it: and contemplating the young man with a moved look, she gently repulsed the timid caresses that his trembling hands attempted.

"Ah! forgive me!" he cried, drawing back.

Emma was seized with a vague fear at this shyness, more dangerous to her than the boldness of Rodolphe when he advanced to her open-armed. No man had ever seemed to her so beautiful. An exquisite candour emanated from his being. He lowered his long fine eyelashes, that curled upwards. His cheek, with the soft skin reddened, she thought; with desire of her person, and Emma felt an invincible longing to press her lips to it. Then, leaning towards the clock as if to see the time—

"Ah! how late it is!" she said; "how we do chatter!"

He understood the hint and took up his hat.

"It has even made me forget the theatre. And poor Bovary has left me here especially for that. Monsieur Lormeaux, of the Rue Grand-Pont, was to take me and his wife."

And the opportunity was lost, as she was to leave the next day.

"Really!" said Léon.

"Yes."

"But I must see you again," he went on. "I wanted to tell you——"

"What?"

"Something—important—serious. Oh, no! Besides, you will not go; it is impossible. If you should—listen to me. Then you have not understood me; you have not guessed——"

"Yet you speak plainly," said Emma.

"Ah! you can jest. Enough! enough! Oh, for pity's sake, let me see you once—only once!"

"Well——" She stopped; then, as if thinking better of it. "Oh, not here!"

"Where you will."

"Will you——" She seemed to reflect; then abruptly. "To-morrow at eleven o'clock in the cathedral."

"I shall be there," he cried, seizing her hands, which she disengaged.

And as they were both standing up, he behind her, and Emma with her head bent, he stooped over her and pressed long kisses on her neck.

"You are mad! Ah! you are mad!" she said, with sounding little laughs, while the kisses multiplied.

Then bending his head over her shoulder, he seemed to beg the consent of her eyes. They fell upon him full of an icy dignity.

Léon stepped back to go out. He stopped on the threshold; then he whispered with a trembling voice, "To-morrow!"

She answered with a nod, and disappeared like a bird into the next room.

In the evening Emma wrote the clerk an interminable letter, in which she cancelled the rendezvous; all was over; they must not, for the sake of their happiness, meet again. But when the letter was finished, as she did not know Léon's address, she was puzzled.

"I'll give it to him myself," she said; "he will come."

The next morning, at the open window, and humming on his balcony, Léon himself varnished his pumps with several coatings. He put on white trousers, fine socks, a green coat, emptied all the scent he had into his handkerchief, then having had his hair curled, he uncurled it again, in order to give it a more natural elegance.

"It is still too early," he thought, looking at the hair-dresser's cuckoo-clock, that pointed to the hour of nine. He read an old fashion journal, went out, smoked a cigar, walked up three streets, thought it was time, and went slowly towards the porch of Notre Dame.

It was a beautiful summer morning. Silver plate sparkled in the jeweller's windows, and the light falling obliquely on the cathedral made mirrors of the corners of the grey stones; a flock of birds fluttered in the grey sky round the trefoil bell-turrets; the square, resounding with cries, was fragrant with the flowers that bordered its pavement, roses, jasmines, pinks, narcissi, and tuberoses, unevenly spaced out between moist grasses, cat-mint, and chickweed for the birds; the fountains gurgled in the centre, and under large umbrellas, amidst melons piled up in heaps, flower-women, bare-headed, were twisting paper round bunches of violets.

The young man took one. It was the first time that he had bought flowers for a woman, and his breast, as he smelt them, swelled with pride, as if this homage that he meant for another had recoiled upon himself.

But he was afraid of being seen; he resolutely entered the church. The beadle, who was just then standing on the threshold in the middle of the left doorway, under the "Dancing Marianne," with feather cap, and rapier dangling against his calves, came in, more majestic than a cardinal, and as shining as a saint on a holy pyx.

He came towards Léon, and, with that smile of wheedling benignity assumed by ecclesiastics when they question children—

"The gentleman, no doubt, does not belong to these parts? The gentleman would like to see the curiosities of the church?"

"No!" said the other.

And he first went round the lower aisles. Then he went out to look at the Place. Emma was not coming yet. He went up again to the choir.

The nave was reflected in the full fonts with the beginning of the arches and some portions of the glass windows. But the reflections of the paintings, broken by the marble rim, were continued farther on upon the flag-stones, like a many-coloured carpet. The broad daylight from without streamed into the church in three enormous rays from the three opened portals. From time to time at the upper end a sacristan passed, making the oblique genuflexion of devout persons in a hurry. The crystal lustres hung motionless. In the choir a silver lamp was burning, and from the side chapels and dark places of the church sometimes rose sounds like sighs, with the clang of a closing grating, its echo reverberating under the lofty vault.

Léon with solemn steps walked along by the walls. Life had never seemed so good to him. She would come directly, charming, agitated, looking back at the glances that followed her, and with her flounced dress, her gold eye-glass, her thin shoes, with all sorts of elegant trifles that he had never enjoyed, and with the ineffable seduction of yielding virtue. The church like a huge boudoir spread around her; the arches bent down to gather in the shade the confession of her love; the windows shone resplendent to illumine her face, and the censers would burn that she might appear like an angel amid the fumes of the sweet-smelling odours.

But she did not come. He sat down on a chair, and his eyes fell upon a blue stained window representing boatmen carrying baskets. He looked at it long, attentively, and he counted the scales of the fishes and the button-holes of the doublets, while his thoughts wandered off towards Emma.

The beadle, standing aloof, was inwardly angry at this individual who took the liberty of admiring the cathedral by himself. He seemed to him to be conducting himself in a monstrous fashion, to be robbing him in a sort, and almost committing sacrilege.

But a rustle of silk on the flags, the tip of a bonnet, a lined cloak—it was she! Léon rose and ran to meet her.

Emma was pale. She walked fast.

"Read!" she said, holding out a paper to him. "Oh, no!"

And she abruptly withdrew her hand to enter the chapel of the Virgin, where, kneeling on a chair, she began to pray.

The young man was irritated at this bigot fancy; then he nevertheless experienced a certain charm in seeing her, in the middle of a rendezvous, thus lost in her devotions, like an Andalusian marchioness; then he grew bored, for she seemed never coming to an end.

Emma prayed, or rather strove to pray, hoping that some sudden resolution might descend to her from heaven; and to draw down divine aid she filled full her eyes with the splendours of the tabernacle. She breathed in the perfumes of the full-blown flowers in the large vases, and listened to the stillness of the church, that only heightened the tumult of her heart.

She rose, and they were about to leave, when the beadle came forward, hurriedly saying—

"Madame, no doubt, does not belong to these parts? Madame would like to see the curiosities of the church?"

"Oh, no!" cried the clerk.

"Why not?" said she. For she clung with her expiring virtue to the Virgin, the sculptures, the tombs—anything.

Then, in order to proceed "by rule," the beadle conducted them right to the entrance near the square, where, pointing out with his cane a large circle of block-stones without inscription or carving—

"This," he said majestically, "is the circumference of the beautiful bell of Ambroise. It weighed forty thousand pounds. There was not its equal in all Europe. The workman who cast it died of the joy——"

"Let us go on," said Léon.

The old fellow started off again; then, having got back to the chapel of the Virgin, he stretched forth his arm with an all-embracing gesture of demonstration, and, prouder than a country squire showing you his espaliers, went on—

"This simple stone covers Pierre de Brézé, lord of Varenne and of Brissac, grand marshal of Poitou, and governor of Normandy, who died at the battle of Montlhéry on the 16th of July, 1465."

Léon bit his lips, fuming.

"And on the right, this gentleman all encased in iron, on the prancing horse, is his grandson, Louis de Brézé, lord of Breval and of Montchauvet, Count de Maulevrier, Baron de Mauny, chamberlain to the king, Knight of the Order, and also governor of Normandy; died on the 23rd of July, 1531 —a Sunday, as the inscription specifies; and below, this figure, about to descend into the tomb, portrays the same person. It is not possible, is it, to see a more perfect representation of annihilation?"

Madame Bovary put up her eyeglasses. Léon, motionless, looked at her, no longer even attempting to speak a single word, to make a gesture, so discouraged was he at this twofold obstinacy of gossip and indifference.

The everlasting guide went on—

"Near him, this kneeling woman who weeps is his spouse, Diane de Poitiers, Countess de Brézé, Duchess de Valentinois, born in 1499, died in 1566, and to the left, the one with the child is the Holy Virgin. Now turn to this side; here are the tombs of the Ambroise. They were both cardinals and archbishops of Rouen. That one was minister under Louis XII. He did a great deal for the cathedral. In his will he left thirty thousand gold crowns for the poor."

And without stopping, still talking, he pushed them into a chapel full of balustrades, some put away, and disclosed a kind of block that certainly might once have been an ill-made statue.

"Truly," he said with a groan, "it adorned the tomb of Richard Cœur de Lion, King of England and Duke of Normandy. It was the Calvinists, sir, who reduced it to this condition. They had buried it for spite in the earth, under the episcopal seat of Monsignor. See! this is the door by which Monsignor passes to his house. Let us pass on quickly to see the gargoyle windows."

But Léon hastily took some silver from his pocket and seized Emma's arm. The beadle stood dumbfounded, not able to understand this untimely munificence when there were still so many things for the stranger to see. So calling him back, he cried—

"Sir! sir! The steeple! the steeple!"

"No, thank you!" said Léon.

"You are wrong, sir! It is four hundred and forty feet high, nine less than the great pyramid of Egypt. It is all cast; it——"

Léon was fleeing, for it seemed to him that his love, that for nearly two hours now had become petrified in the church like the stones, would vanish like a vapour through that sort of truncated funnel, of oblong cage, of open chimney that rises so grotesquely from the cathedral like the extravagant attempt of some fantastic brazier.

"But where are we going?" she said.

Making no answer, he walked on with a rapid step; and Madame Bovary was already dipping her finger in the holy water when behind them they heard a panting breath interrupted by the regular sound of a cane. Léon turned back.

"Sir!"

"What is it?"

And he recognised the beadle, holding under his arms and balancing against his stomach some twenty large sewn volumes. They were works "which treated of the cathedral."

"Idiot!" growled Léon, rushing out of the church.

A lad was playing about the close.

"Go and get me a cab!"

The child bounded off like a ball by the Rue Quatre-Vents; then they were alone a few minutes, face to face, and a little embarrassed.

"Ah, Léon! Really—I don't know—if I ought," she whispered. Then with a more serious air, "Do you know, it is very improper?"

"How so?" replied the clerk. "It is done at Paris."

And that, as an irresistible argument, decided her.

Still the cab did not come. Léon was afraid she might go back into the church. At last the cab appeared.

"At all events, go out by the north porch," cried the beadle, who was left alone on the threshold, "so as to see the Resurrection, the Last Judgment, Paradise, King David, and the Condemned in Hell-flames."

"Where to, sir?" asked the coachman.

"Where you like," said Léon, forcing Emma into the cab.

And the lumbering machine set out. It went down the Rue Grand-Pont, crossed the Place des Arts, the Quai Napoléon, the Pont Neuf, and stopped short before the statue of Pierre Correille.

"Go on," cried a voice that came from within.

The cab went on again, and as soon as it reached the Carrefour Lafayette, set off down-hill, and entered the station at a gallop.

"No, straight on!" cried the same voice.

The cab came out by the gate, and soon having reached the Cours, trotted quietly beneath the elm trees. The coachman wiped his brow, put his leather hat between his knees, and drove his carriage beyond the side alley by the meadow to the margin of the waters.

It went along by the river, along the towing-path paved with sharp pebbles, and for a long while in the direction of Oyssel, beyond the isles.

But suddenly it turned with a dash across Quatremares, Sotteville, La Grande-Chaussée, the Rue d'Elbeuf, and made its third halt in front of the Jardin des Plantes.

"Get on, will you?" cried the voice more furiously.

And at once resuming its course, it passed by Saint-Sever, by the Quai des Curandiers, the Quai aux Meules, once more over the bridge, by the Place du Champ de Mars, and behind the hospital gardens, where old men in black coats were walking in the sun along the terrace all green with ivy. It went up the Boulevard Bouvreuil, along the Boulevard Cauchoise, then the whole of Mont-Riboudet to the Deville hills.

It came back; and then, without any fixed plan or direction, wandered about at hazard. The cab was seen at Saint-Pol, at Lescure, at Mont Gargan, at La Rougue-Marc and Place du Gaillardbois; in the Rue Maladrerie, Rue Dinanderie, before Saint-Romain, Saint-Vivien, Saint-Maclou, Saint-Nicaise —in front of the Customs, at the "Vieille Tour," the "Trois Pipes," and the Monumental Cemetery. From time to time the coachman on his box cast despairing eyes at the public-houses. He could not understand what furious desire for locomotion urged these individuals never to wish to stop. He tried to now and then, and at once exclamations of anger burst forth behind him. Then he lashed his perspiring jades afresh, but indifferent to their jolting, running up against things here and there, not caring if he did, demoralised, and almost weeping with thirst, fatigue, and depression.

And on the harbour, in the midst of the drays and casks, and in the streets, at the corners, the good folk opened large wonder-stricken eyes at this sight, so extraordinary in the provinces, a cab with blinds drawn, and which appeared thus constantly shut more closely than a tomb, and tossing about like a vessel.

Once in the middle of the day, in the open country, just as the sun beat more fiercely against the old plated lanterns, a bared hand passed beneath the small blinds of yellow canvas, and threw out some scraps of paper that scattered in the wind, and farther off alighted like white butterflies on a field of red clover all in bloom.

At about six o'clock the carriage stopped in a back street of the Beauvoisine Quarter, and a woman got out, who walked with her veil down, and without turning her head.

II

ON REACHING THE INN, Madame Bovary was surprised not to see the diligence. Hivert, who had waited for her fifty-three minutes, had at last started.

Yet nothing forced her to go; but she had given her word that she would return that same evening. Moreover, Charles expected her, and in her heart she felt already that cowardly docility that is for some women at once the chastisement and atonement of adultery.

She packed her box quickly, paid her bill, took a cab in the yard, hurrying on the driver, urging him on, every moment inquiring about the time and the miles traversed. He succeeded in catching up the "Hirondelle" as it neared the first houses of Quincampoix.

Hardly was she seated in her corner than she closed her eyes, and opened them at the foot of the hill, when from afar she recognised Félicité, who was on the look-out in front of the farrier's shop. Hivert pulled in his horses, and the servant, climbing up to the window, said mysteriously—

"Madame, you must go at once to Monsieur Homais. It's for something important."

The village was silent as usual. At the corner of the streets were small pink heaps that smoked in the air, for this was the time for jam-making, and every one at Yonville prepared his supply on the same day. But in front of the chemist's shop one might admire a far larger heap, and that surpassed the others with the superiority that a laboratory must have over ordinary stores, a general need over individual fancy.

She went in. The large armchair was upset, and even the "Fanal de Rouen" lay on the ground, outspread between two pestles. She pushed open the lobby door, and in the middle of the kitchen, amid brown jars full of pickled currants, of powdered sugar and lump sugar, of the scales on the table, and of the pans on the fire, she saw all the Homais, small and large, with aprons reaching to their chins, and with forks in their hands. Justin was standing up with bowed head, and the chemist was screaming—

"Who told you to go and fetch it in the Capharnaüm?"

"What is it? What is the matter?"

"What is it?" replied the druggist. "We are making preserves; they are simmering; but they were about to boil over, because there is too much juice, and I ordered another pan. Then he, from indolence, from laziness, went and took, hanging on its nail in my laboratory, the key of the *Capharnaüm*."

It was thus the druggist called a small room under the leads, full of the utensils and the goods of his trade. He often spent long hours there alone, labelling, decanting, and doing up again; and he looked upon it not as a simple store, but as a veritable sanctuary, whence there afterwards issued, elaborated by his hands, all sorts of pills, boluses, infusions, lotions, and potions, that would bear far and wide his celebrity. No one in the world set foot there, and he respected it so, that he swept it himself. Finally, if the pharmacy, open to all comers, was the spot where he displayed his pride, the *Capharnaüm* was the refuge where, egotistically concentrating himself, Homais delighted in the exercise of his predilections, so that Justin's thoughtlessness seemed to him a monstrous piece of irreverence, and, redder than the currants, he repeated—

"Yes, from the *Capharnaüm!* The key that locks up the acids and caustic alkalies! To go and get a spare pan! a pan with a lid! and that I shall perhaps never use! Everything is of importance in the delicate operations of our art! But, devil take it! one must make distinctions, and not employ for almost domestic purposes that which is meant for pharmaceutical! It is as if one were to carve a fowl with a scalpel; as if a magistrate——"

"Now be calm," said Madame Homais.

And Athalie, pulling at his coat, cried "Papa! papa!"

"No, let me alone," went on the druggist, "let me alone, hang it! My word! One might as well set up for a grocer. That's it! go it! respect nothing! break, smash, let loose the leeches, burn the mallow-paste, pickle the gherkins in the window jars, tear up the bandages!"

"I thought you had——" said Emma.

"Presently! Do you know to what you exposed yourself? Didn't you see anything in the corner, on the left, on the third shelf? Speak, answer, articulate something."

"I—don't—know," stammered the young fellow.

"Ah! you don't know! Well, then, I do know! You saw a bottle of blue glass, sealed with yellow wax, that contains a white powder, on which I have even written 'Dangerous!' And do you know what is in it? Arsenic! And you go and touch it! You take a pan that was next to it!"

"Next to it!" cried Madame Homais, clasping her hands. "Arsenic! You might have poisoned us all."

And the children began howling as if they already had frightful pains in their entrails.

"Or poison a patient!" continued the druggist. "Do you want to see me in the prisoner's dock with criminals, in a court of justice? To see me dragged to the scaffold? Don't you know what care I take in managing things, although I am so thoroughly used to it? Often I am horrified myself when I think of my responsibility; for the Government persecutes us, and the absurd legislation that rules us is a veritable Damocles' sword over our heads."

Emma no longer dreamed of asking what they wanted her for, and the druggist went on in breathless phrases—

"That is your return for all the kindnesses we have shown you! That is how you recompense me for the really paternal care that I lavish on you! For without me where would you be? What would you be doing? Who provides you with food, education, clothes, and all the means of figuring one day with honour in the ranks of society? But you must pull hard at the oar if you're to do that, and get, as people say, callosities upon your hands. *Fabricando fit faber, age quod agis.*"

He was so exasperated he quoted Latin. He would have quoted Chinese or Greenlandish had he known those two languages, for he was in one of those crises in which the whole soul shows indistinctly what it contains, like the ocean, which, in the storm, opens itself from the seaweeds on its shores down to the sands of its abysses.

And he went on—

"I am beginning to repent terribly of having taken you up! I should certainly have done better to have left you to rot in your poverty and the dirt in which you were born. Oh, you'll never be fit for anything but to herd animals with horns! You have no aptitude for science! You hardly know how to stick on a label! And there you are, dwelling with me snug as a parson, living in clover, taking your ease!"

But Emma, turning to Madame Homais, "I was told to come here——"

"Oh, dear me!" interrupted the good woman with a sad air, "how am I to tell you? It is a misfortune!"

She could not finish, the druggist was thundering—"Empty it! Clean it! Take it back! Be quick!"

And seizing Justin by the collar of his blouse, he shook a book out of his pocket. The lad stooped, but Homais was the quicker, and, having picked up the volume, contemplated it with staring eyes and open mouth.

"*Conjugal—love!*" he said, slowly separating the two words. "Ah! very good! very good! very pretty. And illustrations! Oh, this is too much!"

Madame Homais came forward.

"No, do not touch it!"

The children wanted to look at the pictures.

"Leave the room," he said imperiously; and they went out.

First he walked up and down with the open volume in his hand, rolling his eyes, choking, tumid, apoplectic. Then he came straight to his pupil, and, planting himself in front of him with crossed arms—

"Have you every vice, then, little wretch? Take care! you are on a downward path. Did you not reflect that this infamous book might fall into the hands of my children, kindle a spark in their minds, tarnish the purity of Athalie, corrupt Napoléon. He is already formed like a man. Are you quite sure, anyhow, that they have not read it? Can you certify to me——"

"But really, sir," said Emma, "you wish to tell me——"

"Ah, yes! madame. Your father-in-law is dead."

In fact, Monsieur Bovary senior had expired the evening before suddenly from an attack of apoplexy as he got up from table, and by way of greater precaution, on account of Emma's sensibility, Charles had begged Homais to break the horrible news to her gradually. Homais had thought over his speech; he had rounded, polished it, made it rhythmical; it was a masterpiece of prudence and transitions, of subtle turns and delicacy; but anger had got the better of rhetoric.

Emma, giving up all chance of hearing any details, left the pharmacy; for Monsieur Homais had taken up the thread of his vituperations. However, he was growing calmer, and was now grumbling in a paternal tone whilst he fanned himself with his skull-cap.

"It is not that I entirely disapprove of the work. Its author was a doctor! There are certain scientific points in it that it is not ill a man should know, and I would even venture to say that a man must know. But later—later! At any rate, not till you are a man yourself and your temperament is formed."

When Emma knocked at the door, Charles, who was waiting for her, came forward with open arms and said to her with tears in his voice—

"Ah! my dear!"

And he bent over her gently to kiss her. But at the contact of his lips the memory of the other seized her, and she passed her hand over her face shuddering.

But she made answer, "Yes, I know, I know!"

He showed her the letter in which his mother told the event without any sentimental hypocrisy. She only regretted her husband had not received the consolations of religion, as he had died at Daudeville, in the street, at the door of a café after a patriotic dinner with some ex-officers.

Emma gave him back the letter; then at dinner, for appearance's sake, she affected a certain repugnance. But as he urged her to try, she resolutely began eating, while Charles opposite her sat motionless in a dejected attitude.

Now and then he raised his head and gave her a long look full of distress. Once he sighed, "I should have liked to see him again!"

She was silent. At last, understanding that she must say something, "How old was your father?" she asked.

"Fifty-eight."

"Ah!"

And that was all.

A quarter of an hour after he added, "My poor mother! what will become of her now?"

She made a gesture that signified she did not know. Seeing her so taciturn, Charles imagined her much affected, and forced himself to say nothing, not to reawaken this sorrow which moved him. And, shaking off his own—

"Did you enjoy yourself yesterday?" he asked.

"Yes."

When the cloth was removed, Bovary did not rise, nor did Emma; and as she looked at him, the monotony of the spectacle drove little by little all pity from her heart. He seemed to her paltry, weak, a cipher—in a word, a poor thing in every way. How to get rid of him? What an interminable evening! Something stupefying like the fumes of opium seized her.

They heard in the passage the sharp noise of a wooden leg on the boards. It was Hippolyte bringing back Emma's luggage. In order to put it down he described painfully a quarter of a circle with his stump.

"He doesn't even remember any more about it," she thought, looking at the poor devil, whose coarse red hair was wet with perspiration.

Bovary was searching at the bottom of his purse for a centime, and without appearing to understand all there was of humiliation for him in the mere presence of this man, who stood there like a personified reproach to his incurable incapacity.

"Hallo! you've a pretty bouquet," he said, noticing Léon's violets on the chimney.

"Yes," she replied indifferently; "it's a bouquet I bought just now from a beggar."

Charles picked up the flowers, and freshening his eyes, red with tears, against them, smelt them delicately.

She took them quickly from his hand and put them in a glass of water.

The next day Madame Bovary senior arrived. She and her son wept much. Emma, on the pretext of giving orders, disappeared. The following day they had a talk over the mourning. They went and sat down with their work-boxes by the water-side under the arbour.

Charles was thinking of his father, and was surprised to feel so much affection for this man, whom till then he had thought he cared little about. Madame Bovary senior was thinking of her husband. The worst days of the past seemed enviable to her. All was forgotten beneath the instinctive regret of such a long habit, and from time to time whilst she sewed, a big tear rolled along her nose and hung suspended there a moment. Emma was thinking that it was scarcely forty-eight hours since they had been together, far from the world, all in a frenzy of joy, and not having eyes enough to gaze upon each other. She tried to recall the slightest details of that past day. But the presence of her husband and mother-in-law worried her. She would have liked to hear nothing, to see nothing, so as not to disturb the meditation on her love, that, do what she would, became lost in external sensations.

She was unpicking the lining of a dress, and the strips were scattered around her. Madame Bovary senior was plying her scissors without looking up, and Charles, in his list slippers and his old brown surtout that he used as a dressing-gown, sat with both hands in his pockets, and did not speak either; near them Berthe, in a little white pinafore, was raking the sand in the walks with her spade.

Suddenly she saw Monsieur Lheureux, the linendraper, come in through the gate.

He came to offer his services "under the sad circumstances." Emma answered that she thought she could do without. The shopkeeper was not to be beaten.

"I beg your pardon," he said, "but I should like to have a private talk with you." Then in a low voice, "It's about that affair—you know."

Charles crimsoned to his ears. "Oh, yes! certainly." And in his confusion, turning to his wife, "Couldn't you, my darling?"

She seemed to understand him, for she rose; and Charles said to his mother, "It is nothing particular. No doubt, some household trifle." He did not want her to know the story of the bill, fearing her reproaches.

As soon as they were alone, Monsieur Lheureux in sufficiently clear terms began to congratulate Emma on the inheritance, then to talk of indifferent matters, of the espaliers, of the harvest, and of his own health, which was always so-so, always having ups and downs. In fact, he had to work devilish hard, although he didn't make enough, in spite of all people said, to find butter for his bread.

Emma let him talk on. She had bored herself so prodigiously the last two days.

"And you're quite well again?" he went on. "*Ma foi!* I saw your husband in a sad state. He's a good fellow, though we did have a little misunderstanding."

She asked what misunderstanding, for Charles had said nothing of the dispute about the goods supplied to her.

"Why, you know well enough," cried Lheureux. "It was about your little fancies—the travelling trunks."

He had drawn his hat over his eyes, and, with his hands behind his back, smiling and whistling, he looked straight at her in an unbearable manner. Did he suspect anything? She was lost in all kinds of apprehensions. At last, however, he went on—

"We made it up, all the same, and I've come again to propose another arrangement."

This was to renew the bill Bovary had signed. The doctor, of course, would do as he pleased; he was not to trouble himself, especially just now, when he would have a lot of worry. "And he would do better to give it over to some one else,—to you, for example. With a power of attorney it could be easily managed, and then we (you and I) would have our little business transactions together."

She did not understand. He was silent. Then, passing to his trade, Lheureux declared that madame must require something. He would send her a black barège, twelve yards, just enough to make a gown.

"The one you've on is good enough for the house, but you want another for calls. I saw that the very moment that I came in. I've the eye of an American!"

He did not send the stuff; he brought it. Then he came again to measure it; he came again on other pretexts, always trying to make himself agreeable, useful, "enfeoffing himself," as Homais would have said, and always dropping some hint to Emma about the power of attorney. He never mentioned the bill; she did not think of it. Charles, at the beginning of her convalescence, had certainly said something about it to her, but so many emotions had passed through her head that she no longer remembered it. Besides, she took care not to talk of any money questions. Madame Bovary seemed surprised at this, and attributed the change in her ways to the religious sentiments she had contracted during her illness.

But as soon as she was gone, Emma greatly astounded Bovary by her practical good sense. It would be necessary to make inquiries, to look into mortgages, and see if there were any occasion for a sale by auction or a liquidation. She quoted technical terms casually, pronounced the grand words of order, the future, foresight, and constantly exaggerated the difficulties of settling his father's affairs so much, that at last one day she showed him the rough draft of a power of attorney to manage and administer his business, arrange all loans, sign and endorse all bills, pay all sums, &c. She had profited by Lheureux's lessons.

Charles naïvely asked her where this paper came from.

"Monsieur Guillaumin"; and with the utmost coolness she added, "I don't trust him overmuch. Notaries have such a bad reputation. Perhaps we ought to consult——We only know—no one."

"Unless Léon——" replied Charles, who was reflecting.

But it was difficult to explain matters by letter. Then she offered to make the journey, but he thanked her. She insisted. It was quite a contest of mutual consideration. At last she cried with affected waywardness—

"No, I will go!"

"How good you are!" he said, kissing her forehead.

The next morning she set out in the "Hirondelle" to go to Rouen to consult Monsieur Léon, and she stayed there three days.

III

THEY WERE THREE FULL, exquisite days—a true honeymoon. They were at the Hôtel-de-Boulogne, on the harbour; and they lived there, with drawn blinds and closed doors, with flowers on the floor, and iced syrups that were brought them early in the morning.

Towards evening they took a covered boat and went to dine on one of the islands. It was the time when one hears by the side of the dockyard the caulking-mallets sounding against the hulls of vessels. The smoke of the tar rose up between the trees; there were large fatty drops on the water, undulating in the purple colour of the sun, like floating plaques of Florentine bronze.

They rowed down in the midst of moored boats, whose long oblique cables grazed lightly against the bottom of the boat. The din of the town gradually grew distant; the rolling of carriages, the tumult of voices, the yelping of dogs on the decks of vessels. She took off her bonnet, and they landed on their island.

They sat down in the low-ceilinged room of a tavern, at whose door hung black nets. They ate fried smelts, cream and cherries. They lay down upon the grass; they kissed behind the poplars; and they would fain, like two Robinsons, have lived for ever in this little place, which seemed to them in their beatitude the most magnificent on earth. It was not the first time that they had seen trees, a blue sky, meadows; that they had heard the water flowing and the wind blowing in the leaves; but, no doubt, they had never admired all this, as if Nature had not existed before, or had only begun to be beautiful since the gratification of their desires.

At night they returned. The boat glided along the shores of the islands. They sat at the bottom, both hidden by the shade, in silence. The square oars rang in the iron thwarts, and, in the stillness, seemed to mark time, like the beating of a metronome, while at the stern the rudder that trailed behind never ceased its gentle splash against the water.

Once the moon rose; then they did not fail to make fine phrases, finding the orb melancholy and full of poetry. She even began to sing—

"One night, do you remember, we were sailing," &c.

Her musical but weak voice died away along the waves, and the winds carried off the trills that Léon heard pass like the flapping of wings about him.

She was opposite him, leaning against the partition of the shallop, through one of whose raised blinds the moon streamed in. Her black dress, whose drapery spread out like a fan, made her seem more slender, taller. Her head was raised, her hands clasped, her eyes turned towards heaven. At times the shadow of the willows hid her completely; then she reappeared suddenly, like a vision in the moonlight.

Léon, on the floor by her side, found under his hand a ribbon of scarlet silk. The boatman looked at it, and at last said—

"Perhaps it belongs to the party I took out the other day. A lot of jolly folk, gentlemen and ladies, with cakes, champagne, cornets—everything in style! There was one especially, a tall handsome man with small moustaches, who was that funny! And they all kept saying, 'Now tell us something, Adolphe—Dolpe,' I think."

She shivered.

"You are in pain?" asked Léon, coming closer to her.

"Oh, it's nothing! No doubt, it is only the night air."

"And who doesn't want for women, either," softly added the sailor, thinking he was paying the stranger a compliment.

Then, spitting on his hands, he took the oars again.

Yet they had to part. The adieux were sad. He was to send his letters to Mère Rollet, and she gave him such precise instructions about a double envelope that he admired greatly her amorous astuteness.

"So you can assure me it is all right?" she said with her last kiss.

"Yes, certainly."

"But why," he thought afterwards as he came back through the streets alone, "is she so very anxious to get this power of attorney?"

IV

LÉON soon put on an air of superiority before his comrades, avoided their company, and completely neglected his work.

He waited for her letters; he re-read them; he wrote to her. He called her to mind with all the strength of his desires and of his memories. Instead of lessening with absence, this longing to see her again grew, so that at last one Saturday morning he escaped from his office.

When, from the summit of the hill, he saw in the valley below the church-spire with its tin flag swinging in the wind, he felt that delight mingled with triumphant vanity and egoistic tenderness that millionaires must experience when they come back to their native village.

He went rambling round her house. A light was burning in the kitchen. He watched for her shadow behind the curtains, but nothing appeared.

Mère Lefrançois, when she saw him, uttered many exclamations. She thought he "had grown and was thinner," while Artémise, on the contrary, thought him stouter and darker.

He dined in the little room as of yore, but alone, without the tax-gatherer; for Binet, tired of waiting for the "Hirondelle," had definitely put forward his meal one hour, and now he dined punctually at five, and yet he declared usually the rickety old concern "was late."

Léon, however, made up his mind, and knocked at the doctor's door. Madame was in her room, and did not come down for a quarter of an hour. The doctor seemed delighted to see him, but he never stirred out that evening, nor all the next day.

He saw her alone in the evening, very late, behind the garden in the lane; —in the lane, as she had the other one! It was a stormy night, and they talked under an umbrella by lightning flashes.

Their separation was becoming intolerable. "I would rather die!" said Emma. She was writhing in his arms, weeping. "Adieu! adieu! When shall I see you again?"

They came back again to embrace once more, and it was then that she promised him to find soon, by no matter what means, a regular opportunity for seeing one another in freedom at least once a week. Emma never doubted she should be able to do this. Besides, she was full of hope. Some money was coming to her.

On the strength of it she bought a pair of yellow curtains with large stripes for her room, whose cheapness Monsieur Lheureux had commended; she dreamed of getting a carpet, and Lheureux, declaring that it wasn't "drinking the sea," politely undertook to supply her with one. She could no longer do without his services. Twenty times a day she sent for him, and he at once put by his business without a murmur. People could not understand either why Mère Rollet breakfasted with her every day, and even paid her private visits.

It was about this time, that is to say, the beginning· of winter, that she seemed seized with great musical fervour.

One evening when Charles was listening to her, she began the same piece four times over, each time with much vexation, while he, not noticing any difference, cried—

"Bravo! very good! You are wrong to stop. Go on!"

"Oh, no; it is execrable! My fingers are quite rusty."

The next day he begged her to play him something again.

"Very well; to please you!"

And Charles confessed she had gone off a little. She played wrong notes and blundered; then, stopping short—

"Ah! it is no use. I ought to take some lessons; but——" She bit her lips and added, "Twenty francs a lesson, that's too dear!"

"Yes, so it is—rather," said Charles, giggling stupidly. "But it seems to me that one might be able to do it for less; for there are artists of no reputation, and who are often better than the celebrities."

"Find them!" said Emma.

The next day when he came home he looked at her shyly, and at last could no longer keep back the words.

"How obstinate you are sometimes! I went to Barfuchères to-day. Well, Madame Liégeard assured me that her three young ladies who are at La Miséricorde have lessons at fifty sous apiece, and that from an excellent mistress!"

She shrugged her shoulders and did not open her piano again. But when she passed by it (if Bovary were there), she sighed—

"Ah! my poor piano!"

And when any one came to see her, she did not fail to inform them that she had given up music, and could not begin again now for important reasons. Then people commiserated her—

"What a pity! she had so much talent!"

They even spoke to Bovary about it. They put him to shame, and especially the chemist.

"You are wrong. One should never let any of the faculties of nature lie fallow. Besides, just think, my good friend, that by inducing madame to study, you are economising on the subsequent musical education of your child. For my own part, I think that mothers ought themselves to instruct their children. That is an idea of Rousseau's, still rather new perhaps, but that will end by triumphing, I am certain of it, like mothers nursing their own children and vaccination."

So Charles returned once more to this question of the piano. Emma replied bitterly that it would be better to sell it. This poor piano, that had given her vanity so much satisfaction—to see it go was to Bovary like the indefinable suicide of a part of herself.

"If you liked," he said, "a lesson from time to time, that wouldn't after all be very ruinous."

"But lessons," she replied, "are only of use when followed up."

And thus it was she set about obtaining her husband's permission to go to town once a week to see her lover. At the end of a month she was even considered to have made considerable progress.

V

SHE WENT ON THURSDAYS. She got up and dressed silently, in order not to awaken Charles, who would have made remarks about her getting ready too early. Next she walked up and down, went to the windows, and looked out at the Place. The early dawn was broadening between the pillars of the market, and the chemist's shop, with the shutters still up, showed in the pale light of the dawn the large letters of his signboard.

When the clock pointed to a quarter past seven, she went off to the "Lion d'Or," whose door Artémise opened yawning. The girl then made up the coals covered by the cinders, and Emma remained alone in the kitchen. Now and again she went out. Hivert was leisurely harnessing his horses, listening, moreover, to Mère Lefrançois, who, passing her head and nightcap though a grating, was charging him with commissions and giving him explanations that would have confused any one else. Emma kept beating the soles of her boots against the pavement of the yard.

At last, when he had eaten his soup, put on his cloak, lighted his pipe, and grasped his whip, he calmly installed himself on his seat.

The "Hirondelle" started at a slow trot, and for about a mile stopped here and there to pick up passengers who waited for it, standing at the border of the road, in front of their yard gates.

Those who had secured seats the evening before kept it waiting; some even were still in bed in their houses. Hivert called, shouted, swore; then he got down from his seat and went and knocked loudly at the doors. The wind blew through the cracked windows.

The four seats, however, filled up. The carriage rolled off; rows of apple trees followed one upon another, and the road between its two long ditches, full of yellow water, rose, constantly narrowing towards the horizon.

Emma knew it from end to end; she knew that after a meadow there was a sign-post, next an elm, a barn, or the hut of a lime-kiln tender. Sometimes even, in the hope of getting some surprise, she shut her eyes, but she never lost the clear perception of the distance to be traversed.

At last the brick houses began to follow one another more closely, the earth resounded beneath the wheels, the "Hirondelle" glided between the gardens, where through an opening one saw statues, a periwinkle plant, clipped yews, and a swing. Then on a sudden the town appeared. Sloping down like an amphitheatre, and drowned in the fog, it widened out beyond the bridges confusedly. Then the open country spread away with a monotonous movement till it touched in the distance the vague line of the pale sky. Seen thus from above, the whole landscape looked immovable as a picture; the anchored ships were massed in one corner, the river curved round the foot of the green hills, and the isles, oblique in shape, lay on the water, like large motionless, black fishes. The factory chimneys belched forth immense brown fumes that were blown away at the top. One heard the rumbling of the foundries, together with the clear chimes of the churches that stood out in the midst. The leafless trees on the boulevards made violet thickets in the midst of the houses, and the roofs, all shining with the rain, threw back unequal reflections, according to the height of the quarters in which they were. Sometimes a gust of wind drove the clouds towards the Saint-Catherine hills, like aerial waves that broke silently against a cliff.

A giddiness seemed to her to detach itself from this mass of existence, and her heart swelled as if the hundred and twenty thousand souls that palpitated there had all at once sent into it the vapour of the passions she fancied theirs. Her love grew in the presence of this vastness, and expanded with tumult to the vague murmurings that rose towards her. She poured it out upon the square, on the walks, on the streets, and the old Norman city outspread before her eyes as an enormous capital, as a Babylon into which she was entering. She leant with both hands against the window, drinking in the breeze; the three horses galloped, the stones grated in the mud, the diligence rocked, and Hivert, from afar, hailed the carts on the road, while the bourgeois who had spent the night at the Guillaume woods came quietly down the hill in their little family carriages.

They stopped at the barrier; Emma undid her overshoes, put on other gloves, rearranged her shawl, and some twenty paces farther she got down from the "Hirondelle."

The town was then awakening. Shop-boys in caps were cleaning up the shop-fronts, and women, with baskets against their hips, at intervals uttered sonorous cries at the corners of streets. She walked with downcast eyes, close to the walls, and smiling with pleasure under her lowered black veil.

For fear of being seen, she did not usually take the most direct road. She plunged into dark alleys, and, all perspiring, reached the bottom of the Rue Nationale, near the fountain that stands there. It is the quarter for theatres, public-houses, and whores. Often a cart would pass near her, bearing some shaking scenery. Waiters in aprons were sprinkling sand on the flag-stones between green shrubs. It all smelt of absinthe, cigars, and oysters.

She turned down a street; she recognised him by his curling hair that escaped from beneath his hat.

Léon walked along the pavement. She followed him to the hotel. He went up, opened the door, entered— What an embrace!

Then, after the kisses, the words gushed forth. They told each other the sorrows of the week, the presentiments, the anxiety for the letters; but now everything was forgotten; they gazed into each other's faces with voluptuous laughs, and tender names.

The bed was large, of mahogany, in the shape of a boat. The curtains were in red levantine, that hung from the ceiling and bulged out too much towards the bell-shaped bedside; and nothing in the world was so lovely as her brown head and white skin standing out against this purple colour, when, with a movement of shame, she crossed her bare arms, hiding her face in her hands.

The warm room, with its discreet carpet, its grey ornaments, and its calm light, seemed made for the intimacies of passion. The curtain-rods, ending in arrows, their brass pegs, and the great balls of the fire-logs shone suddenly when the sun came in. On the chimney between the candelabra there were two of those pink shells in which one hears the murmur of the sea if one holds them to the ear.

How they loved that dear room, so full of gaiety, despite its rather faded splendour! They always found the furniture in the same place, and sometimes hairpins, that she had forgotten the Thursday before, under the pedestal of the clock. They lunched by the fireside on a little round table, inlaid with rosewood. Emma carved, put bits on his plate with all sorts of coquettish ways, and she laughed with a sonorous and libertine laugh when the froth of the champagne ran over from the glass to the rings on her fingers. They were so completely lost in the possession of each other that they thought themselves in their own house, and that they would live there till death, like two spouses eternally young. They said "our room," "our carpet," she even said "my slippers," a gift of Léon's, a whim she had had. They were pink satin, bordered with swansdown. When she sat on his knees, her leg, then too short, hung in the air, and the dainty shoe, that had no back to it, was held in only by the toes to her bare foot.

He for the first time enjoyed the inexpressible delicacy of feminine refinements. He had never met this grace of language, this reserve of clothing, these poses of the weary dove. He admired the exaltation of her soul and the lace on her petticoat. Besides, was she not "a lady" and a married woman —a real mistress, in fine?

By the diversity of her humour, in turn mystical or mirthful, talkative, taciturn, passionate, careless, she awakened in him a thousand desires, called up instincts or memories. She was the mistress of all the novels, the heroine of all the dramas, the vague "she" of all the volumes of verse. He found again on her shoulder the amber colouring of the "odalisque bathing"; she had the long waist of feudal châtelaines, and she resembled the "pale woman of Barcelona." But above all she was the Angel!

Often looking at her, it seemed to him that his soul, escaping towards her, spread like a wave about the outline of her head, and descended drawn down into the whiteness of her breast. He knelt on the ground before her, and with both elbows on her knees looked at her with a smile, his face upturned.

She bent over him, and murmured, as if choking with intoxication—

"Oh, do not move! do not speak! look at me! Something so sweet comes from your eyes that helps me so much!"

She called him "child." "Child, do you love me?"

And she did not listen for his answer in the haste of her lips that fastened to his mouth.

On the clock there was a bronze cupid, who smirked as he bent his arm beneath a golden garland. They had laughed at it many a time, but when they had to part everything seemed serious to them.

Motionless in front of each other, they kept repeating, "Till Thursday, till Thursday."

Suddenly she seized his head between her hands, kissed him hurriedly on the forehead, crying, "Adieu!" and rushed down the stairs.

She went to a hairdresser's in the Rue de la Comédie to have her hair arranged. Night fell; the gas was lighted in the shop. She heard the bell at the theatre calling the mummers to the performance, and she saw, passing opposite, men with white faces and women in faded gowns going in at the stage-door.

It was hot in the room, small, and too low, where the stove was hissing in the midst of wigs and pomades. The smell of the tongs, together with the greasy hands that handled her head, soon stunned her, and she dozed a little in her wrapper. Often, as he did her hair, the man offered her tickets for a masked ball.

Then she went away. She went up the streets; reached the "Croix-Rouge," put on her overshoes, that she had hidden in the morning under the seat, and sank into her place among the impatient passengers. Some got out at the foot of the hill. She remained alone in the carriage. At every turning all the lights of the town were seen more and more completely, making a great luminous vapour about the dim houses Emma knelt on the cushions, and her eyes wandered over the dazzling light. She sobbed; called on Léon, sent him tender words and kisses lost in the wind.

On the hillside a poor devil wandered about with his stick in the midst of the diligences. A mass of rags covered his shoulders, and an old staved-in beaver, turned out like a basin, hid his face; but when he took it off he discovered in the place of eyelids empty and bloody orbits. The flesh hung in red shreds, and there flowed from it liquids that congealed into green scales down to the nose, whose black nostrils sniffed convulsively. To speak to you he threw back his head with an idiotic laugh; then his bluish eye-balls, rolling constantly, at the temples beat against the edge of the open wound. He sang a little song as he followed the carriages—

"*Maids in the warmth of a summer day*
Dream of love, and of love alway."

And all the rest was about birds and sunshine and green leaves.

Sometimes he appeared suddenly behind Emma, bareheaded, and she drew back with a cry. Hivert made fun of him. He would advise him to get a booth at the Saint Romain fair, or else ask him, laughing, how his young woman was.

Often they had started when, with a sudden movement, his hat entered the diligence through the small window. while he clung with his other arm to the footboard, between the wheels splashing mud. His voice, feeble at first and quavering, grew sharp; it resounded in the night like the indistinct moan of a vague distress; and through the ringing of the bells, the murmur of the trees, and the rumbling of the empty vehicle, it had a far-off sound that disturbed Emma. It went to the bottom of her soul, like a whirlwind in an abyss, and carried her away into the distances of a boundless melancholy. But Hivert, noticing a weight behind, gave the blind man sharp cuts with his whip. The thong lashed his wounds, and he fell back into the mud with a yell. Then the passengers in the "Hirondelle" ended by falling asleep, some with open mouths, others with lowered chins, leaning against their neighbour's shoulder, or with their arm passed through the strap, oscillating regularly with the jolting of the carriage; and the reflection of the lantern swinging without, on the crupper of the wheeler, penetrating into the interior through the chocolate calico curtains, threw sanguineous shadows over all these motionless people. Emma, drunk with grief, shivered in her clothes, feeling her feet grow colder and colder, and death in her soul.

Charles at home was waiting for her; the "Hirondelle" was always late on Thursdays. Madame arrived at last, and scarcely kissed the child. The dinner was not ready. No matter! She excused the servant. This girl now seemed allowed to do just as she liked.

Often her husband, noting her pallor, asked if she were unwell.

"No," said Emma.

"But," he replied, "you seem so strange this evening."

"Oh, it's nothing! nothing!"

There were even days when she had no sooner come in than she went up to her room; and Justin, happening to be there, moved about noiselessly, quicker at helping her than the best of maids. He put the matches ready, the candlestick, a book, arranged her nightgown, turned back the bedclothes.

"Come!" said she, "that will do. Now you can go."

For he stood there, his hands hanging down and his eyes wide open, as if enmeshed in the innumerable threads of a sudden reverie.

The following day was frightful, and those that came after still more unbearable, because of her impatience to once again seize her happiness; an ardent lust, inflamed by the images of past experience, and that burst forth feebly on the seventh day beneath Léon's caresses. His ardours were hidden beneath outbursts of wonder and gratitude. Emma tasted this love in a discreet, absorbed fashion, maintained it by all the artifices of her tenderness, and trembled a little lest it should be lost later on.

She often said to him, with her sweet, melancholy voice—

"Ah! you too, you will leave me! You will marry! You will be like all the others."

He asked, "What others?"

"Why, like all men," she replied. Then added, repulsing him with a languid movement—

"You are all evil!"

One day, as they were talking philosophically of earthly disillusions, to experiment on his jealousy, or yielding, perhaps, to an over-strong need to pour out her heart, she told him that formerly, before him, she had loved some one. "Not like you," she went on quickly, protesting by the head of her child that "nothing had passed between them."

The young man believed her, but none the less questioned her to find out what *he* was.

"He was a ship's captain, my dear."

Was this not preventing any inquiry, and, at the same time, assuming a higher ground through this pretended fascination exercised over a man who must have been of warlike nature and accustomed to receive homage?

The clerk then felt the lowliness of his position; he longed for epaulettes, crosses, titles. All that would please her,—he gathered that from her spend-thrift habits.

Emma nevertheless concealed many of these extravagant fancies, such as her wish to have a blue tilbury to drive into Rouen, drawn by an English horse and driven by a groom in top-boots. It was Justin who had inspired her with this whim, by begging her to take him into her service as *valet-de-chambre*, and if the privation of it did not lessen the pleasure of her arrival at each rendezvous, it certainly augmented the bitterness of the return.

Often, when they talked together of Paris, she ended by murmuring, "Ah! how happy we should be there!"

"Are we not happy?" gently answered the young man, passing his hands over her hair.

"Yes, that is true," she said. "I am mad. Kiss me!"

To her husband she was more charming than ever. She made him pistachio-creams and played him waltzes after dinner. So he thought himself the most fortunate of men, and Emma was without uneasiness, when, one evening, suddenly he said—

"It is Mademoiselle Lempereur, isn't it, who gives you lessons?"

"Yes."

"Well, I saw her just now," Charles went on, "at Madame Liégeard's. I spoke to her about you, and she doesn't know you."

This was like a thunderclap. However, she replied quite naturally—

"Ah! no doubt she forgot my name."

"But perhaps," said the doctor, "there are several Demoiselles Lempereur at Rouen who are music-mistresses."

"Possibly!" Then quickly—"But I have my receipts here. See!"

And she went to the writing-table, ransacked all the drawers, rummaged the papers, and at last lost her head so completely that Charles earnestly begged her not to take so much trouble about those wretched receipts.

"Oh, I will find them," she said.

And, in fact, on the following Friday, as Charles was putting on one of his boots in the dark cabinet where his clothes were kept, he felt a piece of paper between the leather and his sock. He took it out and read—

"Received, for three months' lessons and several pieces of music, the sum of sixty-three francs.—FELICIE LEMPEREUR, professor of music."

"How the devil did it get into my boots?"

"It must," she replied, "have fallen from the old box of bills that is on the edge of the shelf."

From that moment her existence was but one long tissue of lies, in which she enveloped her love as in veils to hide it It was a want, a mania, a pleasure carried to such an extent that if she said she had the day before walked on the right side of a road, one might know she had taken the left.

One morning, when she had gone, as usual, rather lightly clothed, it suddenly began to snow, and as Charles was watching the weather from the window, he caught sight of Monsieur Bournisien in the chaise of Monsieur Tuvache, who was driving him to Rouen. Then he went down to give the priest a thick shawl that he was to hand over to Emma as soon as he reached the "Croix-Rouge." When he got to the inn, Monsieur Bournisien asked for the wife of the Yonville doctor The landlady replied that she very rarely came to her establishment. So that evening, when he recognised Madame Bovary in the "Hirondelle," the curé told her his dilemma, without, however, appearing to attach much importance to it, for he began praising a preacher who was doing wonders at the Cathedral, and whom all the ladies were rushing to hear.

Still, if he did not ask for any explanation, others, later on, might prove less discreet. So she thought well to get down each time at the "Croix-Rouge," so that the good folk of her village who saw her on the stairs should suspect nothing.

One day, however, Monsieur Lheureux met her coming out of the Hôtel de Boulogne on Léon's arm; and she was frightened, thinking he would gossip. He was not such a fool. But three days after he came to her room, shut the door, and said, "I must have some money."

She declared she could not give him any. Lheureux burst into lamentations, and reminded her of all the kindnesses he had shown her.

In fact, of the two bills signed by Charles, Emma up to the present had paid only one. As to the second, the shopkeeper, at her request, had consented to replace it by another, which again had been renewed for a long date. Then he drew from his pocket a list of goods not paid for; to wit, the curtains, the carpet, the material for the armchairs, several dresses, and divers articles of dress, the bills for which amounted to about two thousand francs.

She bowed her head. He went on—

"But if you haven't any ready money, you have an estate." And he reminded her of a miserable little hovel situated at Barneville, near Aumale, that brought in almost nothing. It had formerly been part of a small farm sold by Monsieur Bovary senior; for Lheureux knew everything, even to the number of acres and the names of the neighbours.

"If I were in your place," he said, "I should clear myself of my debts, and have some money left over."

She pointed out the difficulty of getting a purchaser. He held out the hope of finding one; but she asked him how she should manage to sell it.

"Haven't you your power of attorney?" he replied.

The phrase came to her like a breath of fresh air. "Leave me the bill," said Emma.

"Oh, it isn't worth while," answered Lheureux.

He came back the following week and boasted of having, after much trouble, at last discovered a certain Langlois, who, for a long time, had had an eye on the property, but without mentioning his price.

"Never mind the price!" she cried.

But they would, on the contrary, have to wait, to sound the fellow. The thing was worth a journey, and, as she could not undertake it, he offered to go to the place to have an interview with Langlois. On his return he announced that the purchaser proposed four thousand francs.

Emma was radiant at this news.

"Frankly," he added, "that's a good price."

She drew half the sum at once, and when she was about to pay her account the shopkeeper said—

"It really grieves me, on my word! to see you depriving yourself all at once of such a big sum as that."

Then she looked at the bank-notes, and dreaming of the unlimited number of rendezvous represented by those two thousand francs, she stammered—

"What! what!"

"Oh!" he went on, laughing good-naturedly, "one puts anything one likes on receipts. Don't you think I know what household affairs are?" And he looked at her fixedly, while in his hand he held two long papers that he slid between his nails. At last, opening his pocket-book, he spread out on the table four bills to order, each for a thousand francs.

"Sign these," he said, "and keep it all!"

She cried out, scandalised.

"But if I give you the surplus," replied Monsieur Lheureux impudently, "is not that helping you?"

And taking a pen he wrote at the bottom of the account, "Received of Madame Bovary four thousand francs."

"Now who can trouble you, since in six months you'll draw the arrears for your cottage, and I don't make the last bill due till after you've been paid?"

Emma grew rather confused in her calculations, and her ears tingled as if gold pieces, bursting from their bags, rang all round her on the floor. At last Lheureux explained that he had a very good friend, Vinçart, a broker at Rouen, who would discount these four bills. Then he himself would hand over to madame the remainder after the actual debt was paid.

But instead of two thousand francs he brought only eighteen hundred, for the friend Vinçart (which was *only fair*) had deducted two hundred francs for commission and discount. Then he carelessly asked for a receipt.

"You understand—in business—sometimes. And with the date, if you please, with the date."

A horizon of realisable whims opened out before Emma. She was prudent enough to lay by a thousand crowns, with which the first three bills were paid when they fell due; but the fourth, by chance, came to the house on a Thursday, and Charles, quite upset, patiently awaited his wife's return for an explanation.

If she had not told him about this bill, it was only to spare him such domestic worries; she sat on his knees, caressed him, cooed to him, gave a long enumeration of all the indispensable things that had been got on credit.

"Really, you must confess, considering the quantity, it isn't too dear."

Charles, at his wit's end, soon had recourse to the eternal Lheureux, who swore he would arrange matters if the doctor would sign him two bills, one of which was for seven hundred francs, payable in three months. In order to arrange for this he wrote his mother a pathetic letter. Instead of sending a reply she came herself; and when Emma wanted to know whether he had got anything out of her, "Yes," he replied; "but she wants to see the account." The next morning at daybreak Emma ran to Lheureux to beg him to make out another account for not more than a thousand francs, for to show the one for four thousand it would be necessary to say that she had paid two-thirds, and confess, consequently, the sale of the estate—a negotiation admirably carried out by the shopkeeper, and which, in fact, was only actually known later on.

Despite the low price of each article, Madame Bovary senior of course thought the expenditure extravagant.

"Couldn't you do without a carpet? Why have re-covered the armchairs? In my time there was a single armchair in a house, for elderly persons,—at any rate it was so at my mother's, who was a good woman, I can tell you. Everybody can't be rich! No fortune can hold out against waste! I should be ashamed to coddle myself as you do! And yet I am old. I need looking after. And there! there! fitting up gowns! fallals! What! silk for lining at two francs, when you can get jaconet for ten sous, or even for eight, that would do well enough!"

Emma, lying on a lounge, replied as quietly as possible—"Ah! Madame, enough! enough!"

The other went on lecturing her, predicting they would end in the workhouse. But it was Bovary's fault. Luckily he had promised to destroy that power of attorney.

"What?"

"Ah! he swore he would," went on the good woman.

Emma opened the window, called Charles, and the poor fellow was obliged to confess the promise torn from him by his mother.

Emma disappeared, then came back quickly, and majestically handed her a thick piece of paper.

"Thank you," said the old woman. And she threw the power of attorney into the fire.

Emma began to laugh, a strident, piercing, continuous laugh; she had an attack of hysterics.

"Oh, my God!" cried Charles. "Ah! you really are wrong! You come here and make scenes with her!"

His mother, shrugging her shoulders, declared it was "all put on."

But Charles, rebelling for the first time, took his wife's part, so that Madame Bovary senior said she would leave. She went the very next day, and on the threshold, as he was trying to detain her, she replied—

"No, no! You love her better than me, and you are right. It is natural. For the rest, so much the worse! You will see. Good-day—for I am not likely to come soon again, as you say, to make scenes."

Charles nevertheless was very crestfallen before Emma, who did not hide the resentment she still felt at his want of confidence, and it needed many prayers before she would consent to have another power of attorney. He even accompanied her to Monsieur Guillaumin to have a second one, just like the other, drawn up.

"I understand," said the notary; "a man of science can't be worried with the.practical details of life."

And Charles felt relieved by this comfortable reflection, which gave his weakness the flattering appearance of higher preoccupation.

And what an outburst the next Thursday at the hotel in their room with Léon. She laughed, cried, sang, sent for sherbets, wanted to smoke cigarettes, seemed to him wild and extravagant, but adorable, superb.

He did not know what recreation of her whole being drove her more and more to plunge into the pleasures of life. She was becoming irritable, greedy, voluptuous; and she walked about the streets with him carrying her head high, without fear, so she said, of compromising herself. At times, however, Emma shuddered at the sudden thought of meeting Rodolphe, for it seemed to her that, although they were separated forever, she was not completely free from her subjugation to him.

One night she did not return to Yonville at all. Charles lost his head with anxiety, and little Berthe would not go to bed without her mamma, and sobbed enough to break her heart. Justin had gone out searching the road at random. Monsieur Homais even had left his pharmacy.

At last, at eleven o'clock, able to bear it no longer, Charles harnessed his chaise, jumped in, whipped up his horse, and reached the "Croix-Rouge" about two o'clock in the morning. No one there! He thought that the clerk had perhaps seen her; but where did he live? Happily, Charles remembered his employer's address, and rushed off there.

Day was breaking, and he could distinguish the escutcheons over the door, and knocked. Some one, without opening the door, shouted out the required information, adding a few insults to those who disturb people in the middle of the night.

The house inhabited by the clerk had neither bell, knocker, nor porter. Charles knocked loudly at the shutters with his hands. A policeman happened to pass by. Then he was frightened, and went away.

"I am mad," he said; "no doubt they kept her to dinner at Monsieur Lormeaux's." But the Lormeaux no longer lived at Rouen.

"She probably stayed to look after Madame Dubreuil. Why, Madame Dubreuil has been dead these ten months! Where can she be?"

An idea occurred to him. At a café he asked for a Directory, and hurriedly looked for the name of Mademoiselle Lempereur, who lived at No. 74 Rue de la Renelle-des-Maroquiniers.

As he was turning into the street, Emma herself appeared at the other end of it. He threw himself upon her rather than embraced her, crying—

"What kept you yesterday?"

"I was not well."

"What was it? Where? How?"

She passed her hand over her forehead and answered, "At Mademoiselle Lempereur's."

"I was sure of it! I was going there."

"Oh, it isn't worth while," said Emma. "She went out just now; but for the future don't worry. I do not feel free, you see, if I know that the least delay upsets you like this."

This was a sort of permission that she gave herself, so as to get perfect freedom in her escapades. And she profited by it freely, fully. When she was seized with the desire to see Léon, she set out upon any pretext; and as he was not expecting her on that day, she went to fetch him at his office.

It was a great delight at first, but soon he no longer concealed the truth, which was, that his master complained very much about these interruptions.

"Pshaw! come along," she said.

And he slipped out.

She wanted him to dress all in black, and grow a pointed beard, to look like the portraits of Louis XIII. She wanted to see his lodgings; thought them poor. He blushed at them, but she did not notice this, then advised him to buy some curtains like hers, and as he objected to the expense—

"Ah! ah! you care for your money," she said, laughing.

Each time Léon had to tell her everything that he had done since their last meeting. She asked him for some verses—some verses "for herself," a "love poem" in honour of her. But he never succeeded in getting a rhyme for the second verse; and at last ended by copying a sonnet in a "Keepsake." This was less from vanity than from the one desire of pleasing her. He did not question her ideas; he accepted all her tastes; he was rather becoming her mistress than she his. She had tender words and kisses that thrilled his soul. Where could she have learnt this corruption almost incorporeal in the strength of its profanity and dissimulation?

VI

DURING THE JOURNEYS he made to see her, Léon had often dined at the chemist's, and he felt obliged from politeness to invite him in turn.

"With pleasure!" Monsieur Homais replied; "besides, I must invigorate my mind, for I am getting rusty here. We'll go to the theatre, to the restaurant; we'll make a night of it!"

"Oh, my dear!" tenderly murmured Madame Homais, alarmed at the vague perils he was preparing to brave.

"Well, what? Do you think I'm not sufficiently ruining my health living here amid the continual emanations of the pharmacy? But there! that is the way with women! They are jealous of science, and then are opposed to our taking the most legitimate distractions. No matter! Count upon me. One of these days I shall turn up at Rouen, and we'll go the pace together."

The druggist would formerly have taken good care not to use such an expression, but he was cultivating a gay Parisian style, which he thought in the best taste; and, like his neighbour, Madame Bovary, he questioned the clerk curiously about the customs of the capital; he even talked slang to dazzle the bourgeois, saying *bender, crummy, dandy, maccaroni, the cheese, cut my stick* and "*I'll hook it,*" for "I'm going."

So one Thursday Emma was surprised to meet Monsieur Homais in the kitchen of the "Lion d'Or," wearing a traveller's costume, that is to say, wrapped in an old cloak which no one knew he had, while he carried a valise in one hand and the foot-warmer of his establishment in the other. He had confided his intentions to no one, for fear of causing the public anxiety by his absence.

The idea of seeing again the place where his youth had been spent no doubt excited him, for during the whole journey he never ceased talking, and as soon as he had arrived, he jumped quickly out of the diligence to go in search of Léon. In vain the clerk tried to get rid of him. Monsieur Homais dragged him off to the large "Café de la Normandie," which he entered majestically, not raising his hat, thinking it very provincial to uncover in any public place.

Emma waited for Léon three quarters of an hour. At last she ran to his office, and, lost in all sorts of conjectures, accusing him of indifference, and reproaching herself for her weakness, she spent the afternoon, her face pressed against the window-panes.

At two o'clock they were still at table opposite each other. The large room was emptying; the stove-pipe, in the shape of a palm-tree, spread its gilt leaves over the white ceiling, and near them, outside the window, in the bright sunshine, a little fountain gurgled in a white basin, where, in the midst of watercress and asparagus, three torpid lobsters stretched across to some quails that lay heaped up in a pile on their sides.

Homais was enjoying himself. Although he was even more intoxicated with the luxury than the rich fare, the Pomard wine all the same rather excited his faculties; and when the omelette *au rhum* appeared, he began propounding immoral theories about women. What seduced him above all else was *chic*. He admired an elegant toilette in a well-furnished apartment, and as to bodily qualities, he didn't dislike a young girl.

Léon watched the clock in despair. The druggist went on drinking, eating, and talking.

"You must be very lonely," he said suddenly, "here at Rouen. To be sure your lady-love doesn't live far away."

And as the other blushed—

"Come now, be frank. Can you deny that at Yonville——"

The young man stammered something.

"At Madame Bovary's, you're not making love to——"

"To whom?"

"The servant!"

He was not joking; but vanity getting the better of all prudence, Léon, in spite of himself protested. Besides, he only liked dark women.

"I approve of that," said the chemist; "they have more passion."

And whispering into his friend's ear, he pointed out the symptoms by which one could find out if a woman had passion. He even launched into an ethnographic digression: the German was vapourish, the French woman licentious, the Italian passionate.

"And negresses?" asked the clerk.

"They are an artistic taste!" said Homais. "Waiter! two cups of coffee!"

"Are we going?" at last asked Léon impatiently.

"*Ja!*"

But before leaving he wanted to see the proprietor of the establishment and made him a few compliments. Then the young man, to be alone, alleged he had some business engagement.

"Ah! I will escort you," said Homais.

And all the while he was walking through the streets with him he talked of his wife, his children, of their future, and of his business; told him in what a decayed condition it had formerly been, and to what a degree of perfection he had raised it.

Arrived in front of the Hôtel de Boulogne, Léon left him abruptly, ran up the stairs, and found his mistress in great excitement. At mention of the chemist she flew into a passion. He, however, piled up good reason; it wasn't his fault; didn't she know Homais—did she believe that he would prefer his company? But she turned away; he drew her back, and, sinking on his knees, clasped her waist with his arms in a languorous pose, full of concupiscence and supplication.

She was standing up, her large flashing eyes looked at him seriously, almost terribly. Then tears obscured them, her red eyelids were lowered, she gave him her hands, and Léon was pressing them to his lips when a servant appeared to tell the gentleman that he was wanted.

"You will come back?" she said.

"Yes."

"But when?"

"Immediately."

"It's a trick," said the chemist, when he saw Léon. "I wanted to interrupt this visit, that seemed to me to annoy you. Let's go and have a glass of *garus* at Bridoux's."

Léon vowed that he must get back to his office. Then the druggist joked him about quill-drivers and the law.

"Leave Cujas and Barthole alone a bit. Who the devil prevents you? Be a man! Let's go to Bridoux's. You'll see his dog. It's very interesting."

And as the clerk still insisted—

"I'll go with you. I'll read a paper while I wait for you, or turn over the leaves of a 'Code.'"

Léon, bewildered by Emma's anger, Monsieur Homais's chatter, and, perhaps, by the heaviness of the luncheon, was undecided, and, as it were, fascinated by the chemist, who kept repeating—

"Let's go to Bridoux's. It's just by here, in the Rue Malpalu."

Then, through cowardice, through stupidity, through that indefinable feeling that drags us into the most distasteful acts, he allowed himself to be led off to Bridoux's, whom they found in a small yard, superintending three workmen, who panted as they turned the large wheel of a machine for making seltzer-water. Homais gave them some good advice. He embraced Bridoux; they took some *garus*. Twenty times Léon tried to escape, but the other seized him by the arm saying—

"Presently! I'm coming! We'll go to the 'Fanal de Rouen' to see the fellows there. I'll introduce you to Thomassin."

At last he managed to get rid of him, and rushed straight to the hotel. Emma was no longer there. She had just gone in a fit of anger. She detested him now. This failing to keep their rendezvous seemed to her an insult, and she tried to rake up other reasons to separate herself from him. He was incapable of heroism, weak, banal, more spiritless than a woman, avaricious too, and cowardly.

Then, growing calmer, she at length discovered that she had, no doubt, calumniated him. But the disparaging of those we love always alienates us from them to some extent. We must not touch our idols; the gilt sticks to our fingers.

They gradually came to talking more frequently of matters outside their love, and in the letters that Emma wrote him she spoke of flowers, verses, the moon and the stars, naïve resources of a waning passion striving to keep itself alive by all external aids. She was constantly promising herself a profound felicity on her next journey. Then she confessed to herself that she felt nothing extraordinary. This disappointment quickly gave way to a new hope, and Emma returned to him more inflamed, more eager than ever. She undressed brutally, tearing off the thin laces of her corset that nestled around her hips like a gliding snake. She went on tiptoe, barefooted, to see once more that the door was closed, then, pale, serious, and, without speaking, with one movement, she threw herself upon his breast with a long shudder.

Yet there was upon that brow covered with cold drops, on those quivering lips, in those wild eyes, in the strain of those arms, something vague and dreary that seemed to Léon to glide between them subtly as if to separate them.

He did not dare to question her; but, seeing her so skilled, she must have passed, he thought, through every experience of suffering and of pleasure. What had once charmed now frightened him a little. Besides, he rebelled against his absorption, daily more marked, by her.personality. He begrudged Emma this constant victory. He even strove not to love her; then, when he heard the creaking of her boots, he turned coward, like drunkards at the sight of strong drinks.

She did not fail, in truth, to lavish all sorts of attentions upon him, from the delicacies of food to the coquetries of dress and languishing looks. She brought roses in her breast from Yonville, which she threw into his face; was anxious about his health, gave him advice as to his conduct; and, in order the more surely to keep her hold on him, hoping perhaps that heaven would take her part, she tied a medal of the Virgin round his neck. She inquired like a virtuous mother about his companions. She said to him—

"Don't see them; don't go out; think only of ourselves; love me!"

She would have liked to be able to watch over his life, and the idea occurred to her of having him followed in the streets. Near the hotel there was always a kind of loafer who accosted travellers, and who would not refuse. But her pride revolted at this.

"Bah! so much the worse. Let him deceive me! What does it matter to me? As if I cared for him!"

One day, when they had parted early and she was returning alone along the boulevard, she saw the walls of her convent; then she sat down on a form in the shade of the elm trees. How calm that time had been! How she longed for the ineffable sentiments of love that she had tried to figure to herself out of books! The first month of her marriage, her rides in the wood, the viscount that waltzed, and Lagardy singing, all repassed before her eyes. And Léon suddenly appeared to her as far off as the others.

"Yet I love him," she said to herself.

No matter! She was not happy—she never had been. Whence came this insufficiency in life—this instantaneous turning to decay of everything on which she leant? But if there were somewhere a being strong and beautiful, a valiant nature, full at once of exaltation and refinement, a poet's heart in an angel's form, a lyre with sounding chords ringing out elegiac epithalamia to heaven, why, perchance, should she not find him? Ah! how impossible! Besides, nothing was worth the trouble of seeking it; everything was a lie. Every smile hid a yawn of boredom, every joy a curse, all pleasure satiety, and the sweetest kisses left upon your lips only the unattainable desire for a greater delight.

A metallic clang droned through the air, and four strokes were heard from the convent-clock. Four o'clock! And it seemed to her that she had been there on that form an eternity. But an infinity of passions may be contained in a minute, like a crowd in a small space.

Emma lived all absorbed in hers, and troubled no more about money matters than an archduchess.

Once, however, a wretched-looking man, rubicund and bald, came to her house, saying he had been sent by Monsieur Vinçart of Rouen. He took out the pins that held together the side-pockets of his long green overcoat, stuck them into his sleeve, and politely handed her a paper.

It was a bill for seven hundred francs, signed by her, and which Lheureux, in spite of all his professions, had paid away to Vinçart. She sent her servant for him. He could not come. Then the stranger, who had remained standing, casting right and left curious glances, that his thick, fair eyebrows hid, asked with a naïve air—

"What answer am I to take Monsieur Vinçart?"

"Oh," said Emma, "tell him that I haven't it. I will send it next week: he must wait; yes, till next week."

And the fellow went without another word.

But the next day at twelve o'clock she received a summons, and the sight of the stamped paper, on which appeared several times in large letters, "Maître Hareng, bailiff at Buchy," so frightened her that she rushed in hot haste to the linendraper's. She found him in his shop, doing up a parcel.

"Your obedient!" he said; "I am at your service."

But Lheureux, all the same, went on with his work, helped by a young girl of about thirteen, somewhat hunchbacked, who was at once his clerk and his servant.

Then, his clogs clattering on the shop-boards, he went up in front of Madame Bovary to the first door, and introduced her into a narrow closet, where, in a large bureau in sapanwood, lay some ledgers, protected by a horizontal padlocked iron bar. Against the wall, under some remnants of calico, one glimpsed a safe, but of such dimensions that it must contain something besides bills and money. Monsieur Lheureux, in fact, went in for pawnbroking, and it was there that he had put Madame Bovary's gold chain, together with the earrings of poor old Tellier, who, at last forced to sell out, had bought a meagre store of grocery at Quincampoix, where he was dying of catarrh amongst his candles, that were less yellow than his face.

Lheureux sat down in a large cane armchair, saying: "What news?"

"See!"

And she showed him the paper.

"Well, how can I help it?"

Then she grew angry, reminding him of the promise he had given not to pay away her bills. He acknowledged it.

"But I was pressed myself; the knife was at my own throat."

"And what will happen now?" she went on.

"Oh, it's very simple; a judgment and then a distraint—that's about it!"

Emma kept down a desire to strike him, and asked gently if there was no way of quieting Monsieur Vinçart.

"I dare say! Quiet Vinçart! You don't know him; he's more ferocious than an Arab!"

Still Monsieur Lheureux must interfere.

"Well, listen. It seems to me so far I've been very good to you." And opening one of his ledgers, "See," he said. Then running up the page with his finger, "Let's see! let's see! August 3d, two hundred francs; June 17th, a hundred and fifty; March 23d, forty-six. In April——"

He stopped, as if afraid of making some mistake.

"Not to speak of the bills signed by Monsieur Bovary, one for seven hundred francs, and another for three hundred. As to your little instalments, with the interest, why, there's no end to 'em; one gets quite muddled over 'em. I'll have nothing more to do with it."

She wept; she even called him "her good Monsieur Lheureux." But he always fell back upon "that rascal Vinçart." Besides, he hadn't a brass farthing; no one was paying him now-a-days; they were eating his coat off his back; a poor shopkeeper like him couldn't advance money.

Emma was silent, and Monsieur Lheureux, who was biting the feathers of a quill, no doubt became uneasy at her silence, for he went on—

"Unless one of these days I have something coming in, I might——"

"Besides," said she, "as soon as the balance of Barneville——"

"What!"

And on hearing that Langlois had not yet paid he seemed much surprised. Then in a honied voice—

"And we agree, you say?"

"Oh! to anything you like."

On this he closed his eyes to reflect, wrote down a few figures, and declaring it would be very difficult for him, that the affair was shady, and that he was being bled, he wrote out four bills for two hundred and fifty francs each, to fall due month by month.

"Provided that Vinçart will listen to me! However, it's settled. I don't play the fool; I'm straight enough."

Next he carelessly showed her several new goods, not one of which, however, was in his opinion worthy of madame.

"When I think that there's a dress at threepence-half-penny a yard, and warranted fast colours! And yet they actually swallow it! Of course you understand one doesn't tell them what it really is!" He hoped by this confession of dishonesty to others to quite convince her of his probity to her.

Then he called back to show her three yards of guipure that he had lately picked up "at a sale."

"Isn't it lovely?" said Lheureux. "It is very much used now for the backs of armchairs. It's quite the rage."

And, more ready than a juggler, he wrapped up the guipure in some blue paper and put it in Emma's hands.

"But at least let me know——"

"Yes, another time," he replied, turning on his heel.

That same evening she urged Bovary to write to his mother, to ask her to send as quickly as possible the whole of the balance due from the father's estate. The mother-in-law replied that she had nothing more, the winding up was over, and there was due to them besides Barneville an income of six hundred francs, that she would pay them punctually.

Then Madame Bovary sent in accounts to two or three patients, and she made large use of this method, which was very successful. She was always careful to add a postscript: "Do not mention this to my husband; you know how proud he is. Excuse me. Yours obediently." There were some complaints; she intercepted them.

To get money she began selling her old gloves, her old hats, the old odds and ends, and she bargained rapaciously, her peasant blood standing her in good stead. Then on her journey to town she picked up nicknacks secondhand, that, in default of any one else, Monsieur Lheureux would certainly take off her hands. She bought ostrich feathers, Chinese porcelain, and trunks; she borrowed from Félicité, from Madame Lefrançois, from the landlady at the "Croix-Rouge," from everybody, no matter where. With the money she at last received from Barneville she paid two bills; the other fifteen hundred francs fell due. She renewed the bills, and thus it was continually.

Sometimes, it is true, she tried to make a calculation, but she discovered things so exorbitant that she could not believe them possible. Then she recommenced, soon got confused, gave it all up, and thought no more about it.

The house was very dreary now. Tradesmen were seen leaving it with angry faces. Handkerchiefs were lying about on the stoves, and little Berthe, to the great scandal of Madame Homais, wore stockings with holes in them. If Charles timidly ventured a remark, she answered roughly that it wasn't her fault.

What was the meaning of all these fits of temper? He explained everything through her old nervous illness, and reproaching himself with having taken her infirmities for faults, accused himself of egotism, and longed to go and take her in his arms.

"Ah, no!" he said to himself; "I should worry her."

And he did not stir.

After dinner he walked about alone in the garden; he took little Berthe on his knees, and unfolding his medical journal, tried to teach her to read. But the child, who never had any lessons, soon looked up with large, sad eyes and began to cry. Then he comforted her; went to fetch water in her can to make rivers on the sand path, or broke off branches from the privet hedges to plant trees in the beds. This did not spoil the garden much, as it was all choked now with long weeds. They owed Lestiboudois for very many days. Then the child grew cold and asked for her mother.

"Call the servant," said Charles. "You know, dearie, that mamma does not like to be disturbed."

Autumn was setting in, and the leaves were already falling, as they did two years ago when she was ill. Where would it all end? And he walked up and down, his hands behind his back.

Madame was in her room, which no one entered. She stayed there all day long, torpid, half dressed, and from time to time burning Turkish pastilles which she had bought at Rouen in an Algerian's shop. In order not to have at night this sleeping man stretched at her side, by dint of manœuvring, she at last succeeded in banishing him to the second floor, while she read till morning extravagant books, full of pictures of orgies and thrilling situations. Often, seized with fear, she cried out, and Charles hurried to her.

"Oh, go away!" she would say.

Or at other times, consumed more ardently than ever by that inner flame to which adultery added fuel, panting, tremulous, all desire, she threw open her window, breathed in the cold air, shook loose in the wind her masses of hair, too heavy, and, gazing upon the stars, longed for some princely love. She thought of him, of Léon. She would then have given anything for a single one of those meetings that surfeited her.

These were her gala days. She wanted them to be sumptuous, and when he alone could not pay the expenses, she made up the deficit liberally, which happened pretty well every time. He tried to make her understand that they would be quite as comfortable somewhere else, in a smaller hotel, but she always found some objection.

One day she drew six small silver-gilt spoons from her bag (they were old Rouault's wedding present), begging him to pawn them at once for her, and Léon obeyed, though the proceeding annoyed him. He was afraid of compromising himself.

Then, on reflection, he began to think his mistress's ways were growing odd, and that they were perhaps not wrong in wishing to separate him from her.

In fact, some one had sent his mother a long anonymous letter to warn her that he was "ruining himself with a married woman," and the good lady at once conjuring up the eternal bugbear of families, the vague pernicious creature, the siren, the monster, who dwells fantastically in depths of love, wrote to Lawyer Dubocage, his employer, who behaved perfectly in the affair. He kept him for three quarters of an hour trying to open his eyes, to warn him of the abyss into which he was falling. Such an intrigue would damage him later on, when he set up for himself. He implored him to break with her, and, if he would not make this sacrifice in his own interest, to do it at least for his, Dubocage's, sake.

At last Léon swore he would not see Emma again, and he reproached himself with not having kept his word, considering all the worry and lectures this woman might still draw down upon him, without reckoning the jokes made by his companions as they sat round the stove in the morning. Besides, he was soon to be head-clerk; it was time to settle down. So he gave up his flute, exalted sentiments, and poetry; for every bourgeois in the flush of his youth, were it but for a day, a moment, has believed himself capable of immense passions, of lofty enterprises. The most mediocre libertine has dreamed of sultanas; every notary bears within him the débris of a poet.

He was bored now when Emma suddenly began to sob on his breast, and his heart, like the people who can only stand a certain amount of music, dozed to the sound of a love whose delicacies he no longer noted.

They knew one another too well for any of those surprises of possession that increase its joys a hundred-fold. She was as sick of him as he was weary of her. Emma found again in adultery all the platitudes of marriage.

But how to get rid of him? Then, though she might feel humiliated at the baseness of such enjoyment, she clung to it from habit or from corruption, and each day she hungered after them the more, exhausting all felicity in wishing for too much of it. She accused Léon of her baffled hopes, as if he had betrayed her; and she even longed for some catastrophe that would bring about their separation, since she had not the courage to make up her mind to effect it herself.

She none the less went on writing him love letters, in virtue of the notion that a woman must write to her lover.

But whilst she wrote it was another man she saw, a phantom fashioned out of her most ardent memories, of her finest reading, her strongest lusts, and at last he became so real, so tangible, that she palpitated wondering, without, however, the power to imagine him clearly, so lost was he, like a god, beneath the abundance of his attributes. He dwelt in that azure land where silk ladders hang from balconies under the breath of flowers, in the light of the moon. She felt him near her; he was coming, and would carry her right away in a kiss.

Then she fell back exhausted, for these transports of vague love wearied her more than great debauchery.

She now felt constant ache all over her. Often she even received summonses, stamped paper that she barely looked at. She would have liked not to be alive, or to be always asleep.

On Mid-Lent she did not return to Yonville, but in the evening went to a masked ball. She wore velvet breeches, red stockings, a club wig, and three-cornered cocked hat on one side. She danced all night to the wild tones of the trombones; people gathered round her, and in the morning she found herself on the steps of the theatre together with five or six masks, *débardeuses* and sailors, Léon's comrades, who were talking about having supper.

The neighbouring cafés were full. They caught sight of one on the harbour, a very indifferent restaurant, whose proprietor showed them to a little room on the fourth floor.

The men were whispering in a corner, no doubt consulting about expenses. There were a clerk, two medical students, and a shopman—what company for her! As to the women, Emma soon perceived from the tone of their voices that they must almost belong to the lowest class. Then she was frightened, pushed back her chair, and cast down her eyes.

The others began to eat; she ate nothing. Her head was on fire, her eyes smarted, and her skin was ice-cold. In her head she seemed to feel the floor of the ballroom rebounding again beneath the rhythmical pulsation of the thousands of dancing feet. And now the smell of the punch, the smoke of the cigars, made her giddy. She fainted, and they carried her to the window.

Day was breaking, and a great stain of purple colour broadened out in the pale horizon over the Saint-Catherine hills. The livid river was shivering in the wind; there was no one on the bridges; the street lamps were going out.

She revived, and began thinking of Berthe asleep yonder in the servant's room. Then a cart filled with long strips of iron passed by, and made a deafening metallic vibration against the walls of the houses.

She slipped away suddenly, threw off her costume, told Léon she must get back, and at last was alone at the Hôtel de Boulogne. Everything, even herself, was now unbearable to her. She wished that, taking wing like a bird, she could fly somewhere, far away to regions of purity, and there grow young again.

She went out, crossed the Boulevard, the Place Cauchoise, and the Faubourg, as far as an open street that overlooked some gardens. She walked rapidly, the fresh air calming her; and, little by little, the faces of the crowd, the masks, the quadrilles, the lights, the supper, those men and women, all disappeared like mists fading away. Then, finally reaching the "Croix-Rouge," she threw herself on the bed in her little room on the second floor, where there were pictures of the "Tour de Nesle." At four o'clock Hivert awoke her.

When she got home, Félicité showed her behind the clock a grey paper. She read—

"In virtue of the seizure in execution of a judgment."

What judgment? As a matter of fact, the evening before another paper had been brought that she had not yet seen, and she was stunned by these words—

"By order of the king, law, and justice, to Madame Bovary." Then, skipping several lines, she read, "Within twenty-four hours, without fail——" But what? "To pay the sum of eight thousand francs." And there was even at the bottom, "She will be constrained thereto by every form of law, and notably by a writ of distraint on her furniture and effects."

What was to be done? In twenty-four hours,—to-morrow. Lheureux, she thought, wanted to frighten her again; for she saw through all his devices, the object of his kindnesses. What reassured her was the very magnitude of the sum.

However, by dint of buying and not paying, of borrowing, signing bills, and renewing these bills, that grew at each new falling-in, she had ended by preparing a capital for Monsieur Lheureux which he was impatiently awaiting for his speculations.

She presented herself at his place with an offhand air.

"You know what has happened to me? No doubt it's a joke!"

"No."

"How so?"

He turned away slowly, and, folding his arms, said to her—

"My good lady, did you think I should go on to all eternity being your purveyor and banker, for the love of God? Now be just. I must get back what I've laid out. Now be just."

She cried out against the debt.

"Ah! so much the worse. The court has admitted it. There's a judgment. It's been notified to you. Besides, it isn't my fault. It's Vinçart's."

"Could you not——?"

"Oh, nothing whatever."

"But still, now talk it over."

And she began beating about the bush; she had known nothing about it; it was a surprise.

"Whose fault is that?" said Lheureux, bowing ironically. "While I'm slaving like a nigger, you go gallivanting about."

"Ah! no lecturing."

"It never does any harm," he replied.

She turned coward; she implored him; she even pressed her pretty white and slender hand against the shopkeeper's knee.

"There, that'll do! Any one'd think you wanted to seduce me!"

"You are a wretch!" she cried.

"Oh, oh! go it! go it!"

"I will show you up. I shall tell my husband."

"All right! I too, I'll show your husband something."

And Lheureux drew from his strongbox the receipt for eighteen hundred francs that she had given him when Vinçart had discounted the bills.

"Do you think," he added, "that he'll not understand your little theft, the poor dear man?"

She collapsed, more overcome than if felled by the blow of a pole-axe. He was walking up and down from the window to the bureau, repeating all the while—

"Ah! I'll show him! I'll show him!" Then he approached her, and in a soft voice said—

"It isn't pleasant, I know; but, after all, no bones are broken, and, since that is the only way that is left for you paying back my money—"

"But where am I to get any?" said Emma, wringing her hands.

"Bah! when one has friends like you!"

And he looked at her in so keen, so terrible a fashion, that she shuddered to her very heart.

"I promise you," she said, "to sign——"

"I've enough of your signatures."

"I will sell something."

"Get along!" he said, shrugging his shoulders; "you've not got anything."

And he called through the peep-hole that looked down into the shop—

"Annette, don't forget the three coupons of No. 14."

The servant appeared. Emma understood, and asked how much money would be wanted to put a stop to the proceedings.

"It is too late."

"But if I brought you several thousand francs—a quarter of the sum—a third—perhaps the whole?"

"No; it's no use!"

And he pushed her gently towards the staircase.

"I implore you, Monsieur Lheureux, just a few days more!"

She was sobbing.

"There! tears now!"

"You are driving me to despair!"

"What do I care?" said he, shutting the door.

VII

SHE WAS STOICAL the next day when Maître Hareng, the bailiff, with two assistants, presented himself at the house to draw up the inventory for the distraint.

They began with Bovary's consulting-room, and did not write down the phrenological head, which was considered an "instrument of his profession"; but in the kitchen they counted the plates, the saucepans, the chairs, the candlesticks, and in the bedroom all the nicknacks on the whatnot. They examined her dresses, the linen, the dressing-room; and her whole existence, to its most intimate details, was, like a corpse on whom a post-mortem is made, outspread before the eyes of these three men.

Maître Hareng, buttoned up in his thin black coat, wearing a white choker and very tight foot-straps, repeated from time to time—"Allow me, madame. You allow me?" Often he uttered exclamations. "Charming! very pretty." Then he began writing again, dipping his pen into the horn inkstand in his left hand.

When they were done with the rooms they went up to the attic. She kept a desk there in which Rodolphe's letters were locked. It had to be opened.

"Ah! a correspondence," said Maître Hareng, with a discreet smile. "But allow me, for I must make sure the box contains nothing else." And he tipped up the papers lightly, as if to shake out napoleons. Then she grew angered to see this coarse hand, with fingers red and pulpy like slugs, touching these pages against which her heart had beaten.

They went at last. Félicité came back. Emma had sent her out to watch for Bovary in order to keep him off, and they hurriedly installed the man in possession under the roof, where he swore he would remain.

During the evening Charles seemed to her careworn. Emma watched him with a look of anguish, fancying she saw an accusation in every line of his face. Then, when her eyes wandered over the chimney-piece ornamented with Chinese screens, over the large curtains, the armchairs, all those things, in a word, that had softened the bitterness of her life, remorse seized her, or rather an immense regret, that, far from crushing, irritated her passion. Charles placidly poked the fire, both his feet on the fire-dogs.

Once the man, no doubt bored in his hiding-place, made a slight noise.

"Is any one walking upstairs?" said Charles.

"No," she replied; "it is a window that has been left open, and is rattling in the wind."

The next day, Sunday, she went to Rouen to call on all the brokers whose names she knew. They were at their country-places or on journeys. She was not discouraged; and those whom she did manage to see she asked for money, declaring she must have some, and that she would pay it back. Some laughed in her face; all refused.

At two o'clock she hurried to Léon, and knocked at the door. No one answered. At length he appeared.

"What brings you here?"

"Do I disturb you?"

"No; but——" And he admitted that his landlord didn't like his having "women" there.

"I must speak to you," she went on.

Then he took down the key, but she stopped him.

"No, no! Down there, in our home!"

And they went to their room at the Hôtel de Boulogne.

On arriving she drank off a large glass of water. She was very pale. She said to him—

"Léon, you will do me a service?"

And, shaking him by both hands that she grasped tightly, she added—

"Listen, I want eight thousand francs."

"But you are mad!"

"Not yet."

And thereupon, telling him the story of the distraint, she explained her distress to him; for Charles knew nothing of it; her mother-in-law detested her; old Rouault could do nothing; but he, Léon, he would set about finding this indispensable sum.

"How on earth can I?"

"What a coward you are!" she cried.

Then he said stupidly, "You are exaggerating the difficulty. Perhaps with a thousand crowns or so the fellow could be stopped."

All the greater reason to try and do something; it was impossible that they could not find three thousand francs. Besides, Léon could be security instead of her.

"Go, try, try! I will love you so!"

He went out, and came back at the end of an hour, saying, with solemn face—

"I have been to three people with no success."

Then they remained sitting face to face at the two chimney corners, motionless, in silence. Emma shrugged her shoulders as she stamped her feet. He heard her murmuring—

"If I were in your place I should soon get some."

"But where?"

"At your office." And she looked at him.

An infernal boldness looked out from her burning eyes, and their lids drew close together with a lascivious and encouraging look, so that the young man felt himself growing weak beneath the mute will of this woman who was urging him to a crime. Then he was afraid, and to avoid any explanation he smote his forehead, crying—

"Morel is to come back to-night; he will not refuse me, I hope" (this was one of his friends, the son of a very rich merchant); "and I will bring it you to-morrow," he added.

Emma did not seem to welcome this hope with all the joy he had expected. Did she suspect the lie? He went on, blushing—

"However, if you don't see me by three o'clock, do not wait for me, my darling. I must be off now; forgive me! Good-bye!"

He pressed her hand, but it felt quite lifeless. Emma had no strength left for any sentiment.

Four o'clock struck, and she rose to return to Yonville, mechanically obeying the force of old habits.

The weather was fine. It was one of those March days, clear and sharp, when the sun shines in a perfectly white sky. The Rouen folk, in Sunday-clothes, were walking about with happy looks. She reached the Place du Parvis. People were coming out after vespers; the crowd flowed out through the three doors like a stream through the three arches of a bridge, and in the middle one, more motionless than a rock, stood the beadle.

Then she remembered the day when, all anxious and full of hope, she had entered beneath this large nave, that had opened out before her, less profound than her love; and she walked on weeping beneath her veil, giddy, staggering, almost fainting.

"Take care!" cried a voice issuing from the gate of a courtyard that was thrown open.

She stopped to let pass a black horse, pawing the ground between the shafts of a tilbury, driven by a gentleman in sable furs. Who was it? She knew him. The carriage darted by and disappeared.

Why, it was he—the Viscount. She turned away; the street was empty. She was so overwhelmed, so sad, that she had to lean against a wall to keep herself from falling.

Then she thought she had been mistaken. Anyhow, she did not know. All within her and around her was abandoning her. She felt lost, sinking at random into indefinable abysses, and it was almost with joy that, on reaching the "Croix-Rouge," she saw the good Homais, who was watching a large box full of pharmaceutical stores being hoisted on to the "Hirondelle." In his hand he held tied in a silk handkerchief six *cheminots* for his wife.

Madame Homais was very fond of these small, heavy turban-shaped loaves, that are eaten in Lent with salt butter; a last vestige of Gothic food that goes back, perhaps, to the time of the Crusades, and with which the robust Normans gorged themselves of yore, fancying they saw on the table, in the light of the yellow torches, between tankards of hippocras and huge boars' heads, the heads of Saracens to be devoured. The druggist's wife crunched them up as they had done—heroically, despite her wretched teeth. And so whenever Homais journeyed to town, he never failed to bring her home some that he bought at the great baker's in the Rue Massacre.

"Charmed to see you," he said, offering Emma a hand to help her into the "Hirondelle." Then he hung up his *cheminots* to the cords of the netting, and remained bareheaded in an attitude pensive and Napoleonic.

But when the blind man appeared as usual at the foot of the hill he exclaimed—

"I can't understand why the authorities tolerate such culpable industries. Such unfortunates should be locked up and forced to work. Progress, my word! creeps at a snail's pace. We are floundering about in mere barbarism."

The blind man held out his hat, that flapped about at the door, as if it were a bag in the lining that had come unnailed.

"This," said the chemist, "is a scrofulous affection."

And though he knew the poor devil, he pretended to see him for the first time, murmured something about "cornea," "opaque cornea," "sclerotic," "facies," then asked him in a paternal tone—

"My friend, have you long had this terrible infirmity? Instead of getting drunk at the public, you'd do better to diet yourself."

He advised him to take good wine, good beer, and good joints. The blind man went on with his song; he seemed, moreover, almost idiotic. At last Monsieur Homais opened his purse—

"Now there's a sou; give me back two liards, and don't forget my advice; you'll be the better for it."

Hivert openly cast some doubt on the efficacy of it. But the druggist said that he would cure himself with an antiphlogistic pomade of his own composition, and he gave his address: "Monsieur Homais, near the market, pretty well known."

"Now," said Hivert, "for all this trouble you'll give us your performance."

The blind man sank down on his haunches, with his head thrown back, whilst he rolled his greenish eyes, lolled out his tongue, and rubbed his stomach with both hands, as he uttered a kind of hollow yell like a famished dog. Emma, filled with disgust, threw him over her shoulder a five-franc piece. It was all her fortune. It seemed to her very fine thus to throw it away.

The coach had gone on again when suddenly Monsieur Homais leant out through the window, crying—

"No farinaceous or milk food, wear wool next the skin, and expose the diseased parts to the smoke of juniper berries."

The sight of the well-known objects that defiled before her eyes gradually diverted Emma from her present trouble. An intolerable fatigue overwhelmed her, and she reached her home stupefied, discouraged, almost asleep.

"Come what may come!" she said to herself. "And then, who knows? Why, at any moment could not some extraordinary event occur? Lheureux even might die!"

At nine o'clock in the morning she was awakened by the sound of voices in the Place. There was a crowd round the market reading a large bill fixed to one of the posts, and she saw Justin, who was climbing on to a stone and tearing down the bill. But at this moment the rural guard seized him by the collar. Monsieur Homais came out of his shop, and Mère Lefrançois, in the midst of the crowd, seemed to be perorating.

"Madame! madame!" cried Félicité, running in, "it's abominable!"

And the poor girl, deeply moved, handed her a yellow paper that she had just torn off the door. Emma read with a glance that all her furniture was for sale.

Then they looked at one another silently. The servant and mistress had no secret one from the other. At last Félicité sighed—

"If I were you, madame, I should go to Monsieur Guillaumin."

"Do you think——"

And this question meant to say—

"You who know the house through the servant, has the master spoken sometimes of me?"

"Yes, you'd do well to go there."

She dressed, put on her black gown, and her hood with jet beads, and that she might not be seen (there was still a crowd on the Place), she took the path by the river, outside the village.

She reached the notary's gate quite breathless. The sky was sombre, and a little snow was falling. At the sound of the bell, Theodore in a red waistcoat appeared on the steps; he came to open the door almost familiarly, as to an acquaintance, and showed her into the dining-room.

A large porcelain stove crackled beneath a cactus that filled up the niche in the wall, and in black wood frames against the oak-stained paper hung Steuben's "Esmeralda" and Schopin's "Potiphar." The ready-laid table, the two silver chafing-dishes, the crystal door-knobs, the parquet and the furniture, all shone with a scrupulous, English cleanliness; the windows were ornamented at each corner with stained glass.

"Now this," thought Emma, "is the dining-room I ought to have."

The notary came in pressing his palm-leaf dressing-gown to his breast with his left arm, while with the other hand he raised and quickly put on again his brown velvet cap, pretentiously cocked on the right side, whence looked out the ends of three fair curls drawn from the back of the head, following the line of his bald skull.

After he had offered her a seat he sat down to breakfast, apologizing profusely for his rudeness.

"I have come," she said, "to beg you, sir——"

"What, madame? I am listening."

And she began explaining her position to him. Monsieur Guillaumin knew it, being secretly associated with the linendraper, from whom he always got capital for the loans on mortgages that he was asked to make.

So he knew (and better than she herself) the long story of the bills, small at first, bearing different names as endorsers, made out at long dates, and constantly renewed up to the day, when, gathering together all the protested bills, the shopkeeper had bidden his friend Vinçart take in his own name all the necessary proceedings, not wishing to pass for a tiger with his fellow-citizens.

She mingled her story with recriminations against Lheureux, to which the notary replied from time to time with some insignificant word. Eating his cutlet and drinking his tea, he buried his chin in his sky-blue cravat, into which were thrust two diamond pins, held together by a small gold chain; and he smiled a singular smile, in a sugary, ambiguous fashion. But noticing that her feet were damp, he said—

"Do get closer to the stove; put your feet up against the porcelain."

She was afraid of dirtying it. The notary replied in a gallant tone—

"Beautiful things spoil nothing."

Then she tried to move him, and, growing moved herself, she began telling him about the poorness of her home, her worries, her wants. He could understand that; an elegant woman! and, without leaving off eating, he had turned completely round towards her, so that his knee brushed against her boot, whose sole curled round as it smoked against the stove.

But when she asked for a thousand écus, he closed his lips, and declared he was very sorry he had not had the management of her fortune before, for there were hundreds of ways very convenient, even for a lady, of turning her money to account. They might, either in the turf-pits of Gaumesnil or building-ground at Havre, almost without risk, have ventured on some excellent speculations; and he let her consume herself with rage at the thought of the fabulous sums that she would certainly have made.

"How was it," he went on, "that you didn't come to me?"

"I hardly know," she said.

"Why, hey? Did I frighten you so much? It is I, on the contrary, who ought to complain. We hardly know one another; yet I am very devoted to you. You do not doubt that, I hope?"

He held out his hand, took hers, covered it with a greedy kiss, then held it on his knee; and he played delicately with her fingers whilst he murmured a thousand blandishments. His insipid voice murmured like a running brook; a light shone in his eyes through the glimmering of his spectacles, and his hand was advancing up Emma's sleeve to press her arm. She felt against her cheek his panting breath. This man oppressed her horribly.

She sprang up and said to him—

"Sir, I am waiting."

"For what?" said the notary, who suddenly became very pale.

"This money."

"But——" Then, yielding to the outburst of too powerful a desire, "Well, yes!"

He dragged himself towards her on his knees, regardless of his dressing-gown.

"For pity's sake, stay! I love you!"

He seized her by her waist. Madame Bovary's face flushed purple. She recoiled with a terrible look, crying—

"You are taking a shameless advantage of my distress, sir! I am to be pitied—not to be sold."

And she went out.

The notary remained quite stupefied, his eyes fixed on his fine embroidered slippers. They were a love gift, and the sight of them at last consoled him. Besides, he reflected that such an adventure might have carried him too far.

"What a wretch! what a scoundrel! what an infamy!" she said to herself, as she fled with nervous steps beneath the aspens of the path. The disappointment of her failure increased the indignation of her outraged modesty; it seemed to her that Providence pursued her implacably, and, strengthening herself in her pride, she had never felt so much esteem for herself nor so much contempt for others. A spirit of warfare transformed her. She would have liked to strike all men, to spit in their faces, to crush them, and she walked rapidly straight on, pale, quivering, maddened, searching the empty horizon with tear-dimmed eyes, and as it were rejoicing in the hate that was choking her.

When she saw her house a numbness came over her. She could not go on; and yet she must. Besides, whither could she flee?

Félicité was waiting for her at the door. "Well?"

"No!" said Emma.

And for a quarter of an hour the two of them went over the various persons in Yonville who might perhaps be inclined to help her. But each time that Félicité named some one Emma replied—

"Impossible! they will not!"

"And the master'll soon be in."

"I know that well enough. Leave me alone."

She had tried everything; there was nothing more to be done now; and when Charles came in she would have to say to him—

"Go away! This carpet on which you are walking is no longer ours. In your own house you do not possess a chair, a pin, a straw, and it is I, poor man, who have ruined you."

Then there would be a great sob; next he would weep abundantly, and at last, the surprise past, he would forgive her.

"Yes," she murmured, grinding her teeth, "he will forgive me, he who would give me a million if I would forgive him for having known me! Never! never!"

This thought of Bovary's superiority to her exasperated her. Then, whether she confessed or did not confess, presently, immediately, to-morrow, he would know the catastrophe all the same; so she must wait for this horrible scene, and bear the weight of his magnanimity. The desire to return to Lheureux's seized her—what would be the use? To write to her father—it was too late; and perhaps she began to repent now that she had not yielded to that other, when she heard the trot of a horse in the alley. It was he; he was opening the gate; he was whiter than the plaster wall. Rushing to the stairs, she ran out quickly to the square; and the wife of the mayor, who was talking to Lestiboudois in front of the church, saw her go in to the tax-collector's.

She hurried off to tell Madame Caron, and the two ladies went up to the attic, and, hidden by some linen spread across props, stationed themselves comfortably for overlooking the whole of Binet's room.

He was alone in his garret, busy imitating in wood one of those indescribable bits of ivory, composed of crescents, of spheres hollowed out one within the other, the whole as straight as an obelisk, and of no use whatever; and he was beginning on the last piece—he was nearing his goal. In the twilight of the workshop the white dust was flying from his tools like a shower of sparks under the hoofs of a galloping horse; the two wheels were turning, droning; Binet smiled, his chin lowered, his nostrils distended, and, in a word, seemed lost in one of those complete happinesses that, no doubt, belong only to commonplace occupations, which amuse the mind with facile difficulties, and satisfy by a realisation of that beyond which such minds have not a dream.

"Ah! there she is!" exclaimed Madame Tuvache.

But it was impossible because of the lathe to hear what she was saying.

At last these ladies thought they made out the word "francs," and Madame Tuvache whispered in a low voice—

"She is begging him to give her time for paying her taxes."

"Apparently!" replied the other.

They saw her walking up and down, examining the napkin-rings, the candlesticks, the banister rails against the walls, while Binet stroked his beard with satisfaction.

"Do you think she wants to order something of him?" said Madame Tuvache.

"Why, he doesn't sell anything," objected her neighbour.

The tax-collector seemed to be listening with wide-open eyes, as if he did not understand. She went on in a tender, suppliant manner. She came nearer to him, her breast heaving; they no longer spoke.

"Is she making him advances?" said Madame Tuvache.

Binet was scarlet to his very ears. She took hold of his hands.

"Oh, it's too much!"

And no doubt she was suggesting something abominable to him; for the tax-collector—yet he was brave, had fought at Bautzen and at Lutzen, had been through the French campaign, and had even been recommended for the cross—suddenly, as at the sight of a serpent, recoiled as far as he could from her, crying—

"Madame! what do you mean?"

"Women like that ought to be whipped," said Madame Tuvache.

"But where is she?" continued Madame Caron, for she had disappeared whilst they spoke; then catching sight of her going up the Grande Rue, and turning to the right as if making for the cemetery, they were lost in conjectures.

"Nurse Rollet," she said on reaching the nurse's,. "I am choking; unlace me!" She fell on the bed sobbing. Nurse Rollet covered her with a petticoat and remained standing by her side. Then, as she did not answer, the good woman withdrew, took her wheel and began spinning flax.

"Oh, leave off!" she murmured, fancying she heard Binet's lathe.

"What's bothering her?" said the nurse to herself. "Why has she come here?"

She had rushed thither, impelled by a kind of horror that drove her from her home.

Lying on her back, motionless, and with staring eyes, she saw things but vaguely, although she tried to with idiotic persistence. She looked at the scales on the walls, two brands smoking end to end, and a long spider crawling over her head in a rent in the beam. At last she began to collect her thoughts. She remembered—one day—Léon—— Oh! how long ago that was—the sun was shining on the river, and the clematis were perfuming the air. Then, carried away as by a rushing torrent, she soon began to recall the day before.

"What time is it?" she asked.

Mère Rollet went out, raised the fingers of her right hand to that side of the sky that was brightest, and came back slowly, saying—

"Nearly three."

"Ah! thanks, thanks!"

For he would come; he would have found some money. But he would, perhaps, go down yonder, not guessing she was here, and she told the nurse to run to her house to fetch him.

"Be quick!"

"But, my dear lady, I'm going, I'm going!"

She wondered now that she had not thought of him from the first. Yesterday he had given his word; he would not break it. And she already saw herself at Lheureux's spreading out her three bank-notes on his bureau. Then she would have to invent some story to explain matters to Bovary. What should it be?

The nurse, however, was a long while gone. But, as there was no clock in the cot, Emma feared she was perhaps exaggerating the length of time. She began walking round the garden, step by step; she went into the path by the hedge, and returned quickly, hoping that the woman would have come back by another road. At last, weary of waiting, assailed by fears that she thrust from her, no longer conscious whether she had been here a century or a moment, she sat down in a corner, closed her eyes, and stopped her ears. The gate grated; she sprang up. Before she had spoken Mère Rollet said to her—

"There is no one at your house!"

"What?"

"Oh, no one! And the doctor is crying. He is calling for you; they're looking for you."

Emma answered nothing. She gasped as she turned her eyes about her, while the peasant woman, frightened at her face, drew back instinctively, thinking her mad. Suddenly she struck her brow and uttered a cry; for the thought of Rodolphe, like a flash of lightning in a dark night, had passed into her soul. He was so good, so delicate, so generous! And besides, should he hesitate to do her this service, she would know well enough how to constrain him to it by re-waking, in a single moment, their lost love. So she set out towards La Huchette, not seeing that she was hastening to offer herself to that which but a while ago had so angered her, not in the least conscious of her prostitution.

VIII

She asked herself as she walked along, "What am I going to say? How shall I begin?" And as she went on she recognised the thickets, the trees, the sea-rushes on the hill, the château yonder. All the sensations of her first tenderness came back to her, and her poor aching heart opened out amorously. A warm wind blew in her face; the melting snow fell drop by drop from the buds to the grass.

She entered, as she used to, through the small park-gate. Then came to the avenue bordered by a double row of dense lime trees. They were swaying their long whispering branches to and fro. The dogs in their kennels all barked, and the noise of their voices resounded, but brought out no one.

She went up the large straight staircase with wooden balusters that led to the corridor paved with dusty flags, into which several doors in a row opened, as in a monastery or an inn. His was at the top, right at the end, on the left. When she placed her fingers on the lock her strength suddenly deserted her. She was afraid, almost wished he would not be there, though this was her only hope, her last chance of salvation. She collected her thoughts for one moment, and, strengthening herself by the feeling of present necessity, went in.

He was in front of the fire, both his feet on the mantelpiece, smoking a pipe.

"What! it is you!" he said, getting up hurriedly.

"Yes, it is I, Rodolphe. I should like to ask your advice." And, despite all her efforts, it was impossible for her to open her lips.

"You have not changed; you are charming as ever!"

"Oh," she replied bitterly, "they are poor charms since you disdained them."

Then he began a long explanation of his conduct, excusing himself in vague terms, in default of being able to invent better.

She yielded to his words, still more to his voice and the sight of him, so that she pretended to believe, or perhaps believed, in the pretext he gave for their rupture; this was a secret on which depended the honour, the very life of a third person.

"No matter!" she said, looking at him sadly. "I have suffered much."

He replied philosophically—

"Such is life!"

"Has life," Emma went on, "been good to you at least, since our separation?"

"Oh, neither good nor bad."

"Perhaps it would have been better never to have parted."

"Yes, perhaps."

"You think so?" she said, drawing nearer, and she sighed. "Oh, Rodolphe! if you but knew! I loved you so!"

It was then that she took his hand and they remained some time, their fingers intertwined, like that first day at the Show. With a gesture of pride he struggled against this emotion. But sinking upon his breast she said to him—

"How did you think I could live without you? One cannot lose the habit of happiness. I was desolate. I thought I should die. I will tell you about all that and you will see. And you—you fled from me!"

For, all the three years, he had carefully avoided her in consequence of that natural cowardice that characterises the stronger sex. Emma went on with dainty little nods, more coaxing than an amorous kitten—

"You love others, confess it! Oh, I understand them, dear! I excuse them. You probably seduced them as you seduced me. You are indeed a man; you have everything to make one love you. But we'll begin again, won't we? We will love one another. See! I am laughing; I am happy! Oh, speak!"

And she was charming to see, with her eyes, in which trembled a tear, like the rain of a storm in a blue corolla.

He had drawn her upon his knees, and with the back of his hand was caressing her smooth hair, where in the twilight was mirrored like a golden arrow one last ray of the sun. She bent down her brow; at last he kissed her on the eyelids quite gently with the tips of his lips.

"Why, you have been crying! What for?"

She burst into tears. Rodolphe thought this was an outburst of her love. As she did not speak, he took this silence for a last remnant of resistance, and then he cried out—

"Oh, forgive me! You are the only one who pleases me. I am imbecile and cruel. I love you. I will love you always. What is it? Tell me!" He was kneeling by her.

"Well, I am ruined, Rodolphe! You must lend me three thousand francs."

"But—but——" said he, getting up slowly, while his face assumed a grave expression.

"You know," she went on quickly, "that my husband had placed his whole fortune at a notary's. He ran away. So we borrowed; the patients don't pay us. Moreover, the settling of the estate is not yet done; we shall have the money later on. But to-day, for want of three thousand francs, we are to be sold up. It is to be at once, this very moment, and, counting upon your friendship, I have come to you."

"Ah!" thought Rodolphe, turning very pale, "that was what she came for." At last he said with a calm air—

"Dear madame, I have not got them."

He did not lie. If he had had them, he would, no doubt, have given them, although it is generally disagreeable to do such fine things: a demand for money being, of all the winds that blow upon love, the coldest and most destructive.

First she looked at him for some moments.

"You have not got them!" she repeated several times. "You have not got them! I ought to have spared myself this last shame. You never loved me. You are no better than the others."

She was betraying, ruining herself.

Rodolphe interrupted her, declaring he was "hard up" himself.

"Ah! I pity you," said Emma. "Yes—very much."

And fixing her eyes upon an embossed carabine that shone against its panoply, "But when one is so poor one doesn't have silver on the butt of one's gun. One doesn't buy a clock inlaid with tortoiseshell," she went on, pointing to a buhl timepiece, "nor silver-gilt whistles for one's whips," and she touched them, "nor charms for one's watch. Oh, he wants for nothing! even to a liqueur-stand in his room! For you love yourself; you live well. You have a château, farms, woods; you go hunting; you travel to Paris. Why, if it were but that," she cried, taking up two studs from the mantelpiece, "but the least of these trifles, one can get money for them. Oh, I do not want them; keep them!"

And she threw the two links away from her, their gold chain breaking as it struck against the wall.

"But I! I would have given you everything. I would have sold all, worked for you with my hands, I would have begged on the highroads for a smile, for a look, to hear you say 'Thanks!' And you sit there quietly in your armchair, as if you had not made me suffer enough already! But for you, and you know it, I might have lived happily. What made you do it? Was it a bet? Yet you loved me—you said so. And but a moment since—— Ah! it would have been better to have driven me away. My hands are hot with your kisses, and there is the spot on the carpet where at my knees you swore an eternity of love! You made me believe you; for two years you held me in the most magnificent, the sweetest dream! Eh! Our plans for the journey, do you remember? Oh, your letter! your letter! it tore my heart! And then when I come back to him—to him, rich, happy, free—to implore the help the first stranger would give, a suppliant, and bringing back to him all my tenderness, he repulses me because it would cost him three thousand francs!"

"I haven't got them," replied Rodolphe, with that perfect calm with which resigned rage covers itself as with a shield.

She went out. The walls trembled, the ceiling was crushing her, and she passed back through the long alley, stumbling against the heaps of dead leaves scattered by the wind. At last she reached the ha-ha hedge in front of the gate; she broke her nails against the lock in her haste to open it. Then a hundred steps farther on, breathless, almost falling, she stopped. And now turning round, she once more saw the impassive château, with the park, the gardens, the three courts, and all the windows of the façade.

She remained lost in stupor, and having no more consciousness of herself than through the beating of her arteries, that she seemed to hear bursting forth like a deafening music filling all the fields. The earth beneath her feet was more yielding than the sea, and the furrows seemed to her immense brown waves breaking into foam. Everything in her head, of memories, ideas, went off at once like a thousand pieces of fireworks. She saw her father, Lheureux's closet, their room at home, another landscape. Madness was coming upon her; she grew afraid, and managed to recover herself, in a confused way, it is true, for she did not in the least remember the cause of the terrible condition she was in, that is to say, the question of money. She suffered only in her love, and felt her soul passing from her in this memory, as wounded men, dying, feel their life ebb from their bleeding wounds.

Night was falling, crows were flying about.

Suddenly it seemed to her that fiery spheres were exploding in the air like fulminating balls when they strike, and were whirling, whirling, to melt at last upon the snow between the branches of the trees. In the midst of each of them appeared the face of Rodolphe. They multiplied and drew near her, penetrating her. It all disappeared; she recognized the lights of the houses that shone through the fog.

Now her situation, like an abyss, rose up before her. She was panting as if her heart would burst. Then in an ecstasy of heroism, that made her almost joyous, she ran down the hill, crossed the cow-plank, the footpath, the alley, the market, and reached the chemist's shop. She was about to enter, but at the sound of the bell some one might come, and slipping in by the gate, holding her breath, feeling her way along the walls, she went as far as the door of the kitchen, where a candle stuck on the stove was burning. Justin in his shirt-sleeves was carrying out a dish.

"Ah! they are dining! I will wait."

He returned; she tapped at the window. He went out.

"The key! the one for upstairs where he keeps the——"

"What?"

And he looked at her, astonished at the pallor of her face, that stood out white against the black background of the night. She seemed to him extraordinarily beautiful and majestic as a phantom. Without understanding what she wanted, he had the presentiment of something terrible.

But she went on quickly in a low voice, in a sweet, melting voice, "I want it; give it to me."

As the partition wall was thin, they could hear the clatter of the forks on the plates in the dining-room.

She pretended that she wanted to kill the rats that kept her from sleeping.

"I must tell master."

"No, stay!" Then with an indifferent air, "Oh, it's not worth while; I'll tell him presently. Come, light me upstairs."

She entered the corridor into which the laboratory door opened. Against the wall was a key labelled *Capharnaüm*.

"Justin!" called the druggist impatiently.

"Let us go up."

And he followed her. The key turned in the lock, and she went straight to the third shelf, so well did her memory guide her, seized the blue jar, tore out the cork, plunged in her hand and withdrawing it full of a white powder, she began eating it.

"Stop!" he cried, rushing at her.

"Hush! some one will come."

He was in despair, was calling out.

"Say nothing, or all the blame will fall on your master."

Then she went home, suddenly calmed, and with something of the serenity of one that had performed a duty.

When Charles, distracted by the news of the distraint, returned home, Emma had just gone out. He cried aloud, wept, fainted, but she did not return. Where could she be? He sent Félicité to Homais, to Monsieur Tuvache, to Lheureux, to the "Lion d'Or," everywhere, and in the intervals of his agony, he saw his reputation destroyed, their fortune lost, Berthe's future ruined. By what?—Not a word! He waited till six in the evening. At last, unable to bear it any longer, and fancying she had gone to Rouen, he set out along the highroad, walked a mile, met no one, again waited, and returned home. She had come back.

"What was the matter? Why? Explain to me."

She sat down at her writing-table and wrote a letter, which she sealed slowly, adding the date and the hour. Then she said in a solemn tone—

"You are to read it to-morrow; till then, I pray you, do not ask me a single question. No, not one!"

"But——"

"Oh, leave me!"

She lay down full length on her bed. A bitter taste that she felt in her mouth awakened her. She saw Charles, and again closed her eyes.

She was studying herself curiously, to see if she were not suffering. But no! nothing as yet. She heard the ticking of the clock, the crackling of the fire, and Charles breathing as he stood upright by her bed.

"Ah! it is but a little thing, death!" she thought. "I shall fall asleep and all will be over."

She drank a mouthful of water and turned to the wall. The frightful taste of ink continued.

"I am thirsty; oh! so thirsty," she sighed.

"What is it?" said Charles, who was handing her a glass.

"It is nothing! Open the window; I am choking."

She was seized with a sickness so sudden that she had hardly time to draw out her handkerchief from under the pillow.

"Take it away," she said quickly; "throw it away."

He spoke to her; she did not answer. She lay motionless, afraid that the slightest movement might make her vomit. But she felt an icy cold creeping from her feet to her heart.

"Ah! it is beginning," she murmured.

"What did you say?"

She turned her head from side to side with a gentle movement full of agony, while constantly opening her mouth as if something very heavy were weighing upon her tongue. At eight o'clock the vomiting began again.

Charles noticed that at the bottom of the basin there was a sort of white sediment sticking to the sides of the porcelain.

"This is extraordinary—very singular," he repeated.

But she said in a firm voice, "No, you are mistaken."

Then gently, and almost as caressing her, he passed his hand over her stomach. She uttered a sharp cry. He fell back terror-stricken.

Then she began to groan, faintly at first. Her shoulders were shaken by a strong shuddering, and she was growing paler than the sheets in which her clenched fingers buried themselves. Her unequal pulse was now almost imperceptible.

Drops of sweat oozed from her bluish face, that seemed as if rigid in the exhalations of a metallic vapour. Her teeth chattered, her dilated eyes looked vaguely about her, and to all questions she replied only with a shake of the head; she even smiled once or twice. Gradually, her moaning grew louder; a hollow shriek burst from her; she pretended she was better and that she would get up presently. But she was seized with convulsions and cried out—

"Ah! my God! It is horrible!"

He threw himself on his knees by her bed.

"Tell me! what have you eaten? Answer, for heaven's sake!"

And he looked at her with a tenderness in his eyes such as she had never seen.

"Well, there—there!" she said in a faint voice. He flew to the writing-table, tore open the seal and read aloud: "Accuse no one." He stopped, passed his hands across his eyes, and read it over again.

"What! help—help!"

He could only keep repeating the word: "Poisoned! poisoned!" Félicité ran to Homais, who proclaimed it in the market-place; Madame Lefrançois heard it at the "Lion d'Or"; some got up to go and tell their neighbours, and all night the village was on the alert.

Distraught, faltering, reeling, Charles wandered about the room. He knocked against the furniture, tore his hair, and the chemist had never believed that there could be so terrible a sight.

He went home to write to Monsieur Canivet and to Doctor Larivière. He lost his head, and made more than fifteen rough copies. Hippolyte went to Neufchâtel, and Justin so spurred Bovary's horse that he left it foundered and three parts dead by the hill at Bois-Guillaume.

Charles tried to look up his medical dictionary, but could not read it; the lines were dancing.

"Be calm," said the druggist; "we have only to administer a powerful antidote. What is the poison?"

Charles showed him the letter. It was arsenic.

"Very well," said Homais, "we must make an analysis."

For he knew that in cases of poisoning an analysis must be made; and the other, who did not understand, answered—

"Oh, do anything! save her!"

Then going back to her, he sank upon the carpet, and lay there with his head leaning against the edge of her bed, sobbing.

"Don't cry," she said to him. "Soon I shall not trouble you any more."

"Why was it? Who drove you to it?"

She replied, "It had to be, my dear!"

"Weren't you happy? Is it my fault? I did all I could!"

"Yes, that is true—you are good—you."

And she passed her hand slowly over his hair. The sweetness of this sensation deepened his sadness; he felt his whole being dissolving in despair at the thought that he must lose her, just when she was confessing more love for him than ever. And he could think of nothing; he did not know, he did not dare; the urgent need for some immediate resolution gave the finishing stroke to the turmoil of his mind.

So she had done, she thought, with all the treachery, and meanness, and numberless desires that had tortured her. She hated no one now; a twilight dimness was settling upon her thoughts, and, of all earthly noises, Emma heard none but the intermittent lamentations of this poor heart, sweet and indistinct like the echo of a symphony dying away.

"Bring me the child," she said, raising herself on her elbow.

"You are not worse, are you?" asked Charles.

"No, no!"

The child, serious, and still half-asleep, was carried in on the servant's arm in her long white nightgown, from which her bare feet peeped out. She looked wonderingly at the disordered room, and half-closed her eyes, dazzled by the candles burning on the table. They reminded her, no doubt, of the morning of New Year's day and Mid-Lent, when thus awakened early by candlelight she came to her mother's bed to fetch her presents, for she began saying—

"But where is it, mamma?" And as everybody was silent, "But I can't see my little stocking."

Félicité held her over the bed while she still kept looking towards the mantelpiece.

"Has nurse taken it?" she asked.

And at this name, that carried her back to the memory of her adulteries and her calamities, Madame Bovary turned away her head, as at the loathing of another bitterer poison that rose to her mouth. But Berthe remained perched on her bed.

"Oh, how big your eyes are, mamma! How pale you are! how hot you are!"

Her mother looked at her.

"I am frightened!" cried the child, recoiling.

Emma took her hand to kiss it; the child struggled.

"That will do. Take her away," cried Charles, who was sobbing in the alcove.

Then the symptoms ceased for a moment; she seemed less agitated; and at every insignificant word, at every respiration a little more easy, he regained hope. At last, when Canivet came in, he threw himself into his arms.

"Ah! it is you. Thanks! You are good! But she is better. See! look at her."

His colleague was by no means of this opinion, and, as he said of himself, "never beating about the bush," he prescribed an emetic in order to empty the stomach completely.

She soon began vomiting blood. Her lips became drawn. Her limbs were convulsed, her whole body covered with brown spots, and her pulse slipped beneath the fingers like a stretched thread, like a harp-string nearly breaking.

After this she began to scream horribly. She cursed the poison, railed at it, and implored it to be quick, and thrust away with her stiffened arms everything that Charles, in more agony than herself, tried to make her drink. He stood up, his handkerchief to his lips, with a rattling sound in his throat, weeping, and choked by sobs that shook his whole body. Félicité was running hither and thither in the room. Homais, motionless, uttered great sighs; and Monsieur Canivet, always retaining his self-command, nevertheless began to feel uneasy.

"The devil! yet she has been purged, and from the moment that the cause ceases——"

"The effect must cease," said Homais, "that is evident."

"Oh, save her!" cried Bovary.

And, without listening to the chemist, who was still venturing the hypothesis, "It is perhaps a salutary paroxysm," Canivet was about to administer some theriac, when they heard the cracking of a whip; all the windows rattled, and a post-chaise drawn by three horses abreast, up to their ears in mud, drove at a gallop round the corner of the market. It was Doctor Larivière.

The apparition of a god would not have caused more commotion. Bovary raised his hands; Canivet stopped short; and Homais pulled off his skull-cap long before the doctor had come in.

He belonged to that great school of surgery begotten of Bichat, to that generation, now extinct, of philosophical practitioners, who, loving their art with a fanatical love, exercised it with enthusiasm and wisdom. Every one in his hospital trembled when he was angry; and his students so revered him that they tried, as soon as they were themselves in practice, to imitate him as much as possible. So that in all the towns about they were found wearing his long wadded merino overcoat and black frock-coat, whose buttoned cuffs slightly covered his brawny hands—very beautiful hands, and that never knew gloves, as though to be more ready to plunge into suffering. Disdainful of honours, of titles, and of academies, like one of the old Knight-Hospitallers, generous, fatherly to the poor, and practising virtue without believing in it, he would almost have passed for a saint if the keenness of his intellect had not caused him to be feared as a demon. His glance, more penetrating than his bistouries, looked straight into your soul, and dissected every lie athwart all assertions and all reticences. And thus he went along, full of that debonair majesty that is given by the consciousness of great talent, of fortune, and of forty years of a laborious and irreproachable life.

He frowned as soon as he had passed the door when he saw the cadaverous face of Emma stretched out on her back with her mouth open. Then, while apparently listening to Canivet, he rubbed his fingers up and down beneath his nostrils, and repeated—

"Good! good!"

But he made a slow gesture with his shoulders. Bovary watched him; they looked at one another; and this man, accustomed as he was to the sight of pain, could not keep back a tear that fell on his shirt-frill.

He tried to take Canivet into the next room. Charles followed him.

"She is very ill, isn't she? If we put on sinapisms? Anything! Oh, think of something, you who have saved so many!"

Charles caught him in both his arms, and gazed at him wildly, imploringly, half-fainting against his breast.

"Come, my poor fellow, courage! There is nothing more to be done."

And Doctor Larivière turned away.

"You are going?"

"I will come back."

He went out only to give an order to the coachman, with Monsieur Canivet, who did not care either to have Emma die under his hands.

The chemist rejoined them on the Place. He could not by temperament keep away from celebrities, so he begged Monsieur Larivière to do him the signal honour of accepting some breakfast.

He sent quickly to the "Lion d'Or" for some pigeons; to the butcher's for all the cutlets that were to be had; to Tuvache for cream; and to Lestiboudois for eggs; and the druggist himself aided in the preparations, while Madame Homais was saying as she pulled together the strings of her jacket—

"You must excuse us, sir, for in this poor place, when one hasn't been told the night before——"

"Wine glasses!" whispered Homais.

"If only we were in town, we could fall back upon stuffed trotters."

"Be quiet! Sit down, doctor!"

He thought fit, after the first few mouthfuls, to give some details as to the catastrophe.

"We first had a feeling of siccity in the pharnyx, then intolerable pains at the epigastrium, super-purgation, coma."

"But how did she poison herself?"

"I don't know, doctor, and I don't even know where she can have procured the arsenious acid."

Justin, who was just bringing in a pile of plates, began to tremble.

"What's the matter?" said the chemist.

At this question the young man dropped the whole lot on the ground with a crash.

"Imbecile!" cried Homais, "awkward lout! blockhead! confounded ass!"

But suddenly controlling himself—

"I wished, doctor, to make an analysis, and *primo* I delicately introduced a tube——"

"You would have done better," said the physician, "to introduce your fingers into her throat."

His colleague was silent, having just before privately received a severe lecture about his emetic, so that this good Canivet, so arrogant and so verbose at the time of the club-foot, was to-day very modest. He smiled without ceasing in an approving manner.

Homais dilated in Amphytrionic pride, and the affecting thought of Bovary vaguely contributed to his pleasure by a kind of egotistic reflex upon himself. Then the presence of the doctor transported him. He displayed his erudition, cited pell-mell cantharides, upas, the manchineel, vipers.

"I have even read that various persons have found themselves under toxicological symptoms, and, as it were, thunderstricken by black-pudding that had been subjected to a too vehement fumigation. At least, this was stated in a very fine report drawn up by one of our pharmaceutical chiefs, one of our masters, the illustrious Cadet de Gassicourt!"

Madame Homais reappeared, carrying one of those shaky machines that are heated with spirits of wine; for Homais liked to make his coffee at table, having, moreover, torrefied it, pulverised it, and mixed it himself.

"*Saccharum*, doctor?" said he, offering the sugar.

Then he had all his children brought down, anxious to have the physician's opinion on their constitutions.

At last Monsieur Larivière was about to leave, when Madame Homais asked for a consultation about her husband. He was making his blood too thick by going to sleep every evening after dinner.

"Oh, it isn't his blood that's too thick," said the physician.

And, smiling a little at his unnoticed joke, the doctor opened the door. But the chemist's shop was full of people; he had the greatest difficulty in getting rid of Monsieur Tuvache, who feared his spouse would get inflammation of the lungs, because she was in the habit of spitting on the ashes; then of Monsieur Binet, who sometimes experienced sudden attacks of great hunger; and of Madame Caron, who suffered from tinglings; of Lheureux, who had vertigo; of Lestiboudois, who had rheumatism; and of Madame Lefrançois, who had heartburn. At last the three horses started;

and it was the general opinion that he had not shown himself at all obliging.

Public attention was distracted by the appearance of Monsieur Bournisien, who was going across the market with the holy oil.

Homais, as was due to his principles, compared priests to ravens attracted by the odour of death. The sight of an ecclesiastic was personally disagreeable to him, for the cassock made him think of the shroud, and he detested the one from some fear of the other.

Nevertheless, not shrinking from what he called his mission, he returned to Bovary's in company with Canivet, whom Monsieur Larivière, before leaving, had strongly urged to make this visit; and he would, but for his wife's objections, have taken his two sons with him, in order to accustom them to great occasions; that this might be a lesson, an example, a solemn picture, that should remain in their heads later on.

The room when they went in was full of mournful solemnity. On the work-table, covered over with a white cloth, there were five or six small balls of cotton in a silver dish, near a large crucifix between two lighted candles.

Emma, her chin sunken upon her breast, had her eyes inordinately wide open, and her poor hands wandered over the sheets with that hideous and soft movement of the dying, that seems as if they wanted already to cover themselves with the shroud. Pale as a statue and with eyes red as fire, Charles, not weeping, stood opposite her at the foot of the bed, while the priest, bending one knee, was muttering words in a low voice.

She turned her face slowly, and seemed filled with joy on seeing suddenly the violet stole, no doubt finding again, in the midst of a temporary lull in her pain, the lost voluptuousness of her first mystical transports, with the visions of eternal beatitude that were beginning.

The priest rose to take the crucifix; then she stretched forward her neck as one who is athirst, and glueing her lips to the body of the Man-God, she pressed upon it with all her expiring strength the fullest kiss of love that she had ever given. Then he recited the *Misereatur* and the *Indulgentiam*, dipped his right thumb in the oil, and began to give extreme unction. First, upon the eyes, that had so coveted all worldly pomp; then upon the nostrils, that had been greedy of the warm breeze and amorous odours; then upon the mouth, that had uttered lies, that had curled with pride and cried out in lewdness; then upon the hands that had delighted in sensual touches; and finally upon the soles of the feet, so swift of yore, when she was running to satisfy her desires, and that would now walk no more.

The curé wiped his fingers, threw the bit of cotton dipped in oil into the fire, and came and sat down by the dying woman, to tell her that she must now blend her sufferings with those of Jesus Christ and abandon herself to the divine mercy.

Finishing his exhortations, he tried to place in her hand a blessed candle, symbol of the celestial glory with which she was soon to be surrounded. Emma, too weak, could not close her fingers, and the taper, but for Monsieur Bournisien would have fallen to the ground.

However, she was not quite so pale, and her face had an expression of serenity as if the sacrament had cured her.

The priest did not fail to point this out; he even explained to Bovary that the Lord sometimes prolonged the life of persons when he thought it meet for their salvation; and Charles remembered the day when, so near death, she had received the communion. Perhaps there was no need to despair, he thought.

In fact, she looked around her slowly, as one awakening from a dream; then in a distinct voice she asked for her looking-glass, and remained some time bending over it, until the big tears fell from her eyes. Then she turned away her head with a sigh and fell back upon the pillows.

Her chest soon began panting rapidly; the whole of her tongue protruded from her mouth; her eyes, as they rolled, grew paler, like the two globes of a lamp that is going out, so that one might have thought her already dead but for the fearful labouring of her ribs, shaken by violent breathing, as if the soul were struggling to free itself. Félicité knelt down before the crucifix, and the druggist himself slightly bent his knees, while Monsieur Canivet looked out vaguely at the Place. Bournisien had again begun to pray, his face bowed against the edge of the bed, his long black cassock trailing behind him in the room. Charles was on the other side, on his knees, his arms outstretched towards Emma. He had taken her hands and pressed them, shuddering at every beat of her heart, as at the shaking of a falling ruin. As the death-rattle became stronger the priest prayed faster; his prayers mingled with the stifled sobs of Bovary, and sometimes all seemed lost in the muffled murmur of the Latin syllables that tolled like a passing bell.

Suddenly on the pavement was heard a loud noise of clogs and the clattering of a stick; and a voice rose—a raucous voice—that sang—

> *"Maids in the warmth of a summer day*
> *Dream of love and of love alway."*

Emma raised herself like a galvanised corpse, her hair undone, her eyes fixed, staring.

> *"Where the sickle blades have been,*
> *Nannette, gathering ears of corn,*
> *Passes bending down, my queen,*
> *To the earth where they were born."*

"The blind man!" she cried. And Emma began to laugh, an atrocious, frantic, despairing laugh, thinking she saw the hideous face of the poor wretch that stood out against the eternal night like a menace.

> *"The wind is strong this summer day,*
> *Her petticoat has flown away."*

She fell back upon the mattress in a convulsion. They all drew near. She was dead.

IX

THERE is always after the death of any one a kind of stupefaction; so difficult is it to grasp this advent of nothingness and to resign ourselves to believe in it. But still, when he saw that she did not move, Charles threw himself upon her, crying—

"Farewell! farewell!"

Homais and Canivet dragged him from the room.

"Restrain yourself!"

"Yes," said he, struggling, "I'll be quiet. I'll not do anything. But leave me alone. I want to see her. She is my wife!"

And he wept.

"Cry," said the chemist; "let nature take her course; that will solace you."

Weaker than a child, Charles let himself be led downstairs into the sitting-room, and Monsieur Homais soon went home. On the Place he was accosted by the blind man, who, having dragged himself as far as Yonville in the hope of getting the antiphlogistic pomade, was asking every passer-by where the druggist lived.

"There now! as if I hadn't got other fish to fry. Well, so much the worse; you must come later on."

And he entered the shop hurriedly.

He had to write two letters, to prepare a soothing potion for Bovary, to invent some lie that would conceal the poisoning, and work it up into an article for the "Fanal," without counting the people who were waiting to get the news from him; and when the Yonvillers had all heard his story of the arsenic that she had mistaken for sugar in making a vanilla cream, Homais once more returned to Bovary's.

He found him alone (Monsieur Canivet had left), sitting in an armchair near the window, staring with an idiotic look at the flags of the floor.

"Now," said the chemist, "you ought yourself to fix the hour for the ceremony."

"Why? What ceremony?" Then, in a stammering, frightened voice, "Oh, no! not that. No! I want to see her here."

Homais, to keep himself in countenance, took up a waterbottle on the whatnot to water the geraniums.

"Ah! thanks," said Charles; "you are good."

But he did not finish, choking beneath the crowd of memories that this action of the druggist recalled to him.

Then to distract him, Homais thought fit to talk a little horticulture: plants wanted humidity. Charles bowed his head in sign of approbation.

"Besides, the fine days will soon be here again."

"Ah!" said Bovary.

The druggist, at his wit's end, began softly to draw aside the small window-curtain.

"Hallo! there's Monsieur Tuvache passing."

Charles repeated like a machine—

"Monsieur Tuvache passing!"

Homais did not dare to speak to him again about the funeral arrangements; it was the priest who succeeded in reconciling him to them.

He shut himself up in his consulting-room, took a pen, and after sobbing for some time, wrote—

"I wish her to be buried in her wedding-dress, with white shoes, and a wreath. Her hair is to be spread out over her shoulders. Three coffins, one of oak, one of mahogany, one of lead. Let no one say anything to me. I shall have strength. Over all there is to be placed a large piece of green velvet. This is my wish; see that it is done."

The two men were much surprised at Bovary's romantic ideas. The chemist at once went to him and said—

"This velvet seems to me a superfetation. Besides, the expense——"

"What's that to you?" cried Charles. "Leave me! You did not love her. Go!"

The priest took him by the arm for a turn in the garden. He discoursed on the vanity of earthly things. God was very great, he said; he was very good: one must submit to his decrees resignedly, without a murmur; nay, one must even thank him.

Charles burst out into blasphemies: "I hate your God!"

"The spirit of rebellion is still upon you," sighed the ecclesiastic.

Bovary was far away. He was walking with great strides along by the wall, near the espalier, and he ground his teeth; he raised to heaven looks of malediction, but not so much as a. leaf stirred.

A fine rain was falling: Charles, whose chest was bare, at last began to shiver; he went in and sat down in the kitchen.

At six o'clock a noise like a clatter of old iron was heard on the Place; it was the "Hirondelle" coming in, and he remained with his forehead against the window-pane, watching all the passengers get out, one after the other. Félicité put down a mattress for him in the drawing-room. He threw himself upon it and fell asleep.

Although a philosopher, Monsieur Homais respected the dead. So bearing no grudge to poor Charles, he came back again in the evening to sit up with the body, bringing with him three volumes and a pocket-book for the purpose of taking notes.

Monsieur Bournisien was there, and two large candles were burning at the head of the bed, that had been taken out of the alcove. The druggist, on whom the silence weighed, was not long before he began formulating some regrets about this "unfortunate young woman," and the priest replied that there was nothing to do now but pray for her.

"Yet," Homais went on, "one of two things; either she died in a state of grace (as the Church has it), and then she has no need of our prayers; or else she departed impenitent (that is, I believe, the ecclesiastical expression), and then——"

Bournisien interrupted him, replying testily that it was none the less necessary to pray.

"But," objected the chemist, "since God knows all our needs, what can be the good of prayer?"

"What!" cried the ecclesiastic, "prayer! Why, aren't you a Christian?"

"Excuse me," said Homais; "I admire Christianity. To begin with, it enfranchised the slaves, introduced into the world a morality——"

"That isn't the question. All the texts——"

"Oh! oh! As to texts, look at history; it is known that all the texts have been falsified by the Jesuits."

Charles came in, and advancing towards the bed, slowly drew the curtains.

Emma's head was turned towards her right shoulder, the corner of her mouth, which was open, seemed like a black hole at the lower part of her face; her two thumbs were bent into the palms of her hands; a kind of white dust besprinkled her lashes, and her eyes were beginning to disappear in that viscous pallor that looks like a thin web, as if spiders had spun it over. The sheet sunk in from her breast to her knees, and then rose at the tips of her toes, and it seemed to Charles that infinite masses, an enormous load, were weighing upon her.

The church clock struck two. They could hear the loud murmur of the river flowing in the darkness at the foot of the terrace. Monsieur Bournisien from time to time blew his nose noisily, and Homais's pen was scratching over the paper.

"Come, my good friend," he said, "withdraw; this spectacle is tearing you to pieces."

Charles once gone, the chemist and the curé recommenced their discussions.

"Read Voltaire," said the one, "read D'Holbach, read the 'Encyclopædia'!"

"Read the 'Letters of some Portuguese Jews,'" said the other; "read 'The Meaning of Christianity,' by Nicolas, formerly a magistrate."

They grew warm, they grew red, they both talked at once without listening to each other. Bournisien was scandalised at such audacity; Homais marvelled at such stupidity; and they were on the point of insulting one another when Charles suddenly reappeared. A fascination drew him. He was continually coming upstairs.

He stood opposite her, the better to see her, and he lost himself in a contemplation so deep that it was no longer painful.

He recalled stories of catalepsy, the marvels of magnetism, and he said to himself that by willing it with all his force he might perhaps succeed in reviving her. Once he even bent towards her, and cried in a low voice, "Emma! Emma!" His strong breathing made the flames of the candles tremble against the wall.

At daybreak Madame Bovary senior arrived. Charles as he embraced her burst into another flood of tears. She tried, as the chemist had done, to make some remarks to him on the expenses of the funeral. He became so angry that she was silent, and he even commissioned her to go to town at once and buy what was necessary.

Charles remained alone the whole afternoon; they had taken Berthe to Madame Homais's; Félicité was in the room upstairs with Madame Lefrançois.

In the evening he had some visitors. He rose, pressed their hands, unable to speak. Then they sat down near one another, and formed a large semicircle in front of the fire. With lowered faces, and swinging one leg crossed over the other knee, they uttered deep sighs at intervals; each one was inordinately bored, and yet none would be the first to go.

Homais, when he returned at nine o'clock. (for the last two days only Homais seemed to have been on the Place), was laden with a stock of camphor, of benzine, and aromatic herbs. He also carried a large jar full of chlorine water, to keep off all miasmata. Just then the servant, Madame Lefrançois, and Madame Bovary senior were busy about Emma, finishing dressing her, and they were drawing down the long stiff veil that covered her to her satin shoes.

Félicité was sobbing—"Ah! my poor mistress! my poor mistress!"

"Look at her," said the landlady, sighing; "how pretty she still is! Now, couldn't you swear she was going to get up in a minute?"

Then they bent over her to put on her wreath. They had to raise the head a little, and a rush of black liquid issued, as if she were vomiting, from her mouth.

"Oh, goodness! The dress; take care!" cried Madame Lefrançois. "Now, just come and help," she said to the chemist. "Perhaps you're afraid?"

"I afraid?" replied he, shrugging his shoulders. "I daresay! I've seen all sorts of things at the hospital when I was studying pharmacy. We used to make punch in the dissecting room! Nothingness does not terrify a philosopher; and, as I often say, I even intend to leave my body to the hospitals, in order, even after my death, to serve science."

The curé on his arrival inquired how Monsieur Bovary was, and, on the reply of the druggist, went on— "The blow, you see, is still too recent."

Then Homais congratulated him on not being exposed, like other people, to the loss of a beloved companion; whence there followed a discussion on the celibacy of priests.

"For," said the chemist, "it is unnatural that a man should do without women! There have been crimes——"

"But, good heaven!" cried the ecclesiastic, "how do you expect an individual who is married to keep the secrets of the confessional, for example?"

Homais fell foul of the confessional. Bournisien defended it; he enlarged on the acts of restitution that it brought about. He cited various anecdotes about thieves who had suddenly become honest. Military men on approaching the tribunal of penitence had felt the scales fall from their eyes. At Fribourg there was a minister—

His companion was asleep. Then he felt somewhat stifled by the over-heavy atmosphere of the room; he opened the window; this awoke the chemist.

"Come, take a pinch of snuff," he said to him. "Take it, it'll relieve you."

A continual barking was heard in the distance. "Do you hear that dog howling?" said the chemist.

"They smell the dead," replied the priest. "It's like bees; they leave their hives on the decease of any person."

Homais made no remark upon these prejudices, for he had again dropped asleep. Monsieur Bournisien, stronger than he, went on moving his lips gently for some time, then insensibly his chin sank down, he let fall his big black book, and began to snore.

They sat opposite one another, with protruding stomachs, puffed-up faces, and frowning looks, after so much disagreement uniting at last in the same human weakness, and they moved no more than the corpse by their side, that seemed to be sleeping.

Charles coming in did not wake them. It was the last time; he came to bid her farewell.

The aromatic herbs were still smoking, and spirals of bluish vapour blended at the window-sash with the fog that was coming in. There were a few stars, and the night was warm. The wax of the candles fell in great drops upon the sheets of the bed. Charles watched them burn, tiring his eyes against the glare of their yellow flame.

The watering on the satin gown shimmered white as moonlight. Emma was lost beneath it; and it seemed to him that, spreading beyond her own self, she blended confusedly with everything around her—the silence, the night, the passing wind, the damp odours rising from the ground.

Then suddenly he saw her in the garden at Tostes, on a bench against the thorn hedge, or else at Rouen in the streets, on the threshold of their house, in the yard at Bertaux. He again heard the laughter of the happy boys beneath the apple trees: the room was filled with the perfume of her hair; and her dress rustled in his arms with a noise like electricity. The dress was still the same.

For a long while he thus recalled all his lost joys, her attitudes, her movements, the sound of her voice. Upon one fit of despair followed another, and even others, inexhaustible as the waves of an overflowing sea.

A terrible curiosity seized him. Slowly, with the tips of his fingers, palpitating, he lifted her veil. But he uttered a cry of horror that awoke the other two.

They dragged him down into the sitting-room. Then Félicité came up to say that he wanted some of her hair.

"Cut some off," replied the druggist.

And as she did not dare to, he himself stepped forward, scissors in hand. He trembled so that he pierced the skin of the temple in several places. At last, stiffening himself against emotion, Homais gave two or three great cuts at random that left white patches amongst that beautiful black hair.

The chemist and the curé plunged anew into their occupations, not without sleeping from time to time, of which they accused each other reciprocally at each fresh awakening. Then Monsieur Bournisien sprinkled the room with holy water and Homais threw a little chlorine water on the floor.

Félicité had taken care to put on the chest of drawers, for each of them, a bottle of brandy, some cheese, and a large roll; and the druggist, who could not hold out any longer, about four in the morning sighed—

"My word! I should like to take some sustenance."

The priest did not need any persuading; he went out to go and say mass, came back, and then they ate and hobnobbed, giggling a little without knowing why, stimulated by that vague gaiety that comes upon us after times of sadness, and at the last glass the priest said to the druggist, as he clapped him on the shoulder—

"We shall end by understanding one another."

In the passage downstairs they met the undertaker's men, who were coming in. Then Charles for two hours had to suffer the torture of hearing the hammer resound against the wood. Next day they lowered her into her oak coffin, that was fitted into the other two; but as the bier was too large, they had to fill up the gaps with the wool of a mattress. At last, when the three lids had been placed down, nailed, soldered, it was placed outside in front of the door; the house was thrown open, and the people of Yonville began to flock round.

Old Rouault arrived, and fainted on the Place when he saw the black cloth.

X

HE HAD ONLY RECEIVED the chemist's letter thirty-six hours after the event; and, from consideration for his feelings, Homais had so worded it that it was impossible to make out what it was all about.

First, the old fellow had fallen as if struck by apoplexy. Next, he understood that she was not dead, but she might be. At last, he had put on his blouse, taken his hat, fastened his spurs to his boots, and set out at full speed; and the whole of the way old Rouault, panting, was torn by anguish. Once even he was obliged to dismount. He was dizzy; he heard voices round about him; he felt himself going mad.

Day broke. He saw three black hens asleep in a tree. He shuddered, horrified at this omen. Then he promised the Holy Virgin three chasubles for the church, and that he would go barefooted from the cemetery at Bertaux to the chapel of Vassonville.

He entered Maromme shouting for the people of the inn, burst open the door with a thrust of his shoulder, made for a sack of oats, emptied a bottle of sweet cider into the manger, and again mounted his nag, whose feet struck fire as it dashed along.

He said to himself that no doubt they would save her; the doctors would discover some remedy surely. He remembered all the miraculous cures he had been told about. Then she appeared to him dead. She was there, before his eyes, lying on her back in the middle of the road. He reined up, and the hallucination disappeared.

At Quincampoix, to give himself heart, he drank three cups of coffee one after the other. He fancied they had made a mistake in the name in writing. He looked for the letter in his pocket, felt it there, but did not dare to open it.

At last he began to think it was all a joke; some one's spite, the jest of some wag; and besides, if she were dead, one would have known it. But no! There was nothing extraordinary about the country; the sky was blue, the trees swayed; a flock of sheep passed. He saw the village; he was seen coming bending forward upon his horse, belabouring it with great blows, the girths dripping with blood.

When he had recovered consciousness, he fell, weeping, into Bovary's arms: "My girl! Emma! my child! tell me——"

The other replied, sobbing, "I don't know! I don't know! It's a curse!"

The druggist separated them. "These horrible details are useless. I will tell this gentleman all about it. Here are the people coming. Dignity! Come now! Philosophy!"

The poor fellow tried to show himself brave, and repeated several times, "Yes! courage!"

"Oh," cried the old man, "so I will have, by God! I'll go along o' her to the end!"

The bell began tolling. All was ready; they had to start. And seated in a stall of the choir, side by side, they saw pass and repass in front of them continually the three chanting choristers.

The serpent-player was blowing with all his might. Monsieur Bournisien, in full vestments, was singing in a shrill voice. He bowed before the tabernacle, raising his hands, stretched out his arms. Lestiboudois went about the church with his whalebone stick. The bier stood near the lectern, between four rows of candles. Charles felt inclined to get up and put them out.

Yet he tried to stir himself to a feeling of devotion, to throw himself into the hope of a future life in which he should see her again. He imagined to himself she had gone on a long journey, far away, for a long time. But when he thought of her lying there, and that all was over, that they would lay her in the earth, he was seized with a fierce, gloomy, despairful rage. At times he thought he felt nothing more, and he enjoyed this lull in his pain, whilst at the same time he reproached himself for being a wretch.

The sharp noise of an iron-ferruled stick was heard on the stones, striking them at irregular intervals. It came from the end of the church, and stopped short at the lower aisles. A man in a coarse brown jacket knelt down painfully. It was Hippolyte, the stable-boy at the "Lion d'Or." He had put on his new leg.

One of the choristers went round the nave making a collection, and the coppers chinked one after the other on the silver plate.

"Oh, make haste! I am in pain!" cried Bovary,. angrily throwing him a five-franc piece. The churchman thanked him with a deep bow.

They sang, they knelt, they stood up; it was endless! He remembered that once, in the early times, they had been to mass together, and they had sat down on the other side, on the right, by the wall. The bell began again. There was a great moving of chairs; the bearers slipped their three staves under the coffin, and every one left the church.

Then Justin appeared at the door of the shop. He suddenly went in again, pale, staggering.

People were at the windows to see the procession pass. Charles at the head walked erect. He affected a brave air, and saluted with a nod those who, coming out from the lanes or from their doors, stood amidst the crowd.

The six men, three on either side, walked slowly, panting a little. The priests, the choristers, and the two choir-boys recited the *De profundis*, and their voices echoed over the fields, rising and falling with their undulations. Sometimes they disappeared in the windings of the path; but the great silver cross rose always between the trees.

The women followed in black cloaks with turned-down hoods; each of them carried in her hands a large lighted candle, and Charles felt himself growing weaker at this continual repetition of prayers and torches, beneath this oppressive odour of wax and of cassocks. A fresh breeze was blowing; the rye and colza were sprouting, little dewdrops trembled at the roadsides and on the hawthorn hedges. All sorts of joyous sounds filled the air; the jolting of a cart rolling afar off in the ruts, the crowing of a cock, repeated again and again, or the gambolling of a foal running away under the apple trees. The pure sky was fretted with rosy clouds; a bluish haze rested upon the cots covered with iris. Charles as he passed recognised each courtyard. He remembered mornings like this, when, after visiting some patient, he came out from one and returned to her.

The black cloth bestrewn with white beads blew up from time to time, laying bare the coffin. The tired bearers walked more slowly, and it advanced with constant jerks, like a boat that pitches with every wave.

They reached the cemetery. The men went right down to a place in the grass where a grave was dug. They ranged themselves all round; and while the priest spoke, the red soil thrown up at the sides kept noiselessly slipping down at the corners.

Then when the four ropes were arranged the coffin was placed upon them. He watched it descend; it seemed descending for ever. At last a thud was heard; the ropes creaked as they were drawn up. Then Bournisien took the spade handed to him by Lestiboudois; with his left hand all the time sprinkling water, with the right he vigorously threw in a large spadeful; and the wood of the coffin, struck by the pebbles, gave forth that dread sound that seems to us the reverberation of eternity.

The ecclesiastic passed the holy water sprinkler to his neighbour. This was Homais. He swung it gravely, then handed it to Charles, who sank to his knees in the earth and threw in handfuls of it, crying, "Adieu!" He sent her kisses; he dragged himself towards the grave, to engulf himself with her. They led him away, and he soon grew calmer, feeling perhaps, like the others, a vague satisfaction that it was all over.

Old Rouault on his way back began quietly smoking a pipe, which Homais in his innermost conscience thought not quite the thing. He also noticed that Monsieur Binet had not been present, and that Tuvache had "made off" after mass, and that Theodore, the notary's servant, wore a blue coat, "as if one could not have got a black coat, since that is the custom, by Jove!" And to share his observations with others he went from group to group. They were deploring Emma's death, especially Lheureux, who had not failed to come to the funeral.

"Poor little woman! What a trouble for her husband!"

The druggist continued, "Do you know that but for me he would have committed some fatal attempt upon himself?"

"Such a good woman! To think that I saw her only last Saturday in my shop."

"I haven't had leisure," said Homais, "to prepare a few words that I would have cast upon her tomb."

Charles on getting home undressed, and old Rouault put on his blue blouse. It was a new one, and as he had often during the journey wiped his eyes on the sleeves, the dye had stained his face, and the traces of tears made lines in the layer of dust that covered it.

Madame Bovary senior was with them. All three were silent. At last the old fellow sighed—

"Do you remember, my friend, that I went to Tostes once when you had just lost your first deceased? I consoled you at that time. I thought of something to say then, but now——" Then, with a loud groan that shook his whole chest, "Ah! this is the end for me, do you see! I saw my wife go, then my son, and now to-day it's my daughter."

He wanted to go back at once to Bertaux, saying that he could not sleep in this house. He even refused to see his granddaughter.

"No, no! It would grieve me too much. Only you'll kiss her many times for me. Good-bye! you're a good fellow! And then I shall never forget that," he said, slapping his thigh. "Never fear, you shall always have your turkey."

But when he reached the top of the hill he turned back, as he had turned once before on the road to Saint-Victor when he had parted from her. The windows of the village were all on fire beneath the slanting rays of the sun sinking behind the field. He put his hand over his eyes, and saw in the horizon an enclosure of walls, where trees here and there formed black clusters between white stones; then he went on his way at a gentle trot, for his nag had gone lame.

Despite their fatigue, Charles and his mother stayed very long that evening talking together. They spoke of the days of the past and of the future. She would come to live at Yonville; she would keep house for him; they would never part again. She was ingenious and caressing, rejoicing in her heart at gaining once more an affection that had wandered from her for so many years. Midnight struck. The village as usual was silent, and Charles, awake, thought always of her.

Rodolphe, who, to distract himself, had been rambling about the wood all day, was sleeping quietly in his château, and Léon, down yonder, also slept.

There was another who at that hour was not asleep.

On the grave between the pine trees a child was on his knees weeping, and his heart, rent by sobs, was beating in the shadow beneath the load of an immense regret, sweeter than the moon and fathomless as the night. The gate suddenly grated. It was Lestiboudois; he came to fetch his spade, that he had forgotten. He recognised Justin climbing over the wall, and at last knew who was the culprit who stole his potatoes.

<h1 style="text-align:center">XI</h1>

THE NEXT DAY Charles had the child brought back. She asked for her mamma. They told her she was away; that she would bring her back some playthings. Berthe spoke of her again several times, then at last thought no more of her. The child's gaiety broke Bovary's heart, and he had to bear besides the intolerable consolations of the chemist.

Money troubles soon began again, Monsieur Lheureux urging on anew his friend Vinçart, and Charles pledged himself for exorbitant sums; for he would never consent to let the smallest of the things that had belonged to *her* be sold. His mother was exasperated with him; he grew even more angry than she did. He had altogether changed. She left the house.

Then every one began "taking advantage" of him. Mademoiselle Lempereur presented a bill for six months' teaching, although Emma had never taken a lesson (despite the receipted bill she had shown Bovary); it was an arrangement between the two women. The man at the circulating library demanded three years' subscriptions; Mère Rollet claimed the postage due for some twenty letters, and when Charles asked for an explanation, she had the delicacy to reply—

"Oh, I don't know. It was for her business affairs."

With every debt he paid Charles thought he had come to the end of them. But others followed ceaselessly. He sent in accounts for professional attendance. He was shown the letters his wife had written. Then he had to apologise.

Félicité now wore Madame Bovary's gowns; not all, for he had kept some of them, and he went to look at them in her dressing-room, locking himself up there; she was about her height, and often Charles, seeing her from behind, was seized with an illusion, and cried out—

"Oh, stay, stay!"

But at Whitsuntide she ran away from Yonville, carried off by Theodore, stealing all that was left of the wardrobe.

It was about this time that the widow Dupuis had the honour to inform him of the "marriage of Monsieur Léon Dupuis her son, notary at Yvetot, to Mademoiselle Léocadié Lebœuf of Bondeville." Charles, among the other congratulations he sent him, wrote this sentence—

"How glad my poor wife would have been!"

One day when, wandering aimlessly about the house, he had gone up to the attic, he felt a pellet of fine paper under his slipper. He opened it and read: "Courage, Emma, courage. I would not bring misery into your life." It was Rodolphe's letter, fallen to the ground between the boxes, where it had remained, and that the wind from the dormer window had just blown towards the door. And Charles stood, motionless and staring, in the very same place where, long ago, Emma, in despair, and paler even than he, had thought of dying. At last he discovered a small R at the bottom of the second page. What did this mean? He remembered Rodolphe's attentions, his sudden disappearance, his constrained air when they had met two or three times since then. But the respectful tone of the letter really deceived him.

"Perhaps they loved one another platonically," he said to himself.

Besides, Charles was not of those who go to the bottom of things; he shrank from the proofs, and his vague jealousy was lost in the immensity of his woe.

Every one, he thought, must have adored her; all men assuredly must have coveted her. She seemed but the more beautiful to him for this; he was seized with a lasting, furious desire for her, that inflamed his despair, and that was boundless, because it was now unrealisable.

To please her, as if she were still living, he adopted her predilections, her ideas; he bought patent leather boots and took to wearing white cravats. He put cosmetics on his moustache, and, like her, signed notes of hand. She corrupted him from beyond the grave.

He was obliged to sell his silver piece by piece; next he sold the drawing-room furniture. All the rooms were stripped; but the bedroom, her own room, remained as before. After his dinner Charles went up there. He pushed the round table in front of the fire, and drew up *her* armchair. He sat down opposite it. A candle burnt in one of the gilt candlesticks. Berthe by his side was painting prints.

He suffered, poor man, at seeing her so badly dressed, with laceless boots, and the arm-holes of her pinafore torn down to the hips; for the char-woman took no care of her. But she was so sweet, so pretty, and her little head bent forward so gracefully, letting the dear fair hair fall over her rosy cheeks, that an infinite joy came upon him, a happiness mingled with bitter-ness, like those ill-made wines that taste of resin. He mended her toys, made her puppets from cardboard, or sewed up half-torn dolls. Then, if his eyes fell upon the work-box, a ribbon lying about, or even a pin left in a crack of the table, he began to dream, and looked so sad that she became as sad as he.

No one now came to see them, for Justin had run away to Rouen, where he was a grocer's assistant, and the druggist's children saw less and less of the child, Monsieur Homais not caring, seeing the difference of their social position, to continue the intimacy.

The blind man, whom he had not been able to cure with the pomade, had gone back to the hill of Bois-Guillaume, where he told the travellers of the vain attempt of the druggist, to such an extent, that Homais when he went to town hid himself behind the curtains of the "Hirondelle" to avoid meeting him. He detested him, and wishing, in the interests of his own reputation, to get rid of him at all costs, he directed against him a secret battery, that betrayed the depth of his intellect and the baseness of his vanity. Thus, for six consecutive months, one could read in the "Fanal de Rouen" editorials such as these—

"All who bend their steps towards the fertile plains of Picardy have, no doubt, remarked, by the Bois-Guillaume hill, a wretch suffering from a horrible facial wound. He importunes, persecutes one, and levies a regular tax on all travellers. Are we still living in the monstrous times of the Middle Ages, when vagabonds were permitted to display in our public places leprosy and scrofulas they had brought back from the Crusades?"

Or—

"In spite of the laws against vagabondage, the approaches to our great towns continue to be infested by bands of beggars. Some are seen going about alone, and these are not, perhaps, the least dangerous. What are our ediles about?"

Then Homais invented anecdotes—

"Yesterday, by the Bois-Guillaume hill, a skittish horse——" And then followed the story of an accident caused by the presence of the blind man.

He managed so well that the fellow was locked up. But he was released. He began again, and Homais began again. It was a struggle. Homais won it, for his foe was condemned to life-long confinement in an asylum.

This success emboldened him, and henceforth there was no longer a dog run over, a barn burnt down, a woman beaten in the parish, of which he did not immediately inform the public, guided always by the love of progress and the hate of priests. He instituted comparisons between the elementary and clerical schools to the detriment of the latter; called to mind the massacre of St. Bartholomew, àpropos of a grant of one hundred francs to the church, and denounced abuses, aired new views. That was his phrase. Homais was digging and delving; he was becoming dangerous.

However, he was stifling in the narrow limits of journalism, and soon a book, a work was necessary to him. Then he composed "General Statistics of the Canton of Yonville, followed by Climatological Remarks." The statistics drove him to philosophy. He busied himself with great questions: the social problem, moralisation of the poorer classes, pisciculture, caoutchouc, railways, &c. He even began to blush at being a bourgeois. He affected the artistic style, he smoked. He bought two *chic* Pompadour statuettes to adorn his drawing-room.

He by no means gave up his shop. On the contrary, he kept well abreast of new discoveries. He followed the great movement of chocolates; he was the first to introduce "cocoa" and "revalenta" into the Seine-Inférieure. He was enthusiastic about the hydro-electric Pulvermacher chains; he wore one himself, and when at night he took off his flannel vest, Madame Homais stood quite dazzled before the golden spiral beneath which he was hidden, and felt her ardour redouble for this man more bandaged than a Scythian, and splendid as one of the Magi.

He had fine ideas about Emma's tomb. First he proposed a broken column with some drapery, next a pyramid, then a Temple of Vesta, a sort of rotunda, or else a "mass of ruins." And in all his plans Homais always stuck to the weeping willow, which he looked upon as the indispensable symbol of sorrow.

Charles and he made a journey to Rouen together to look at some tombs at a funeral furnisher's, accompanied by an artist, one Vaufrylard, a friend of Bridoux's, who made puns all the time. At last, after having examined some hundred designs, having ordered an estimate and made another journey to Rouen, Charles decided in favour of a mausoleum, which on the two principal sides was to have "a spirit bearing an extinguished torch."

As to the inscription, Homais could think of nothing so fine as *Sta viator*, and he got no further; he racked his brain, he constantly repeated *Sta viator*. At last he hit upon *Amabilem conjugem calcas*, which was adopted.

A strange thing was that Bovary, while continually thinking of Emma, was forgetting her. He grew desperate as he felt this image fading from his memory in spite of all efforts to retain it. Yet every night he dreamt of her; it was always the same dream. He drew near her, but when he was about to clasp her she fell into decay in his arms.

For a week he was seen going to church in the evening. Monsieur Bournisien even paid him two or three visits, then gave him up. Moreover, the old fellow was growing intolerant, fanatic, said Homais. He thundered against the spirit of the age, and never failed, every other week, in his sermon, to recount the death agony of Voltaire, who died devouring his excrements, as every one knows.

In spite of the economy with which Bovary lived, he was far from being able to pay off his old debts. Lheureux refused to renew any more bills. A distraint became imminent. Then he appealed to his mother, who consented to let him take a mortgage on her property, but with a great many recriminations against Emma; and in return for her sacrifice she asked for a shawl that had escaped the depredations of Félicité. Charles refused to give it her; they quarrelled.

She made the first overtures of reconciliation by offering to have the little girl, who could help her in the house, to live with her. Charles consented to this, but when the time for parting came, all his courage failed him. Then there was a final, complete rupture.

All his affections vanished, he clung more closely to the love of his child. She made him anxious, however, for she coughed sometimes, and had red spots on her cheeks.

Opposite his house, flourishing and merry, was the family of the chemist, with whom everything was prospering. Napoléon helped him in the laboratory, Athalie embroidered him a skull-cap, Irma cut out rounds of paper to cover the preserves, and Franklin recited Pythagoras' table in a breath. He was the happiest of fathers, the most fortunate of men.

Not so! A secret ambition devoured him. Homais hankered after the cross of the Legion of Honour. He had plenty of claims to it.

"First, having at the time of the cholera distinguished myself by a boundless devotion; second, by having published, at my expense, various works of public utility, such as" (and he recalled his pamphlet entitled, "Cider, its manufacture and effects," besides observations on the lanigerous plant-louse, sent to the Academy; his volume of statistics, and down to his pharmaceutical thesis); "without counting that I am a member of several learned societies" (he was member of a single one).

"In short!" he cried, making a pirouette, "if it were only for distinguishing myself at fires!"

Then Homais inclined towards the Government. He secretly did the prefect great service during the elections. He sold himself—in a word, prostituted himself. He even addressed a petition to the sovereign in which he implored him to "do him justice"; he called him "our good king," and compared him to Henry IV.

And every morning the druggist rushed for the paper to see if his nomination were in it. It was never there. At last, unable to bear it any longer, he had a grass plot in his garden designed to represent the Star of the Cross of Honour, with two little strips of grass running from the top to imitate the ribband. He walked round it with folded arms, meditating on the folly of the Government and the ingratitude of men.

From respect, or from a sort of sensuality that made him carry on his investigations slowly, Charles had not yet opened the secret drawer of a rosewood desk which Emma had generally used. One day, however, he sat down before it, turned the key, and pressed the spring. All Léon's letters were there. There could be no doubt this time. He devoured them to the very last, ransacked every corner, all the furniture, all the drawers, behind the walls, sobbing, crying aloud, distraught, mad. He found a box and broke it open with a kick. Rodolphe's portrait flew full in his face in the midst of the overturned love letters.

People wondered at his despondency. He never went out, saw no one, refused even to visit his patients. Then they said "he shut himself up to drink."

Sometimes, however, some curious person climbed on to the garden hedge, and saw with amazement this long-bearded, shabbily clothed, wild man, who wept aloud as he walked up and down.

In the evening in summer he took his little girl with him and led her to the cemetery. They came back at nightfall, when the only light left in the Place was that in Binet's window.

The voluptuousness of his grief was, however, incomplete, for he had no one near him to share it, and he paid visits to Madame Lefrançois to be able to speak of *her*. But the landlady only listened with half an ear, having troubles like himself. For Lheureux had at last established the "Favorites du Commerce," and Hivert, who enjoyed a great reputation for successfully doing errands, insisted on a rise of wages, and was threatening to go over "to the opposition shop."

One day when he had gone to the market at Argueil to sell his horse—his last resource—he met Rodolphe.

They both turned pale when they caught sight of one another. Rodolphe, who had only sent his card, first stammered some apologies, then grew bolder, and even pushed his assurance (it was in the month of August and very hot) to the length of inviting him to have a bottle of beer at the public-house.

Leaning on the table opposite him, he chewed his cigar as he talked, and Charles was lost in reverie at this face that she had loved. He seemed to see again something of her in it. It was a marvel to him. He would have liked to have been this man.

The other went on talking agriculture, cattle, pasturage, filling out with banal phrases all the gaps where an allusion might slip in. Charles was not listening to him; Rodolphe noticed it, and he followed the succession of memories that crossed his face. This gradually grew redder; the nostrils throbbed fast, the lips quivered. There was at last a moment when Charles, full of a sombre fury, fixed his eyes on Rodolphe, who, in something of fear, stopped talking. But soon the same look of weary lassitude came back to his face.

"I don't blame you," he said.

Rodolphe was dumb. And Charles, his head in his hands, went on in a broken voice, and with the resigned accent of infinite sorrow—

"No, I don't blame you now."

He even added a fine phrase, the only one he ever made—

"It is the fault of fatality!"

Rodolphe, who had managed the fatality, thought the remark very off-hand from a man in his position, comic even, and a little mean.

The next day Charles went to sit down on the seat in the arbour. Rays of light were straying through the trellis, the vine leaves threw their shadows on the sand, the jasmines perfumed the air, the heavens were blue, Spanish flies buzzed round the lilies in bloom, and Charles was suffocating like a youth beneath the vague love influences that filled his aching heart.

At seven o'clock little Berthe, who had not seen him all the afternoon, went to fetch him to dinner.

His head was thrown back against the wall, his eyes closed, his mouth open, and in his hand was a long tress of black hair.

"Come along, papa," she said.

And thinking he wanted to play, she pushed him gently. He fell to the ground. He was dead.

Thirty-six hours after, at the druggist's request, Monsieur Canivet came thither. He made a post-mortem and found nothing.

When everything had been sold, twelve francs seventy-five centimes remained, that served to pay for Mademoiselle Bovary's going to her grandmother. The good woman died the same year; old Rouault was paralysed, and it was an aunt who took charge of her. She is poor, and sends her to a cotton-factory to earn a living.

Since Bovary's death three doctors have followed one another at Yonville without any success, so severely did Homais attack them. He has an enormous practice; the authorities treat him with consideration, and public opinion protects him.

He has just received the cross of the Legion of Honour.

THE END

SALAMMBÔ

I

THE FEAST

It was in Hamilcar's gardens, at Megara, on the outskirts of Carthage.

The soldiers whom he had commanded in Sicily were celebrating with a great feast the anniversary of the battle of Eryx.

The captains, wearing bronze cothurnes, were seated in the central avenue, beneath a purple canopy fringed with gold, extending from the stable walls on one side to the first terrace of the palace on the other; while the majority of the common soldiers were dispersed under the trees. Farther on in the gardens were a number of flat-roofed structures, comprising wine-presses, wine-cellars, bakeries, warehouses, and arsenals. There were also a court for elephants, pits for ferocious animals, and a prison for slaves.

The kitchens were surrounded by fig-trees; beyond, a sycamore grove extended to masses of verdure, wherein the pomegranate shone in the midst of white tufts of cotton plants; vines laden with grapes encircled the branches of the pines; a field of roses bloomed beneath the plane trees, and here and there, appearing above the green grass, lilies waved gracefully. The pathways were strewn with black sand mixed with powdered coral, and through the centre, from end to end of this vast park, an avenue of cypress trees formed a double colonnade of green obelisks.

Hamilcar's palace, built of yellow-spotted Numidian marble, of four terraced stories, towered above a foundation of huge courses of stone; its grand, straight, ebony stairway, bearing on the corner of each step the prow of a vanquished galley; its red doors quartered with black crosses, protected at the base from scorpions by brass grillages, and the openings at the top masked by the trellises of golden baguettes—seemed to the soldiers, in its display of barbaric opulence, as solemn and impenetrable as the face of Hamilcar.

At daybreak the convalescents who had slept in the temple of Eschmoûn set out to attend the feast, dragging themselves on their crutches to the gardens.

By all the diverse pathways soldiers poured forth incessantly, like torrents precipitated from heights into a lake. Bewildered kitchen-slaves, half-naked, could be seen running about among the trees in confusion, and the startled gazelles fled in terror over the lawns.

The sun was setting, and the perfume of the lemon-trees rendered even heavier and more oppressive the exhalations of this seething, perspiring crowd. Here, upon this festal occasion, men of all nations were gathered together: Ligurians, Lusitanians, Balearic warriors, Negroes, and Roman fugitives. Here could be heard, mingled with the heavy Dorian *patois*, the

Celtic syllables, rattling like battle-chariots; and the Ionian terminations, clashing with the consonants of the desert, harsh as the yelpings of jackals. Greeks could be recognised by their slender figures; Egyptians by their high, square shoulders; Cantabrians by their broad, muscular legs; Carians proudly swayed their helmet plumes; Cappadocian archers were conspicuous by the large flowers painted over their entire bodies; and some Lydians feasted arrayed in women's robes, slippers, and earrings; others had daubed themselves with vermilion, resembling, as they moved about, animated coral statues.

While feasting they stretched themselves out upon cushions, or ate as they squatted around large trays; or even lay flat on their stomachs, and pulled toward themselves pieces of meat, which they munched, leaning on their elbows, in the pacific attitude of lions devouring their prey. The late comers, standing against the trees, looked wistfully at the low tables, half concealed beneath scarlet cloths, and the sumptuous repast, eagerly awaiting their turns.

Hamilcar's kitchens being insufficient for this occasion, the Grand Council had supplied slaves, utensils, and couches. Bright, huge fires blazed in the centre of the gardens, before which oxen were roasting, giving the appearance of a battle-field upon which the dead were being burned. On the tables were placed loaves of bread sprinkled with anise-seed, alternating with large cheeses, heavier than discs. Bowls of wine, and canthari filled with water, were placed by the side of gold filigree baskets containing flowers.

The delight of being able at last, after prolonged privations, to gorge themselves at will, dilated the eyes of these starving warriors, and here and there a song burst forth. The absence of Hamilcar added to the freedom with which they ate, drank, and caroused.

First came birds, covered with green sauce, served in red clay dishes embellished with black designs; then all species of shell-fish caught on the Punic coast, followed by broths of barley, wheat, and beans; and snails dressed with cumin, on plates of yellow amber. Later the tables were covered with every variety of meats: roasted antelopes, with their horns—peacocks in their plumage—whole sheep cooked in sweet wine—legs of camels and buffaloes—hedgehogs, with garum sauce—fried grasshoppers, and preserved dormice. In Tamrapanni wooden bowls, large pieces of fat floated in the midst of saffron—every dish overflowed with pickles, truffles, and assafœtida; pyramids of fruit rolled over honey-cakes; nor were forgotten some of the red-haired, plump little dogs fattened on olive-lees; a Carthaginian dainty which was detested by all other nationalities.

Surprise at these new dishes excited the greed of the multitude. Gauls, with their long hair coiled up on the top of their heads, snatched from each other watermelons and lemons, which they crunched, rinds and all; Negroes, who had never before seen lobsters, tore their faces with the red claws; shaven-faced Greeks, whiter than marble, threw behind them the leavings from their plates, and herdsmen of Bruttium clothed in wolves' skins silently devoured their portions with their faces buried in the food.

Night fell. The canopy that had been spread over the cypress avenue was now withdrawn, and torches were lit. The wavering petroleum lights, burning in porphyry vases, frightened in the tops of the cedars the apes sacred to the moon; the terrified chatterings of these animals filled the soldiers with mirth. Oblong flames trembled over the brazen cuirasses; all manner of scintillations flashed from the dishes incrusted with precious gems. Bowls bordered with convex mirrors multiplied the reflected images, enlarging every object so strangely as to attract the attention of the soldiers, who, in astonishment, crowded around, gazing at themselves, or making grimaces to provoke the laughter of their comrades by the grotesque reflections. They tossed to each other across the tables the ivory stools and the gold spatulas. They swallowed, in gluttonish mouthfuls, all the Greek wine in the wine-skins; the Campanian wines held in amphoras, and that from Cantabria, which was drawn from casks; as well as the jujube, cinnamon, and lotus wines. What was not drunk was spilled upon the ground, forming puddles in which the rioters would slip. In dense vapours, the fumes of the viands, mixing with the heavy breaths, rose in the foliage. In a nameless clatter mingled the crunching of jaws, din of words, outburst of songs, clinking of cups, crashing of Campanian vases—scattered in a thousand fragments—and the limpid ring of large silver plates. As their intoxication increased they recalled to memory more vividly the injustice of Carthage.

The Republic, exhausted by the war, had permitted all the returning troops to gather in the city. General Gisco, however, had taken the precaution of sending them back in detachments, in order to facilitate their speedy payment and discharge; but the Council, believing that they would succeed in getting these warriors to consent to some compromise, had detained them. At present dissatisfaction was caused by the inability to pay them. This war debt was confused in the minds of the people with the three thousand two hundred Eubœan talents exacted by Lutatius; hence these soldiers, like the Romans, were considered enemies to Carthage. The Mercenaries comprehended this feeling, therefore their indignation burst forth in menaces and irruptions. Finally, they demanded a reunion, to celebrate one of their victories: the peace party yielded, hoping at the same time to revenge itself upon Hamilcar, who had so strongly supported the war. It had been terminated contrary to his policy and efforts; so much so that despairing of help from Carthage, he placed Gisco in command of the Mercenaries, himself continuing to march toward the amber country. The Council, desirous of attracting upon Hamilcar some of the hatred the soldiers bore them, appointed his palace gardens as the place for the festival. The excessive expense would have to be defrayed in greater part by Hamilcar.

Proud of having made the Republic obey their demands on this score, the Mercenaries believed that they would also ultimately return to their native countries, with the payment for their blood in the hoods of their cloaks. But now their hardships, seen through the vapours of drunkenness, seemed prodigious, and but poorly recompensed. They displayed their wounds, recounted their combats, their journeys, and the hunts peculiar to the various countries; imitating the cries and leaps of ferocious animals. They made indecent wagers, immersing their heads in amphoras of wine, there remaining drinking like thirsty dromedaries, without intermission. A Lusitanian, of gigantic height, carrying a man upon each arm, ran across the tables, the while spurting out fire from his nostrils. Lacædemonians who had not removed their cuirasses leaped about with heavy strides; others advanced like lewd women making obscene gestures; some, stripped naked, wrestled like gladiators in the midst of the feast; and a company of Greeks danced around a vase upon which were nymphs; meantime a Negro pounded lustily on a brass buckler with a beef-bone.

Suddenly a plaintive song, strong and soft, was heard, rising and falling on the air like the fluttering wings of a wounded bird. It was the voice of the slaves imprisoned in the *ergastulum*.

Some soldiers bounded off, bent upon liberating them. Presently they returned, shouting, and chasing before them, through the dust, a score of men, distinguished by the paler hue of their faces. These slaves wore on their shaven heads little, conical-shaped, black felt caps; their feet were shod in wooden sandals, and as they ran, their chains clattered like the iron felloes of a moving chariot. Thus driven, they finally reached the cypress avenue, where they were lost in the crowd that surrounded and questioned them.

One of them stood apart from the others. Through his tattered tunic could be seen on his shoulders the weals of long gashes; with chin lowered he looked suspiciously about him as he half-closed his eyelids, in the glare of the torches; but when he saw that none of the armed men wanted to harm him, a deep sigh of relief escaped from his breast, and he stammered and mouthed, while tears bathed his face; then, suddenly seizing a full cantharus by its rings, he raised it up on high, straight in the air, revealing chains dangling from his wrists.

He gazed upward, still holding the cup, as he cried: "All hail! first, to thee, Baal Eschmoûn, liberator, whom the people of my country call Æsculapius! Hail! ye, genii of the springs! of the light! and of the woods! and ye, gods, hidden beneath the mountains and in the caverns of the earth! and ye strong men in shining armour, who have released me!"

He dropped the cantharus, and told his story. His name was Spendius; he had been captured by the Carthaginians during the battle of the Ægatian islands. He spoke Greek, Ligurian, and Phœnician. Once more he thanked the Mercenaries, kissed their hands, felicitated them on their feast; but expressed surprise that he did not see the golden cups of the Sacred Legion. These cups were embellished on each of their six golden faces by an emerald vine, and belonged to a militia exclusively comprised of young patricians of the tallest stature. To see them was a privilege, con-

sidered almost a sacerdotal honour, and nothing in the treasury of the
Republic was so coveted by the Mercenaries. They detested the Legion
because of this possession, and had been known to risk their lives for the
ineffable pleasure of merely drinking out of these cups. Incited by the
words of the slave, the soldiers demanded that the cups should be brought
to them. The slaves said that they were deposited with the Syssites, companies of merchants who ate in common; but at this hour all the members
of the Syssites slept.

"Let them be wakened!" responded the Mercenaries.

After another attempt, one of the slaves explained that the cups were
locked up in a temple.

"Let the temple be opened!" replied the soldiers. Then the slaves
trembled, avowing that veritably the cups were in the possession of General
Gisco. They yelled, "Let him bring them!"

Presently Gisco appeared at the end of the garden, with an escort of
the Sacred Legion: his ample black mantle was adjusted on his head by a
gold mitre starred with precious stones; and its folds fell all around him,
reaching down to his horse's hoofs and blending in the distance with the
shadows of night. His white beard, the radiancy of his coiffure, and his
triple collar of wide blue plaques, which, agitated by the motion of his
horse, struck against his breast, alone were visible.

As he appeared, the soldiers saluted him with great cheers, crying out:
"The cups! The cups!"

He began by declaring "that if one only considered their courage, they
certainly merited the cups,"—at which the crowd fairly howled with joy.
"He knew it well, he who had commanded them, and had returned with
the last cohort, on the last galley!"

"It is true! it is true!" they cried out.

"Nevertheless," continued Gisco, "the Republic respects the divisions
of the people, their customs, and their religions; at Carthage they were
free. But the gold cups of the Sacred Legion, they were personal property."

Suddenly, from beside Spendius, a Gaul darted across the tables, making
straight for Gisco, whom he threatened with two naked swords. Without
interrupting himself, the General struck this man over the head with his
heavy ivory staff, felling him to the ground; at this the Gauls all shrieked,
and their fury communicating itself to the other soldiers, they turned upon
the Legionaries.

Gisco shrugged his shoulders as he saw his escort grow pale: his courage would be vain against these foolish, exasperated brutes; whereas, later
perhaps he might avenge himself by some strategy; so he made a sign to
his guards, and they all slowly moved away. When under the gateway,
he turned toward the Mercenaries, and cried out: "You shall repent of
this!"

The feast was resumed; but the revellers were uneasy; Gisco might return,
and by surrounding the suburb which impinged on the last ramparts,
crush them against the walls. They felt alone, despite their numbers; and

the vast city, with its massive piles of stairways and lofty black mansions sleeping under them in the shadow, filled them with terror: but yet more ferocious than the city, or its people, were its mysterious gods. In the distance ships' lanterns glided about the harbour, and lights could be seen in the temple of Khamoûn. Their troubled thoughts reverted to Hamilcar. Where was he? Why had he abandoned them just as peace was declared? Doubtless his dissensions with the Council had been a trick planned for their destruction. They exasperated each other by the recital of their personal wrongs, and their insatiable hatred centred itself upon him.

At this stage a crowd was attracted under the plane trees by a Negro who rolled about beating the ground frantically with his arms and feet, his eyes fixed, his neck contorted, and foaming at the mouth. Some one cried out that the man had been poisoned; then they all believed themselves to be poisoned, and fell upon the slaves. A vertigo of destruction whirled over this drunken army; they struck at random, breaking, maiming, killing. Some, moved by diabolical impulse, hurled torches into the foliage; others leaned over the balustrade of the lions' pit, ruthlessly killing the animals with arrows; and the most venturesome recklessly ran to the elephants, and sought to hew off their trunks and destroy their tusks.

Meanwhile a group of Balearic slingers, to pillage more conveniently, had turned a corner of the palace, but were hindered from proceeding by a high barrier constructed of Indian cane. However, not to be daunted, they severed, by the aid of poniards, the leather thongs holding the hedge together. This obstacle surmounted, they found themselves under the façade that looked toward Carthage, in another garden filled with tall vegetation. Rows of white flowers succeeded one another, throwing shadows on the azure-coloured ground like trails of shooting stars. Shadowy bushes exhaled honey-sweet, warm odours; and the trunks of trees, daubed with cinnabar, resembled blood-stained columns. In the centre were twelve copper pedestals, each one supporting a large glass bowl; the ruddy gleams filled and flickered confusedly in these hollow bowls, like enormous throbbing eye-balls. The soldiers carried torches as they stumbled down a deeply furrowed declivity. They descried a little lake, divided into numerous basins by partitions of blue stone. The water contained therein was so limpid, that the reflected torch flames quivered to the very bottom, striking on a bed of white shells and gold dust. Suddenly the water set up a bubbling, and luminous spangles glistened, as large fish, with precious stones in their gills, came swimming to the surface.

The soldiers, laughing boisterously, thrust their fingers through the fishes' gills, and carried them to the tables. These fish belonged to the Barca family, and were reputed descendants of the primordial eel-pout, which had hatched the mystic egg wherein was hidden the goddess.

The idea of committing a sacrilege revived the gluttony of the Mercenaries. They kindled fires under the brass vases, and entertained themselves by watching the beautiful fish flounder about and perish in the boiling water. The throng of soldiers surged forward. Fear no longer deterred them. They again commenced their carousal and drinking. Perfumes trickled down over their foreheads, falling in large drops, moistening their tattered tunics. They leaned their fists on the tables, that seemed to them to oscillate like ships; while their large, drunken eyes turned and roved about as though seeking to devour with their glances all that they had not the power to take away. Others walked about in the midst of the plates on the crimson table-covers, breaking, with wanton kicks, the Tyrian glass phials and the ivory benches. Songs intermingled with the death-rattle of the attendant slaves, breathing their last amid the shattered cups. Still the soldiers demanded more wine, more meat, more gold. They shouted for women—raving deliriously in a hundred languages. Some believed themselves in the vapour baths, deceived by the fumes floating about them; or even, whilst observing the foliage, fancied that they were engaged in hunting, and thus deluded, would rush violently upon their comrades, thinking them to be ferocious beasts. Steadily the torches were igniting the foliage: the fire spread from tree to tree, until the tall masses of verdure resembled a volcano beginning to smoke. The clamor redoubled, the wounded lions roared, and the elephants trumpeted through the darkness.

By a single flash the palace was suddenly illuminated to its highest terrace; the centre door at the top opened, and a woman—the daughter of Hamilcar—robed in black garments, appeared on the threshold. She descended down the stairway that traversed obliquely the third story, then the second and the first; pausing on the last terrace at the top of the galley staircase, motionless, head drooping, looking down upon the soldiers. Behind her on both sides were two long processions of pale men, clothed in white red-fringed robes, hanging straight to their feet; their heads and eyebrows were shaven; their hands, in which they carried enormous lyres, glittered with rings. In a shrill voice they sang a hymn to the divinity of Carthage. These were the eunuch priests of the temple of Tanit, often summoned by Salammbô to her palace.

At last she descended the stairway of the galleys, followed by the priests; and moved forward under the cypress trees, between the tables at which the captains were seated, who drew back slightly as they watched her pass. Her hair was powdered with violet dust, and, according to the fashion of Canaanite maidens, it was gathered up in the form of a tower on the crown of her head, making her appear still taller: strands of pearls fastened to her temples fell to the corners of her mouth—as rosy as a half-opened pomegranate; on her bosom she wore a collection of luminous gems, which appeared in their medley as the scales of a sea-eel; her sleeveless tunic, made of a black tissue, was starred with red flowers, and exposed her bare arms, bedecked with diamonds. Between her ankles she wore a gold chainlet to regulate the length of her steps; and her voluminous dark purple mantle, of an unknown fabric, trailed, making at each step a wide billow behind her.

From time to time the priests played on their lyres subdued, almost soundless, chords. During the intervals of the music could be detected the clinking of her gold chainlet and the rhythmic patter of her papyrus sandals. No person as yet recognised her. It was only known that she lived in seclusion, devoted to pious practices. During the nights the soldiers had seen her between the curling smoke arising from fuming censers, kneeling before the stars, on the summit of the palace.

At this moment the moon made her appear very pale, and something of the gods seemed to envelope her like a subtle mist. Her eyes seemed to penetrate far away beyond terrestrial space. She advanced with bent head, holding in her right hand a small ebony lyre. They heard her murmur:

"Dead! all dead! No longer will you obey my voice when I sit on the lake shore and throw pips of watermelons into your mouths! In the depths of your eyes, more limpid than the drops of purling streams, rolled the mystery of Tanit!" Then she called her fish by their several names, which were the names of the months—"Siv! Sivan! Tammoûz! Eloul! Tischri! Schebar!—Ah, goddess, have pity on me!"

Without understanding her meaning, the soldiers crowded around her, amazed at her attire. She cast upon them a long, frightened look; then, drooping her head to her bosom, she threw out her arms, repeating many times: "What have you done? What have you done? For your enjoyment bread, meat, oil, and malobathrum were provided from the storehouses; I even had oxen brought from Hecatompylus, and sent hunters into the desert that you might have all sorts of game."

Her voice grew louder, her cheeks blazed, as she continued: "Where, then, think you that you are now? Is this a conquered city, or the palace of a master? And what master! Hamilcar, the Suffet, my father, servitor of the Baalim! Your weapons now reek with the blood of his slaves, when it was he who refused them to Lutatius! Know you of one of your own countries greater in the conduct of battles? Behold! the steps of our palace are laden with the trophies of our victories! Go to, burn it to the ground! I will take away with me the genius of our mansion—my black serpent—who sleeps up there in the lotus leaves; for when I whistle he will follow me, and when I enter my galley he will glide in the wake of the vessel on the foam of the waves."

Her delicate nostrils palpitated. She crushed her nails against the jewels of her bosom. Her eyes became suffused as she continued: "Alas! Carthage! lamentable city! no longer hast thou for thy defence the strong men of former times, who traversed beyond the oceans to build in thine honour temples on foreign shores. All the lands have grown by thee, and wave with thy harvests, and the plains of the seas are ploughed by thine oars!"

Then she began to chant the adventures of Melkarth, the god of the Sidonians and founder of her family. She told how he had ascended the mountains of Ersiphonia, journeyed to Tartessus, and waged war against Masisabal to avenge the Queen of the Serpents.

"He pursued the female monster, whose tail undulated like a rivulet of silver over dead leaves into the forest; and he came to a prairie the colour of blood, over which the moon shone refulgent within a pale circle; and there he found women, half dragons, grouped around a huge fire, poised erect on their tails, thrusting out and curving their scarlet tongues, forked like fishermen's harpoons, to the very edge of the flames."

Then, without pausing, Salammbô recounted how Melkarth, after vanquishing Masisabal, had put the decapitated head of his victim at the prow of his ship: "At each surge of the waves it was immersed under the foam; and it was embalmed by the sun until it became more enduring than gold, yet tears never ceased flowing from the eyes, but dropped continuously into the water." All this she chanted in old Canaanite dialect, which the Barbarians did not understand.

They inquired of one another what she could be saying to them, and why she accompanied her words with such frightful gestures. Mounted upon the tables, the benches, and the branches of sycamores, with open mouths and outstretched necks, they endeavoured to grasp the vague stories that drifted before their imaginations, through the obscurity of the theogonies, like phantoms draped in the clouds.

Only the beardless priests understood Salammbô. Their shrivelled hands tremblingly clutched the strings of their lyres, upon which from time to time they struck a mournful chord; they were more feeble than old women, and shivered as much from fear as with mystic emotion, not knowing what the soldiers might be tempted to do. The Barbarians noticed them not, for they were intent in listening to the chanting maiden.

None watched her more fixedly than a young Numidian chief who sat among the captains, surrounded by the soldiers of his own nation. His girdle so bristled with darts that it made a projection beneath his wide mantle, fastened to his temples by a leather lacing; this garment divided and swung down over his shoulders in such a manner as to keep effectually his face in shadow, concealing all but his gleaming eyes. It was by chance that he attended this feast. His father, conforming to the custom adopted by kings of sending their sons to live in noble families in other dominions, in order to prepare for noble alliances, had sent him to abide with Barca. During the six months that Narr' Havas had been in Carthage, he had never before seen Salammbô; and now sitting on his heels, his head resting against the handles of his javelins, he gazed at her with nostrils distended, like a leopard crouching in a jungle.

At the other side of the tables was a Libyan of colossal stature, with short, curly black hair. He was unarmed, save for his military jacket, the brass plates of which were fraying the purple covering of the couch. A necklace of silver moons was entangled in the hairs of his breast; splashes of blood spotted his face; he leaned on his left elbow, with wide open mouth, and smiled.

Salammbô ceased to use sacred rhythm, resorting successively to the various barbaric dialects, and with delicate subtlety seeking to soften their anger, speaking Greek to the Greeks; then turning toward the Ligurians, the Campanians, and the Negroes in turn, till each, in listening, found in her voice the sweetness of his native tongue.

Carried away by the memories of Carthage, she chanted the old battles against Rome, thus gaining their applause. Becoming excited by the flashing of the naked swords, she cried out, with open arms. Her lyre fell, then relapsing into silence, she pressed her heart with both hands, thus resting for some minutes with closed eyes as though to surfeit the agitation of all these warriors.

Mâtho, the Libyan, leaned toward her; involuntarily she approached him, and moved by recognition of his pride, she poured out for him into a gold cup a long stream of wine in token of her reconciliation with the army.

"Drink!" she said.

He took the proffered cup, and was carrying it to his lips, when a Gaul, the same Gisco had wounded, slapped him across the shoulders, uttering in a jovial manner insinuating pleasantries in his native language. Spendius, who was near by, volunteered to interpret.

"Speak," said Mâtho.

"The gods be with you, for you are about to become rich. When will the bridal be?"

"What bridal?" asked Mâtho.

"Thine; for with us," said the Gaul, "when a woman offers drink to a warrior she proffers him her couch."

Spendius had hardly interpreted before Narr' Havas sprang forward, pulling from his belt a javelin, poised his right foot on the edge of the table, and hurled the weapon at Mâtho. The javelin sped between the cups, and passed through the Libyan's arm, nailing it firmly to the table, with such momentum as to cause the shaft to vibrate in the air. Mâtho quickly jerked it out; but, as he was weaponless, in his rage he lifted up the heavily laden table, and pitched it against Narr' Havas. In the midst of the crowd that rushed between the two infuriated men, Numidians and the soldiers mingled so closely that they could not draw their swords. Mâtho moved forward, dealing heavy blows with his head. Finally, when he lifted his face to look about, Narr' Havas had disappeared; Salammbô had also gone. Turning his eyes toward the palace, he noticed that the red door near the summit, quartered with a black cross, was just closing, and he darted off toward it. He could be seen running between the prows of the galleys, disappearing and reappearing successively the length of the three stairways till he at last reached the red door; this he threw himself against with all his weight, but to no purpose. Panting, breathless, he leaned against the wall to keep from falling.

A man had followed him, and as he crossed the shadows—for the lights of the feast were obscured by an angle of the palace—he recognised Spendius.

"Begone!" he said.

The slave, without answering, began to tear his tunic with his teeth; then kneeling beside Mâtho he took hold of his arm, gently feeling in the dark to discover the wound. Under a ray of moonlight that just then gleamed between the clouds, Spendius perceived in the middle of the arm a gaping wound; he rolled around it the strips he had torn off from his tunic; but Mâtho irritably said:

"Leave me! leave me!"

"No!" replied the slave, "you delivered me from the *ergastulum*. I am yours! you are my master! Command me!"

Keeping close against the wall, Mâtho made a circuit of the terrace, listening at every step; darting at intervals glances through the golden trellises into the silent apartments. At last he paused in despair.

"Listen," said the slave. "Do not despise me for my weakness; I have lived in this palace, I can crawl like a viper between its walls. Come, there is in the Chamber of the Ancestors an ingot of gold under each slab, and an underground passage leading to their tombs."

"Well, what of that?" asked Mâtho.

Spendius was silent.

Standing on the terrace, an immense expanse of shadow spread out before them that seemed full of vague forms, like the gigantic billows of a black, petrified ocean. Toward the east a luminous bar appeared; and to the left, the canals of Megara began to outline with their white sinuosities the verdant gardens. The conical roofs of the heptagonal temples, the stairways, the terraces, the ramparts, all became palely defined in the early dawn; and surrounding the peninsula of Carthage a girdle of white foam curled, and the foam of emerald sea seemed congealing in the coolness of morning. In proportion as the rosy sky widened, the tall mansions climbing up the slope rose higher and massed together, like a herd of black goats descending the mountains. The deserted streets stretched out; motionless palm trees jutted beyond the walls; the overflowing cisterns glistened like silver shields lost in the courtyards; on the promontory of Hermæum the lighthouse beacon grew dimmer. On the summit of the Acropolis in the cypress-groves the horses of Eschmoûn just sensing the light, placed the hoofs of their forefeet upon the marble parapet, neighing toward the rising sun. It appeared. Spendius lifted his arms and uttered a cry of adoration.

All the universe seemed pulsating in a ruddy flood, for the god, as if rending himself, poured forth in fulsome rays upon Carthage the golden rain of his veins. The prows of the galleys glittered, the roof of Khamoûn appeared ablaze, and through the open doors lights could be descried in the interior of the temple. The wheels of large chariots coming from the country to the city marts, rumbled over the pavements; dromedaries loaded with baggage descended the slopes; money-changers in the thoroughfares took down the weather-boards from their shops; storks took to flight, and white sails fluttered, athrill with the glory of day.

From the groves of Tanit could be heard the tambourines of the sacred courtesans; and at the point of Mappals the furnaces for the baking of clay coffins began to smoke.

Spendius leaning over the terrace, gnashed his teeth, repeating, "Ah, yes, . . . yes, . . . master, I understand why you just now disdained to pillage the mansion."

Mâtho was aroused by the murmur of the man's voice, yet he did not seem to understand.

Spendius resumed, "Ah, what wealth! and the men who possess it have not even the weapons to protect it." Then, with his right hand extended, he pointed out some people who were crawling on the sand outside of the pier, seeking for gold dust.

"Look!" he exclaimed, "the Republic is like those wretched ones grovelling on the sea-beach. She also plunges her greedy arms into the sea-sands, and the roar of the billows so fills her ears, that she hears not behind her the step of a master!"

Drawing Mâtho along to the end of the terrace, the slave pointed out the garden wherein the sun shone on the soldiers' swords that were hanging in the trees.

"But here be strong men, made reckless by hatred; and they owe no allegiance to Carthage, neither families, nor oaths, nor gods!"

Mâtho still leaned against the wall. Spendius drew nearer, continuing in a low voice:

"Do you comprehend me, soldier? We shall go about arrayed in purple like satraps. We shall bathe in perfumes. I too shall have my slaves! Do you not weary of drinking camp vinegar, and of the sound of the trumpets? You think to repose later, do you not? When they pull off your cuirass to throw your body to the vultures! or possibly when leaning on a staff, blind, feeble, lame, you hobble about from portal to portal and recount to the pickle vendors and to the little children the tale of your youth! Recall all the injustice of your chiefs, the encampments in the snow, the forced marches, exposure to the sun, the tyrannies of discipline, and the eternal threat of the cross! After so much misery, a collar of honour is given to you, as one hangs a girdle of bells around asses' necks to divert them on their toilsome marches and render them less sensible to their fatigue. A man like you, braver than Pyrrhus! If you desire no more, very good! Ah, but you would be happy in the great, cool halls, listening to the sound of lyres as you repose on flowers, surrounded by buffoons and women! Do not tell me that is impossible! Have not the Mercenaries already taken possession of Rhegium and other strong places in Italy? Who can hinder you? Hamilcar is absent; the people execrate the Rich; Gisco has no power over the cowards who surround him; but you have courage, the soldiers will obey you. Command them! Carthage is ours; let us fall upon it!"

"No!" said Mâtho; "the curse of Moloch weighs upon me. I felt it in her eyes, and just now I saw a black ram recoil in the temple!" then adding, as he looked around him: "Where is she?"

Spendius now understood that a great inquietude absorbed Mâtho, and he dared not speak again.

Behind him the trees still smoked; and from the charred branches carcasses of half-burned apes tumbled down from time to time among the dishes; drunken soldiers with open mouths snored by the side of corpses; and those who were awake lowered their heads, dazzled by the glare of the sun. The trampled earth was covered with bloody pools. The elephants swayed their bleeding trunks between the pickets of their paddocks. In the open granaries could be seen sacks of wheat scattered about, and under the gateways a compact line of chariots heaped up by the Barbarians; in the cedars, peacocks perched, spreading their tails and beginning to utter their cry.

Mâtho's immobility astonished Spendius. He was now even paler than before, and his eyes fixedly followed some object apparently visible on the horizon, as he leaned with both hands on the edge of the terrace, Spendius also, leaning over, discovered what thus occupied him. In the distance a point of gold turned in the dust on the road leading to Utica. It was the axle of a chariot drawn by two mules, guided by a slave who ran at the end of the pole, holding the bridle. Two women were seated in the chariot. The manes of the mules were puffed out in Persian fashion between their ears, beneath a network of blue pearls.

Spendius, recognising them, suppressed a cry. A wide veil floated behind in the breeze.

II

AT SICCA

THE MERCENARIES left Carthage two days later. Each soldier had received a piece of money, upon the stipulated condition that he would go into camp at Sicca, and they had been told, with all manner of fawning:

"You are the saviours of Carthage, but you will certainly starve her if you remain here, for the city will become insolvent. You must, for your own sake withdraw; and by such a consideration you will secure the goodwill of the Republic. We will immediately levy taxes to complete your payment, and galleys shall be equipped to conduct you to your native countries."

The soldiers did not know what to reply to such talk. These men, accustomed to war, weary of sojourning in the city, were not difficult to convince. The entire populace of Carthage mounted on the city walls to watch them depart, as they defiled through the street of Khamoûn by the gate of Cirta, pell-mell—archers with hoplites, captains with common soldiers, Lusitanians with Greeks. They marched boldly, making their heavy cothurnes ring on the pavements. Their armour was dented by the catapults, their faces were sunburnt from long exposure on battle-fields.

From their mouths, covered with heavy beards, rasping yells issued; their torn coats of mail rattled upon the hilts of their swords, and through the rents in the metal were revealed naked limbs as terrible as war-engines. Sarissas, spears, felt caps, and bronze helmets all swayed as by a single motion. This long array of armed men poured forth between the six-storied mansions daubed with bitumen, making the very walls crack as they overflowed the street. From behind iron or wicker grills, the women, veiled and silent, watched the Barbarians pass.

The terraces, the fortifications, and the walls were hidden under the throng of Carthaginians attired in black; the sailors' tunics looked like spots of blood amongst this sombre multitude. Children, almost naked, gesticulated in the foliage of the columns, or between the branches of the palm-trees. The Elders took their position on the platforms of the towers; and no one knew why a man with a long beard kept moving from place to place, in a thoughtful attitude. In the distance he appeared indistinct as a phantom, and at times as motionless as the stones.

All were oppressed by the same fear, dreading lest the Barbarians, perceiving themselves to be so strong, might desire to remain. But they departed with such assurance that the Carthaginians were gradually emboldened to mingle with the soldiers, overwhelming them with gifts and protestations. Some in an access of cunning and audacious hypocrisy, begged them not to leave the city. They threw flowers, perfumes, and pieces of money; others gave away their amulets, worn to ward off illness and harm, but first spat upon them three times in order to dispel their intrinsic charm, and attract death; or, to make the hearts of the recipients cowardly, they enclosed jackal's hair in the talismans; others would invoke aloud the blessing of Melkarth, but in a whisper implore his curse.

Following the soldiers came a mass of baggage, beasts of burden, and stragglers; the sick groaned on the backs of dromedaries, while others limped along, supporting themselves on broken spears. The bibulous carried wine-skins, the gluttonous took quarters of meat, cakes, fruits, and butter done up in fig-leaves, and snow packed in canvas bags. Some were observed holding parasols, and others had parrots perched on their shoulders, or were followed by dogs, gazelles, or panthers. Libyan women, mounted on asses, heaped invectives upon the negresses who had forsaken the brothels of Malqua to go with the soldiers; many suckled the infants suspended from their bosoms in a leather leash. Mules, urged by their drivers with the points of spears, bent under the heavy burden of tents heaped on their backs. The train also included a number of varlets and water-carriers, feeble and yellow from fevers, filthy with vermin, the scum of the plebeian Carthaginians who had attached themselves to the Barbarian troops.

As soon as they had all passed out, the gates were closed behind them. Still the people did not descend from the walls. The army spread quickly over the width of the isthmus, and divided in unequal detachments, until the lances appeared like tall blades of grass; finally all were lost to sight in clouds of dust, and the soldiers, looking back at Carthage, could only distinguish its long wall with the vacant battlements outlined against the sky.

Then the Barbarians heard a great outcry; not knowing the exact number of their troops, they thought that some of their comrades had lingered behind in the city to amuse themselves by plundering a temple; they laughed heartily over this idea as they continued on their way. Once more marching together through the open country, they were full of joy, and the Greeks sang the old song of the Mamertines:

> *"With my lance and my sword I sow*
> *And I reap; I am master of the house!*
> *The disarmed must fall at my feet,*
> *And call me 'Lord' and 'King!'"*

They shouted, leaped, and the gayest narrated stories, for the period of their miseries was past. Upon reaching Tunis, some of the soldiers noticed that a troupe of Balearic slingers were missing; but, assuming that they could not be far behind, no further thought was given to them.

At Tunis some lodged in the houses, others camped at the foot of the walls, and the people of the city came out to chat with them. During the entire night fires blazed on the horizon in the direction of Carthage, and the flames, like gigantic torches, stretched over the surface of the motionless lake: yet no one in the army could divine what festival was being celebrated.

The next day the Barbarians crossed a tract of country under complete cultivation. Patricians' farmhouses succeeded one another along the edge of the route, irrigating ditches flowed through palm-groves, olive-trees formed long green lanes, rosy vapours floated in the gorges of the hills, and blue mountains towered up behind. A warm wind blew. Chameleons crawled over the broad cactus-leaves. The Barbarians marched in isolated detachments one after another, at long intervals and with slackening speed. They ate grapes from the vines, slept on the grass, and looked in dull astonishment at the large artificially twisted horns of the cattle, the sheep covered with skins to protect their wool; the furrows, intercrossing in lozenge-like shape; then they scanned the ploughs, with shares like the flukes of a ship's anchor, and the pomegranates watered with silphium. The opulence of the earth, and the wisdom of all these strange agricultural inventions, truly amazed them.

With faces upturned to the stars, they stretched themselves at night upon their unfolded tents, regretfully thinking of the delights of Hamilcar's feast as they fell asleep.

In the middle of the following day they halted on the banks of a river amidst bushes of laurel-roses. Throwing aside their lances, bucklers, and belts, they plunged into the water, shouting as they bathed, drinking out of their helmets or from the stream as they lay flat on the ground, surrounded by the beasts of burden from whose backs the baggage was falling.

Spendius, seated on a dromedary stolen from Hamilcar's parks, spied

Mâtho at a distance, steadily looking in the running water while his mule drank. His wounded arm was hanging against his chest, he was bareheaded, and his face was downcast. The slave ran through the crowd, calling out: "Master! Master!"

Mâtho gave him slight thanks for his blessings. Spendius, little heeding the repulse, followed on behind him, and from time to time turned his eyes restlessly toward Carthage. Spendius was the son of a Greek rhetorician and a Campanian courtesan. He became rich by selling women: then was ruined by a wreck; after which, with the Samnite shepherds, he made war against the Romans, was captured, escaped, and was then retaken. During his captivity he had worked in the quarries, panted in the sweating-baths, shrieked in the tortures, passed into the hands of various masters, and experienced many misfortunes. One day, in despair, he plunged into the sea off a trireme, in which he was one of a squad pulling the oars. The sailors picked him up as drowning, and took him to Carthage to the *ergastulum* of Megara; but as the fugitives were finally to be delivered back to the Romans, he had profited by the prevailing confusion to fly with the soldiers. During the entire march he remained near Mâtho, attending to his food, assisting him to mount and dismount, and at night placing a carpet under his head. Touched by such persistent attentions, Mâtho became gradually less reserved.

Mâtho was born on the Gulf of Syrtis; his father had taken him on a pilgrimage to the temple of Ammon; he had hunted elephants in the forests of the Garamantians; and afterward had engaged himself in the service of Carthage. After the capture of Drepanum he had been appointed tetrarch. The Republic was in Mâtho's debt for four horses, twenty-three *medimni* of wheat, and his pay for one winter. He feared the gods, and wished to die in his native country.

Spendius talked to him of his travels, his people, and the temples that he had visited; he knew many things: how to make sandals, boar-spears, and nets; how to tame wild animals, and the manner of curing fish. From time to time he stopped his narration to give utterance, from the depths of his chest, to a sharp cry, at which Mâtho's mule quickened its pace and the others followed; then Spendius would resume his tale, always agitated by his grief. On the evening of the fourth day be became calm.

Side by side they marched, at the right of the army on the flank of a hill; the plain below stretching away until indistinguishable in the evening mists. The lines of soldiers, defiling below them, made undulations through the darkness. From time to time, when passing over eminences lit by the moon, a star would quiver on the shining points of the moving spears, or for an instant mirror itself on the helmets, then disappear, to be continually succeeded by others. In the distance, the disturbed flocks bleated, and an infinite sweetness seemed to envelop the earth.

Spendius, with raised head, and eyes half-closed, breathed in the fresh breeze with deep inhalations, throwing out his arms, and moving his fingers restlessly, to feel better the caresses of the air gliding over his body. The thirst for vengeance returned, transporting him. He pressed his hand over his mouth to prevent sobs escaping his lips, and thus, half swooning in a delirium, he dropped the dromedary's halter; but the animal continued to move forward with long, regular strides. Mâtho had relapsed into his former sadness; his long legs hung down to the ground, and the grasses, rubbing against his cothurnes, made a constant rustling.

The road seemed to be without end, for at the extremity of a plain it came to a round plateau, then descended into a valley; and the mountains, that in the distance closed in the horizon, as they were approached were displaced, and slipped away farther into the perspective. Now and then a river might be seen flowing through the verdure of tamarisks, only to lose itself at a turn of the hills. Occasionally an immense rock stood up like the prow of a vessel, or like the pedestal of some vanished statue. At regular intervals they passed little quadrangular temples, serving as shelters for the pilgrims journeying to Sicca. They were as firmly closed as tombs. The Libyans knocked loudly against the doors but no one responded from within.

At this point cultivation became rare. They came upon strips of sand bristling with clumps of thorns; flocks of sheep browsed among the stones, watched over by a woman about whose waist was a blue fleece-girdle. When she saw the soldiers' spears between the rocks, she fled screaming.

They were marching through a wide passage, formed by two chains of reddish hillocks, when a nauseous odour struck their nostrils, and they believed that they saw something extraordinary at the top of a carob tree; a lion's head standing up above the foliage.

Hastening toward it, they found a lion attached to a cross by its four limbs, like a criminal; his enormous muzzle hung to his breast, and his fore-paws, half hidden beneath the abundance of his mane, were widely spread apart, like the wings of a bird; under the tightly drawn skin, his ribs protruded and his hind legs were nailed together, but were slightly drawn up; black blood had trickled through the hairs, and collected in stalactites at the end of his tail, which hung straight down the length of the cross. The soldiers crowded around the beast, amusing themselves by calling him: "Consul!" and "Citizen of Rome!" and threw pebbles into his eyes to drive away the swarming gnats.

A hundred paces farther on they came upon two more lions; then presently appeared a long row of crosses supporting yet other lions. Some had been dead a long time, for nothing remained against the wooden crosses save the débris of their skeletons; and their half-corroded jaws were distorted in horrible grimaces. Others were of such huge size that the shafts of the crosses bent beneath their great weight and swayed in the wind, so that flocks of ravenous vultures circled high in the air without daring to alight.

Thus it was that the Carthaginian peasantry revenged themselves when they captured ferocious beasts, hoping by such examples to terrify others. The Barbarians ceased their laughter, relapsing into a deep amazement.

"What people is this," thought they, "which finds amusement in crucifying lions?"

The men from the north were vaguely disturbed, anxious, and already ill. They tore their hands on the aloe thorns, large mosquitoes buzzed in their ears, and dysentery was attacking the army. They were disheartened because they could not yet see Sicca, and fearful lest they should be lost and perish in the desert—the region of sands and terrors. Many would not advance farther; others turned back on the road to Carthage.

On the seventh evening, after following for a long time the base of a mountain, the road abruptly turned to the right, and beyond loomed up a line of walls, resting upon and blending with white rocks. Suddenly the entire city rose before them. Blue, yellow, and white veils fluttered along on the walls in the blush of the evening, as the priestesses of Tanit came forward to receive the soldiers; there they waited, ranged along the length of the rampart, striking tambourines, playing lyres, clattering castanets, while the sun's rays, as it set behind the Numidian mountains, gleamed between the harpstrings and their bare, outstretched arms. At intervals the instruments were silenced; then a strident cry rang out furious and frenzied, a sort of barking produced by clacking their tongues against the corners of their mouths. Those who were not playing remained motionless, leaning on their elbows with their chins pressed in the palms of their hands, more immobile than sphinxes—darting glances from their large, black eyes at the advancing army.

Sicca was a sacred city, but the temple and its dependencies occupied half of its area, so it could not contain such a multitude: therefore the Barbarians camped on the plain, at their ease. Those who were disciplined took up regular quarters; others arranged themselves by nationalities or according to their own fancies.

The Greeks pitched their tents of skin in parallel rows; Iberians arranged their canvas canopies in a circle; Gauls made wooden huts; Libyans constructed cabins of dry stones; and the Negroes dug with their nails holes in the sand in which they slept; and many, not knowing what to do with themselves, wandered about amongst the baggage, and at night lay on the ground rolled up in their ragged mantles.

The plain spread around them, bounded on all sides by mountains; here and there a palm-tree inclined on the top of a sand-hill; firs and oaks dotted the sides of precipices. Sometimes a rain cloud would hang in one part of the sky like a long scarf, while the rest of the country would stay imbued with azure and serenity; then a warm wind would drive before it whirlwinds of sand. A stream descended in cascades from the heights of Sicca, where upon brazen columns rose the golden-roofed temple of the Carthaginian Venus, ruler of the country. The goddess seemed to fill it with her soul. By the heavings of the earth, by the changes of temperature and the play of lights, she manifested the extravagance of her authority with the beauty of her eternal smile. The summits of the mountains were crescent shaped; others resembled the bosom of a woman offering her swelling breasts. Surmounting their fatigues the Barbarians felt an overwhelming sense of this reigning influence, full of soft delights.

Spendius had bought a slave with the money received from the sale of the stolen dromedary. He slept before Mâtho's tent the whole day long; imagining in his dreams that he heard the whirr of the lash, he would wake and pass his hands over the cicatrices on his legs, caused by having so long worn irons; satisfied of his safety, he would fall asleep again.

Mâtho accepted the companionship of Spendius, who, wearing a long sword at his side, escorted him when he went out like a lictor. Sometimes he would even rest his arm on the shoulder of Spendius, who was a small man.

One evening, as they were traversing the camp streets, they saw a number of men robed in white mantles, and in their midst was Narr' Havas, the Numidian prince. Mâtho trembled. "Your sword!" cried he. "I will kill him!"

"Not yet," replied Spendius, restraining him. Narr' Havas was already coming toward them.

He kissed his thumbs as a sign of an alliance, speaking of the anger he had shown at the feast as being due to drunkenness; then he spoke at length against Carthage, but he did not say what had brought him to the Barbarians.

"Was it to betray them or the Republic?" Spendius wondered to himself; and as he anticipated profit from all disturbances, he felt grateful to Narr' Havas for the future treacheries of which he suspected him.

The Numidian chief remained among the Mercenaries; he seemed desirous to attach Mâtho to himself. He sent him fattened goats, gold-dust, and ostrich-plumes. The Libyan, amazed by these tokens of favour, hesitated whether to respond amicably, or to resent them; but Spendius appeased him. Mâtho seemed irresolute and in an invincible torpor, like one who had partaken of some deadly potion, and he allowed himself to be governed by his slave.

One morning, when the three started off on a lion-hunt, Narr' Havas concealed a poniard under his mantle. Spendius, who observed the act, walked continually behind him; hence they returned without the Numidian having had an opportunity to draw the weapon. Upon another occasion Narr' Havas led them a very long way, in fact, to the boundaries of his own kingdom; they entered a narrow gorge, and Narr' Havas smiled while declaring he no longer knew the road; however, Spendius found it again.

Mâtho more frequently than ever before was as melancholy as an augur; starting at sunrise he would wander into the country, throw himself on the ground, and there remain motionless till evening.

He consulted, one after another, all the soothsayers in the army: those who observed the trails of serpents, those who studied the stars, and those who blew on the ashes of the dead. He swallowed galbanum, meadow-saxifrage, and the venom of vipers, supposed to freeze the heart. He summoned the Negro women, who chanting barbaric words by moonlight pricked the skin of his forehead with golden stilettoes. He loaded himself with amulets and charms; invoking one after another Baal-Khamoûn, Moloch, the seven Kabiri, Tanit, and the Grecian Venus; he engraved a name on a copper plate, and buried it at the threshold of his tent. Spendius could hear him constantly moaning and talking to himself. One night he ventured to enter his master's tent. Mâtho, naked as a corpse, was lying flat on a lion's skin, his face buried in his hands; a suspended lamp lit up his armour, hung against the tent-pole.

"You suffer?" said the slave to him. "What is it? Tell me!" and he shook him by the shoulders, calling him several times "Master! Master!"

Mâtho raised his large, troubled eyes toward him.

"Listen!" he said in a deep voice, with one finger on his lips; "it is the wrath of the gods! The daughter of Hamilcar pursues me! I fear her, Spendius!" then he pressed his hands against his breast, like a child terrified by a phantom. "Speak to me! I am ill! I wish to recover! I have vainly tried everything; but you, mayhap you, know of stronger gods, or some compelling invocation?"

"To what purpose?" asked Spendius.

Mâtho struck his head with his fists: "To liberate me from her!" Then, at long intervals, he said, talking to himself: "I am perhaps the victim of a holocaust she has promised to the gods. . . . She holds me bound by a chain that cannot be seen. . . . If I walk, she is beside me; when I pause, she stops. . . . Her eyes burn me. . . . I hear her voice. . . . She encompasses, she penetrates me. . . . It seems that she has become my soul! And yet, between us flow the invisible waves of a boundless ocean! She is remote and inaccessible! The splendour of her beauty weaves around her a mist of light; at moments I think I never saw her—that she has no existence—that it is all a dream!"

Mâtho wept in despair. Outside, the Barbarians slept.

Spendius, looking at this man, recalled to mind the young men who, with golden vases in their hands, had supplicated him, when he paraded his troops of courtesans through the cities. A feeling of pity touched him, and he said:

"Be strong, my master! Call upon your will, and no longer implore the gods; they do not heed the cries of men! See, you cry out like a coward! Are you not humiliated that a woman should cause you to suffer thus?"

"Am I a child?" said Mâtho. "Believe you that I yet weaken at the sight of women's faces, and at the sound of their songs? We kept them in Drepanum to sweep out our stables. . . . I have possessed them under crumbling walls, while the catapults yet vibrated! . . . But that woman! Spendius, she!" . . .

The slave interrupted him:

"If she were not the daughter of Hamilcar!"

"No!" exclaimed Mâtho. "She has nothing like unto any other daughter of man! Have you not seen her glorious eyes under her great curved eyebrows, like suns beneath triumphal arches? Remember, when she appeared, how all the lamps paled, and between the diamonds of her collar glimpses of her bosom shone resplendently—how behind her floated an odour like the perfumes from a temple, and something came forth from her entire being more fragrant than wine, and more terrible than death! . . . She moves. . . . She stops." He remained open-mouthed, his head lowered, eyes fixed.

"But I desire her! I must have her! I am dying for her! The thought of holding her in my arms fills me with a frenzy of rapture; and yet, withal, I hate her! Spendius, I want to overcome her! How can I do it? I could sell myself to become her slave. You were her slave; you could see her. Tell me of her—does she not go out on the terrace of her palace every night? Ah! the stones must thrill under her sandals, and the stars themselves bend down to gaze at her!"

He fell back in an access of passion, moaning like a wounded bull. Presently he sang: "He pursued the female monster, whose tail undulated over the dead leaves like a rivulet of silver," modulating his voice in imitation of Salammbô's, while his extended hands feigned to touch lightly the strings of a lyre.

To all the consolations offered by Spendius, he kept repeating the same words. The nights were passed in lamentations and exhortations. Mâtho endeavoured to deaden his senses in wine, but after his orgy had passed, he would become sadder than ever. Then he tried to distract his thoughts by playing knuckle-bone, losing in his unlucky wagers, one after another, the gold plaques of his collar. He even visited the handmaidens of the goddess, but afterward descended the hillside in sobs, like one returning from a funeral.

Spendius, on the contrary, became more daring and gay; he might be seen in the leaf-thatched taverns, discoursing with the soldiers. He repaired the old cuirasses. He juggled with swords. He gathered herbs in the fields for the sick. He was facetious, subtle, full of inventions and words; and the Barbarians became accustomed to his services, and grew to like him.

Meanwhile they eagerly awaited the promised messenger from Carthage, who was to bring them, on the backs of mules, baskets filled with gold; and continually making the same calculations, they would figure on the sand with their fingers. Each man arranged his future course of life; one planned to have concubines, another slaves, or lands, and others thought that they would bury their treasures, or risk them on a vessel. But during this protracted season of idleness, the diverse dispositions chafed; there continually arose disputes between the cavalry and infantry, the Barbarians and the Greeks, and above the wrangles of the men could ever be heard the shrill voices of the women.

Day after day men drifted into camp, nearly naked, wearing grasses on their heads to protect them from the sun; they were debtors of rich Carthaginians, and had been forced to till the lands, but had escaped. Libyans arrived in numbers, accompanied by peasants ruined by taxes, exiles and all kinds of malefactors. Then came crowds of merchants, and vendors of oil and wine, all furious because they had not received their money, denouncing the Republic. Spendius declaimed also. Soon the provisions diminished; then they talked of moving in a body on to Carthage, and even entertained an idea of appealing to the Romans.

One evening, during the supper hour, heavy creaking sounds were heard, and in the distance appeared something red moving over the undulations of the soil. It was a grand purple litter, ornamented at the corners with bunches of ostrich plumes; crystal chains, interwoven with garlands of pearls, beat against the closed hangings. Each stride made by the camels rang large bells suspended from their breast-plates, and on all sides of them was to be seen an escort of cavalry, clad from head to feet in an armour of golden scales.

The cavalcade halted three hundred paces from the camp, to draw from the sheaths which they carried behind them, their round bucklers, Bœotian helmets, and broadswords. Some of the men remained with the camels, the others resumed their march. At last appeared the ensigns of the Republic, blue wooden poles, terminated by horses' heads or pine-cones. The Barbarians all arose cheering, and the women rushed toward the Guards of the Legion and kissed their feet.

The litter advanced on the shoulders of twelve Negroes, who marched together with a short, rapid step, going at random from right to left, much embarrassed by the tent-ropes and animals moving about, and by the tripods where meats were cooking. Occasionally a fat hand laden with rings would half open the curtain, and a harsh voice cry out reproaches; then the bearers would halt, turn about, and try another road through the camp.

When the purple curtains were lifted there was disclosed on a large pillow an impassive, bloated human head. The eyebrows, joining over the nose, formed two ebony arches; gold dust glittered in the crimped hair; and the face was so ghastly, that it seemed powdered over with marble-dust; the remainder of the body was hidden under the fleeces that filled the litter. In this man the soldiers recognised the Suffet Hanno, the one whose negligence had helped to lose the battle of the Ægatian islands. In his victory at Hecatompylus over the Libyans, he had acted with seeming clemency, although he was thought by the Barbarians to have been actuated by cupidity, as he had sold to his own profit all the captives, subsequently reporting to the Republic that they were dead.

After looking for some time for a convenient place from which to address the soldiers, Hanno signalled the litter to stop, and assisted by two slaves he alighted and placed his tottering feet on the ground. They were clad in black felt boots, studded with silver moons; bands like those that encase a mummy enwrapped his legs, the flesh protruding where the linen strips crossed. His stomach extended beyond the scarlet jacket that covered his thigh; and the folds of his neck fell down on his breast like the dewlaps of an ox; his tunic, on which flowers were painted, was torn at the armpits; he also wore a scarf, a girdle, and a great black mantle with laced double sleeves. The extent of his vestments, his collar of blue gems, his gold clasps and his heavy earrings rendered even more hideous, if possible, his physical deformities. He appeared like some gross idol, roughly hewn out of a block of stone, for a pale leprosy covered his entire body, imparting to him the aspect of something inert. His nose, however, hooked like a vulture's beak, dilated violently, as he inhaled the air, and his small eyes, with their gummed lashes, flashed with a hard, metallic glitter. He held in one hand an aloe spatula, wherewith to scratch his diseased skin.

Two heralds sounded their silver horns; the tumult subsided, and Hanno began to speak.

He commenced with a eulogy of the gods and the Republic, saying that the Barbarians ought to congratulate themselves on having served Carthage; but they should also be reasonable, for the times were hard: "and if a master had only three olives, was it not just that he keep two for himself?"

Thus the old Suffet interpolated throughout his speech proverbs and apologies, nodding his head all the time to solicit approbation. He spoke in the Punic language, and those who surrounded him—the most alert, who had run thither without their weapons—were Campanians, Gauls, and Greeks, so that no one in the immediate crowd understood him. Perceiving this, Hanno paused to reflect, meanwhile rocking himself heavily from one leg to the other. The idea occurred to him to gather together the captains, and his heralds cried out the order in Greek, the language which had served for word of command in the Carthaginian armies since the time of Xanthippus.

The guards with blows of their whips dispersed the mob of soldiers, and soon the captains of the phalanxes, drilled like the Spartans and the chiefs of the Barbaric cohorts, came forward wearing the insignia of their rank, and the armour of their nation.

Night was falling; here and there blazed the fires; a great tumult stirred the encampment; and they went from one to another, asking, "What has he brought?" and "Why does not the Suffet distribute the money?"

He was explaining the infinite obligations of the Republic to the captains and chiefs; her treasury was empty; the Roman tribute overwhelmed her; in fact: "We do not know what to do! The Republic is deserving of much pity!"

From time to time he rubbed his limbs with his aloe spatula, or even paused to drink, from a silver cup held to his lips by a slave, a decoction of ashes of weasels and asparagus boiled in vinegar; then, after drying his mouth with a scarlet napkin, he resumed:

"That which used to be worth only one shekel of silver costs to-day three shekels of gold, and the farms abandoned during the war yield nothing. Our purple fisheries are almost lost; pearls even have become exorbitant; and it is with difficulty that we can obtain sufficient unguents for service to the gods! and, as for articles for table consumption—this subject is a disaster on which I shall not dwell. For lack of galleys the spices fail, and it will be difficult to procure silphium, in consequence of the rebellions on the frontier of Cyrene. Sicily, whence we used to procure our slaves, is no longer open to us! Yesterday I gave more money for a bath-man and four kitchen-varlets than formerly I should have paid for a pair of elephants!"

He unrolled a long strip of papyrus, and read, without omitting a single figure, all the expenses that the Government had been under, for reparations of the temples, paving streets, constructing vessels, coral-fisheries, the aggrandisement of the Syssites, and construction of engines for the mines in Cantabria.

But the captains had no better understanding of Punic than the soldiers, even though the Mercenaries saluted in that language. Ordinarily numerous Carthaginian officers were interspersed through the Barbaric armies to serve as interpreters, but after the recent war they had hidden, abandoning their posts, fearful of vengeance; and Hanno had not the forethought to provide himself with interpreters before setting out on his mission. His voice too was so low, it became lost in the wind.

The Greeks, girding on their iron sword-belts, listened attentively, striving to fathom his meaning; the mountaineers, covered with skins like bears, looked distrustfully at him, or yawned, leaning on their heavy clubs studded with brass nails. The Gauls inattentively sneered, shaking their tall towers of hair; and the men of the desert, completely muffled up in grey woollen clothing, listened motionless. Men pushed forward from behind, till the Guards, crowded by the surging mob, actually swayed on their horses. Negroes held at arm's length lighted torches of fir-branches; and the big Carthaginian continued his harangue, standing in full view on a grassy mound.

Meanwhile the Barbarians grew impatient, and began to murmur. Each one apostrophised Hanno, who gesticulated with his spatula; those who wished to silence others yelled louder, thereby increasing the din. Suddenly a man of stunted appearance bounded to Hanno's feet, snatched a trumpet from one of the heralds, blew it, and Spendius—for it was he—announced that he had something to say of importance. He rapidly reiterated this declaration in five different languages, Greek, Latin, Gallic, Libyan, and Balearic; the captains, half surprised, half laughing, responded, "Speak! Speak!"

Spendius, hesitating a moment, trembled; at last he commenced by addressing the Libyans, as they were the most numerous:

"You have all heard the horrible threats of this man!"

Hanno made no remonstrance, as he did not comprehend Libyan; so, to continue the experiment, Spendius repeated the same phrase in all the other Barbaric idioms. The soldiers looked at one another in amazement; when all, as by tacit consent, or perhaps believing that they comprehended, bowed their heads to signify agreement.

Then Spendius began in a vehement voice:

"In the first place, he has said that all the gods of other nations were but myths compared with the Carthaginian gods! He has called you all cowards, thieves, liars, dogs and sons of harlots! He has said, that but for you the

Republic would not now be paying the tribute to Rome, and that by your outrages you have drained Carthage of perfumes, aromatics, slaves, and silphium, as you are in league with the Nomads, on the frontiers of Cyrene. You yourselves have heard! Then he has said that the offenders shall be punished, and has read the enumeration of the punishments, such as paving the roads, fitting up the vessels, embellishing the Syssites, and being forced to dig in the mines of Cantabria."

Spendius repeated all this to the Greeks, Gauls, Campanians, and Balearics. They recognised many of the proper names that Hanno had used, so were convinced that he was giving an accurate report of the Suffet's discourse. Some yelled out to him:

"You lie!"

Their voices were lost in the uproar of others, and Spendius went on:

"Do you not see that he has left a reserve force of cavalry outside the camp? At a signal from him, they are prepared to rush upon you and slay you."

At this the Barbarians turned in the direction indicated; and as the crowd was then dispersing, there appeared in their midst, moving slowly as a phantom, a human being, bent over, thin, entirely naked, and hidden almost to his thighs by his long hair, bristling with dry leaves, dust, and thorns. About his loins and knees were wisps of straw and shreds of cloth; his cadaverous skin hung to his fleshless limbs like rags on dry branches; his hands trembled continually, and he advanced leaning on an olive staff. He came toward the Negro torch-bearers. An idiotic grin revealed his pale gums, and his great frightened eyes examined the Barbarians who gathered around him.

Suddenly uttering a cry of fright, he sprang behind the Negroes, hiding himself with their bodies, and stammered out, "Look at them! look at them!" pointing at the Suffet's guards sitting motionless in their glistening armour, their horses pawing the ground, dazzled by the torch-lights that crackled in the darkness. The human spectre struggled and yelled, "They killed them!"

At these words, which were screamed in Balearic, the Balearians drew nearer, and recognised him; but without responding to their questions, he repeated:

"Yes, killed all! all! Crushed like grapes! The fine young men! The slingers! My comrades and yours!"

They gave him wine to drink, overcome by weakness, he wept. Then again he launched forth a volley of words.

With difficulty Spendius managed to conceal his joy; even while explaining to the Greeks and Libyans all the horrible events recounted by Zarxas, he could scarcely credit such an apropos and desirable coincidence. The Balearic soldiers paled on being told of the manner in which their companions had perished. A troop of three hundred slingers had landed at Carthage in the evening and overslept themselves, so that when they arrived the next morning at the square of Khamoûn, the Barbarians had already gone, and they found themselves defenceless, their clay balls having been packed upon the camels with the other army baggage. They were allowed to enter the street of Satheb, and to proceed till they reached the oaken gate lined with brass plates, when the people, by a single movement, sprung upon the helpless troop.

Many of the soldiers recalled the great shouting they had heard; but Spendius, who had fled at the head of the columns, had not heard it.

The corpses of the slingers were placed in the arms of the *Dii-Patœci—*which surrounded the temple of Khamoûn. Then they were reproached for all the crimes committed by the Mercenaries—their gluttonies, thefts, impieties, insults, and the ruthless slaughter of the fishes in Salammbô's garden. The bodies were infamously mutilated; the priests burned their hair, believing this would torture their souls; pieces of their flesh were hung up in the butchers' shops: some of the torturers even buried their teeth in the flesh; and at night, to complete the outrages, the remains were burned on pyres at the cross-ways.

These, then, were the fires that had flashed so brightly in the distance over the lake. Some of the horses took fire, so the remaining bodies and the dying were hurriedly pitched over the walls. Zarxas was one of this number, and until the next day remained in the reeds on the lake shore; then he wandered about, seeking the army by its footsteps in the dust. During the daytime he hid in caverns, continuing his march in the night time. With wounds unstaunched, famishing and ill, he subsisted on roots and carrion. At length one day he saw on the horizon the lances, and followed them. His reason was disturbed by the force and continuance of his terrors and miseries.

While he spoke, the soldiers controlled their indignation with difficulty; when he had finished, however, it burst forth like a storm; they wanted then and there to massacre the Guards and the Suffet. Some less violent objected, saying that at least he should be heard and let them know if they were to be paid.

All yelled "Our money!" Hanno replied that he had brought it.

They made a rush to the advance posts, dragging the Suffet's baggage to the centre of the camp. Without waiting for the slaves, they unfastened the baskets. In those they opened first they found hyacinth-robes, sponges, scratchers, brushes, perfumes, and bodkins of antimony for painting the eyes—all belonging to the Guards, who were rich men accustomed to luxuries.

Then they found on one of the camels a large bronze bath-tub, in which the Suffet bathed during his march; for he took all sorts of precautions, even bringing caged weasels from Hecatompylus, to be burned alive for his decoction. And as his malady imparted to him an enormous appetite, he had brought a plentiful supply of comestibles—wines, pickles, meats and fish preserved in honey, and little Commagène-pots of goose-grease packed in snow and chopped straw. When the baskets were opened and the contents were displayed, the provisions appeared in such considerable quantities as to provoke a laughter that swept over the Barbarians like conflicting waves.

But the wages of the Mercenaries hardly filled two esparto coffers; and even in one of these they saw the leather tokens used by the Republic to save their specie. The Barbarians expressing surprise, Hanno explained that their accounts were very difficult, and that the Elders had not yet found leisure to examine them. In the meantime they had sent this supply. Everything was emptied recklessly and overturned—mules, valets, litter, provisions, and baggage.

The soldiers seized upon the money in the sacks to throw at Hanno. With great difficulty he was mounted upon an ass, and he fled, clutching its mane; howling, crying, jolted, bruised, as he hurled back upon the army the curses of all the gods. His broad, jewelled necklace rebounded to his ears; he held his long, trailing mantle on by clutching it between his teeth, and the Barbarians yelled after him from afar:

"Go, coward! Pig! Sewer of Moloch! Sweat out now your gold and your pestilence. Faster! Faster!" The escort in disorder galloped beside him.

The fury of the Barbarians could not be appeased: they recalled that many of their number who had set out for Carthage had never returned: doubtless they had been killed. So much injustice enraged them, and they began to pull up their tent pegs, roll up their mantles, bridle their horses, each one taking his casque and sword; and in an instant everyone was ready. Those who did not possess weapons rushed into the woods to cut bludgeons.

Day dawned: the people of Sicca awoke, and bestirred themselves in the streets to witness the army leaving.

"They go to Carthage!" it was said; and the rumour ran like wild-fire, spreading throughout the country.

From every pathway, from every ravine, men sprang forth. Shepherds could be seen descending the mountains, running breathlessly. When the Barbarians had gone Spendius circled the plain, mounted on a Punic stallion, accompanied by his slave, who led a third horse. A single tent remained on the field. Spendius entered it, exclaiming:

"Up, master! Awake! We depart!"

"Whither do we go?" demanded Mâtho.

"To Carthage!" cried Spendius.

Mâtho bounded upon the horse which the slave held at the entrance.

III

SALAMMBÔ

ACROSS THE WAVES the rising moon struck a shaft of light and over the city hung vast shadows, interspersed with luminous glints of brilliant whiteness —the pole of a chariot in a courtyard, some vagrant rag of linen, the angle of a wall, or the glitter of a gold necklace on the bosom of a god. On the roofs of the temples the glass globes glittered like enormous diamonds: but half defined ruins, heaps of black earth, and gardens, made more sombre masses in the general obscurity.

At the foot of Malqua, fishermen's nets extended from house to house, like gigantic bats with outspread wings. The creaking of the hydraulic wheels that forced the water to the upper stories of the palaces had ceased. In the centre of the terraces camels tranquilly reposed, lying on their bellies after the manner of ostriches. The porters slept in the streets at the thresholds of the mansions. The colossi cast long shadows over the deserted squares. In the distance, the smoke of a sacrifice still burning escaped through the bronze tiles; and a heavy breeze brought the odour of aromatic perfumes and the scent of the sea, mingled with exhalations from the sun-heated walls.

Around Carthage the motionless waters gleamed resplendent, as the rising moon spread her light, at the same time, over the gulf, enclosed by mountains and over the lake of Tunis, where upon the banks of sand flamingoes formed long, rose-coloured lines; and farther on below the catacombs the large salt lagoon shimmered like a lake of burnished silver. The blue dome of heaven on the one side sank into the horizon down to the powdered plains, and on the other side faded away into the sea-mists; and on the summit of the Acropolis, the pyramidal cypresses bordering the temple of Eschmoûn swayed, murmuring like the swell of the waves that beat slowly along the mole at the foot of the ramparts.

Salammbô ascended to the upper terrace of her palace, supported by a slave, who carried an iron plate filled with burning charcoal.

In the centre of the terrace was a small ivory couch covered with lynx-skins, upon which were pillows made out of the feathers of the prophetic parrots—birds consecrated to the gods—and at the four corners were long cassolettes, filled with spikenard, incense, cinnamon, and myrrh. The slave lit the perfumes.

Salammbô contemplated the polar star, then slowly saluting the four quarters of the heavens knelt on the ground amid the azure powder strewn with gold stars, in imitation of the firmament. Then she pressed her elbows close against her sides, extending her forearms perfectly straight, with hands open, her head turned upward and back under the full rays of the moon, reciting:

"O Rabetna! Baalet! Tanit!" Her tones continued plaintively, as if she called some one: "Anaitis! Astarte! Derceto! Astoreth! Mylitta! Athara! Elissa! Tiratha! . . . By the hidden symbols . . . by the resounding timbrels . . . by the furrows of the earth . . . by the eternal silence . . . by the everlasting fruitfulness. . . . Ruler of the shadowy sea, and of the azure shore, O Queen of the humid world, all hail!"

She swayed her entire body two or three times, then threw herself face downward, with outstretched arms, flat in the dust.

Her slave lifted her up quickly, for it was appointed that after such rites some one should always lift the suppliant from her prostration, as a sign that the service was acceptable in the sight of the gods; Salammbô's nurse never failed in this pious duty. This slave had been brought, when but a child, to Carthage by some merchants of Dara-Getulia, but after her emancipation she had no wish to leave her many masters; as a proof of her willing servitude, according to a recognised custom, in her right ear a large hole was pierced. She wore a many-coloured striped skirt fitting tightly about her hips, falling straight down to her ankles, between which as she walked two tin rings struck against one another; her flat face was as yellow as her tunic; very long silver pins made a halo at the back of her head, and in one nostril was inserted a coral stud. She now stood beside the couch with eyes downcast, more erect than a Hermes.

Salammbô walked to the edge of the terrace; her eyes swept for an instant over the horizon, then she lowered her gaze to the sleeping city. She heaved a sigh from the depths of her bosom, causing her long white simarre to undulate from end to end as it hung unconfined either by girdle or agrafe. Her curved sandals with turned-up toes were hidden beneath a mass of emeralds: her hair was carelessly caught up in a net of purple silk.

She raised her head to contemplate the moon—mingling with her words the fragments of hymns as she murmured:

"How lightly dost thou turn, supported by the impalpable ether! It is luminous about thee, and the movement of thy changes distributes the winds and the fruitful dews; as thou waxest and wanest, the eyes of cats elongate or shorten, and the spots of the leopard are changed. Women scream thy name in the pangs of childbirth! Thou increasest the shell-fish. Thou causest the wine to ferment! Thou putrefiest the dead! Thou shapest the pearls at the bottom of the seas; and all germs, O goddess! are quickened in the profound obscurity of thy humidity! When thou comest forth a calmness spreadeth over the earth; the flowers close; the waves are lulled; wearied men sleep with their faces upturned toward thee; and the entire earth, with its oceans and its mountains, is reflected in thy face, as in a mirror. Thou art white, sweet, lustrous, gentle, immaculate, purifying, serene!"

The crescent moon was just then over the Hot-Springs Mountain; below it in the notch of the two summits on the opposite side of the gulf, appeared a little star, encircled by a pale light. Salammbô continued:

"But thou art a terrible mistress! . . . Likewise produced by thee are monsters, frightful phantoms, and awful dreams; thine eyes devour the stones of the edifices, and during the periods of thy rejuvenescence the sacred apes fall ill. Whither goest thou then? Why continually changest thou thy forms? Sometimes narrow and curved, thou glidest through space as a mastless galley, and again, in the midst of stars thou resemblest a shepherd guarding his flock; anon shining and round, thou grazest the summit of the mounts like a chariot wheel!

"O Tanit, dost thou not love me? I have gazed on thee so often! But, no, thou proceedest in thine azure, whilst I remain on the motionless earth? . . .

"Taanach, take your nebal and play softly on the silver string, for my heart is sad."

The slave lifted a sort of ebony harp, taller than herself, of a triangular shape like a delta, and placing the point in a crystal globe began to play with both hands.

Sounds followed low, precipitous tones, like the buzzing of bees, and growing more and more sonorous, were wafted into the night, and mingled with the lament of the waves and the rustling of the large trees on the summit of the Acropolis.

"Hush!" cried Salammbô.

"What is it, mistress? If a breeze but blow, or a cloud pass, thou art vexed and disturbed."

"I know not," she replied.

"You have exhausted yourself by praying too long," urged the slave.

"Oh! Taanach! I would dissolve myself in prayer like a flower in wine!"

"Perhaps it is the scent of the perfumes?"

"No!" said Salammbô. "The spirit of the gods dwells in sweet odours."

Then the slave talked to her of her father. It was believed that he had gone into the Amber country beyond the pillars of Melkarth.

"But, mistress, if he should not return," she said, "you must choose, as was his will, a husband from among the sons of the Elders; and your unrest will vanish in the embrace of your husband."

"Why?" asked the young girl. All the sons of the Elders she had ever seen horrified her with their wild beast laughter, and their coarse limbs.

"Taanach, sometimes a feeling emanates from the innermost depths of my being, like hot flushes, heavier than the vapours arising from a volcano—voices call to me; a fiery globe rises up in my breast; it suffocates me. I seem to be about to die, when something sweet flows from my brow, extending to my very feet—thrills through every atom of my being—it is a caress which envelops me—I feel myself crushed as if a god spread himself over and upon me. Oh! I long to lose myself in the night mists—in the ripples of the fountains, in the sap of the trees, to leave my body to be but a breath of air—a ray of light, and glide through space unto thee, O Mother!"

She raised her arms to their full height, bending her body backward, pale and delicate in her white robe, as the moon; then in her ecstasy she fell panting on her ivory couch. Taanach placed around her mistress's neck a collar of amber and dolphins' teeth to banish these terrors. Salammbô said, in a voice almost inaudible, "Go and bring Schahabarim here to me."

Salammbô's father had not wished that she should enter the college of priestesses, nor even that she should know aught concerning the popular Tanit. He intended her for some alliance which would serve his political aims: so that Salammbô lived alone in her palace, her mother having been dead for years. She had grown up amid abstinences, fasts, and purifications, and was always surrounded by exquisite and solemn things—her body saturated with perfumes—her soul filled with prayers. She had not tasted wine, or eaten meat, or touched an unclean animal, or put her foot in the house of death.

She was ignorant of obscene images; for each god was manifested in many different forms, and the various rites, often most contradictory, all demonstrated the same principles; and Salammbô had been taught to adore the goddess in her sidereal representation.

An influence had descended from the moon upon this maiden, for whenever the planet waned Salammbô became feeble, languishing all day, only reviving at night; during an eclipse she had nearly died.

But the jealous Rabbetna revenged herself on this chaste maiden, withheld from immolation; obsessing her with allurements all the stronger because they were vague, the outgrowth of faith, strengthened by imagination.

The daughter of Hamilcar was constantly troubled about Tanit. She had learned the goddess's adventures, her journeys, and all her names, which she repeated, without their having any distinct significance for her. In order to penetrate the profundities of her dogma, she longed to know, in the most secret places of the temple, the ancient idol, with the magnificent veil, wherein rested the destiny of Carthage. The idea of a deity was not clearly revealed by her representation, and to possess or even behold her image was to share a part of her power, and in some measure to dominate her.

Salammbô turned as she recognised the tinkling of the gold bells that Schahabarim wore at the hem of his robe.

He ascended the stairs, and pausing as he reached the threshold of the terrace, folded his arms. His sunken eyes burned like lamps in a sepulchre; his long, thin body glided along in its linen robe, which was weighted by bells alternating with emerald balls about his heels. His limbs were feeble, his head oblique, his chin peaked, his skin was cold to the touch, and his yellow face, covered with deeply furrowed wrinkles, seemed as if contracted in a yearning, in an eternal chagrin.

This man was the high priest of Tanit, and he had educated Salammbô.

"Speak!" said he. "What do you wish?"

"I hoped—you almost promised me— . . ." she stammered, half fearing; then suddenly continued: "Why do you despise me? What have I neglected in the rites? You are my teacher, and you have said to me that no person is more learned than I in the mysteries of the goddess; but there are some of which you have not yet told me; is not this true, O father?"

Schahabarim remembering the orders of Hamilcar concerning his daughter's education, responded: "No! I have nothing more to teach you."

"A spirit," she resumed, "urges me to this adoration. I have climbed the steps of Eschmoûn—god of the planets and intelligences; I have slept under the golden olive tree of Melkarth—patron of all Tyrian colonies; I have opened the gates of Baal-Khamoûn—medium of light and fertilisation; I have made sacrifices to the subterranean Kabiri—to the gods of the winds, the rivers, the woods, and the mountains—but they all are too distant, too high, too insensible—you understand? But Tanit mingles in my life, she fills my soul, and I tremble with internal dartings, as if she struggled to escape the confines of my body. I feel I am about to hear her voice, behold her face; a brightness dazzles me, then I fall back again into the shadows."

Schahabarim was silent. She implored him with beseeching glances. At length he made a sign to dismiss the slave, who was not of Canaanite race. Taanach disappeared, and the priest raised one arm in the air, and began:

"Before the gods, only darkness existed, and a breath stirred, heavy and indistinct, like the consciousness of a man in a dream: it contracted itself, creating Desire and Vapour; from Desire and Vapour proceeded primitive Matter. This was a water, black, icy, profound, containing insensible monsters, incoherent parts of forms to be born, such as are painted on the walls of the sanctuaries. Then Matter condensed and became an egg. The egg broke: one half formed the earth, the other half the firmament. The sun, moon, winds, and clouds appeared, and at a crash of thunder the sentient animals awoke. Then Eschmoûn unrolled himself in the starry sphere! Khamoûn shone brilliantly in the sun; Melkarth with his arms pushed him beyond Gades; the Kabiri descended into the volcanoes; and Rabbetna, like one who nourishes, leaned over the world, pouring forth her light like milk, and her night like a mantle."

"And then?" she inquired—for the priest had related the secrets of origins, to distract her by the highest, the most abstract forms; but the desire of the maiden was rekindled at his last words, and Schahabarim, half consenting, resumed:

"She inspires and governs the loves of men."

"The loves of men!" repeated Salammbô, dreamily.

"She is the soul of Carthage," continued the priest. "Although her influence reaches over all, it is here she dwells, beneath the *Sacred Veil*."

"O, father!" exclaimed Salammbô, "I shall see her, shall I not? You will take me to her? For a long time I have hesitated: now the desire to see her form devours me. Pity me; comfort me! Let us go to the temple!"

He repulsed her by a vehement gesture, full of pride.

"Never! Do you not know that to look upon her is death? The hermaphrodite Baals unveil only to us; men that we are in comprehension and women in weakness. Your desire is sacrilege. Be satisfied with the knowledge that is already yours."

She fell upon her knees, placing two fingers against her ears in sign of repentance; sobbing, crushed by the priest's words, at the same time indignant with him—filled equally with fear and humiliation.

Schahabarim remained standing, more insensible than the stones of the terrace. He looked down upon her quivering at his feet, and it afforded him a measure of delight to see her thus suffering for his divinity whom he, himself, could wholly embrace.

Already the birds sang, and a cold wind blew, and little clouds fluttered across the pale sky. Suddenly the priest perceived on the horizon behind Tunis what at first appeared to be a light mist floating over the ground; then it formed a vast curtain of grey dust spreading perpendicularly, and

through the whirling mass, the heads of dromedaries, and the flash of lances
and bucklers could be seen. It was the Barbarian army advancing on
Carthage.

IV

Beneath the Walls of Carthage

Mounted on asses or running on foot, pale, breathless, frantic with terror,
the people from the country around came flocking into the city. They were
flying before the army of the Barbarians, which, within three days, had
accomplished the journey from Sicca, bent on destroying Carthage.

Almost as soon as the citizens closed the gates the Barbarians were seen,
but they halted in the middle of the isthmus on the lake shore. At first they
made no sign whatever of hostility. Some approached with palms in their
hands, only to be driven back by the arrows of the Carthaginians, so intense
was their terror.

During the early morning and at nightfall stragglers prowled along the
walls. A small man, carefully wrapped in a mantle, with his face concealed
under a low visor, was specially noticeable. He lingered for hours gazing
at the aqueduct, and with such concentration that he undoubtedly hoped
to mislead the Carthaginians as to his actual designs. He was accompanied
by another man, of giant-like stature, who was bareheaded.

Carthage was protected throughout the entire width of the isthmus: first
by a moat, then by a rampart of turf; finally by a double-storied wall, thirty
cubits high, built of hewn stones. It contained stables for three hundred
elephants, with accommodation for their caparison's, shackles, and provisions; other stables for a thousand horses with their harness and fodder; also
barracks for twenty thousand soldiers, arsenals for their armour, and all the
materials and necessaries of war. On the second story were towers, with
battlements, provided on the outside with bronze bucklers suspended from
camp irons.

The first line of walls sheltered Malqua, the quarter inhabited by sea-
faring people and dyers of purple. Masts were to be seen on which purple
sails were drying, and beyond, on the last terraces, clay furnaces for cooking saumure. In the background the city was laid out in tiers, like an
amphitheatre; its high dwellings formed like cubes were severally built of
stones, planks, shingles, reeds, shells, and pressed earth. The groves of the
temples were like lakes of verdure in this mountain of diversely-coloured
blocks. The public squares levelled it at unequal distances, and innumerable
streets intercrossed from top to bottom. The boundaries of the three old
quarters, no longer to be found, could be distinguished, and they rose up
like huge rocks or spread out in enormous flat spaces of walls—half covered
with flowers, and blackened by wide streaks where refuse had been thrown
over. Streets passed through the yawning spaces like streams under bridges.

The hill of the Acropolis, in the centre of Byrsa, was hidden under a medley of monuments—there were temples with torsel-columns, bearing bronze capitals and metal chains, cones of uncemented stones banded with azure, copper cupolas, marble architraves, Babylonian buttresses, and obelisks poised on their points like reversed torches. Peristyles reached to frontons; volutes appeared between colonnades; granite walls supported tile partitions. All these mounted one above another, half hidden, in a marvellous, incomprehensible fashion. Here one witnessed the succession of ages, and the memories of forgotten countries were awakened.

Behind the Acropolis, in the red earth, the Mappalian road, bordered by tombs, stretched in a straight line from the shore to the catacombs; then came large dwellings in spacious gardens; and the third quarter, Megara, the new city, extended to the edge of the cliffs, on which was a gigantic lighthouse, where nightly blazed a beacon.

Carthage thus displayed herself before the soldiers now encamped on the plains.

They could recognise the markets and the cross-roads, and disputed among themselves as to the sites of the various temples. Khamoûn faced the Syssites, and had golden tiles; Melkarth, to the left of Eschmoûn, bore on its roof coral branches; Tanit, beyond, curved up through the palm-trees its copper cupola; and the black Moloch stood below the cisterns at the side of the lighthouse.

At the angles of the frontons, on the summit of the walls, at the corners of the squares everywhere, were various divinities with their hideous heads, colossal or dwarfish, with enormous or with immeasurably flattened bellies, open jaws, and outspread arms, holding in their hands pitchforks, chains, or swords. And the blue sea reached away at the end of the streets, rendering the perspective still steeper.

A tumultuous people from morning till night filled the streets: young boys ringing bells cried out before the doors of the bath-houses; shops wherein hot drinks were sold smoked; the air resounded with the clangour of anvils; the white cocks, consecrated to the sun, crowed on the terraces; oxen awaiting slaughter bellowed in the temples; slaves ran hither and thither bearing baskets on their heads; and in the depth of the porticoes now and again a priest appeared clothed in sombre mantle, bare-footed, wearing a conical cap.

This spectacle of Carthage enraged the Barbarians. They admired her; they execrated her; they desired both to inhabit her and annihilate her. But what might there not be in the military harbour, defended by a triple wall? Then again, behind the city, at the back of Megara, higher even than the Acropolis, loomed up Hamilcar's palace.

Mâtho's eyes constantly turned in that direction. He climbed into the olive-trees, and leaned forward, shading his eyes with his hand; but the gardens were deserted, and the red door with the black cross remained closed.

More than a score of times he made the circuit of the ramparts, searching for some breach by which to enter. One night he threw himself into the gulf, and swam for three hours. He ultimately reached the foot of Mappals, tried to cling to and climb up the cliffs, but cruelly tore his knees, and crushed his nails, so he fell back into the water and returned defeated.

His impotence exasperated him: he was jealous of this Carthage that held Salammbô, as of some one who might have possessed her. Maddened by these thoughts, all enervation left him: henceforth he plunged continuously into a frenzy of reckless deeds. His cheeks blazed, his eyes burned, his voice rasped; he strode at a rapid pace across the camp, or sat on the shore rubbing his large sword with the sand; he shot arrows at the passing vultures. His heart overflowed in furious speech.

"Let your wrath course freely like a runaway chariot," said Spendius. "Shout; blaspheme, ravage and kill; sorrow allays itself in blood, and since you cannot satiate your love, gorge your hate; it will sustain you!"

Mâtho resumed command of his soldiers, drilling them unmercifully. They respected him for his courage, and especially for his strength; besides, he inspired in their hearts a mystic fear, for they believed that he communed at night with phantoms.

The other captains were stirred by his example; and thus the army was very soon under fine discipline. The Carthaginians heard from their dwellings the constant sound of trumpet calls, regulating the military exercises. At length the Barbarians advanced. ·

In order to crush them in the isthmus, the Carthaginians would have required two armies to attack them in the rear simultaneously: the one debarking at the end of the Gulf of Utica, and the other at the Hot-Springs Mountain. But, what could the Carthaginians do now, with only the Sacred Legion, consisting at most of but six thousand men? If the Barbarians diverged toward the east they would join the Nomads, intercepting the road to Cyrene and thus the commerce of the desert. If they fell back to the west the Numidians would revolt. Finally, lack of food would force them, sooner or later, to devastate like locusts the surrounding country; the wealthy trembled for their beautiful châteaux, for their vineyards, and for their farms.

Hanno proposed the most atrocious and impracticable measures, such as promising a large sum of money for every Barbarian's head, or that with implements and war engines they should fire the enemy's camp. His colleague Gisco, on the contrary, advised that the Mercenaries should be paid. The Elders detested him on account of his popularity, as they dreaded to incur the risk of a master, and from terror of a monarchy strove to weaken whatever could tend to re-establish such a form of government.

Outside the fortifications were people of another race and of unknown origin, all porcupine hunters, eaters of molluscs and serpents—people who penetrated the caverns, captured live hyenas, and found amusement in chasing them during the evenings on the sands of Megara between the stelas of the tombs. Their cabins made of wrack and mud hung against the cliffs like swallows' nests; they lived without government, without gods, pell-mell, completely naked, and at once both feeble and savage—during all ages cursed by the Carthaginians because of their unclean food. One morning the sentinels perceived that they had all gone.

At length the members of the Grand Council determined that they would go personally to the Barbarians' camp, without collars or girdles, and with their sandals uncovered, like friendly neighbours. Accordingly, one day they advanced with a tranquil step, throwing salutations to the captains, or even stopping to talk with the soldiers, saying that all war was now at an end, and they were prepared to do justice to the demands of the Mercenaries.

Many of these patricians saw for the first time a Mercenarian camp. Instead of finding the confusion that they had imagined, order ruled, and a frightful stillness was over everything. A rampart of turf enclosed the army within a high wall invincible to the shocks of catapults. The camp streets were kept sprinkled with fresh water. Through holes in the tents they saw lurid eyes gleaming mid the shadows. The stacks of spears and the suspended panoplies dazzled them like mirrors. They talked in undertones, and seemed constantly in fear of overturning with their long robes some of the vast medley of objects.

The soldiers asked for provisions, agreeing to pay for them out of the money that the Republic owed them. Oxen, sheep, guinea-fowls, dried fruits, lupins, as well as smoked mackerel—those excellent mackerel which Carthage exported with large revenue to all other ports—were sent to them. But the soldiers disdainfully walked around the magnificent cattle, disparaging that which they coveted, offering for a sheep the price of a pigeon, for three goats the value of a pomegranate. The eaters of unclean things presented themselves as arbitrators, affirming that they were being duped. Then they drew their swords and threatened to slay the ambassadors.

The commissioners of the Grand Council wrote down the number of years' pay due to each soldier; but it was now impossible to know how much the Mercenaries had originally been engaged for, and the Elders were frightened at the immense sums they would be obliged to pay. It would necessitate the sale of the reserve of silphium, and compel them to impose a tax on the trading cities. The Mercenaries would be impatient; already Tunis sympathised with them.

The Rich, stunned by Hanno's fury and by the reproaches of his colleague Gisco, urged the citizens who might perchance know any Barbarians to go and see them immediately, in order to regain their friendship; such confidence would calm them.

Tradesmen, scribes, workers from the arsenals, and entire families visited the Barbarians. The soldiers permitted all the Carthaginians to enter, but by a single passage, so narrow that four men abreast elbowed each other.

Spendius stood against the barrier, and caused each one to be carefully searched. Mâtho faced him, examining the passers, seeking to find some one whom he might have seen at the palace of Salammbô.

The encampment resembled a town, it was so filled with people and movement. Yet the two distinct crowds, military and civic, mingled without being confounded; the one dressed in linen or wool, wearing felt-caps pointed like pine-cones, and the other vested in iron, wearing metal helmets. Amid serving men and vendors strolled about women of all nationalities; brown as ripe dates, green as olives, yellow as oranges. These women had been sold by sailors, or stolen from dens and caravans, or taken during the sacking of cities, that they might be wearied with lust while they were young, or be overwhelmed with blows when they were old, and die neglected on the roadside, during the retreats in the midst of the baggage, along with the abandoned beasts of burden.

The wives of the Nomads dangled over their heels their square cut, tawny coloured robes, of dromedaries' hair. The Cyrenaic musicians, with painted eyebrows, and wrapped in violet gauze, sang as they squatted on mats; old negresses, with their hanging breasts, picked up sun-dried dung for fuel. Syracusians wore golden plates in their hair; Lusitanians were adorned with necklaces made of shells; the Gallic women wore wolves' skins over their white breasts; and sturdy children, covered with vermin, naked, uncircumcised, butted the passers-by with their lusty heads, or crept up behind them, like young tigers, to bite their hands.

The Carthaginians walked through the camp, amazed at the quantity of strange articles with which it teemed. The most miserable were melancholy, while the others strove to dissimulate their anxiety.

Soldiers slapped them familiarly on their shoulders, exhorting them to be gay; and as soon as they perceived some person of note, invited him to join their games; if one perchance consented to play a game of discs, then the soldiers managed to crush his feet; or in boxing, after the first pass, broke his jaw.

The slingers terrified the Carthaginians with their slings, the snake-charmers with their vipers, and the cavalry with their horses. These citizens, used to peaceful occupations, bent their heads and forced a smile at all the outrages. Some, assuming bravery, even made signs that they desired to become soldiers. They were set to cleave wood and to curry mules; or they were buckled in armour, and rolled about like casks through the camp streets. Afterward, when they wanted to take leave, the Barbarians pulled out their own hair, and with grotesque contortions demonstrated their pretended grief.

Many of the Mercenaries, from foolishness or prejudice, really believed that all Carthaginians were very rich; they followed their visitors, begging; they asked for all that they wore that seemed beautiful in their barbaric eyes—a ring, a girdle, sandals, or the fringes off their robes; after the Carthaginians were utterly despoiled and said, "But we have nothing left; what do you want?" they would answer, "Your women! your lives!"

In due time the military accounts were turned over to the captains, read to the soldiers, and definitely approved. Then the soldiers demanded the tents, which were given to them—the Greek polemarchs demanded some of the beautiful suits of armour made in Carthage; the Grand Council voted a sum of money for this purpose. Then the cavalry-men insisted that it would be but fair for the Republic to indemnify them for their horses; one affirmed that he had lost three in such and such a siege, and another five on a certain march, another fourteen over precipices. They were proffered the fine stallions of Hecatompylus; but no, they preferred money.

Finally they demanded their pay in silver, not with leather tokens, for all the grain due to them, and that at the highest prices it had brought during the war, so that they asked for one measure of meal, four hundred times more than had actually been given for a sack of wheat. This injustice and greed exasperated the Council; nevertheless, they had to yield.

Then the delegates of the soldiers and the Council were reconciled, swearing renewed amity by the genius of Carthage and by the gods of the Barbarians. With demonstrations and Oriental verbosity they exchanged excuses and caresses. The soldiers now demanded as a proof of friendship the punishment of the traitors who had estranged them from the Republic.

The Carthaginians feigned that they did not comprehend; the Barbarians, explaining more clearly, boldly declared that they must have Hanno's head. Frequently during the day they would leave their camp and walking along the foot of the walls cry out for some one to throw the Suffet's head down to them, at the same time holding their robes outstretched to receive it.

Perhaps the Grand Council might have yielded, had not a last exaction, more outrageous than all others, followed, for now the Mercenaries demanded in marriage for their chiefs maidens to be chosen from the noble families. This idea had been suggested by Spendius, and many thought it easy to achieve and strongly expedient. However, their audacious presumption in wanting to mix with the Punic blood filled the citizens with such indignation that they brusquely told them they had nothing more to expect or receive from Carthage. Then the soldiers exclaimed that they had been basely deceived, and that if within three days they did not receive their pay they would go themselves and take it in Carthage.

The bad faith of the Mercenaries was not quite so complete as the Carthaginians supposed, for Hamilcar had made them extravagant promises—vague, it is true, but solemn, and oft repeated. They had been led to believe that, when they landed at Carthage, the city would forthwith be given up to them, and that they should share among themselves the city treasure; hence, when they came, only to find their payments were repudiated, or would be paid with great difficulty and delay, the disillusion of their pride, as well as the rebuff to their cupidity, was severe.

Dionysius, Pyrrhus, Agathocles, and the generals of Alexander, had they not furnished examples of marvellous fortunes? The ideal of Hercules, whom the Canaanites confounded with the sun, illumined the horizon of the armies. They knew that soldiers from the ranks had worn diadems, and the re-ēchoing fame of falling empires made the Gauls dream of glory in their oak forests, and inspired with ambition the Ethiopians on their native sands. But here was a nation always ready to utilise the courageous; and the thief driven from his tribe, the parricide skulking on the highways, the sacrilegious pursued by the gods, all the starving, and all desperadoes endeavoured to reach the port, where the agents of Carthage recruited soldiers. Usually the Republic kept its promises; however, in this case the strength of its avarice had dragged it into a perilous infamy. The Numidians, the Libyans, the whole of Africa, would now be ready to throw themselves upon Carthage. The sea only remained open to it, and there it would come into collision with Rome: so, like a man assailed by murderers, it felt death lurking all around.

The Council decided that it would be necessary to have recourse again to Gisco, for the Barbarians would probably look favourably on the intervention of their former general. One morning the chains of the port were lowered, and three flat boats passed through the canal of the Tænia and entered the lake.

At the prow of the first boat Gisco could be seen; behind him, rising higher than a catafalque, loomed up an enormous chest, ornamented with rings like pendant wreaths. Following, appeared the legion of interpreters coiffured like sphinxes, with parrots tattooed on their breasts. Friends and slaves followed, all without arms, and in such a multitude that they touched shoulder to shoulder. These three long, crowded boats solemnly advanced amid the cheers of the expectant army watching them from the shore.

As soon as Gisco landed, the soldiers rushed to meet him. He soon erected, with sacks piled on top of each other, a kind of tribunal, and declared that he would not leave the place until he had paid them all in full.

There was an outburst of applause which prevented his speaking for some time. Then he censured the wrong-doing of the Republic and the wrong-doing of the Barbarians; the great fault had been with those few who had mutinied, with such extreme violence as to have alarmed Carthage. The best proof of the Republic's present good intentions was the fact that it had sent him—the eternal adversary of Hanno—to treat with them. They must not suppose that the people would be so foolish as to anger brave men, or so ungrateful as to discount their services. Gisco prepared to pay the soldiers, beginning with the Libyans. As they declared the lists incorrect, he set them aside.

They defiled before him by nations, and raised their fingers to indicate the term of years they had served. Each man successively was marked on his left arm with green paint; scribes made with a stiletto holes on sheets of lead; while others drew out the money from open coffers.

Presently a man passed tramping heavily, like an ox.

"Come up near to me," said Gisco, suspecting some fraud. "How many years have you served?"

"Twelve," responded the Libyan.

Gisco slipped his fingers under the fellow's chin, as the chin-piece of the helmets produced, after being worn for a long time, two callosities that were called *carroubes*, and "having carroubes" was synonymous to being a veteran.

"Thief!"—exclaimed Gisco. "That which is missing on your face should be on your shoulders!" At this he tore off the man's tunic, disclosing a back covered with bleeding sores. In truth he was a slave labourer of Hippo-Zarytus. Yells arose, and the culprit was beheaded.

When night fell, Spendius went and roused up the Libyans, saying to them:

"When the Ligurians, the Greeks, Balearics, and all the men of Italy shall be paid, they will return to their native countries, but you others must remain in Africa; scattered among the tribes without any means of defence! Then the Republic will revenge itself! Beware of the journey! Are you going to believe all these speeches? The two Suffets are in accord! This one imposes your confidence! Do you recollect the island of bones, and Xanthippus, whom they sent back to Sparta on a rotten galley?"

"How are we to behave?" demanded they.

"Be circumspect," replied Spendius.

The two next days were spent in paying the people of Magdala, Leptis and Hecatompylus. Spendius spread fresh dissensions among the Gauls, saying:

"They are paying the Libyans, afterward they will discharge the Greeks, then the Balearics, then the Asiatics, and all the others! But you, who are but a small number, will receive nothing! You will see your country no more! You have no vessels! They will kill you to save the expense of your keep!"

The Gauls set out to find Gisco. Autharitus, the man whom he had wounded in Hamilcar's gardens, tried to speak with him, but was repulsed by the slaves, and disappeared, swearing revenge.

Demands and complaints multiplied. The most persistent entered the Suffet's tent at night, and to move him to pity, they would take his fingers and make him feel their toothless mouths, their emaciated arms, and the cicatrices of their wounds. Those who were not yet paid became exasperated; those who had received their pay demanded an additional sum for their horses; and the vagabonds and outcasts assumed soldiers' arms and declared that they had been forgotten. Every moment men surged forward in eddies; the tents cracked under the strain, and finally toppled over; the multitude, giving vent to yells, crowded between the ramparts, swaying and surging from the entrance to the centre of the camp. When the tumult became excessive, Gisco rested one elbow on his ivory sceptre, and gazed motionless over the sea of faces, with his fingers buried in his beard.

Mâtho often went aside to talk to Spendius, but ever took his place again facing the Suffet; and Gisco could feel perpetually his eyes like flaming fire-lances darting toward him. Frequently they interchanged words of abuse, above the heads of the crowd, but neither understood the other. Meanwhile, the distribution continued, and the Suffet found ways of removing every obstacle.

The Greeks quibbled about the differences in the currency; but he furnished such satisfactory explanations that they withdrew without a murmur. The Negroes demanded their pay in the white shells used in trading through the interior of Africa; he offered to send there and bring a supply to Carthage; then, like the others, they accepted the silver money. The Balearians had been promised something better—women. The Suffet informed them that an entire caravan of virgins was expected for them; but the road was long, and it would require six moons more. However, when they arrived at their destination, they would be fat, and well rubbed with benzoin, and they would be sent on vessels to the Balearic ports.

Suddenly Zarxas, now fine and vigorous, leaped like a mountebank upon the shoulders of his friends, and cried out, "What have you reserved for the dead?" pointing to the gate of Khamoûn.

Under the last rays of the sun the brass plates that decorated the gate from top to bottom were refulgent, and the Barbarians believed that they saw on them a track of blood. Every time Gisco tried to speak, their yells began again; finally he descended with slow steps, and shut himself up in his tent.

At sunrise, when he went forth again, his interpreters, who slept outside his tent, did not stir. They lay on their backs, eyes fixed, tongues protruding between their teeth, and their faces bluish; white froth oozed from their nostrils, their limbs were stiff, as if they had been frozen during the night, and around the neck of each was drawn a noose of rushes.

From this time the rebellion increased. The murder of the Balearians recalled by Zarxas added fuel to the suspicions set brewing by Spendius. They imagined that the Republic was always seeking to deceive them. It must be ended! They could do without interpreters! Zarxas, with a sling around his head, sang war songs; Autharitus brandished his great sword; Spendius would whisper something to one, and to another give a sword. The most powerful endeavoured to pay themselves; but those less enraged requested that the distribution continue.

During this excitement none laid down their weapons, and their wrath centred upon Gisco in a tumultuous hatred. Some went up beside him. So long as they only vociferated their wrongs, they were patiently listened to; but the moment they uttered the slightest word in his favour they were immediately stoned, or their heads were cut off by a blow from behind. The heap of sacks soon became red as an altar during sacrifice.

They became terrible after eating, and when they had drunk wine! This was an indulgence forbidden under pain of death in the Punic armies; but in derision of her discipline they raised their cups toward Carthage. Afterward they turned on the slaves of the exchequer and began killing them. The word *strike*, different in each language, was understood by all.

Gisco understood that his country had forsaken him, but in spite of this he would not dishonour it. When the soldiers recalled to him that the government had promised them vessels, he swore by Moloch to furnish them himself at his own expense, and pulling off his necklace of blue stones threw it to the crowd as a pledge of his faith.

Then the Africans claimed their grain, according to the arrangement with the Grand Council. Gisco spread out the accounts of the Syssites, traced with violet paint on sheepskins, and read all that had entered into Carthage, day by day, month by month.

Suddenly he paused; his eyes opened wide, as if he had discovered between the figures his own death sentence. In effect the Elders had made fraudulent reductions, and the grain sold during the most calamitous period of the war was rated so low in these accounts that only the blindest person could have been deceived.

"Speak!" cried they; "louder! Oh! he strives to lie, the coward! We distrust you!"

He hesitated for some time; at length he again took up his task.

The soldiers, without suspecting the accounts rendered by the Syssites to be inaccurate, accepted them. The abundance that they found in Carthage threw them into a jealous fury. They broke open the sycamore coffer; it was now three-quarters empty, but having seen such enormous sums taken from it, they had fancied it inexhaustible. Had Gisco hidden some in his tent? The soldiers climbed over the sacks, led on by Mâtho, yelling:

"The money! the money!"

Gisco at last responded.

"Let your general give it to you!"

Without speaking further, he looked at them with his large yellow eyes and long pale face, whiter than his beard. An arrow whistled toward him, and was arrested by its feathered barb, holding fast by his broad gold earring; a thread of blood trickled down from his tiara upon his shoulder.

At a gesture from Mâtho all advanced upon Gisco. He held out his arms; Spendius with a running knot fastened his wrists together; some one pitched him over, and he disappeared in the prevailing disorder of the crowd, which was tumbling over the sacks. They completely ransacked his tent, finding nothing but the necessities of life; and on further search, three images of Tanit, and in a monkey's hide, a black stone, said to have fallen from the moon.

The numerous Carthaginians who had accompanied Gisco were all of the war party, and were men of importance. They were taken outside of the tents, and thrown into the pit for filth. They were attached by chains to stakes driven in the earth, and their food was held out to them on the points of javelins.

Over all of these captives Autharitus kept surveillance, heaping invectives upon them; but as they did not comprehend his language, they made no response, and the Gaul would, from time to time, throw stones in their faces, to make them cry out.

The next day a languor possessed the army. According as their rage subsided they became anxious. Mâtho suffered from a strange melancholy. It seemed to him that he had indirectly insulted Salammbô: these rich men were like a dependence of her person. He sat at night on the edge of their pit, and in their moans fancied he heard something akin to the voice, of which his heart was full.

Meanwhile, all reproached the Libyans, who alone were paid. But though national antipathies and personal hatreds were reviving, everyone felt the present danger of yielding to them. Reprisals after such an outrage would be formidable. They must by common adhesion ward off the vengeance of Carthage. Conventions and harangues were continuous; everyone talked; no one was listened to; and Spendius, ordinarily so fluent, now at all proposals shook his head.

One evening he carelessly asked Mâtho if there were any springs in the interior of the city.

"Not one!" responded Mâtho.

The next day Spendius led him to the lake shore. "Master, if your heart is brave, I will conduct you to Carthage."

"How?" breathlessly asked Mâtho.

"Swear to execute my orders, and to follow me like a shadow," said Spendius.

Mâtho raised his arm toward the planet Kabira, saying:

"By Tanit I swear it!"

Spendius resumed:

"To-morrow, after sunset, await me at the foot of the aqueduct between the ninth and tenth arcades. Bring with you an iron pike, a crestless helmet, and leathern sandals." The aqueduct to which he referred traversed obliquely the entire isthmus—a work much enlarged later by the Romans. Notwithstanding the disdain of Carthage for other peoples, she had awkwardly borrowed this new invention from Rome; even as Rome herself had imitated the Punic galleys. It was of a broad low architecture of five ranges of superposed arches, with buttresses at the base and lions' heads at the summit, which abutted on the western side of the Acropolis, where it plunged under the city, pouring almost a river into the cisterns of Megara.

At the hour agreed upon, Spendius found Mâtho waiting. He fastened a sort of harpoon to the end of a long rope, and whirled it rapidly like a sling; as the iron caught in the masonry, moving one behind the other, they climbed up along the wall. After reaching the first story, each time that the harpoon was thrown it fell back; hence, in order to discover some fissure, they were compelled to walk on the edge of the cornice. On each row of arches they found it became narrower. At times the rope slackened, and again it threatened to break. At length they attained the upper platform. Spendius leaned over, sounding the stones from time to time with his hands.

"It is here"—said he—"we will begin!" and pressing on the pike Mâtho had brought, he disjoined one of the stones.

In the distance below them they perceived a troop of cavalry galloping, without bridles on their horses, their gold bracelets bounding in the loose draperies of their ample mantles. In advance could be distinguished a man crowned with ostrich-plumes, holding a lance in each hand as he galloped.

"Narr' Havas!" exclaimed Mâtho.

"What matter?" replied Spendius, leaping into the hole he had just made by displacing a stone. Mâtho, by his orders, tried to prize out one of the blocks of stone, but on account of lack of space he could not move his elbows.

"We shall return,"—said Spendius—"go first."

Then they ventured into the water-channel. It reached up to their waists; soon they staggered, and were obliged to swim. Their limbs knocked against the inner walls of the very narrow duct and as they progressed, the water gradually rose till it almost reached the superior stones, against which they tore their faces, as the swift current carried them along. An air heavy as that of a sepulchre pressed upon their lungs, and with their heads under their arms, their knees together, elongating themselves as much as possible, they passed like arrows through the denseness, stifled, gasping for breath, nearly dead. Suddenly all was dark before them—the speed of the water redoubled. They sank. When they rose to the surface again they remained for some minutes floating on their backs, inhaling the delicious pure air. Arcades one behind another opened out amid wide walls separating the basins; all were full, and the water continued as one unbroken sheet the length of the cisterns. Through the air-holes in the cupola of the ceiling, a pale brightness spread over the water like discs of light; the darkness thickened toward the walls as they retreated to an indefinite extent—here the slightest noise made a tremendous echo.

Spendius and Mâtho began swimming again, and passing the openings of the arches, crossed numerous chambers in succession: two similar but much smaller rows of basins extended parallel on each side. They lost themselves, and were compelled to turn and swim back for some distance. Something offered a footing under their feet: it was the pavement of the gallery running the length of the cistern. With great caution they proceeded to feel the walls, striving to detect an issue; but their feet slipped, and they fell into the deep basin; they struggled up, but again fell back. As they struck out once more they experienced a frightful fatigue in swimming—their limbs seemed about to dissolve in the water—their eyes closed—they seemed in a death agony.

Spendius struck his hand against the bar of a grating; both men shook it vigorously; it yielded, and they found themselves on the steps of a stairway closed at the top by a bronze door. With the point of a dagger they wrested free the bolt, which was opened from the outside, and at once gained access to pure, fresh air.

The night was full of silence, and the sky seemed an immeasurable height; clumps of trees projected beyond the long lines of walls; the entire city was sleeping; and the fires of the advance posts shone through the night like lost stars.

Spendius, who had spent three years confined in the *ergastulum*, knew the city but imperfectly. Mâtho, however, conjectured that in order to reach Hamilcar's palace they must go to the left and cross the Mappalian section.

"No!" said Spendius; "take me to the temple of Tanit."

Mâtho tried to speak.

"Remember!" said the former slave, as he lifted his right arm, and pointed to the resplendent planet of Kabira.

Mâtho silently turned toward the Acropolis. They crept cautiously along the enclosures of cactus bordering the pathways. The water trickled from their limbs upon the dust; their wet sandals were soundless. Spendius, with eyes more gleaming than torches, peered into the bushes at every step. He groped his way behind Mâtho, constantly clutching in his hands, ready for immediate action, the two daggers he wore attached to his arms by a leather band below the armpits.

V

TANIT!

MATHO AND SPENDIUS now left the gardens, but soon found themselves confronted by the ramparts of Megara. In a little while, however, they discovered a breach in the wall, through which they passed.

The ground descended, forming a broad valley. It was an excellent point for a reconnaissance.

"Listen," said Spendius; "and above all, fear nothing: I will fulfil my promise"; and with an air of reflection he paused, as if to measure his words. "You remember, just at sunrise, when we stood on the terrace of Salammbô's palace, and I pointed out Carthage to you? We were strong that day, but you would not listen to me." Then in a graver voice he pursued: "Master, there is, in the sanctuary of Tanit, a mysterious veil, fallen from Heaven, that covers the goddess."

"I know that," replied Mâtho.

Spendius resumed: "It is divine, because it is a part of Tanit. . . . The gods reside where their images dwell. It is because Carthage possesses it that Carthage is great." Then leaning forward he whispered, "I have brought you with me, to take this veil!"

Mâtho recoiled with horror. "Go! get some one else! I will not aid in such an abominable crime."

"But Tanit is your enemy," said Spendius. "She persecutes you, and is destroying you with her anger. You can thus revenge yourself. She will obey you. You will become almost immortal and invincible!"

Mâtho bowed his head low at this suggestion, and Spendius continued: "If we succumb, the army will become self-annihilated. We have neither escape, succour, nor pardon to hope for! What punishment of the gods can you dread when once you possess, in your own person, their strength? Do you prefer to perish miserably the night of a defeat under the shelter of a bush, or be burned at the stake amid the outrages heaped upon you by the populace? Master, some day you will enter Carthage between the colleges of pontiffs, who will kiss your sandals; and if the veil of Tanit then weighs upon you, reëstablish it in her temple. Follow me! Come, take it!"

A terrible longing consumed Mâtho: he would have liked to abstain from the sacrilege, and yet desired to possess the veil. He thought to himself that perhaps he did not desire to take it merely to monopolise its virtues. However, he did not probe to the foundation of his intentions, but paused at the limit where his thoughts frightened him.

"We will go on," he said; and they moved forward with rapid strides, side by side, without speaking.

The ground ascended, and the habitations were closer together; they turned aside amid the darkness in the narrow streets. The esparto-hangings closing the doorways beat against the walls; camels ruminated before heaps of cut grass in a square; then they passed under a gallery covered over with foliage, where a pack of dogs barked at them. The space suddenly grew wider, and they recognised the western façade of the Acropolis. At the foot of Byrsa extended a long, black mass; it was the temple of Tanit, a collection of monuments and gardens, courts and forecourts, hemmed in by a low wall of loose stones, over which Spendius and Mâtho vaulted.

This first enclosure surrounded a grove of plane-trees, planted as a precaution against the pest and infections of the air. Here and there were scattered tents in which, during the day, were sold depilatory pastes, perfumes, clothing, crescent-shaped cakes, images of the goddess, and models of the temple carved in blocks of alabaster. They had now nothing to fear, as, on the nights that the planet did not appear, all rites were suspended; still Mâtho slackened his pace; he stopped before the three ebony steps leading to the second enclosure.

"Proceed!" urged Spendius.

Pomegranates, almonds, cypresses, and myrtles, alternated regularly, and were as motionless as bronze foliage; the path, paved with blue stones, creaked under their feet; and roses in full bloom hung in a bower over the long alley. They came to an oval opening, protected by a grating. Then Mâtho, who was alarmed by the silence, said to Spendius:

"It is here that the Sweet and the Bitter Waters are mingled."

"I have seen all that," replied the former slave, "in the town of Maphug, in Syria."

By a flight of six silver steps, they entered the third enclosure. An enormous cedar occupied the centre; its lowest branches were covered with scraps of fabrics and necklaces appended by the faithful. They went a few steps more, and the façade of the temple appeared before them.

Two long porticoes, with architraves reposing on dwarfish pillars, flanked a quadrangular tower, adorned on the platform by a crescent moon. At the angles of the particoes, and at the four corners of the tower, were vases full of burning aromatics. Pomegranates and colocynths loaded the capitals: interlacements and lozenges alternated regularly with garlands of pearls, festooning the walls, and a hedge of silver filigree formed a wide semicircle before a brass stairway leading down from the vestibule.

At the entrance, between a stela of gold and a stela of emerald, was a stone cone; Mâtho kissed his right hand as he passed it.

The first room was very lofty; innumerable openings pierced the vaulted ceiling, through which the stars could be seen. All around the wall reed-baskets were heaped up with beards and hair, first indications of adolescence; and in the centre of the circular apartment the body of a woman rose from a pedestal which was covered with breasts. Fat, bearded, with eyelids lowered, she appeared to be smiling; her hands crossed the lower part of her gross abdomen—polished by the kisses of her votaries.

Then they found themselves in the open air in a transverse corridor, where a small alter stood against an ivory gate, barring the passage. Beyond this the priests alone might pass—for the temple was not a place for the congregation of the people, but the particular abode of its divinity.

"The undertaking is impossible," exclaimed Mâtho. "You did not remember this; let us go back."

Spendius was carefully examining the walls. He coveted the veil: not that he reposed confidence in its virtues, for Spendius believed only in the Oracle; but he was persuaded that if the Carthaginians were deprived of the veil they would fall into great consternation.

To discover some outlet, they went round to the back. Under the turpentine trees could be seen little buildings of various shapes. Here and there appeared a stone phallus; and large stags tranquilly wandered about, crushing under their cloven hoofs the fallen pine-cones.

They retraced their steps between two long parallel galleries, from which tiny cells opened out. Tambourines and cymbals hung on the cedar columns. Extended on mats outside were women asleep. Their bodies were so greased with unguents that they exhaled an odour of aromatics and extinguished perfuming pans; and they were so covered with tattooing, collars, bracelets, vermilion, and antimony, that, but for the movement of their breasts, they might easily have been mistaken for idols.

Lotuses were clustered round a fountain, where swam fish like Salammbô's; then in the background, against the wall of the temple, spread a vine, with tendrils of glass bearing clusters of emerald grapes; rays from the precious stones made a play of light between the painted columns over the faces of the sleeping women.

Mâtho felt suffocated in the warm atmosphere that pressed upon him from the cedar compartments. All these symbols of fecundation, the lights, the perfumes, and the exhalations overcame him. Through this mystic bewilderment he dreamed of Salammbô; she was confused in his mind with the goddess herself, and his passion grew stronger, unfolding and spreading itself from the depths of his being, as the great lotuses blossoming on the surface of the water.

Spendius calculated what sums of money he could have made in former days by the sale of these sleeping women, and with a rapid glance in passing, he computed the value of the gold necklaces.

The temple, on this side as on the other, was impenetrable. They retraced their steps behind the first chamber. While Spendius sought to ferret out an entrance, Mâtho, prostrate before the ivory gate, implored Tanit, supplicating her not to permit their contemplated sacrilege. He endeavoured to appease her by caressing words such as one might address to an angry being. Meanwhile Spendius descried above the door a narrow aperture.

"Stand up!" said Spendius.

Mâtho complied, putting his back against the wall, standing erect, while Spendius, placing one foot in his hands and the other on his head, was enabled to reach the air-hole, through which he crawled and disappeared. Then Mâtho felt the knotted rope that Spendius had wound about his body before entering the cisterns, strike his shoulder. Clutching it with both hands, he drew himself up until he reached the opening, through which he crawled, and found himself beside Spendius, in a large hall full of shadow.

An attempt like this was unthought-of. The inadequacy of the means to prevent it showed that it was deemed impossible. The inspired terrors, more than the walls, defend such sanctuaries. Mâtho at every step expected to die.

A light gleamed in the extremity of the darkness; they drew nearer. It was a lamp burning in a shell placed on the pedestal of a statue wearing the cap of the Kabiri. Diamond discs were strewn over her long blue robe, and chains, passing under the pavement stones, attached her heels to the ground. At the sight of this idol, Mâtho suppressed a scream, stammering, "Ah! behold her! behold her!" . . . Spendius took up the lamp, moving it about to light himself.

"How impious you are!" murmured Mâtho; and yet he followed him.

They entered an apartment containing nothing except a black painting representing woman. Her legs reached to the top of one of the walls; her body filled the entire ceiling; from her naval hung suspended by a thread an enormous egg, and the remainder of her body, her head downward, descended the other wall to the level of the pavement, where her finger-points touched.

To pass on farther they drew aside a tapestry; a puff of wind entinguished the light, and they groped about, bewildered by the complications of the architecture. Suddenly they felt under their feet something strangely soft. Sparks crackled and sprang; they seemed to tread on fire. Spendius patted the floor with his hands, and could feel that it was carefully carpeted with lynx-skins. Then it seemed to them that a thick, moist rope, cold and clammy, slid between their legs. Through the fissures cut in the wall, thin rays of whiteness entered; they moved on by these uncertain streaks of light; presently they distinguished a large black serpent, as it darted quickly away and disappeared.

"Let us fly!" exclaimed Mâtho. "It is she! I felt her! She comes!"

"No! no," responded Spendius, "the temple is empty."

A dazzling light made them lower their eyes; all about them were innumerable beasts, emaciated, panting, extending their claws; those above were confused with those beneath in a horrible disorder, most frightful to behold. Serpents had feet; bulls had wings; fishes with human heads devoured fruits; flowers blossomed in crocodiles' jaws; and elephants, with their trunks elevated, floated through the air as freely and proudly as eagles. A terrible exertion distended their imperfect or manifold members. They seemed as they thrust out their tongues to be fain to exhale their souls with their breath. All forms were found there, as if the receptacle of germs had burst and emptied itself over the walls of the hall.

Twelve blue crystal globes encircled the room, supported on monsters resembling tigers. Their eyeballs protruded like those of snails, and menacingly curving their thick-set backs, they turned toward the farther part of the hall, where, radiant on an ivory chariot, was enthroned the supreme Rabbet, the Omnifecund, the last-imagined.

Tortoise shells, plumes, flowers, and birds were profusely heaped up about the idol, reaching to her waist. Silver cymbals hung from her ears and touched her cheeks. Her large fixed eyes stared upon the intruders, a luminous gem set in an obscene symbol on her forehead lighted the hall, and was reflected above the entrance in the red copper mirrors.

Mâtho took a step forward, a stone receded under the pressure of his heels, and behold! all the spheres revolved, the monsters roared, music rose melodious, swelling forth like the harmony of the planets; the tumultuous soul of Tanit gushed and expanded. She was about to rise, and with outstretched arms fill the sanctuary. Suddenly the monsters closed their jaws, and the crystal globes revolved no longer.

Then a solemn modulation coursed through the air, lasting for some time, and finally died away.

"The veil!" exclaimed Spendius. Nowhere could it be seen. Where was it to be found? How discover it? And if the priests had hidden it! Mâtho experienced an anguish of his heart, like a deception in his faith.

"Come this way!" whispered Spendius. Guided by an inspiration, he led Mâtho behind Tanit's chariot, where a slit a cubit wide penetrated the wall from the top to the bottom. Through this they entered into a small, round room, so lofty that it resembled the interior of a column. In the centre was a large black stone, semi-spherical, like a tambourine; flames burned above it, and an ebony cone was erected at the back, bearing a head and two arms. Beyond appeared a cloud wherein stars scintillated; in the depths of its folds were figures representing Eschmoûn, the Kabiri, many of the monsters they had already seen, the sacred beasts of the Babylonians, and numerous other unknown creatures. This passed like a mantle under the face of the idol, and ascending it spread out over the wall, hanging by the corners; it was at the same time bluish—like night; yellow—like dawn; and crimson—like the sun; harmonious, diaphanous, glittering, and light.

This was the mantle of the goddess, the sacred Zaïmph, which no one might behold! Both men grew pale.

"Take it!" said Mâtho. Spendius did not hesitate, but, leaning on the idol, unfastened the veil, which sank upon the ground. Mâtho placed one hand beneath it, and put his head through the opening in the middle; then he completely enveloped himself in the Zaïmph, and spread out his arms the better to contemplate its splendour.

"Let us go!" said Spendius.

Mâtho stood panting, with his eyes riveted on the pavement. Suddenly he exclaimed:

"But, what if I now go to her? I no longer need fear her beauty! What can she compass against me? Behold, I am more than a man! I can traverse flames! I can walk on the sea! Transport possesses me! Salammbô! Salammbô! I am thy master!"

His voice thundered. He appeared to Spendius of greater height, and transfigured.

Footsteps drew near; a door opened and a man appeared, a priest with a tall cap peering about with wide-open eyes. Before he could make a sign, Spendius rushed upon him, grappled him and buried the two daggers in his sides. His head rang upon the stone pavement.

They paused, as motionless as the body, listening. They heard nothing but the moaning of the wind through the half-open door. It led into a narrow passage. Spendius entered, followed by Mâtho. They almost immediately found themselves in the third enclosure, between the lateral porticoes among the quarters occupied by the priests. They hastened, hoping there might be some short way out behind the cells.

Spendius, crouching on the edge of the fountain, washed his blood-stained hands. The women still slept; the emerald vine shone. They resumed their way.

Something ran behind them under the trees, and Mâtho, who wore the veil, frequently felt a gentle tug at the fringe; it was a large cynocephalus, one of those that lived at liberty in the precincts of the temple. This creature clung to the veil as if it were conscious of the theft; nevertheless they did not dare to strike it, fearful that it might cry more loudly. Suddenly its anger seemed to subside, and it trotted beside them, swinging its body and its long hanging arms.

On reaching the barrier it bounded into a palm-tree.

Leaving the last enclosure, they diverged toward Hamilcar's palace, Spendius seeing that it would be useless to endeavour to dissuade Mâtho from his course.

They went by the Tanners' street, through the square of Muthumbal, the vegetable-market, and the cross-roads of Cynasyn. At the corner of a wall a man recoiled, frightened by the sparkling object that passed through the darkness.

"Hide the Zaïmph," whispered Spendius.

Other people passed, but they were unobserved.

At length they reached the mansions of Megara. The lighthouse, built at the back on the summit of the cliff, lit up the sky with a large, clear, red light; and the shadow of the palace, with its rising terraces, projected over the gardens like an immense pyramid. They entered the gardens through a hedge of jujube trees, cutting off obstructing branches with their poniards. Everything bore evidence of the Mercenaries' recent feast and depredations: the paddocks were broken down; the watercourses were dried up; the doors of the *ergastulum* stood open; no one was visible about the kitchens or cellars. They were surprised at the silence, broken only by the hoarse breathing of the elephants moving about in their paddocks, and the crepitations from the lighthouse, where a pile of aloes was burning.

Mâtho continued, repeating: "Where is she? I must see her; take me to her."

"It is madness," replied Spendius; "she will summon her slaves, and, in spite of your strength, you will be slain!"

They attained the stairway of the galleys. Mâtho raised his head, and imagined he could see high above a dim light softly radiating. Spendius tried to detain him, but he sprang swiftly up the steps.

In being again in these places where he had previously seen her, the interval that had elapsed was instantly effaced from his memory. A moment ago she was chanting between the tables—she had just disappeared—and ever since he seemed to have been climbing that stairway. The sky was covered with fire; the sea filled the horizon; and at every step an increasing immensity surrounded him; he continued to climb with that strange facility that one feels in dreams.

The rustling of the veil touching against the stones recalled his new power, but, in the excess of his hope, he no longer knew what to do; this uncertainty alarmed him. From time to time he pressed his face against the quadrangular openings in the closed apartments, and in many he fancied he could faintly see sleepers within.

The last story was narrower, and formed a sort of thimble on the top of the terraces. Mâtho slowly walked around it. A milky light filled the talc-sheets which closed the little openings in the wall, and, in their symmetrical arrangement resembled in the darkness rows of fine pearls. Mâtho's heart thrilled as he recognised the red door with the black cross. He felt as if he must fly. He pushed the door, and it opened.

A suspended lamp, fashioned like a galley, burned at the extreme end of the room, and three rays escaping from its silver keel, trembled over the high red wainscoting, which was decorated with black bands. A number of small gilded beams formed the ceiling, with amethysts and topazes set in the knots of the wood. Stretched against the wall of both sides of the room were very low couches made of white leathern straps; and shell-like arches opened in the depth of the wall, from which many garments in disorder hung down to the floor.

An onyx step surrounded an oval basin, on the edge of which rested a pair of dainty serpent-skin slippers, and beside them an alabaster pitcher. Wet footprints were clearly defined on the pavement beyond, and the vapours of exquisite perfumes floated everywhere.

Mâtho glided over the pavement, encrusted with gold, mother-of-pearl, and glass; and, despite the highly polished surface, it seemed to him that his feet sank, as if he were walking in sand. Behind the silver lamp he noticed a large azure square, suspended in the air by four cords; he drew toward it, with back bent and mouth open. Strewn about the room among purple cushions were flamingoes' wings, with handles of black coral branches, tortoise-shell combs, cedar caskets, and ivory spatulas. There were rows of rings, and bracelets hanging from antelopes' horns; and in a cleft in the walls, on a reed lattice, were clay vases, filled with water cooled by the incoming breezes. Frequently Mâtho struck his foot, as the floor was of unequal heights, making the chamber like a succession of apartments. At the far end a silver balustrade surrounded a carpet, painted with beautiful flowers. He reached the suspended couch, beside which stood an ebony stool, serving as a step.

The light was arrested at the edge of the couch, and the shadow, like a thick curtain, concealed all objects, save a little bare foot peering from under a white robe, resting on the corner of a red mattress. Mâtho very softly drew down the lamp. She slept, her cheek resting on one hand, the other arm thrown out and exposed. The curls of her wavy black hair tumbled about her in such abundance that she appeared actually to lie on a mass of black plumes; her white, wide tunic was crushed in soft draperies to her feet, indistinctly defining the outlines of her form; and her eyes were partially revealed between the half-closed lids. The perpendicular couch-hangings enshrouded her in a bluish atmosphere, and the swaying movement, imparted to the cords by her breathing, rocked her suspended couch in mid-air. An enormous mosquito buzzed.

Mâtho stood motionless, holding the silver lamp at arm's-length. Suddenly the airy mosquito nettings took fire and disappeared. Salammbô awoke. The fire had extinguished itself. She did not speak. The lamp flickered over the wainscoting in wave-like splashes of light.

"What is it?" she exclaimed.

He responded: "It is the veil of Tanit."

"The veil of Tanit?" cried Salammbô, as, supporting herself on her hands, she leaned tremblingly over the side of the couch.

He continued: "I have sought it for you in the depths of the sanctuary! Behold!" The Zaïmph glittered, covered with rays.

"You remember, then?" queried Mâtho. "In the night you came in my dreams; but I could not divine the mute command in your eyes."

She placed one foot on the ebony stool.

"Had I understood, I should have hastened, I should have abandoned the army, I should not have left Carthage. To obey you I would descend by the cavern of Hadrumetum into the realms of the Shades! Forgive me! Mountains have seemed to weigh upon my days, and yet something drew me on. I yearned to reach you; but without the aid of the gods I should never have dared! Let us depart; you must follow me, or if you do not desire to go I will remain. It makes no difference! Drown my soul in the sweetness of your breath! let my lips be crushed in kissing your hands!"

"Let me see it!" she exclaimed. "Nearer! nearer!"

As the dawn broke, a wine-coloured hue spread over the talc-sheets in the walls. Salammbô leaned back fainting on the pillows.

"I love you!" cried Mâtho.

"Give it to me!" and they drew nearer together.

She moved forward, robed in her white trailing simarre, her large eyes riveted on the veil. Mâtho contemplated her, dazzled by the splendour of her head. Holding toward her the Zaïmph, he endeavoured to envelop her in an embrace. She extended her arms. Suddenly she paused; and they stood, silently regarding each other with open mouths.

Without knowing what he solicited, a horror seized her. She raised her delicate eyebrows, her lips parted, and she trembled; at length recovering, she struck one of the brass pateras hanging at the corner of the red mattress, screaming:

"Help! Help! Back! Sacrilegious! Infamous! Accursed! Come to me, Taanach, Kroûm, Ewa, Micipsa, Schaoûl!"

Spendius' scared face appeared in the wall between the flagons, as he cried with alarm, "Fly! they are coming!"

A great uproar broke out, shaking the stairway, and a host of women, valets, and slaves burst into the apartment, carrying spears, maces, cutlasses, and poniards. They were paralysed with indignation at finding a man in Salammbô's room. The female servants uttered funereal wails, and the eunuchs fairly paled under their black skins.

Mâtho stood behind the balustrade, the Zaïmph enveloping him; he resembled a sidereal god, environed by the firmament. The slaves were about to throw themselves upon him, but Salammbô stopped them.

"Do not touch him! It is the mantle of the goddess!"

She had retreated into a corner, but now she stepped toward Mâtho, and extending her bare arm cursed him:

"Malediction on you, who have plundered Tanit! Hate, vengeance, massacre, and sorrow! May Gurzil, god of battles, rend you! May Mastiman, god of death, strangle you! and may the Other—whom I dare not name—burn you!"

Mâtho uttered a cry, like one wounded by a spear.

Frequently she repeated, "Go! Go!"

The throng of servants parted as Mâtho with downcast eyes slowly passed out through the group. At the door he was stopped by the fringe of the Zaïmph becoming entangled on one of the golden stars adorning the pavement, but by an abrupt movement of his shoulders he detached it and descended the stairs.

Spendius, bounding from terrace to terrace, leaping over the hedges and ditches, escaped from the gardens and reached the foot of the lighthouse; here the wall was abandoned, as the cliff was inaccessible. He advanced to the edge, then lying down on his back, slid to the bottom; then swimming, he reached the Cape of the Tombs, whence he made a wide circuit of the lagoon, reëntering the Barbarians' camp at evening.

The sun had risen as Mâtho descended the roads, glaring about him with terrible eyes, like an escaping lion. An indistinct murmur, emanating from the palace, and reëchoed in the distance from the direction of the Acropolis, struck his ears. It was rumoured that some one had taken from the temple of Moloch the treasure of Carthage; others spoke of the assassination of a priest; elsewhere it was imagined that the Barbarians had entered the city.

Mâtho, not knowing how to get out of the enclosures, followed a straight path; as soon as he was seen a clamour was raised. The people understood; consternation ensued; then an immense rage possessed them. From the back part of the Mappalian quarter, from the heights of the Acropolis, from the catacombs, from the lake shore, multitudes ran. The patricians left their palaces, tradesmen their shops, women abandoned their children; some seized swords, axes, and clubs; but the same superstitious obstacle that had hindered Salammbô likewise checked the mob.

How could they retake the veil? Only to look upon it was a crime; it was of the nature of the gods, and mere contact was death.

On the peristyles of the temples the priests wrung their hands in sheer desperation. The guards of the Legion galloped at random; people went up on the house-tops, thronged the terraces, and climbed upon the shoulders of the colossi and into the ships' riggings. Still Mâtho proceeded, and at every step the rage and terror of the people increased. The streets cleared at his approach, and the human torrent receded on both sides to the top of the walls. Mâtho saw everywhere only glaring eyes, wide open as if to devour him, and defiant, clenched fists, and he heard gnashing teeth between threatening lips; but above all Salammbô's maledictions resounded in his ears, in multiplied echoes.

Suddenly a long arrow whirred past, then another, and still another; stones also flew by, only to rebound about him on the ground; the missiles, all indifferently directed, for the throwers feared to strike the Zaïmph, passed over his head. Recognising this fact, Mâtho made the veil serve as a shield, holding it first to the right, then to the left; then before, then behind him; thus thwarted, they could invent no expedient. He walked faster and faster; finding the street openings all impassable, barred by ropes, chariots, and snares, his attempts to effect egress were balked, and he had again and again to retrace his steps; at length he entered the Square of Khamoûn, where the Balearic slingers had perished. Mâtho stopped, and grew as pale as death. This time he surely was lost. The multitude, witnessing his dilemma, clapped their hands with joy.

He ran up to the huge, closed gate. It was very high and most formidably constructed of heart of oak sheathed with brass, and studded with iron nails. Mâtho flung himself with all his might against it; the people stamped their feet, wild with delight at witnessing the impotence of his fury. Then he removed his sandal, spat upon it, and struck the immovable panels with it; again the entire concourse of people yelled, forgetting the veil in their transport.

They were about to rush forward to crush him. Mâtho gazed with large vague eyes at the crowd. His temples throbbed giddily; he felt invaded by such enervation as besets a drunken man. All at once he saw dangling the long chain that served to work the lever of the gate. With a fierce bound he grasped, and forcibly pulled the chain, at the same time using his feet as a buttress; the enormous valves, yielding to his mad strength, half-opened.

Once outside, he took the sublime Zaïmph from his neck, and lifted it over his head as high as possible. Distended and borne up by the sea breeze, the glittering material became resplendent in the sunshine, displaying its wondrous medley of inshot colours and precious stones; and over all its sheen could be described the faint images of its gods.

Thus Mâtho bore his trophy across the entire plain until he reached the camp of the Barbarians, and from the walls the irate people watched the fortune of Carthage pass into the hands of the enemy.

VI

HANNO

"I SHOULD have brought her with me!" Mâtho kept muttering to Spendius that evening. "I should have seized and carried her from her palace! No one would have dared stop me!"

Spendius paid no attention as he lay on his back enjoying himself beside a large jar of honey-water, wherein he would from time to time dip his head, in order to drink more copiously.

Mâtho resumed: "What is to be done? . . . How can we gain entrance again into Carthage?"

"I do not know," answered Spendius.

This impassibility exasperated Mâtho, who exclaimed:

"What! The fault is yours! You led me; then you desert me, coward that you are! Why then should I obey you? Do you believe yourself my master? Oh! panderer, slave, son of slaves!" He ground his teeth in wrath, and lifted his large hand over Spendius.

The Greek did not reply. A clay lamp burned low against the tent-pole, where the Zaïmph glittered in the suspended panoply.

All at once Mâtho drew on his cothurnes, buckled on his jacket of plates of brass, and put on his helmet.

"Where are you going?" asked Spendius.

"I shall return to the palace! Let me alone! I shall carry her off! And if they oppose me I shall crush them like vipers! I shall put her to death, Spendius! Yes," he repeated, "I shall kill her! You will see, I shall kill her!"

But Spendius, who was listening attentively, hurriedly pulled down the Zaïmph, threw it into a corner, and covered it with fleeces.

A murmur of voices was heard; torches blazed; and Narr' Havas entered, followed by about twenty men. They wore white woollen mantles, leather collars, wooden earrings, and hyena-skin shoes, and were armed with daggers. Pausing at the threshold, they leaned upon their lances, like shepherds resting.

Narr' Havas was the handsomest of the group. The leather straps encircling his slender arms were ornamented with pearls. His wide mantle was fastened round his head by a gold band, from which an ostrich plume fell drooping on his shoulders. A continual smile revealed his teeth; his eyes were sharp as arrows; his entire bearing was observant, and yet cool and indifferent.

He declared that he had come to join the Mercenaries, as the Republic had for a long time menaced his kingdom; consequently, he was interested in aiding the Barbarians, and he possessed the power to be of service to them. "I will give you elephants, for my forests are full of them; with wine, oil, barley, dates, pitch, and sulphur for sieges; with twenty thousand foot soldiers, and ten thousand horses. If I now address you, Mâtho, it is because the possession of the Zaïmph has rendered you of the first importance in the army; we were also friends at one time," he added.

Meanwhile Mâtho looked at Spendius, who listened intently, sitting on a heap of sheep-skins, all the time making little signs of assent with his head. Narr' Havas talked on, calling upon the gods to witness his sincerity. Then he cursed Carthage. To attest the violence of his imprecations, he broke a javelin, and all his men uttered in unison a deafening howl.

Mâtho, carried away by so much rage, cried out that he accepted the proffered alliance.

Then they brought a white bull and a black sheep—symbolical of day and night—which they slaughtered on the edge of a pit, and, when it became full of blood, they plunged their arms into it. Afterward Narr' Havas placed his outspread hand on Mâtho's breast, and Mâtho placed his hand on Narr' Havas' breast; then they repeated the stigmata on their tent-cloths. Subsequently the night was passed in eating. The remnants of meat, with all the skins, bones, horns, and hoofs, were burned.

Mâtho, at the time he returned to the camp wearing the veil of the goddess, had been greeted with tremendous acclamation. Even those who were not of the Canaanite religion felt in their vague enthusiasm the advent of a genius. As for seeking to capture the Zaïmph, no one thought of such a thing; the mysterious manner whereby he had acquired it sufficed in the minds of the Barbarians to make his possession of it legitimate. Thus thought the soldiers of African race; but others, whose hatred against the Republic was of more recent origin, knew not what to think. If they had only possessed vessels, they would have immediately set sail for their own countries.

Spendius, Narr' Havas, and Mâtho sent envoys to all the tribes of the Punic territory. Carthage had exhausted the strength of these people by exorbitant taxes; punishing delinquents, and even those who murmured, by chains, the executioner's axe, or the cross. It was compulsory to cultivate that which pleased the Republic, and furnish what she demanded. No one had the right to own a weapon. Whatever villages rebelled, the inhabitants were sold as slaves, the governors were estimated like wine-presses, according to the quantity of taxes they were able to extort.

Beyond the region immediately subject to Carthage were their allies, who were burdened with only a moderate tribute; beyond these allies wandered the Nomads, who could be let loose upon them. By this system the harvests were always abundant, the breeding studs skilfully conducted, the plantations superb. Old Cato, a master in agriculture and slave-raising, ninety-two years later was amazed at it, and the death cry, *"Delenda est Carthago,"* repeated by him in Rome, was but an exclamation of jealous cupidity.

During the last war the exactions had been doubled, so that nearly all the towns of Libya had surrendered to Regulus. As punishment, the Republic exacted from them one thousand talents, twenty thousand head of cattle, three hundred sacks of gold-dust, and considerable advances of grain; and the chiefs of tribes had been crucified or thrown to the lions.

Carthage was especially execrated by Tunis, which was an older city than the metropolis. Tunis could not forgive the grandeur of the Republic, as she lay fronting its walls, crouching in the mud on the water's edge, like a malignant beast watching its prey. Transportations, massacres, epidemics, had not enfeebled her; moreover, she had supported Archagathus, son of Agathocles. The Eaters-of-Unclean-Things soon found arms there.

The couriers had not as yet set out on their mission when a universal joy spread abroad throughout the provinces. Without waiting for provocation they strangled the stewards of the houses and the functionaries of the Republic in the baths; old weapons were brought forth from caverns, where they had formerly been hidden, and the iron of ploughs was forged into swords; children deftly whetted javelins on the doorsteps; and the women contributed their necklaces, rings, earrings, and, in fact, everything that could be transposed or employed in any manner for the desired destruction of Carthage. Each one wished to give something. Stacks of lances accumulated in the country towns like sheaves of maize. Cattle and money were sent to Mâtho, who at once paid all arrears to the Mercenaries, and this, which had been suggested by Spendius, resulted in Mâtho being named Schalischim of the Barbarians.

Meanwhile men trooped in from all quarters. First came the aborigines, who were followed by the slaves from the fields. Caravans of Negroes were seized and armed, and the merchants who were going to Carthage, calculating on a more certain and speedy profit, joined in with the Barbarians. Unceasingly numerous bands arrived, and from the heights of the Acropolis the Carthaginians could see the army rapidly growing.

On the platform of the aqueduct the Guards of the Legion were posted as sentinels, and near them, at certain distances, were erected huge brazen vats, in which boiled quantities of asphalt. Below, on the plain, the vast concourse stirred about tumultuously. They were uncertain, experiencing that embarrassment with which Barbarians are always filled whenever they encounter walls.

Utica and Hippo-Zarytus withheld their alliance. Phœnician colonies, like Carthage, were self-governed, and in the treaties which the Republic concluded had always caused to be subjoined clauses to distinguish them from it. Yet they respected this strongest sister, who protected them, and they did not believe that a mass of Barbarians was able to vanquish her, but on the contrary, that Carthage could annihilate the enemy. They desired to remain neutral and live peacefully.

But the position of these two colonies rendered them indispensable. Utica, at the end of a gulf, was convenient to bring assistance from without into Carthage. If Utica alone should be captured, then Hippo-Zarytus, six hours farther along on the coast, could replace the loss, and the metropolis, being thus revictualled, would be found impregnable.

Spendius wanted the siege to be begun immediately. Narr' Havas strongly opposed such hasty action, as it was necessary an attack should first be made on the frontier. This was the opinion of the veterans called in council, and approved by Mâtho. It was decided that Spendius should attack Utica; Mâtho, Hippo-Zarytus; that the third army corps, commanded by Autharitus, resting upon Tunis, should occupy the plain of Carthage, and that Narr' Havas should return to his own kingdom to procure elephants, and with his cavalry hold the roads.

The women clamoured violently against this decision; they coveted the jewels of the Punic dames. The Libyans also protested, declaring that they had been summoned to engage in a siege against Carthage, and now they were ordered away from it. The soldiers departed almost alone.

Mâtho commanded his own companions, also the Iberians and Lusitanians, the men from the West and from the islands; while those who spoke Greek requested that they might be placed under Spendius's command, because of his astuteness.

The Carthaginians were stupefied when they saw this army all at once in motion, stretching away under the mountain of Ariana, by the road to Utica on the seacoast. A detachment remained before Tunis; the rest disappeared, to reappear on the other shore of the gulf, on the outskirts of the woods, in which it was again lost to view.

Possibly this army numbered eighty thousand men. The two Tyrian cities would offer no resistance, and they would return against Carthage. Already a considerable army cut her off, occupying the base of the isthmus, and soon Carthage would be in a state of famine, as the people were dependent on the aid of the provinces, the citizens paying no contributions, as at Rome.

Carthage was weak in political genius. Her eternal strife for gain had prevented her from exercising that prudence which encourages the highest ambition. She was like a galley anchored on the Libyan sands, maintained there by force of labour. The nations, like billows, roared about her, and the least storm shook this formidable machine to the foundation.

Her treasury had been depleted by the Roman war and all that had been squandered and lost during the bargaining with the Barbarians. However, she must have soldiers, and not a government now reposed trust in the Republic! Ptolemy, a short time before, had refused to loan Carthage two thousand talents. And yet another significant cause of discouragement was the rape of the Veil. Spendius had wisely foreseen this.

But the nation, which felt itself detested, clasped to its heart its money and its gods, and its patriotism was maintained by the constitution of its government.

In the first place, the power belonged to all, without anyone being able to monopolise it. Personal debts were considered as public debts. The men of Canaanite race had the monopoly of commerce. In multiplying the profits of piracy by the practice of usury, and by rigorously exacting to the extreme limit from the slaves, the lands and the poor, men sometimes became wealthy. Wealth alone opened all the magistracies, and even though the power and money were perpetuated in the same families, the oligarchy was tolerated because each had the hope of some day sharing in it.

The societies of commerce, wherein the laws were elaborated, elected the inspectors of finance, to whose discretion it was left, on quitting office, to nominate the hundred members of the Council of Elders who belonged to the Grand Assembly, a general convention of all the Rich.

As for the two Suffets, the relics of monarchy and inferior to consuls, they were elected on the same day, from two distinct families. It was desirable that they should be divided by various animosities, and thus mutually enfeebled. They were not empowered to deliberate on the war, and when they were conquered the Grand Council crucified them.

Hence the strength of Carthage emanated from the Syssites, who were established in a grand court in the centre of Malqua, the spot where it was supposed the first bark manned by Phœnician sailors had landed. Since that period the sea had retreated greatly. It was a group of small chambers of an archaic architecture, built from the trunks of palm-trees, with stone cornerpieces, separated one from another, affording to each chamber complete isolation for the various companies in their conferences. The Rich gathered therein daily to discuss their own affairs, as well as those of the Government, from the procuring of pepper to the conquest of Rome.

Three times every moon they had their couches carried up on the high terrace, bordering the wall of the court; and from below they could be seen sitting at table in the open air, without cothurnes or mantles; their diamonds flashing on their fingers as they handled their food, and their large earrings glittering as they dangled between the flagons. They were all strong and fat, half-naked, happy, and laughing, eating in the open under the blue sky, like huge sharks disporting in the sea.

This time, however, they could not dissemble their anxiety; they were too pale. The crowd below waited to escort them to their palaces, in the hope of ascertaining some news. As during times of the plague, all the houses were closed; occasionally the streets would suddenly swarm with people, and just as suddenly empty and become deserted. Some ascended the Acropolis, others ran toward the harbour. Every night the Grand Council deliberated. At last the people were convened in the square of Khamoûn, and it was officially announced that they had decided to place in command Hanno, the great conqueror of Hecatompylus.

He was a pious, crafty man, merciless to the Africans—a true Carthaginian.

His revenues equalled those of the Barcas, and no other man had such experience in administrative affairs.

Hanno decreed the enrolment of all able-bodied citizens, placed catapults upon the towers, demanded exorbitant supplies of weapons, ordered the construction of fourteen galleys, which were not required; and commanded that everything be registered and accurately set down in writing. He was carried by his slaves to the lighthouse, the arsenal, and into the treasury of the temples; and was continually to be seen in his large litter, as it rocked from step to step, ascending or descending the stairways of the Acropolis. At night, in his palace, being unable to sleep, he prepared himself for the coming battle by shouting in a terrible voice orders for military manœuvres.

Everyone, by reason of extreme terror, became brave. The Rich at cockcrow would assemble along the length of Mappals, turning up their robes as they practised the use of the pike. But having no instructor, they disputed among themselves as to methods. They would sit panting on the tombs, then begin again their exercises after resting. Many even dieted themselves. Some imagined that to acquire strength it was necessary to eat large quantities, and gorged themselves; others, incommoded by corpulence, endeavoured to reduce themselves by fastings.

Utica had already frequently asked the assistance of Carthage; but Hanno would not move until the last screw was set in every war machine. He lost three more moons of time in the equipment of the hundred and twelve elephants, stabled in the ramparts. These vanquishers of Regulus, so loved by the people, certainly could not be treated too well. Hanno ordered their brazen breastplates to be recast, their tusks gilded, their towers enlarged, and had made for them most beautiful purple caparisons, bordered with very heavy fringes. Inasmuch as their leaders were called Indians (the first doubtless having come from the Indies), he ordered that they should wear Indian costumes, consisting of a white turban, and little breeches of byssus, which, with their transverse pleats, looked like two valves of a shell, fastened on their hips.

During all these preparations, the army commanded by Autharitus remained stationed before Tunis, concealed behind a mud wall, and protected on the top by thorn-bushes. The Negroes erected, in various places, on large stakes, frightful images, human masks composed of birds' feathers, heads of jackals and serpents, which gaped toward the enemy to frighten them; by such measures the Barbarians considered themselves to be utterly invincible, and danced, wrestled, and juggled, convinced that Carthage before long would be destroyed.

Any other general than Hanno could have crushed with facility this multitude, embarrassed by herds and women, and who, furthermore, were not versed in any military tactics; and Autharitus had grown discouraged and no longer required his men to drill.

They scattered before him, as he passed by, rolling his large blue eyes. Then when he arrived at the lake shore, he would remove his seal-skin tunic, untie the cord holding back his long red locks, and soak them in the water. He regretted that he had not deserted to the Romans with the two thousand Gauls of the temple of Eryx.

Frequently during the middle of the day the sun's rays suddenly vanished, then the gulf and open sea seemed as motionless as molten lead. A cloud of brown dust rising perpendicularly, would course along in whirling eddies, under the force of which the palm trees bowed, the sky became obscured, stones could be heard rebounding on the backs of the animals, and the Gaul would glue his lips against the holes in his tent, gasping from exhaustion and melancholy. In fancy he inhaled the perfumes of his native pastures on autumn mornings, he saw the snowflakes, and again heard the lowing of the aurochs lost in the fog; then closing his eyes, he seemed to see the fires in the long cabins thatched with straw, as they quivered on the marshes at the edge of the woods.

There were others who regretted their native country as much as he, though it might not be so far away. The Carthaginian captives could indeed distinguish, at the other side of the gulf, on the declivities of Byrsa, the canopies spread over the courts of their dwellings. Sentinels patrolled around these prisoners perpetually. Each man wore an iron yoke, by which all were attached to one chain. The crowd never tired of coming to look at these patrician captives. The women showed their little children the beautiful Punic robes hanging in tatters upon their shrunken limbs.

Every time that Autharitus saw Gisco, a fury possessed him at the thought of the old general's insult to him, and he would certainly have killed him but for the oath he had made to Narr' Havas. He would then return to his tent and drink a mixture of barley and cumin, till he became drunk to unconsciousness: at noontime the following day he would awake, consumed by a horrible thirst.

Mâtho, in the meantime, besieged Hippo-Zarytus. This town was protected by a lake communicating with the sea. It had three lines of fortifications, and on the heights which overlooked it, a wall extended, fortified by towers.

Mâtho had never before commanded such an undertaking. Moreover, the thought of Salammbô beset him, and he dreamed of the pleasures of her beauty, as in the sweetness of a revenge that transported him with pride. His desire to see her again was bitter, furious, unceasing. He even thought of offering himself as a bearer of a flag of truce, in the hope that once in Carthage he might make his way to her. Often he would sound the signal for assault, and without waiting for aught, would dart on to the pier that they were endeavouring to construct in the sea. Here he tore up the stones with his hands, turned everything upside down, plunging and striking about in every direction with his broad sword. The Barbarians followed his leadership, and dashed pell-mell upon the works; the overcrowded ladders would break with a loud crash, and masses of men tumble into the water, which leaped in reddened waves against the walls. At last the tumult would lessen and the soldiers withdraw to renew the assault. Mâtho would seat himself outside his tent, wipe his blood-spattered face, and, looking toward Carthage, wistfully gaze at the horizon.

Facing him, among the olive, palm, myrtle, and plane trees, were two wide pools, which joined another lake, the outline of which was not perceptible from this point of view. Behind a mountain rose other mountains, and in the middle of the immense lake stood an island, perfectly black, of a pyramidal shape. On the left, at the extremity of the gulf, the sand heaps resembled great golden billows arrested in their course, and the sea, flat as a pavement of lapis-lazuli, ascending imperceptibly to the sky. The verdure of the country in places disappeared under long yellow patches, the carobs shone bright as coral buttons, the vines hung in festoons from the top of sycamores. The faint murmuring of the water was audible, the tufted skylarks hopped about, and the last flashes of the sun gilded the carapaces of the tortoises as they came out of the rushes to inhale the sea breezes.

Mâtho, sighing deeply, lay flat on the ground, digging his nails into the sand, and wept, feeling wretched, mean, and forsaken. He could never possess Salammbô; and he could not even succeed in capturing a town. At night, alone in his tent, he contemplated the Zaïmph, querying of what use was this thing of the gods to him? And doubts sprang up in the Barbarian's mind. Then it seemed to him, on the contrary, that the vestment of the goddess belonged to Salammbô, and that part of her soul floated in it, more subtle than a breath; and he caressingly patted it, breathed with his face buried in its folds, kissed it with sobs. He drew it over his shoulders to intensify the illusion that he was embracing her.

Sometimes, by the light of the stars, he would suddenly leave his tent, stepping over the sleeping soldiers wrapped in their mantles; then at the gates of the camp he would leap upon a horse, gallop away, and two hours afterwards be at Utica in the tent of Spendius. At first he would talk of the siege, but his real motive was to ease his sadness by talking about Salammbô.

Spendius exhorted him to wisdom.

"Expel from your soul these mysteries that but degrade it! Formerly you obeyed, but now you command an army; and if Carthage is not conquered, at least we shall have provinces granted to us, and we shall become as kings!"

But why was it that the possession of the Zaïmph had failed to give them victory?

According to Spendius it was necessary to wait. Mâtho imagined that perhaps the veil concerned exclusively those of the Canaanite race, and with Barbarian subtilty said to himself:

"The Zaïmph will avail me nothing; but, because they have lost it, it avails them nothing."

Then came a scruple that disturbed him; he feared in adoring the Libyan god Aptouknos to offend Moloch, and timidly asked Spendius to which of these gods it would be well to sacrifice a man.

"Always sacrifice!" said Spendius, laughing.

Mâtho did not understand such indifference, and suspected that the Greek had a genius of whom he did not wish to speak.

All religions, as all races, met together in these Barbarian armies, and they were ever considerate of the gods of others, for they also inspired terrors. Many mingled in their native religion foreign practices. It was not fitting to adore the stars, but this or that constellation being fatal or helpful, they made sacrifices to it. An unknown amulet, found by chance in a moment of peril, became a divinity. Or perhaps it was a name—nothing but a name—which they repeated without ever attempting to understand its meaning.

But the result of having pillaged numerous temples, and seen many nations and massacres, was that many ended by believing only in destiny and death, and every night they slept with the perfect placidity of wild beasts.

Spendius would have spat upon the images of Jupiter Olympus; notwithstanding, he dreaded to speak aloud in the dark, and never failed to put on his right sandal first.

He raised a long quadrangular terrace fronting Utica, but in proportion as it was built up the ramparts were also heightened. That which was beaten down by one army, was almost immediately reërected by the other.

Spendius looked carefully to his troops; he constantly devised plans, and endeavoured to recall the stratagems he had heard recounted in his travels.

Why did not Narr' Havas return? The delay filled them with anxiety.

Hanno had at last completed his preparations.

During one moonless night he moved his elephants and soldiers on rafts across the Gulf of Carthage. They then turned around the Hot-Springs Mountain, to avoid Autharitus, and proceeded so slowly that, instead of surprising the Barbarians the next morning, as the Suffet had planned, they only arrived at noon on the third day.

On the eastern side of Utica a plain reached as far as the great lagoon of Carthage; behind it extended at a right angle a valley, cutting between two low mountains, which suddenly closed in. Further off, to the left, the Barbarians were encamped in such a manner as to blockade the harbour. They were sleeping in their tents—as on this day besieged and besiegers were too weary to enter into combat, and had sought repose—when at the curve of the hills the Carthaginian army appeared.

The camp followers, armed with slings, were stationed on the wings. The Guards of the Legion, wearing armour of golden scales, formed the first line: their large horses, which had neither manes, hair, nor ears, wore a silver horn in the centre of their foreheads, to make them resemble rhinoceroses. Between their squadrons, young men, wearing on their heads small helmets, balanced in both hands ashwood javelins; the heavy infantry, armed with long pikes, marched in the rear. All the traders were laden with as many weapons as they could possibly carry: some bore a lance, an axe, a mace, and two swords: others, like porcupines, bristled with darts, and their arms stood out from their cuirasses of sheets of horn, or plaques of metal. Finally the scaffoldings of the lofty war engines appeared: *carro-balistas*, onagers, catapults and *scorpions*, rocking on cars, drawn by mules and quadrigas of oxen.

As the army unfolded itself, the captains ran breathlessly from right and left, giving orders, closing up the lines, and maintaining proper spaces.

The Elders who were in command had come decked in purple casques, the magnificent fringes of which became entangled in the straps of their cothurnes. Their faces, greased over with vermilion, glistened under enormous helmets, surmounted by images of the gods. They carried shields bordered with ivory, and studded with jewels; as they passed in glittering array, they appeared like suns traversing brass walls.

The Carthaginians manœuvred so awkwardly, that the Barbarians, in derision, invited them to be seated: and shouted that they would soon empty their huge bellies, dust the gilding from their skins, and make them drink iron.

At the top of a pole planted before the tent of Spendius, a strip of green cloth fluttered as a signal. The Carthaginians responded to it by a great bluster of trumpets, cymbals, drums, and flutes made of asses' bones.

Already the Barbarians had leaped beyond the palisades, and now were face to face with their enemies, within a javelin's length of them.

A Balearic slinger advanced a step, placed in his sling one of his clay balls, and waved his arm; an ivory shield was shattered, and the two armies mingled together.

The Greeks with their long lances pricked the horses' nostrils, making them fall back on their riders; the slaves whose duty it was to sling stones had chosen those which were too large, and they fell close to them. The Punic foot soldiers, in striking out with their long swords to cut down the enemy, exposed their right sides; the Barbarians broke into their lines, thrusting at them with their broad swords: they madly stumbled over the dying and dead, blinded by the blood that spurted into their faces. The confused mass of pikes, helmets, cuirasses, swords, and human limbs quivered and writhed, widening and narrowing in elastic contractions.

The Carthaginian cohorts showed wider and wider gaps; their heavy war engines could not be extricated from the sands: and finally the Suffet Hanno's litter—his grand litter, with the crystal pendulums, that had been seen since the very beginning of the attack swaying among the soldiers like a barque on the ocean—suddenly foundered. He doubtless was killed! The Barbarians found themselves alone. They burst forth into song.

The dust was beginning to settle, when Hanno reappeared on the back of an elephant. He sat bareheaded while a Negro carried over him an umbrella of byssus. His collar of blue plaques struck on the painted flowers of his black tunic, circles of diamonds surrounded his enormous arms; he advanced, mouth wide open, brandishing an enormous spear which expanded at the end like a lotus, and was more brilliant than a mirror.

The earth trembled, and suddenly the Barbarians saw, bearing down upon them in one straight line, all the Carthaginian elephants, with their tusks gilded, ears painted blue, sheathed in bronze, shaking above their purple caparisons the leather towers, in each of which were three archers holding large, drawn bows.

The soldiers scarcely had time to seize their arms, they were ranged at random, frozen with terror, and helpless from indecision.

Already from the towers volleys of arrows and javelins, fire-lances and masses of lead were being hurled down on them. Some clung on to the fringes of the caparisons, in an effort to climb up, but their hands were hewn off with cutlasses, and they fell backward on the drawn swords of their own comrades.

Their pikes were too frail and broke. The elephants plunged into the phalanxes like wild boars through clumps of grasses. They uprooted the palisades with their trunks, and traversed the camp from end to end, over-turning the tents with their breasts.

Panic-stricken, the Barbarians took to flight, hiding themselves in the hills that bordered the valley whence the Carthaginians had issued.

Hanno presented himself before the gates of Utica as conqueror, and sounded his trumpet. The three judges of the city appeared in the opening of the battlements, on the summit of a tower. The people of Utica did not care to receive as guests so many armed men. Hanno was furious. Finally they consented to admit him with a small escort.

The streets were too narrow to admit the elephants, so they had to be left outside the city gates.

As soon as the Suffet entered the town, the principal men came to welcome him. He demanded to be immediately conducted to the bath-house, and there summoned his cooks.

Three hours later he was still immersed in the oil of cinnamon with which the bath-tub had been filled, and while bathing he ate from off an ox-hide stretched across the tub flamingoes' tongues and poppy-seeds, seasoned with honey. His Greek doctor, in a long, yellow robe, stood beside him, immobile, from time to time directing the temperature of the bath; and two young boys leaned on the steps of the bath rubbing the leper's legs. But the care of his body did not interfere with his love for public affairs, for he occupied himself with the dictation of a letter to the Grand Council; and, as some prisoners had been taken, he pondered as to what terrible new torture could be invented for them.

"Stop!" said he to the slave who stood near, writing on the palm of his hand. "Let them be brought to me! I wish to see them."

And from the end of the hall, which was now filled with a whitish vapour, on which the torches cast red spots, some one pushed forward three Barbarians: a Samnite, a Spartan, and a Cappadocian.

"Proceed!" said Hanno. "Rejoice, light of the Baals! your Suffet has exterminated the ravenous dogs; Benedictions on the Republic! Order prayers to be said!" He perceived the captives, and then burst into laughter.

"Ha! ha! ha! my braves of Sicca. You do not shout so loud to-day. It is I! Do you recognize me? Where then are your swords? What terrible men are these!"—and he feigned to hide as if he experienced great fear.— "You asked for horses, women, lands, magistracies, and doubtless also for priesthoods! Why not? Ah, well, I will give you the lands, and you shall never leave them. You shall be married to gallows that are new! For your pay, ingots of lead shall be melted in your mouths, and I will put you in the very best places, far up and exalted, among the clouds, near the eagles!"

The three Barbarians, long-haired and tattered, looked at him without understanding what he said. Wounded in the knees, they had been lassoed and captured, and the ends of the heavy chains on their hands dragged on the stones. Hanno was indignant at their impassibility.

"On your knees! On your knees! Jackals! Dirt! Vermin! Excrement! And they do not reply? Enough! Silence! Let them be flayed alive! No! not now, presently!"

He snorted like a hippopotamus, and rolled his eyes about. The perfumed oil trickled down his gross body, sticking to the scales on his skin; and the torchlights threw over him a pink hue.

He resumed his official letter: "During four days we suffered intensely from the sun. In the passage of the Macar we lost some mules. Despite the enemies' position, the extraordinary courage . . . Oh! Demonades, how I suffer! Have the bricks reheated till they are red hot."

A raking noise was heard in the furnaces. The incense smoked in the large perfume-pans, and the shampooers, entirely naked, dripping like sponges, anointed his joints with a paste composed of wheat, sulphur, black-wine, bitches'-milk, myrrh, galban, and storax.

An incessant thirst consumed him. The man dressed in the yellow robe, however, did not yield to his patient's desire; he held to him a golden cup in which steamed a broth of vipers.

"Drink!" urged he, "that the strength of the serpents, born of the sun, may penetrate the marrow of your bones. And take courage! O reflection of the gods! You know, moreover, that a priest of Eschmoûn watches the cruel stars around the Dog whence you derive your malady. They pale like the spots on your skin; therefore you will not die."

"Ah, yes! That is true!" repeated the Suffet—"I ought not to die of them!" And from his violet purple lips escaped a breath more nauseous than the exhalations of a corpse.

His eyes, which were without lashes, resembled two burning coals; heavy folds of skin hung on his forehead; his ears stood out from his head, and began to swell; and the deep wrinkles that formed semicircles around his nostrils gave him a strange, frightful aspect, the air of a savage brute.

His unnatural voice resembled a roar as he said: "Perhaps you are right, Demonades. Look, even now some of the ulcers are closed; I feel stronger! See how I eat!"

And, less from gluttony than ostentation—and to convince himself that he was really improving—he first ate of the minced cheese and marjoram, then the boned-fish, pumpkin, oysters with eggs, horseradish, truffles and brochettes of little birds.

As he looked at the prisoners while he ate, he delighted in the imagination of their tortures. Then he recalled Sicca; and his rage for all his sufferings was showered, in a volley of insults, on these three men.

"Ah, traitors! Wretches! Infamous! Accursed! And you outraged me! Me!—the Suffet Hanno! Their services, the price of their blood, as they have said. Ah! yes! their blood! their blood!" Then he talked to himself: "All shall perish! Not one shall be sold! It would be best to bring them to Carthage. No, let me see . . . without doubt I have not brought enough chains. . . . Write: 'Send to me' . . . How many prisoners are there? Let some one go and ask Muthumbal. Go! No pity! And have all their hands cut off, and brought to me in baskets!"

But strange cries, at once hoarse and shrill, penetrated the hall, above Hanno's voice and the clatter of the dishes which were being placed around him. The cries increased; and in an instant a furious trumpeting of elephants burst forth, as if the battle had broken out anew. A tremendous tumult encompassed the town.

The Carthaginians had not attempted to pursue the Barbarians. They had established themselves at the foot of the walls with their baggage, valets, and all their satraps' train, to rejoice under their beautiful pearl-embroidered tents. The Mercenaries' camp was nothing but a heap of ruins on the plain.

In the meantime Spendius had regained his courage. He despatched Zarxas to Mâtho, and hastened through the woods to rally his men. Their losses were not great, and enraged at having been thus conquered without fighting, they were reforming their lines, when a vat of petroleum, doubtless left by the enemy, was discovered. Spendius had swine carried off from the neighbouring farmhouses, besmeared them with the bitumen, and setting fire to them, turned them loose toward Utica.

The elephants, frenzied by these running flames, stampeded over the rising ground. The ground inclined upwards; a volley of javelins was hurled upon the infuriated creatures; they turned back upon the Carthaginians, ripped them up with strokes of their tusks, and trampling them beneath their massive feet, suffocated and crushed them. The Barbarians descended the hill behind them; the Punic camp, being without entrenchments, was sacked at the first attack, and the Carthaginians found themselves crushed against the city gates, which were kept closed from fear of the Mercenaries.

At daybreak Mâtho's foot soldiers were seen advancing from the west, and at the same time the Numidian cavalry of Narr' Havas appeared, bounding over the ravines and underbrush, running down the fugitives like hounds chasing hares.

This change of fortune interrupted the Suffet, and he screamed for some one to assist him to leave the vapour bath.

Before him still stood the three captives. A Negro, the same who had carried his umbrella during the battle, leaned over and whispered something in his ear.

"What then?" slowly asked the Suffet. "Ah, well, kill them!" he added, in a brusque tone.

The Ethiopian drew from his belt a long dagger, and the three heads fell. One rebounded into the midst of the recent feast, then rolled into the tub of oil, and floated for sometime with open mouth and fixed eyes.

The morning light entered the slits in the walls; the three bodies lay on their breasts. Great streams gurgled from the headless trunks like fountains, and a sheet of blood flowed over the mosaics, which were sanded with blue powder. The Suffet dipped his hands in the warm pool, rubbing the blood over his knees, this being considered a remedy for his malady.

Evening came. He escaped from Utica with his escort, making his way to the mountains to rejoin his army. He found only the remnants of it. Four days later he was at Gorza, on the top of a defile, when Spendius' troops showed themselves below. Had twenty good lancers attacked the front of their advancing column, they could easily have checked them; but the paralysed Carthaginians watched them pass by. Hanno recognised in the rear guard the Numidian king. Narr' Havas bowed his head in salutation, making a sign that he could not interpret.

Hanno's forces returned toward Carthage in terror, marching only at night, and hiding by day in the olive woods. During every stage some of the men died. They frequently thought themselves to be lost. Finally they attained the Cape of Hermæum, where vessels came for them. Hanno was so fatigued, so desperate, and especially so overwhelmed by the loss of the elephants, that he besought Demonades to administer poison to him, and thereby put an end to his existence. Besides, he already imagined himself extended on his cross.

Carthage, however, did not possess the strength to be indignant with him. The losses amounted to four hundred thousand nine hundred and seventy-two shekels of silver, fifteen thousand six hundred and twenty-three shekels of gold, eighteen elephants, fourteen members of the Grand Council, three hundred patricians, eight thousand citizens, corn enough for three moons, considerable baggage, and all their war engines.

The defection of Narr' Havas was undoubted. The two sieges recommenced, and now Autharitus' army extended from Tunis to Rhades. From the top of the Acropolis could be seen, over the surrounding country, wide columns of smoke ascending to the sky from the burning mansions of the patricians.

One man only had the power to save the Republic. The Carthaginians repented that they had misunderstood him, and even the peace faction voted holocausts for Hamilcar's return.

The sight of the Zaïmph had utterly prostrated Salammbô. At night she believed she could hear the footsteps of the goddess, and would awake terrified and screaming. Every day she sent food to the temples. Taanach was wearied executing her orders, and Schahabarim left her no more.

VII

HAMILCAR BARCA

NIGHTLY, from the summit of the temple of Eschmoûn, the Announcer-of-the-Moons proclaimed through his trumpet the disturbances of the planet. One morning he saw in the west what appeared to be a bird, skimming its long wings over the surface of the sea. It was a ship with three tiers of oars, the prow ending in a sculptured horse.

The sun rose; the Announcer-of-the-Moon shaded his eyes, and seizing his clarion at arm's length, sent a ringing blast over Carthage.

The people issued from every house, unable to believe the announcement, and disputing amongst themselves the probability of its truth. The pier was soon crowded with the curious. Finally, Hamilcar's trireme was recognized by all.

The vessel advanced in proud and haughty fashion, her yard perfectly straight, her sail bulging the entire length of the mast. Cleaving the foam about her, her gigantic oars struck the water in cadence. From time to time the extremity of her keel, formed like a ploughshare, was seen as she plunged; and under the beak at the end of the prow, the sculptured horse with ivory head, rearing both its feet, seemed to course over the plains of the sea.

As she rounded the promontory her sail fell; the wind had ceased; and now, near the pilot, could be distinguished a man standing bare-headed. It was the Suffet Hamilcar himself! About his sides he wore shining plates of steel; a red mantle, attached to his shoulders, exposed his arms; two very long pearls hung from his ears, and his black bushy beard rested on his breast.

The galley, tossed between the rocks, coasted the mole, and the excited crowd followed her along on the flagstones, shouting:

"Welcome! Greeting! Eyc of Khamoûn! Oh, deliver us! It is the fault of the Rich! They desire your death! Guard yourself, Barca!"

He made no response, as if the clamour of the oceans and the din of battles had completely deafened him. But as the vessel came under the stairway which descended from the Acropolis, Hamilcar raised his head, crossed his arms, and looked at the temple of Eschmoûn. He gazed still higher, up into the dome of the pure sky, and in a harsh tone cried out an order to his sailors. The trireme bounded through the water. She grazed the idol set up at the corner of the pier to ward off storms; and into the merchant port, full of filth, splinters of wood, and fruit-rinds, she crowded, ripping open the sides of vessels moored to piles ending in crocodiles' jaws.

The people hastened to follow the vessel. Some excitedly plunged into the water and swam alongside of her. Soon the galley reached the head of the port, before the formidable gate, bristling with spikes. The gate lifted, to allow the trireme to pass, and it vanished under the deep vault.

The Military Harbour was completely separated from the town, and when ambassadors came, they were obliged to enter between two walls into a passage emerging to the left in front of the temple of Khamoûn. This large basin of water was round, like a cup, and surrounded by quays, where docks were built to shelter vessels. Before each dock were two columns, bearing on their capitals the horns of Ammon, which formed a continuous portico all around the basin. In the centre, on an isle, was a house for the Suffet of the sea. The water was so limpid that the bottom of the basin, paved with white shells, was visible.

The noise from the streets did not penetrate thus far, and Hamilcar, in passing, recognised the triremes which he had formerly commanded. There now remained scarcely twenty vessels in shelter on the shore—leaning over on their sides, or straight on their keels, with their poops high in the air, displaying their bulging prows covered with gilding and mystic symbols. The chimeras had lost their wings, the Patæcian gods their arms, the bulls their silver horns; yet all, though half defaced, inert, and rotten, were full of associations, and still exhaled the aroma of past voyages; now, like disabled soldiers who again meet their old commander, these old vessels seemed to say to him:

"Here we are! 'Tis we! And you also—you are vanquished!"

No one excepting the marine Suffet had the right to enter the admiralty. Until proof of his death was certainly established, he was always considered to be alive. By this observance the Elders avoided an additional master. Hence, despite their disaffection toward Hamilcar, they had not failed to respect the custom.

The Suffet entered the deserted apartments, at every step recognising armour, furniture, and familiar objects, all of which, however, astonished him; even in the vestibule there yet remained in a perfuming-pan the ashes of the perfumes burned at the time of his departure, as an offering to conjure Melkarth. It was not thus that he had hoped to return!

All that he had done and that he had seen—the assaults, the incendiary fires, the legions, the tempests—came back to his mind: Drepanum, Syracuse, Lilybreum, Mount Etna, the plateau of Eryx, his five years of battle, till the fatal day when, laying down their arms, they had lost Sicily. Once more he saw the citron-woods, the herdsmen tending their goats on the grey mountains, and his heart beat wildly at the thought of another Carthage established down yonder. His projects and his memories buzzed in his brain, yet dizzy from the pitching of the vessel. An overwhelming pang seized him, and suddenly becoming weak, he felt the need of drawing closer to the gods. He ascended to the highest story of his mansion; then, after withdrawing, from a gold shell suspended on his arm, a spatula studded with nails, he opened the door of a small oval room. The narrow black discs, encased in the walls, were as transparent as glass, and admitted a soft light. Between these regular rows of discs, hollows were made like the niches used for urns in a *Columbarium*. Each one of these hollows contained a round, dark-coloured stone, apparently very heavy. Only people of deep understanding honoured these *abaddirs*, fallen from the moon. By their fall these stones signified the planets, the sky, the fire; by their colour, the darkness of night; and by their density, the cohesion of terrestrial things.

A stifling atmosphere filled this mystic place. The round stones in the niches were slightly whitened by the sea-sand, which the wind had driven through the door. Hamilcar counted them, one by one, touching each with the tip of his finger; then hiding his face under a saffron-coloured veil, fell upon his knees, and, with outstretched arms, laid himself prone on the ground.

Outside, the daylight struck against the laths of the black lattices; in their diaphanous thickness shrubberies, hillocks, whirlwinds, and indistinct outlines of animals were discerned. Within, the light entered, fearful and yet peaceful, as it must be behind the sun in the gloomy spaces of future creations.

Hamilcar endeavoured to banish from his thoughts all the forms, symbols, and appellations of the gods, in order better to grasp the immutable spirit which these appearances concealed. Something of the planetary vitalities penetrated his being, causing him to feel for death, and all dangers, a disdain intimate and personal.

When he arose he experienced a serene intrepidity, indifferent alike to mercy or fear; and feeling half-suffocated he ascended to the top of the tower, overlooking Carthage.

The city descended in a sweeping curve, with her cupolas, temples, golden roofs, mansions, clumps of palms, and here and there glass globes, from which refracted lights sparkled; and surrounding this horn of plenty opening out toward him was the gigantic border of the ramparts. Below, he could see the harbours, the squares, the interior of the courts, and the outlines of the streets; and from this height men appeared as mites, and almost level with the pavement.

"Ah! if Hanno had not arrived too late on the morning of the battle of the Ægatian islands!" Thus thinking, he turned his eyes to the extreme horizon, extending his arms tremblingly toward Rome.

A multitude thronged the steps of the Acropolis. In the square of Khamoûn, people jostled each other, waiting to see the Suffet; the terraces gradually became thronged with eager gazers, some of whom recognised and saluted him. In order, however, to rouse their impatience more effectually, he withdrew from sight.

Hamilcar found awaiting him below in the hall the most important men of his faction—Istatten, Subeldia, Hictamon, Yeoubas, and others. They recounted to him all that had happened since the conclusion of the peace—the cupidity of the Elders; the departure and subsequent return of the soldiers; their demands; the capture of Gisco; the rape of the Zaïmph; the succour, and subsequent desertion, of Utica; but not one ventured to tell him of the events which concerned him personally. Finally they separated, to meet again that night at the Assembly of Elders in the temple of Moloch.

The deputation had but just gone, when a tumult was heard outside the gate. Some one attempted to enter, in spite of the servants' protests; and as the uproar redoubled Hamilcar ordered that the unknown person should be shown in.

An old Negress appeared, broken, wrinkled, trembling in a stupid manner, and enveloped to her heels in wide blue veils. She came forward, facing the Suffet. They looked at one another for some moments. Suddenly Hamilcar started; at a gesture of his hand his slaves withdrew; and he signed to the negress to move with caution, drawing her by the arm to a distant room.

She threw herself on the floor to kiss Hamilcar's feet; roughly raising her, he asked:

"Where have you left him, Iddibal?"

"Away down there, master!"

Throwing aside the veils, she rubbed the black from her face with one of the sleeves of her tunic; the senile, trembling, stooping figure was transformed, revealing a robust old man, whose skin seemed somewhat tanned by sand, wind, and sea. A tuft of white hair stood up on the crown of his head, like a bird's aigrette. With an ironical glance he pointed to the discarded disguise on the floor.

"You have done well, Iddibal. It is well!" Then, with a piercing look, Hamilcar added, "Does anyone yet suspect?"

The old man swore by the Kabiri that the secret had not been divulged. They never left their cabin, which was three days from Hadrumetum; the shores were peopled with tortoises, and the dunes were covered with palm trees. "And, obedient to your commands, master, I am teaching him to hurl javelins, and to manage teams."

"He is strong, is he not?"

"Yes, master, and intrepid, also; he fears neither serpents, nor thunder, nor phantoms. He runs barefooted, like a herdsman, on the very brink of the precipices."

"Speak! Speak!"

"He invents snares to capture wild beasts. The other moon—would you believe it?—he surprised an eagle. He clutched it; and the blood of both child and struggling bird spattered through the air in large drops, like the wind-driven roses. The furious bird enveloped him with the beating of its strong wings; but the dauntless boy seized it more firmly, and clasped it against his chest; and, in proportion as its death agony increased, his laughter redoubled, till it rang out glorious, like the clash of swords."

Hamilcar lowered his head, dazzled by these presages of greatness.

"But, for some days he has been restless and agitated. He watches the far-off sails passing by at sea; he is melancholy, and refuses his food! he asks questions about the gods, and he desires to know Carthage."

"No! no! not yet!" exclaimed the Suffet.

The old slave seemed to understand the peril that disturbed Hamilcar, and resumed:

"But how is he to be restrained? Already he has made me promise; and I should not have come to Carthage except to buy him a dagger with a silver handle, encircled by pearls."

Then the slave described how, having espied the Suffet on the terrace, he had managed to pass the guards of the harbour in the guise of one of Salammbô's women, in order to reach his master's presence.

Hamilcar remained a long time lost in meditation. At last he said:

"To-morrow, at sunset, present yourself at Megara, behind the purple factory, and imitate a jackal cry three times. If you do not see me, the first day of each moon you are to return to Carthage. Forget nothing! Cherish him! You may speak to him now of Hamilcar."

The slave resumed his disguise, and they left the house and the harbour together. Hamilcar continued his way on foot without an escort, as the conferences of the Elders were, on all extraordinary occasions, secret, and attended mysteriously.

At first he skirted the eastern face of the Acropolis, then passed by, in succession, the vegetable-market, the galleries of Kinisdo, and the suburb of the perfumers. The scattered lights were being extinguished; silence settled on the wider streets, and shadowy forms gliding through the darkness followed him: others came up—all, like him, directing their steps toward the Mappalian district.

The Temple of Moloch stood at the foot of a steep gorge, in a sinister spot. From below only the high walls could be perceived, rising indefinitely, like the sides of an immense tomb. The night was sombre; a grey fog seemed to weigh upon the sea waves, as they beat against the cliffs, with a sobbing and moaning like a death rattle; and the human shadows gradually disappeared, as if they had glided through the walls.

Just beyond the entrance was a vast quadrangular court, bordered by arcades; in the centre rose a massive structure, with eight uniform sides. Cupolas surmounted it, ranged around the second story, which supported a form or rotunda, from which sprang a cone with a returning curve, terminating on the summit in a ball.

In filigree cylinders fastened on standards and borne by men, fires burned. These lights flickered in the gusts of wind, and reddened the golden combs holding the braided tresses at the nape of the necks of the servitors. They ran forward, calling to each other to receive the Elders. Here and there on the flags enormous lions crouched like sphinxes—the living symbols of the Sun, the Devourer. They dozed with half-closed eyes; but, roused by the tramp of feet and sound of voices, they slowly rose and approached the Elders, whom they recognised by their costumes; they rubbed against their thighs, curving their backs, and yawning sonorously, and the vapour of their breaths passed like mist across the flames of the torches.

The excitement increased; the gates were closed; all the priests fled, and the Elders disappeared under the columns, which formed a deep vestibule around the temple. These columns were arranged in a manner to reproduce in circular ranges, comprised one within another, the Saturnian period, containing the years, the months within the years, and the days within the months—finally reaching to the walls of the sanctuary.

In this vestibule the Elders laid aside their narwhal-tusk staves—as a law, which was always observed, punished with death anyone who should enter a session with any weapon.

At the hem of their robes many displayed a rent mended by a strip of purple braid, as evidence that they were too preoccupied mourning their relatives to bestow time in the arrangement of their clothing, and this testimony of their bereavement prevented the rent from enlarging. Others, as a sign of mourning, enclosed their beards in a small bag of violet-coloured skin, attached by two cords to their ears.

Their first act on assembling was to embrace one another, breast to breast. They surrounded Hamilcar to offer congratulations; they appeared like brothers meeting a brother again.

The majority were thick-set, with hooked noses, resembling the Assyrian Colossi; some, by their projecting cheekbones, their greater height, and narrow feet, betrayed an African origin and Nomad ancestors. Those who lived constantly in their counting-houses had pale faces; others retained about them the severity of the desert, and strange jewels sparkled on all their fingers, tanned by unknown suns. The navigators were distinguished by their rolling gait, and the agriculturists had about their persons the odours of wine-presses, dried grasses, and the sweat of mules. These old pirates had farms under tillage; these money-makers equipped vessels; and these proprietors of plantations kept slaves who followed various trades. All were learned in the religious disciplines, expert in stratagems, unmerciful and rich. Protracted cares had imparted to them an air of weariness; their flaming eyes expressed defiance, and the habit of travel, and of lying, and of trading, and of command, gave to their persons an aspect of cunning and violence—a sort of circumspect and calculated brutality. Besides, the influence of Moloch made them solemn.

At first they walked through a long, vaulted hall, shaped like an egg. Seven doors, corresponding to the seven planets, displayed against the wall seven squares of different colours. After passing through the long room, they entered another similar hall, in which, at the far end, was a lighted candelabrum, covered with chased flowers, and each one of its eight golden branches bore in a chalice of diamonds a wick of byssus. This candelabrum was placed on the last of the long steps leading to a grand altar, terminating at the corners in brazen horns. Two lateral stairways led up to its flattened summit, where the stones were covered under a mountain of accumulated ashes. Something indistinct smouldered slowly upon it. Then beyond, higher than the candelabrum, and even higher than the altar, towered up the iron Moloch with his man's breast, in which yawned seven apertures; his wings stretched out over the walls; his tapering hands reached to the floor; three

black stones, encircled in yellow, represented three eyeballs in his forehead; and his bull's head was raised by a terrible effort, as if to bellow.

All around the hall were ebony benches; behind each was a bronze standard, which rested on three claws, and supported a torch. All these lights
were reflected in the polished surface of the mother-of-pearl lozenges
paving the hall. The room was so lofty that the red walls, as they neared
the dome, appeared black, and the three eyes of the idol far above seemed
like stars half lost in the night.

The Elders sat on the ebony benches, having thrown over their heads the
trains of their long robes. They remained motionless, with their hands
crossed in their wide sleeves; and the mother-of-pearl pavement was like a
luminous stream, running under their bare feet from the altar toward the
door.

In the centre the four pontiffs sat back to back on four ivory chairs, forming a cross. The pontiff of Eschmoûn robed in hyacinth, the pontiff of
Tanith in a white linen robe, the pontiff of Khamoûn in a reddish woollen
garment, and the pontiff of Moloch in purple.

Hamilcar walked forward to the candelabrum, and making a circuit of
it, examined the burning wicks, then threw upon them a scented powder.
Instantly violet flames sprang up at the extremities of the branches.

Then a shrill voice broke forth, another responded, and the hundred
Elders, the four pontiffs, and Hamilcar, all standing, intoned a hymn,
always repeating the same syllables and reswelling the sounds; their voices
continued to rise until they became terrible, when, simultaneously, all were
silent.

They paused some minutes. At last Hamilcar drew from his breast a small
three-headed statuette, blue as a sapphire, and placed it before him. It was
the image of Truth, the very genius of his speech. He replaced it in his
breast, and all, as though seized by a sudden fury, screamed out:

"These Barbarians are your good friends! Traitor! Wretch! You have
come to see us perish, have you not? . . . Let him speak! . . . No!
No! . . ."

They were revenging themselves for the constraint which had been
imposed on them by the official ceremony; and though they had longed
for the return of Hamilcar, they were now indignant that he had not prevented their disasters, or, rather, that he also had not suffered under them,
like themselves.

As soon as the tumult was calmed, the pontiff of Moloch arose, saying:
"Explain why you have not returned to Carthage before."

"What is that to you?" disdainfully responded the Suffet.

Their outcries redoubled.

"Of what do you accuse me? Perhaps, that I have conducted the war
badly? You have seen the ordinances of my battles, you who conveniently
leave to the Barbarians . . ."

"Enough! Enough!" they yelled.

He continued in a deep voice, to make himself better heard:

"Oh, that is true! I deceive myself! Lights of the Baal. Here in your midst are braves! Gisco, rise!" And, moving before the altar step, half-closing his eyes, seemingly in search of some one, he repeated: "Rise up, Gisco! You can accuse me; they will support you! But where is he?" Then, pausing as though to remind himself: "Ah! in his dwelling, without doubt. Surrounded by his sons, commanding his slaves, happy, and enumerating on the walls the necklaces of honour that his country has conferred upon him!"

They writhed about, shrugging their shoulders, as if lashed with thongs. "You do not even know whether he is dead or alive!" And, without heeding their clamour, he told them that in abandoning the Suffet they had deserted the Republic. Likewise that the treaty of peace with Rome, advantageous though they thought it was, was more fatal than twenty battles.

Some—the least wealthy of the Council, who were always suspected to incline toward the people or toward tyranny—applauded.

Their adversaries, the chiefs of the Syssites and administrators, triumphed over them by force of numbers; the most important had gathered near Hanno, who sat at the other end of the hall before the high door, that was closed by a hyacinth tapestry.

The ulcers on Hanno's face were covered with paint; the gold-powder from his hair had fallen upon his shoulders, where it made two brilliant patches; and his hair appeared white, fine, and crinkled, like lamb's wool. His hands were wrapped in linen bandages saturated with perfumed grease, that trickled down and dropped on the pavement; and his disease seemed considerably worse, for his eyes were so covered by the folds of his eyelids that, in order to see, he was compelled to tip his head backwards.

His partisans urged him to speak. At length he said, in a harsh, hideous voice:

"Less arrogance, Barca! We have all been conquered! Each one bears his own misfortune; therefore be resigned!"

"Inform us, rather," Hamilcar smilingly said, "how you steered your galleys into the Roman fleet?"

"I was driven by the wind out of my course," responded Hanno.

"You are like the rhinoceros, who treads in his own dung; you expose your own folly! Be silent!" and they began mutual recriminations respecting the battle of the islands of Ægates. Hanno accused Hamilcar of not having come to join forces with him.

"But that would have entailed leaving Eryx. You should have stood out from the coast. What prevented you? Oh! I forgot—the elephants are afraid of the sea!"

Hamilcar's partisans found this jest so good that they laughed heartily; the dome of the temple reëchoed as to the beating of drums.

Hanno denounced the indignity of such an outrage, protesting that his malady had attacked him as the result of a chill during the siege of Hecatompylus; and the tears coursed down his face as winter rain over a ruined wall.

Hamilcar continued: "If you had loved me as much as you do that man, there would to-day be great joy in Carthage! How many times have I not implored you for aid, and you have always refused to give me money!"

"We needed it here," said the chief of the Syssites.

"And when my affairs were desperate—for we have been compelled to drink the urine of our mules cooled in our helmets, and have eaten the thongs of our sandals; when I fairly longed that the blades of grass were soldiers, or that I could form battalions with our rotting dead—you called back the vessels yet remaining with me!"

"We could not risk everything," interrupted Baat-Baal, owner of gold mines in Darytian-Getulia.

"And now, what have you done here in Carthage, in your dwellings, behind your walls? There were the Gauls on the Eridanus that should have been stirred; the Canaanites at Cyrene, who would have come to our help; and while the Romans were sending ambassadors to Ptolemy . . ."

"He lauds the Romans to us now!" some one cried out. "How much have they paid you to defend them?"

"Ask that of the plains of Bruttium, or the ruins of Locri, Metapontum, and Heraclea! I have burned all their trees, have robbed all their temples, and even to the death of the grandsons of their grandsons. . . ."

"Truly, you declaim like an orator!" interrupted Kapouras, an illustrious merchant. "What is it you want?"

"I say that you must be more ingenious, or more formidable! If all Africa rejects your yoke, it will be because you do not know how to fasten it on her shoulders—feeble masters that you are! Agathocles, Regulus, Cœpio, any of the daring men, have only to land in order to capture the Republic; and when the Libyans in the east combine with the Numidians in the west, and the Nomads shall have come from the south, and the Romans from the north . . ."

A cry of horror burst out.

"Oh! you will strike your breasts, roll in the dust, and tear your mantles! What matter? You will be forced to turn the millstones in Suburra, and gather grapes on the hills of Latium."

They struck their right thighs to show their offence at such a suggestion, lifting the sleeves of their robes like the wings of frightened birds.

Hamilcar, carried away by an inspiration, continued in the same strain as he stood alone on the topmost step of the altar, quivering with terrible emotion. He raised his arms, and the rays from the candelabrum burning behind him, passed in streaks between his fingers, like javelins of gold.

"You will lose your vessels, your fields, your chariots, your suspended couches, and the slaves who rub your feet! The jackals will make their lairs in your palaces, the plough pass over your tombs; all that will remain will be the cry of the eagles and a heap of ruins! Carthage, thou shalt fall!"

The four pontiffs threw out their hands to ward off this anathema. All had risen; but the Suffet of the sea was a sacerdotal magistrate under the protection of the sun and inviolable, so long as the assembly of the Rich had not judged him. Terror was connected with the altar on which he stood. They drew back.

Hamilcar said no more. With eyes fixed and face as pale as the pearls in his tiara, he panted, almost terrified at himself, and his spirit lost in dismal visions. From the height on which he stood, the torches on the bronze standards appeared to him to be a vast crown of fire laid flat on the pavement, from which a black smoke escaped and rolled up through the darkness of the dome. The intensity of the silence for some moments was such that the distant roar of the sea could be plainly heard.

Then the Elders counselled among themselves. Their interests, their very existence, were attacked by the Barbarians. But they could not conquer them without the Suffet's aid; and despite their pride this fact made them overlook every other. They called his friends aside, and in a parley made interested reconciliations, understandings, and promises.

Hamilcar protested that he no longer desired any command. All implored him to reconsider his decision. When the word treason escaped their lips, he was angry, retorting that the only traitor to Carthage was the Grand Council. The engagements with the soldiers expired with the war, hence they became free as soon as the war ended. He even extolled their bravery, and depicted all the advantages that would accrue if the soldiers could be permanently attached to the Republic by donations and privileges.

At this, Magdassan, an old governor of provinces, rolling his yellow eyes, said:

"Truly, Barca, while travelling you have become a Greek, a Latin, and I know not what else! Why do you talk of advantages for these men? Better let ten thousand Barbarians perish than one of us."

The Elders nodded their approval, and murmured: "Yes; why trouble on that score? We can always get Mercenaries when needed."

"Yes, and you can easily get rid of them, is it not so? Abandon them, as you did in Sardinia. Advise the enemy the road they must take, as was done for those Gauls in Sicily, or else debark them in the open sea. While returning, I saw the rocks white with their bones!" retorted Hamilcar.

"What a pity!" impudently ejaculated Kapouras.

"Have they not gone over a hundred times to the enemy?" exclaimed others.

"Why, then," answered Hamilcar, "notwithstanding your laws, have you recalled them to Carthage? And why, when once here in your city, poor and numerous amidst your wealth, did you not think to weaken them by some division? You dismissed them with their women and children—without keeping a single hostage! Did you imagine that they would assassinate each other and spare you the annoyance of fulfilling your pledges? You hate them because they are strong! You hate me even more, because I am their master! Oh! I just now felt, when you kissed my hands, that you all restrained yourselves with difficulty from biting them!"

If the sleeping lions had entered at this moment from the outer court, howling wildly, the uproar could not have been more awful. But the pontiff of Eschmoûn rose, and with his knees tightly pressed together, his elbows straight, and hands half open, said:

"Barca, Carthage requests you to take the general command of the Punic forces against the Barbarians!"

"I refuse!" replied Hamilcar.

"We will give you full authority," screamed out the chiefs of the Syssites.
"No!"

"Without any control! Without division! All the money that you want! All the captives, all the booty, fifty zerets of land for each enemy's corpse."

"No! no! With you it is impossible to vanquish them!"

"He is afraid!"

"Because you are cowards, avaricious, ungrateful, pusillanimous, and fools!"

"He makes terms with the enemies! To put himself at their head," cried out some.

"And return against us," screamed others.

And from the end of the hall Hanno yelled, "He desires to be king!"

Then they all jumped up, overturning the benches and torches, and pressed in a crowd toward the altar, brandishing daggers.

Hamilcar, diving under his sleeves, drew forth two large cutlasses. Advancing his left foot, he confronted and defied them all, as, with flashing eyes and bending forward, he stood immovable under the golden candelabrum.

Thus, as a precaution, every member of the conference had carried concealed weapons into the temple: it was crime; they looked at one another with guilty terror. As all were culpable, each became quickly reassured, and gradually turned his back to the Suffet, retreating to the body of the hall, enraged and humiliated. For the second time they had recoiled before Hamilcar.

They remained for some moments standing. Some, who had carelessly wounded their fingers, held them in their mouths, or rolled them up gently in the ends of their mantles, and, as they were dispersing, Hamilcar heard these words:

"It is a matter of delicacy. He does not wish to afflict his daughter!"

A voice, in a louder tone, answered: "Doubtless, since she takes her lovers from amongst the Mercenaries!"

At first he staggered; then his eyes searched rapidly over the throng for Schahabarim. The pontiff of Tanit alone had remained seated. Hamilcar could only perceive in the distance his tall cap. All sneered at the Suffet to his very face, and, as his agony increased, their joy redoubled, while amid the confused yells he could hear those who were last to depart, screaming back at him:

"He was seen leaving her bed-chamber!"

"One morning in the month of Tammouz!"

"He is the thief of the Zaïmph!"

"A very handsome man!"

"Taller than Hamilcar!"

At this he jerked off his tiara, the badge of his dignity—his tiara of eight mystic rows, with an emerald shell in the centre—and with both hands dashed it fiercely to the ground. The gold circles broke and rebounded, and the pearls rang out on the pavement.

On his pale forehead now appeared a long scar that moved like a serpent between his eyebrows; his limbs trembled; he went up one of the lateral stairways leading to the altar, and stepped on the top. It was to consecrate himself to the gods by offering himself as a holocaust. The movement of his flowing mantle agitated the lights of the candelabrum, which was lower than his sandals, and a fine powder was raised by his steps, and floated about him like a cloud, as high up as his waist. He stopped between the legs of the brass colossus, took up two handfuls of the ashes, the very sight of which alone made all the Carthaginians tremble with terror, and said:

"By the hundred torches of your Intelligences! By the eight fires of the Kabiri! By the stars! By the meteors! And by the volcanoes! By all that which burns! By the thirst of the desert! By the saltness of the Ocean! By the cavern of Hadrumetum, the realm of Souls! by the extermination! By the ashes of your sons, and the ashes of the brothers of your ancestors, with which I now commingle my own! You, the hundred Councillors of Carthage, have lied in accusing my daughter! And I, Hamilcar Barca, Suffet of the sea, Chief of the Rich and Ruler of the people, before Moloch with the bull's head, I swear . . ." They waited for something awful; but he resumed in a much louder and calmer voice—"That I will not even speak of it to her!"

The sacred servitors, wearing golden combs, entered, some carrying sponges of purple, and others palm branches. They raised the hyacinth curtain spread before the doorway, and through the opening was visible at the end of the other halls the vast rose-coloured sky, which seemed to be but a continuation of the temple's vault, and to rest at the horizon upon the blue sea.

The sun was rising from the billows, striking in full radiance against the breast of the brazen idol, which was divided into seven compartments, closed by gratings. Moloch's jaws, revealing his red teeth, opened in a horrible yawn; his enormous nostrils were dilated; the broad daylight seemed to animate and impart to him a terrible air of impatience, as if he would have liked to bound outside to mix with the sun and the god, and speed with him through the immensities of space.

Meanwhile the still burning torches, scattered on the mother-of-pearl pavement, gleamed like splashes of blood.

The Elders reeled from exhaustion, and filled their lungs with long inhalations of fresh air; perspiration ran down their livid faces; their fierce outcries had left them almost voiceless; but their wrath against the Suffet had not subsided, and their adieus were parting threats, to which Hamilcar responded.

"To-morrow night, Barca, in the temple of Eschmoûn!"

"I shall be there——!"

"We will have you condemned by the Rich!"

"And I you by the people!"

"Be warned, lest you end on a cross!"

"And you, that you are not torn in the streets!"

As soon as they reached the threshold of the court they resumed a calm deportment.

Their runners and charioteers awaited them at the gate. Most departed on white she-mules. The Suffet sprang into his chariot, taking the reins himself; the two horses arched their necks, struck rhythmically the stones, which rebounded under their hoofs, and ascended the entire length of the Mappalian Way at such a fleet gallop that the silver vulture on the end of the pole seemed to fly as the chariot swept past.

The road crossed a field set with long stones which had pointed pyramidal tops; on each was carved an open hand, as if the dead reposing beneath had reached out of their tombs toward heaven to claim something. Further along were scattered cone-shaped cabins, built of clay, branches, and reed wattles. Little stone walls, runnels of water, esparto ropes, and hedges of cactus irregularly separated these habitations, which became denser as the road approached the Suffet's gardens.

But Hamilcar kept his eyes fixed on a large tower of three stories, forming three enormous cylinders, the first built of stone, the second of brick, and the third entirely of cedar, supporting a copper cupola on twenty-four juniper columns, over which fell like garlands the interlacings of slender brass chainlets. This lofty edifice overlooked the buildings that extended to the right, consisting of the warehouses and counting-house, while the palace of the women loomed up at the end of the avenue of cypresses, which stood in line like two bronze walls.

When the rumbling chariot had entered through the narrow gate, it halted under a wide shed, where horses were fastened feeding from heaps of cut grass.

All the servants ran forward. They were indeed a host; for those who worked in the adjacent country in terror of the soldiers had fled to Carthage. The farm labourers, clothed in animals' skins, dragged behind them chains riveted to their ankles; the workers in the purple factories had arms stained red as those of executioners; the sailors wore green caps; the fishermen coral necklaces; the hunters bore a net across their shoulders, and the people of Megara wore white or black tunics, leather breeches, and skull-caps of straw, felt, or linen, according to their different employment or industries.

Behind pressed a populace in rags, who lived without employment, far from the dwelling houses, sleeping on the ground, sheltered only by the trees in the gardens, eating the scraps from the kitchens—human excrescences vegetating in the shadow of the palace.

Hamilcar tolerated them from prudence, even more than from disdain.

Many of them had never before seen the Suffet, but all, as a sign of their joy, wore flowers in their ears.

Men, with head-dresses like sphinxes, carrying large clubs, brandished them about in the crowd, striking right and left to keep back the slaves over-curious to see their master, so that he might not be inconvenienced by their numbers or incommoded by their smell.

Then they all threw themselves flat on the ground, crying out: "Eye of Baal! May your house flourish for ever!" and between the men thus prostrated in the avenue of cypresses, the intendant of the intendants, Abdalonim, wearing a white mitre, advanced toward Hamilcar, carrying a censer in his hand.

Salammbô descended the stairway of the galleys. All her slave-women followed her, and at each step she advanced they also descended.

The heads of the negresses made large black spots amid the line of bands of golden plaques which bound the foreheads of the Roman women. Others wore in their hair silver arrows, emerald butterflies, or long pins spreading like the rays of the sun. Over the confusion of their white, yellow, and blue garments, their fringes, agraffes, necklaces, rings, and bracelets glittered. The robes rustled, and the clattering of sandals could be heard, accompanied by the dull sound of the naked feet upon the wood. Here and there a tall eunuch, whose shoulders overtopped the women, smiled with his face uplifted.

As soon as the acclamations of the men were quieted, the women, hiding their faces in the sleeves of their dresses, uttered in unison a strange cry, like the howl of a she-wolf, so furious and strident that it seemed to make the grand ebony stairway, now covered with women, vibrate like a lyre from top to bottom.

The wind fluttered their long veils and gently waved the slender papyrus stems.

It was the month of *Schebaz*, and the depth of winter; the pomegranate trees, at this season in flower, stood out against the azure sky; through the branches the sea appeared, with an island in the distance, half lost in the mist.

Hamilcar paused when he perceived Salammbô.

Born after the death of several male children, she had not been welcomed, for the birth of a daughter was considered a calamity in the religions of the sun. The gods had given him a son later; but he never forgot his blighted hopes, and, as it were, the shock of the malediction he had pronounced against her.

Meanwhile, Salammbô continued to advance. Pearls of various colours fell in long clusters from her ears over her shoulders, down to her elbows; her hair was crimped to simulate a cloud. Around her neck she wore small quadrangular gold plaques representing a woman between two lions rampant, and her costume reproduced completely the attire of the Goddess Tanit. Her hyacinth robe, with flowing sleeves, drawn tightly in at the waist, widened out at the bottom. The vermilion of her lips made her pearly teeth even whiter than they actually were; the antimony on her eyelids lengthened her eyes and made them almond shape. Her sandals, made of a bird's plumage, had very high heels. She was extraordinarily pale, doubtless because of the cold.

At length she arrived before Hamilcar, and, without looking up, or raising her head, she addressed him, saying:

"All hail, Eye of Baalim! Eternal glory! Triumph! Contentment! Peace! Wealth! A long time has my heart been sad, and the household languished, but the master who returns is like Tammuz restored to life; and under thy gaze, O father, joyousness and a new existence will expand over all!"

And taking from Taanach's hand a little oblong vase, in which fumed a mixture of meal, butter, cardamon, and wine, she continued: "Drink a full draught of the welcome cup prepared by thy servant."

"Benediction on thee!" he replied, mechanically grasping the golden vase she proffered to him.

All the while he examined her with a scrutiny so keen that Salammbô, troubled thereat, stammered out:

"Thou hast been told, O master! . . ."

"Yes! I know!" answered Hamilcar, in a low voice. Was this a confession? Or did she merely allude to the Barbarians? And he added a few vague words concerning the public embarrassment that he himself hoped now to dispel.

"O father!" exclaimed Salammbô, "thou canst never repair that which is irreparable!"

At this he started back, and Salammbô was astonished at his amazement, as she did not dream of Carthage, but of the sacrilege in which she felt herself involved. This man, who made legions fear, and whom she scarcely knew, frightened her like a god. He had divined it; he knew all; something terrible was about to befall her; she cried out—"Mercy!"

Hamilcar lowered his head slowly. Disposed as Salammbô was to accuse herself, she dared not now open her lips, though she was almost suffocated with the desire to complain to, and be comforted by, her father. Hamilcar struggled against his inclination to break his oath. However, he kept it from pride, or through dread of putting an end to his uncertainty, and scanned her full in the face, trying with all his might to discover what she hid at the bottom of her heart.

Salammbô, panting, buried her head gradually in her bosom, crushed by his austere scrutiny. He was now sure that she had yielded to the embrace of a Barbarian. He shuddered, lifting both his fists over her. She shrieked and fell back among her women, who eagerly pressed about her.

Hamilcar turned on his heels, followed by all of his attendants. The door of the warehouses was thrown open, and he entered into a vast, round hall, whence long passages led like the spokes of a wheel from its hub into other halls. A stone disc stood in the centre, surrounded by a railing for holding the cushions that were heaped upon the carpets. The Suffet walked with long rapid strides, breathing heavily, striking the ground sharply with his heels. He drew his hand across his forehead like one tormented by flies; then he shook his head; and as he perceived the accumulation of his wealth he became calmer. His thoughts were attracted to the perspective of the passages and to the adjoining halls filled with the rarest treasures. Therein were amassed bronze plates, ingots of silver, and pigs of iron alternating with blocks of tin brought from the Cassiterides, by way of the Shadowy Sea; gums from the countries of the Blacks overflowed their sacks of palm-bark; and gold dust, heaped in leather bottles, imperceptibly filtered through the worn seams; delicate filaments, drawn from marine plants, hung amid the flax from Egypt, Greece, Taprobane, and Judea. Madrepores, as broad as bushes, bristled at the base of the walls, and an indefinable odour floated about, evidently proceeding from the abundant store of perfumes, spices, hides, and ostrich plumes, tied in large bunches at the very top of the roof. Before each passage elephants' tusks stood, joined at the points, forming an arch above the doorway.

Finally, he mounted the stone disc. All the intendants stood with their arms crossed and heads bent, while Abdalonim lifted his pointed mitre with a regal air.

Hamilcar questioned the Chief of the Ships. He was an old pilot, with eyelids reddened by the wind; his white locks fell to his hips, as if the foam of tempests had lingered in his beard.

He answered that he had sent a fleet by Gades and Thymiamata to endeavour to reach Eziongeber by rounding the South Horn and the promontory of Aromata.

Other vessels had sailed continuously to the west during four moons, without making land; but the prows of the vessels became entangled in the weeds; the horizon resounded continually with the noise of cataracts; blood-coloured mists obscured the sun, and a breeze, laden with perfumes, put the crews to sleep, and their memories had been thereby so much disturbed that at present they could tell naught concerning the region. Meantime, other vessels had ascended the streams of Scythia, penetrating Colchis to the Jugrians and the Estians; had carried away from the archipelago fifteen hundred virgins; and sent to the bottom all foreign vessels navigating beyond the cape of Æstrymon, in order that the secret of the routes might not be known. King Ptolemy had kept back the incense from Schesbar, Syracuse, and Elatea. Corsica and the islands had furnished nothing. Then the old pilot dropped his voice to announce that one trireme had been taken at Rusicada by the Numidians—"For they are with them, master."

Hamilcar knitted his brows, then signed to the Chief of the Journeys to speak. This man was wrapped in a brown ungirdled robe, and his head was bound round by a long scarf of white material, which passed over his mouth and fell back on his shoulders.

The caravans had gone out regularly at the winter equinox. But out of fifteen hundred men bound to the further Ethiopia with excellent camels, new leather bottles, and stocks of painted linen, one only had returned to Carthage; all the others had died from fatigue, or become mad through the terrors of the desert. He said that he had seen far beyond the Black Harosch, beyond at Atarantes, and the country of the big apes, immense kingdoms where even the ordinary utensils were of gold; a river the colour of milk and spreading out like the sea, forests of blue trees, hills of aromatics, monsters with human faces, vegetating on rocks, whose eyes opened like flowers to look at you; then, behind lakes covered with dragons, mountains of crystal supporting the sun. Other caravans had returned from the Indies, bringing peacocks, pepper, and some new materials. As for those who went to purchase chalcedonies, by the road of the Syrtis and the temple of Ammon, they had doubtless perished in the sands. The caravans of Gaetulia and Phazzana had furnished their usual supplies, but he, the Chief, did not at present dare to equip any other expeditions.

Hamilcar, comprehending by this that the Mercenaries occupied the country, moaned as he leaned on his other elbow.

The Chief of Farms, who was summoned next in order, was in such fear that he trembled violently, in spite of his thick-set shoulders and great red eyes; his flat-nosed face resembled a mastiff's, and was surmounted by a network of bark-fibres; he wore a girdle of hairy leopard skin, in which shone two formidable cutlasses.

As soon as Hamilcar turned toward him, he uttered a cry invoking all the Baals, protesting he was not to blame! He could do nothing! He had watched the temperature, the land, the stars; had made the plantations at the solstice of winter; had pruned at the wane of the moon; and had inspected the slaves, and provided them with clothing.

Hamilcar, irritated by such loquacity, clacked his tongue, and the man with the cutlasses continued in a rapid voice:

"Ah! master! They have plundered everything! sacked everything! destroyed everything! Three thousand feet of timber were cut down at Maschala, and at Ubada the granaries were broken open and the cisterns filled up! At Tedes they carried off fifteen hundred gomers of wheat; at Marazzana they killed the herdsmen, ate the flocks, and burned your house, your beautiful house of cedar beams, where you spend your summers. The slaves of Tuburbo, who reaped the barley, fled to the mountains; and of the asses, riding and working mules, the cattle of Taormina, and the antelopes, not one remains; all were taken away. It is a curse. I cannot survive it!"

He began to cry, adding: "Ah, if you only knew how full the cellars were, and how the ploughshares shone! Ah, the fine rams! Ah, the fine bulls!"

Hamilcar's rage suffocated him; he burst forth: "Be still! Am I then a pauper? No lies! Speak the truth! I wish to know all that I have lost, to the last shekel, to the last cab! Abdalonim, bring me the accounts of the vessels, of the farms, of the caravans, and of my household! And if any of your consciences be not clear, sorrow on your heads! . . . Leave!"

All the attendants retired, walking backward, touching their fingers to the ground.

Abdalonim took from the middle of a nest of pigeon-holes in the wall the accounts, which were kept on knotted cords, bands of linen or of papyrus, and shoulder-blades of sheep covered with fine writing. He laid them all at Hamilcar's feet, and placed in his hands a wooden frame, strung with three interior wires on which gold, silver, and horn balls were strung, and began:

"One hundred and ninety-two houses in the Mappals, let to the new Carthaginians at the rentals of one beka per moon."

"Hold! That is too much! Be charitable to the poor. Write me the names of those whom you believe to be the most courageous, and ascertain if they are attached to the Republic. What next?"

Abdalonim hesitated, surprised by such generosity.

Hamilcar impatiently snatched from his hands the linen bands, saying, as he looked:

"What, then, is this? Three palaces around Khamoûn at twelve kesitath per month! Raise it to twenty. I do not wish to be devoured by the Rich."

Abdalonim after a long salute resumed: "Loaned to Tigilas, until the end of the season, two kikars at thirty-three and a third per cent. maritime interest; advanced to Bar-Malkarth fifteen hundred shekels on the security of thirty slaves, but twelve have died in the salt marshes."

"In other words, they were not strong," laughingly said the Suffet. "No matter! if he needs money, let him have it! One must always lend, and at different rates of interest, according to the wealth of the person."

Then the servitor hastened to read all that had been brought in by the iron mines of Annaba, the coral fisheries, the purple factories, the yield of the tax on the resident Greeks, and the exportation of silver to Arabia, where it was ten times the value of gold; then on the captures of vessels, allowing for the deduction of a tenth, being tithes for the temple of Tanit: "Each time I have declared one-fourth less, master."

Hamilcar reckoned, rattling the balls under his fingers. "Enough! What have you paid?"

"To Stratonicles of Corinth, and three merchants of Alexandria, on the letters, which have been cashed, ten thousand Athenian drachmas and twelve Syrian talents of gold. The provisions for the crews rising to twenty minæ per month for each trireme. . . ."

"I know it! How much are the losses?"

"Here is the account on these sheets of lead," said the intendant. "With reference to the ships chartered in common, as throwing the cargoes overboard, was often unavoidable, the unequal losses were divided according to the number of partners. For ropes borrowed from the arsenals which it has been impossible to return, the Syssites exacted eight hundred kesitath before the expedition to Utica."

"The Syssites again!" said Hamilcar, bending his head, and remaining for a while as if crushed under the weight of all the hatreds he felt levelled at him. "But I do not see here the Megara expenses."

Abdalonim turned pale, as he brought from another pigeon-hole the sycamore-wood tablets filed in bundles, and tied together with leather straps.

Hamilcar listened, curious as to the domestic details, and calmed by the monotony of the man's voice as he enumerated the accounts, while Abdalonim read slower and slower. Suddenly, letting the wooden tablets fall to the ground, he threw himself flat on his face with arms extended, in the position of one condemned.

Hamilcar, without evincing any emotion, picked up the tablets; his lips parted and his eyes opened wide as he saw charged for the expenses of one day an exorbitant consumption of meats, fish, birds, wines, and aromatics, vases broken, slaves killed, and napery destroyed.

Abdalonim, remaining prostrate, told him of the Barbarians' feast and that he had been unable to escape from obeying the commands of the Elders. Salammbô, too, had commanded that money should be lavished to receive the soldiers.

At the name of his daughter Hamilcar jumped up; then compressing his lips, he sank back amid the cushions, tearing the fringes with his nails, his eyes fixed, panting.

"Arise!" said the Suffet.

Then he descended from the dais, followed by Abdalonim, whose knees trembled. But seizing an iron bar, he went to work like a madman to unseal the pavement. A disc of wood flew out and revealed under the entire length of the passage, numerous broad covers that concealed pits where grain was stored.

"Eye of Baal! You see by this," said the servant, trembling, "they have not taken everything! For these pits are deep, each one fifty cubits, and full to the brim! During your absence I have had similar pits dug in the arsenals and in the gardens, so that your mansion is as full of grain as your heart is of wisdom."

A smile passed over Hamilcar's face.

"It is well, Abdalonim." Afterward he whispered: "You must obtain grain from Etruria and Bruttium, and from whatever place you can and at any price. Amass it and keep it stored. It is important that I alone possess all the grain in Carthage."

Then, when they reached the end of the passage, Abdalonim, with one of the keys hanging from his girdle, opened a large quadrangular room, divided in the centre by cedar pillars. Gold, silver, and brass coins were piled on tables, or stacked in niches that extended the length of the four walls, reaching up to the beams of the roof; enormous coffers of hippopotamus hide stood in the corners, supporting rows of smaller bags; and bullion heaped up, made hillocks on the pavement, while here and there piles too high had toppled over, appearing like columns in ruins. The large pieces of Carthaginian money, stamped on the face with a representation of Tanit and a horse under a palm tree, were mixed with those of the colonies on which were stamped the figure of a bull, a star, a globe, or a crescent. Then, disposed about in unequal amounts, were pieces of all values, and dimensions, and ages, from the ancient ones of Assyria, that were slender as a finger-nail, to the old ones of Latium, that were thicker than a hand; there were also the buttons of Ægina, the tablets of Bactria, and the short bars of ancient Lacædemonia. The coins were rusty, greasy with dirt; many were covered with verdigris, having been fished up out of water in nets; others were blackened by fire, having been found after sieges in the midst of the ruins.

The Suffet had quickly calculated whether the present sums corresponded with the gains and losses that had just been submitted to him, and he was about proceeding when he discovered three brass jars completely empty. Abdalonim averted his head with a sign of horror, and Hamilcar resigned himself in silence.

They crossed other passages and other halls, coming at last before a door where, to guard it the better, a man was fastened about the waist to a long chain, riveted in the masonry of the wall—a Roman custom but lately introduced into Carthage. His beard and nails had grown excessively long, and he swayed from right to left, with a continued oscillation, like that of a captive animal.

As soon as he recognised Hamilcar, he cried out: "Mercy, Eye of Baal! Pity! Kill me! It is now ten years since I have seen the sun! In the name of your father, mercy!"

Without answering him, Hamilcar clapped his hands. Three men appeared, who, with the assistance of Abdalonim, set at once to work, straining their arms in the effort to release from its ring the enormous bar securing the door. Hamilcar took a torch, and disappeared in the darkness.

This was believed to be a passage leading to the family sepulchre; but only a wide pit would have been found, which was excavated to mislead thieves, and in reality concealed nothing.

Hamilcar passed it, then, leaning down, turned aside on its rollers a very heavy millstone; there was revealed an opening, through which he entered an apartment built in the form of a cone. The walls were covered with brass scales. In the centre, on a granite pedestal, was a statue of one of the Kabiri, bearing the name of Aletes, the discoverer of the mines in Celtimeria. Against the base of this statue, on the ground, were placed crosswise, broad golden bucklers, and monstrous silver vases with closed necks, all of such an extravagant form as to make them useless, it being the custom to cast such quantities of metal in these objects as to render it next to impossible to embezzle or even move them.

With his torch he lighted a small miner's lamp fixed in the idol's cap. Immediately, the hall was illuminated with green, yellow, blue, violet, wine and blood coloured lights; for it was filled with precious stones placed in golden calabashes hanging like sconces to brass plates, or in their native blocks ranged along at the base of the walls. Here were to be found in abundance turquoises shot away from the mountains by the swirl of a sling; carbuncles formed by lynxes' urine, tongue-liked stones fallen from the moon, *tyanos*, diamonds, *sandastrum*, beryls, the three varieties of rubies, the four species of sapphires, and the twelve kinds of emeralds. These precious stones flashed variously like splashes of milk, blue icicles, or silver dust, and threw their rays in sheets, in beams, or like twinkling stars. The ceraunia engendered by the thunder scintillated near the chalcedonies, which nullified the effect of poisons. There were topazes from Zabarca, effective in warding off terrors; opals from Bactria, employed to prevent abortions, and horns of Ammon, which are placed under the beds to invite dreams.

The fantastic fires from the gems and the flames from the lamp were mirrored in the broad, gold shields. Hamilcar stood with folded arms, smiling—and he revelled less in the spectacle than in the consciousness of his riches. They were inaccessable, inexhaustible, infinite. The thought of his ancestors sleeping beneath his feet sent thrilling to his heart some conception of their eternity: he felt drawn very near to the subterranean spirits. He experienced an emotion akin to the joy of a Kabira, and the large luminous rays striking his face, resembled the end of an invisible network that crossed abysses, and attached him to the centre of the world.

An idea came which made him shiver: he went behind the idol, and walked straight therefrom to the wall; he searched on his arm amid numerous tattooings; examining a horizontal line with two perpendicular lines, which in Canaanite figures expressed thirteen; then he counted to the thirteenth brass plate on the wall, when he again lifted his sleeve, and with his right hand traced on another part of his arm other lines more complicated, delicately moving his fingers as if he played upon a lyre. Finally, he struck seven blows with his thumb, at which one entire section of the wall turned around as a single block. This concealed a sort of cellar, in which were enclosed mysterious things that possessed no names, but of an incalculable value. Hamilcar descended the three steps, took from a silver vat an antelope's skin that floated in a black liquid, and then reascended.

Abdalonim then walked before him. At each step he struck the pavement with his tall staff, the handle of which was ornamented with bells, and before the door of each room cried Hamilcar's name, accompanied with praises and benedictions.

In the circular gallery, from which branched all the lobbies, were small beams of algum-trees; piled along the walls were sacks of henna, cakes of Lemnos-earth, and tortoise shells filled with pearls. The Suffet in passing brushed unheedingly with his robe gigantic pieces of amber, formed by the sun's rays and almost divine.

A mist of odorous vapour arose.

"Open that door!" the Suffet commanded.

They entered. Naked men were laboriously engaged kneading pulp, pressing herbs, stirring the fires, pouring oil into jars, opening and closing little oval cells excavated all around in the walls, which were so numerous that the room resembled the interior of a bee-hive. Myrobalans, bdellium, saffron, and violets overflowed the place, and all about were gums, powders, roots, glass phials, branches of dropwort and rose petals; the scents were stifling, in spite of the clouds from the storax that crackled in the centre on a brass tripod.

The Chief of Perfumes, pale and very tall, like a wax torch, came forward to greet Hamilcar, by crushing over his hands a roll of aromatic ointment, whilst two slaves rubbed his heels with harewort leaves. The Suffet repulsed them, for they were Cyrenians of infamous morals, but valued because of their secret knowledge of concocting perfumes.

To display his vigilance, the Chief of Perfumes offered to the Suffet, in an electrum spoon, a little malobalthrum to taste; then with an awl pierced three Indian bezoars. Hamilcar, who was familiar with the artifices of the craft, took a hornful of balm, and after holding it near the fire, spilled it on his robe, when a brown stain appeared, which proved it was adulterated. At this he looked fixedly at the Chief, and, without saying a word, threw the gazelle-horn in his face.

Indignant as he was that these adulterations should be committed to his own detriment, yet upon perceiving some packages of spikenard that were being packed for exportation to the countries beyond the seas, he ordered antimony to be added to make them heavier. Then he inquired for three boxes of *psagas* destined for his own personal use.

The Chief of Perfumes avowed that he knew nothing of them; the soldiers had invaded the distillery with drawn knives, and coerced him by threats to open the three boxes.

"You, then, fear their wrath more than mine?" cried the Suffet, and through the fumes his eyeballs flashed like torches upon the tall, pale man, who began to comprehend the situation. "Abdalonim, before sunset have him flogged, and torture him!"

This loss, though less important than the others, had exasperated him. In spite of his efforts to banish the Barbarians from his thoughts, he was continually reminded of them. Their excesses were confused with his daughter's shame, and he was angered to think that his household knew, and had not mentioned it to him. But something impelled him to plunge deeper in his misfortune, and, taken with an inquisitorial rage, he paid visits of inspection to the hangars, behind the house of commerce, examining the stores and supplies of bitumen, wood, anchors, cordage, honey, and wax; then the magazines of fabrics, the reserves of provisions, not forgetting the marble yards and the barn of silphium.

He crossed to the opposite side of the gardens, inspecting with keen scrutiny in their cabins the domestic artisans whose productions were sold; watched the tailors as they embroidered mantles, others as they knotted the nets, and others who combed the wool for cushions or cut out sandals. He viewed the Egyptian workers polishing papyrus with a shell, as shuttles of the weavers clacked, and the armourers' anvils clanged. To these craftsmen he said:

"Forge swords! Always forge! I shall need them." And he took from his breast the antelope skin that had been macerated in poisons, and ordered them to cut and fashion from it a breastplate for him, that would be more solid than brass, and impervious alike to weapons or flames.

As soon as he got near the various workers, Abdalonim, in order to divert the Suffet's anger from himself, sought to anger him against them by disparaging their work, murmuring:

"What a piece of work! It is a shame! Truly the master is too good!" Hamilcar, without heeding, went on his way.

He slackened his pace, as the path was barred by large, noble trees, completely charred, such as may be seen in woods where herdsmen have camped. The roads were barricaded, the palisades were broken, the water was lost in the ditches; fragments of glass and bones of apes appeared in the midst of muddy puddles. On the bushes scraps of cloth hung, and under the citrons decaying flowers formed a rotten heap. The servants had neglected everything, believing that Hamilcar would never return.

At each step he discovered some new disaster, more proofs of the very thing he had forbidden himself to learn. Lo! even now, as he walked about, he soiled his purple boots, crushing under foot the very filth of the Barbarians; and yet he had not these wretches at the end of a catapult to make them fly into pieces. He experienced a sense of humiliation for having defended them in the Assembly: it was treachery and treason; but as he could not avenge himself on the soldiers, or on the Elders, or on Salammbô, or on any person, and his wrath needed some victim, he condemned to the mines all the garden slaves by a single decree.

Each time that Abdalonim saw his master approach the parks he shuddered. But Hamilcar first took the road to the mill, whence issued a most mournful melopœia.

In the midst of clouds of flour-dust turned the heavy mills, constructed of two porphyry-cones, placed one upon the other; the uppermost one was of funnel-shape and revolved as it ground the grain on the second cone by the aid of strong bars pushed by men. They held their chests and arms firmly against them, or pulled with all their might, harnessed to the bars. The friction of the breast-strap had formed around their armpits purulent sores, such as might be seen on asses' withers; and black, filthy rags, hardly covering their loins, flapped over the thighs like long tails. Their eyes were red, the shackles on their feet clattered as they panted, heaved and tugged in unison. On their mouths were muzzles, fastened by little bronze chains, rendering it impossible for them to eat the meal, and gauntlets, made without fingers, preventing them from pilfering.

At the entrance of the Suffet the wooden bars creaked still more loudly, the grain grated in grinding. Many of these slaves, upon seeing him, fell down on their knees, while the others continued their drudgery, treading heedlessly over their kneeling companions.

The Suffet asked for Giddenem, the governor of the slaves, who appeared, displayed the dignity of his office by the richness of his costume: his tunic, which was slit at the sides, was of fine purple; heavy rings weighed down his earlobes; and the bands of material enveloping his legs were joined by a gold lacing, like a serpent coiling around a tree, reaching from his ankles to his hips. In his hands, covered with rings, he held a string of jet beads, to identify the men subject to the accursed malady.

Hamilcar signed to him to unfasten the slaves' muzzles. They all, with cries like famished animals, rushed upon the meal, burying their faces in the heaps and devouring it.

"You starve and exhaust them!" said the Suffet. Giddenem replied that it was necessary in order to subdue them.

"Then it was scarcely worth while sending you to the training-school for slaves at Syracuse. Bid others come before me."

And the cooks, butlers, grooms, runners, porters of the litters, men from the vapour-baths, and the women with their children, all ranged themselves in the gardens in a single file, from the house of commerce as far as the deer park. They all held their breaths terror-stricken, and a vast silence reigned over Megara. The sun lengthened its rays over the Lagoon below the catacombs. The peacocks began to screech. Hamilcar moved step by step, before this long array of slaves.

"Of what use are these old slaves?" said he. "Sell them; there are too many Gauls; they are drunkards! and too many Cretans, they are liars! Buy for me Cappadocians, Asiatics, and Negroes."

He was astonished at the small number of children. "Every year, Giddenem, the establishment should have some births. You must leave the huts open every night, so that they may mix freely."

The governor then pointed out to him the thieves, the lazy, and the mutinous, and he distributed chastisements, with reproaches to Giddenem, who, like a bull, drooped his low forehead, with its thick intercrossed eyebrows.

"Look, Eye of Baal," said the governor, pointing to a robust Libyan, "there; behold one who was discovered with a rope around his neck."

"Ah! so you want to die?" scornfully said the Suffet.

And the slave, in an intrepid tone, answered "Yes!"

Without caring either for the example or pecuniary loss, Hamilcar ordered—"Away with him!"

Perhaps he had in his mind the idea of a sacrifice. It was a misfortune that he inflicted upon himself in order to ward off more terrible ones.

Giddenem had hidden the mutilated slaves behind the others, but Hamilcar perceived them, and demanded of one:

"Who cut your arm?"

"The soldiers, Eye of Baal."

Then addressing himself to a Samnite, who staggered like a wounded heron, he said:

"And you—who did that to you?"

The governor had broken his leg with an iron bar. Such atrocious imbecility exasperated the Suffet, and he jerked away from Giddenem the string of jet.

"Curses be upon the dog who wounds the herds! Crippler of slaves—

gracious Tanit! Ah, thus would you ruin your master! Let him be smothered in a dung-heap! And those who are missing, where are they? Have you assisted the soldiers to assassinate them?"

His face became so terrible that all the women fled, and the slaves drew back, making a wide circle; meantime Giddenem frantically kissed Hamilcar's feet, who stood with his hands raised over him.

But his mind, now clear as during the most critical moment of battle, recalled a thousand odious things, the ignominies from which he had turned, and by the gleam of his anger, as by the lightnings of a terrible storm, he instantly realised his disasters. The governors of the country estates had fled from terror, possibly by connivance with the soldiers; all were deceiving him. For a long time he had restrained himself; but now he cried out:

"Let them be brought and branded on their foreheads with red-hot iron, as cowards!"

The fetters, pillories, knives, and chains for those condemned to the mines, the *cippes* to grip their legs, the *numella* to confine their shoulders, and the scorpions, or whips of three thongs terminating in brazen claws, all were brought and spread out in the middle of the gardens.

The slaves were placed facing the sun, toward Moloch the Devourer, extended on the ground flat on their faces, or on their backs; and those condemned to flagellation were fastened against trees with two men beside them, the one who struck the blows and the other who counted the stripes. The former wielded the whip with both arms, the thongs whistling sharply through the air at each blow, and making the bark fly off the plane-trees; the blood would spurt from the culprit's body like rain over the foliage; and red masses writhed, howling, at the foot of the trees.

Those who were branded tore their faces with their nails. The wooden screws creaked, dull thuds were heard, and sometimes over all, a sharp scream from the victim suddenly pierced the air.

In the direction of the kitchens, amid ragged clothing and dishevelled hair, men could be seen with bellows reviving the fires, and the atmosphere was charged with the odour of burning flesh.

The whipped creatures fainted; but retained by the cords around their arms, helplessly with closed eyes, rolled their heads on their shoulders. Those who were looking on uttered screams of fright; and the lions, perhaps recalling the recent feast, yawned and stretched themselves against the narrow confines of their dens.

Salammbô was now seen on the platform of her terrace: she walked wildly from right to left in terror. Hamilcar saw her, and it seemed to him that she lifted her arms toward him to beseech pardon. With a gesture of horror he straightway passed into the elephant paddocks.

These animals were the pride of the noble Punic families. They had borne their ancestors, had triumphed in the wars, and they were reverenced as favourites of the sun. Those of Megara were the strongest in Carthage.

Before his departure on his last expedition, Hamilcar had charged Abdalonim under oath that he would ever watch over these creatures. But they had died from their mutilations, and now only three were left, lying in the dust in the middle of the court, before the remnants of their manger.

Recognising Hamilcar, the elephants came toward him. One had his ears dreadfully slit; another a large gaping wound on his knee; and the third had his trunk cut off. They looked at him with a pitiful air, like reasoning persons; and the one that had lost his trunk lowered his enormous head, and bending his knees, endeavored to strike his master gently with the hideous extremity of its stump. At this attempted caress from the wounded animal, tears gushed from the Suffet's eyes, and he sprang upon Abdalonim.

"Oh, wretch! to the cross! to the cross!" Abdalonim fainted, falling backward to the ground.

From behind the purple factories, whence blue smoke slowly curled up to the heavens, the yelp of a jackal rang out. Hamilcar paused.

The thought of his son, like contact with a god, calmed him at once. It was a prolongation of his strength, an indefinite continuation of his personality, which now appeared before his mind; and the slaves could not comprehend from what source came this sudden appeasement to their master.

He diverged toward the purple factories; he passed before the *ergastulum*, a long, black stone structure built in a square pit, with a little passage around it, and four stairways at the corners.

To complete his signal, Iddibal was doubtless waiting for nightfall. Nothing was yet pressing, Hamilcar thought. As he descended into the prison some cried out to him:

"Return!" The most daring followed him.

The open door swung to and fro in the wind. Twilight entered through the narrow loopholes, revealing in the interior broken chains hanging to the walls. Behold, these were all that remained of the war captives! Then Hamilcar grew extraordinarily pale, and those who lingered outside in the ditch saw him put one hand against the wall for support. But the jackal yelped three times in succession. Hamilcar lifted his head, he did not speak a word, he did not move. As soon as the sun had completely set he disappeared behind the cactus hedge; and at night, as he entered the assembly of the Rich convened in the temple of Eschmoûn, he said:

"Lights of the Baalim, I accept the command of the Punic forces against the Barbarians!"

VIII

THE BATTLE OF THE MACAR

HAMILCAR, on the day following, drew two hundred and twenty-three thousand kikars of gold from the Syssites and imposed a tax of fourteen shekels on the Rich. The women also were made to contribute, and a tax had to be paid for the children; and foreign to all Carthaginian customs—he forced the colleges of priests to furnish money.

He demanded all the horses, mules, and weapons. The possessions of those who misrepresented their wealth were confiscated and sold; and, in order to abash the avaricious, he personally contributed sixty suits of armour, and twelve hundred gomers of meal—as much as was given by the Ivory Company.

He sent to Liguria to hire as soldiers, three thousand mountaineers, accustomed to fight bears, advancing to them six moons' pay, at four minæ a day.

Though it was necessary to form an army, he did not accept, like Hanno, all the citizens. In the first place he rejected those of sedentary occupations; next, those whose bellies were too large, or whose appearance was cowardly; while, on the other hand, he admitted dishonoured men, the dissolute of Malqua, the sons of Barbarians, and freed slaves. As reward, he promised to the New Carthaginians all the rights of the city.

His first undertaking was to reform the Legion—those fine young men, who considered themselves the military majesty of the Republic, and were self-governed. He reduced all the officers to the ranks; he treated the men roughly, making them run, leap, and ascend without halting the acclivity of Byrsa; hurl javelins, wrestle, and even sleep out of doors in the public squares. Their families came to see and pity them.

He directed that the swords should be made shorter, and the buskins stouter; he restricted the number of attendants, and reduced the baggage.

In the temple of Moloch there was kept a treasure of three hundred Roman pilums, which he took despite the pontiff's protests.

With the elephants that had returned from Utica, and those that were the personal property of citizens, he organized a phalanx of seventy-two, and used every device to render them formidable. Their drivers were provided with a mallet and chisel to split open the animals' skulls if during a mêlée they tried to run away.

He would not permit the Grand Council to elect his generals. The Elders endeavored to oppose the laws to him, but he overrode them, and not one dared murmur: all bent under the vehemence of his genius. He assumed the sole direction of the war, the government, and the finances; and, to prevent accusations against him, he insisted that the Suffet Hanno should be made examiner of his accounts.

To procure sufficient stones to repair the rampart he demolished the old interior walls, which were at present useless. But difference of fortune replacing the hierarchy of races still made an unsurmountable barrier between the sons of the vanquished and those of the victors; and the patricians watched with an irritated eye the destruction of these ruins, while the plebeians, hardly knowing why, rejoiced over it.

Armed troops marched from morning till night through the streets; every moment the sound of trumpets was heard; chariots passed laden with bucklers, tents, and pikes; the courts were thronged with women making bandages; the ardour of one communicated itself to another; the soul of Hamilcar inspired the Republic.

He had distributed the soldiers in equal numbers of pairs, placing along the lines alternately a strong and a weak man, so that the less vigorous or more cowardly would be led and impelled by two others. But with his three thousand Ligurians and the best of the Carthaginians, he could only form a simple phalanx of four thousand and ninety-six hoplites, protected by bronze casques, and wielding ashwood sarissas fourteen cubits long. Two thousand young men were armed with slings and a poniard, and shod in sandals. These he reënforced with eight hundred others, armed with round bucklers and Roman swords.

The heavy cavalry consisted of the nineteen hundred remaining guards of the Legion, mailed in vermilion bronze like the Assyrian Clinabarians. He had four hundred mounted archers, called Tarentines, wearing weasel-skin caps and leather tunics, and armed with a double-edged battle-axe. Finally, mixed with the Clinabarians were twelve hundred Negroes from the quarter of the caravans, who were to run alongside of the stallions, clutching their manes with one hand.

All was ready; yet Hamilcar did not start.

Frequently at night he would leave Carthage and, unaccompanied, go a distance beyond the Lagoon, toward the mouths of the Macar. Did he intend to join the Mercenaries? The Ligurians camped in the Mappalian district surrounded his mansion.

The apprehensions entertained by the Rich appeared justified when one day they beheld three hundred Barbarians approach the walls. The Suffet ordered the gates to be opened to them; they were deserters, and, impelled either by fear or fidelity, they came to their master.

Hamilcar's return did not astonish the Mercenaries, for they did not believe this man could die. He was returning to fulfil his promises—a hope which had in it nothing absurd, considering how deep the abyss was between the Republic and the Army. Besides, they did not consider themselves culpable; they had already forgotten the feast.

The spies whom they surprised undeceived them. It was a triumph for the desperate; even the lukewarm became furious. The two sieges had overwhelmed them with weariness; nothing was being achieved, it were far better to have a battle! Thus, many of the men, disbanding, had taken to wandering over the country, but at the news of the armament they returned.

Mâtho leaped with joy, crying out:

"At last! At last!"

The resentment which he had centred upon Salammbô now turned against Hamilcar. His hatred had for its object a settled prey; and as vengeance became more easy to conceive, he almost fancied he had attained it, and already gloated over it. At the same time he was possessed by a deeper tenderness and devoured by a keener desire.

At one time he saw himself in the midst of the soldiers, brandishing the

Suffet's head upon a pike. At another time in the chamber with the purple couch, holding the maiden in his arms, covering her face with kisses, stroking her splendid long black hair; and this vision, which he knew could never be realised, tortured him. He swore to himself, since his comrades had named him Schalischim, to command the war, and the certainty that he would never return from it determined him to render it pitiless.

He sought out Spendius in his tent, and said to him:

"You get your men! I shall bring mine! Warn Autharitus! We are lost if Hamilcar attacks us! Do you hear me? Arise!"

Spendius was stupefied by this authoritative air. Mâtho had so long permitted himself to be led, and the fits of passion he had previously evinced had always quickly subsided. But now he seemed at once calmer and more terrible; a superb will flashed in his eyes like the flames of sacrifice.

The Greek did not heed Mâtho's reasons. He occupied one of the pearl-embroidered Carthaginian tents, spending his time drinking cool drinks from silver cups, playing at cottabus; letting his hair grow long, and conducting the siege indolently. Also he had established secret communications with the city, and did not wish to depart, believing that before many days it would open its gates.

Narr' Havas, who constantly wandered between the three armies, at this juncture was with Spendius. He supported his opinion, and even blamed Mâtho for being willing through an excess of courage to abandon their enterprise.

"Leave, then, if you are afraid!" cried Mâtho, "you promised us pitch, sulphur, elephants, foot soldiers and horses—where are they?"

Narr' Havas reminded him that he had exterminated Hanno's last cohorts; as for the elephants, his men were now hunting for them in his forests; he was equipping the infantry, and the horses were already on the way.

As he talked the Numidian kept stroking the ostrich plume that fell over his shoulder, rolling his eyes like a woman and all the time smiling in an aggravating manner. Mâtho stood before him unable to reply.

Just then an unknown man entered, dripping with sweat, terrified, his feet bleeding, his girdle unfastened; and his laboured breathing shook his thin sides enough to burst them; he launched forth in an unintelligible dialect, with wide open eyes, as if he were telling of a battle.

The Numidian king sprang outside the tent and summoned his horsemen. They ranged themselves on the plain in the form of a circle before Narr' Havas, who was now mounted; he bent his head and bit his lips. At last he divided his men in two divisions, ordering the first section to await him; then, with an imperious gesture, he led the other section at a gallop, and disappeared on the horizon in the direction of the mountains.

"Master!" said Spendius—"I do not like these extraordinary chances—the Suffet who returns, and Narr' Havas who goes off!"

"Well! what matters it?" said Mâtho disdainfully.

It was but another reason why they must forestall Hamilcar and rejoin

Autharitus. But if they abandoned the siege of the cities the inhabitants would come out and attack them in the rear, while they would have the Carthaginians in front of them. After many discussions they resolved upon the following plan, which was immediately put in execution.

Spendius with fifteen thousand men proceeded as far as the bridge over the Macar, three miles from Utica. The corners of it were fortified by four enormous towers upon which were planted catapults. With trunks of trees and masses of rock, barricades of thornbushes and stone walls, all the mountain paths and gorges were blocked. On the summits heaps of grass were piled up ready to be fired as signals; and shepherds accustomed to see at long distances were posted at regular intervals.

Hamilcar doubtless would not take the road by the Hot-Springs Mountain as Hanno had. He would certainly conclude that Autharitus, being master of the interior, would close the road against him. Then a check at the beginning of the campaign would ruin Hamilcar, while a victory would only result in soon having to begin over again, as the Mercenaries would be farther off. Again, he could land at the Cape of Grapes and then march on to one of the cities; but he would find himself between the two armies: an imprudence which he could not risk with such a small number of troops. Therefore he was bound to proceed along the base of the Ariana and turn to the left to avoid the mouths of the Macar, and march straight to the bridge. It was at this point Mâtho waited for him.

At night by torchlight he inspected the pioneers; anon he hastened to Hippo-Zarytus, to inspect the works in the mountains; returning so full of his plans that he could not rest.

Spendius envied his tireless energy, but for all details as to directing the spies, the choice of sentinels, the construction of machines, and all measures for defence, Mâtho listened docilely to his companion. They talked no more of Salammbô—one not thinking of her and the other restrained by a sense of shame.

Often Mâtho went in the direction of Carthage, striving to see Hamilcar's army. He darted his eyes along the horizon, threw himself flat on the earth, and in the throbbing of his own arteries believed that he could hear the tramp of troops.

He declared to Spendius that if before three days Hamilcar was not in sight he should march with all his men to meet him and offer battle. Two days more passed, still Spendius contrived to detain him; but the morning of the sixth day he departed.

The Carthaginians were just as impatient for battle as the Barbarians. In the tents and in the houses all felt the same desire, the same pangs; all were asking what kept Hamilcar back.

From time to time, the Suffet ascended the cupola of the temple of Eschmoûn and stood beside the Announcer-of-the-Moons to observe the winds. One day, the third of the month of Tibby, he was seen descending the Acropolis with hurried steps. A great clamor arose in the Mappals, the streets were filled with commotion, and everywhere soldiers began to arm themselves, amid the cries of distracted women, who threw themselves upon their breasts; then they ran to the square of Khamoûn and fell into their ranks. No one was permitted to follow or speak to the soldiers, or to approach the ramparts: during some minutes the entire town was as silent as a vast tomb. The soldiers leaned on their lances thoughtfully, and those in the houses sighed.

At sunset the army marched through the western gate, but instead of taking the road to Tunis or starting for the mountains in the direction of Utica, they went along the sea-coast, and by this road they soon reached the Lagoon, where large round spots whitened with salt glistened like gigantic silver plates forgotten on the shores. Farther on, the puddles of water multiplied, the ground gradually became softer, the soldiers' feet sank in it; yet Hamilcar went on. He always moved at the head of the troops, mounted on his horse, spotted yellow like a dragon, that kept tossing the froth about as he advanced, straining his loins, through the mire. Night came, misty and moonless. Some of the soldiers cried out that they would perish; he snatched away their weapons and gave them to the serving men.

At every step the mud became deeper and deeper; it was necessary for the men to mount the beasts of burden, others clung to the horses' tails; the robust pulled up the weak, and the Ligurians drove forward the infantry at the points of their spears. The obscurity increased: the road was lost: all halted.

Then the Suffet's slaves advanced to seek for the buoys planted at certain distances by his orders; they shouted back through the darkness and the army followed them.

Soon the resistance of firm ground was felt. Then a whitish curve became vaguely outlined, and they found themselves on the banks of the Macar. Notwithstanding the cold, no fires were lighted.

In the middle of the night squalls of wind arose. Hamilcar commanded the officers to arouse the soldiers, but no trumpets were sounded; the captains moved quietly about, tapping the men on their shoulders.

A very tall man waded into the water; it did not reach to his girdle; the army could ford it.

The Suffet ordered thirty-two of the elephants to be placed in the stream, one hundred paces apart, whilst others stationed below would stay the lines of men being swept away by the current; and all the troops, holding their weapons above their heads, crossed the Macar as between two walls. Hamilcar's observations had revealed the fact, that when the westerly winds blew they drove the sand in such a way as to obstruct the stream by forming across it a natural causeway.

He was now on the left bank facing Utica, and on a vast plain, an advantage for the elephants, which constituted the main strength of his army.

This stroke of genius aroused the enthusiasm of the soldiers; an extraordinary confidence returned to them; they wanted to fall immediately upon the Barbarians; but the Suffet ordered them to rest for at least two hours.

As soon as the sun appeared the troops marched into the plain, in three lines; the elephants first, then the light infantry with the cavalry behind them, and lastly the phalanx.

The Barbarians encamped at Utica, and the fifteen thousand around the bridge, were surprised to see in the distance the ground undulating. The wind, which blew very strongly, chased tornadoes of dust, they lifted themselves up, as if detached from the soil, in large golden pillars, then parted asunder, always beginning again, and thus hiding from the view of the Mercenaries the Punic army. The effect produced by the horns placed on the side of the casques caused some to believe that they perceived a herd of cattle; others, deceived by the fluttering mantles, pretended to distinguish wings; and those who had travelled much shrugged their shoulders, saying that it was the illusion of the mirage. Still something subtle of enormous size continued to advance. Little vapours, as breaths, floated over the surface of the desert. The sun, now much higher, shone powerfully; a fierce glare, which seemed to quiver, made the depth of the sky more profound, and permeating objects rendered the distance incalculable.

The immense plain developed on all sides beyond the reach of vision; and the almost invisible undulations of the ground were prolonged to the extreme horizon, closed in by the long blue line which they knew to be the sea. The two armies went forth from their tents to gaze; and the people of Utica crowded upon the ramparts.

They distinguished many transverse bars bristling with even points; these became thicker and larger; black hillocks swayed; suddenly square bushes appeared: they were the elephants and the lances. A single yell burst forth: "The Carthaginians!" and, without signal or command, the soldiers at Utica and those stationed at the bridge made a dash pell-mell to fall in one body upon Hamilcar.

Spendius shuddered and breathlessly repeated—"Hamilcar! Hamilcar!" And Mâtho was not there! What should be done? No means for flight!

The surprise of this event, his terror of the Suffet, and above all the urgency for an immediate resolution, upset him: he could see himself slashed by a thousand swords, decapitated, dead.

Meanwhile they called for him. Thirty thousand men were ready to follow his leadership; a fury against himself seized him and he fell back upon the hope of victory; it was full of delight, and he fancied himself braver than Epaminondas. To hide his pallor he smeared his cheeks with vermilion, then he buckled on his greaves and cuirass, swallowed a cup of pure wine, and ran hotly after his troops, who had hastened toward those of Utica.

They united so rapidly that the Suffet had not time to range his men in line of battle. Gradually he slackened his pace.

The elephants stopped, swaying their heavy heads, covered with ostrich-plumes, and striking their shoulders with their trunks.

At the back through the intervals could be distinguished the cohorts of

velites, and farther on, the large helmets of the Clinabarians with polished
weapons that glittered under the sun's rays; cuirasses, plumes, and waving
standards.

But the Punic army all told numbering only eleven thousand three hundred and ninety-six men, seemed scarcely to contain so many, for it formed
a long square, narrowed at the flank and closed up on itself. Seeing them so
weak the Barbarians were possessed with a riotous joy, for they were three
times the number of the enemy.

As yet no one had discerned Hamilcar; he had perhaps remained behind?
What difference, after all? The disdain that they had for these merchant
soldiers reënforced their courage; and before Spendius could command
the manœuvre, it had all been anticipated and already executed.

They deployed in a long straight line that overlapped the wings of the
Punic army, in order to completely encompass it. But when they were
not more than three hundred paces apart, the elephants, instead of advancing, turned back; then behold, the Clinabarians wheeled round and followed them, and the surprise of the Mercenaries was great when they
perceived all the archers running to rejoin them. The Carthaginians were
afraid; they were flying! A formidable hooting burst out among the Barbarian troops, and from the back of his dromedary Spendius cried out:

"Ah, I knew it well! Advance! Forward!"

Then launched forth instantaneously through the air, streams of javelins
and darts, and balls from whirring slings. The elephants, galled on their
haunches by the flying arrows, galloped rapidly and stirred up a great dust,
presently vanishing like shadows in a cloud.

Far beyond could be distinguished a loud noise of tramping, predominated
by the shrill blare of trumpets blown furiously. The spaces before the
Barbarians, full of eddies and tumult, drew them in like a whirlpool, and
some dashed headling into it. The cohorts of infantry appeared; they
closed their ranks, and simultaneously all the others saw the foot soldiers
running with the galloping cavalry.

Hamilcar had ordered the phalanx to break its sections, for the elephants,
light infantry, and cavalry to pass through these intervals, in order to take
up their stations quickly on the wings; and he had so exactly calculated
the distance from the Barbarians that at the moment when they came
within reach, the entire Carthaginian army was re-formed in a long straight
line. In the centre bristled the phalanx, formed in syntagmata or perfect
squares, having sixteen men on each side. All the file leaders appeared
between the long sharp points, which jutted unequally beyond them, for
the first six ranks crossed their sarissas, holding them in the middle, and
the ten lower ranks supported theirs on the shoulders of their comrades immediately before them.

Their faces were half hidden under the visors of their casques, bronze
greaves covered their right legs, and broad cylindrical shields reached down
to their knees; and this awful quadrangular mass, moving as a single piece,
seemed to possess the life of an animal and the functions of a machine. Two

cohorts of elephants bordered it, and the huge creatures kept quivering, to detach the splinters of the arrows sticking in their black hides. The Indians crouching on their necks amidst tufts of white plumes, guided them with the spoon-shaped end of the harpoons they wielded; while in the towers men concealed as far as their shoulders, waved, behind the great bent bows, iron holders containing burning tow.

On the right and left of the elephants hovered the slingers, each with a sling around his head, another about his loins, and a third in his right hand. Then came the Clinabarians, each one flanked by a Negro, holding their lances between the ears of their horses, covered, like their riders, with gold. Following at intervals came the light-armed soldiers, with bucklers of lynx-skin, over which projected the points of the javelins which they held in their left hands; and the Tarentines, each managing two horses coupled together, finished off at both extremities this wall of soldiers.

The Barbarian army, on the contrary, had not been able to maintain its line. Its enormous length wavered and opened out in gaps. All panted, breathless from running. The phalanx swayed heavily as it thrust forward all its sarissas; under this tremendous weight the Mercenaries' thin lines gave way in the middle.

The Carthaginian wings opened out to seize them; the elephants followed: with lances held obliquely the phalanx cut the Barbarians in two; both the enormous bodies were shaken; the wings, with volleys of arrows and balls, drove them back against the phalangites. The cavalry failed to disengage itself, with the exception of two hundred Numidians, who charged the right squadron of the Clinabarians. All the others were hemmed in and could not escape from the lines. Destruction was imminent and the necessity of coming to some resolution urgent.

Spendius commanded an attack on both flanks of the phalanx to be made simultaneously, so as to force a passage right through it. But the narrowest ranks glided within the longer ones, returned to their position, and the phalanx wheeled to meet the Barbarians, as terrible on its flanks as it had been just before on its front.

They struck against the staves of the sarissas; the cavalry in the rear foiled their attack, and the phalanx, supported by the elephants, kept closing up and extending, and presented successively a square, a cone, a rhombus, a trapezium, and a pyramid. A double interior movement was continually being made from its front to its rear, as those who were at the end of the files ran toward the first ranks, while those who were fatigued or wounded fell back to the base. The Barbarians found themselves crowded on to the phalanx. It was impossible for it to advance; the field of action appeared like an ocean whereon were tossing red plumes and bronze scales, while the bright bucklers rolled like silver foam. Sometimes from end to end wide currents would descend and then ascend, while in the centre a dense mass remained motionless.

The lances bent and rose alternately. Elsewhere was so rapid a movement of naked blades that only the points could be distinguished, and the turms of cavalry swept in wide circles which closed up behind them in eddies. Above the captains' voices, the blare of the clarions and the twanging of lyres, leaden bullets and almond-shaped pellets of clay whistled through the air, smiting swords from hands and making brains leap from the skulls. The wounded, sheltering themselves with one arm under their shields, pointed their swords while the pommel rested on the ground, and others, writhing in pools of blood, turned to bite the passers' heels. The multitude was so compact, the dust so thick, the tumult so deafening, that it was impossible to distinguish anything clearly; the cowards who offered to surrender were not even heard. When men were disarmed they gripped body to body, and breasts cracked against the cuirasses, and the heads of the corpses hung backward between nerveless arms.

There was a company of sixty Umbrians who, firm on their legs, their pikes advanced before their eyes, unshaken and grinding their teeth, cut down and forced back two syntagmata at once. The Epirote shepherds ran to the left squadron of the Clinabarians, seized their horses by the manes, twisting their clubs in them, till the tortured animals, throwing their riders, fled across the plain. The Punic slingers, scattered here and there, stood agape. The phalanx began to waver, the captains ran about distracted, the rear ranks pressed on the soldiers, and the Barbarians had reformed their lines. They returned to the charge; the victory was within reach.

But a cry, one frightful shriek, burst out, a roar of pain and rage; it came from the seventy-two elephants charging down in a double line. Hamilcar had waited until the Mercenaries were massed in a single spot, before loosing the elephants upon them; the Indians had goaded them so cruelly that the blood ran over their large ears. Their trunks were bedaubed with minium, and they held them straight in the air like red serpents; their breasts were accoutred with a boar-spear, their backs with a cuirass, their tusks elongated with iron blades curved like sabres; and to render them more ferocious, they had been intoxicated with a mixture of pepper, pure wine, and incense. They shook their necklaces of bells, shrieking, and the elephant-archers lowered their heads to avoid the stream of flaming darts which began to fly from the tops of the towers.

In order to resist the charge more effectually, the Barbarians closed up in a compact body; the elephants dashed themselves impetuously into the middle of it. The boar-spears attached to their breasts like the prows of ships clove through the cohorts, which fell back in great waves; with their trunks the elephants kept strangling men, or, snatching them from the ground, held them over their heads and delivered them to the soldiers in the tower; with their tusks they disembowelled their victims and tossed their bodies in the air, while long entrails hung from their ivory tusks like bundles of cordage from masts. The Barbarians endeavoured to blind them or hamstring them; others glided under their bodies and plunged their blades up to the hilts, but were crushed beneath the falling animals and perished; the more intrepid clutched on to their girths, under the downpouring volley of flames, balls, and arrows, and continued to sever the leather till the wicker towers rolled off like a tower of stones. Fourteen elephants on the extreme right, maddened by their wounds, turned on the second line; the Indians seized their mallets and chisels, and applying them to the neck-joint, with all their force struck one mighty blow.

Down the enormous animals sank, falling one upon another, forming almost a mountain, and on the heap of carcasses and armour a monstrous elephant, called Fury of Baal, caught by the leg among the chains, trumpeted till evening with an arrow in his eye.

Meanwhile the others, like conquerors who delight in the extermination of foes, were overthrowing, crushing, stamping, venting their fury on the corpses and on the wrecks. In order to repel them, the companies pressed around them in close circles, but they turned on their hind feet in a continual rotary movement, always advancing. The Carthaginians felt a renewal of vigour, and the battle raged again.

The Barbarians weakened; some Greek hoplites threw away their weapons; a panic seized the others. Spendius was seen leaning forward on his dromedary as he spurred it on the shoulders with two javelins. Then all made a dash toward the wings and ran in the direction of Utica.

The Clinabarians, whose horses were exhausted, made no effort to overtake them. The Ligurians, overcome by thirst, screamed to be carried to the stream. But the Carthaginians, placed in the middle of the syntagmata, had suffered least, and stamped their feet with eagerness when they saw their vengeance escaping; already they were starting in pursuit of the Mercenaries, when Hamilcar appeared.

He held in with silver reins his spotted horse, all covered with foam. The bandlets attached to the horns of his casque clattered in the wind behind him, and he had placed under his left thigh his oval shield. With a movement of his three-pointed pike he checked the army.

The Tarentines sprang quickly upon their spare horses, and departed to the right and left toward the water and the city.

The phalanx easily exterminated all the remaining Barbarians. When the swords came near, they closed their eyes and stretched out their throats. Others defended themselves to the death; they were struck down from far off under a shower of stones, like mad dogs. Hamilcar had ordered his men to take prisoners; but the Carthaginians obeyed him with rancour, as it gave them pleasure to plunge their swords into the Barbarians' bodies. As they got heated they set to work with naked arms like mowers, and when they stopped to take breath, they followed with their eyes across the country a horseman in pursuit of a runaway soldier. He would succeed in catching him by the hair and hold him thus some moments, then cut him down with a blow of his battle-axe.

Night fell. The Carthaginians and Barbarians had disappeared. The elephants that had fled were roaming on the horizon, with their towers on fire, burning in the darkness here and there, like moving beacons, half lost in the mist; and no other movement was noticeable over the plain than the rippling of the stream swollen by the corpses which were drifting out to sea.

Two hours later, Mâtho arrived. By the starlight he caught sight of long unequal heaps lying upon the ground. They were files of Barbarians. He stooped down; all were dead. He called afar; not one voice replied.

That same morning he had quitted Hippo-Zarytus with his soldiers to march on Carthage; he reached Utica, to find that Spendius's army had just left, and the inhabitants had begun to fire the war-machines. All had fought furiously. But the tumult that was raging in the direction of the bridge redoubled in an incomprehensible manner. Mâtho hurried by the shortest route across the mountain, but as the Barbarians were flying by the plain, he had met no one.

Before him small pyramidal masses stood out in shadow, and nearer, on this side of the stream, were motionless lights level with the ground. In fact, the Carthaginians had fallen back behind the bridge, and to deceive the Barbarians, the Suffet had established numerous posts on the other bank.

Mâtho continued to press forward, believing that he distinguished Punic ensigns, for horses' heads which did not move appeared in the air fixed on the top of staves, thrust in invisible stacks of arms, and he heard in the distance a great uproar, the noise of songs and clinking of cups.

Then, unable to find out where he was, or how to reach Spendius, and quite overcome by anguish, terrified and lost in the darkness, he impetuously retraced his steps by the same route. The dawn was breaking, when from the mountain height he saw the town, with the frames of the engines blackened by the flames and leaning like giant skeletons against the walls.

All was hushed in an unusual silence and dejection. Amongst his soldiers on the edge of the tents slept men almost naked, stretched out on their backs, or with their foreheads on their arms, supported by their cuirasses. Some of them were unfastening the bloody bandages from their legs. Those who were dying rolled their heads gently; others dragged themselves along to fetch their comrades a drink. Along the narrow paths, sentinels patrolled to keep themselves warm, or stood, their faces turned savagely toward the horizon, and their pikes on their shoulders.

Mâtho found Spendius sheltered under a piece of canvas that was hung from two poles driven into the ground, his knees between his hands, his head bent.

They remained awhile without speaking. Finally Mâtho murmured:

"Vanquished!"

Spendius replied in a sombre voice:

"Yes; vanquished!"

And to all questions he answered only by gestures of despair.

Meanwhile, moans and death-rattles were heard on all sides. Mâtho partially opened the canvas. Then the sight of the soldiers reminded him of another disaster in the same place, and grinding his teeth, he exclaimed:

"Wretch! once already . . ."

Spendius interrupted him:

"But you were not there, either!"

"It is a curse!" cried Mâtho. "At last, nevertheless, I shall reach him. I shall vanquish him! I shall slay him! Ah, if I had only been there! . . ." The idea of having missed the battle stung him to greater desperation than the defeat. He pulled off his sword and threw it to the ground. "But how did the Carthaginians defeat you?"

The former slave recounted the manœuvres. Mâtho felt that he saw them, and was exasperated. The army of Utica, instead of running toward the bridge, should have fallen upon Hamilcar in the rear.

"Alas! I know it," said Spendius.

"You ought to have doubled the depths of your ranks, not to have engaged the phalanx with the light troops, and have made way for the elephants. Up to the last moment you could have regained the field; there was no need to retreat."

Spendius answered:

"I saw Hamilcar pass by in his large red mantle, his arms raised above the dust like an eagle flying on the flanks of the cohorts, and at every gesture of his head they closed in or extended their ranks; the multitude drew us the one toward the other; he was looking at me; I felt in my heart a cold steel!"

"Perhaps he chose the day?" Mâtho said in an undertone to himself.

They questioned each other, trying to fathom what had brought the Suffet at the most untoward juncture. They talked of the situation, and to extenuate his fault, or reimbue himself with courage, Spendius declared that there was still some hope.

"And if there were none it would be of no consequence," retorted Mâtho. "All alone I should continue the war!"

"And I, also!" cried the Greek. Bounding to his feet, he walked with long strides, his eyes flashing, and a strange smile wrinkled his jackal face.

"We will make a new start; do not leave me again! I am not made for battles in the daylight; the flash of swords troubles my vision; it is a malady; I lived too long in the *ergastulum*. But give me walls to scale at night, and I will penetrate to the citadels, and the corpses shall be cold before cock-crow! Show me some one—something—an enemy, a treasure, a woman," he repeated—"a woman, be she the daughter of a king, and I will quickly bring your desire to your feet. You reproach me for having lost the battle against Hanno; nevertheless it was I who regained it—confess it! My drove of swine did better service than a phalanx of Spartans." And yielding to the desire to extol himself and take his revenge, he enumerated all that he had done for the cause of the Mercenaries.

"It was I, in the gardens of the Suffet, who incited the Gauls! Later at Sicca I maddened them all with fear of the Republic; Gisco was about to send the interpreters back, but I did not choose that they should be able to speak. Ah, how their tongues hung out of their mouths! Do you remember? I led you to Carthage; I stole the Zaïmph; I guided you to her; I will do still more; you shall see!" He burst into laughter like a madman.

Mâtho looked at him with wide open eyes. He experienced a sort of embarrassment before this man, who was at once so cowardly and so terrible.

The Greek resumed in a jovial tone, snapping his fingers:

"By Bacchus! After the rain the sun! I have worked in the quarries, and I have drunk Massic wine, in a ship which I owned, beneath a golden canopy like a Ptolemy. Misfortune ought to render us more capable. By force of toil one bends fortune. She loves the crafty; she will yield!"

He went over to Mâtho and took him by the arm.

"Master, at present the Carthaginians are sure of their victory. You have a whole army which has not been in combat, and your men obey *you!* Place them in the front. Be certain that my men, for vengeance's sake, will follow. I have yet remaining three thousand Carians, twelve hundred slingers and archers, complete cohorts! We might even form a phalanx: let us return!"

Mâtho, stunned by the disaster, until now had thought of no way of regaining what had been lost. He listened with open mouth; the bronze plates encircling his sides rose and fell with the throbbing of his heart. He picked up his sword and cried out:

"Follow me! We will march!"

But the scouts, when they returned, reported that the Carthaginian dead had been carried away, the bridge was in ruins, and Hamilcar was nowhere to be seen.

IX

THE CAMPAIGN

THINKING that the Mercenaries would await him at Utica, or might return against him, Hamilcar, knowing that his army was not strong enough to deliver or receive an attack, had gone southward of the right bank of the river, which protected him from the danger of a surprise.

From the first, shutting his eyes to their revolt, he wished to detach all the tribes from the cause of the Barbarians; then, when they should be safely isolated in the middle of the provinces, he would fall upon and exterminate them.

In fourteen days he pacified the region comprised between Thouccaber and Utica, with the towns of Tignicabah, Tessourah, Vacca, and others to the west. Zounghar, built in the mountains, Assouras, celebrated for its temple, Djeraado, fruitful in juniper-trees, Thapitis, and Hagour sent ambassadors to him.

The country people came laden with provisions, imploring his protection, kissing his feet and the feet of his soldiers, and uttering bitter complaints against the Barbarians. Some offered in sacks the decapitated heads of Mercenaries whom they claimed to have killed, but which in fact they had cut from the corpses that they found, as numberless soldiers were lost in the retreat, and were afterward picked up dead in different places, some under the olive trees, others in the vineyards.

To dazzle the people, Hamilcar, the day after his victory, sent to Carthage the two thousand captives taken on the battle-field. They arrived in long companies, each consisting of a hundred men, their arms fastened behind their backs by a bronze bar which caught them at the nape of their necks; even the wounded, yet bleeding, were forced to run, driven along by cuts from the whips of the horsemen riding behind them.

There was a delirium of joy! It was reported that six thousand Barbarians had been killed, the others could not hold out, and that the war was over. People embraced one another in the streets, and rubbed butter and cinnamon on the faces of the *Dii-patæci*, to express their thankfulness. These gods, with their big eyes and their gross bellies, with their arms raised to their shoulders, seemed under the access of fresh paint to be alive, and to participate in the happiness of the people.

The Rich left their doors open; the city resounded with the beating of tambourines; the temples were illuminated nightly, and the handmaidens of the goddess descended to Malqua, and established at the cross-roads tressels of sycamore where they prostituted themselves. Lands were voted to the conquerors; holocausts to Melkarth; three hundred golden crowns to the Suffet, and his partisans suggested that new prerogatives and fresh honours be given to him.

Hamilcar had solicited the Elders to make overtures to Autharitus, offering to exchange all the Barbarian prisoners, if necessary, for the aged Gisco and the other Carthaginians taken by him. The Libyans and the Nomads who composed Autharitus's army scarcely knew the Mercenaries, who were men of Italiote or Greek race; and inasmuch as the Republic offered so many Barbarians in exchange for so few Carthaginians, they decided that it must be because the Barbarian captives possessed no value, in proportion to the others. They feared a trap. Autharitus refused.

Forthwith the Elders issued a decree for the execution of their prisoners, although the Suffet had written that they were not to be put to death, as he had planned to incorporate the best with his own troops, hoping by this step to encourage defection. But hatred swept away all prudence.

The two thousand Barbarians were fastened against the stelas of the tombs in the Mappals; then the pedlars, kitchen scrubs, embroiderers, and even women, the widows of the dead warriors, with their children, joined by all who cared, came to kill them with arrows. In order to prolong their agony they slowly took deliberate aim. Each lowered his weapon, and raised it again by turns. The multitude crowded forward, hooting and howling.

The paralytics had themselves brought on stretchers; many prudently came with provisions and stayed till evening; others passed the night there. Drinking booths had been set up. Many gained large sums by hiring out their bows.

The crucified bodies were allowed to stand, appearing like so many red statues on the tombs; and the exultation reached even as far as the people of Malqua, descendants of the aboriginal tribes, who ordinarily were indifferent to events in the Republic. Out of gratitude for the present pleasure afforded to them by the government, they were now concerned in her fortunes, feeling themselves to be Punic; and the Elders considered it shrewd thus to have merged the entire people in the same vengeance.

The sanction of the gods was not wanting, for from every quarter of the sky ravens descended, beating their wings as they circled in the air, with loud, hoarse croaks, and making an enormous cloud which continually wheeled over itself. It was visible from Clypea, from Rhades, and from the promontory of Hermæum. Sometimes this mass would suddenly rift, widening afar its black spirals, as an eagle would swoop into the middle, and then soar away. On the terraces, on the domes, on the points of the obelisks, and on the pediments of the temples, here and there, big birds were perched holding in their reddened beaks fragments of human flesh.

In consequence of the odour the Carthaginians resigned themselves to the release of the bodies. Some were burned, others were thrown into the sea, and, driven by the north wind on the waves, were washed upon the beach at the end of the gulf before the camp of Autharitus.

This revenge had doubtless terrified the Barbarians; as from the roof of Eschmoûn they could be seen hastily pulling up their tents, rounding up their herds, and packing the baggage upon the asses, so that by the evening of the same day the entire army had withdrawn.

It was intended, by marching and countermarching between the Hot-Springs Mountain and Hippo-Zarytus, to prevent the Suffet approaching the Tyrian cities, and thus returning to Carthage.

In the meantime the two other armies endeavoured to reach him in the south, Spendius by the east, Mâtho by the west, so as to unite the three armies and then surprise and entrap him. An unlooked-for reënforcement astonished them, for Narr' Havas reappeared with three hundred camels laden with bitumen, twenty-five elephants, and six thousand horsemen.

To weaken the Mercenaries the Suffet had deemed it well to give Narr' Havas enough to keep him busy in his own distant kingdom. From the heart of Carthage he had to come to an understanding with Masgaba, a Getulian brigand who sought to make a realm for himself. Supported with Carthaginian silver, the adventurer had stirred the Numidian states to revolt, by promises of freedom. But Narr' Havas, warned by the son of his nurse, had surprised Cirta, poisoned the conquerors with the water in the cisterns, struck off some heads, and set everything in order: and he now returned more furious than the Barbarians against the Suffet.

The chiefs of the four armies agreed as to the conduct of the war. As it would be long, it was necessary to provide against every contingency.

It was agreed first to ask the assistance of the Romans, and this mission was offered to Spendius; but as a fugitive he did not dare to take charge of it, therefore twelve men from Greek colonies were selected to execute it, and embarked on a Numidian shallop at Annaba.

Then the chiefs exacted from all of the Barbarians an oath of absolute obedience. Each day the captains inspected the clothing and shoes; even the use of shields was forbidden to the sentinels, for they often had been found to prop them against their lances and thus sleep whilst standing upright. Those who dragged about any baggage were ordered to get rid of it; everything, according to Roman custom, must be carried on the back. As a precaution against the elephants Mâtho instituted a corps of panoplied cavalry, in which both man and horse were concealed under a cuirass of hippopotamus hide bristling with nails; and to protect the horses' hoofs, they wore shoes of plaited esparto-grass.

It was forbidden to pillage the villages, or to tyrannise over the inhabitants of non-Punic race. As the country was becoming exhausted, Mâtho ordered the distribution of rations to the soldiers individually, without heeding the women; at first the men shared with them, and from lack of sufficient food, many became weak. It was the occasion of incessant quarrels and invectives, many attracting the companions of others by bribes, or even by the promise of their rations. Seeing this, Mâtho commanded that all women should be driven away without pity. They took refuge in the camp of Autharitus; but the women of the Gauls and Libyans, by force of outrages, compelled them to leave.

At length they arrived under the walls of Carthage, imploring the protection of Ceres and of Proserpine; for there was in Byrsa a temple and priests, consecrated to these goddesses, in expiation of the horrors committed formerly during the siege of Syracuse. The Syssites, alleging their right to all strays, claimed the youngest to sell; and the New Carthaginians took some of the blonde Lacædemonian women in marriage.

Others of the women persistently followed the armies. They ran on the flank of the syntagmata beside the captains. They called to their men, and pulled them by their cloaks, struck themselves on their breasts as they uttered curses, and held out at arms' length their crying naked little babies. This sight weakened the hearts of the Barbarians; the women were obviously a hindrance, a peril even. Frequently they were rudely pushed back, but they would obstinately return. Mâtho ordered the cavalry of Narr' Havas to charge them with their lances, and when the Balearic warriors cried out to him that they must have women—"But, I myself have none!" he replied.

The genius of Moloch possessed him. Despite the rebellion of his conscience, he executed frightful deeds, and imagined that in so doing he obeyed the voice of a god. When he could not ravage the fields, he threw stones into them to render them unfruitful.

By continual messages he pressed Autharitus and Spendius to hasten on. But the operations of the Suffet were incomprehensible. He encamped successively at Eidous, at Monchar, at Tehent; the scouts believed that they espied him in the direction of Ischiil, near the frontier of Narr' Havas's dominion; and it was rumoured that he had crossed the stream above Tebourba, as if to return to Carthage. Scarcely was he in one place, when he moved to another. The routes that he followed always remained unknown. Without giving battle, the Suffet held his advantages; while pursued by the Barbarians, he seemed to lead them on.

These marches and counter-marches fatigued the Carthaginians yet more; and Hamilcar's forces, not being renewed, day by day diminished. The people from the country brought provisions to him more reluctantly. Everywhere he met a hesitation, a taciturn hatred; and in spite of his supplications to the Grand Council no help came from Carthage.

Some said—and perhaps believed—that he did not require succour. It was a ruse, or a useless complaint, and Hanno's partisans, in order to do an ill office to Hamilcar, exaggerated the extent of his victory. The troops that he had they were content to sacrifice, but they were not going to supply continually all his demands. The war was quite expensive enough! it had cost too much; and, actuated by pride, the patricians of his faction supported him half-heartedly.

Then, despairing of the Republic, Hamilcar levied by force on the tribes for all that was needed for the war: grain, oil, wood, animals, and men. At these demands the inhabitants were not long in taking to flight. The villages that he traversed were deserted, cabins were ransacked without anything being found, and soon a frightful solitude encompassed the Punic army.

The Carthaginians were furious; they pillaged the provinces, filled up the cisterns, burned the houses, the sparks setting fire to entire forests, bordering the valleys with a crown of flames: to pass beyond, the troops were compelled to wait until they subsided. Then they resumed their march under the full sun, over the hot ashes.

Sometimes they saw by the roadside lurid gleams in the bushes like the eyes of a tiger-cat. This would be a Barbarian crouching on his haunches, daubed with dust that he might blend with the colour of the foliage; or when they went along a ravine, those who were on the wings would suddenly hear stones rolling, and, lifting their eyes, would perceive in the opening of the gorge a bare-footed man fleetly bounding by.

Inasmuch as the Mercenaries did not besiege them again, Utica and Hippo-Zarytus were free. Hamilcar commanded them to come to his aid. Not caring to compromise themselves, they replied by vague words, compliments, and excuses.

He abruptly marched northward, determined to obtain possession of one of the Tyrian towns, even if he had to besiege it. It was necessary for him to have a station on the coast in order to draw from the islands, or from Cyrene, supplies and soldiers, and he coveted the port of Utica as being the nearest to Carthage.

The Suffet accordingly left Zouitin, and cautiously skirted the lake of Hippo-Zarytus. But soon he was obliged to extend his regiments in a column, to climb up the mountain separating the two valleys. At sunset they descended into its summit, hollowed out like a funnel; suddenly they perceived before them, level with the ground, bronze she-wolves, which appeared to be running over the grass.

Then large plumes of feathers rose into view; and to the rhythm of flutes a formidable chant burst forth. It was the army commanded by Spendius: for the Campanians and Greeks, in their abhorrence of Carthage, had adopted Roman ensigns. At the same time on the left appeared long pikes, shields of leopard's skin, linen cuirasses, and naked shoulders. They were Mâtho's Iberians, Lusitanians, Balearics, and Getulians; the neighing of the horses of Narr' Havas was heard: they spread around the hill. Then came the irregular mob commanded by Autharitus, made up of Gauls, Libyans, and Nomads; and in their midst the Eaters-of-Unclean-Things could be recognised by the fishbones they wore in their hair.

Thus the Barbarians had so exactly regulated their marches that they came together simultaneously. But, surprised themselves, they halted for some minutes motionless, and consulted.

The Suffet had collected his men in an orbicular mass, which offered on every side equal resistance. Their high-pointed shields, stuck in the turf one against another, surrounded the infantry. The Clinabarians remained outside; and farther off, at intervals, the elephants were stationed. The Mercenaries were exhausted with fatigue: it would be better to wait until the following day; and, sure of their victory, the Barbarians occupied themselves during the entire night in eating.

They lighted immense bright fires, which while dazzling them, left the Punic army beneath them in the shade. Hamilcar caused a trench to be excavated Roman fashion around his encampment, fifteen feet wide and ten cubits deep; and a parapet to be massed up with the earth thus dug out, on which were planted interlacing sharp stakes. At sunrise the Mercenaries were amazed to behold the Carthaginians thus entrenched as in a fortress.

They recognised Hamilcar in the midst of the tents walking about giving orders. His body was encased in a brown cuirass fashioned of small scales. He was followed by his horse, and from time to time he stopped, extending his right arm to point out something.

Then more than one recalled similar mornings when amid the din of clarions he had passed slowly before them, and how his looks had fortified them as cups of wine. A sort of emotion seized them. Those, on the contrary, who did not know Hamilcar, were delirious with joy at having caught him.

Still, if all attacked at the same time they would inflict mutual damage in the narrow space. The Numidians might charge across, but the Clinabarians, protected by their cuirasses, would crush them; then how could they pass the palisades? As for the elephants, they were not sufficiently trained.

"You are all cowards!" cried Mâtho.

And with picked troops he dashed against the entrenchments. A volley of stones repulsed them, for the Suffet had taken on the bridge their abandoned catapults.

This defeat abruptly turned the unstable spirit of the Barbarians. Their excessive bravado disappeared; they wished to conquer, but with the smallest possible risk. According to Spendius, they should carefully guard the position they had secured, and starve out the Punic army. But the Carthaginians began to dig wells, and as mountains surrounded the hill they discovered water.

From the summit of their palisade they fired arrows, hurled earth, dung, and stones, which they picked up from the ground; whilst the six catapults were wheeled constantly the length of the entrenchment.

But the springs would naturally dry up, the provisions would not last, the catapults would wear out; the Mercenaries were ten times their number, and would certainly triumph in the end. As a subterfuge to gain time, the Suffet opened negotiations, and one morning the Barbarians found within their lines a sheep-skin covered with writing. He justified himself for his victory: the Elders had forced him into the war; and, to show them that he kept his word, he now offered to them the plunder of Utica or Hippo-Zarytus, whichever they chose. Hamilcar, in conclusion, declared that he did not fear them, because he had won over some traitors, and with their help he would easily make an end of them all.

The Barbarians were troubled; this offer of immediate booty made them ponder; they feared treason, not suspecting a snare in the boasting of the Suffet; and they began to regard each other with distrust. Every word was observed, every movement watched; and at night terrors kept them awake. Many left their comrades, following their personal fancy in choosing the army to which they attached themselves: and the Gauls with Autharitus joined the men of the Cisalpine province, whose language they understood.

The four chiefs conferred every night in Mâtho's tent, and, squatting around a shield, they moved forward and backward attentively the little wooden dummies, invented by Pyrrhus for representing military manœuvres. Spendius would show the resources of Hamilcar, entreating them by all the gods not to throw away this opportunity. Mâtho in vexation walked about gesticulating. For him the war against Carthage was a personal affair, and he felt indignant that the others interfered without being willing to obey him. Autharitus divined his words from his face, and applauded. Narr' Havas raised his chin as a sign of disdain; not one measure was offered but he judged it fatal. Mâtho smiled no more: sighs escaped him as if he had forced back the anguish of an impossible dream, the despair of an unattainable enterprise.

While the Barbarians deliberated in their uncertainty, the Suffet increased his defences, dug a second trench on the inside of the palisades, erected a second wall, and constructed wooden towers at the corners; his slaves went to the middle of the advance-posts to bury caltrops in the ground. But the elephants, whose allowances were lessened, struggled in their shackles. To economise the fodder, he ordered the Clinabarians to kill the weakest of the stallions. Some of the men refused to comply, and were at once beheaded. The horses were eaten. The memory of this fresh meat was a great sorrow in the days that followed.

From the bottom of the amphitheatre, where the Punic army was confined, they saw all around them on the heights the four busy Barbarian camps. Women moved about balancing leathern bottles on their heads; goats wandered bleating under the stacks of pikes; the sentinels were going on or off duty, and men were eating around the tripods. In fact, the various tribes furnished them with abundant supplies, and they had no idea how greatly their inaction disturbed the Punic army.

From the second day, the Carthaginians had remarked in the camp of the Nomads a troop of three hundred men remote from the others. They were the Rich, held as prisoners since the beginning of the war.

The Libyans ranged them on the edge of the ditch, and, posted behind them, threw javelins, while making a rampart of their bodies. Scarcely could these wretched creatures be recognised, to such a degree were their faces disfigured by vermin and filth. Their hair had been pulled out in spots, leaving bare ulcers on their scalps; and they were so thin and hideous that they resembled mummies in tattered shrouds. Some trembled and sobbed in a stupid manner; others screamed out to their friends to fire upon the Barbarians.

There was one among the prisoners perfectly motionless, with head bent, and speaking no word; his flowing white beard reached to his hands, which were covered with chains. The Carthaginians felt from the depths of their hearts the downfall of the Republic as they recognised Gisco. Though the place was dangerous they crowded to see him. Some one had placed on his head a grotesque tiara, made of hippopotamus-skin studded over with pebbles. This had been a fancy of Autharitus that was thoroughly displeasing to Mâtho.

Hamilcar was infuriated, and ordered the palisades to be opened, determined to cut a way at any cost, and in a mad rush the Carthaginians charged half-way up, about three hundred paces. Such a torrent of Barbarians poured down that they were driven back on their own lines.

One of the guards of the Legion was left outside, having stumbled over the stones. Zarxas ran up, knocked him down, and plunged his dagger into his throat; he drew out the weapon and threw himself upon the wound— gluing his lips to it; with ejaculations of delight and wild starts that shook him to his very heels, he sucked the blood in deep draughts, then calmly sat on the body with face uplifted, holding his head back to inhale the air, like a hind that has just drunk from a torrent. He struck up in a shrill voice a Balearic song, a vague melody, full of prolonged modulations, breaking off and replying to himself, like echoes answering echoes in the mountains; he called upon his dead brothers and invited them to a feast; then, he let his hands fall listlessly between his knees, slowly bent his head and wept. This atrocity filled the Barbarians, and especially the Greeks, with horror.

From this time the Carthaginians made no sortie; but they had no thought of surrender, knowing that they would perish under tortures.

Meanwhile, despite Hamilcar's care, the provisions decreased frightfully. For each man there remained not more than ten *k'hommer* of corn, three *hin* of millet, and twelve *betza* of dried fruits. No more meat, oil, or salt provisions, not one grain of barley for the horses; they could be seen bending down their emaciated necks to seek in the dust for trampled bits of straw.

Often the sentinels patrolling the terrace would see in the moonlight a dog belonging to the Barbarians prowling below the entrenchments in heaps of filth. They would fell it with a stone, and then, by the aid of straps of a shield, lower themselves down the length of the palisade, and without a word devour it. Occasionally a horrible baying would be heard, and the venturesome never returned. In the fourth dilochia of the twelfth syntagma, three phlangites quarrelling about a rat killed each other with blows of their knives.

All longed for their families and their homes: the poor for their cabins shaped like bee-hives with shells placed at the thresholds, and a net suspended outside; and the patricians for their grand halls full of bluish shadows, wherein, during the warmest hour of the day, they sought repose, listening to the indistinct voices in the street, mingled with the rustling of leaves in their gardens, stirred by the breeze; and, to better enter into these reveries, and thoroughly enjoy them, they half-closed their eyelids until the shock of a wound would awake them.

Every moment there was some engagement, some new alarm; the towers blazed, the Eaters-of-Unclean-Things leaped upon the palisades—their hands were chopped off with axes; others ran up; a hail of iron fell upon the tents. Galleries of reed hurdles were erected to protect them from the projectiles. The Carthaginians shut themselves up and went out no more.

Each day the sun in its course deserted from the early hours the depth of the gorge and left them in shadow. In front and behind rose the grey slopes of earth, covered with stones spotted with scanty lichens, and over their head the sky, always cloudless, spread out more steely cold to the eye than a metal cupola. Hamilcar was so indignant against Carthage that he felt strongly disposed to join the Barbarians and lead them against her. Besides, now, even the porters, the sutlers, and slaves began to murmur; and neither the people, the Grand Council, nor anyone sent a word of hope. The situation was unbearable, and especially so because of the fear that it would become worse.

At the news of the disaster Carthage throbbed with anger and hatred; the citizens perhaps would have execrated the Suffet less if early in the war he had allowed himself to be vanquished.

But to hire other Mercenaries there was neither time nor money. As for recruiting soldiers in the town, how could they equip them? Hamilcar had already taken all the weapons! And who would command new troops? The best captains were with him. Meanwhile, messengers despatched by the Suffet arrived in the streets and cried out for help. The Grand Council was disturbed, and made arrangements for their disappearance.

This was an unnecessary precaution: all accused Barca for having acted with too much leniency. He should have annihilated the Mercenaries after his victory. Why had he ravished the tribes? They already had imposed on themselves sacrifices enough! And the patricians repented their contribution of fourteen shekels, the Syssites theirs of two hundred and twenty-three thousand kikar of gold, and those who had given nothing lamented as bitterly as the others.

The populace was jealous of the New Carthaginians, to whom Hamilcar had promised the complete rights of the city; and even the Ligurians, who had fought so bravely, were confounded with the Barbarians, and like them were cursed; their race became a crime, the sign of complicity. The shopkeepers on the door-sills of their shops, journey-men who walked about with their leaden rules in their hands, pedlars of pickle rinsing their baskets, bath-men in the vapour baths, and the vendors of hot drinks, all discussed the management of the campaign. They traced in the dust with their fingers the plans of battle; and there was not a vagabond so low that he could not correct Hamilcar's military errors.

The priests averred that all his misfortunes were a punishment for his long impiety. He had offered no holocausts, he had not purified his troops, he had even refused to take augurs with him; and the scandal of the sacrilege intensified the violence of restrained hatreds, the rage of hopes betrayed. They recalled the disaster of Sicily, and all the burden of his pride that they had borne so long. The colleges of pontiffs could not pardon him for seizing their treasure, and they exacted from the Grand Council a pledge to crucify him should he ever return.

This year the heat of the month of Eloul, which was most excessive, was another calamity. From the lake shore nauseous odours arose and were diffused through the atmosphere with the smoke of the spices circling up at the street corners. Hymns constantly resounded. Streams of people crowded the stairways to the temples; the walls were draped with black veils; tapers burned constantly in front of the *Dii-patæci;* and the blood of the camels slaughtered as sacrifices ran along the flights of steps, forming red cascades.

Carthage was stirred with a funereal delirium. From the extremity of the narrowest alleys, and from the blackest dens, pale faces appeared—men with profiles like vipers, who ground their teeth. The shrill screams of women filled the dwellings, and escaping through the lattices, made those who stood chatting about the squares turn around. Sometimes it was believed that the Barbarians were coming: they had been seen behind the Hot-Springs Mountain. Then it was rumoured that they were encamped at Tunis. And the voices multiplied, swelling till they were merged in one confusing clamour. Then a universal silence would reign. Some of the people remained clinging to the pediments of the edifices with one hand shielding their eyes, while others, lying flat at the foot of the ramparts, strained their ears. The fear having passed, their fury broke out afresh. But the knowledge of their powerlessness soon threw them back into the same profound sadness.

It redoubled every evening, when all, ascending the terraces, uttered, while bowing nine times, a vast cry of salutation to the sun, as it sank slowly behind the Lagoon, then suddenly disappeared in the mountains in the direction of the Barbarians.

They were anticipating the thrice holy feast, when from the top of a pyre an eagle soared toward the sky—a symbol of the resurrection of the year, a message from the people to its supreme Baal which they regarded as a kind of union, a means of attaching themselves to the majesty of the Sun.

Filled as they were with hatred, the people naturally turned toward Moloch, the Man-Slayer, and all deserted Tanit. In effect, the Rabbetna, no longer possessing her veil, was despoiled of a part of her power. She refused the blessing of her waters. She had forsaken Carthage; she was a deserter, an enemy. Some, to insult her, threw stones at her. But even while cursing many pitied her. She was still cherished, and perhaps more intensely than ever.

All their misfortunes came from the rape of the Zaïmph. Salammbô had indirectly participated in this crime; therefore she was included in the same bitterness; she must be punished. The vague idea of an immolation quickly circulated amongst the people. To appease the Baalim, undoubtedly they must offer something of incalculable value—a beautiful being, young, a virgin of an ancient family, descended from the gods—a human Star.

Daily strange men invaded the gardens of Megara, and the slaves, fearing for themselves, did not dare resist them. However, they did not pass on to the stairway of the galleys, but always stopped below with eyes raised to the last terrace; they waited for Salammbô, and for hours cried out against her, like dogs baying at the moon.

X

The Serpent

The daughter of Hamilcar was not alarmed by the clamourings of the populace; she was troubled by loftier anxieties—for her great serpent, the black Python, was failing: and for the Carthaginians a serpent was not only a national but a personal fetich. They believed every serpent to be an offspring of the slime of the earth, inasmuch as it emerged from its depths, and needed no feet to walk upon; its movements were as the undulations of streams; its temperature was ancient darkness, clammy and fecund; and the orb that it described when biting its tail, the complete planetary system, the intelligence of Eschmoûn.

Salammbô's serpent had many times of late refused the four living sparrows offered to it at the new and full of each moon. Its beautiful skin, covered like the firmament with spots of gold on a dead black surface, was now yellow, flabby, wrinkled, and too large for its body; over its head was spreading a downy mould; and in the corners of its eyes appeared little red spots that seemed to move.

Salammbô repeatedly drew near to its silver filigree basket, and drew aside the purple curtain, the lotus leaves and bird's down—but it was continually coiled upon itself, stiller than a withered vine. As a result of her intense observation she ended by feeling in her heart a spiral like another serpent, which was gradually rising up to her throat and strangling her.

She was in despair at having seen the Zaïmph; and yet she felt a sort of joy, a peculiar pride. A mystery eluded her in the splendour of its folds; it was the mist surrounding the gods, the secret of universal existence; and Salammbô, while horrified at herself, regretted that she had not raised it.

Almost always she was crouching on the floor of her apartment, her hands clasped around her left knee, her mouth half open, chin sunken, and eyes fixed. She recalled with terror her father's face. She longed to make a pilgrimage in the mountains of Phœnicia, to the temple of Aphaka, where Tanit had descended in the form of a star. All manner of imaginations allured and alarmed her; besides, each day a greater solitude environed her. She did not even know what had become of Hamilcar.

Wearied of her thoughts, she would rise; and the soles of her tiny sandals would clatter against her heels at every step as she walked at random in the large, silent room. The amethysts and topazes in the ceiling quivered here and there in luminous points, and Salammbô, as she walked, turned her head slightly to view them. She took the suspended amphoras by their necks; she refreshed herself under the broad fans, or amused herself by burning cinnamon in hollowed pearls.

At sunset Taanach would draw back the lozenges of black felt which closed the openings in the wall; then Salammbô's doves, rubbed with musk like the doves of Tanit, flew into her presence, and their pink feet slipped over the glass pavement in the midst of the grains of barley which Salammbô scattered to them in handfuls, like a sower in a field. But in a moment she would burst out in sobs, and remain extended full length on the great couch of cow-hide straps, motionless, repeating one word, always the same, with wide-open eyes, pale as death, insensible, cold; and yet she could hear the cries of the apes in the clumps of palm trees, and the continuous grinding of the great wheel raising through the stories a stream of pure water up into the porphyry basin.

Sometimes for many days she refused to eat. She dreamed that she saw dim stars passing beneath her feet. She would summon Schahabarim; and when he came she had nothing to say to him.

She could not live without the comfort of his presence; but her spirit rebelled against this domination; she felt for the priest, at the same time, terror, jealousy, hatred, and an emotion akin to love, in recognition of the sensuous delight she experienced whenever she found herself near to him.

He had recognised the influence of Rabbet, skilled as he was to distinguish the gods who sent illnesses; and to cure Salammbô he had her room sprinkled with lotions of vervain and maidenhair, and ordered that she should eat mandrake every morning, and sleep with her head on a sachet of aromatics mixed by the pontiffs. He had even employed hazelwort, a fiery-coloured root, by which fatal spirits are driven back in the north. Finally, he turned toward the polar star, and murmured thrice the mysterious name of Tanit. But Salammbô continued to suffer, and her anguish deepened.

No one in Carthage was as learned as this priest. In his youth he had studied in the college of the Mogbeds at Barsippa, near Babylon; then had visited Samothrace, Pessinus, Ephesus, Thessaly, Judea, and the temples of the Nabathæans, which are lost in the sands; and he had traversed on foot the banks of the Nile, from the cataracts to the sea. His face covered with a veil, and waving torches, he had cast a black cock on a fire of sandarack before the breast of the Sphinx—Father-of-the-Terror. He had descended into the caverns of Proserpine; he had witnessed the five hundred columns of Lemnos revolve, and had seen the brightness of the candelabrum of Tarentum, which carried on its standard as many sconces as there are days in the year.

Sometimes at night he would receive Greeks to question them. The constitution of the world concerned him no less than the nature of the gods; with the armillary placed in the portico of Alexandria he had observed the equinoxes, and accompanied as far as Cyrene the bematists of Euergates, who measured the heavens by calculating the number of their paces. So now there was growing up in his thoughts a subjective religion, with no defined formula, and for this very reason full of ecstasies and fervour.

He no longer believed that the earth was shaped like a .pine-cone; he believed it to be round, and eternally falling in space with such prodigious velocity that no one could perceive its fall.

From the position of the sun above the moon, he judged that Baal was supreme; the orb was only his reflection and visage. Moreover, all terrestrial things which he then saw forced him to recognise as supreme the male exterminating principle. Then, he secretly held Rabbet responsible for the misfortune of his life. Was it not for her that the grand pontiff had advanced amid a tumult of cymbals and taken his future virility? And he followed with a melancholy gaze the men who abandoned themselves to pleasures with priestesses in the depths of the turpentine groves.

His days were spent in inspecting the censers and gold vases, tongs and rakes used for the ashes of the altar, and all the robes of the statues, even to the bronze pins used to curl the hair of an old Tanit in the third chapel, close to the emerald vine. Regularly at certain hours, he raised before the same entrances the grand tapestries, which fell back behind him again. He remained with his arms open in the same attitude, prayed prostrated upon the same stones; and about him, through the lobbies filled with eternal twilight, moved only a population of barefooted priests.

But over the barrenness of his life Salammbô came as a flower in the cleft of a sepulchre. Yet he was harsh to her, and spared her neither penances nor bitter speeches. His condition established between them the equality of a common sex; and yet, his desire toward the maiden would have been rather to have the power of possessing her than to find her so fair, and above all, so pure. Often he saw that she wearied, trying in vain to follow his thoughts. Then he turned away sadly, and felt himself more forsaken, more lonely, and more useless.

Strange words frequently escaped him, and passed before Salammbô like broad flames illuminating abysses.

It would be night, on her terrace, when alone these two would observe the stars, while Carthage spread itself below their feet, and the gulf and open sea were vaguely obscured in the colour of the darkness.

He revealed to her the theory of souls which descended on the earth, following the same route as the sun through the signs of zodiac. With extended arm he pointed out in Aries the entrance of the human generation; in Capricorn the return toward the gods; and Salammbô strove to perceive them, for she took these conceptions for realities, accepting as realities pure symbols, and even figures of speech, a distinction no longer clearly defined even to the priest.

"The souls of the dead," he said, "resolve themselves into the moon as do the corpses into the earth. Their tears compose her humidity; it is a dark abode full of mire, wrecks, and tempests."

She asked what then would become of her.

"At first you will languish, light as a vapour that floats on the waves; and after trials and most prolonged agonies, you will enter the centre of the sun, the very source of Intelligence!"

As he did not mention Tanit, Salammbô imagined he refrained through shame for his vanquished goddess, and therefore called her by a commonplace name, that designated the moon. But she continued to pour forth blessings upon the planet so fertile and benign. At last he exclaimed:

"No! no! she draws from the sun all her fruitfulness! Have you not seen her wandering around him like an amorous woman who runs after a man in a field?"—and unceasingly he exalted the virtues of light.

Far from lessening her mystic desires, on the contrary, he stimulated them, and he even seemed to take pleasure in troubling her by his revelations of a pitiless doctrine. Salammbô, despite the throes of her love, threw herself upon them with rapture.

But the more Schahabarim felt doubts concerning Tanit the more he desired to believe in her. In the depths of his soul remorse checked him. It was necessary that he should have some proof, a manifestation of the gods; and in the hope to attain such, he devised an undertaking that should at the same time save his country and his belief.

From this moment he set himself to deplore before Salammbô the sacrilege and the consequent misfortunes even in the regions of the sky. Then abruptly he announced the peril threatening the Suffet, who was assailed by three armies commanded by Mâtho—for, because of Mâtho's possession of the veil, he was, in the eyes of the Carthaginians, king of the Barbarians; and he added that the preservation of the Republic, as well as her father, depended upon her alone.

"Upon me!" she exclaimed. "What can I do?"

But the priest, with a smile of disdain, said:

"Never will you consent!"

She entreated him to explain. Finally Schahabarim said to her:

"It is necessary that you go to the Barbarians' camp and bring back the Zaïmph."

She sank down upon the ebony stool, and remained with her arms stretched out between her knees, shuddering throughout her entire frame like a victim at the foot of an altar awaiting the blow of the axe. Her temples throbbed; she saw circles of fire burning before her eyes, and in her stupor comprehended nothing more than that she must die soon.

But if Rabbetna triumphed—if the Zaïmph was recovered and Carthage delivered—of what importance the life of one woman! thought Schahabarim. Then she might perhaps obtain the veil and not perish.

For three days he stayed away from her; the evening of the fourth day she sent for him.

To inflame her heart more surely, he reported all the invectives that were openly hurled in the Council upon Hamilcar; he told her she had sinned, and that she should make reparation for her crime; that Rabbetna commanded this sacrifice.

A great clamour crossed over the Mappals, and reached Megara. Schahabarim and Salammbô went quickly out, and looked from the top of the galley stairway.

It was occasioned by the people congregated in the square of Khamoûn, who yelled out for arms. The Elders did not wish to furnish them, as they esteemed this effort unavailing; others who had gone without a general had been massacred. At last the crowd was permitted to sally forth; and as a kind of homage to Moloch, or a vague wish for destruction, they pulled up in the groves of the temple large cypress trees, and having lighted them in the torches of the Kabiri, carried them through the streets while they sang. These monstrous flames advanced swaying gently, casting reflections on the glass globes at the crest of the temples, on the ornaments of the colossi, on the beak-heads of the ships, passing beyond the terraces, and appearing like suns revolving in the city. They descended the Acropolis. The gate of Malqua opened.

"Are you ready?" exclaimed Schahabarim, "or have you told them to say to your father that you abandon him?" She hid her face in her veil, and the great lights receded, gradually sinking to the edge of the waves.

An indefinable terror held her; she was afraid of Moloch, afraid of Mâtho. That man of giant stature, who was master of the Zaïmph, dominated Rabbetna, even as the Baal did, and he appeared to her surrounded with the same splendours. Then she remembered that the spirit of the gods sometimes visited the bodies of men. Had not Schahabarim, in speaking of him, declared that she ought to conquer Moloch? They were confused the one with the other: she confounded them: both pursued her.

Wishing to know the future, she approached her serpent—for auguries were often drawn from the attitude of the serpents. The basket was empty. Salammbô was troubled.

She found it coiled up by its tail to one of the silver balustrades near the suspended couch, rubbing itself, to get free from its old yellowish skin;

meanwhile its body, shining and bright, was gradually appearing, like a blade being drawn from the scabbard.

The following days, in proportion as she allowed herself to be convinced and was more disposed to succour Tanit, the Python grew better and larger, and seemed to revive.

The certainty that Schahabarim expressed the will of the gods established itself in her conscience. One morning she arose decided, and asked the priest what it was necessary for her to do to compel Mâtho to give back the veil.

"Claim it," said Schahabarim.

"But if he refuses?" she resumed.

The priest gazed at her attentively, and with such a smile as she had never before seen.

"Yes; what shall I do?" repeated Salammbô.

He rolled between his fingers the ends of the bandlets that fell down from his tiara over his shoulders, his eyes downcast; finally perceiving that she did not comprehend, he said:

"You will be alone with him."

"And then?"

"Alone in his tent."

"And what then?"

Schahabarim bit his lips; he sought for some indefinite phrase.

"If you are to die it will be later," said he; "much later! fear nothing; and whatever he attempts, do not call out! do not be frightened! You must be humble, you understand, and submissive to his desire, for it is ordained of Heaven!"

"But the veil?"

"The gods will care for it," responded Schahabarim.

She added:

"Oh, father, if you would only accompany me?"

"No!"

He made her kneel, and keeping her left hand raised and her right one extended, he swore in her behalf to bring back to Carthage the veil of Tanit. With fearful imprecations, she consecrated herself to the gods, and each time that Schahabarim pronounced a word she tremblingly repeated it.

He indicated to her all the purifications and fasts she ought to perform, and what paths to follow, in order to reach Mâtho's tent; besides, he told her that a servitor familiar with the roads should accompany her.

She felt herself freed. She dreamed of naught but the happiness of finding the Zaïmph; and now she blessed Schahabarim for his exhortations.

The doves of Carthage at this season migrated to the mountain of Eryx in Sicily, there nesting about the temple of Venus. Previous to their departure, during many days, they sought each other, and cooed to reunite themselves; finally one evening they flew away, driven by the wind, and the large white cloud blew across the heavens very high above the sea.

The horizon was crimson. They seemed gradually to descend to the waves, then to disappear as if swallowed up and falling, of their own accord, into the jaws of the sun. Salammbô, who watched them go, drooped her head. Taanach, believing that she surmised her mistress's grief, tenderly said:

"But, mistress, they will return."

"Yes! I know it."

"And you will see them again."

"Perhaps!" Salammbô said, as she sighed.

She had not confided to anyone her resolution, and for its secret accomplishment she sent Taanach to purchase, in the suburbs of Kinisdo (instead of requiring them of the stewards), all the articles it was necessary she should have: vermilion, aromatics, a linen girdle, and new garments. The old slave was amazed at these preparations, but dared not ask any questions; and so the day arrived fixed by Schahabarim for Salammbô's departure.

Toward the twelfth hour, she perceived at the end of the sycamores an old blind man, who rested one hand on the shoulder of a child who walked before him, and in the other hand he held, against his hip, a species of cithara made of black wood.

The eunuchs, the slaves, the women had been sent away; no one could possibly know the mystery that was being prepared.

Taanach lighted in the corners of the room four tripods full of *strobus* and cardamom, then she spread out great Babylonian tapestries, and hung them on cords all round the room—for Salammbô did not wish to be seen even by the walls. The player of the kinnor waited crouching behind the door, and the young boy, standing up, applied a reed flute to his lips. In the distance the clamour of the streets died away, the violet shadows lengthened before the peristyles of the temples, and on the other side of the gulf the base of the mountain, the olive fields, and the waste yellow ground undulated, till they finally blended in a bluish vapour; not a sound could be heard, and an indescribable oppression filled the air.

Salammbô crouched on the onyx step on the edge of the porphyry basin; she lifted her wide sleeves fastening them behind her shoulders, and began her ablutions in a methodical manner, according to the sacred rites.

Next Taanach brought to her an alabaster phial, in which was something liquid, yet coagulated; it was the blood of a black dog, strangled by barren women on a winter night amid the ruins of a sepulchre. She rubbed it on her ears, her heels, and the thumb of her right hand, and even the nail remained tinged a trifle red, as if she had crushed a berry. The moon rose, and then the cithara and the flute began to play. Salammbô removed her earrings, her necklace, bracelets, and her long white simarre; unknotted the fillet from her hair, and for some minutes shook her tresses gently over her shoulders to refresh and disentangle them. The music outside continued; there were always the same three notes, precipitous and furious; the strings grated, the flute was high-sounding and sonorous. Taanach marked time by striking her hands; Salammbô, with a swaying of her entire body, chanted her prayers, and one by one her garments fell around her on the floor.

The heavy tapestry trembled, and above the cord that sustained it the head of the Python appeared. He descended slowly, like a drop of water trickling along a wall, and glided between the stuffs scattered about, then poised himself on his tail; suddenly he lifted himself perfectly straight, and darted his eyes, more brilliant than crimson carbuncles, upon Salammbô. A shudder of cold, or a feeling of modesty perhaps, at first made her hesitate. But she recalled the order of Schahabarim, so she advanced; the Python lowered himself, alighting in the middle of his body upon the nape of her neck, allowing his head and tail to hang down like a broken necklace, with the two ends trailing on the floor. Salammbô rolled them around her sides, under her arms, between her knees; then taking him by the jaw, she drew his little triangular mouth close to her teeth; and with half-closed eyes she threw herself back under the moon's rays. The white light seemed to enshroud her in a silvery fog; the tracks of her wet feet shone on the flagstones; stars twinkled in the depths of the water; the serpent tightened around her his black coils, speckled with spots of gold. Salammbô panted under this great weight; her loins gave way, she felt that she was dying: the Python patted her thighs softly with his tail; then the music ceased, and he fell down.

Taanach returned to Salammbô, and after arranging two candelabra, the lights of which burned in two crystal globes filled with water, she tinted with henna the inside of the hands of her mistress, touched her cheeks with vermilion, put antimony on her eyelids, and lengthened her eyebrows with a mixture of gum, musk, ebony, and crushed flies' feet.

Salammbô, sitting in a chair mounted with ivory, abandoned herself to the care of her slave. But the soothing touches, the odour of the aromatics, and the fasts she had kept, enervated her: she became so pale that Taanach paused.

"Continue!" said Salammbô; and as she drew herself up in spite of her fatigue, she felt all at once reanimated. Then an impatience seized her; she urged Taanach to hasten her movements, and the old slave growled:

"Well! well! mistress! . . . You have no one waiting for you!"

"Yes!" responded Salammbô, "some one waits for me."

Taanach started with surprise, and in order to learn more, she said:

"What do you order me to do, mistress, if you should remain away?" . . .

But Salammbô sobbed, and the slave exclaimed:

"You suffer! What is it? Do not go! Take me! When you were a little one and wept, I held you to my heart and suckled you, and made you laugh by tickling you with my nipples. Mistress!" she struck her withered breasts, "you sucked them dry. Now I am old! I can do nothing for you! You do not love me any more! You hide your troubles from me, you despise your nurse!" With fondness and vexation the tears coursed down her face, in the scars of her tattooing.

"No!" said Salammbô, "no; I love you; be comforted!"

Taanach, with a smile like a grimace of an old ape, continued her task. Following the directions of the priest, Salammbô ordered her slave to make her magnificent. Taanach complied, with a barbaric taste full of elaboration and ingenuity.

Over a first fine wine-coloured tunic she placed a second one, embroidered with birds' plumes. Golden scales rested on her hips, from her wide girdle flowed the folds of her blue, silver-starred trousers. Then Taanach adjusted an ample robe of rare stuff from the land of the Seres, white, variegated with green stripes. She fastened over Salammbô's shoulders a square of purple, made heavy at the hem with beads of *sandastrum;* and at the top of all these robes she arranged a black mantle with a long train. Then she contemplated her, and, proud of her work, she could not keep from saying:

"You will not be fairer the day of your bridal!"

"My bridal!' repeated Salammbô in a reverie, as she leaned her elbow on the ivory chair.

Taanach held up before her mistress a copper mirror, wide and long enough for her to view herself completely. She stood up, and with a light touch of a finger put back a curl that drooped too low on her forehead. Her hair was powdered with gold dust, waved in front, hanging down her back in long twists, terminating in pearls. The light from the candelabra heightened the colour on her cheeks, the gold throughout her garments, and the whiteness of her skin. She wore around her waist, on her arms, hands, and feet such a number of jewels that the mirror, reflecting like a sun, flashed back prismatic rays upon her: and Salammbô standing beside Taanach, leaned and turned around on all sides to view herself, smiling at the dazzling effect.

Then she walked to and fro, embarrassed by the time that she needs must wait.

Suddenly the crow of a cock was heard. She quickly pinned over her hair a long yellow veil, passed a scarf around her neck, and buried her feet in blue leather boots, saying to Taanach:

"Go, see under the myrtles, if there be not a man with two horses."

Taanach had scarcely reëntered before Salammbô descended the stairway of the galleys.

"Mistress!" called out the slave. Salammbô turned around and placed one finger on her lips, in sign of discretion and silence.

Taanach crept softly the length of the prows as far as the foot of the terrace, and in the distance by the moonlight she discerned in the cypress avenue a gigantic shadow moving obliquely to the left of Salammbô: this was a presage of death.

Taanach went back to her room, cast herself on the floor, tore her face with her finger-nails, pulled out her hair, and uttered piercing yells at the top of her voice.

Finally the thought came to her that she might be heard; then she was quiet, sobbing very low, with her head between her hands and her face laid flat on the pavement.

XI

IN THE TENT

SALAMMBÔ was led by the guide Schahabarim had appointed, up the road toward the Catacombs and then down the long suburb of Molouya, full of steep lanes.

The sky began to grow grey. Sometimes palm-branches jutting beyond the walls obliged them to bend their heads. The two horses, walking carefully, kept slipping; and they thus arrived at the Teveste gate.

Its heavy valves were half open; they passed through, and it slowly swung to behind them.

For some time they followed the foot of the ramparts, and at the top of the cisterns they took a road by the Tænia, a narrow strip of yellow land, which separating the gulf from the lake, extended as far as Rhades.

No one was visible in or about Carthage, either on the sea or in the surrounding country. The clay-coloured waves rippled softly, as the gentle wind tossed the foam over the sweep of the breakers and flecked them with broken splashes of white.

Notwithstanding her numerous wraps, Salammbô shivered in the freshness of the morning; she felt dizzy from the unaccustomed motion of the horse and the open air. Then the sun rose; its rays fell on the back of her head, and involuntarily she became drowsy. The two horses ambled along side by side, burying their hoofs in the silent sand.

When they passed the Hot-Springs Mountain, they gained speed as the ground became firmer.

Although it was the season for ploughing and sowing, the fields as far as the eye could see were as forsaken as a desert; heaps of grain were spread out from place to place; elsewhere the reddened barley shed itself from the ear; and on the clear horizon, villages showed black, with incoherent and mutilated outlines.

Now and again a half-calcined piece of wall stood erect on the roadside. The cabin roofs were falling in, exposing the interiors, where could be seen fragments of pottery, tatters of clothing, all sorts of utensils, and unrecognisable shattered objects. Frequently a being covered with rags emerged from the ruins, its face incrusted with dirt, and eyes flaming, but always quickly took to its heels, or disappeared in a hole. Salammbô and her guide did not pause.

Abandoned plains succeeded each other. Over wide stretches of yellow earth spread out in uneven streaks, a black charcoal dust, raised by the horses' feet, rose behind them in clouds. Sometimes they came to peaceful nooks, where a brook ran amid long grasses, and as they climbed up the opposite bank, Salammbô, to refresh her hands, would pluck the wet leaves.

At the corner of a wood of laurel-roses she was nearly unseated by her horse shying at a corpse in the roadway. The slave readjusted her on the cushions. He was one of the servitors of the temple of Tanit, a man whom Schahabarim employed in perilous missions. With extreme caution he now went on foot beside her, between the two horses, now and then touching them up with the end of a leather lash, wound around his arm; or pulling from a pannier hung on his breast balls of wheat, dates, and yolks of eggs, wrapped up in lotus leaves, he would proffer them to Salammbô, without speaking or pausing.

In the middle of the day, three Barbarians dressed in animals' skins crossed their path; gradually others appeared, wandering in bands of ten, twelve, or twenty-five, many driving she-goats or limping cows. Their heavy clubs were studded with brass points; cutlasses glittered on their filthy savage clothing. Seeing the riders, they opened their eyes wide with a threatening and amazed air.

As they passed along, some shouted after them a commonplace benediction, others obscene pleasantries; and the guide answered each group in their own idiom, telling them that he was conducting a sick youth to be healed at a distant temple.

Meantime the day fell. The baying of a dog was heard, and they proceeded toward the sound. Through the twilight they perceived an enclosure of uncemented stones surrounding a shapeless building. A dog ran along on the wall; the slave threw a stone at it, and they entered a high, vaulted hall. In the centre a crouching woman was warming herself at a brushwood fire, the smoke from which escaped through a hole in the roof. Her white hair fell to her knees, half concealing her, and not wishing to answer the guide, she mumbled in an idiotic manner words of vengeance against the Barbarians and the Carthaginians.

After the guide had ferreted about from right to left, he came back to the old woman, and demanded something to eat. She shook her head, keeping her eyes fixed on the fire, and murmured:

"I was the hand; the ten fingers are cut off. The mouth can eat no more."

The guide showed her a handful of gold pieces; she threw herself upon them, but quickly resumed her motionless attitude.

Finally he drew a dagger from his girdle, and pointed it at her throat; then she tremblingly lifted up a large slab, and brought out from concealment an amphora of wine and some fish preserved in honey from Hippo-Zarytus.

Salammbô turned away from this unclean food, and, being weary, slept on the caparisons taken from her horse, and heaped in a corner of the hall.

Before daybreak the guide awoke her.

The dog growled, and the guide stole softly up behind it, and with a single blow of his dagger, cut off its head. He rubbed the blood on the horses' nostrils to reanimate them. The old hag threw a curse after them. Salammbô heard it, and pressed the amulet she wore to her heart.

They resumed their journey. Urged by impatience, now and again she asked the guide if they should not soon reach their destination. The road led over little hills. The chirping of the cicadas was alone audible. The sun heated the yellowed grasses. The ground was riven by crevices, which divided it into immense slabs.

Sometimes a viper crawled by, or an eagle flew overhead. The guide ran alongside of Salammbô, who mused beneath her veils, and, despite the heat, refrained from casting them aside, fearful of soiling her beautiful vestments.

At regular distances towers loomed up, built by the Carthaginians for the purpose of watching the tribes. Occasionally they entered one of these, to avail themselves of the shade, but, once refreshed, started on again.

The previous day, by way of precaution, they had made a wide détour, but at present they were meeting no one; the region was barren, the Barbarians had not passed that way.

Gradually the devastation appeared again; and sometimes in the midst of a field there appeared a mosaic floor, the sole relic of a vanished mansion. The olive-trees, stripped of foliage, seemed in the distance like broad thorn-bushes. They passed through a town in which all the houses had been burnt flat to the ground. Along on the wall-sides could be seen human skeletons, as well as those of dromedaries and mules; and half-devoured carrion blocked many of the streets.

Night fell; the sky hung low, and was covered with clouds.

For two hours more they ascended in a westerly direction; when all at once appeared quantities of small flames.

At the bottom of an amphitheatre, here and there golden plates gleamed as they moved about. These were the cuirasses of the Clinabarians in the Punic camp. Then they distinguished in the same vicinity other and more numerous lights, for the armies of the Mercenaries were now combined and massed together, covering a vast area.

Salammbô made a movement to advance, but the guide led her farther on, and they skirted the terrace that enclosed the Barbarians' camp. A breach was discovered: the slave disappeared.

At the top of the entrenchments patrolled a sentinel, carrying a bow in his hand and a pike over his shoulder.

Salammbô continued to advance. The sentinel knelt down, and a long arrow pierced the end of her mantle. Then she halted motionless; he asked her what she wanted.

"To speak to Mâtho," she replied. "I am a fugitive from Carthage."

He whistled; the signal was repeated many times in the distance.

Salammbô waited; her frightened horse snorted and wheeled.

When Mâtho arrived, the moon was rising behind her, but her face was concealed under a yellow veil covered with black flowers, and so many draperies enveloped her, it was impossible to recognise her. From the top of the terrace he contemplated this vague form rising like a phantom through the evening shadows.

At length she said to him:

"Conduct me to your tent. I wish it."

A recollection which he could not define passed through his memory. He felt his heart beat. This air of command intimidated him.

"Follow me!" said he.

The barrier was lowered; she was within the camp of the Barbarians.

It was replete with a great tumult and a surging crowd. Fires burned brightly under suspended camp kettles, and their crimson reflections cast weird shadows in certain places, while permitting others to remain in complete darkness.

People were shouting and calling on all sides; the horses were tethered in long, straight rows between the tents, that were round or square, constructed of leather or canvas; there were also reed huts, and holes dug in the ground, like burrows of animals.

The soldiers were carting faggots for the fires, or were squatting on the ground, or, wrapped up in their mats, were preparing themselves for sleep; and Salammbô's horse, in order to step over their forms, sometimes was forced to stretch out its legs and leap.

Salammbô recalled having seen these very same men before; but now their beards were much longer, their faces more tanned, and their voices harsher. Mâtho walked in front of her, and waved them away with a gesture of his arm that lifted his red mantle. Some kissed his hands, others bowed down and accosted him, to request his commands, for he was now veritable and only Chief of the Barbarians: Spendius, Autharitus, and Narr' Havas had been discouraged, but he had shown such audacity and determination that all obeyed him.

Salammbô, following him, traversed the entire length of the camp, as his tent was pitched at the end, only three hundred paces from Hamilcar's entrenchments.

She noticed on the right a broad pit, and it seemed to her that faces leaned on the edge, level with the ground, resembling decapitated heads; yet their eyes moved, and from their half-opened mouths moans in the Punic language escaped.

Two Negroes, holding cressets filled with burning resin, stood on either side of Mâtho's tent. He advanced, and brusquely drawing aside the canvas, entered. She followed him. It was a deep tent, supported by a pole in the middle, and lighted by a large sconce in the form of a lotus, filled with yellow oil, on which floated handfuls of burning tow; in the shadows were shining military accoutrements. A naked sword leaned against a stool, beside a shield; whips of hippopotamus hide, cymbals, little bells and collars, were thrown pell-mell into baskets of esparto-grass; crumbs of black bread soiled a felt rag; in one corner, on a round stone, copper money was carelessly heaped; and through the rents of the tent-canvas the wind brought from without the dust, and the scent of the elephants, which could be heard feeding and rattling their chains.

"Who are you?" commanded Mâtho.

Without a reply she slowly looked round the tent, and her glance was arrested at the background, where, on a bed of palm-branches, lay something bluish and scintillating.

She advanced quickly: a cry escaped her. Mâtho, behind her, stamped his foot.

"What brings you here? Why do you come?"

She replied, pointing to the Zaïmph:

"To take it!" and with the other hand she pulled off her veils. Mâtho recoiled, his elbows thrown back, gaping, almost terrified.

She felt herself sustained as if by the power of the gods, and gazing at him face to face, she demanded the Zaïmph, claiming it with profuse and haughty words.

Mâtho did not hear: he was staring at her, and her garments, that were to him blended with her body: the sheen of the fabrics was like the splendour of her skin, something special, peculiar to her alone: her eyes and her diamonds sparkled; the polish of her finger-nails was a continuation of the lustre of the jewels that bedecked her fingers; the two clasps fastening her tunic raised her breasts a trifle up and pressed them closer; and he, in a reverie, lost himself in the narrow space between them as his eye followed the slender thread to which was suspended an emerald medallion that revealed itself lower down under the violet gauze. She wore for earrings two tiny balances of sapphires, supporting a hollow pearl filled with liquid perfume, which percolated through minute perforations, moistening her bare shoulders. Mâtho watched it slowly trickle down.

An irresistible curiosity attracted him, and like a child who puts its hand on an unknown fruit, tremblingly he touched her lightly with the tip of his finger on the upper part of her bosom; the flesh, slightly cold, yielded with an elastic resistance.

This contact, although scarcely perceptible, penetrated Mâtho to the depths of his soul. An insurrection of his whole being impelled him toward her. He desired to envelop her, absorb her, drink her. His bosom heaved, his teeth chattered.

Taking her by the wrists he gently drew her to him, and then sat down on a cuirass beside the couch of palm-branches, covered with a lion's skin; she remained standing. Thus holding her between his knees, he scanned her from head to foot, repeating:

"How beautiful you are! How beautiful you are!"

His eyes continually fixed on hers made her suffer, and this embarrassment, this repugnance, increased in a manner so keen that Salammbô had to restrain herself from screaming out. The thought of Schahabarim came to her; she resigned herself.

Mâtho kept her little hands in his, and from time to time, in spite of the priest's orders, she averted her face, and tried to throw him off by shaking her arms. He dilated his nostrils to breathe more freely the perfume exhaled from her person—a fresh indefinable emanation which yet made him dizzy, like the fumes from a censer—a diffusion of honey, pepper, incense, roses, and yet another odour.

But, how came she to be thus beside him in his tent, at his discretion? Some one doubtless had brought her. She had not come for the Zaïmph? His arms fell, and he bent his head, overwhelmed by a sudden reverie.

In order to move him, Salammbô said, in a plaintive voice:

"What, then, have I done to you, that you wish my death?"

"Your death!" he exclaimed.

She resumed:

"I saw you one night, by the flames of my burning gardens, between the steaming cups and my slain slaves; and at that time your wrath was so fierce that you bounded toward me, and made me fly! Then a terror entered Carthage—devastation of the cities—burning of the countries—massacre of the soldiers. It is you who have ruined them! It is you who have assassinated them! I abhor you! Your name alone gnaws me like remorse! You are more execrable than the plague! Aye, than the Roman war! The provinces quake before your fury; the ditches are full of corpses! I have followed the trace of your fires as if I walked behind Moloch!"

Mâtho bounded up; a tremendous pride swelled his heart; he felt himself lifted to the stature of a god.

With palpitating nostrils and clenched teeth, she continued:

"As if there had not already been enough sacrilege, you came to my palace while I slept, enveloped in the Zaïmph! Your words I did not comprehend; but I saw that you desired to drag me toward something frightful —to plunge me to the bottom of an abyss!"

Mâtho, wringing his hands, cried out:

"No! no! It was to give the Zaïmph to you! To render it back to you! For it seemed to me that the goddess had left her vestment for you, and that it was yours! In her temple or in your mansion, what matter? Are you not all-powerful, immaculate, radiant and beautiful as Tanit?" And with a look full of adoration:

"At least—perhaps—if you may not be Tanit herself?"

"I, Tanit!" Salammbô thought, wondering.

They spoke no more. The distant thunder rumbled. The sheep bleated, frightened by the storm.

"Oh! come near!" he resumed. "Come near; fear nothing!

"Formerly, I was but a soldier, among the common Mercenaries, and even carried upon my back the wood for my comrades. Do I trouble myself about Carthage? The crowd of Carthage tosses to and fro as if lost in the dust of your sandals, and all the Carthaginian treasures, with her provinces, her waters, and her islands, do not tempt me like the freshness of your lips and the turn of your shoulders. But I wanted to pull down her walls, that I might come near to you and possess you! Besides, while I wait I revenge myself! At present, I crush men like shells. I throw myself on the phalanxes; I scatter the sarissas with my hands, and arrest the stallions by their nostrils; a catapult is powerless to kill me! Oh! if you only knew how in the midst of this war I have thought of you! Sometimes the memory of a gesture—of a fold in your garments, has suddenly seized me and entangled me like a

net! I see your eyes in the flames of the fire-lances and above the gilding
of the shields. I hear your voice in the sounding of the cymbals; I turn
around—you are not there! And then I plunge again into the thick of
battle!"

He lifted his arms, and the swollen veins intercrossed like ivy creeping
over the branches of trees; the perspiration rolled down on his chest between his squared muscles, while his rapid breathing made his sides palpi-
tate beneath his belt of bronze, fitted with straps that hung to his knees,
which were firmer than marble. Salammbô, accustomed to the eunuchs,
yielded to the force of this man.

It was the chastisement of the goddess, or the influence of Moloch, circulating around her in the five armies. Overwhelmed by a certain lassitude,
she indistinctly heard through her stupor the intermittent call of the sentinels answering one another.

The flames of the lamp wavering fitfully under gusts of warm air, became
at moments bright flashes of light, then almost died out, intensifying the
obscurity; and she saw only Mâtho's eyeballs like two glowing coals in the
night. Now she felt, indeed, that a fatality encompassed her, that she had
attained a supreme moment which was irrevocable, and with one effort
she went toward the Zaïmph, and raised her hands to seize it.

"What are you doing?" cried Mâtho.

She answered calmly:

"I am going back to Carthage with the Zaïmph."

He advanced, and folded his arms with an air so terrible that she was
immediately as one nailed to the ground.

"You return with it to Carthage!" he stammered; and repeated, grinding
his teeth: "You return with it to Carthage! Ah! you came to take the
Zaïmph, to conquer me, then to disappear! No! no! you belong to me!
and no one can now tear you from here! Ah! I have not forgotten the
insolence of your large, tranquil eyes, and how you crushed me with your
haughty beauty! It is my turn now! You are my captive, my slave, my
servant! Call, if you will, on your father, and his army, the Elders, the
Rich, and your entire accursed people! I am the master of three hundred
thousand soldiers! I will go and seek them in Lusitania, among the Gauls,
and in the depths of the desert. I will overthrow your town, and burn all
its temples! The triremes shall float on waves of blood! I do not choose
that a single house, a stone, or a palm-tree remain! And if men fail me,
I will draw the bears from the mountains, and turn the lions upon your
people! Do not seek to fly, or I shall kill you!"

Ghastly, and with fists clenched, he quivered like a harp when the over-
tense strings are about to snap. Suddenly sobs suffocated him, and he sank
down before her.

"Ah! forgive me, I am a wretch, viler than the scorpions, than the mud
or the dust! Just now, as you were speaking, your breath passed over my
face, and I revelled in it as a dying man who, prone on his face, drinks
at the edge of a stream. Crush me, that I may feel your feet! Curse me, that

I may hear your voice! Do not go! Have pity! I love you! I love you!" He was on his knees on the ground before her, and he encircled her waist with his arms, his head thrown back and his hands wandering about her; the gold discs suspended from his ears shone on his bronzed throat; large tears rolled in his eyes, like silver balls; he sighed caressingly, and murmured vague speeches lighter than a breeze, sweet as a kiss.

Salammbô was overcome by a softness in which she lost all consciousness of herself. Something at once from within, and from on high, an order of the gods, forced her to yield herself; clouds uplifted her, and, fainting, she fell back on the couch in the midst of the lion's skin. Mâtho seized her in a frantic embrace; her golden chainlet snapped, and the two ends flew apart, striking against the tent like two leaping vipers. The Zaïmph fell and enveloped her. Seeing Mâtho's face bending over her, she exclaimed:

"Moloch, thou burnest me!" and the kisses of the soldier, more devouring than fire, covered her. She was as if lifted up in a storm, or as consumed by the force of the sun.

He kissed all her fingers, her arms, her feet, and the long tresses of her hair from end to end.

"Take the Zaïmph," he said; "how can I resist? Take me also with it! I will renounce everything! Beyond Gades, twenty days' journey by the sea, there is an island covered with gold-dust, with verdure, and birds. On the mountains flowers full of smoking perfume swing like eternal censers; in citron trees taller than cedars, milk-white serpents with the diamonds of their jaws toss the fruit to the ground. The air is so soft that you cannot die. Aye, I will seek it; you shall see this haven. We shall live in crystal grottoes hewn out at the foot of the hills. No one inhabits this country; I shall become king."

He brushed the dust from his cothurnes; then besought her to allow him to put a quarter of a pomegranate between her lips; he piled up garments behind her head to make a pillow; in fact he sought in every imaginable way to serve her, to humble himself, and even went so far as to spread over her knees the Zaïmph as if it were a simple rug.

"Do you still keep," said he, "those little gazelle horns on which your necklaces are suspended? Give them to me! I love them!" Joyous laughter escaped him; he talked as if the war were at an end; the Mercenaries, Hamilcar, and all obstacles, had disappeared.

Through an opening in the tent they saw the moon gliding between two clouds.

"Ah! what nights I have spent in contemplating her! She seemed to me a veil which hid your face; you looked at me through it; memories of you were mingled with her rays. Then I could see you there no more!" And with his head upon her bosom, he wept freely.

"And this is he," she thought, "the formidable man who makes Carthage tremble!"

Finally he slept; then, disengaging herself from his arms, she placed one foot on the ground, and she saw that her chainlet was broken.

In great families the virgins were accustomed to respect these little shackles with almost the same reverence as if they were religious symbols. Salammbô, blushing, rolled around her ankles the two ends of her dishonoured gold chainlet. Carthage, Megara, her mansion, her room and the tract of country through which she had recently traversed, rushed in whirlwinds through her memory, in images tumultuous, and yet distinct. But an abyss removed them far from her, to an infinite distance.

The storm was clearing; occasional heavy drops of rain, spattering one by one, made the tent-top sway.

Mâtho slept as a man intoxicated, extended on his side, one arm flung out beyond the edge of the couch; his pearl bandeau, raised a trifle, exposed his forehead. A smile parted his lips, disclosing his glittering teeth in the midst of his black beard, and in his half-closed eyes lurked a silent, almost outrageous gaiety. Salammbô regarded him, her head bent, her hands clasped, motionless.

At the head of the couch a dagger lay on a cypress table; the sight of this shining blade inflamed her with murderous desire. Lamenting voices came from afar through the darkness, and like a choir of spirits urged her. She drew near and seized the haft of the weapon, but at the rustle of her robe Mâtho partially opened his eyes, moved his· lips over her hands, and the dagger dropped.

Shouts burst out; a frightful light flashed behind the tent. Mâtho lifted the tent cloth; a vast conflagration enveloped the Libyan camp. Their reed cabins were burning, the stems twisting, splintered through the smoke, flying like arrows; against the red horizon black shadows ran frantically about. Yells issued from those within the cabins; the elephants, the cattle, and the horses leaped and plunged among the· distracted crowd, crushing the soldiers with the munitions and baggage that they dragged out of the fire. Trumpets sounded. Voices called out:

"Mâtho! Mâtho!" Men tried to enter, shouting:

"Come! come! Hamilcar is burning the camp of Autharitus."

At this he made one bound. Salammbô· now found herself alone.

Then she examined the Zaïmph; after she had contemplated it well, she was surprised not to experience that degree of happiness she had formerly thought would be hers. She remained melancholy before her dream accomplished.

Just then the end of the tent was lifted and a hideous form appeared. At first Salammbô could only discern two eyes, and a long white beard, which hung down to the ground, for the rest of the body, entangled in the rags of a tawdry garment, trailed along the earth: and at every forward movement the two hands were buried in his beard, and then fell back. Crawling thus he gradually arrived at Salammbô's feet, and she recognised the aged Gisco.

In fact, the Mercenaries, to prevent the captive Elders from escaping, had broken their legs with a metal bar, then had thrown them all promiscuously to rot in a ditch of filth. The most robust, when they heard the rattle of the platters, used to raise themselves up and yell: it was thus that Gisco had seen Salammbô.

When Mâtho led Salammbô across the camp to his tent Gisco had conjectured her to be a Carthaginian woman by the little beads of *sandastrum* that clattered on her buskins,. and actuated by the presentment of some important mystery, with the aid of his companions he had succeeded in getting out of the pit, and he dragged himself on his hands and elbows twenty yards or more to Mâtho's tent; he had heard everything.

"It is you!" she said, almost appalled.

Lifting himself up on his hands, he replied:

"It is I! All believe me to be dead, is it not so?"

She bowed her head, and he continued:

"Ah! why have not the Baals granted me this mercy!"—and he drew so close that he touched her robe—"they would have spared me the pain of cursing you!"

Salammbô drew herself quickly back; she was afraid of this unclean being, who seemed as hideous as a larva and as terrible as a phantom.

"I shall soon be one hundred years old," he said. "I have seen Agathocles, I have also seen Regulus and the Roman eagles pass over the Punic harvest fields! I have seen all the horrors of battles and the sea encumbered with the wrecks of our fleets! The Barbarians whom I once commanded have captured and chained me by my four limbs like a murderous slave; my companions are dying about me; the odours of their corpses awaken me at night; I drive away the birds that swoop down to peck out their eyes; and yet not for one single day have I despaired of Carthage! Though I had seen the armies of the world pitted against her and the flames of the siege overtop the temples, I should still have believed in her eternity! But now all is ended! All is lost! The gods curse her! Malediction on you who have hastened her ruin by your dishonour!"

She opened her lips.

"Ah! I was there!" cried he. "I heard you panting with lust like a prostitute, and when he told you of his passion, you permitted him to kiss your hands! But if the madness of your unchastity impelled you, at least you should have done as the wild beasts,. which hide themselves to couple, and not thus have displayed your shame almost before the very eyes of your father!"

"What?" she exclaimed.

"Ah, then you do not know that the two entrenchments are within sixty cubits of each other—that your Mâtho, from excess of audacious pride, has established himself in front of Hamilcar? Your father is just there behind you, and if I could only have climbed up the pathway leading to the platform I could have cried, 'Come now, see your daughter in the embrace of a Barbarian! She has put on the vestments of the goddess to please him, and abandons her body to his lust; thus she betrays the honour of your name and the majesty of the gods, the vengeance of her country, even the salvation of Carthage!'"

The movements of his toothless mouth agitated his long white beard to its very end; his eyes were fastened upon her and seemed to devour her, as he said:

"Oh! Sacrilegious one! Be accursed! Accursed! Accursed!"

Salammbô had drawn back the tent cloth, and held it uplifted without answering Gisco. She looked in the direction of Hamilcar's encampment.

"It is this way, is it not?" she asked.

"What matters that to you? Turn aside! Away! Rather crush your face against the earth! It is a holy place, which your look would pollute!"

She threw the Zaïmph around her waist, gathered up her veils, mantle, and scarf—"I go there!" she ejaculated, and disappeared.

At first she moved along in the darkness without meeting anyone, as all had hastened toward the fire, and the uproar increased as the far-reaching flames of the conflagration impurpled the sky behind. Presently a long terrace stopped her progress. She turned from right to left at hazard, searching for a rope, a ladder, a stone, anything, in fact, to enable her to mount over the wall. She was afraid of Gisco, and it seemed that cries and steps pursued her. Day was beginning to dawn. She discerned by the feeble light a pathway in the entrenchments; taking the hem of her robe between her teeth, in three bounds she attained the platform.

A sonorous shout sounded below her in the shade, the same signal that she had heard at the foot of the stairway of the galleys. Leaning over the terrace, she recognised the man sent by the priest Shahabarim, holding the two saddled horses.

All night he had wandered between the two entrenchments, but becoming disquieted by the conflagration, he had gone back, trying to discover what was happening in Mâtho's camp; and as he knew that this place was nearest to his tent, in obedience to the priest's orders he had not left the spot, but there awaited Salammbô.

He mounted and stood upright on the back of one of the horses, and Salammbô slipped down from the terrace to him; they spurred their horses into a sharp gallop, circling the Punic camp in search for an entrance.

Mâtho reëntered his tent. The smoking lamp scarcely burned; as he believed Salammbô was sleeping, he patted delicately all over the lion's skin spread out on the couch of palm-branches. He called, and she answered not; he quickly tore down a strip of canvas to admit the daylight. The Zaïmph was gone.

The earth trembled beneath the tread of the multitude. Yells, neighs, and clash of armours sounded through the air, and the fanfare of the clarions rung out the signal for a charge. All was like a fierce hurricane whirling around him. An inordinate fury seized him; he grasped his weapons and madly dashed outside.

Long files of Barbarians were descending the mountain sides at a run, and the Punic squares were advancing against them with a heavy, regular oscillation. The fog, rifted by the sun's rays, formed little detached clouds that hung in the air, and gradually rising, disclosed standards, helmets, and the points of pikes. Under the rapid evolutions, portions of the field still in shadow, seemed to change place as a single piece. Elsewhere it appeared as if torrents were crossing each other, and between them thorny masses stood motionless. Mâtho distinguished the captains, soldiers, heralds, and even the varlets in the rear who were mounted on asses. But Narr' Havas, instead of holding his position and covering the foot-soldiers, abruptly wheeled to the right, as if he deliberately desired to be crushed by Hamilcar's troops.

His cavalry outsped the elephants, which had slackened their speed, and all the horses stretched out their heads, uncurbed by reins, galloping at a pace so furious that their bellies fairly seemed to graze the earth. Then suddenly Narr' Havas rode resolutely toward a sentinel, threw down his sword, his lance, his javelins, and disappeared, unarmed, in the midst of the Carthaginians.

The king of the Numidians entered Hamilcar's tent and said to him, pointing out his men, who had halted at a distance:

"Barca! I bring them to you—they are yours!"

Then he prostrated himself in sign of obedience; and recalled, as proof of his fidelity to Hamilcar, all his conduct since the beginning of the war.

First he recounted how he had prevented the siege of Carthage and the massacre of the Punic captives; then, how he had refrained from profiting by the victory over Hanno after the defeat at Utica. As to the Tyrian cities, they were on the frontier of his own realm. Finally, he had not participated at the battle of Macar, had even purposely absented himself, to avoid the obligation of combating the Suffet.

In truth, Narr' Havas had ever desired to aggrandise himself by encroachments on the Punic provinces, and, according to the chances of victory, he had succoured or deserted the Mercenaries. But seeing that Hamilcar would ultimately be the stronger, he had determined to ally himself to him; and perhaps there might also be in his present defection a grudge against Mâtho, either because he was in command, or by reason of his former love.

Without interruption the Suffet listened. This man who presented himself thus with all his forces in an army to which he owed a debt of vengeance, was an auxiliary not to be despised. Hamilcar divined at once the utility of such an alliance for the advancement of his great projects. With the Numidians he would at once free himself from the Libyans; then he could draw with him the West to the conquest of Iberia: hence, without asking why he had not come sooner, or commenting on any of his falsehoods, Hamilcar kissed Narr' Havas, clasping him thrice to his breast.

As a last resort and in despair Hamilcar had fired the Libyans' camp. This army came to him like help from the gods; but dissimulating his joy, the Suffet craftily replied:

"May the Baals favour you! I know not what the Republic will do for you, but know this, that Hamilcar is not ungrateful."

The tumult redoubled; captains entered; he armed himself as he spoke: "Let us go! Return! Your cavalry will destroy their infantry between your elephants and mine! Courage! Exterminate them!"

Narr' Havas was rushing forth just as Salammbô appeared. She quickly dismounted and threw open her wide mantle; spreading out her arms she displayed the Zaïmph.

The leathern curtain of the tent, looped up at the four corners, made visible the entire circuit of the mountains covered with soldiers, and as it stood in the centre, from all sides Salammbô could be seen. An immense clamour burst forth, a long cry of triumph and of hope. Those who were marching stopped; the dying leaned on their elbows, and turned round to bless her.

All the Barbarians now knew that she had recovered the Zaïmph; from the distance they saw her, or believed that they saw her, and their yells of rage and vengeance resounded, despite the applause of the Carthaginians. Thus these five armies in tiers upon the mountains stamped and howled with joy or rage on all sides of Salammbô.

Hamilcar, powerless to speak, thanked her by nodding his head. His eyes alternately scanned her and the Zaïmph; and he noticed that her chainlet was broken. Then he quivered, seized by a terrible suspicion. But quickly resuming his impassibility, he looked at Narr' Havas askance without turning his face.

The king of the Numidians held himself apart in a discreet attitude; on his forehead was a little dust where he had touched the ground when prostrating himself. Finally the Suffet advanced toward him, and, with an air full of gravity:

"In recognition of the services that you have rendered me, Narr' Havas, I give you my daughter!" adding, "Be my son, and protect your father!"

Narr' Havas made a gesture of great surprise, then throwing himself on Hamilcar's hands, he covered them with kisses.

Salammbô, calm as a statue, seemed not to comprehend: she blushed slightly and cast down her eyes, and her long lashes made shadows upon her cheeks. Hamilcar desired to unite them immediately in an indissoluble betrothal. In Salammbô's hand a lance was placed, which she offered to Narr' Havas; their thumbs were tied together with a thong of leather; then corn was poured over their heads, and the grains which fell around them rang, like rebounding hail.

XII

THE AQUEDUCT

TWELVE HOURS LATER, there remained of the Mercenaries only heaps of wounded, dying, and dead.

Hamilcar had suddenly come forth from the bottom of the gorge, and descended again upon the western slope looking toward Hippo-Zarytus, whither, as the space broadened out, he had managed to attract the Barbarians. Narr' Havas with his cavalry encompassed them; the Suffet meanwhile drove them back, and crushed them. Furthermore, they were conquered in advance by the loss of the Zaïmph; even those who had no real faith in it felt a distress akin to weakness. Hamilcar, not gratifying his pride by remaining in possession of the battle-field, had drawn off a little to the left upon the heights, whence he commanded the enemy.

The outline of the camps could be recognised by the bent-down palisades. A long mass of black cinders smoked on the site of the Libyans' camp; the upturned ground undulated like the waves of the sea, and the tents, with their flapping canvas, resembled rudderless ships, half lost among the breakers. Cuirasses, pitchforks, clarions, fragments of wood, iron, and brass, grain, straw, were mingling with the corpses. Here and there some stray fire-lance on the point of extinction was burning against a pile of baggage. The earth in some places was hidden under the shields; the carcasses of horses succeeded each other in heaps, like a chain of hillocks. Large sandals, arms, coats of mail and heads in their helmets, kept together by the chin-pieces, which rolled about like balls, were everywhere visible. Human hair hung on the thorn-bushes. In pools of blood disembowelled elephants lay struggling in death-agonies, with their towers yet upon their backs. One stepped upon glutinous things; and though the rain had not fallen, there were pools of mud.

This confusion of corpses covered the entire surface of the mountain from top to bottom.

Those who survived did not stir more than the dead, but crouched in irregular groups, gazing at one another, too much terrified to speak.

At the end of a long meadow, the lake of Hippo-Zarytus shone under the rays of the setting sun; to the right, close-packed groups of white houses stood out above a girdle of walls; the sea beyond spread out indefinitely; and with their chins in their hands, the Barbarians sighed as they thought of their native lands. A cloud of grey dust settled down. The evening wind blew, refreshing and inflating their lungs. As it grew colder, the vermin could be seen leaving the dead bodies, which were growing cold, and crawling along on the warm sand; and ravens perched motionless on the top of large stones, looking toward the dying.

When night fell, dogs with yellow hair, the unclean beasts which follow armies, came stealing softly amidst the Barbarians. At first they licked the clotted blood from the yet warm stumps of limbs, but soon they set to devour the corpses, always beginning on the bowels first.

One by one, like shadows, the fugitives reappeared; the women also ventured to return, for there were still some of them left, especially with the Libyans, despite the frightful massacre of them by the Numidians.

Some lighted the ends of ropes to serve as torches; others held their pikes crossed, upon which they placed their dead and carried them apart.

The dead were extended on their backs in long rows, open-mouthed, with their lances hard by, or else they were piled up in confusion; and often, in the endeavour to discover the missing, it became necessary to dig through quite a heap. Then the torches were moved slowly over their faces: the hideous weapons had inflicted complicated wounds; greenish shreds of flesh hung from their foreheads: they were cut in pieces, or clove into the marrow, bluish from strangulation, or deeply gashed by the elephants' tusks.

Even though they had expired almost at the same time, there were marked differences in the progress of decomposition. Men from the north were bloated with livid swellings; and the Africans, who were more wiry, seemed to have been smoked, and were already drying up.

The Mercenaries were recognisable by the tattooings on their hands; the veterans of Antiochus displayed a sparrow-hawk; those who had served in Egypt, the head of a cynocephalus; those who had served under the princes of Asia, a battle-axe, a pomegranate, or a hammer; and those who had served in the Greek Republics, the profile of a citadel or the name of an Archon; and there were some whose arms were entirely covered by numerous symbols, blending with the scars of old and new wounds.

For the bodies of men of Latin race—namely, the Samnites, Etruscans, Campanians, and the Bruttians—four large funeral pyres were erected.

The Greeks dug pits for their dead with the points of their swords; the Spartans took off their red cloaks to wrap about their fallen comrades; the Athenians turned the bodies so as to face the rising sun; the Cantabrians buried their slain under heaps of pebbles; the Nasamones doubled the corpses in two, lashing them together with leathern thongs; and the Garamantians went away to bury upon the shore, that the waves might perpetually lave them. But the Latins were in despair, because they could not collect the ashes in urns; the Nomads regretted the hot sands in which bodies were mummified; and the Celts missed the three rough stones under a rainy sky at the end of a gulf full of islets.

Loud cries were raised, followed by a long silence. This was to compel the departed souls to return. Then the clamour was perseveringly resumed at regular intervals.

They excused themselves to the dead for being unable to accord them honours, as the rites prescribed; for owing to this privation they were doomed to wander during infinite periods through all manner of perils and metamorphoses. They questioned them, asking what they desired, while others poured abuse on them for allowing themselves to be conquered.

The light from the great funeral pyres cast a weird pallor over the bloodless faces, upturned here and there upon fragments of armour; tears induced tears, till sobs became more poignant, recognitions and embraces more frantic. The women threw themselves upon the bodies, mouth to mouth and brow against brow; they were only forced away with blows when the earth was thrown into the pits over the bodies. They blackened their cheeks; cut their hair; drew their blood and shed it in the graves. They even gashed upon themselves wounds similar to those disfiguring their dead husbands and lovers.

Groans burst through the clashing uproar of the cymbals. Some pulled off their amulets and spat upon them. The dying rolled in the bloody mire, furiously biting their mutilated fists; and forty-three Samnites, a devoted band, all in the sacred springtime of their youth, cut each other's throats like gladiators. Presently the wood for the funeral pyres failed; the flames died down; all the ditches were filled; and, wearied with weeping, enfeebled, tottering, they slept beside their dead brethren, some clinging tenaciously to a life full of troubles, and others desirous that they might never awaken again.

In the grey of the dawn there appeared, beyond the lines of the Barbarians, soldiers filing past with their helmets uplifted on the points of spears; saluting the Mercenaries, they inquired if they had no message to send back to their countries.

Others advanced, and the Barbarians recognised many of their old comrades.

The Suffet had proposed to all of the captives to serve in his troops. Many had fearlessly refused; and as he was determined not to feed them, or hand them over to the Grand Council, he had dismissed them with a warning not to fight again against Carthage. He had distributed the enemies' weapons to those whom fear of torture had rendered tractable, and now they presented themselves to the vanquished, less to win them over than from an impulse of pride and curiosity.

They began with a recital of the good treatment bestowed upon them by the Suffet. Much as the Barbarians despised these traitors, they listened to them with envy. Then, at the first words of reproach, the cowards got angry, displaying from afar their own captured swords and cuirasses, daring them with insults to come and take them. The Barbarians picked up stones: all fled; and nothing more could be seen at the top of the mountain than their spear-points projecting above the palisades.

Then a grief heavier than that caused by the humiliation of a defeat overwhelmed the Barbarians; they reflected upon the futility of their courage, and they remained with their eyes fixed, grinding their teeth.

The same idea took possession of all: they rushed in a tumultuous crowd upon the Carthaginian prisoners whom by chance the soldiers of the Suffet had failed to find; and as he had withdrawn from the battle-field, they were still secure in the deep pit. These victims were now ranged on a flat stretch of ground, while sentinels made a circle around them, and the women were permitted to enter the enclosure by thirties and forties successively. Eager to make the most of the short time permitted to each group, they ran from one victim to another, uncertain, palpitating; then leaning over the poor wretches, they pounded them with all their might, like washerwomen beating linen; crying aloud their husbands' names, they tore them with their nails and dug out their eyes with their hairpins.

After this the men tortured them: from their feet, which they cut off at the ankles, to their foreheads, from which they tore crowns of skin to place upon their own heads. The Eaters-of-Unclean-Things were atrocious in their devices: they inflamed the wounds by pouring into them dust, vinegar, and bits of pottery; others were waiting behind them; the blood flowed, and they made merry as do the vintagers around the fuming vats.

All this time Mâtho was seated on the ground in the same place as when the battle ended. His elbows on his knees, and his temples pressed between his hands, he saw nothing, heard nothing, and thought no more.

At the shouts of joy uttered by the crowd, he raised his head. Before him, upon a pole, hung a strip of canvas trailing on the ground, partially screening disordered baskets, rugs, and a lion's skin. He recognised his tent; and he riveted his eyes upon the ground, as if on that spot the daughter of Hamilcar, in vanishing from him, had been engulfed in the earth.

The tattered canvas flapped in the wind; sometimes the long strips fluttered across his face, whereon he could see a red mark like the print of a hand—the imprint of the hand of Narr' Havas, the token of their alliance. Then Mâtho arose; he seized a yet smoking brand, and threw it contemptuously upon the wreck of his tent. Then with the toe of his cothurn he kicked into the flames the things which were scattered about, so that all should be consumed.

Suddenly, without anyone knowing whence he sprang, Spendius appeared. The former slave had bound two splints of a broken lance-butt upon his thighs, and he limped about in a piteous way, giving vent to dolorous moans.

"Take those off," said Mâtho to him. "I know that you are brave!" He was so crushed by the injustice of the gods that he had not sufficient energy to be indignant with mortals.

Spendius, beckoning, led him to the hollow of a peak, where Zarxas and Autharitus were in concealment.

They had taken flight like the slave—the one, cruel as he was, and the other despite his valour. But who, said they, could have expected the treason of Narr' Havas, or the burning of the Libyans' camp, or the loss of the Zaïmph, or the sudden attack of Hamilcar, and above all, his manœuvres, compelling them to return to the heart of the mountain, under the direct fire of the Carthaginians? Spendius would not acknowledge his terror, and persisted in the assertion that his leg was broken.

Finally the three chiefs and the *Schalischim* consulted as to what course would be best in their present strait.

Hamilcar had closed their road to Carthage; they were trapped between his soldiers and the provinces of Narr' Havas; the Tyrian towns would join the conquerors. They would be driven to the sea-coast; and all the united forces would crush them. This was what would inevitably befall them.

No means suggested themselves for avoiding the war, hence they must pursue it to the uttermost. But, how could they make the necessity for an interminable struggle comprehensible to those discouraged people with their bleeding wounds?

"I charge myself with that," said Spendius.

Two hours later a man who came from the direction of Hippo-Zarytus climbed the mountain at a run. He waved tablets at arm's-length, and as he shouted loudly the Barbarians surrounded him.

He bore despatches from the Greek soldiers of Sardinia, advising their comrades in Africa to keep a close watch over Gisco and the other captives. A merchant of Samos, a certain Hipponax, coming from Carthage, had apprised them that a plot was being organised for their rescue, and the Barbarians were notified to provide against the emergency, as the Republic was powerful.

Spendius's strategy did not at first succeed as he had anticipated. This assurance of a new peril, far from exciting fury, raised fears. They remembered Hamilcar's warning, thrown but lately in their midst; they now expected something unforeseen and terrible. The night was passed in great anxiety; many even removed their arms, to mollify the Suffet whenever he might present himself.

But on the morrow, at the third watch of the day, a second courier appeared, still more breathless and begrimed with dust than the first. Spendius jerked from his hands a papyrus scroll covered with Phœnician characters, wherein the Mercenaries were supplicated not to be discouraged, for the braves of Tunis were coming with large reënforcements.

Spendius read this letter three times successively; and sustained by two Cappadocians, who held him sitting upon their shoulders, he was carried from place to place, reading it. For seven consecutive hours he harangued.

He reminded the Mercenaries of the promises made by the Grand Council; the Africans of the cruelties of the intendants; and all the Barbarians of the general injustice of Carthage. The Suffet's gentleness was a trap to capture them. Those who surrendered would be sold as slaves; the vanquished would perish in tortures. As for flight, what road was open? No nation would receive them. Whereas, if they persisted in their efforts, they would obtain at once their liberty, revenge, and money! And they would not have to wait long, since all the people of Tunis and of Libya were hurrying to their assistance.

He displayed the unrolled papyrus, saying, "Look upon this! Read! Here is what they promise! I do not lie!"

Dogs prowled about, their black muzzles plastered with red. The high sun heated the bare heads of the men. A nauseous odour exhaled from the imperfectly buried dead; some of the corpses protruded from the ground as far as the waists. Spendius called on them to bear witness to the truth of what he said; then menacingly he raised his fists in the direction of Hamilcar.

Mâtho was watching him, and, in order to cover his cowardice, he made a display of anger, by which he was himself gradually impressed: he dedicated himself to the gods, while he heaped curses upon Carthage. "The torture of captives was mere child's-play. Why, therefore, spare them, only to drag after the army useless cattle? No! we must make an end of them! their projects are known. Only one escaping could betray us! No quarter!

The worthy men will be recognised by the fleetness of their legs, and the strength of their blows."

Then they returned to the captives, many of whom were still in death-throes; they finished them by thrusting their heels into the victims' mouths, or stabbing them with javelins. Finally they thought of Gisco; no one had seen him anywhere; this caused them anxiety. All desired to be convinced of his death, and to participate in its consummation. At last three Samnite herdsmen discovered him at a distance of twelve paces from the site where recently Mâtho's tent had stood; they recognised him by his long beard, and called the others.

Lying down on his back, his arms against his hips, and his knees pressed together, he had the appearance of one dead, laid out for the tomb. However, his thin sides rose and fell, and his eyes opened widely, contrasting with the pallor of his face, as he glared with a fixed, intolerable stare.

At first the Barbarians looked at him with great astonishment. During the time that he had been in the pit almost everyone had forgotten him; disturbed by old memories, they stood at a distance, not daring to lift a hand against him.

But those who were behind, murmured and thrust themselves forward; a Garamantian passed through the crowd, brandishing a sickle; all understood his intent; their faces grew crimson, and seized with shame, they yelled, "Yes! yes!"

The man with the curved steel went up to Gisco, took him by the head, and placing it on his knee, he reaped it with a few rapid strokes; it fell, and two great gushing jets of blood made a hole in the dust. Zarxas sprung upon it, and, more agile than a leopard, he ran toward the Carthaginians.

Then, when he was two thirds up the mountain, he pulled Gisco's head from his breast, and holding it by the beard, revolved his arm rapidly many times, and the head finally launched forth, describing a long parabola, and disappeared behind the Punic entrenchments.

Soon on the edge of the palisades were erected two standards intercrossed, an understood sign for reclaiming the dead. Then four heralds, chosen because of their deep voices, came forward with large clarions, and through the brass trumpets they declared that henceforth there could be nothing between the Carthaginians and the Barbarians, neither faith, nor pity, nor gods; that they refused in advance all overtures, and that messengers of truce would be returned with their hands cut off.

Immediately afterward, Spendius was deputed to Hippo-Zarytus, in order to arrange for provisions. The Tyrian city sent them supplies the same evening. They ate greedily; and when thus comforted, they quickly packed up the remnants of their baggage and their broken weapons, placing the women in the centre, and, without heeding the wounded wailing behind them, they set out by the river-bank at a quick march, like a pack of departing wolves.

They were marching upon Hippo-Zarytus, determined to take it, for they very much needed a town.

Hamilcar saw the Barbarians depart from the distance, and was filled with despair, in spite of the pride he felt to see them fly before him. He should have been able to attack them at once with fresh troops. Another such a day, and the war was at an end! If matters dragged, the enemy would return stronger, as the Tyrian towns would doubtless join them. His clemency to the vanquished had served no purpose; henceforth he would be merciless.

The same evening he sent to the Grand Council a dromedary laden with bracelets taken from the dead; and, with horrible threats, he ordered that they should despatch another army to him.

For a long time all had believed him to be lost, so that when they learned of his victory, they experienced a stupefaction that amounted almost to terror. The vaguely announced return of the Zaïmph completed the marvel. Thus the gods and the power of Carthage seemed now to belong to Hamilcar.

Not one amongst his enemies dared venture a complaint or a recrimination. By the enthusiasm of his friends, and the pusillanimity of his enemies, an army of five thousand men was ready before the prescribed time.

This reënforcement promptly made for Utica to support the Suffet in the rear, while three thousand of the most important citizens embarked on vessels which were to land at Hippo-Zarytus, whence they purposed to drive the Barbarians back.

Hanno had accepted the command, but he confined the army to his lieutenant, Magdassan, in order to conduct the naval forces himself, as, in consequence of his malady, he could no longer endure the jolting of his litter. His disease had eaten away his lips and nostrils, and made a large hole in his face, so that at ten paces the back part of his throat was visible. Knowing that he was hideous, he wore a veil, like a woman, over his head.

Hippo-Zarytus heeded not his summons, neither that of the Barbarians; but each morning the inhabitants lowered to them baskets filled with provisions, and calling from the height of the towers, excused themselves on account of the exigencies of the Republic, and implored them to withdraw. They addressed by signs the same protestations to the Carthaginians stationed on the sea.

Hanno contented himself with blockading the port, without risking an attack. Meantime, he persuaded the judges of Hippo-Zarytus to receive in the city three hundred soldiers. Afterward, he sailed toward the cape of Grapes, making a long détour in order to encompass the Barbarians—an inopportune and even dangerous proceeding. His jealousy prevented him from aiding Hamilcar: he arrested the Suffet's spies, interfered in all his plans, and compromised his enterprise. At length Hamilcar wrote to the Grand Council to deprive Hanno of his command, and the latter was therefore recalled to Carthage, furious at the baseness of the Elders and the folly of his colleague. Then, after so much hope, they found themselves in a situation even more deplorable; but they all tried not to reflect or even speak on the topic.

As if they had not enough misfortunes, they learned that the Mercenaries of Sardinia had crucified their general, seized the fortified towns, and everywhere had slain the men of Canaanite race. The Romans threatened the Republic with immediate hostilities unless she gave them twelve hundred talents, with the entire island of Sardinia. Rome had accepted an alliance with the Barbarians, and had sent to them flat boats freighted with flour and dried meats. The Carthaginians pursued these, and captured five hundred men; but, three days later, a fleet coming from the country of Byzacium, carrying provisions to Carthage, foundered in a storm. The gods evidently were against Carthage.

Then the citizens of Hippo-Zarytus, pretending an alarm, made Hanno's three hundred men mount on the walls; then coming behind them they seized them by the legs, and suddenly hurled them over the ramparts. Those who were not instantly killed, were pursued, and drowned themselves in the sea.

Utica also was suffering from the presence of soldiers, for Magdassan had acted like Hanno, and according to his orders he surrounded the city, deaf to Hamilcar's prayers. His soldiers were given wine mixed with mandrake, and during their sleep they were slaughtered. At the same time the Barbarians arrived, and Magdassan took flight. The gates were opened, and from this moment the two Tyrian towns showed a persistent devotion for their new friends, and an inveterate hatred for their former allies.

This abandonment of the Punic cause was a warning and an example. Hopes of future deliverance were rekindled. Populations heretofore uncertain, hesitated no longer. All gave way. The Suffet learned it, and expected no assistance. He was now irrevocably lost.

He dismissed Narr' Havas at once, for he had to defend, henceforth, the boundaries of his own kingdom. For his own part he resolved to return to Carthage and obtain soldiers to resume the war.

The Barbarians established at Hippo-Zarytus perceived his army as it descended the mountain.

Whither were the Carthaginians going? Doubtless hunger urged them; and maddened by their sufferings, despite their weakness, they were coming to offer battle. But they turned to the right: then it must be that they were retreating. They might be followed and utterly crushed. The Barbarians dashed in pursuit.

The Carthaginians were retarded by the stream; it was swollen wide, and the west wind had not been blowing. Some swam across, others floated on their shields, and they resumed their march. Night fell. They were no longer visible.

The Barbarians did not pause, but ascended the stream, searching for a shallow place to ford. The people of Tunis hastened to help, bringing those of Utica with them. At every clump of bushes their number increased, and the Carthaginians, lying on the ground, could hear the tramp of feet in the darkness. From time to time, in order to make their pursuers slacken their pace, Barca fired back upon them a volley of arrows, thereby killing many. When day broke they were in the Mountains of Ariana, at the point where the road makes a bend.

Then Mâtho, marching at the head of his troops, believed that he distinguished in the horizon something green on the summit of an eminence. The earth sloped; obelisks, domes, and houses appeared! It was Carthage! His heart beat so furiously that he leaned against a tree to keep from falling.

He thought of all that had occurred in his existence since that last time that he had passed there! It was an infinite surprise, an amazement. Then joy possessed him at the idea that he should again see Salammbô. His past reasons for execrating her flooded his memory, but he peremptorily rejected them. Quivering in every fibre, and with straining eyes, he gazed beyond Eschmoûn at the high terrace of a palace above the palms. An ecstatic smile illumined his face, as if some great radiant light had fallen over him; he opened his arms, and sent kisses on the breeze, murmuring, "Come! Come!" A sigh swelled his bosom, and two tears, long, like pearls, fell upon his beard.

"What stops you?" cried Spendius. "Hasten! March on! The Suffet will escape us! But your knees shake, and you look at me like a drunken man!"

Stamping his feet with impatience, he urged Mâtho to advance, and blinking his eyes, as at the approach to an end seen far away, he cried: "Ah! we are there! We are there! I hold them!"

He had such a convincing, triumphant air, that Mâtho, wakened out of his torpor, felt himself drawn on. These words coming unexpectedly in the crisis of his distress, drove his despair to vengeance, and made an opening for his wrath. He mounted one of the camels in the baggage train, tore off the halter, and with the long cord struck with his full force the laggards, running alternately from right to left in the rear of the troops, like a dog driving a flock.

At his voice of thunder the men closed up the lines, and those on crutches hastened their steps: half-way across the isthmus the interval lessened. The vanguard of the Barbarians marched in the dust of the Carthaginians. The two armies drew nearer and nearer, until they almost touched. But the gates of Malqua and Tagaste, and the great gate of Khamoûn, threw open their ponderous valves. The Punic squares divided; three columns were swallowed up and eddied under the porches. Soon the masses closed in too much upon themselves, and were choked in the entrances, so that they could not move. Spears struck against spears in the air, and the Barbarians' arrows splintered against the walls.

Hamilcar appeared on the threshold of Khamoûn; he turned, and ordered his men to scatter; then he dismounted, and with his sword pricked his horse on the crupper, letting him loose upon the Barbarians. It was an Orynx stallion, nourished on balls of meal, and would bend his knees to permit his master to mount him. Why, then, did he send it away? Was this a sacrifice?

The noble horse galloped amidst the lances, knocking down men; entangling his feet in his halter, he fell, then struggled up on his feet with furious bounds; and while they scattered, endeavoured to arrest him, or looked at him in surprise, the Carthaginians reunited and entered the enormous gate, that resoundingly closed behind them.

It did not yield; the Barbarians plunged and battered against it; and during the lapse of some minutes the entire length of the army presented an oscillation that became weaker and weaker, and at last entirely subsided.

The Carthaginians having stationed soldiers on the aqueduct, began hurling stones, balls, and beams. Spendius acknowledged that it was useless to persist; therefore they pitched their encampment at a greater distance from the walls, fully resolved to besiege Carthage.

The rumour of the war in the meantime had reached beyond the confines of the Punic dominion; and from the Pillars of Hercules, to the other side of Cyrene, the herdsmen guarding their herds thought of it, and the caravans talked about it at night in the starlight. This noble Carthage, Mistress of the Sea, wonderful as the sun, awful as a god, had found men who dared to attack her! Even her downfall had frequently been reported, and all had believed it, as all were longing for it—the subject peoples, tributary villages, allied provinces, and independent tribes: those who cursed her for her tyranny, or who were jealous of her power, or who coveted her wealth.

The bravest had promptly joined themselves to the Mercenaries. The defeat at the Macar, however, discouraged all the others. Finally they regained confidence, and gradually making advances, had come nearer; and now the inhabitants of the eastern regions, the sand-hills of Clypea, were located on the other side of the gulf. As soon as the Barbarians appeared, they showed themselves.

These were not the Libyans from the vicinity of Carthage, who had for a long time constituted the third army, but the Nomads from the plateau of Barca, bandits from Cape Phiscus and the promontory of Derne, and others from Phazania and Marmarica. They had crossed the desert, sustaining themselves by drinking from the brackish wells built of camels' bones: the Zuæces, covered with ostrich plumes, had come in their quadrigæ; the Garamantians, masked with black veils, rode in the rear on their painted mares; others mounted on asses, on onagers, on zebras, or on buffaloes; and some dragged the roofs of their cabins, shaped like a shallop, with their families and idols.

There were Ammonians, with limbs wrinkled by the hot water of the fountains; Atarantes, who curse the sun; Troglodytes, who laughingly inter their dead under branches of trees; and the hideous Auseans, who eat locusts; the Achrymachidas, who eat lice; and the Gysantes, painted over with vermilion, who eat monkeys.

All were ranged along the sea-coast in a great, straight line. They advanced in succession, like whirlwinds of sand raised by the wind. In the centre of the isthmus the crowd stopped; the Mercenaries established in front of them near the walls did not wish to move.

Then from the direction of Ariana came the men of the west, the people of Numidia—for, in fact, Narr' Havas only governed the Massylians; and furthermore, as custom permitted them, after a reverse, to abandon their king, they had assembled on the Zainus, and at the first movement Hamilcar had made, they crossed it. First were seen running up all the hunters of the Malethut-Baal and of the Garaphos, dressed in lions' skins, and driving with the shafts of their pikes little, thin horses with long manes; after these came the Getulians, encased in breast-plates of serpents' skins; then the Pharusians, wearing tall crowns made of wax and resin; following these were the Caunians, Macares, and Tillabares, each holding two javelins and a round shield of hippopotamus hide. They halted at the foot of the Catacombs, near the first pools of the great Lagoon.

But when the Libyans had moved away, on the ground that they had occupied there appeared, like a cloud, lying level with the earth, a multitude of Negroes: they had come from White-Harousch and Black-Harousch, from the desert of Augîla, and even from the vast country of Agazymba, four months' journey to the south of the Garamantians, and regions even more distant! In spite of their redwood ornaments, the filth on their black skins made them look like mulberries that had rolled a long time in the dust.

They wore breeches made from fibres of bark, tunics of dried grass, and on their heads the muzzles of wild animals: they howled like wolves, as they shook triangles ornamented with dangling rings, and brandished cowtails on the end of sticks by way of banners.

Behind the Numidians, the Maurusians, and the Getulians, crowded the yellow men who were scattered over the country beyond Taggir in the cedar forests. Cat-skin quivers flapped over their shoulders, and they led in leashes enormous dogs as tall as asses, which never barked.

And then, as if Africa had not sufficiently emptied itself, and in order to collect together more furies, they had even recruited the lowest races: in the rear of all the others they could be seen; men with profiles of animals, grinning in an idiotic manner, wretches ravaged by hideous diseases, deformed pigmies, mulattoes of doubtful sex, Albinos blinking their pink eyes in the sunlight—all stammering unintelligible sounds, and putting a finger in their mouths to signify hunger. The medley of weapons was not less remarkable than the people, or their apparel. Not a deadly invention was absent, from wooden poniards, stone battle-axes, ivory tridents, to long sabres toothed like saws, slender, and made of a pliable sheet of copper. They wielded cutlasses divided in many branches, like antelopes' horns; they carried bill-hooks attached to cords, iron triangles, clubs, and stilettoes.

The Ethiopians of Bambotus secreted in their hair tiny poisoned darts. Many had brought stones in sacks; others, who were empty-handed, gnashed their teeth.

A continual surging moved this multitude. Dromedaries, daubed with tar like the hulls of ships, knocked over the women who carried their children on their hips. Provisions were spilling out of their baskets; and in walking one stepped on morsels of rock salt, packages of gum, rotten dates, and gourou-nuts. Sometimes on a bosom covered with vermin could be seen, suspended from a fine cord, a diamond, a fabulous gem worth an entire empire, for which satraps had sought. The majority of these people did not even know what they desired: a fascination, a curiosity urged them: the Nomads, who had never seen a town, were frightened by the shadows cast by the massive walls.

The isthmus was obscured by this multitude of men, and the long stretch of tents, resembling cabins during an inundation, spread out to the first lines of the other Barbarians, who were streaming with steel, and symmetrically posted on the two flanks of the aqueduct.

The Carthaginians were still in terror of those who had already arrived, when they saw, making straight for Carthage, huge monsters, like edifices, with their shafts, weapons, cordage, articulations, capitals, and carapaces—the siege engines sent by the Tyrian cities: sixty *carrobalistas,* eighty *onagers,* thirty *scorpions,* fifty *tollenones,* twelve rams, and three gigantic catapults, able to throw rocks weighing fifteen talents. Masses of men clutched at their base, pushed and pulled to propel the engines, that quivered and shook at each step: in time the throng arrived in front of the walls.

But a few days would still be required to complete the preparations for the siege. The Mercenaries, forewarned by their previous defeats, did not wish to risk themselves in fruitless engagements; and on neither side was there any hurry, as all knew that a terrible conflict was about to ensue, which would result either in absolute victory or complete extermination.

Carthage would hold out for a long time; her broad walls offered a series of salient and reëntering angles—an arrangement full of advantages for repelling assaults.

However, on the side of the Catacombs a portion of the wall had crumbled; and during dark nights, between the disjointed blocks could be seen lights in the dens of Malqua. In certain places these overlooked the top of the ramparts, and here lived many who had taken for new wives the women of the Mercenaries driven by Mâtho out of the camp. When the women saw their own men, their hearts melted, and they waved from the distance long scarves; then they came in the darkness to chat with the soldiers through the rift in the walls, and the Grand Council were told one morning that they had all fled. Some had crawled between the stones; others, more daring, had descended by ropes.

Spendius finally resolved to accomplish his cherished project.

The war, by keeping him at a distance, had, up to this time, debarred him from it; and since they had returned before Carthage, it seemed to him that the townsmen suspected his enterprise; but soon they diminished the sentinels on the aqueduct, as they did not possess too many guards for the defence of the walls. During many days the former slave practised aiming arrows at the flamingoes on the lake shore. Then one moonlight evening he entreated Mâtho to have lighted in the middle of the night a huge bonfire of straw, and order all his men simultaneously to utter shrieks; then taking Zarxas, he went off by the edge of the gulf in the direction of Tunis.

When abreast of the last arches, they returned, going straight toward the aqueduct. As the road was exposed, they crept along to the base of the pillars. The sentinels on the platform patrolled calmly.

High flames shot up; clarions were sounded. The soldiers in the watch-towers, believing that it was an assault, rushed toward Carthage.

One man remained. He stood like a black figure against the dome of the sky; the moonlight was behind him, and his disproportionate shadow fell on the plain, like a moving obelisk. They waited until he was exactly in front of them. Zarxas seized his sling, but Spendius stopped him, moved by prudence or ferocity, and whispered: "No! the whirring of the ball would make a noise! Leave it to me!" Then he bent his bow with all his might, supporting the end against his left instep, took aim, and the fatal arrow flew.

The man did not fall. He disappeared.

"If he were wounded we should hear him," said Spendius, and he sprang quickly up, story after story, as he had done the first time, by the aid of the harpoon and cord. When he reached the top, beside the corpse, he let the cord fall. The Balearian fastened to it a pick and mallet, and returned. The trumpets no longer sounded: all was now perfect quiet. Spendius had lifted one of the flagstones, entered the water, and replaced the stone over himself.

Estimating the distance by paces, he reached the exact spot where he had previously noticed a slanting fissure, and for three hours—in fact, till morning—he worked continuously and furiously, breathing with great difficulty through the interstices of the upper stones; racked with violent pains, twenty times he believed he was dying.

At last a cracking was heard, an immense stone bounded on the lower arches and rolled down to the bottom—and all at once a cataract, an entire river, fell as from the sky into the plain! The aqueduct, cut in the centre, was emptying itself. This meant the death of Carthage and the victory of the Barbarians.

In an instant, the aroused Carthaginians appeared on the walls, the house-tops and the temples. The Barbarians gave vent to joyous shouts, dancing around the vast waterfall in delirium, and in the enthusiasm of their delight wetted their heads in the rushing water.

At the summit of the aqueduct a man was perceived wearing a torn, brown tunic. Leaning over the edge, his hands upon his hips, he gazed beneath him, as if astonished at his own work.

Then he stood erect, scanning the horizon with a proud, haughty air, which seemed to say—"Behold! this is what I have accomplished!" Applause burst from the Barbarians. At last the Carthaginians comprehended the cause of their disaster, and howled in despair. Spendius ran from end to end of the platform, mad from pride, raising his arms, like the driver of a victorious chariot in the Olympian games.

XIII

MOLOCH

ON THE SIDE toward Africa the Barbarians did not need to circumvallate, as it was already theirs; but to make the approach to the walls less difficult they tore down the entrenchments bordering the moat. Mâtho then divided the army into large semicircles, so as to more effectually beleaguer Carthage. The hoplites of the Mercenaries were stationed in the front rank; behind them, the slingers and horsemen; behind were the baggage, the chariots, and the horses; and in front of this multitude, at three hundred paces from the towers, bristled the war-engines, known by an infinity of names that changed frequently in the course of the ages; however, they could always be reduced to two systems—those which acted like slings, and the others which operated like bows.

The first, the catapults, consisted of a square frame with two vertical standards and a horizontal bar. At its anterior portion a cylinder furnished with cables held down a large beam carrying a ladle to receive the projectiles; the base of the beam was caught in a hank of twisted horsehair; when the cords were loosened, the beams flew up, struck against the bar, which, checking it by a sudden shock, multiplied its force.

The second system was a more complicated mechanism. On a small pillar a cross-piece was attached by its centre, at which point ended a channel at right angles to it: at the ends of the cross-piece rose two frames, containing a twisted hank of hair: two small beams were fastened therein to hold the extremities of the cord, which was drawn to the bottom of the channel over a bronze tablet; by a spring, this plate of metal was released, and, sliding over grooves, shot out the arrows in all directions.

Catapults were frequently called onagers, because they were like wild asses which throw stones by kicking; and the ballistas were called scorpions because of a hook fastened on the tablet, which, on being lowered with a blow of the fist, disengaged the spring.

Their construction required expert calculation. The timber selected had to be of the hardest grain; the gearing was all of brass. They were stretched with levers, pulleys, capstans, or drums; strong pivots changed the direction of their aim. They were moved forward on cylinders; and those of the largest size, which were transported in sections, were set up in front of the enemy.

Spendius placed the three large catapults opposite the three principal angles; before each gate he placed a ram, before each tower a ballista; and farther back were wheeled the *carrobalistas*. But it was necessary to prevent their being fired by the besieged, and also to fill up the trench which separated them from the walls.

They pushed forward galleries made of green wattles and oaken ribs, like enormous shields sliding on three wheels; little cabins, covered with fresh hides and padded with wrack, sheltered the workmen. The catapults and ballistas were protected by curtains of rope that had been soaked in vinegar to render them incombustible. The women and children went to the beach to gather stones, which they collected with their hands and brought to the soldiers.

The Carthaginians also made preparations for the siege.

Hamilcar had reassured them, by declaring that there yet remained enough water in the cisterns for one hundred and twenty-three days. This statement, his presence in their midst, and the recovery of the Zaïmph, above all, imparted great hope. Carthage recovered from her dejection, and those who were not of Canaanite origin were carried away by the enthusiasm of the others.

The slaves were armed, the arsenals emptied, each citizen had his allotted post and employment. Twelve hundred of the refugees had survived: the Suffet made them all captains; and the carpenters, armourers, blacksmiths, and the silversmith were appointed to superintend the engines. The Carthaginians had retained some, notwithstanding the conditions of the Roman peace. Understanding their construction, they repaired them readily.

The northern and eastern sides, being protected by the sea and the gulf, were inaccessible. On the wall facing the Barbarians were piled up trunks of trees, mill-stones, vases full of sulphur, and vats of oil, and furnaces were built. Stones were heaped up on the platforms of the towers, and the houses immediately connecting with the rampart were crammed with sand to increase its strength and thickness.

The sight of all these preparations angered the Barbarians. They wanted to engage in combat at once. The weights they put into the catapults were of such an exorbitant size that their beams broke, thereby delaying the attack.

Finally, on the thirteenth day of the month of Schmar, at sunrise, a tremendous blow was heard at the gate of Khamoûn.

Seventy-five soldiers were hauling ropes arranged at the base of a gigantic beam horizontally suspended by chains, descending from a gallows, and terminating in a brazen ram's head. It was swathed in hides; bands of iron encircled it from place to place, and it was three times thicker than a man's body, one hundred and twenty cubits long, and it advanced or receded under the crowd of naked arms, pushing it forward or hauling it backward, with a regular swing.

The rams before the other gates also began to move; in the hollow wheels of the drums men might be seen ascending step by step. Pulley and capitals creaked; the rope screens were lowered, and volleys of stones and arrows simultaneously shot forth. All the scattered slingers ran up; some of them approached the ramparts, carrying hidden under their shields pots of ignited resin; then they hurled them with all their might upon the enemy. The terrific hail of balls, darts, and fire passed beyond the front ranks, forming a curve which fell within the walls. But on their summits were erected huge cranes such as were used for masting vessels; from them descended enormous pinchers, ending in two semicircles, toothed on the inside edge. These bit the rams. The soldiers, clinging to the beam, dragged it back. The Carthaginians panted in their efforts to haul it up, and the struggle continued till evening.

When the Mercenaries resumed their task the next day they found the tops of the walls packed with bales of cotton, cloth, and cushions; the battlements were closed with mattings, and between the cranes could be distinguished lines of pitchforks and sharp blades set in sticks. A furious resistance began immediately.

Tree-trunks fastened to cables fell and rose alternately, battering the ram; grappling-irons, shot by the ballistas, tore the roofs off the cabins; and from the platforms of the towers fell torrents of flint and pebbles.

At length the rams burst the gate of Khamoûn and that of Tagaste; but the Carthaginians had heaped the inner side with such an abundance of materials that the leaves could not open: they remained upright.

Tenebras were then forced against the walls, and applied to the joints of the massive blocks until they were loosened. The engines were handled better because their crews worked in relays; from morning till evening they plied uninterruptedly, with the monotonous precision of a weaver's loom.

Spendius never tired attending to these engines. He personally tautened the cordage of the ballistas. In order that there should be an exact equality in their twin tensions, their cords were wound up and struck in turn on the right and left side till both sounded in unison. Spendius mounted on their frames, and delicately tapped them with the end of his foot, straining his ear, like a musician tuning a lyre. Then when the beam of the catapult rose, when the pillar of the ballista trembled at the shock of the spring, as the stones poured out in streams, and the arrows darted forth like rays, he leaned his entire body over the platform, throwing his arms up in the air, as if he would follow the flight of the missiles.

Admiring his skill, the soldiers willingly obeyed his orders. In the gaiety of their labour they made jokes on the names of the engines. Thus the plyers for seizing the rams were called "wolves," and the covered galleries, "vines"; they were lambs, they were going to the vintage; and as they were loading their pieces they would say to the onagers, "Go now, kick well!"—and to the scorpions, "Pierce through the enemies' hearts!" This facetiousness, always the same, sustained their courage.

Still, the engines did not demolish the rampart. It was formed of a double wall and completely filled with earth; they battered down its upper works, but the besieged each time raised them again. Mâtho ordered the construction of wooden towers of an equal height with the enemies' stone towers. Into the moat were thrown turf, stakes, and chariots with the wheels on, to fill it up more rapidly; before it was completed the immense crowd of Barbarians undulated over the plain in a single movement, and advanced to beat against the base of the walls like an inundating sea.

They brought forward rope-ladders, straight ladders, and *sambucæ*, which consisted of two masts from which were lowered by tackles a series of bamboos ending in a movable bridge. They were in numerous straight lines, supported against the walls, and the Mercenaries mounted them in file, one after another, holding their weapons in their hands. Not one Carthaginian appeared until they had attained two-thirds of the height of the ramparts. Then the battlements opened, vomiting forth like dragons' jaws, fire and smoke; sand scattered, filtering through the joints of their armour; the petroleum fastened on their clothing, the molten lead skipped over their helmets, burning cruel holes in their flesh; a shower of sparks flashed into their faces—the eyeless orbits seemed to weep tears as large as almonds. The hair of some, yellow with oil, was blazing. They started to run, and set the others on fire. From a distance cloaks soaked in blood were thrown over their faces and extinguished the flames. Some who were not wounded remained motionless, stiffer than stakes, with open mouth and both arms thrown out in the last agony.

For many successive days the assault continued, the Mercenaries hoping to triumph by excess of force and audacity.

Sometimes a man, standing on the shoulders of another, would drive an iron pin between the stones to serve as a step to reach higher, where he drove a second, and a third, and so on, protected by the overhanging battlements; in this way they gradually climbed up: but always at a certain height they were smitten and fell. The broad ditch became so full of human beings that it overflowed; under the feet of the living the wounded were heaped pell-mell with the dead and dying. Amid entrails, oozing brains, and pools of blood, calcined trunks made black spots; arms and legs, half protruding from the heap, stood straight up like vine-stakes in a burning vineyard.

As the ladders proved insufficient, they employed the *tollenones*—instruments consisting of a long beam placed transversely on an upright post, and carrying at the extremity a square basket, which held thirty foot-soldiers fully equipped.

Mâtho wanted to ascend in the first that was ready, but Spendius prevented him.

Men turned a small wheel, and responsively the large beam became horizontal, then reared itself almost vertically; but being too heavily laden at the end, it bent like a reed. The soldiers, concealed up to their chins, crowded together; nothing but their helmet plumes could be seen. Finally, when the basket was fifty cubits in the air, it swayed from right to left several times, then fell; and like the arm of a giant holding on his hand a cohort of pigmies, it deposited on the edge of the wall the basketful of men. They leaped out in the midst of the enemies, but never returned.

All the other *tollenones* were speedily prepared; but it would require a hundred times as many to capture the town. They were utilised in a murderous manner: Ethiopian archers were ordered in the baskets; then the cables were so adjusted that they should remain suspended in mid-air, while the occupants fired poisoned arrows. The fifty *tollenones* thus dominated the battlements surrounding Carthage like monstrous vultures, and the Negroes laughed to see the guards on the ramparts dying in horrible convulsions.

Hamilcar despatched hoplites thither, and made them each morning drink the juices of certain herbs which were antidotes for poisons.

One evening, during a dark period, Hamilcar embarked the best of his soldiers on lighters and rafts, and turned to the right of the harbour, landing on the Tænia. From there they advanced as far as the first lines of the Barbarians, and, taking them in the flank, made a terrible carnage. Men suspended by ropes descended the walls during the night, and set fire to the Mercenaries' works, remounting in safety.

Mâtho was enraged; each obstacle, in fact, plunged him deeper in wrath, causing him to do terrible and extravagant things. Mentally he entreated Salammbô for a rendezvous; then waited for her. She did not come: this was a new treason, and henceforth he cursed her. Perhaps if he had seen her dead body he might have gone away.

He doubled his outposts, planted pitchforks at the base of the rampart, buried caltrops in the ground, and commanded the Libyans to bring to him an entire forest, in order to set fire to Carthage and burn it like a den of foxes.

Spendius persisted in the siege, striving to invent frightful machines such as had never been constructed before. The other Barbarians who were encamped at a distance on the isthmus were amazed at these delays. They complained; they were let loose.

Then they rushed forward, battering against the gates with their cutlasses and javelins. But the nakedness of their bodies made it easy to wound them, and the Carthaginians freely massacred them, while the Mercenaries rejoiced over it, doubtless from greed of the plunder. There resulted quarrels and contentions between themselves. The country being now laid waste, they were stung by hunger and soon were wresting the provisions from each other. They became discouraged. Numerous hordes went away; but the crowd was so dense that their absence was not noticed.

The best of the men endeavoured to dig mines; the ground, badly propped, caved in; then they would begin again elsewhere. Hamilcar always discovered the direction of their operations by applying his ear to a bronze shield. He dug counter-mines under the road over which the wooden towers had to be wheeled, so that when they were moved they would sink in the holes.

At length all acknowledged that the city was impregnable unless they erected a long terrace to the height of the city walls, permitting them to fight on the same level; the top should be paved, in order to facilitate the moving of the engines. Then Carthage could not possibly resist.

The town was suffering from thirst. Water sold at the outbreak of the siege at two *kesitah* a barrel now brought a shekel of silver. The supplies of meat and grain were also becoming exhausted; they feared a famine; some even spoke of useless mouths, which terrified everyone.

From the square of Khamoûn as far as the temple of Melkarth, corpses cumbered the streets; and as it was the end of summer, large black flies pestered the combatants. Old men carried the wounded off the field, and the devout continually performed fictitious funeral rites for their relatives and friends who had died far away during the wars. Statues of wax with hair and clothes were laid out before the house entrances. They melted in the heat of the tapers burning close to them, and the paint trickled down over their shoulders; and tears coursed the cheeks of the living as they intoned sad hymns beside these effigies. The crowd meanwhile ran hither and thither; troops were constantly passing; captains shouted orders, and the shocks of the rams battering the rampart were constantly heard.

The temperature became so heavy that the corpses swelled and could not be placed in the coffins, so they were burned in the middle of the courts. These fires in the narrow spaces ignited the neighbouring walls, and long flames suddenly escaped from the houses, like blood spurting from an open artery. Thus Moloch possessed Carthage, he embraced the ramparts, he rolled through all the streets, and he consumed the dead.

Men who wore in sign of despair mantles of rags, stationed themselves at the corners of the streets, declaiming against the Elders and against Hamilcar, predicting total ruin for the people, and inviting them to general destruction and license. The most dangerous were the drinkers of henbane, who in their crises fancied themselves to be wild beasts, and sprang upon the passers-by, to tear them to pieces. Mobs collected around them, forgetting the defence of Carthage. The Suffet conceived the idea of paying others of their class to support his policy.

In order to retain the Genii of the gods in the town, their images were covered with chains, black veils were thrown over the *Dii-patæci*, and hair cloths around the altars. Endeavours were made to excite the pride and jealousy of the Baals by dinning in their ears, "You will be conquered! The other gods are more powerful than you! Show your might! Aid us! that the peoples may not say, 'Where are now their gods?' "

A constant anxiety disturbed the pontiffs; those of Rabbetna were especially alarmed, for the reëstablishment of the Zaïmph had not sufficed; they remained sequestered in the third enclosure, as impregnable as a fortress; only one of their number, the high priest, Schahabarim, risked going out.

He went to Salammbô's palace, but remained silent, ever looking at her with fixed gaze; or else pouring upon her words of reproach, harder than ever.

By an inconceivable inconsistency, he could not pardon this young girl for having obeyed his orders. Schahabarim had divined all—and this besetting idea strengthened the jealousy of his impotency. He accused her of being the cause of the war. Mâtho, according to his account, was besieging

Carthage to recapture the Zaïmph; and he poured forth imprecations and sarcasms upon this Barbarian for essaying to possess sacred things. That, however, was not what the priest desired to say.

But Salammbô had no further terror of the priest. The agonies she formerly suffered had all vanished, being replaced by an ineffable calm; even her gaze was less wandering, and burned with a limpid light.

Meanwhile the Python had again fallen ill, and as, on the contrary, Salammbô appeared to recover, the aged Taanach rejoiced over it, feeling sure that by its decline it had taken the weakness from her mistress.

One morning the slave found it behind the cow-hide couch, coiled up on itself, colder than marble, its head covered by a mass of worms. At her screams Salammbô came. She turned it over for some time with the toe of her sandal; her indifference amazed the slave.

Hamilcar's daughter no longer fasted with her former fervour or rigour. She spent whole days on the top of her terrace, leaning on her elbows over the balustrade, amusing herself watching the objects before her. The top of the walls at the end of the town cut. against the sky irregular zigzags, and the sentinels' lances all along formed what looked like a border of corn-ears. Beyond, between the towers, she could see the manœuvres of the Barbarians. On days when the siege was suspended she could even distinguish their occupations, as they mended their weapons, or oiled their hair, or washed their blood-stained arms in the sea. Their tents were closed, and the beasts of burden were eating; far away the scythes of the chariots, ranged in a semicircle, looked like a silver scimitar extended at the base of the hills.

Schahabarim's talk revolved through her brain. She waited for her betrothed, Narr' Havas. Despite her hatred, she had a wish to see Mâtho again. Of all the Carthaginians, she was, perhaps, the only person who would have spoken to him without fear.

Frequently her father came into her room and sat on the cushions, considering her with an air almost tender, as if he found in looking at her an immunity from his fatigues. Sometimes he questioned her as to the incidents of her journey to the camp of the Mercenaries, asking her if no one had by chance compelled her to go thither; and with a shake of the head, she answered, "No," so proud was Salammbô of having rescued the Zaïmph.

But the Suffet always reverted to Mâtho, under the pretext of acquiring military information. He could not understand how she had employed the hours passed in his tent. Salammbô did not mention Gisco; for as words contain in themselves an effective power, curses that are repeated to anyone else might return to their injury. She likewise kept silent concerning her impulse to assassinate Mâtho, fearful lest she should be censured for not having yielded to it. She said that the *Schalischim* appeared furious, that he had shouted a good deal, and afterward went to sleep. Salammbô told' nothing more, perhaps from shame, or possibly from an excess of innocence, which caused her to attach no importance to the kisses of the soldier. Besides, it all floated through her melancholy and misty brain like the remembrance of an overpowering dream, and she would not have known in what manner or by what words to express it.

One evening, when father and daughter were thus facing each other in conversation, Taanach, all amazement, entered announcing that an old man, accompanied by a child, was in the courts, and asking to see the Suffet.

Hamilcar turned pale, but promptly replied:

"Let him come up."

Iddibal entered, without prostrating himself, holding by the hand a young boy covered with a cloak of goat's skin, and at once raising the hood which concealed the boy's face, said:

"Here he is, master! Take him!"

The Suffet and the slave retired to a corner of the room. The boy remained standing in the centre with a gaze more attentive than astonished; he looked at the ceiling, the furniture, the pearl necklaces hung over purple draperies, and at the majestic maiden who leaned forward toward him.

He was, perhaps, ten years old, and no taller than a Roman sword; his curly hair overshadowed his convex forehead; his eyes seemed to penetrate space; his thin nostrils dilated widely, and over all his person was that indefinable splendour characterising those beings destined for grand careers. When he had thrown aside his heavy cloak, he remained clad in a lynx-skin fastened around his waist, and stood resolutely pressing his small, bare feet, white with dust, upon the pavement. Doubtless he surmised that important topics were being discussed, as he maintained a motionless posture, holding one hand behind his back, his chin lowered and a forefinger in his mouth.

At last Hamilcar attracted Salammbô's attention by a sign, and said in a low voice:

"Keep him with you. Do you understand? No one, not even of the household, must know of his existence."

Then, behind the door, he again asked Iddibal if he were certain that no one had noticed them.

"No one," said the slave; "the streets were deserted."

As the war filled all the provinces, he had feared for the safety of his master's son. Then, not knowing where to hide him, Iddibal had brought him along the coast in a shallop, and for three days they had cruised about in the gulf, watching the ramparts; finally, that evening, when the neighbourhood of Khamoûn seemed deserted, he had ventured to quickly cross the channel and land in the vicinity of the arsenal—the entrance to the harbour being free to all.

But soon the Barbarians established, opposite it, an immense raft, to prevent the Carthaginians getting out. They built up the proposed terrace, and erected the wooden towers.

Communication between the towns and the outside was cut off, and an intolerable famine began.

All the dogs, mules, and asses were killed; and then the fifteen elephants that the Suffet had brought back. The lions of the temple of Moloch became savage, and the keepers no longer dared approach them; at first they were fed with wounded Barbarians; then corpses yet warm were thrown to them; but these they refused; and finally they all died. At twilight people wandered along the old enclosures, gathering from between the stones grasses and flowers, which they boiled in wine, as wine was less costly than water. Others slipped up to the outposts of the enemy, and, crawling under the tents, stole food. Sometimes the Barbarians were so stupefied by this audacity that they allowed them to return.

At length a day came when the Elders resolved to slaughter the horses of Eschmoûn privately; they were sacred animals in whose manes the pontiffs braided gold ribbons, and whose existence signified the movements of the sun—the idea of fire in its most exalted form. Their flesh was divided into equal portions, and hidden behind the altar; then every evening the Elders, alleging some religious service, ascended to the temple, regaled themselves in secret, and each brought back, concealed under his tunic, some morsel for his children.

In the deserted quarters distant from the walls, the less miserable inhabitants, from fear of the others, had barricaded themselves.

The stones from the catapults, and the demolitions ordered for their defences, had accumulated heaps of ruins in the streets.

During the most peaceful hours, masses of people would suddenly rush out, yelling at the top of their voices; and from the top of the Acropolis fires appeared, like purple rags blown by the wind, dispersed over the terraces.

The three great catapults did not stop: their ravages were extraordinary; a man's head rebounded from the pediment of the Syssites; in the street of Kinisdo a woman in childbirth was crushed by a block of marble, and her infant, with her couch, was carried as far as the forum of Cynasyn, where the coverlet was found.

The slingers' bullets proved to be the most vexatious missiles; these fell upon the roofs, into gardens, and in the middle of courtyards, where people were at table before their meagre repasts, with their hearts heavy with anguish. These horrible projectiles were engraved with letters that left an imprint on the victim's flesh; on the dead could be read such appellations as *"swine," "jackal," "vermin,"* and sometimes such pleasantries as *"catch!"* or *"I have quite deserved it!"*

That portion of the rampart extending from the angle of the harbours abreast of the cisterns was battered in. Then the people of Malqua found themselves caught between the old enclosure of Byrsa in the rear, and the Barbarians in front. Hamilcar had enough to do to strengthen the wall and raise it as high as possible, without troubling himself about the troubles of these people. They were abandoned, and all perished; and although they were generally hated, in consequence of this desertion the Carthaginians conceived a great abhorrence of Hamilcar.

The following day he opened the pits wherein he had stored his corn: his intendants gave it freely to the people. For three days they gorged themselves. Their thirst in consequence became more intolerable, and they always saw before them the long cascade of pure water falling from the aqueduct: while under the sunshine, the fine mist floated up from its base with a rainbow beside it, and a little serpentine stream curved over the plain and emptied itself into the gulf.

Hamilcar did not weaken, for he was counting upon an event—something decisive and extraordinary. His own slaves tore off the silver plates from the temple of Melkarth. Four long boats were taken from the harbour and dragged by means of capstans to the foot of Mappals, the wall abutting on the shore was bored, and they departed to Gallia, to hire Mercenary soldiers at any price.

Nevertheless Hamilcar was disturbed at his inability to communicate with the Numidian king, as he knew full well that he was stationed behind the Barbarians, and ready to fall upon them. But Narr' Havas's forces were too weak to risk making any venture alone.

The Suffet had the rampart heightened twelve palms, all the munitions of war in the arsenals collected in the Acropolis, and the engines repaired once more.

They were wont to use for the cordage of the catapults tendons taken from the necks of bulls, or else stags' hamstrings; but in Carthage there were no longer either bulls or stags. Hamilcar demanded from the Elders their wives' tresses; and though all made the sacrifice, the quantity was insufficient. There were, in the buildings of the Syssites, twelve hundred marriageable slaves, intended for prostitution in Greece and Italy, and their hair had become peculiarly elastic from the constant use of unguents, and was admirably suited for the war machines. But afterward the loss would be too considerable. Then it was determined to select the finest heads of hair among the wives of the plebeians. Indifferent to their country's needs, all the women cried out in despair when the servitors of the Hundred came with scissors to lay hands upon them.

An increased fury animated the Barbarians, for from a distance they could be seen taking fat from the dead, to oil their machines, and pulling out the finger and toe nails of the corpses, which they sewed one over-lapping another, to make breastplates for themselves.

They conceived the idea of charging their catapults with vases full of serpents brought by the Negroes; these clay vessels shattered in falling upon the flagstones, and the serpents crawling about were so numerous that they seemed to swarm, and to come naturally out of the walls. Discontented with this invention they improved upon it, and threw all kinds of filth—such as human excrement, morsels of carrion, and corpses—upon their enemy. The plague broke out. The teeth of the Carthaginians dropped out, and their gums became discoloured, like those of camels after too protracted a journey.

The Barbarians' war machines were mounted upon the new terrace, even though it failed as yet to reach at every point the height of the rampart. In front of the twenty-three towers on the fortifications were erected twenty-three wooden towers; all the *tollenones* were remounted, and in the centre, a little farther back, loomed up the formidable *helepolis* of Demetrius Poliorcetes, which Spendius had at last reconstructed. Pyramidal, like the lighthouse at Alexandria, it was one hundred and thirty cubits high and twenty-three wide, with nine stories diminishing towards the top; they were protected by brass scales pierced by numerous sally-ports, and filled with soldiers; on the topmost stage a catapult flanked by two ballistas was erected.

Hamilcar planted crosses upon which to crucify all those who talked of surrender. Even the women were formed in brigades. People slept in the streets, and waited, full of anguish.

Then one morning, a little before sunrise, on the seventh day of the month of Nyssan, they heard a loud shout uttered simultaneously by all the Barbarians; the lead trumpets blared, and the great Paphlagonian horns bellowed like bulls. There was an immediate rush for the rampart.

A forest of lances, pikes, and spears bristled at its base; it leaped against the walls, ladders were grappled on, and in the openings of the battlements Barbarians' heads appeared.

Beams, carried by long files of men, battered the gates; and in places where the terrace was wanting, the Mercenaries, in order to breach the wall, came up in close cohorts, the first line crouching down, the second bending their hips, while the others rose in succession, by gradual inclinations of their bodies, until the last stood bolt upright; while elsewhere, to climb up, the tallest advanced at the head, the shortest in the rear; and they all supported with their left arms above their helmets their shields, locked together so tightly by the rims that they appeared like an assemblage of large tortoises. The projectiles slid over these slanting masses.

The Carthaginians hurled mill-stones, pestles, vats, casks, couches, everything, in fact, that could make a weight and crush. Some watched in the embrasures with fishing nets, and when a Barbarian came up he found himself caught in the meshes, and struggled like a floundering fish. They themselves demolished their own battlements; portions of the walls fell down, stirring up a blinding dust. The catapults on the platform and those on the ramparts shot one against the other, the stones clashed together and shattered into a thousand fragments, falling in a wide shower upon the combatants.

Soon the two crowds formed but one thick chain of human bodies, overflowing into the intervals of the terrace, and a little relaxed at the two ends, swayed perpetually without advancing.

They grappled each other, lying flat on the ground like wrestlers, and were crushed. Women leaned over the battlements and shrieked. They were dragged forward by their veils, and the whiteness of their sides, suddenly uncovered, shone between the arms of the Negroes, as they plunged their daggers into them.

Some corpses were too closely packed in the crowd to fall, but, borne up by the shoulders of their comrades, they moved forward for some minutes quite upright, their eyes staring wide open.

Some, pierced through both temples with javelins, swayed their heads like bears; their mouths opened to scream, but remained silently agape; severed hands flew through the air. There were mighty blows, of which the survivors spoke many a long day afterward.

Meanwhile arrows darted from the tops of the wooden and stone towers. The long yards of the *tollenones* moved rapidly; and as the Barbarians had pillaged the ancient cemetery of the Autochthones beneath the Catacombs, they hurled the tombstones upon the Carthaginians. Under the weight of the baskets, too heavily laden, the cables sometimes broke, and numbers of men, wildly throwing up their arms, fell from the sky.

Until the middle of the day the veterans of the hoplites had fiercely attacked the Tænia, in order to penetrate into the harbour and destroy the fleet. Hamilcar had lighted on the roof of Khamoûn a fire of humid straw, the smoke from which blinded them; they fell back to the left, increasing the horrible crowd which pressed forward in Malqua. Some syntagmata, composed of strong men expressly chosen, had forced three of the gates. Then high barriers, constructed with boards studded with nails, barred their way; a fourth entrance readily yielded; they darted beyond, and ran forward, only to roll into a pit in which snares had been hidden.

At the south-east angle Autharitus and his men beat down the rampart, the fissure of which had been stopped up with bricks. The ground behind rose; they slowly climbed up, but found on top a second wall, composed of stones and long beams lying flat, alternating like the squares on a chessboard. This was a Gallic method adapted by the Suffet to the requirements of the situation. The Gauls thought themselves in front of a town of their own country. Their attack was languidly made, and they were repulsed.

From the street of Khamoûn to the Vegetable Market, now belonged to the Barbarians, and the Samnites finished the dying with blows of their spears, or else with one foot on the wall contemplated beneath them the smoking ruins, and the battle which had begun again in the distance.

The slingers distributed in the rear fired incessantly, but from long use the springs of the Arcananian slings were broken, so, like shepherds, many slung the stones with their hands; others shot the lead balls with the handles of whips. Zarxas, with his long black hair covering his shoulders, was everywhere and led on the Balearians; two pouches were suspended from his hips; into one he kept plunging his left hand, while his right arm whirled like the wheel of a chariot.

Mâtho had at first withheld from the combat, to command more effectually all his forces at once. He had been seen along the gulf shore with the Mercenaries; near the Lagoon with the Numidians; then on the shore of the lake amongst the Negroes; at the end of the plain he pushed forward masses of soldiers, who came incessantly against the line of the fortifications. Gradually he drew nearer; the odour of blood, the sight of carnage, and the fanfare of clarions, had finally made his heart bound. Then he entered his tent, threw aside his cumbersome breastplate, taking instead his lion-skin, which was more convenient for battle. The muzzle fitted on his head, and surrounded his face with a circle of fangs; the two fore-paws crossed over his breast, and the claws of the hind-paws reached down to his knees.

He kept on his strong waist-belt, in which flashed a double-edged battle-axe; then, holding his large sword in both hands, he plunged impetuously through the breach. Like a pruner lopping off willow branches, endeavouring to cut as many as possible in order to gain the more money, he moved about, mowing down Carthaginians on all sides of him. Those who tried to seize him by the sides he knocked down with blows of the pommel of his sword; when they attacked him in front he pierced them through; and if they took flight he slashed them down.

Two men simultaneously jumped upon his back: he jumped backward at one bound against a door, crushing them. His sword rose and fell; at last it shattered against an angle of the wall. Then he took his heavy axe, and from behind and in front he disembowelled the Carthaginians like a flock of sheep. They scattered more and more before him; slaying right and left, he arrived alone, before the second enclosure, at the foot of the Acropolis.

Materials that had been flung from the summit encumbered the steps, and overflowed beyond the walls. Mâtho, in the midst of these ruins, turned around to call his comrades; he saw their crests scattered through the multitude—they were being surrounded: they would perish. He dashed toward them; then the vast crowd of red plumes uniting, quickly rejoined and surrounded him. But the side streets disgorged an enormous throng, and he was taken up by his hips and carried away to the outside of the rampart, to a spot where the terrace was high.

Mâtho shouted a command: all the shields were levelled above the helmets; he leaped on them to catch hold of something that might enable him to scale the walls and reënter Carthage, and brandished his terrible battle-axe as he ran over the shields, that resembled bronze waves, like a marine god on the billows shaking his trident.

Meanwhile a man in a white robe walked on the edge of the rampart, impassive and indifferent to the death surrounding him. At times he extended his right hand to shade his eyes, as if he sought for some one. Mâtho passed beneath him. All at once his eyes flamed, his livid face contracted, and, lifting his meagre arms, he shouted out words of abuse.

Mâtho heard them not; but he felt a look so cruel and furious enter his heart that he gave vent to a moan. He hurled his long axe toward this man; people threw themselves about Schahabarim, and Mâtho, losing sight of him, fell backward exhausted.

A fearful creaking drew near, mingled with the rhythm of hoarse voices singing in unison.

A vast throng of soldiers surrounded the *helepolis;* they dragged it with both hands, hauled it with ropes, and pushed it with their shoulders—for the slope rising from the plain to the platform, though it was extremely gentle, proved impracticable for machines of such prodigious weight. It had eight iron-bound wheels, and since morning it had advanced thus slowly; it was like a mountain being elevated to the top of a mountain.

From the base of this machine an enormous ram projected; along the three sides facing the city the doors were lowered, and inside appeared mailed soldiers, like iron columns, who could be seen climbing and descending the two stairways that traversed the stories. Some of these men were in readiness to spring the moment the grapples of the doors should touch the wall. In the middle of the upper platform the skeins of the ballistas were turning and the great beam of the catapult kept descending.

Hamilcar was at this moment standing on the roof of Melkarth; he judged that the beam would come directly toward him, against the most invulnerable portion of the wall, which on that account was denuded of sentinels. For a long time his slaves had been carrying leather water-bottles to the circular road, where two transverse partitions of clay had been constructed to form a sort of basin. The water insensibly ran over the terrace, and yet Hamilcar did not seem to be disturbed by this waste.

But when the *helepolis* was about thirty paces off, he commanded that boards should be placed between the houses over the streets, from the cisterns to the rampart, and that the people should form in a file and pass from hand to hand helmets and amphoras filled with water, that were continually emptied. The Carthaginians waxed indignant at this extravagant waste of water. The ram was demolishing the wall; suddenly a fountain sprang up from the disjointed stones, and the brazen structure of nine stages, containing more than three thousand soldiers, began to sway gently, like a ship rocking on the billows.

In fact, the water had penetrated the terrace and undermined the road before the machine; the wheels were imbedded in mire. Between the leather curtains on the first stage, Spendius's head appeared, blowing lustily through an ivory horn. The mammoth machine convulsively moved about ten more paces; but the ground became softer and softer, the mire reached up to the axle-trees, then the huge *helepolis* stopped, leaning frightfully on one side. The catapult rolled to the edge of the platform, and, carried away by the weight of its beam, toppled off, crushing the lower stages in pieces beneath it. The soldiers who were standing in the doors slid into the abyss, or held on to the extremities of the long beam, and by their weight increased the inclination of the *helepolis*, which was now going to pieces and cracking in all its joints.

The other Barbarians rushed to the rescue, crowding in a compact mass. The Carthaginians descended over the rampart and attacked them from behind, killing them at their ease. But the chariots armed with scythes came speedily up, galloping around the outside of this multitude, causing them to remount the walls. Night fell, and the Barbarians gradually retired.

Nothing could be seen over the plain but a black, swarming mass, from the bluish gulf to the glittering white Lagoon; and the lake, into which streams of blood had flowed, spread out beyond like a great purple pool.

The terrace was now so encumbered with corpses that it might have been constructed out of human bodies. In the centre stood the *helepolis* covered with armour, and from time to time enormous fragments became detached from it, like stones from a crumbling pyramid. Broad tracks made by the streams of molten lead could be distinguished on the walls; a burning wooden tower here and there had tumbled over, and the houses appeared dimly like the tiers in a ruined amphitheatre. Heavy clouds of smoke curled up, through which whirled trails of sparks that lost themselves in the black sky.

Meantime the Carthaginians, who were consumed by thirst, had rushed to the cisterns. They broke open the doors: a muddy swamp spread over the bottom.

What could be done now? The Barbarians were innumerable, and when they had recovered from their fatigue, would begin again.

All night the people deliberated in groups at the corners of the streets. Some said that they must send away the women, the sick, and the aged. Others proposed to abandon the town, and establish a new colony far away. But ships were wanting; the sun rose and no decision had been reached.

That day there was no fighting, everyone being exhausted. The people slept as if they were dead.

When the Carthaginians reflected upon the cause of their disasters, they remembered that they had neglected to send to Phœnicia the annual offering due to the Tyrian Melkarth, and an immense terror came over them. The gods were indignant with the Republic, and would doubtless pursue her with vengeance.

The divinities were considered in the light of cruel masters, only to be appeased with supplications, and bribed by gifts. All were weak before Moloch—the devourer. Human existence, even the flesh of mankind, belonged to him; therefore, to preserve it, the Carthaginians were wont to offer a portion of it to him, which calmed his wrath. Children were burned on their foreheads, or on the nape of their necks, with woollen wicks; and this custom of seeking to satisfy the Baal brought considerable money to the priests; they rarely failed to recommend the easiest and least painful method of sacrifice.

But now it was a question of the very existence of the Republic. And as every profit must be purchased by some loss, and every transaction is regulated by the requirements of the weaker and the demands of the stronger, there was no suffering too great for the god, since he took delight in the most horrible, and they all were now at his mercy. He must therefore be completely satiated. Precedents showed that carnal sacrifices to him had compelled the scourge to disappear. Besides, it was believed an immolation by fire would purify Carthage. The ferocity of the people was in favour of it beforehand, inasmuch as the choice of victims must fall exclusively on the grand families.

The Elders assembled. Their session was long. Hanno was present, but as he was now unable to sit up, he remained lying near the entrance, half hidden in the fringes of the lofty tapestry; and when the pontiff of Moloch asked if those convened consented to deliver up their children, his voice suddenly broke forth from the shadows as the roaring of a spirit out of the depths of a cavern. He regretted, he said, that he had none of his own blood to give, and he significantly looked at Hamilcar, who faced him at the other end of the hall.

The Suffet was so disturbed by this gaze that he lowered his eyes. All approved by nodding their heads successively; and, according to the rites, he had to reply to the high priest, "Yes, so be it!" Then the Elders decreed the sacrifice by a traditional periphrasis—for there are things more troublesome to speak than to execute.

Almost immediately this decision was made known throughout Carthage, and lamentation resounded. Everywhere the women were heard crying; their husbands either consoled them or heaped invectives upon them for offering remonstrance.

Three hours afterward extraordinary news was spread among the people: the Suffet had discovered springs at the base of the cliff. All rushed to the place; holes had been dug in the sand, showing water; and already some were lying flat on their bellies drinking.

Hamilcar did not himself know whether it was an inspiration from the gods or the indistinct recollection of a revelation his father had formerly made to him; but, on leaving the conference of Elders, he had gone down to the beach with his slaves, and begun digging in the gravel.

He distributed clothing, shoes, and wine, and the balance of the grain stored in his vaults; he even made the populace enter his palace, opening the kitchens, magazines, and all the rooms except Salammbô's. He announced that six thousand Gallic Mercenaries were coming, and that the king of Macedonia was also sending soldiers.

On the second day after the discovery of the springs, the volume of water had considerably diminished, and on the evening of the third day they were completely dry. Then the Elders' former decree circulated anew on all lips, and the priests of Moloch began preparations for the sacrifice.

Men in black robes presented themselves at the houses; many of the inhabitants had deserted them on pretence of business, or of some dainty that they must buy. The servitors of Moloch took the children. Others, stupidly scared, delivered them up. They were all conveyed to the temple of Tanit, to the priestesses, who were ordered to amuse and feed them until the solemn day.

They arrived suddenly at Hamilcar's palace, and finding him in his gardens, said:

"Barca! we come for that you know of—your son!" They added, that some people had met the boy one night during the last moon, in the middle of Mappals, led by an old man.

At first he felt as if suffocating; but quickly realising that denial would be in vain, he inclined his head, and introduced them into his house of commerce. His slaves, at a gesture from him, ran to keep watch around it.

He entered Salammbô's room, bewildered, seized Hannibal by one hand, and with the other tore from a trailing robe some strings, with which he fastened the boy's hands and feet together, placing the ends of the strings in his mouth as a gag, and hid him under the cowhide couch, arranging some wide drapery so that it fell all about the couch to the floor.

Then he paced the room from right to left, raised his arms, turned around, bit his lips; then he halted, with his eyes fixed, and gasping as if he were dying.

At length, he clapped his hands three times. Giddenem appeared.

"Listen!" said he. "Go and take from amongst the slaves a male child of eight or nine years, with black hair and projecting forehead! Bring him here! Hasten!"

Giddenem soon returned, and presented a boy.

He was a wretched child, at the same time thin and bloated; his skin greyish, like the loathsome rags that clung to his loins. He hung his head, and rubbed his eyes, which were full of flies, with the back of his hands.

"How could anyone possibly take him for Hannibal! and there was no time to choose another!" Hamilcar looked at Giddenem with the desire to strangle him.

"Go!" cried he; and the Master of Slaves fled.

The sorrow which the Suffet had for so long a time apprehended had come, and he sought with immeasurable efforts to discern if there were no manner, no way of averting it.

Abdalonim spoke from the other side of the door: the servitors of Moloch were becoming impatient, and asked for the Suffet.

Hamilcar suppressed a cry; he experienced a pang akin to the seething burn from a red-hot iron; he began anew to pace the floor like a madman; then he sank down near the balustrade, and with his elbows on his knees, pressed his temples between his clenched hands.

The porphyry basin still contained a small quantity of clean water for Salammbô's ablutions. Despite his repugnance and all his pride, the Suffet plunged the child into the basin, and like a slave merchant washed and scrubbed the boy with strigils and red earth. Then he took from the cases surrounding the walls two squares of purple; of these he put one on the child's breast, the other on his back, pinning them over the collar-bone with two diamond agrafes; he poured perfumes over his head, clasped an electrum necklace around his throat, and thrust his plebeian feet into sandals with pearl heels—his daughter's own sandals; but he stamped with shame and anger. Salammbô, who was earnestly assisting him, was quite as pale as he. The child smiled, pleased with these splendours, and even growing bolder, began to clap his hands and jump, when Hamilcar led him forth.

He held him firmly by the arm, as if he feared he should lose him; and the child, hurt by the fierce grasp, whimpered slightly as he ran beside the Suffet.

Abreast of the *ergastulum,* under a palm tree, a voice rose, a lamenting, supplicating voice, murmuring, "Master! oh, master!"

Hamilcar turned, and saw at his side a man most abject in appearance—one of the wretches who lived a haphazard existence in his gardens. "What do you want?" asked the Suffet. The slave, trembling horribly, stammered:

"I am his father!"

Hamilcar kept on walking; the slave followed, with bent back, and head thrust forward; his face was convulsed by an indescribable agony, and his suppressed sobs stifled him, so anxious was he at once to question him and to cry out "Mercy!"

At length he dared to touch the Suffet's elbow lightly with one finger. "Do you take him to the . . . ?" He had not the strength to finish, and Hamilcar stopped, amazed at such grief.

He had never thought—so immense was the gulf separating the one from the other—that there could be anything in common between them. It even appeared to him to be a sort of outrage, an encroachment on his own privileges. He replied by a look, colder and heavier than the axe of an executioner; the slave fainted and dropped in the dust at his feet. Hamilcar stepped over him.

The three black-robed men waited in the great hall, standing against the stone disc. All at once the Suffet tore his garments, and rolled upon the stones, uttering sharp cries.

"Ah, poor little Hannibal! Oh! my son! my consolation! my hope! my life! kill me also! Take me! Misery! misery!" he ploughed his face with his finger-nails, and tore out his hair, howling like the mourners at funerals. "Take him away! I suffer too much! Go! go! kill me with him!" The servitors of Moloch were astonished that the great Hamilcar possessed such a faint heart. They were almost touched.

Just then, the noise of naked feet was heard, and with a jerking rattle, like the panting of a ferocious beast when running in pursuit, on the threshold of the third gallery, between the ivory door-posts, a man appeared, pallid, terrible, with outstretched arms, screaming:

"My child!"

With a bound Hamilcar fell upon him, covering his mouth with his hands, and exclaiming still more loudly:

"He is the old slave who reared Hannibal! he calls him 'my child'! he will become mad! Enough! enough!" And pushing out the three priests and their victim, he went out with them, and closed the door behind him with a tremendous kick.

For some time Hamilcar listened attentively, fearing they might return. He next thought of killing the slave, to make quite sure of his not speaking; but the peril had not completely passed, and his death, if the gods were angered by it, might return upon his own son. Then changing his purpose, he sent to him by Taanach the best things from his kitchen—a quarter of a goat, some beans, and preserved pomegranates. The slave, who had not eaten for a long time, flung himself upon the food, whilst his tears fell into the dishes.

Hamilcar now returned to Salammbô, and unknotted Hannibal's cords. The child was in such a state of exasperation that he bit the Suffet's hand until he drew blood; he repressed him with a caress.

To keep the boy quiet, Salammbô tried to frighten him with stories of Lamia—an ogress of Cyrene. "Where then is she?" he asked. He was told that the brigands would come to put him in prison; to which he replied, "When they come I shall kill them."

Hamilcar then told him the frightful truth, but he grew angry with his father, declaring that he was able to exterminate the people, since he was the master of Carthage.

At last, exhausted by his struggles and anger, he slept a savage sleep, talking in his dreams, as he lay with his back propped up against a scarlet pillow, his head thrown a trifle backward, and his little arm extended out straight from his body in an imperious attitude.

When the night grew dark Hamilcar lifted the child in his arms, and descended the stairway of the galleys without a torch. In passing through the commercial house he took a bunch of grapes and a jug of pure water. The child awakened before the statue of Aletes, in the vault of gems, and smiled, as the other child had smiled, in the arms of the Suffet, at the splendours surrounding him.

Hamilcar was very certain that no one could now take his son. It was an impenetrable spot, communicating with the shore by a subterranean passage, that he alone knew: he cast his eyes about him, inhaling a long breath, and placed the boy on a stool beside some golden shields.

No one at present could see them; he had nothing more to heed, and he gave way to his feelings. Like a mother who finds her lost firstborn, he embraced his son, pressing him to his heart; he laughed and wept at the same time, called him by the most endearing names, and covered him with kisses. Little Hannibal, frightened by this terrible tenderness, remained silent.

Hamilcar returned with slow steps, feeling along the walls around him, until he reached the large hall, wherein the moonlight entered through one of the slits in the dome: in the middle the slave slept, lying at full length on the marble. He regarded him, and was moved by a kind of pity. With the toe of his buskin he pushed a rug under his head. Then he lifted his eyes and gazed at Tanit, whose slender crescent was shining in the sky. He felt himself stronger than the Baals, and full of contempt for them.

The preparations were already being made for the sacrifice.

A portion of the wall in the temple of Moloch was removed in order to pull the brazen god through without disturbing the ashes on the altar. As soon as the sun rose the sacred slaves of the temple pushed it to the square of Khamoûn.

It moved backward, sliding over cylinders; its shoulders overtopped the walls; from the farthest distance the Carthaginians who perceived it fled with speed, for the Baal could not be contemplated with impunity save in the exercise of his wrath.

An odour of aromatics was wafted through the streets. All the temples were thrown open simultaneously, and tabernacles upon chariots, or on litters which pontiffs carried, came forth. Great plumes of feathers nodded at their corners, and rays flashed from their pointed spires, terminated by globes of crystal, gold, silver, or copper.

These were the Canaanitish Baalim, reproductions of the supreme Baal, returning toward their essence to humble themselves before his might, and be lost in his magnificence. The canopy of Melkarth, of fine purple, sheltered a flame of bitumen oil; while upon that of Khamoûn, which was of hyacinth colour, was erected an ivory phallus bordered with a circle of gems: between the curtains of Eschmoûn, blue as the ether, a python slept, describing a circle with its tail; and the *Dii-patæci*, held in the arms of the priests, their heels dragging on the ground, resembled large infants in swaddling clothes.

Following came all the inferior forms of divinity: Baal-Samin, god of celestial spaces; Baal-Peor, god of sacred mountains; Baal-Zeboub, god of corruption; and those of the neighbouring countries and of cognate races; the Iarbal of Libya; the Adrammelech of Chaldea; the Kijun of the Syrians; Derceto, with her maiden's face, creeping upon her fins; and the body of Tammouz was transported on a catafalque between torches and heads of hair. To subdue the kings of the firmament to the sun, and prevent their individual influence from impeding his, metal stars of divers colours were brandished on the ends of long staves. In this collection all were found, from the black Nebo, which was the genius of Mercury, to the hideous Rahab, the constellation of the Crocodile.

The Abaddirs, stones fallen from the moon, revolved in silver filigree slings; small loaves representing the female sex were carried in baskets by the priests of Ceres; others brought their fetiches, their amulets; forgotten idols reappeared; and they had even taken from the ships their mystic symbols, as though Carthage was desirous to concentrate herself completely in one thought of death and desolation.

Before each of the tabernacles a man balanced on his head a vase of smoking incense; cloudlets hovered here and there, and through the dense vapours could be discerned the hangings, the pendants, and the embroideries of the sacred pavilions.

In consequence of their enormous weight, they advanced slowly. The axle-trees of the chariots occasionally got caught in the narrow streets; then the devotees profited by the opportunity to touch the Baalim with their clothing, which they afterward preserved as something sacred. The brazen statue continued to advance toward the square of Khamoûn. The Rich, carrying sceptres with emerald balls, started from the far end of Megara; the Elders, crowned with diadems, assembled in Kinisdo; and the masters of finance, the governors of provinces, merchants, soldiers, sailors, and the numerous horde employed at funerals, all displaying the insignia of their magistry or the instruments of their calling, converged toward the tabernacles that descended from the Acropolis between the colleges of pontiffs. In deference to Moloch, they were all adorned with their most splendid jewels. Diamonds sparkled on their black apparel; but their rings, now too large, fell loosely from their emaciated hands, and nothing could be more mournful than that silent concourse, where brilliant earrings touched against pallid faces, and where gold tiaras encircled foreheads wrinkled by a profound despair.

Finally the Baal attained the centre of the square. His pontiffs made an enclosure with trellises to keep back the multitude, and prostrated themselves at his feet, surrounding him.

The priest of Khamoûn, in reddish woollen robes, aligned before their temple under the columns of the portico; those of Eschmoûn, in white linen mantles, with necklaces of the heads of hoopoes and conical tiaras, established themselves on the steps of the Acropolis; the priests of Melkarth, in violet tunics, took their position on the western side; the priests of the Abaddirs, encircled in bands of Phrygian stuffs, placed themselves on the eastern side; and ranged on the southern side with the necromancers, all covered with tattooings, were the shriekers in patched mantles, the priests of the Dii-patæci, and the Yidonim, who foretold the future by placing a bone of a dead body in their mouths. The priests of Ceres, habited in blue robes, had prudently stopped in Satheb street, and were intoning in a low voice a thesmophorion in Megarian dialect.

From time to time files of men arrived, completely naked, with arms stretched out, holding each other by the shoulders, giving vent from the depths of their chests to hoarse, cavernous intonations; their eyes were turned toward the Colossus, which glittered through the dust, and at intervals they swayed their bodies all together, as if shaken by a single movement. These men were so frenzied that, in order to establish quiet among them, the sacred slaves struck them roughly with clubs, making them lie flat on the ground with their faces against the brazen trellises.

At this moment, from the back of the square, a man in a white robe came forward. As he slowly penetrated the throng, he was recognised as a priest of Tanit—the high-priest Schahabarim. Yells were raised, for the tyranny of the male principle prevailed upon this occasion in all minds, and the goddess was so completely forgotten that no one had even noticed the absence of her pontiffs. But the amazement redoubled when her high-priest was seen to open one of the gates of the trellis, intended only to admit those who would offer victims for the sacrifice.

The priests of Moloch, believing that he came to offer an insult to their god, with violent gestures endeavoured to expel him. Nourished as they were by the viands of the holocausts, clothed in purple like kings, and wearing triple crowns, they held in contempt this pale eunuch priest, attenuated by macerations; an insolent laughter shook their black beards, spread out over their breasts in the sunlight.

Schahabarim, without response, continued to walk forward, crossing, step by step, the whole enclosure, until he arrived beneath the legs of the Colossus; then he threw out his arms and touched it on both sides: this was a solemn act of adoration.

For a long period the Rabbet had tortured him, and in despair, or perhaps for need of a god completely satisfying his thoughts, he had decided at last to accept Moloch.

The crowd, shocked by this apostasy, uttered a prolonged murmur. There was a feeling that the last tie had been severed that attached their souls to a merciful Deity.

But Schahabarim, because of his mutilation, could not participate in the cult of the Baal. The men in red mantles expelled him from the enclosure; then, when he was outside, he turned around to all the other colleges successively, and the priest, now having no god, disappeared in the crowd, which scattered at his approach.

Meantime a fire of aloes, cedar, and laurel wood burned between the legs of the Colossus. Its long wings buried their points in the flame; the unguents with which it had been rubbed trickled like sweat over its brazen limbs. About the circular stone on which its feet rested, children, enveloped in black veils, formed a motionless circle; and its inordinately long arms allowed the palms of the hands to reach down to them, as if to seize this crown and convey it to the sky.

The Rich, the Elders, the women, and in fact the entire multitude, thronged behind the priests, and on the terraces of the houses. The large, painted stars revolved no longer; the tabernacles were set on the ground, and the smoke from the censers rose on high perpendicularly, like gigantic trees spreading their bluish boughs to the centre of the azure. Many fainted; others became inert and petrified in their ecstasy; infinite agony oppressed their hearts. The noises one by one died out, and the people of Carthage waited in silence, absorbed in the terror of their desire.

At last the high-priest of Moloch passed his right hand beneath the children's veils, and pulled out a lock of hair from each of their foreheads, which he threw into the flames. Then the men in red mantles intoned a sacred hymn:

"Homage to thee, O Sun! King of the two Zones! Creator, self-begotten! Father and Mother! Father and Son! God and Goddess! Goddess and God!" and their voices were lost in the outburst of countless instruments, sounding in unison to smother the cries of the victims. The scheminith with eight strings, the kinnor with ten, and the nebel with twelve, all twanged, whistled, and thundered forth. Enormous leathern bottles stuck full of tubes made a sharp, clashing noise; the tambourines, beaten with all possible force, resounded with heavy, rapid blows; and despite the fury of the clarions, the salsalim clicked like the wings of locusts.

The sacred slaves with a long hook opened the seven compartments contained in the body of the Baal. Into the highest division meal was introduced; into the second, two turtle-doves; into the third, an ape; into the fourth, a ram; into the fifth, a lamb; and into the sixth, as they did not possess an ox, a tanned hide from the sanctuary was substituted; the seventh aperture remained gaping and empty.

Before a human victim should be offered, it was well to test the arms of the god. Slender chainlets, passing from the fingers over the shoulders, descended at the back; these men pulled downward, raising to the height of its elbows two open hands that, in approaching each other, closed over its belly. They worked them several times successively with little jerks. Then the musical instruments were dumb, and the fire roared fiercely.

The pontiffs of Moloch walked to and fro on the large stone slab, inspecting the multitude.

The first offering must be an individual sacrifice, an oblation perfectly voluntary, which would include the others along with it. But no one came forward, and the seven alleys leading from the barrier to the Colossus remained completely empty. To stimulate the people, the priests pulled from their girdles little stilettoes, with which they slashed their faces. The Devotees, who were stretched on the ground outside, were brought into the enclosure, and a bundle of horrible irons was thrown to them: each one chose his torture. They passed spits through their breasts, slit their cheeks, put upon their heads crowns of thorns; then they enlaced their arms together, and surrounding the children, they formed another great circle, ever contracting and expanding. When they reached the balustrade, they threw themselves back, only to eddy outward again, continually attracting to them the crowd, by the dizziness of their movements, accompanied by blood and cries.

Gradually the people, thus incited, came into the end of the alleys, and threw into the flames, pearls, gold vases, cups, all their treasures, and torches.

These offerings became more and more splendid, and kept multiplying. Presently a man who staggered, a man pale and hideous from terror, thrust forward a child; then could be distinguished between the hands of the Colossus a little black mass—it disappeared into the dark opening. The priests leaned over the edge of the large slab, and a new chant burst out, celebrating the joys of death and of new birth into eternity.

The children mounted slowly, and as the smoke rose in lofty, whirling masses, they seemed from afar to disappear in a cloud. Not one moved. All had been bound hand and foot, and the dark drapery prevented them from seeing anything, and from being recognised.

Hamilcar, in a red mantle, like the priests of Moloch, stood near the Baal, upright before the great toe of its right foot. When the fourteenth child was put in, all saw that he made a gesture of horror; but quickly resuming his attitude of composure, he crossed his arms, and gazed on the ground. On the other side of the Colossus the grand pontiff likewise remained motionless, bowing his head, upon which was an Assyrian mitre, and watching on his breast the gold plaque covered with prophetic stones, which threw out iridescent lights as the flame struck across them. He grew pale and abstracted.

Hamilcar inclined his head, and they were both so near the funeral pyre that the hem of their robes in rising from time to time swept it.

Moloch's brazen arms moved more rapidly; they no longer paused. Each time a child was placed upon them, the priests of Moloch extended their hands over the victim to lay upon it the sins of the people, vociferating: "These are not men, but oxen!" and the multitude around repeated, "Oxen! Oxen!" The Devotees screamed out, "Lord! Eat!" and the priests of Prosperine, conforming in terror to Carthage's need, mumbled their Eleusinian formula: "Pour forth rain! conceive!" No sooner were the victims placed on the edge of the aperture than they vanished, like a drop of water on a red-hot plate, and white smoke curled up through the scarlet glow.

Yet the appetite of the god was not appeased: he still wanted more. In order to supply him, the children were piled on his hands, and were held there by a great chain.

In the beginning, Devotees tried to count them, in order to see if the total number corresponded to the days of the solar year; but now so many were piled on that it was impossible to distinguish them in the dizzy motion of those horrible arms. All this lasted a long time, until nightfall. Then the interior divisions gave a sombre glare. For the first time, the burning flesh was visible. Some even fancied that they recognised hair, limbs, and entire bodies.

Night fell; clouds gathered over the head of the Baal. The pyre, now flameless, made a pyramid of glowing embers that reached to his knees; and all crimson, like a giant covered with blood, with head bent backward, he seemed to reel under the weight of his intoxication. According as the priests hastened, the frenzy of the people increased; as the number of victims diminished, some cried out to spare them, others that Moloch must have more. It seemed as if the walls, with their masses of spectators, would crumble beneath the yells of horror and of mystic voluptuousness. Then came into the passages some faithful ones, dragging their children, who clung to them; and they beat the little hands to make them loose their hold, that they might deliver them to the red men.

Occasionally the musicians stopped from sheer exhaustion; and in the lull could be heard the screams of mothers and the crackling of the grease falling on the coals. The mandrake-drinkers crept on all-fours around the Colossus, roaring like tigers. The Yidonim prophesied; the Devotees sang with their cleft lips. The trellis-work was broken, for all wanted to participate in the sacrifice; and fathers whose children were long since deceased cast into the yawning furnace their effigies, toys, and preserved bones. Those who possessed knives rushed upon the others; they cut each other's throats in their voracious rage. The sacred slaves, with bronze winnowing-baskets, took from the edge of the stone slab the fallen cinders, which they tossed high in the air, that the sacrifice should be dispersed over the entire city, and ascend to the region of the stars.

The tumultuous noise and vast illumination had attracted the Barbarians to the very foot of the walls. Climbing upon the ruins of the *helepolis*, to have a better view, they looked on, gasping with horror.

XIV

THE PASS OF THE BATTLE-AXE

ALMOST before the Carthaginians had time to reach their homes the clouds gathered thickly, and those who looked up toward the Colossus felt great drops—and the rain fell.

All night it rained unceasingly—in floods; the thunder growled; it was the voice of Moloch triumphant over his vanquishment of Tanit; and being now fecundated, she opened from high heaven her vast breast. Occasionally she was seen in a luminous light extended on pillows of clouds, then the darkness reclosed, as though, still too weary, she would sleep again. The Carthaginians, all believing water to be brought forth by the moon, uttered piercing cries to facilitate her travail.

The deluging rain beat upon the terraces, overflowing everywhere, forming lakes in the courts, cascades over the stairways, and whirlpools at the street corners. It poured down in heavy, warm masses and spouting streams; from the corners of all the buildings gleamed great, foaming jets; against the walls it was like white sheets vaguely suspended, and the roofs of the temples shone brilliantly black under the flashes of lightning. By a thousand channels torrents descended from the Acropolis; houses suddenly crumbled; beams, rubbish, and furniture swept by in the streams gushing impetuously over the pavements.

Amphoras, jugs, and canvases were exposed to catch the water: the torches were extinguished; and to light their pathways they took brands from the pyre of the Baal. In order that they might drink, they turned up their faces and opened their mouths. Some, by the edges of miry pools, plunged their arms in up to their armpits, and gorged themselves with water which they vomited like buffaloes.

Gradually a freshness spread abroad; all breathed the humid air, giving full play to their limbs; and in the happiness of their intoxication boundless hope sprang up. All their miseries were forgotten. Their country was revived anew.

They felt a desire to direct upon others the excess of their fury, which they had been unable to employ against themselves. Such a sacrifice ought not to be useless—even though they had no remorse, they found themselves carried away by that frenzy caused by complicity in irreparable crimes.

The storm fell upon the Barbarians in their poorly closed tents; and the next day, still benumbed, they were floundering about in the deep mud, searching for their munitions and weapons, which were spoiled and lost.

Hamilcar himself went to seek Hanno, and in pursuance of his full powers, entrusted to him the command. The old Suffet hesitated some minutes between his rancour and his appetite for authority; however, he accepted.

Subsequently Hamilcar sent out a galley, equipped with a catapult on both ends, and anchored her in the gulf, facing the raft. Then on all the disposable vessels he embarked the most robust of his troops. He was apparently flying; and making sail toward the north, he gradually disappeared in the mist.

But three days later, when they were about to renew the attack, some people from the Libyan coast arrived in a tumultuous state. Barca had come upon them. He had levied for provisions on all sides, and was spreading his troops throughout the country.

The Barbarians were as indignant as if he had betrayed them. However, those who were most tired of the siege, and especially the Gauls, did not hesitate to leave the walls in order to endeavour to rejoin the Suffet. Spendius wanted to reconstruct the *helepolis*. Mâtho had traced an imaginary line from his tent to Megara, and inwardly pledged himself to follow it; and not one of their men stirred. But Autharitus's soldiers departed, deserting the western portion of the ramparts. The indifference was so profound that no one even thought of replacing them.

Narr' Havas spied them from the distance in the mountains. He moved his troops during the night along the exterior side of the Lagoon by the sea-coast, and entered Carthage.

He presented himself like a saviour, with six thousand men, all carrying meal under their mantles, and bringing forty elephants laden with forage and dried meats. Soon the people flocked around them, giving them names. The arrival of such a succour rejoiced the Carthaginians even less than the sight of these strong animals sacred to Baal: it was a pledge of his favour, a proof that at last he came to defend them, and to intervene in the war in their behalf.

Narr' Havas received the compliments of the Elders; then he ascended toward Salammbô's palace. He had not seen her since the time when, in Hamilcar's tent, between the five armies, he had felt her little, cold, soft hand bound to his. After the betrothal she had returned to Carthage. His love, diverted by other ambitions, had come back to him, and now he anticipated enjoying his rights by marrying and taking possession of her.

Salammbô did not understand how this young man could ever become her master! Though she prayed nightly to Tanit for the death of Mâtho, her horror of the Libyan was decreasing. She dimly felt that the hatred with which he had persecuted her was something almost religious; and she would gladly have seen in Narr' Havas some reflection of that violence which fascinated her. She yearned to know more of him; nevertheless, his presence would have embarrassed her, and she sent word that she could not receive him.

Besides, Hamilcar had forbidden his people to admit the Numidian king to his daughter; he withheld this reward till the conclusion of the war, hoping thereby to preserve his devotion; and Narr' Havas, fearing Hamilcar, retired.

But he bore himself haughtily toward the Hundred, changing their plans, demanding privileges for his men, and having them appointed to important posts.

With wide-open eyes, the Barbarians discerned the Numidians on the towers.

However, the Carthaginians' surprise was even greater when there came sailing into their harbour an old Punic trireme bearing four hundred of their men, who had been taken prisoners during the Sicilian war. In fact, Hamilcar had secretly sent back to the Quirites the crews of the Latin vessels taken before the defection of the Tyrian towns, and Rome, in exchange for this fair dealing, had now returned to him these captives. Rome scorned the overtures of the Mercenaries in Sardinia, refusing even to recognise as subjects the inhabitants of Utica.

Hiero, who ruled at Syracuse, was impressed by this example. In order to preserve his own States, he required a balance of power between the two peoples; hence he was interested in the welfare of the Canaanites, and he declared himself their friend by sending to them twelve hundred head of cattle and fifty-three thousand nebels of wheat.

A deeper reason brought help to Carthage: it was thoroughly realised that, if the Mercenaries triumphed, all, from the soldiers to the scullions, would rise in revolt, and that no government, no household, would be able to resist them.

In the meantime Hamilcar reduced the eastern countries. He drove back the Gauls; and the Barbarians found themselves besieged on every side.

Then he set himself to harass them. He would march up, then depart, continually renewing this manœuvre, until gradually he drew them out from their encampments. Spendius was obliged to follow; and Mâtho, in the end, yielded also.

He did not pass beyond Tunis. He shut himself within its walls. This obstinacy was full of sagacity; for soon they saw Narr' Havas coming through the gate of Khamoûn with his elephants and soldiers. Hamilcar recalled him. But already the other Barbarians were wandering about the provinces in pursuit of the Suffet.

At Clypea he had received three thousand Gauls. He had horses brought to him from Cyrenaica and suits of armour from Bruttium, and reopened the war.

Never had his genius been so impetuous and fertile. For five months he drew them in his track. He had a goal to which he wished to lead them.

The Barbarians had at first tried to surround him with small detachments, but he always escaped them. They separated no more. Their army now numbered forty thousand men all told, and many times they rejoiced to see the Carthaginians driven back.

That which tormented them most was the cavalry of Narr' Havas. Often in the most oppressive hours of the day as they traversed the plains, dozing under the weight of their weapons, a great line of dust would suddenly rise on the horizon, horsemen would gallop up, and from out of the depths of a cloud full of flaming eyes, a shower of darts would be launched upon them. The Numidians, in their white mantles, would utter loud yells, lift up their arms, press their knees against their rearing stallions, make them wheel suddenly, and then disappear. They always held in reserve provisions and javelins, at some distance off, packed upon dromedaries; and they would return more terrible, howling like wolves, flying like vultures.

The Barbarians who were posted at the extremities of the files fell one by one: this would continue till the evening, when an endeavour would be made to enter the mountains.

Although they were perilous for the elephants, Hamilcar had involved himself in them. He followed the long chain which extended from the promontory of Hermæum to the summit of Zagouan. This they believed was a plan to hide the weakness of his troops. But the continual uncertainty in which he kept them ended by exasperating them more than a defeat. Nevertheless, they were not discouraged, but marched after him.

One evening, behind the Silver Mountain and the Lead Mountain, in the midst of huge rocks, and at the mouth of a defile, they surprised a corps of velites and thought that certainly the whole Punic army was before them, for they could hear the tramp of feet and bluster of clarions; the Carthaginians immediately fled through the gorge. This defile sloped down to a plain, formed like an iron axe, environed by high cliffs. To overtake the velites the Barbarians dashed into it; right at the farther end other Carthaginians were rushing about tumultuously among galloping oxen. A man in a red mantle could be discerned: it was the Suffet; the pursuers yelled out, transported by an increase of fury and joy. Many, either from languor or caution, had remained at the entrance of the pass; but cavalry, debouching from a wood, with blows of lances and sabres drove them down upon the others, until finally all the Barbarians were below in the plain.

After this vast mass of men had fluctuated about for some time, they halted; they could discover no outlet.

Those who were adjacent to the pass turned back, but the passage had in the meantime entirely disappeared. They hailed those in front to make them proceed; the latter crushed themselves against the mountain, and from afar they abused their comrades, who could not find the passage again.

In fact, scarcely had the Barbarians descended, before men lying in ambush behind the rocks had heaved them up with beams and overset them; and as the slope of the ground was very abrupt the enormous blocks of rocks, rolling down in confusion, completely choked up the narrow opening.

At the other extremity of the plain extended a long passage, here and there split by crevices, that led to a ravine beyond, rising to the upper plateau, where the Punic army was stationed. In this passage, against the walls of the cliff, scaling-ladders had previously been placed; and, protected by the circuitous turnings of the crevices, the velites, before being overtaken, were able to seize the ladders and mount the walls; nevertheless, many became entangled at the bottom of the ravine, and these were drawn aloft with cables, as the earth in that quarter was covered by quicksand, and of such a declivity that it would be impossible for any man to crawl up, even on his hands and knees.

Almost immediately the Barbarians reached this spot; but a portcullis, forty cubits high, made to fit exactly in the intervening space, suddenly dropped before them, like a rampart that had fallen from the sky. Thus the strategic combinations of the Suffet were successfully accomplished. None of the Mercenaries knew the mountain, and, marching at the head of the column, they had thus led the others into the trap. The rocks, a little narrower at the base, were easily knocked over, and whilst they all were running, his army in the horizon had yelled as if in distress. Hamilcar, it is true, might have lost all his velites—half of whom only remained; but he would willingly have sacrificed twenty times as many men for the success of such an enterprise.

Until morning the Barbarians marched in compact files, from one end to the other of this circumscribed plain. They tapped the mountain with their hands, seeking some passage; but all to no purpose.

Finally, day broke; they then saw a large, white, perpendicularly hewn wall; and not a visible means of escape, not a hope! The two natural passages from this alley were closed by the portcullis on one side, and by rocks on the other.

They all looked at each other without a word. They collapsed, feeling an icy cold in their loins and an overwhelming weight upon their eyelids.

They rose and bounded against the rocks; but those at the base, held down by those above, were immovable. Then they tried to clutch on to the rocky sides so as to reach the top; but the tun-bellied form of these huge masses refused all hold. They tried to split the earth at the sides of the gorge, but their weapons broke; then, as a last resort, they made a vast fire with their tent-poles, but the mountain would not burn.

Now they went back to the portcullis; it was garnished with long spikes, thick as boar-spears, and sharp as porcupine quills, set closer together than bristles in a brush. But their rage infuriated them so blindly, that they threw themselves upon it: the first were spiked to the very backbone, the second fell backward over each other, and all recoiled, leaving human shreds and blood-stained scalps on the horrible spikes.

When their discouragement was a little abated, they examined their provisions. The Mercenaries, whose baggage was lost, possessed but enough for two days, and all the others found themselves absolutely destitute, as they had been waiting for a promised convoy from the southern villages.

Meanwhile, the cattle loosened by the Carthaginians in the gorge to decoy the Barbarians into this trap wandered about: these they killed with their lances; when their stomachs were full, their thoughts were less dismal.

The next day they slaughtered the mules, forty in number; then they scraped the hides, boiled the entrails, and pounded the bones. As yet they did not despair: the army at Tunis would assuredly hear of their position, and come promptly to their rescue.

But on the evening of the fifth day their hunger redoubled: they gnawed the shoulder-belts of their swords and the little sponges edging the bottoms of their helmets.

These forty thousand men were crowded in a sort of hippodrome formed by the mountain; some of them persistently remained before the portcullis, or at the base of the rocks; the rest confusedly covered the plain of the basin. The strong avoided each other, and the timid sought out the brave, who, however, could not save them.

From fear of infection, the bodies of the velites had been quickly buried, and the location of the graves remained no longer distinguishable.

Lying on the ground, all the Barbarians languished. Here and there between their lines, a veteran sometimes passed, and they shouted curses against the Carthaginians, against Hamilcar, and against Mâtho, although he was innocent of their present disaster. But it seemed to them that the calamity would have been less if he had also shared it. Then they moaned; some even wept softly, like little children.

They would go to the captains and implore them to give them something to appease their sufferings. The officers made no reply, or, seized with rage, picked up stones and threw them into their faces.

In truth, many kept carefully hidden in a hole in the ground a reserve of food, possibly only a few handfuls of dates, or a little meal; this they ate stealthily during the night, with their heads cautiously covered by their mantles; those who possessed swords held them drawn, and the more defiant stood upright, with their backs to the mountain.

They accused and threatened their chiefs. Autharitus had no fear in showing himself; with the tenacity peculiar to the Barbarians, which nothing could rebut, twenty times a day he went forth to the rocks, each time hoping to find them displaced, and, swinging his heavy shoulders covered with furs, he reminded his companions of a bear leaving its cavern in the spring to see if the snow has melted.

Spendius, surrounded by Greeks, hid himself in one of the crevices; and, as he was afraid, he caused a rumour of his death to be noised about.

By this time they were all hideously meagre; their skin was mottled with bluish patches. The evening of the ninth day three Iberians died, whereupon their frightened comrades left the place. The bodies were stripped, and the white, naked corpses remained on the sand exposed to the sun.

Then some Garamantians began to prowl about these bodies. They were men accustomed to a life of solitude in the desert, and reverenced no god. At length the oldest one of the band made a sign, and bending over the corpses, with their knives they cut off strips and devoured them, squatting on their heels. The others looked on, standing aloof. Cries of horror were raised. Many of these men, notwithstanding, in the depth of their hearts were jealous of their frightful courage.

In the middle of the night some of these approached, and, dissimulating their eagerness, asked for a tiny morsel, only to taste. Some braver ones followed; their number increased; soon a crowd collected. But almost all, feeling the cold flesh on their teeth, let their hands fall, others, on the contrary, devoured their portions with delight.

In order to be encouraged by example, they stimulated each other. Those who had at first refused, came to see Garamantes, and did not leave; their pieces were cooked over the embers on the point of a spear, and salted with the dust; they even contended among themselves as to the best bits. When nothing remained of the three corpses, their eyes roved over the plain to find others.

But did they not possess some Carthaginians—twenty captives taken in the last skirmish—and whom no one until now had remembered? They disappeared; moreover, it was a piece of revenge. Then, as they needs must live, and the taste for such food developed itself, and as they were dying, they killed the water-carriers, the grooms, and all the servants of the Mercenaries. Some of them were killed every day. A few ate lustily, regained their strength, and were no longer sad.

Soon this resource failed them; then their desire turned toward the sick and wounded: since they could not recover, it was well to deliver them from their agony. Hence, as soon as a man tottered, all cried out that he was lost, and should serve the others. To accelerate their deaths they employed all manner of schemes. They stole from them the last remnants of their foul portion: as if by accident, they trod upon them. The dying, to induce a belief in their strength, endeavoured to lift their arms, or to rise up, or to laugh. Men who had swooned were roused by the cold contact of a notched blade sawing off a limb; and they killed still others out of ferocity, without need, in order to appease their fury.

On the fourteenth day a warm, heavy mist, such as frequents those regions at the end of winter, settled down upon the army. This change of temperature caused many deaths, and corruption was developed with frightful speed in the warm humidity retained by the mountain walls. The drizzle, which fell upon the corpses and softened them, soon made of the whole plain one great mass of rottenness. White vapour floated above, stinging the nostrils, penetrating the skin, and troubling the eyes: and the Barbarians fancied that through the exhalations of the breath they could see the souls of their dead comrades. An immense disgust overwhelmed them. They would have no more of it. They desired to die.

Two days later the air became pure again, and hunger reseized them. It seemed at times that their stomachs were clawed with hooks; then they rolled over in convulsions, stuffing their mouths full of dirt, biting their own arms, and bursting into frantic spasms of laughter.

Yet more, if possible, did their thirst torment them, as they had not a drop of water—for their leathern water-bottles since the ninth day had been completely dry. To deceive this need, they resorted to the trick of applying on their tongues the metal scales of their sword-belts, the ivory hafts, or the steel of their swords, while experienced camel-drivers tightened their bellies with ropes; others sucked a stone; many drank urine cooled in their brazen helmets.

And they still looked for the army from Tunis! The length of time that it took in coming, according to their conjecture, made its speedy arrival certain. Besides, Mâtho, who was so brave, would not desert them. "He will come to-morrow!" they said to each other. The morrow came and passed.

In the early days they had prayed, made vows, and all sorts of incantations; but now they did not feel for their divinities other than hatred, and out of vengeance endeavoured not to believe in them.

Men of violent characters perished first; the Africans resisted longer than the Gauls. Zarxas, amid the Balearians, remained extended full length, his hair tossed over his arms, inert. Spendius had found a plant with broad leaves full of juice, and in order to scare the others declared it to be poisonous; then he fed himself upon it.

They were too weak to knock down with stones the ravens that flew about. Sometimes, when a bearded vulture perched on a corpse, and had been for a long time tearing it, a man would crawl toward it with a javelin between his teeth, lean upon his arm, and, taking a good aim, would throw the weapon. The bird with white plumage, disturbed by the noise, would pause, look about in a tranquil manner, like a cormorant on a reef, then would plunge again its hideous yellow beak into its prey; while the man, in despair, would fall flat on his face in the dust. Some discovered chameleons and serpents. But it was the love of life that kept them alive. They concentrated their minds exclusively on this idea—and clung to existence by an effort of will that in itself prolonged it.

The most stoical kept close together, sitting about in the centre of the plain, here and there between the dead; and, wrapped in their mantles, abandoned themselves silently to their sorrow.

Those who had been born in towns recalled the bustling streets full of noise, the taverns, the theatres, the baths, and the barbers' shops, where stories were told: others, again, saw fields at sunset, where the yellow grain waved and the huge oxen ascended the hills with the ploughshares on their necks. Travellers dreamed of cisterns, hunters of their forests, veterans of battles; and in the torpor that benumbed them, their fancies jostled one another with all the power and clearness of dreams. Hallucinations came over them; they sought a gate in the mountain side to escape, and tried to pass through. Others, believing that they were navigating in a storm, gave orders for the handling of a ship; some even recoiled in terror, perceiving in the clouds Punic battalions; others fancied that they were at a feast, and sang songs.

Many in a strange mania repeated the same word, or continually made the same gesture; then, when they raised their heads and looked at one another, sobs suffocated them, on discovering the horrible ravages depicted on their faces. Some had ceased to suffer, and sought to employ the tedious hours by recounting the various perils from which they had miraculously escaped.

Death seemed certain and imminent to all. How often had they not tried to open a passage! As for imploring terms from the conquerors, by what means could they? They did not even know where Hamilcar was.

The wind blew from the direction of the ravine, making the sand flow continuously over the portcullis in cascades, and the mantles and hair of the Barbarians were completely covered with falling sand, as if the earth were rising and desirous to engulf them. Nothing moved; the eternal mountain each morning seemed higher. Sometimes flocks of birds flew swiftly overhead, spreading out their wings across the open blue sky, in the freedom of the air: the men closed their eyes to avoid seeing them. They felt at first a buzzing in their ears; their finger-nails blackened; the cold seized their breasts. They lay upon their sides, and expired without a cry.

On the nineteenth day two thousand Asiatics were dead, and fifteen hundred men from the Archipelago, eight thousand Libyans, the youngest Mercenaries, and whole tribes—in all, twenty thousand soldiers, one half of the army.

Autharitus, who had only fifty Gauls surviving, was about to kill himself, thereby putting an end to it all, when at the summit of the mountain facing him, he thought he saw a man. The great height made him look like a dwarf. However, Autharitus recognised on his left arm a trefoil-shaped shield, and cried out, "A Carthaginian!" In the plain below the portcullis, and under the rocks, all instantly rose to their feet. The soldier marching on the edge of the precipice was eagerly watched by the Barbarians.

Spendius picked up an ox skull, and with two girdles fashioned a diadem, placing it on the horns at the end of a pole, to signify peaceful intentions. The Carthaginian disappeared. They waited a long time.

At last, in the evening, like a stone loosened from the cliffs, there suddenly fell from above a sword-belt made of red leather covered with embroidery and three diamond stars; in the centre it bore stamped upon it the seal of the Grand Council—a horse beneath a palm tree. This was Hamilcar's response, the safe conduct that he sent.

They had nothing to fear; any change of fortune brought with it an end to their ills. A measureless rapture agitated them; they embraced and wept. Spendius, Autharitus, Zarxas, four Italians, one Negro, and two Spartans, offered themselves as envoys. They were promptly accepted; however, they knew no way by which to gain exit.

In the midst of this dilemma, a crash resounded in the direction of the rocks, and the topmost crag, having swayed on its base, bounded down to the bottom. In fact, though from the side of the Barbarians they were immovable—for it would have been necessary for them to ascend an inclined plane: besides, they were closely packed by the narrowness of the gorge—from the other side, on the contrary, a vigorous push was enough to make them descend.

The Carthaginians pushed them, and at daybreak they had fallen into the plain, looking like the steps of a gigantic stairway in ruins.

Still the Barbarians could not climb up, so ladders were thrown over.

All rushed for these; but the prompt discharge of a catapult drove them back; and only the Ten were taken up.

They marched between Clinabarians, leaning their hands on the cruppers of the horses to support themselves. Now that their first joy was over, they began to feel uneasiness. The demands of Hamilcar would be cruel; but Spendius reassured his companions, saying:

"It is I who will speak!" Then he vaunted his knowledge of admirable things to say for the welfare of the army.

Behind all the bushes they encountered sentinels in ambush, who prostrated themselves before the sword-belt which Spendius had put over his shoulder.

When finally they arrived at the Punic encampment, the crowd pressed about them, and they heard significant whispers and laughter.

The door of a tent opened; Hamilcar was at the back part, seated on a bench near a low table, on which shone a naked blade. His captains stood about him. When he saw these men, he started back, then leaned forward to examine them.

The pupils of their eyes were extraordinarily large, and a wide black ring encircled them, extending to the lower part of their ears; their bluish noses projected between their hollow cheeks, furrowed by deep wrinkles; the skin of their bodies, too large for their flabby muscles, was hidden under a coat of slate-coloured dust; their lips were glued against their yellow teeth; they exhaled an infectious odour, they appeared like half-open tombs intended for living sepulchres.

In the middle of the tent, on a mat, round which the captains were about to sit down, there was a smoking dish of pumpkins. The Barbarians riveted their gaze on it, shivering in every limb, and tears started to their eyes. Nevertheless they restrained themselves.

Hamilcar turned away to speak to some one. Instantly they all rushed upon the dish, throwing themselves flat on the ground, their faces steeped in the grease; noises of deglutition mingled with sobs of delight, which they could not suppress. Rather from astonishment than pity, they were permitted to finish the contents of the bowl. Then, when they again stood up, Hamilcar commanded by a sign that the man who wore the sword-belt should speak. Spendius was frightened and stammered.

Hamilcar, while listening, constantly twirled around on one finger a large gold ring, the same which had imprinted the seal of Carthage on the sword-belt; he accidentally let it fall on the ground. Spendius at once stooped down and picked it up: before his master the servile habits of a slave returned to him. The others shuddered indignantly at this contemptible baseness.

But the Greek raised his voice, and recounted the crimes of Hanno, whom he knew to be a foe of Barca. He tried to move Hamilcar's pity with the details of their sufferings, and spoke on for a long time in a style, rapid, insidious, and violent. Toward the end he became forgetful of self, and was carried away by the fervour of his imagination.

Hamilcar replied that he accepted their excuses. Peace, therefore, was about to be concluded, and this time it would be definitive! But he required that ten Mercenaries chosen by himself, without weapons and without tunics, should be delivered to him.

They had not expected such clemency, and Spendius exclaimed:

"Yes! twenty, if you will, master!"

"No! ten will suffice," mildly replied Hamilcar.

In order that they could deliberate, they were dismissed from his tent. As soon as they were alone, Autharitus objected to the sacrifice of their companions, and Zarxas said to Spendius:

"Why did you not kill him?—his sword was within your reach!"

"Him!" exclaimed Spendius, and repeated frequently, "Him! him!" as if the thing had been an impossibility, and Hamilcar were a divinity.

So thoroughly were they overcome by their protracted fatigue, that they stretched themselves on their backs upon the ground; sorely perplexed as to what course to follow.

Spendius urged them to yield; after some parley they consented, and they returned to the Suffet.

Then the Suffet put his hand in the hands of the ten Barbarians one after another, and pressed their thumbs; afterward he rubbed his hands on his garment, for their clammy skins had presented to his touch a sensation harsh and soft, that made a slimy, creeping impression. Subsequently he said:

"You all, then, are the chiefs of the Barbarians, and you have sworn for them?"

"Yes!" they replied.

"Without reservation, from the bottom of your souls, with the intention of fulfilling your promises?"

They assured him that they would return to the others, and fulfil their pledges.

"Ah! well!" said the Suffet, "according to the convention which has passed between me, Barca, and you, the ambassadors of the Mercenaries, it is you whom I choose, and shall keep!"

Spendius fell fainting on the mat. The Barbarians, as if abandoning him, pressed close together; and there was not a word nor a murmur.

Their comrades who awaited them, when they did not return, believed themselves betrayed. Without doubt the envoys had given themselves up to the Suffet.

They waited two days longer; then, on the morning of the third, their resolution was taken. With ropes, picks, and arrows fitted like rungs of a ladder between strips of canvas, they succeeded in scaling the rocks; and leaving behind them the weaker ones, about three thousand in number, they marched off to rejoin the army at Tunis.

At the top of the gorge spread a prairie, lightly sprinkled with shrubs, the buds of which the Barbarians devoured; then they came upon a field of beans: these also disappeared as if a cloud of locusts had passed. Three hours later they came to a second plateau, bounded by a belt of green hills.

Between the undulations of these hillocks silvery sheaves shone, stacked at regular intervals: the sun so dazzled the Barbarians that they could but confusedly discern under them large, black masses; these sprang up, as if they were ascending out of the earth. They were lances in towers, on the backs of formidably equipped elephants.

Besides the spears of their breastplates, the pointed ferrules on their tusks, the brazen plates which covered their sides, and the daggers fastened to their knee-caps, they had on the end of their trunks a band of leather, in which was fixed the hilt of a broad cutlass. Starting all at the same time from the bottom of the plain, they advanced from each side in parallel lines. A nameless terror froze the Barbarians; they did not try to escape. Already they found themselves surrounded.

The elephants entered this mass, and with the spears on their breastplates clove it; the lance-like tusks overturned it like ploughshares. They cut, they hewed, they hacked with the scythes extending from their trunks; the towers full of fiery darts seemed like moving volcanoes. Nothing could be distinguished but a broad heap, on which were visible white patches of human flesh, grey spots of fragments of brass, and red splashes of blood. The horrible animals passed through it all, digging out black furrows.

The most furious were led by a Numidian, crowned with a diadem of plumes. He hurled javelins with terrific speed, while uttering at intervals a long, shrill whistle; the huge beasts, docile as dogs, in the midst of the carnage kept turning an eye in his direction.

Their circle gradually narrowed. The weakened Barbarians could make no resistance: soon the elephants reached the centre of the plain. There was not room enough, and the animals crowded together, half rearing up, and clashed their tusks. Suddenly Narr' Havas quieted them, and turning round they trotted back toward the hills.

Meanwhile two syntagmata, taking refuge at the right in a hollow, had thrown down their weapons, and were now upon their knees: turning toward the Punic tents, with uplifted arms, they implored mercy.

Their arms and legs were tied; then, when they were flat on the ground, close together, the elephants were led over them.

Their breast-bones cracked like coffers being broken; the huge animals at each step crushed two men; their cumbrous feet sank into the bodies with a movement of their haunches, that made them appear lame. They continued to the very end.

The level of the plain became motionless; night fell. Hamilcar was exulting before the spectacle of his vengeance, when suddenly he started.

He saw, and all saw, six hundred paces distant, on the left at the summit of a peak, some more Barbarians! In fact, four hundred of the stoutest Mercenaries, Etruscans, Libyans, and Spartans, early in the fray had gained the heights, and until now had been uncertain what to do. After the massacre of their comrades, they resolved to cut through the Carthaginians; already they were descending in close columns in a marvellous and formidable fashion.

A herald was instantly despatched by the Suffet, stating that he required soldiers, and would receive them unconditionally, so much did he admire their bravery. They could even, added the man of Carthage, come a little nearer, to a certain spot, which he pointed out, and where they would find provisions.

The Barbarians ran thither and passed the night in eating; then the Carthaginians burst into murmurs against the partiality of the Suffet for the Mercenaries. Did he yield to the promptings of an insatiable hatred, or was it possibly a refinement of treachery?

The day after he came himself, unarmed, bareheaded, with an escort of Clinabarians, and declared to the Barbarians that, having more men than he could afford to feed, his intention was not to keep them. However, as he required good soldiers, and knew not by what method to choose the best, they must fight among themselves till death, and he would admit the victors to his own body-guard. Such a mode of death was preferable to any other. Then he parted his troops—for the Punic standards hid the horizon from the Mercenaries—and showed them Narr' Havas's one hundred and ninety-two elephants, forming a single straight line, and brandishing with uplifted trunks cutlasses, like giant arms holding axes over their heads.

The Barbarians looked at each other silently. It was not the fear of death that made them pale, but the horrible compulsion to which they found themselves reduced.

The community of their hazardous life had established between these men profound friendships. For the most part the camp took the place of country; and living without families, they transferred to a comrade their instincts of tenderness, and they slept side by side under the same mantle, beneath the starlight. They exchanged their necklaces and earrings, gifts they had formerly bestowed upon each other after some great peril.

All begged to die, but no one would strike the blow. Here and there a youth said to another man, whose beard was grey: "No! no! you are more robust! You will revenge us! Kill me!" and the elder answered: "I have fewer years to live! Strike to the heart, and think no more about it!"

Brothers gazed on each other, with hands clasped; friend uttered to friend eternal farewells, standing upright, weeping on each other's shoulders. They took off their breastplates, that the sword points might bury themselves more quickly, revealing the scars of terrific blows received for Carthage, resembling historic inscriptions on columns.

Placing themselves in four rows, in the fashion of gladiators, they began by timid engagements; some even bound up their eyes; moving their swords gently, like the sticks of the blind, The Carthaginians yelled, crying out that they were cowards. The Barbarians grew excited, and soon the conflict became general, headlong and terrible.

Sometimes two men stopped, covered with blood, fell into each other's arms, and expired kissing. Not one recoiled. They rushed determinedly upon the extended blades. Their delirium became so furious that the Carthaginians even at a distance were afraid.

At length they stopped. A loud, hoarse noise was emitted from their chests; and their eyeballs could be seen amidst their long hair, which hung down as if they had emerged from a bath of purple dye. Some turned rapidly round and round, like panthers wounded in the forehead. Others stood motionless, regarding a corpse at their feet; then suddenly they tore their faces with their finger-nails, seized their swords with both hands, and buried them in their own bodies. Sixty yet remained. They asked for drink. They were bidden to throw down their swords; when they had done so, water was brought to them.

While they were drinking, their faces buried in the vessels, sixty Carthaginians leaped upon them, and stabbed them with stilettoes in the back.

Hamilcar had permitted this, to gratify the instincts of his troops, and by this treason, to attach them to him personally.

Thus was the war ended, or so at least he believed it to be. Mâtho would certainly not resist, and in his impatience, the Suffet gave command for immediate departure.

His scouts came to inform him that a convoy had been observed, going toward the Lead Mountain. Hamilcar did not care—for, once the Mercenaries were annihilated, the Nomads would make no trouble. The important thing was to take Tunis; so by forced marches he advanced toward it.

He had sent Narr' Havas back to Carthage, to carry the news of his victory. And the king of the Numidians, proud of his success, presented himself at Salammbô's palace.

Salammbô received him in her gardens, under a large sycamore tree, sitting between pillows of yellow leather, with Taanach beside her. Her face was covered with a white scarf, that passed over her mouth and forehead, allowing only her eyes to be seen: but through the transparency of the tissue, her lips shone like the gems on her fingers—for Salammbô kept both hands likewise covered, and all the time they conversed never made a gesture.

Narr' Havas announced to her the defeat of the Barbarians. She thanked him, with a blessing, for the services he had rendered to her father. Then he recounted the whole campaign.

The doves in the palms around them cooed softly, and other birds, such as the ringed galeoles, quails from Tartessus, and Punic guinea-fowls, fluttered in the grass. The gardens, uncultivated for so long a time, were thick with verdure; the colocynth sprang up through the branches of the cassia trees; the dragon-wort sprinkled the rose-fields; all species of vegetation formed tangled bowers, and the sun's rays, descending slantingly, outlined here and there upon the ground, as in a wood, the shadow of a leaf.

The domestic animals, having grown wild, bounded away at the slightest noise. Sometimes a gazelle might be seen dragging with its little black hoofs the peacocks' feathers scattered about. The noise of the distant town was lost in the murmur of the waves. The sky was perfectly blue, and not a sail appeared on the sea.

Narr' Havas ceased speaking. Without responding, Salammbô looked at him. He wore a linen robe upon which flowers were painted, with a golden fringe at the hem; two silver arrows held back his hair, braided close against his ears. His right hand rested on the wooden shaft of a pike ornamented with bands of electrum and tufts of hair.

As she looked at him a host of thoughts absorbed her. This young man, with a sweet voice and feminine figure, captivated her eyes by the grace of his fine person, and he seemed like an elder sister sent by the Baals to protect her. The memory of Mâtho seized her, nor did she resist the desire to inquire what had become of him.

Narr' Havas responded that the Carthaginians were advancing on Tunis to capture him. While he explained their chances of success and Mâtho's weakness, she appeared to rejoice with an extraordinary hope; her lips quivered, her breast panted. When at last he vowed to kill Mâtho himself, she cried out:

"Yes! Kill him! It must be so!"

The Numidian replied that he ardently desired his death, inasmuch as when the war was over he should marry her.

Salammbô trembled, and bent her head.

But Narr' Havas went on to compare his love and his desires to the powers that languished for rain; to travellers lost in the night awaiting the dawn. He told her that she was more beautiful than the moon; more to be preferred than the morning breezes, or than the face of a guest. He would have rare objects, not to be found in Carthage, brought for her from the country of the Blacks, and the apartments of their house should be sprinkled with gold dust.

Evening fell. Odours of balsam filled the air. For a long time they looked at one another in silence, and Salammbô's eyes, in the depth of her long, ample draperies, had the appearance of two stars in the rift of a cloud. Before sunset, he retired.

The Elders felt relieved from a vast anxiety when he left Carthage; the people had received him with even more enthusiastic acclamations than upon the former occasion. If Hamilcar and the Numidian king triumphed alone over the Mercenaries, it would be impossible to resist them. Then they resolved to weaken Barca, by making old Hanno, the one whom they loved, participate in the deliverance of Carthage.

Hanno went immediately toward the western provinces, so as to revenge himself in the same regions which had witnessed his shame: but the inhabitants, as well as the Barbarians, were dead, hidden, or fled. Then his wrath poured itself forth upon the country; he burned the ruins of ruins, leaving not a solitary tree, not a spear of grass: the children and the infirm whom they met with were tortured; he gave the women to the soldiers, to violate before slaying them, having the most beautiful always thrown into his own litter—for his atrocious malady inflamed his desires, and he would gloat over his victims with all the passion of a madman.

Often, on the crest of the hills, black tents sank down, as if overthrown by the wind, and broad discs with shining edges, which were recognised as the wheels of chariots, revolved with a plaintive sound as they gradually disappeared in the valleys.

The tribes which had abandoned the siege of Carthage were thus wandering through the provinces, waiting for an opportunity or for some victory of the Barbarians, to return. But from terror, or because of famine, they all followed the roads leading to their own countries, and disappeared.

Hamilcar was not jealous of Hanno's successes, nevertheless he hastened to end matters; he ordered him to fall back on Tunis; and Hanno, who loved his country, on the appointed day was under the walls of that town.

Tunis had for her defence her aboriginal population, twelve thousand Mercenaries, and all the Eaters-of-Unclean-Things. They, like Mâtho, had their eyes riveted on the horizon of Carthage, and the populace, as well as the *Schalischim*, beheld her lofty walls from afar, dreaming of the infinite joys behind them. With this harmony of hatred, the resistance was quickly organised. Leather bottles were used to make helmets, all the palms in the gardens were cut down to furnish lances, cisterns were excavated; and as for food, they fished along the lake shore, catching large white fish which fed on the corpses and filth.

Their ramparts, kept in ruins by the jealousy of Carthage, were so weak that one might throw them over with a push of the shoulder. Mâtho ordered the breaches to be filled up with the stones from dwellings. It was the final struggle; he hoped for nothing, and yet he reminded himself that Fortune was fickle.

As the Carthaginians drew near, they noticed a man on the rampart, who from his waist overtopped the battlements. The arrows flying about him seemed to frighten him no more than a flight of swallows. Most extraordinarily, not one of them touched him.

Hamilcar pitched his camp on the southern side; Narr' Havas on his right occupied the plain of Rhades; Hanno was stationed on the lake shore; and the three generals were to retain their respective positions so that all should attack the walls simultaneously.

But Hamilcar, in the first place, desired to show the Mercenaries that he would punish them like slaves, therefore he had the ten ambassadors crucified close together on a hillock facing the city.

At this sight the besieged abandoned the ramparts.

Mâtho had believed, that if he could pass between the walls and Narr' Havas's tents so expeditiously that the Numidians would not have time to sally forth, he would fall on the rear of the Carthaginian infantry, who would thus be caught between his division and the troops within the town. He dashed out with his veterans.

Narr' Havas saw him; he crossed the lake shore, and went to warn Hanno to despatch his men to Hamilcar's aid. Did he think Barca too weak to resist the Mercenaries? Was this treachery or folly? No one ever knew.

Hanno, desiring to humiliate his rival, did not hesitate; he ordered the trumpets to be sounded, and all his troops rushed upon the Barbarians. The latter wheeled round and charged straight upon the Carthaginians; they overthrew them, trampled them under foot, and driving them back, reached the tent of Hanno, who then was surrounded by thirty Carthaginians, the most illustrious of the Elders.

Hanno appeared stupefied by their audacity; he called for his captains; the assaulters thrust their fists forward to seize him by the throat, vociferating abuse. The crowd pushed each other, and those who had their hands on him could scarcely hold him. However, he tried to whisper to them: "I will give you all you want! I am rich! Save me!" They dragged him away, and, heavy as he was, his feet did not touch the ground. They also dragged away the Elders. His terror increased.

"You have defeated me! I am your captive! I will ransom myself! Listen to me, my friends!" and, carried along by their shoulders pressed against his sides, he repeated: "What are you going to do? What do you want? You see well, I do not resist! I have always been complaisant!"

A gigantic cross stood at the gate; the Barbarians howled out, "Here! here!" Then he raised his voice higher, and in the name of their gods he entreated them to take him to their *Schalischim*, because he had something to confide to him, upon which depended their safety.

They paused, some declaring it would be wise to call Mâtho; and he was sent for.

Hanno sank down upon the grass, and he saw around him still more crosses, as if the torture under which he was about to perish had multiplied itself. He made efforts to believe that he was deceived, that there was only one cross, and even that there were none at all. Finally, the Mercenaries lifted him up as Mâtho appeared.

"Speak!" said Mâtho.

He offered to deliver over Hamilcar: then they would enter Carthage, and both be kings.

Mâtho turned away, making a sign for the men to hasten; he thought this was a stratagem to gain time.

The Barbarian was mistaken, for Hanno was in one of those dire extremities where a man no longer considers anything but self-preservation. Besides, he hated Hamilcar so thoroughly, that for the slightest reason he would have sacrificed him and all his soldiers.

At the foot of thirty crosses the Elders languished upon the ground; already ropes had been passed under their armpits. Then the old Suffet, realising that he was to be put to death, wept bitterly.

His captors pulled off what remained of his clothing, revealing the horrors of his person. Ulcers covered this nameless mass; the fat of his legs hid his toe-nails; the flesh hung like green rags to his fingers; the tears which ran between the tubercles of his cheeks made his visage something shockingly deplorable, for they seemed to occupy more space than on any other human face. His royal bandeau, half untied, trailed with his long white hair in the dust.

Believing that the ropes were not sufficiently strong to haul him up to the top of the cross, they nailed him to it before it was erected, in the Punic fashion. But his pride was aroused in his pain; he began to overwhelm them with abuse. He frothed and writhed like a marine monster stranded and killed on the shore. He predicted that they should all end even more horribly than he, and that he should be revenged. He was right: for on the other side of the town, whence now escaped jets of flames mingled with columns of smoke, the envoys of the Mercenaries were in the agonies of death.

Some who had fainted at first, were revived by the coolness of the breeze; but they remained with their chins on their breasts, their bodies fallen a little, in spite of the nails through their arms, which were fastened above their heads. From their hands and heels blood slowly fell in big drops, like ripe fruit falling from the branches of a tree; and Carthage, the gulf, the mountains, and the plains, appeared to them to be all revolving like an immense wheel; sometimes a cloud of dust lifted from the earth, and enveloped them in its eddies. They were consumed by a horrible thirst; their tongues curled up in their mouths, and they felt an icy sweat trickling over them with their departing souls. Meanwhile, they could see at an infinite depth, streets, soldiers marching, swords swinging; and, the tumult of battle came indistinctly to them, as the noise of the sea to shipwrecked sailors dying in the rigging of their ships. The Italiots, more robust than the rest, continued to shriek; the Lacædemonians kept silent, with eyes closed; Zarxas, formerly so vigorous, drooped like a broken reed; the Ethiopian alongside of him had his head thrown backward over the arm of the cross; Autharitus, motionless, rolled his eyes; his heavy, long hair was caught in a crack in the wood and drawn straight over his forehead, and his death-rattle seemed rather like a growl of wrath.

As for Spendius, a strange courage had come to him; he despised life now, because of the certainty that he should have an almost immediate and eternal release; he awaited death with impassibility.

In the midst of their swoonings, sometimes they shuddered at the touch of feathers as they grazed against their lips. Huge wings cast long, waving shadows about them, croakings sounded in the air; and as the cross of Spendius was the highest, it was thereon the first vulture alighted. Then he turned his face towards Autharitus, saying slowly, with a strange smile:

"Do you recall the lions on the road to Sicca?"

"They were our brothers!" answered the Gaul, as he expired.

The Suffet, in the meantime, had broken through the walls and gained the citadel. Under a gust of wind the smoke suddenly disappeared, disclosing the horizon as far as the walls of Carthage; he believed even that he could distinguish the people watching from the platform of Eschmoûn;

then he turned his eyes, and perceived to the left, on the lake shore, thirty immense crosses.

In fact, to render the crosses still more frightful, they had constructed them out of tent-poles, lashed end to end; so that the thirty bodies of the crucified Elders appeared high up in the sky. On their bosoms gleamed, like white butterflies, the feathers of the arrows which had been shot at them from below.

On the summit of the highest shone a broad, gold fillet; it hung upon the shoulder of the crucified one, for the arm on that side was wanting; and Hamilcar with difficulty recognised Hanno. His spongy bones giving way under iron nails, portions of his limbs had become detached, and there only remained on the cross shapeless fragments, like portions of animals hung upon a hunter's door.

The Suffet had been unable to learn anything of Mâtho's sally: the town in front of him concealed all that lay beyond at the back; and the captains sent successively to the two generals had not returned. Then the fugitives came, recounting the rout; and the Punic army halted. This catastrophe coming in the midst of their victory, stupefied them. They no longer heeded Hamilcar's orders. Mâtho profited by this to continue his ravages upon the Numidians.

Hanno's camp having been overthrown, he had turned again on them. The elephants charged; but the Mercenaries, shaking firebrands snatched from the burning wall, advanced on the plain; the huge animals were frightened, and fled, precipitating themselves into the gulf, killing one another in their struggles, or drowning under the weight of their breastplates. Already Narr' Havas had ordered his cavalry to charge; the Mercenaries threw themselves face downward against the ground, then, when the horses were within three steps of them, they sprang under their bellies and ripped them open with daggers; half of the Numidians had thus perished when Barca came up.

The Mercenaries, now exhausted, could not hold out against his troops. They retreated in good order as far as the Hot-Springs Mountain. The Suffet had the prudence not to follow them. He moved toward the mouth of the Macar.

Tunis was his; but the city was now nothing but a heap of smoking rubbish. The ruins had tumbled down through the breaches in the walls out into the plain; beyond, between the shores of the gulf, the elephants' carcasses, driven by the wind, collided, like an archipelago of black rocks floating on the water.

Narr' Havas, in order to sustain this war, had exhausted his forests, taking alike young and old, male and female elephants, and the military strength of his kingdom could not be reënforced. The people, who saw these animals perish from afar, were in despair; many lamenting in the streets, calling them by their names, as if deceased friends: "Ah! Invincible! Victor! Thunderbolt! Swallow!" And during the first day everyone spoke only of the dead citizens. The next day, seeing the Mercenaries' tents pitched on the Hot-Springs Mountain, their despair became so deep that many of the people, especially the women, flung themselves headlong from the top to the bottom of the Acropolis.

None knew of Hamilcar's designs; he lived alone in his tent, with no one near him but a young boy, never admitting anyone, not even Narr' Havas, to eat with them. Nevertheless, he showed him much deference since Hanno's defeat; and the king of the Numidians had too much interest in becoming his son to be distrustful.

This inaction veiled crafty plans. By all sorts of artifices he won over the chiefs of the villages; and the Mercenaries were hunted, repulsed, and tracked like wild beasts. As soon as they entered a wood, the trees were fired about them, the waters of the springs they drank from were poisoned; they were walled up in caverns wherein they had taken refuge to sleep. People who had formerly protected them, even their recent accomplices, now pursued them; they could always recognise in these bands Carthaginian armour.

Numbers of the Mercenaries' faces were consumed with red-tetter; this they thought had attacked them from touching Hanno. Others imagined it was because they had eaten the fish of Salammbô; and, far from repenting, they dreamed of yet more abominable sacrileges, that the humiliation of the Punic gods might be yet greater. They would have liked to exterminate them.

Thus, for three months, they lingered wearily along the eastern coast, from behind the mountain of Selloum, and as far as the first sands of the desert, seeking a place of refuge, no matter where. Utica and Hippo-Zarytus alone had not betrayed them; but alas, Hamilcar surrounded both of these cities. Then they went to the north at hazard, without knowing the roads. By stress of miseries, their brains were disturbed.

Their only sentiment was one of exasperation, which continued developing itself. One day they found themselves again in the gorges of Cobus, once more before Carthage! Then the engagements multiplied. Fortune favoured neither side; both armies were so worn out that they wished, instead of skirmishing, to engage in a great pitched battle, provided that it should certainly be the last.

Mâtho was desirous of carrying the challenge himself to the Suffet. However, one of his Libyans devoted himself to the mission. At his departure all were firmly convinced that he would never return to them.

He returned the same evening.

Hamilcar accepted the challenge. They would meet the next day at sunrise, on the plain of Rhades.

The Mercenaries wanted to know if he had said anything more, and the Libyan added:

—"As I stood before him, he asked me why I waited. I answered,—'To be killed!' Then he replied:—'No! go now; that shall be to-morrow, with the rest.'"

This generosity astonished the Barbarians; some were terrified at it, and Mâtho regretted that the envoy had not been killed.

Mâtho's army still contained three thousand Africans, twelve hundred Greeks, fifteen hundred Campanians, two hundred Iberians, four hundred Etruscans, five hundred Samnites, forty Gauls, and a band of Naffurs— Nomad bandits met with in the date region: all told, seven thousand two hundred and nineteen soldiers; but not one complete syntagma. They stopped up the holes in their breastplates with the shoulder-blades of animals, and they replaced their brass cothurnes with ragged sandals. Copper or iron plates weighed down their garments; their coats-of-mail hung in tatters about them, revealing scars that seemed like purple threads, between the hair on their arms and faces.

The resentment for their dead comrades came back upon their souls, and increased their energy. They felt confusedly that they were the ministers of a god who dwelt in the hearts of the oppressed, like the pontiffs of a universal vengeance! Then the misery of an exorbitant injustice enraged them, especially as they gazed at Carthage on the horizon. They swore the most solemn oaths to fight for one another to the death.

They slaughtered the beasts of burden, eating as much as possible in order to gain strength; afterward they slept. Some prayed, turning toward different constellations.

The Carthaginians arrived first on the battle-field. They rubbed the faces of their shields with oil, to make the arrows glance off more easily; the foot-soldiers who had long hair prudently cut it off close over the forehead; and Hamilcar, as early as the fifth hour, ordered his men to overturn all the bowls, knowing the disadvantage of entering a battle with too full stomachs. His army consisted of fourteen thousand men, about double the entire number of the Barbarians. Still he had never been more anxious: if he succumbed, it would certainly be the annihilation of the Republic, and he would perish on the cross; if he triumphed, on the contrary, he would conquer Italy by the Pyrenees, Gaul, and the Alps, and the empire of the Barcas would become eternal. Twenty times during the night he got up to inspect everything personally, even to the most minute details. As for the Carthaginians, they were exasperated by the prolonged terror.

Narr' Havas doubted the fidelity of his Numidians; furthermore, the Barbarians might conquer them; a strange weakness possessed him, and every moment he drank large cups of water.

A man whom he did not know opened his tent and placed on the ground a crown of rock salt, ornamented with hieratic designs made in sulphur and lozenges of mother-of-pearl. Sometimes a marriage-crown was sent to a betrothed husband as a proof of love or manner of invitation.

Nevertheless, Hamilcar's daughter had no affection for Narr' Havas. The memory of Mâtho embarrassed her in an intolerable way; it seemed to her that the death of this man could alone clear her thoughts: like seeking to cure the sting of a viper by crushing the viper on the wound.

The king of the Numidians was at her disposal. He waited impatiently for his wedding, and as it was to follow the victory Salammbô had sent him this present in order to inspire his courage. Then his distress disappeared, and he thought only of the happiness of possessing so beautiful a woman.

The same vision had assailed Mâtho; but he rejected it at once; and his love, which he drove back, was expended on his comrades-in-arms. He cherished them like a portion of his own person—aye, of his hate—and he felt his spirit loftier, his arm more powerful; all that he must do appeared now clearly before him. If occasionally sighs escaped from him, it was because he recalled the fate of Spendius.

He ranged the Barbarians in six equal ranks, stationing the Etruscans in the centre, all fastened to one bronze chain; the archers were kept in the rear, and on the wings he distributed the Naffur, mounted on short-haired camels covered with ostrich plumes.

The Suffet arranged his soldiers in similar order; outside of the infantry, beside the velites, he placed the Clinabarians, and beyond them the Numidians. When day appeared, the two armies were thus drawn up in line of battle, face to face. All looked at each other with large, wild eyes. At first, there was some hesitation; at length the two armies moved. The Barbarians advanced slowly, to avoid getting out of breath, beating the ground with their feet. The centre of the Punic army formed a convex curve. Then came a terrible shock, like the crashing of two fleets in collision. The first rank of the Barbarians was soon opened, and the archers, sheltered behind the others, hurled their balls, arrows, and javelins. Meanwhile, the curve of the Punic army gradually straightened: it became a straight line, then curved inwards; next, the two sections of velites approached each other in parallel lines like the branches of closing compasses.

The Barbarians, charging the phalanx furiously, entered into the break: they were losing themselves. Mâtho halted them, and whilst the Carthaginian wings continued to advance he commanded the three interior ranks of his army to retire outwardly; soon they overlapped his flanks; his army then appeared in a long line of three ranks. But the Barbarians placed at the extremities were the weakest, especially those on the left, who had exhausted their quivers; and the troop of velites, which had at last come up against them, slaughtered them freely.

Mâtho drew them back. His right wing contained the Campanians, armed with battle-axes; these he pushed against the left of the Carthaginians; the centre forces attacked the enemy, and those on the other extremity, out of danger, kept the velites at bay.

Then Hamilcar divided his cavalry into squadrons, set the hoplites between them, and let them charge the Mercenaries.

These conical masses presented a front of horses, and their broader sides bristled with lances. It was impossible for the Barbarians to resist, for only the Greek foot-soldiers were equipped in brazen-armour, all the rest being merely armed with cutlasses on the end of poles, scythes taken from the farmhouses, and swords made from the felloes of wheels; the blades, too soft, bent in striking, and while they were straightening them under their heels, the Carthaginians easily massacred them right and left.

But the Etruscans, riveted to their chain, did not swerve. Those who were slain, unable to fall, made a barrier with their corpses; and this vast line of bronze alternately spread out and closed in, supple as a serpent, and as impregnable as a wall. The Barbarians came behind it to re-form, took breath for a minute, and rushed on again, with their shattered weapons in their hands.

Many already were weaponless, and they sprang upon the Carthaginians, biting them in their faces like rabid dogs. The Gauls with pride stripped off their tunics, showing from afar their fine, large, white bodies, and endeavoured to terrify the enemy by enlarging their wounds. In the midst of the Punic syntagma, the voice of the crier repeating the orders was no longer heard. The standards above the dust repeated their signals, and everyone was swept along, impelled by the movement of the vast mass surrounding him.

Hamilcar commanded the Numidians to advance, but the Naffurs precipitated themselves to meet the encounter. These men, habited in ample black robes, with a tuft of hair on the top of their heads, carrying rhinoceros leather shields, wielded a blade without haft, held by a rope; and their camels, stuck all over with feathers, gave vent to long, loud, gurgling plaints. Their blades fell in exact places, and then were lifted up with a sharp stroke, each time carrying off a limb. The fierce camels galloped through the syntagma; those with broken legs hopped awkwardly, like wounded ostriches.

The entire Punic infantry fell again on the Barbarians, and broke their line. Their maniples wheeled, separating one from another. The more glittering Carthaginian weapons encircled them like crowns of gold; a swarming agitation filled the centre; the sun shone down on them, tipping the sword-points with white, dancing gleams. Files of the slain Clinabarians lay stretched on the plain; the Mercenarians stripped off their armour and put it on themselves; then they returned to the combat. The Carthaginians, deceived, constantly entangled themselves in the midst of them. Stupefaction kept them motionless, or else they fell back and the triumphant cheers which arose from a distance seemed to drive them like derelicts in a storm. Hamilcar was in despair, for all was going to be wrecked by the genius of Mâtho and the invincible courage of the Mercenaries!

A noise of tambourines rang out on the horizon. It was a crowd of old men, invalids, and youths fifteen years old, and even women, who, no longer able to restrain their anxiety, had left Carthage. In order to place themselves under the protection of something formidable, they had taken out of Hamilcar's park the only elephant left to the Republic—the one whose trunk had been cut off.

Then it seemed to the Carthaginians that their country, abandoning her walls, came to command them to die valiantly for her. Redoubled fury seized upon them, and the Numidians led on all the others.

In the middle of the plain the Barbarians were standing with their backs to a hillock. They had no chance of success, nor even of surviving; but they were the best, the most intrepid, and the strongest.

The people of Carthage began to throw over the Numidians' heads, spits, larding-pins, and hammers; and those who had made consuls tremble died beneath sticks thrown by women: the Punic populace was exterminating the Mercenaries.

The Barbarians took refuge on the top of the hill: their circle at every fresh breach closed in. Twice they descended, but at each encounter were repulsed, and the Carthaginians, pell-mell, extended their arms, and reached out their spears between their comrades' legs, and thrust at random in front of them. They slipped in the blood, and the steep decline of the hill caused the corpses to roll down. The elephant, in trying to climb the beleaguered hill, trod upon them up to his belly, and seemed to spread himself over them with delight. The large end of his amputated trunk from time to time was lifted up like an enormous blood-sucker.

All halted. The Carthaginians ground their teeth as they contemplated the top of the hill, where the Barbarians held their position, standing firmly; finally, they rallied, and charged abruptly forward: the fray began again.

Often the Mercenaries allowed the enemy to approach near, crying out that they would surrender, then with frightful sneers, at one blow they killed themselves; and as the dead fell, others jumped on them to defend themselves. The hill became like a pyramid that gradually grew higher.

Soon only fifty Barbarians were left, then twenty, then but three, then two only survived—a Samnite armed with an axe, and Mâtho, who still had his sword.

The Samnite, bent on his haunches, swung his axe from right to left, constantly warning Mâtho of blows directed at him: "Master! this way! that way! stoop down!"

Mâtho had lost his shoulder-pieces, helmet, and breastplate; he was completely naked, and more livid than the dead; his hair was perfectly erect, the corners of his mouth were covered with froth, and his sword whirled with such speed, that it made an aureole about him. A stone shattered it close up to the guard; the Samnite was killed; the mass of Carthaginians closed in; they were touching him. Then he raised his empty hands toward the sky, closed his eyes, and with arms thrown wide open, like a man about to leap from the summit of a promontory into the sea, he hurled himself into the midst of the lances.

The foe scattered before him. Frequently he rushed against the Carthaginians; but they always recoiled, turning aside their weapons.

Mâtho's foot struck against a sword, and as he bent to seize it, he felt himself trammelled by the wrists and knees, and he fell.

Narr' Havas had followed him for some time, step by step, with a large net used for trapping wild beasts, and taking advantage of the moment when Mâtho bent he ensnared him in it.

He was then fastened on the elephant's back, his four limbs cross-wise, and all those who were not wounded escorted him, hurrying with great tumult towards Carthage.

The news of this victory had already travelled there—an inexplicable thing—as early as the third hour of the night, and the water-clock of Khamoûn marked the fifth hour as they reached Malqua. Then Mâtho reopened his eyes; there were so many lights in the houses that the town appeared to be all in flames.

An immense clamour came dimly to him, and lying on his back he gazed at the stars.

Then a door closed, and darkness enveloped him.

The following day, at the same hour, the last of the men who had remained in the Pass of the Battle-axe expired.

The day that their comrades had departed, some Zuæces who were returning home had rolled away the rocks, and had supplied them with food for some time.

The Barbarians always expected to see Mâtho appear—and they would not leave the mountain, from dejection, from weakness, and that obstinacy of sick men who refuse to stir. At length, the provisions were exhausted, and the Zuæces went away. It was known that they numbered hardly thirteen hundred, and that there was no need to employ soldiers to make an end of them.

Wild beasts, especially lions, in the three years of the war had greatly multiplied. Narr' Havas made an extensive bushbeat, then chasing them, after having baited them by tethering goats at regular distances, he had drawn them into the Pass of the Battle-axe; and all these animals were still living there when the man arrived who had been sent by the Elders to find out what was left of the Barbarians.

Over the extent of the plain lions and corpses were mixed with clothing and armour. From almost all, the face, or else an arm, was missing. Some appeared still untouched; others were completely dried up, and the dusty skulls filled the helmets; fleshless feet stuck straight out of the graves; skeletons still wore their mantles; bones bleached by the sun made shining patches on the sand.

The lions rested, their chests against the ground, their two fore-paws stretched out, blinking their eyes in the glare of daylight, which was intensified by its reflection from the white rocks. Others, sitting on their haunches, stared fixedly before them, or, half lost in their profuse manes, slept, rolled up like a ball. All appeared to be satiated, wearied, and dull. They were as motionless as the mountain, or as the dead. Night was falling; wide red bands streaked the western sky.

In one of the heaps irregularly embossing the plain, something more weird than a spectre arose; then one of the lions began to move, cutting with his monstrous form a black shadow on the background of the purple sky. When he got near to the man he felled him with a single blow of his paw. Then, stretched flat on his belly, he slowly drew out the entrails.

Afterwards he opened his jaws wide, and for some minutes uttered a long, deep roar, which reëchoed in the mountains, and was finally lost in the solitude.

All at once gravel rolled from above; then came the pattering of rapid steps, and from the side of the portcullis and from the gorge appeared pointed snouts and straight ears, with yellow gleaming eyeballs. These were the jackals, coming to devour the remains.

The Carthaginian who leaned over the edge of the precipice, returned to Carthage.

XV

Mâtho

In carthage there was joy—a deep, universal, uncontrolled, frantic joy. The statues of the gods had been repainted, the holes in the ruins repaired, and the streets strewn with branches of myrtle; at the corners of the streets incense burned; and the multitude, crowding on the terraces in their motley apparel, resembled masses of flowers blooming in the air.

The continual din of voices was dominated by the cry of the water-carriers as they sprinkled the pavements. Hamilcar's slaves, in his name, distributed roasted barley and pieces of raw meat. People accosted each other, and embraced in tears; the Tyrian towns were taken, the Nomads were dispersed, and all the Barbarians annihilated. The Acropolis was hidden beneath coloured canopies; the beaks of the triremes, drawn up outside of the mole, glittered like a bank of diamonds; everywhere there was a feeling of order reëstablished, a new existence beginning. A vast happiness spread over all! it was the wedding day of Salammbô and the king of the Numidians.

On the terrace of the temple of Khamoûn, gigantic gold plate covered three long tables, where the priests, the Elders, and the Rich were to sit; and a fourth table, still higher, was arranged for Hamilcar, Narr' Havas, and Salammbô: for by the restoration of the Zaïmph she had saved her country, therefore the people made her wedding a national rejoicing, and on the square below they awaited her appearance.

But another longing, much keener, excited their impatience; the death of Mâtho was promised for this ceremony.

It had been at first proposed to flay him alive, to run molten lead into his bowels, or to starve him to death; others wished to attach him to a tree with a monkey fastened behind him, to beat his brains out with a stone— for he had offended Tanit, and it was but just that the cynocephales of Tanit should avenge her. Some advised placing him on the back of a dromedary, and after having inserted in various parts of his body flaxen wicks steeped in oil, that he should be paraded about; and they were amused at the idea of the large animal wandering through the streets with this man writhing under the fire, like a lighted candelabrum blown about by the wind.

But to which of the citizens should his torture be committed, and why disappoint the others? They desired to find a mode of death wherein the entire city could participate, that all hands, all weapons, all things Carthaginian, even to the paving stones of the streets, and the water of the gulf, should unite to rend him, crush him, annihilate him. Therefore the Elders decided that he shoud go from his prison to the square of Khamoûn without any escort, his arms fastened behind his back; the people were forbidden to strike him to the heart, as it was desired to prolong his life; or to put out his eyes, for they would have him see his torture until the end; or to hurl anything against his person, or strike him with more than three fingers at a single blow.

Although he was not to appear until the close of the day, frequently the crowd fancied they caught sight of him, and they would rush toward the Acropolis, deserting the streets: then they returned with a prolonged murmur. Since the previous day many people had remained standing in the same places, and from a distance called out to each other, displaying their finger-nails, which they had let grow long to more surely lacerate the victim's flesh. Others walked about restlessly. Some were pale, as if they awaited their own execution.

Suddenly, behind the Mappals, great feather fans rose above the heads. It was Salammbô leaving her palace: a sigh of relief went forth.

But the cortège occupied a long time coming, moving step by step.

First defiled the priests of the *Dii-Patæci*, then those of Eschmoûn, and of Melkarth, successively followed by all the other colleges, with the same insignia and in the same order as they had observed at the time of the procession to the sacrifice. The pontiffs of Moloch passed by with heads bent, and the multitude, as in a kind of remorse, shrank back from them. But the priests of the Rabbetna advanced with a proud step, their lyres in their hands: the priestesses, wearing transparent robes of yellow or black, followed, uttering cries like birds, writhing like vipers, or to the sound of flutes they whirled about, imitating the dance of the stars, and their light, fluttering vestments wafted delicate puffs of perfume through the streets. The people wildly applauded. Among these women were hailed with applause the Kedeschim with their painted eyelids, symbolic of the hermaphrodism of the Divinity; perfumed and clothed like the women, they resembled them, in spite of their flat breasts and their narrower hips.

The female principle dominated, overpowering all else. A mystic voluptuousness floated in the heavy air; already the torches were lighted in the depths of the sacred woods, for during the night a grand debauchery would be held there—three vessels had brought courtesans from Sicily, and others had come from the desert.

As the various colleges arrived they took their places in the courts of the temple, on the outer galleries, or on the length of the double stairway that ascended against the walls, meeting at the top. Rows of white robes appeared between the colonnades, and the entire architecture was peopled with human statues, motionless as stone.

After the priests came the masters of finance, the governors of provinces, and all the Rich. Below, surged a vast tumult. From the neighbouring streets the crowd poured forth; the sacred slaves beat them back with their staves; and then, in the midst of the Elders, crowned with gold tiaras, Salammbô appeared upon a litter, over which a purple canopy was borne.

A tremendous shout arose; the cymbals and castanets sounded louder and louder, and the tambourines thundered as the grand purple canopy passed out of sight between the two gate-towers.

It reappeared on the first landing. Salammbô walked slowly beneath it; then she crossed the terrace to take her seat at the back part, on a throne carved out of a tortoise shell. An ivory stool with three steps was placed under her feet; on the edge of the first step two Negro children kneeled, and occasionally she rested her arms, which were weighted with heavy bracelets, upon their heads.

From her ankles to her hips she was enveloped in a network of tiny links, in imitation of the scales of a fish, and lustrous as polished mother-of-pearl. A blue zone clasped her waist, allowing her breasts to be seen through two crescent-shaped slashes, where carbuncle pendants hid the nipples. Her headdress was made of peacocks' plumage, starred with jewels; a wide, ample mantle, white as snow, fell behind her—her elbows were close against her body; her knees pressed together; circlets of diamonds were clasped on her arms; she sat perfectly upright in a hieratic attitude.

Her father and the bridegroom occupied lower seats. Narr' Havas was robed in a golden-coloured simarre, and wore his crown of rock-salt, from beneath which escaped two locks of hair, twisted like the horns of Ammon; Hamilcar was attired in a tunic of violet, brocaded with golden vine leaves, and wore his battle-sword girt to his side. In the space enclosed by the tables, the python of the temple of Eschmoûn lay on the ground between puddles of rose-oil; biting its tail, it described a large black circle, in the centre of which was a copper column supporting a crystal egg, and as the sun shone upon it, prismatic rays emitted on all sides.

Behind Salammbô spread the priests of Tanit, in flaxen robes. At her right the Elders, bedecked with their tiaras, formed a great golden line. On the left, the Rich, with their emerald sceptres, made a long green line; and in the extreme background the priests of Moloch were ranged, and seemed, because of their mantles, like a purple wall. The other colleges occupied the lower terraces. The multitude filled the streets or were mounted on the house-tops, and reached in long rows to the summit of the Acropolis.

Having thus the people at her feet, the firmament above her head, and around her the immensity of the sea, the gulf, the mountains, and the distant provinces, Salammbô, resplendent, seemed one with Tanit, and herself the prevailing genius of Carthage—its soul incarnate.

The festival was to last all night, and candelabra with many branches were planted like trees on the painted woollen tapestries that covered the low tables. Large flagons of electrum, amphoras of blue glass, tortoise-shell spoons, and small round loaves, crowded between the double row of plates bordered with pearls; clusters of grapes with their leaves like thyrsi entwined vine-stocks; blocks of snow were melting on ebony salvers; lemons, pomegranates, gourds, and watermelons, were piled in hillocks beneath the tall, massive argentries; wild boars with open jaws wallowed in the dust of spices; hares cooked whole, covered with fur, seemed to leap among the flowers; shells were filled with forced-meat; pastries were in symbolic forms; and when the dish-covers were removed doves flew out.

Meanwhile, slaves with their tunics tucked up moved about on tip-toe; from time to time the lyres sounded a hymn, or a chorus of voices arose. The hum of the people, continuous like the roar of the sea, floated vaguely over the feast, and seemed to lull it in a vast harmony. Many recalled the banquet of the Mercenaries; they abandoned themselves to dreams of happiness; the sun now began to decline, and the crescent moon was already rising in another part of the sky.

Salammbô turned her head, as if some one had called her; the concourse, who watched her every movement, followed the direction of her gaze.

At the summit of the Acropolis the door of the dungeon, cut in the rock at the foot of the temple, had just opened; a man stood on the threshold of this black hole.

He came forth bent double, with the frightened air of a captive wild beast suddenly set free. The light dazzled him; he remained some minutes motionless. All had recognised him, and they held their breath.

The body of this victim was for the populace something specially their own, imbued with a splendour almost religious.

They leaned forward, straining to see him, particularly the women, who burned to look upon the one who had caused the death of their children and husbands; yet, despite themselves, in the depths of their souls there arose an infamous curiosity—a desire to know him completely, a longing blended with remorse, which turned into an excess of execration.

Finally he advanced; the bewilderment of surprise vanished. Numberless arms were raised, and for the moment he was lost to sight.

The stairway of the Acropolis had sixty steps; he descended them, as if he were rolled in a torrent from the top of a mountain. Thrice he was seen to bound, then at the bottom he came down on his feet.

His shoulders bled, his chest heaved with deep pulsations, and he made such efforts to break the shackles, that his arms, which were crossed on his naked loins, swelled like the coils of a serpent.

The place into which he now walked presented many streets. Along each street a triple-barrier of bronze chains, attached to the navel of the *Dii-Patæci*, extended in parallel lines from end to end. The crowd was packed against the walls and houses; in the midst of the throng, the slaves of the Elders moved about, brandishing whip-thongs.

One of these pushed Mâtho before him with a powerful blow; he began to move forward.

The people stretched out their arms beyond the chains, shouting that he had been allowed too wide a path. He passed along, struck, pricked, mangled by all these revengeful fingers; when he reached the end of one street another appeared. Sometimes he threw himself to the side, striving to bite his tormentors; they would quickly draw back, and when the chains restrained him, they would burst out in peals of laughter.

A child tore his ear; a young girl concealing under her sleeve a spindle, with the point of it slit his cheek; they pulled out handfuls of his hair, tore strips from his flesh, and others held sticks on which were fastened sponges saturated in filth, with which they buffeted his face.

A stream of blood gushed from the right side of his throat; immediately a frenzy began. This last Barbarian represented to them all the Barbarians, all the army; they took revenge on him for all their disasters, terrors and shame. The rage of the people increased with its gratification; the chains strained too tight as they leaned against them, threatening to part asunder. They were insensible to the blows the slaves dealt to force them back; some clung to the projections of the houses; all the openings in the walls were choked up by heads, and the evil they were incapable of doing to his person they howled upon him.

Their maledictions teemed with atrocities of obscene abuse, with ironical encouragements and imprecations; and as they were dissatisfied with his present agonies they prophesied to him others more terrible yet for eternity.

This vast howling filled Carthage with a stupid monotony. Often a single syllable, one intonation, harsh, profound, frantic, would be repeated for several minutes by the entire people. The walls vibrated from top to bottom, and both sides of the streets seemed to Mâtho to come against him, and rise from the ground like two immense arms, which suffocated him in the air.

He remembered that he had previously experienced something similar. There was the same crowd on the terraces, the same fierce looks, the same rage; but then he walked at liberty—all scattered before him, for the power of a god shielded him. This memory, gradually becoming distinct, brought to him a crushing sadness. Shadows passed before his eyes. The town whirled in a vertigo through his brain; blood streamed from a wound in his thigh; he felt himself to be dying; his legs doubled under him, and he sank gently upon the pavement.

Some of his persecutors took from a tripod in the peristyle of the temple of Melkarth a red-hot bar, slipped it under the first chain, and pressed it against his wound. The flesh was seen to smoke; the yells of the people drowned his voice; again he stood up and advanced.

Six paces farther on, and a third, and yet a fourth time he fell: always some new torture goaded him up and on. Boiling oil was squirted through tubes upon him; fragments of broken glass were strewn under his feet; still he continued to walk. At the corner of the street of Satheb he leaned beneath the pent-house of a shop, with his back against the wall, and moved no farther.

The slaves of the Council struck him with whips of hippopotamus hide so furiously and long that the fringes of their tunics were soaked with sweat. Mâtho appeared insensible. Suddenly he started to run at random, emitting from his lips a shuddering noise, like one suffering from intense cold. Thus he passed through the streets of Boudès, the street of Sœpo, crossed the vegetable-market, and came into the square of Khamoûn.

From this point he belonged to the priests, and the Elders' slaves scattered the crowd; here he had more space. Mâtho gazed around him, and his eyes encountered Salammbô.

At the first step that he had taken she had risen; then involuntarily, according as he drew nearer, she had advanced gradually to the edge of the terrace. Soon, for her, all other external things were effaced: she saw only Mâtho. A silence possessed her soul, one of those abysses wherein the whole world disappears under the impression of a single thought, of one memory —of one look. This man who was walking toward her fascinated her.

There remained nothing except his eyes which retained a human appearance; he was a long form completely red; his broken bonds, hanging the length of his thighs, were so bloody that they could no longer be distinguished from the tendons of his wrists, denuded of flesh; his mouth remained open; from his orbits issued two flames, which had the appearance of mounting to his hair—and yet this wretched creature still moved on.

He arrived at the foot of the terrace. Salammbô was leaning over the balustrade; those frightful eyeballs were staring at her; and within her awoke the consciousness of all that he had suffered for her. Although he was now agonised in his death-agony, she saw him in his tent, on his knees as he encircled her waist with his arms, babbling sweet speeches; she yearned to feel those arms again, and hear those words. She did not desire him to die. At this moment Mâtho was seized with a great tremor. She was about to shriek out, when he fell backward to the earth, and moved no more.

Salammbô almost swooned; she was carried back to her throne by the priests who pressed around her. They congratulated her: it was her work. All clapped their hands and stamped their feet, and yelled her name in universal acclamation.

A man darted upon the corpse; although he was beardless, he wore on his shoulders the mantle of the priests of Moloch, and in his belt a sort of knife used to cut up the sacred meat, the haft terminating in a golden spatula.

By a single stroke he split open Mâtho's chest, tore out his heart, and placed it on the spatula; and Schahabarim—for it was he—raised his arm, offering it to the Sun.

The sun was sinking behind the waves; his rays fell like long arrows athwart the crimson heart. He sank beneath the sea as the throbbing diminished and as the last pulsation disappeared. Then from the gulf to the Lagoon, and from the isthmus to the lighthouse, in all the streets, over all the house-tops, and over all the temples, there went forth a single cry; sometimes it paused, only to be renewed; the edifice trembled—Carthage was convulsed in the spasm of a Titanic joy, and a boundless hope.

Narr' Havas, intoxicated with pride, passed his left arm about Salammbô's waist, in sign of possession; and in the right hand he took a gold patera, and drank to the genius of Carthage.

Salammbô arose, like her consort, grasping a cup in her hand, to drink also. She fell, with her head lying over the back of the throne, pallid, stiff, her lips parted—and her loosened hair hung to the ground.

Thus died Hamilcar's daughter, for having touched the Veil of Tanit.

THE TEMPTATION OF
SAINT ANTHONY

THE TEMPTATION OF
SAINT ANTHONY

PART I

EVENING, on a mountain; desert on the horizon; to the right hand is S. Anthony's hut; near the door is a bench; to the left is a small chapel. A lamp is hung thereto above a painting of the Blessed Virgin.
In front of the hut, on the ground, are a few baskets of palm-leaves.
In a cleft of the rock lies the hermit's pig, asleep in the shade.
S. Anthony is alone, seated on the bench, busy with his baskets. He raises his head and looks at the sun.

S. ANTHONY. Enough have I laboured so. Let us to prayer. [He moves towards the chapel, then pauses.] Yet a little and it will be the hour. When the shadow of the cross shall touch yonder stone, then will I begin my prayers.
[He paces slowly up and down, his arms hanging loose.]
The sky paleth. The gier eagle wheeleth hither and thither, the palm-trees shiver, anon will the moon rise, . . . and to-morrow? the sun will return! then will he set. And ever thus, ever. I, I shall awake, I shall pray, I shall finish these baskets that I deliver unto the shepherds that they may bring me bread. Then shall I pray, shall I awaken, . . . and ever thus, ever. . .
[He sighs.]
Ah God! do the rivers weary them of the flow of their waters? Doth the sea tire of beating upon her shores? Have the trees that writhe in the great winds no longing to depart with the birds that raze their topmost boughs? [He looks at the shadow of the cross.] Yet the breadth of two sandals, and it will be the hour for prayer; it must be so.
[A tortoise crawls out from between the rocks, S. Anthony looks at it.]
Of a truth the beast is most fair to look upon.
[He then drowses.]
I am greatly wearied to-night. My hair-shirt doth irk me; how heavy it is!
[He turns round and perceives the shadow of the cross; it is past the rock.]
Ah! woe on me! what have I done? up, up, make speed!
[He strikes two pebbles together and kindles a dry leaf and lights the little lamp, which he then hangs up again on the wall; the night is almost fully come; he kneels down.]
There be they that pray for this alone that it pleaseth them to pray, that humble them for the sake of lowliness; but I? is it for need or for duty? enough, enough, away with these thoughts.
Hail, Mary, fulfilled of grace. How greatly do I love Thee! wherefore might I not have walked in the dust of the roadway, and followed Thy long floating blue veil what time, to the measured pace of the ass whereon Thou didst fare, it rose behind Thee and disappeared under the plane-trees.

[He breaks off; the tortoise moves forward, the pig wakes up.]

Ah! the face of Her! it is as though I had never beheld it! I would it were larger.

A VOICE. [Murmuring, almost inaudible.] Raised up on high, so wouldest thou?

S. ANTHONY. [Starts.] Who speaketh? [He listens.] Nay, it was my thought.

THE VOICE. [Again.] Raised up on high, graven outward even as an image that thou mightest seize it with thine hands.

S. ANTHONY. Art Thou not the Beloved of them that know no love?

THE VOICE. Pray unto Her, Anthony, and She shall love thee; lo, She maketh sign unto thee.

[The picture shakes.]

S. ANTHONY. Nay! She moved; peradventure it was the wind.

THE VOICE. Ay, the wind of the evening that bloweth from the hot seas.

S. ANTHONY. Accursed be it if it soften the heart of the solitary!

THE VOICE. What? art thou not humble, art thou not pure, art thou not strong?

S. ANTHONY. I?

THE VOICE. Ay, thou. Thou hast despised all joys, all feasting, all women, the sound of the chariots and the praises of the multitude.

S. ANTHONY. [Smiling.] It is truth; naught that tempted other men hath beguiled me.

[He sets him again to prayer.]

THE PIG. I behold my lusty body in the pools as it were in a mirror; I delight to look upon myself. My paws are lean, mine ears are long, mine eyes are small, my belly is fat.

THE VOICE. [Stronger.] Noah was drunk with wine, Jacob lied, Moses doubted, Solomon was found wanting, Peter denied, but thou? . . .

S. ANTHONY. Wherewithal should I be drunken? To whom should I lie? Did I doubt, then should I not be here; less than any other have I failed; never have I denied the Lord.

THE PIG. In very truth I see no beast created that exceedeth mine own self in worth.

[Vague shadows appear deep down in the scene; whisperings are heard; the wind blows, the lamp sways.]

S. ANTHONY. [Resuming his prayers.] Blessed art Thou among all women.

THE VOICE. [Repeats.] All women.

S. ANTHONY. May Thy name . . .

THE VOICE. Softer than a kiss, sorrowful as a sigh. . . .

S. ANTHONY. Mary, Mary.

THE VOICE. See Her delicate eyelashes that lower, Her hands white as altar candles; Her eyes roll, Her lips tremble.

[A gust of wind tears off the picture of the Blessed Virgin, who rises up, tall as a living woman.]

S. ANTHONY. Lo! Lo! She waxeth great! what is this aileth me?

THE VOICE. Nought. It is a woman.

S. ANTHONY. [Striking his brow.] The thought of it!

THE VOICE. See.

S. ANTHONY. Lo! She casteth back Her head; Her loins writhe.

THE VOICE. Ay, and Her locks fly forth. . . . Ah! the long locks, the locks of gold! breathe in their sweetness, kiss them!

S. ANTHONY. Enough! enough! In the name of the Lord depart, thou vision of hell!

[All disappears. The pig groans. S. Anthony gazes into the distance melancholy.]

(VARIANT: *Note: The 1856 MS. contains the following variant, on a page gummed to p. 5.*)

THE VOICE. [Resumes.] One night—it was at the City of the Sun, on the Nile—thou didst watch, even as now, hearkening to the clear fall into the porphyry basons of the fountains that the lions blew from out their nostrils; two torches there were, two torches at a bed-head, and nigh the bed myrrh smoked in a brazen tripod. A long veil stretched out covered a slender shape, and the middle thereof was hollow—even as the soft curve of a wave that giveth place; it swelled gently towards the head thereof, and the straight folds of it flowed down on either side even unto the ground; that was the daughter of Martiallus the quaestor, dead that same morn, the morrow of her wedding day.

As thine eyes passed to and fro upon her, it seemed unto thee now and then that the cloth trembled from one end even to the other, and thou didst step three paces forward to look upon her face, thou liftedst the veil.

The funeral wreath was knotted tightly; it girt her ivory forehead; her eyeballs waned in the milky colour of her hollow eyes. She seemed to sleep; her mouth was open, for her tongue passed over the edge of her teeth.

And thou saidst unto thyself: but yesterday she was alive, she spake, her arms had held him therein, her unmoving heart had beaten; the very walls still held in their angles the oppression of yesternight and the broken speech thereof.

Thou didst approach, thou didst bow thee above her; upon the right side of her neck was a red spot; thou didst divine it.

Aha! In a myrtle bush the lark cried aloud; the boatmen upon the river took up their song again, and thou didst betake thee once more to prayer.

S. ANTHONY. Ay, ay. I remember.

THE VOICE. The nipples of her breast lifted up her gown.

S. ANTHONY. Yea, and the gold ring on her finger, stricken by the light of one of the torches, it sent forth a great ray. Just such a night as this it was; the air was heavy, my breast failed me.

[*End of Variant.*]

THE VOICE. [Resumes.] Yonder, in the sand, the purple litter doth approach, swaying softly on the black arms of the eunuchs. Within it is the daughter of the consuls, sighing for weariness beneath the great pine-trees of her houses, there is the Lydian woman, worn with weariness, nor hath she desire any more for Adonis; there is the daughter of Judah, disquieted, seeking for her Messias.

S. ANTHONY. [Slowly.] Yea. They are sick.

THE VOICE. They are come to tell thee of their sufferings. Some there be who die for the love of dancers, others that faint at the sound of the flutes, nor say they that it is the dancers that they love, nor is their ravishment by reason of the music. They believe not the oracle, yet have they bent their ear at the edge of the valleys of Thessaly, they have bought of the sorcerers plates of metal that they wear upon their womb. They deny them unto their husbands, they laugh now at the sacrifices, they are weary of all the gods, yet would they know wherefore Mary of Magdalene followed Christ over the ways. Do not the simplest among them ask thee if it sufficeth to cherish his servant that they may please the Crucified?

S. ANTHONY. [Greatly troubled.] Ah! God! is the fault mine? They came and I received them; should I not renew their life unto sinners, strengthen them that believed, convert the idolatrous women?

THE VOICE. Nay, wherefore couldest thou not follow the idolatress in the great hall, and kneel down by the side of her that believed on the cool stones of the sanctuary? But the sinner, the sinner shouldest thou not have forsaken, O Anthony. Little by little wouldest thou have weaned her of men, thou wouldest have taken from off her forehead the purple bands, and snatched from off her breast the prideful necklace, and drawn from off her fingers the heavy rings.

S. ANTHONY. [Wrathful.] Let her pray, let her weep, let her fast, for her the hair-shirt, the thorns!

THE VOICE. She assayeth it, she shutteth her in; lo, she is alone, she hath cast off her raiment, she untieth her shoe-latchet, the hanging urn swayeth shadows upon the whiteness of her naked side. But she dareth not yet, she shuddereth; she taketh the little chain with the barbed points, the blood starteth forth, her eyes grow pale, she swooneth away.

[S. Anthony sighs and stretches out his arms; the pig rubs his belly against the ground. The shapes hardly visible hitherto now begin to grow greater; they are the Seven Deadly Sins—Envy, Avarice, Lust, Anger, Greed, Sloth, Pride. There is an eighth figure, smaller than these—Logic. They hover, like shadows, lightly, all round S. Anthony, and the outline of them is cast forward on to the rocks.]

S. ANTHONY. [Looking at his pig.] What herb hath he eaten that he slavereth in that wise? Yet thou art wont to seem happy, and every morning, when I awaken . . .

ENVY. Others, at that same hour, hear the laughter of children.

S. ANTHONY. [Sighing.] Ay, of a truth!

ENVY. The ants have their brood. On the surface of the waters the dolphins swim together, the male with the female. Hast thou seen the wandering she-wolves that gallop in the forest, bearing their young in their jaws?

S. ANTHONY. But I—I am more solitary than the wild beasts in the woods or the monsters underneath the sea.

LOGIC. Who desired it? Who constraineth thee?

ENVY. Thou sufferest, thou art athirst. Others even now lie upon ivory beds and eat snow in silver saucers.

S. ANTHONY. Yea. Indeed, so is it.

AVARICE. Hadst thou not given thy goods to the poor . . .

GREED. Thou wouldst have cellars full.

IDLENESS. And thou wouldest sleep stretched out upon the fleeces of thy flocks. [Silence.]

ENVY. [Resumes.] Why didst thou not buy the charge of a tax-gatherer at the gate of some bridge? Then wouldest thou have seen, now and then, wayfarers who would have told thee new tidings . . . strangers in curious vesture, soldiers who love laughter.

AVARICE. Thou wouldest have shaped holy images, to sell them unto pilgrims, and thou wouldest have stored the price thereof in a jar, and buried it in the ground, within thy hut.

S. ANTHONY. Nay. Nay. Never.

ANGER. Thou shouldest have had an heavy sword beating against thy bare leg. Then wouldest thou have passed through the dark forests with thy stout comrades; thou wouldest have pitched upon the heath and drunk of the waters of strange lands.

S. ANTHONY. Nay. Nay.

PRIDE. Had not the pride of thy merit cast thee into the ignorance that shutteth thee in, thou wouldest be this day a wise man, a doctor, a master!

LOGIC. Thou wouldest know the cause of eclipses and of sicknesses, the virtue of plants, the reckoning of the stars, the earth, the heavens.

PRIDE. Kings, curious for speech of thee, would make thee sit by their side.

AVARICE. Ay, and they would send thee away laden with great gifts that men would pack in chests.

[Silence.]

LOGIC. [Resumes.] Who hindered thee from being a priest?

PRIDE. Canst thou dream of the unspeakable joy that with words thou canst cause the Most High to come down from Heaven?

LUST. Ay, and shake the hearts of fearful women as it were the wind?

ENVY. Get thee back unto Alexandria, preach unto the converts, make oration in the Councils. . . . Why shouldest not thou, even as any other, be a bishop?

S. ANTHONY. Nay, but the sight of those great followings would affright me—I who at times feel within mine heart infinite doubt to discern what is just.

LOGIC. Ay, so thou sinnest often for lack of counsel.

IDLENESS. Better to have remained among the holy men.

LOGIC. In such wise should a man live happily, be fat and well-liking, and saintly.

S. ANTHONY. [Sighing.] Ay, indeed.

THE SINS. [Repeating, one after the other.] Ay, indeed, indeed.

LOGIC. Bethink thee of thy life as it now is.

S. ANTHONY. Ay, well I know it. Rather is it a death-bed. Howbeit, at times I have had lights of blessedness wherein it seemed unto me . . .

LOGIC [Interrupting him.] Nay, thy memory leadeth thee astray. For happiness, when a man shall turn his head to see it once again, doth bathe its summit in a vapour of gold and seemeth to attain unto the heavens even as the mountains who lengthen their shadows unto the twilight, yet are they none the higher thereby.

S. ANTHONY. [Begins to weep quietly.] Alas, alas! Even as one who would sleep, but lice torment him who passeth his hands about his face, who groaneth and sobbeth, awakened continually in the bosom of the darkness—even so am I aware of somewhat that I may not grasp nor count, that runneth, that returneth, that burneth me, angering me, itching, devouring me. What shall I do, O Lord? whither shall I fly, or where shall I abide? Command me, O Lord. I weep even as a fool who hath been beaten, I turn at random as it were the wheel loosed from a chariot.

LOGIC. Because of thy sufferings art thou lost more and more daily.

S. ANTHONY. How?

LOGIC. On the altar men place candlesticks of gold with flowers in bloom, they shut in the bones of the martyrs beneath fine pearls and topazes. Why then dost thou refuse happiness and spread unceasingly upon thy soul as it were a pall of mourning nor thinkest thou that the heel of God is upon it?

S. ANTHONY. [Abashed.] Is then penance of none avail?

LOGIC. Fret not thyself so greatly for works! What matter deeds! Before the Most High the cedars and the blades of grass are of equal stature. Where then is the worth of thy holiness and the greatness of thy lowliness?

S. ANTHONY. Howbeit . . . the Law. . . .

LOGIC. Do not the Jews say . . . the Law? the Sadducees who preach it, and the Pharisees who sell it? Came not Jesus to destroy it? Said He not that He was the sword? Hath the Law fed the multitudes, or calmed the raging waters, or flamed upon the Mount Tabor? The Law! In the name of the Law were the prophets slain; the Law crucified Jesus, the Law stoned Stephen. Of the Law died Peter and also Paul and all the martyrs. The Law is the curse of the serpent, and the Son of God came to redeem the nations therefrom. The Spirit that was aforetime once imprisoned in Israel is now freed and can be increased at His ease in His fulness. Let Him fly toward the south and toward the north, toward the west and toward the east. For Samaria is no longer accursed; nay, even Babylon hath been raised up from her sadness.

S. ANTHONY. Lord, Lord, I feel as it were a flood arise within me.

LOGIC. Let it rise! It cleanseth thee. [Silence.]

S. ANTHONY. [Trying to collect his ideas.] Howbeit . . . the Son was sent by the Father in order that . . .

LOGIC. Why not the Father by the Son?

S. ANTHONY. He was to come after!

LOGIC. Being created of Him without doubt?

S. ANTHONY. Nay.

LOGIC. Who created the world?

S. ANTHONY. The Father.

LOGIC. And where was the Son then?

[Opposite the Deadly Sins, behind the chapel, appear other shadows, lesser in stature and more numerous.]

And where was the Son then? Was He the Christ inasmuch as Christ was man and men were not? And the Spirit, what did He?

S. ANTHONY. They were one.

LOGIC. One! three Gods!

S. ANTHONY. Nay, they were one.

LOGIC. But inasmuch as Christ Jesus was God albeit He was man, where was God while He lived? What did God when He died? Where was God when He was dead?—for He died.

S. ANTHONY. [Making the sign of the cross.] Yea, and rose again.

LOGIC. But if He was before life was, there was no need that He should rise again, whereby He should once again have being after death. What did He with His mortal body? What befell His human soul? Did He bind it to His Godhead soul? Then would He be a man who should be God, who should be added unto God, a God who should be flesh; and inasmuch as He is but One with the Father and the Spirit, the Father and the Spirit would be flesh and all would be flesh; there would be nought but flesh?

S. ANTHONY. Nay, nay, wholly spirit.

LOGIC. Of a truth, for Christ Jesus is God. But Jesus was born, He ate, walked, slept, suffered and died; can the Spirit be born, doth He eat, doth He walk, can He die? Then did Christ Jesus suffer neither birth nor death—else was He not spirit.

S. ANTHONY. The man in Him it was that suffered.

LOGIC. Ay, not the God, of a surety! Had He been God . . .

S. ANTHONY. Nay, but He was God.

LOGIC. Then did He not suffer, He feigned suffering; He was not born of Mary, He seemed to be born. When they nailed Him upon the cross, He from on high beheld His body that men tormented. When on the third day He raised the stone of His sepulchre, it was as it were a vapour that went forth therefrom—a phantom, who shall say? Thomas doubted, who would touch His wounds; but it was easy for Him to feign wounds, inasmuch as He feigned a body; had it been a real body like unto thine, could He have passed through the walls and been borne to and fro in the firmament? Nay, if it were not a body, if it were not a man. . . . Jesus is indeed Christ? Thou dost not believe that Christ was Melchisedek nor Shem nor Theodotus nor Vespasian?

S. ANTHONY. Yea, Jesus is the Christ.

LOGIC. Ay, and the Christ is Jesus. . . . Howbeit, that He may live He must have a body, He must be, and inasmuch as He had not that body, therefore He was not, and the Christ is a lie.

S. ANTHONY. [Despairing.] Woe is me! In despite of myself hath all this entered into mine head, thought after thought. Pardon me, O Lord, pardon, how evil is it!

LOGIC. [Interrupting him.] What is evil?

S. ANTHONY. [Astonished.] That which is not good.

LOGIC. Ha! thou hast cunning discourse even as that of a Greek! Thou sayest good, evil, ill, well. Now, O wise man, evil is that which is not good, and good is doubtless that which is not evil—and after?

S. ANTHONY. [Irritated.] Nay, nay, evil is that which is forbidden by God.

LOGIC. Of a surety! of such is slaughter of men, adultery, worship of idols, theft, treason, and rebellion against the law. Therefore did He command unto Abraham that he should offer up Isaac who was his son, and unto Judith that she should slay Holofernes who was her lover, unto Jael that she should smite Sisera who was her guest within her tent; therefore commanded He unto all His people that they should make an end of all other nations, that they should slaughter beasts, and rip open the wombs of women in travail; therefore did He cause Abraham to commit fornication with Agar, and Ozeas with the harlot; therefore did Jacob steal from Laban, and Moses spoiled the king of Egypt, and David was the greatest of all robbers; therefore did the dwellers in the city rob the stranger within their gates, and the people of the Lord stole from the cities of their allies and plundered the towns they had overcome; therefore, from the days of Aaron even unto the days of Zedekias men worshipped the brazen serpent, and gave gifts unto Rahab the harlot, and rewarded the traitor of Bethel, and He, even He, sent His son who should destroy the law that He had made. If it were good, wherefore should He overthrow it? and if it were evil, wherefore did He give it? Is there aught good that is not evil or aught evil that is not good? Canst thou say that evil is, or that good is? Is there any truth? Where is untruth? The wise men have searched but have discovered nought, the prophets have spoken but have said nothing; thou shalt do even as they did, and the generations shall do even as thou doest. Tush! fret not thyself for the task, turn thou the mill of life and sing as thou toilest thereat!

S. ANTHONY. What matter to me? Do I know the counsels of God?

LOGIC. Wherefore then dost thou worship in Him what thou wouldest abhor in man, inasmuch as thou dost bow down before evil.

S. ANTHONY. Nay, all evil is in the Evil One.

LOGIC. Who then made the Evil One?

S. ANTHONY. God.

LOGIC. If the Evil One were created of God and the creation went forth from His word then was the word in Him or ever that word were spoken, and before the Evil One came into the world he was in the world, and with him was all his hell: hath he a body?

S. ANTHONY. The Evil One! a body!

LOGIC. Had he a body, he would not be everywhere at one moment, even as is God, Who, being spirit, is in all places at once. But if he be spirit then is he God, nay, rather is he a part of God. But if thou takest away a part from the whole, dost thou not destroy the whole? Wherefore, if thou dost sever from God a part of God, thou deniest God; but thou dost not deny God, thou dost worship God.

[Then Logic, in the shape of a black dwarf, clothed in parchment, with monstrous cock's spurs on his hands and feet, balancing now on one foot, now on the other, upon a rolling globe, bends down to S. Anthony's ear.] Thou dost worship God; worship the Devil!

PRIDE. [Calling out.] Hither, my daughters!

[She appears behind the hermit. Her hair bristles, her eyes are red, her complexion pale; she is of great stature; her eyebrows are raised. A great purple cloak in which she is wrapped hides the ulcers on her legs, and she lowers her chin to look into her bosom at a serpent that is gnawing it. The sound of whistling is heard, of barking, of cymbals ringing, of little bells tinkling; and the Heresies advance, in long separate files, bearing on their heads serpents or flowers, and carrying in their hands whips, books, zodiacs, swords, idols; they wear necklaces of amulets round their necks; their faces are tattooed; they are clad in costumes of Chaldaea, Persia, and India. The faces of some are inflamed like a furnace, others are paler than shadows. There are long-bearded magicians, prophetesses with dishevelled hair, dwarfs that howl. Their breath forms a vapour in the night, and their eyes sparkle even as the eyeballs of wild cats.

They crowd into a mass, climbing upon one another's shoulders; Logic, who beats the measure with a rod of iron, leads their march, and Pride laughs, strident, sneering. S. Anthony in his cell shudders. As they approach, one by one the former shadows appear in their proper shapes and mingle with the group.

First comes Lust, red-haired, white of skin, very fat, clad in a yellow gown enriched with pearls and diamonds. She is blind.

With her emerald-loaded fingers she gently lifts up her gown as far as her ankles.

Follows Greed, thin-necked, with violet lips and blue nose. Her cankered teeth droop on her chin, and her smock, stained with grease and wine, gives to her protruding belly that falls over her thighs. Then Anger, in brazen hauberk, streaming with blood; flames spout from her vizored casque; her arms end in two leaden balls.

Then Envy, with huge ears; she pinches her lips, she gnaws her nails, she scratches her face; she lies down behind all the other Sins, wallows on the earth, and bites their heels.

Then Avarice, an old woman in re-sewn rags; she waves her right hand in the air unceasingly; it has ten fingers. With her left hand she keeps back the pieces of silver that would fall out of her pockets that are full to over-flowing.

Sloth, armless and legless, drags herself painfully along the ground on her belly, sighing.

By now all the Heresies are in a confused throng. The Sins, taller than they, push them on from behind.

Brown clouds roll on to the moon that appears here and there between the rifts in them, and lights up the scene with a greenish glimmer.

The Heresies increase in number, and surround the hut; they come even to the threshold of the chapel; they soften their voices and say:]

Wherefore tremble, good hermit? We are the selfsame thoughts with whom thou didst hold converse but a moment past; fear nought, good Anthony, fear nought.

S. ANTHONY. Ah me! the multitude of them! I fear!

THE PATRICIANISTS. For the flesh, of a surety? Ay, the flesh is evil.

S. ANTHONY. Yea.

THE PATRICIANISTS. By it we are accursed.

S. ANTHONY. Yea, of a truth.

THE PATRICIANISTS. And accursed are we by the Father of the Word, from Whom is all spirit, and Whose enemy is the flesh, even as the Evil One is His enemy. Yet, if He had created it, would He have called His handi-work accursed? Bodies make bodies, Spirit maketh Spirit; therefore hath the Devil made the body and he hath made man; Satan is the author thereof.

THE PATERNIANS. Nay, not wholly! From the breast alone even to the parts below. God hath fashioned the head wherein groweth thought and the heart wherein beateth life. But the Devil hath made the travail of the stomach and the organs of gendering and the longing of the wayfarer that goeth about in the feet.

ONE HERESY. Yea, man is of two parts so far as concerneth his body, and of one only so far as concerneth his spirit; that is to say, three parts in all. Even so God is of three parts whereof the Father is the first, the Son is the second, the Holy Spirit is the third, and the Trinity is the whole thereof.

S. ANTHONY. [Dreamily.] The whole! . . .

THE SABELLIANS. Nay! nay! Father, Son, and Spirit are one and the same person.

S. ANTHONY. [Alert.] Yea! indeed, yea! It is so.

THE SABELLIANS. They are the God-Unity. And forasmuch as the Son hath suffered Who is God, therefore have the Father and the Holy Spirit suffered Who are that same God. [They advance.]

S. ANTHONY. [Drawing back.] Nay! nay!

ALL THE HERESIES. What then is God?

S. ANTHONY. [Dreamily.] God?

AUDIUS. Of His unknown substance He hath drawn forth the worlds and the souls. He is a great spirit who hath a body.

S. ANTHONY. Leave me, leave me!

THE HERESIES. What then is the soul?

S. ANTHONY. [Dreamily.] The soul?

THE TERTULLIANISTS. It is made of flame and of air. It dwelleth in a body, it hath a place, it suffereth in hell pain beyond bearing upon the tongue. But the spirit hath neither seat nor place; it knoweth not pain nor pleasure. God alone is therefore without substance and the soul is indeed a body.

S. ANTHONY. A body! Who hath said this?

TERTULLIAN. [His cloak on his back.] I!

S. ANTHONY. Thou, illustrious Septimus, thou who didst so sternly persecute idolaters! And now art thou clothed even as one of the wise men of the Porch!

TERTULLIAN. Ay, I have written a book thereon; thou shouldest have read it.

THE HERESIES. He is an unbeliever! Shame be upon him!

TERTULLIAN. [Vanishing.] Thou deniest the master! May all light depart from thee!

THE HERESIES. [Ever pressing upon S. Anthony.] But we will not forsake thee; we abide. Who was Christ? Whence came His flesh? Was it man or God?

S. ANTHONY. God! [Correcting himself.] Nay, man!

THE HERESIES. [All together.] That is truth, that is truth!

THE APOLLINARISTS. It was the flesh of the Word and not the flesh of Mary. Should He, the Spirit, have sojourned in the womb of a woman?

THE ANTIDICOMARISTS. Wherefore not?

THE MENANDRIANS, THE CORINTHIANS. Forasmuch as Christ was no more than a wise man!

ARIUS. Horror! Desolation! He was God the Son, created by the Father and Creator Himself of the Holy Spirit.

THE THEODOTISTS. He was Theodotus. There be men that knew him.

THE SETHIANIANS. He was Shem, the son of Noah.

THE GNOSTICS. He was the child of the Ages, the mate of Arhamoth repentant, the Father of the Maker of Nations who made Him who ruleth the world and man.

[S. Anthony stands motionless, bewildered; the Ophites advance; they bear an immense python, gold-coloured with sapphire patches and black patches. That they may uphold him horizontally, the children raise him with straight-stretched arms, the women clasp him to their breast, the men press him against their bellies. They halt before S. Anthony, and with the serpent whom they unfold they form a great semi-circle at whose entrance stands an old man in a white robe, thrumming on a lyre; with him is a naked child playing on the flute an air that is sweet and merry though fully slow in measure.]

THE OPHITES. [Beginning.] He it was! This was known unto Moses!

S. ANTHONY. [Cries out.] Nay! nay! how could that be?

THE OPHITES. Moses knew it, who raised the brazen serpent in the wilderness.

[S. Anthony opens his eyes, stupefied; they recommence.]

His coils are the circles of the worlds; the metals have taken their colours from the patches on his skin; of whatsoever he eateth nothing is rendered, he maketh all of it to be a part of him.

Seated under a terebinth tree, she watched him rise. His slimy body clung fast to the bark and the green leaves were enkindled at his breath.

When he had passed through every branch he appeared again; the bones of his jaw parted, the fruit fell.

He held it upon his teeth, and hanging by his tail to the trunk of the great tree, he swayed his hissing head and his ravished eyelids before the face of Eve.

She gazed eagerly upon him; he stayed him. Her breast heaved, the tail of the serpent writhed, a lotus flower opened, the dates of the palm-trees ripened. She held forth her hand.

It was good, the noble fruit. She gathered up the rind thereof to perfume her bosom.

Had they tasted more fully thereof, they would now be gods, according to the promise of the Tempter.

Be thou worshipped, thou great black serpent, who hast golden spots even as the sky hath stars! Fair serpent whom the daughters of Eve cherish, to the torch of the nail on the tightened chord, awake!; to the murmur of the hollow reed, arouse thee!; swell out thy rings!—up, up, come to our altars and lick the sacred bread that we offer unto the Lord.

[The Ophites enclose S. Anthony in the circle of the serpent. He leaps over it with joined feet. Everything vanishes.]

S. ANTHONY. [Alone, slowly.] Therein was the most abhorred abomination that ever man could think upon! Furthermore, wherefore should the Son of God choose, among all faces, that of yonder cold beast, flat-headed, who seemeth to guard the mystery of evil within the speechlessness of his winding shape? Nay! never could He have wished that, He who was all love and sacrifice. "Take, eat," said He, "this is my body; and drink this," said He. . . .

[A wine-skin falls at the feet of S. Anthony.]

THE ASCITES. [Drunken men and women, running round in a dance.] Hail, wine! overflow, wine! flood the world, wine! Wine is the Christ. When His side was pierced, it was wine that flowed, the wine of the Good Tidings that we honour in this goat-skin.

S. ANTHONY. [Exasperated.] Nay! the very unbelievers never committed such abominable wickedness.

THE SEVERIANS. Nay! never. Wine was born of the strength of Satan. Wine is madness, wine is lust.

THE AQUARIANS. So do we drink nought save water, which is the sign of the Word.

THE ASTOTYRITES. Accursed be the flesh, and they that use it, and they that preach it!

S. ANTHONY. Nay, but I preach it not, I use it not.

[Applause bursts forth behind S. Anthony. He turns round and sees.]

THE MANICHAEANS. [Clothed in black robes, sown with silver moons; in their ears are golden rings; they are very lean and their hair is held up by combs.]

Captive in the matter wherein it gendereth, Godhead. . . .

S. ANTHONY. [Cries out.] Nay! that cannot be!

THE MANICHAEANS. But in the Host, O Anthony, who is the Host? [He bows his head.]

Godhead assayeth to go forth from it, whereby it may be joined again unto its beginning. It escapeth from rest, from doing, from the movement of the hands and the look of the eyes, and thus flying through so many diverse occasions, there remaineth in us nought save a gross residue, the root of evil whence bodies are made. For Saclas, prince of darkness, imagined the ways of birth whereby he should enclose the least parts of Godhead; then created he two children, Adam and Eve.

But, forasmuch as the flesh constraineth God within her, let us take thought for the captivities wherein He doth languish, let us destroy in the seed of it the cause that doth crush Him. He whose loins are not proven thereto must abstain from women; rather should he draw from out himself the parts of light that be bound therein and let him take pleasure, without haste, in the delight of his loneliness. Then will his heart rejoice within him, for the thought that he hath delivered God.

S. ANTHONY. Woe is me! Meseemeth I slip, I stay not, even upon the stairs of Hell.

THE GNOSTICS. [A vast quire, composed of different groups; Saturnians, Marcosians, Valentinians, Nicolaists, Elxaites, &c. . . .] Hearken not unto those sorrowful men; they are unbelievers from Asia. Their great prophet Manes was flayed with the point of a reed, for his false pretending, and his skin was filled with straw and hung upon the gates of Ctesiphon.

We will teach thee, we who are wise and learned and pure—we will teach thee that that great God, the Eternal, Whom none may approach, Whom nought may disturb, He is not the creator of the world. Wouldest thou know the life of Jesus before He appeared upon earth, the exact measure of His stature, the name of the star wherein is His throne? Here is the book of Norra, the wife of Noah. She wrote it in the Ark, in the nighttime, seated upon the back of an elephant, by the flame of the lightnings. Here is the book, open it! Assay it! A line only! . . .

PRIDE. What peril is there?

S. ANTHONY. Nay, peradventure. . . .

LOGIC. It may be the thoughts that oppress thee will flee away.

PRIDE. [Passes him the open book over his shoulder. His eyes fall on this phrase.]

"In the beginning the Abysm was. Of His thought was born Understanding who took Truth to wife. And of Truth and Understanding issued the Word and Life who begat five pairs like unto one another. Of the Word and of Life came forth Man and the Church who begat yet another six pairs, of whom The Comforter and Belief begat Wisdom and The Perfected. These fifteen couples are the fifteen lesser Yokes who are of thirty supreme Ages who are the Fulfilment or Highest Whole, and who are God."

THE HERESIES. [Aside.] He readeth! He readeth! He is ours!

S. ANTHONY. [Continuing.] "Barbelo, Son of Baal, is the prince of the eighth heaven. Ialdamoth hath made the angels, the earth and the six heavens below him. He hath the shape of an ass."

[S. Anthony throws aside the book in a fury.]

THE GNOSTICS. [Closing in again about him.] Wherefore? Begin again; thou hast not understood.

THE VALENTINIANS. [Tracing with their fingers figures upon the sand.] Behold the 365 heavens that match with the limbs of the body.

S. ANTHONY. [Closing his eyes.] I have no wish to know them.

THE BASILIDIANS. The word ABPAKAC signifieth . . .

S. ANTHONY. [Stopping his ears.] I will not hear it.

THE SATURNIANS. We will tell thee the name of the seven angels who have made . . .

S. ANTHONY. Nay! nay!

THE COLORBASIANS. The name of the seven stars whence issueth the life of men.

S. ANTHONY. Nay! nay!

THE THERAPEUTES. Stay! stay! we shall dance the dance of the passage of the Red Sea and sing the hymn of the Sun.

THE RABDALISTS. [Pointing out with their wands several points in Space.] Seest thou the Beingless, the Universal, flowing through the hidden veins of all the worlds as it were the blood in a great body?

S. ANTHONY. [In the midst of the Heresies.] By what path shall I fly? Voices howl in mine ears! Where am I? Whereon thought I? Ay! I recall it, upon that which is the Word. What now?

[The Heresies form a great circle around him and stand on tiptoe, open-mouthed.]

But I understand nought of all this. My soul is whirled and torn in these thoughts even as the sail of a ship in the tempest. Nay! I will no more. Back! back! [All vanishes. Silence.]

But Damnation standeth behind thy back, woe unto thee! Woe! the terror of Eternity freezeth me even unto the bowels, as it were the dark vault of a great sepulchre.

[Vague lamentations are heard afar off; he listens.] Who is it that weep-eth? Is it some wayfarer slain in the mountain?

[He picks up a trail of bindweed and kindles it at the little lamp of the chapel; he searches, lowering and raising his torch; the sounds of weeping seem to draw nearer.]

Ha! it is a woman.

[He sees a woman approaching; her black headbands fall all adown her face; her torn purple smock shows her wasted arm whereon rings a coral bracelet. Under her eyes are red swellings, and on her cheeks the marks of bites, on her arms the traces of blows. She leans, weeping, on the arm of a bald-headed man who is clad in a long robe all of one red colour. He has a long grey beard; in his hand he holds a little bronze vase, which he places upon the ground.]

SIMON THE MAGICIAN. (Simon Magus.) [To Helen.] Stay thy feet.

HELEN. [Groaning on Simon's bosom.] Father, father, I am athirst.

SIMON. Thy thirst be removed from thee!

HELEN. Father, I would sleep.

SIMON. Awake!

HELEN. Ah! Father, when may I be seated?

SIMON. Stand up!

S. ANTHONY. [Bewildered.] What hath she done?

SIMON. [Calling three times.] O Understanding! Understanding! Understanding! He asketh what thou hast done; tell that thou hast to say.

HELEN. [As though awakening from a long sleep.] What I have to say, my father?

SIMON. Whence comest thou?

HELEN. [Casts her eyes in every direction round her, raises her head toward the clouds, collects herself a moment, then begins in veiled tones.] I have memory of a far country, of a forgotten land. The peacock's tail, vast, outspread, closeth the bounds thereof, and through the spaces between the feathers ye may see a sky green as a sapphire. In the cedars the birds, whose crests are of diamond and their wings are the colour of gold, cry aloud, and their cry is as the sound of a breaking harp string. I was the light of the moon; I passed through the leaves of the trees; with my face I lit up the pale blue firmament of the summer nights.

S. ANTHONY. [To Simon, signing to him that she is mad.] Ay! I understand! some poor child whom thou hast found by chance and taken unto thee.

SIMON. [His finger on his lips.] Hush, hush!

HELEN. [Resumes.] At the prow of the galley near to the ram's head that dipped beneath the waters whensoever the waves smote it, there stood I and I moved not. The wind blew, the keel cleaved the foam. He said unto me "what matter to me if I bring disturbance upon mine own land, what though I lose my crown! thou shalt be mine, within mine house."

Menelaus wept; he aroused the dwellers in the islands; they set sail, they and their bucklers, their lances, and their horses that snorted for terror upon the decks of the ships.

How sweet was the chamber within his palace! He laid him down on purple coverings, on beds of ivory; he toyed with the ends of my tresses, he sang love songs unto me.

At eventide I went up on to the wall, I beheld the two camps and the beacons that were being kindled, Odysseus speaking with his friends at the door of his tent, Achilles fully armed driving his chariot along the shore of the sea.

S. ANTHONY. But she is mad, wholly mad; wherefore then? . . .

SIMON. [His finger upon his lips.] Hush, hush!

HELEN. I was in a forest and men passed by. They took me and bound me with ropes; they bore me away upon their camels. They entered in unto me by stealth as I slept—first of all the prince, then the captains, then the men-at-arms, then the footmen who tend the asses.

They washed me in the fountain, but my blood that flowed reddened the waters, and my dusty feet troubled the spring. They anointed me with oils, they rubbed me with ointments, and they sold me to the folk that I might make sport for them.

It was at Tyre of Syria, hard by the harbour, at a narrow crossing of the ways. . . . One night I stood up naked, the timbrel was in mine hand, I played and the Greek sailors danced. The rain of the tempest poured down upon the house, the vapour of wine rose with the breath of men and the smoke of the lamps. On a sudden a man entered, yet the door was not open. He lifted his left arm and parted two fingers. The wind made the walls to crack, the tripods were aflame, and I ran unto him.

SIMON. Ay, I was seeking thee, but I found thee, I redeemed thee. She it is, O Anthony, whom men call Grace, Silence, Understanding, Barbelo Mother of God. She was the thought of the Father, the Mind that may not be destroyed, Who created the worlds. But the angels, her sons, drove her from out her dominion. Then was she the moon, she was Woman, the perfect Agreement, the Pointed Angle. Then, that they might take their ease more fully in the infinite, whence they had driven her forth, they prisoned her at the last in a woman's shape.

She hath been Helen of the Trojans, whose memory was cursed by the poet Stesichorus. She hath been Lucretia, the fair lady ravished by the kings. She hath been that Delilah who cut the hair of Samson. She hath been that daughter of the Hebrews who departed from the tents that she might give herself unto the goats; she it was whom the twelve tribes stoned. She hath loved fornication, lies, worship of idols, and folly. She hath abased herself in all corruption, she hath wallowed in all wretchedness, she hath lain with all nations, she hath sung at every cross-road and hath kissed all faces. At Tyre she was the harlot of the thieves. She drank with them during the night-time and she hid the slayers of men amid the lice of her warm bed.

I! even I! The Father unto the Samaritans, the Son unto the Jews, the Holy Spirit unto the Gentiles, I came that I should make her to arise again in her splendour, and stablish her once again in the bosom of the Father. And now, indivisible the one from the other, we go, freeing the Spirit and terrifying the Gods.

I have preached in Ephraim and in Issachar, in Samaria and in the cities, in the valley of Megiddo and on the banks of the swift river Bizor, from Zoata even unto Arnon, and beyond the mountains in Bostra and Damascus.

I am come to destroy the law of Moses, to overthrow the ordinances, to purify the impurities. I call the souls of the sons of Adam unto the greater love that they may be mad with lust or drunk with repentance. Come unto me all ye that are clothed in mire, ye that are drowned in blood, ye that are steeped in wine! By the new baptism, even as by the torch of pine-wood that men trail in the house of the leper that it may burn away from off the walls the red stains that devour them, thereby will I wash you clean even unto the bowels, even to the innermost parts of your being.

Be kindled, O fire! Leap, run, lay waste, purify, thou blood of Understanding, thou soul of Very God.

[A white flame appears on the surface of the vase, escapes therefrom, hovers from side to side, and pursues S. Anthony.]

At the court of Nero I flew in the circus; so high flew I that none ever saw me again. My statue standeth upright in the island of the Tiber. I am Strength, Beauty, the Master! She, Understanding, is Athene. I am Apollo the god of the daylight! I am Hermes the Blue! I am Zeus the Thunderer. I am the Christ. I am the Comforter. I am the Lord. I am that which is in God. I am Very God.

S. ANTHONY. Ah! had I holy water!

[The fire goes out. The woman utters a piercing cry and vanishes with Simon.]

S. ANTHONY. [Gasps and looks around him.] Nay! . . . nought remaineth! . . . ah me! [He wipes his brow with his sleeve.]

Ah me! How the flames ran! [He laughs.]

Out on it! These be vain imaginations! The Spirit of God is not abased so low. If once the soul be yoked to evil, it ceaseth to be, say they what they will.

Yet . . . if by some mighty striving it should shake off that burden of substance that doth overwhelm it, . . . wherefore should it not rise again even unto God? . . . then . . . then would the space of life vanish . . . and the works thereof would be of little matter.

[Thereupon appear the Elxaites, cloaked in great violet mantles, their faces hidden under masks of wild beasts.]

Believe! What mattereth all else! Eat of unclean meats if so be that the Spirit hungereth for the Word. Phineas bowed him down before Diana, and Peter denied Jesus; for martyrdom is unholy and desire of suffering is a temptation of evil.

S. ANTHONY. [Repeats.] A temptation?

[The Cainites appear; their hair is knotted with vipers that twine round their necks and droop their heads back on their shoulders.]

THE CAINITES. Let us exalt them that are accursed, let us worship them that are abhorred! More than Abraham and the prophets, more than Paul, and more than all the saints, they have laboured for thy soul, they have been damnèd for thee. Glory be to Cain! Glory be to Sodom! Glory be to Judas! Cain begat the race of the strong, Sodom affrighted the earth by her chastisement, through Judas was it that the Son of God saved the world!

S. ANTHONY. [Slowly.] Judas? . . . Yea, indeed, yea . . . it is so.

THE CARPOCRATIANS. [Naked down to the girdle, bearing flowers in their hands, long-haired, full-bearded, with long nails. They all have on their ears a red mark, and on their chests suns are tattooed.] Fulfil the task of the body! This must be!

The spirit bewildered wandereth amid the chances of life, nor shall it return unto the unmoved bosom of Concupiscence until it hath fulfilled in its flesh all the works of the flesh. . . .

Come with us to the love-feasts by night. The naked women, crowned with hyacinths, eat by the light of the torches that are mirrored in the golden plates. They are free for all, as are our goods, as are our books, as is the sun, and as is God. At meat we sing songs of burial, we cut ourselves with knives, we drink the blood from our arms. We mount upon the altar. We cense ourselves with the incense from our censers.

THE FALSE PROPHETESS OF CAPPADOCIA. [Her great mass of red hair falls even to her heels. She waves a flaming pine brand, she leans with her left hand on the muzzle of a tigress who rubs herself against her thigh.] Spirit is in the flame, in the flesh, in the whirlwind. The Spirit shall leap forth for thee at the Invocation of Terror. Hearken thereunto! I will roll thee within my love even to the depths of the abysm. Hither, hither!

[She shakes her torch and its drops of fire fall at the feet of S. Anthony. The tigress arches her back. S. Anthony draws back, affrighted.]

S. ANTHONY. Woe, woe! they will take me! I fear! The beast roareth! How came they even unto me! My fault it was, O God! Have pity, have pity!

[He grasps his scourge and whirls it rapidly round and round like a sling. The Heresies withdraw, lowering their heads between their shoulders, and with gestures of fright.]

Ah! I was persuaded thereof! The sign of Penitence putteth them to flight. It is thought alone that worketh evil. Away with these dreams wherein the soul doth lose itself. Deeds, deeds!

[He scourges himself, and the Montanists advance, clad in dark frocks, their heads covered with ashes, their arms folded.]

THE MONTANISTS. Courage, O Anthony! Do as we do; six times in a month we fast wholly, three times in a year keep we Lenten fast, every night do we scourge our bodies. Moreover, we baptize the dead, we veil virgins, we forbid second wedlock.

THE TATIANS. [Their heads are shaven, and they have prisoned themselves in black sacks. They cry out.]

Forbid all! . . . the tree of Eden that bore each year twelve fruits red as blood, this, even this, is woman! He who sleepeth in the shade thereof shall not awaken, save in hell.

S. ANTHONY. [Sorrowfully.] It is to save me from that slumber that I have sought out loneliness.

[The group of Montanists opens and two women are seen advancing; they are very pale, and are clad in brown mantles. MAXIMILLA is dark, PRISCILLA is fair. They throw back their hoods and say:]

What time we dwelt in the house of our husbands we went out early in

the morning without our litter, without our followers, that we might go
into the taverns and corrupt the jailers. We visited the confessors, we sang
psalms, we spake of angels. Our husbands the while were sore troubled in
their houses. Ah! Mother of God, their kisses troubled the calm depth of
faith as it were stones that one throweth into a well, the one after the other.

[St. Anthony steps forward the better to see them.]

PRISCILLA. [Begins to speak.] I was in the bath, the walls streamed, the
water flowed, and I drowsed to the vague murmur of the streets that rose
even unto mine ears.

On a sudden I heard much clamour; men cried, "He is a wizard, he is
the devil!" and the multitude stayed before our house, over against the
temple of Aesculapius. I rose up, unshod, and raised myself with mine
hands unto the height of the casement.

On the hall of the columns of the temple stood a man robed as a freed
slave, having an iron collar on his neck. He took live coals from a chafing-
dish and upon his breast he drew great lines therewith, calling aloud the
while "Jesus, Jesus!" The people said, "It is not permitted; let us stone him."
Others praised him. But he ceased not, and when he was weary of moving
his right hand he moved his left hand.

It was wondrous, mine heart was uplifted! Great open flowers turned
as wheels before mine eyes, and I heard in space as it were the music of
a golden bow. Mine hands loosed hold of the bars and my body fell. I know
not if he had ceased to speak or if I had ceased to hear him; but the pool
of the bath was empty, and the moon, entering, cast clear lengthening rays
upon the pavement that was strewn with blue sand.

S. ANTHONY. [Listening with attention.] Of whom speak they?

MAXIMILLA. We were on our way back from Tarsus, over the mountains,
when we saw a man at a turning of the road under a fig-tree.

He was plucking the leaves and casting them to the wind.

He tore off the fruits and crushed them upon the earth. He cried out unto
us from afar, "Halt! ye!" and he ran upon us, cursing us. The slaves
hastened unto us. He laughed aloud with great laughter. The horses reared
up, and the great hounds howled, every one of them.

He stood up, on the edge of the precipice. The sweat flowed upon his
dark face. His black cloak flapped in the wind of the mountains.

He called us by our names, he reproved us for the vanity of our works
and for the foulness of our bodies; he lifted his hand in wrath toward the
dromedaries by reason of the silver bells that they bare under their jaws.
His wrath affrighted me even to mine innermost parts; his speech was
strange rapture, it was mingled with soft winds and sweet odours; it soothed
me to sleep, it made me drunk as with wine. First the slaves drew nigh:
"Master," said they, "the beasts are wearied"; then came the women: "The
night is at hand, we are afeared"; and the slaves departed. The children
cried aloud: "We are an-hungered"; and as none made answer unto the
women, they also departed. But he spake on; his voice whistled, his words

454   WORKS OF GUSTAVE FLAUBERT

fell headlong; sharp-edged as daggers they made my heart bleed, they voided it.

I was aware of one near unto me; it was my husband; but I hearkened unto the other. He wept aloud, he drew himself on his knees over the stones and cried out, "Thou dost forsake me!" and I made answer, "Yea, get thee gone!"

[S. Anthony opens his mouth, but Priscilla and Maximilla begin to sing.] The Father hath dominion, the Son suffereth, the Spirit is a burning flame! The Comforter is ours! The Spirit is ours! for we are the beloved of the great Montanus!

[They point to a black eunuch standing near them, clad in a cloak fawn-coloured with gold braid, clasped over his breast by two human bones.]

MONTANUS. It is not Montanus whom ye love, but the Spirit of God that filleth his soul. For I am no man; that ye know, ye who faint with desire upon mine hairless breast.

Ye, my beloved, ye are Love that cannot be satisfied, forasmuch as at this present ye delight in pain, and life giveth pain unto you, as it were a running sore. Weep ye, shed tears! Let your eyes be pale even as a blue cloak that hath lost its colour in the tempest. Call upon me! I will lay you upon racks! Scourge ye the white skin of our bodies with green thistles! When the blood shall flow, then shall I come. Ay, I shall hasten . . . that I may suck it with my mouth!

[Maximilla and Priscilla pass their arms round his waist and remain with their heads resting on his shoulder, making a sign the while to S. Anthony.]

S. ANTHONY. In the name of Christ! In the name of the Virgin! By the excellence of all the angels. . . .

THE MONTANISTS. Nay! thou shalt not drive us hence! Zotimus of Co-manus was conquered by Maximilla, and Sotas, the bishop of Anquiala, was overcome by Priscilla. We have saints who be holier than thy saints, we have martyrs whose testimony is greater than that of thy martyrs. Knowest thou Alexander, Theodotus, Thermison? They tore out the eyes, the teeth, and the nails of Alexander of Phrygia; they rubbed his skin with honey, and upon it they cast raging wasps; they bound him with a rope to the tail of a bull that went slowly through a pasture. Thermison they tore with knives of wood; they made the blood of his entrails to flow over his face. But Satan upon a mountain-top beat Thermison during six nights with the trunk of a cedar-tree that had all its branches: then did he cast him away, as it were a stone, into the valley. Up! come! Jesus hath suffered; what is thy suffering after His?

S. ANTHONY. [Bitterly.] Nought, nought, I know it. The tears of all generations of man that would make a great sea, were they united, are but a drop of water upon a leaf before those His everlasting tears. [Silence.]

THE MONTANISTS. [Resuming.] Love overfloweth from out the bleeding heart. The closed eyes of the ravished behold the splendours of Heaven; in the agony of the body shall the fulness of understanding come upon thee, even as the lightning that appeareth not save in the openings of the clouds.

S. ANTHONY. Yea, verily! My body doth irk me, it doth crush me, it doth choke me.

THE VALERIANS. [They are very tall, and very lean, they have daggers in their girdles and crowns of thorns on their foreheads; they seize their daggers in one hand and their crowns in the other, and they say:] Here is that shall cleave lust in sunder! Here is that shall give pain unto pride! Is it pain that thou fearest, O thou of little courage? Dost thou tremble for thy flesh, thou hypocrite? Thou liest down near unto it, thou dost watch it in its sleep; it shall awaken more ravenous than a lion. Choke thou it, cut it in pieces, make an end of it!

S. ANTHONY. I have a loathing for myself! I abhor life, and the earth, and the sun.

[Ferocious outcries burst forth and the DONATIST CIRCONCELLIONS appear: they are filthy, hideous, clothed in goat-skins, and they bear iron clubs upon their shoulders.]

Accursed be the whole world! Accursed be we ourselves! Accursed be man! Accursed be woman! Accursed be children! Trample upon the fruit, trouble the spring! Plunder the rich man who is happy, who eateth his fill; beat the poor man who coveteth the housing of the ass and the meal of the dog and the nest of the bird, who mourneth in his loneliness for that all men are not miserable even as he is. Feed the bears, call unto the vultures, whistle unto the crocodiles and to the lizard by the riverside!

We are the Captains of the Saints: we destroy substance whereby we may hasten the end of the world; we slay, we burn, we slaughter! We break down the dykes, we cast money abroad into the sea.

None may be saved except they suffer martyrdom; we give martyrdom unto ourselves; we flay the skin from off our feet and we run upon the shingle. We thrust spits of iron into our entrails. We roll naked in the snow.

We slay ourselves with knives, crying out, "Praise be to God!" We go up to the roofs of high houses that we may cast ourselves down headlong. We lie down under the wheels of chariots, we cast ourselves into the mouths of furnaces.

Reviled be baptism, reviled be the Bread and Wine, reviled be marriage, reviled be the anointment of the dying!

Repentance alone cleanseth the soul.

Jesus cannot be touched, Jesus cannot be eaten. Damnation upon adultery sanctified! with suffering must ye be wedded!

Damnation upon the vanity of man who must die, yet thinketh he that the flesh is eternal! Damnation upon the folly of them that hope, upon the wickedness of them that teach! Damnation upon thee! Damnation upon us! Damnation upon all, and glory be unto Death!

S. ANTHONY. Horror!

[There is a clap of thunder; a dense smoke covers the scene; S. Anthony can no longer distinguish anything.]

Yet I dreamt not? . . . nay . . . they were there! . . . they roared round about me, and my thoughts crumbled to dust beneath their feet even as the lesser islands of sand in the rivers that fall in great masses beneath the heavy feet of the crocodiles. They spake all together and so swiftly that I could not tell their voices the one from the other. [He collects himself little by little.] Yet some there were of them who were not wholly hateful. How was this? I should have made answer unto them. I have not seen all.

[He glances vaguely from side to side, and utters a cry as he perceives in the fog two men covered with long mantles that fall even to their feet. The foremost is of great stature, of mild countenance and grave demeanour; his fair locks, severed by a parting even as those of Christ, fall in regular lines upon his shoulders. He casts down a white staff that he held in his hand, and his companion picks it up, bowing after the manner of the men of the East. This latter is clothed similarly, in a white tunic, unembroidered; he is small and fat, snub-nosed, of squat figure; he has woolly hair and is of simple aspect. Both are bare-footed and bare-headed, and covered with dust like men who have just come from a journey.]

What would ye? Speak! . . . begone!

DAMIS. [The little man.] Nay, nay, good hermit! What would I? I know not! Here is the Master. Touching our departure, charity at least should require . . .

S. ANTHONY. Nay, pardon me! Mine head is sorely troubled! . . . what is your need?—be ye seated.

[Damis sits down—the other remains standing.]

And thy master?

DAMIS. [Smiling.] Nay, he hath need of nought! He is a wise man! But for me, good hermit, I would pray thee give me a little water, for my thirst is great.

[S. Anthony fetches a crock from his cell, raises it himself, and offers Damis to drink. Little by little the smoke vanishes.]

DAMIS. [After having drunk.] Pah! how evilly it tasteth! thou shouldest have covered it with leaves!

S. ANTHONY. My Lord, there is not even a blade of grass at hand.

DAMIS. Hast thou nought for me to eat? My hunger is great.

[S. Anthony goes into his hut and returns with a piece of dried-up black bread. Damis bites it.]

How hard it is!

S. ANTHONY. I have none other, My Lord.

DAMIS. Ah! [He breaks the bread, tears out the crumb, and throws away the crusts. The pig makes for them: S. Anthony makes an angry gesture as if to beat him.]

Nay! Suffer him! Surely all must live! [Silence.]

S. ANTHONY. [Resumes.] And ye come?

DAMIS. From afar . . . from a great distance. . . .

S. ANTHONY. And . . . ye go?

DAMIS. [Pointing to the other.] Whither his will leadeth.

S. ANTHONY. Who then is he?

DAMIS. Apollonius!

[S. Anthony makes a gesture of ignorance.]

Apollonius! [louder.] Apollonius of Tyana!

S. ANTHONY. I have never heard speak of him.

DAMIS. [In anger.] What! Never! . . . Ah! I see clearly, good man, that thou hast no knowledge whatsoever of what passeth in the world.

S. ANTHONY. Of a truth, My Lord, for my days are given over to worship.

DAMIS. Even so is it with him.

S. ANTHONY. [To himself.] With him! [He considers Apollonius.]

Indeed, he hath the look of an holy man. . . . I would fain hold converse with him . . . it may be that I deceive myself . . . for . . .

[The smoke has vanished; the air is quite clear, the moon shines brightly.]

DAMIS. Whereon thinkest thou that thou sayest never a word?

S. ANTHONY. I ponder . . . nay, it is nothing.

[Damis approaches S. Anthony and walks round him several times, stooping, nor ever raising his head;—at length—]

APOLLONIUS. [Still motionless.] What is it?

DAMIS. Master, it is a Galilean hermit who would know whence wisdom cometh.

APOLLONIUS. Let him draw nigh! [S. Anthony hesitates.]

DAMIS. Draw nigh!

APOLLONIUS. [In a voice of thunder.] Draw nigh! Thou wouldest know who I am, what I have done, what are my thoughts; is it not so, my child?

S. ANTHONY. [Embarrassed.] If haply these things may further my salvation.

APOLLONIUS. Rejoice! I will tell them unto thee.

DAMIS. [In a low voice, to S. Anthony.] Can this be! Surely, at the first sight of thee, he hath perceived that thou art wondrously disposed unto wisdom. [He rubs his hands.] I also will profit therefrom.

APOLLONIUS. First I will tell thee of the long path I have trodden that I might possess the Doctrine—and shouldest thou discover in all my life but one evil deed, then shalt thou bid me stay. For he who hath offended in his deeds, his words shall be a stumbling-block.

DAMIS. [To S. Anthony.] A just man, is he not!

S. ANTHONY. Verily I think he speaketh truth.

APOLLONIUS. On the night of my birth my mother dreamed that she gathered flowers on the shores of a lake. The lightning flashed and she brought me forth to the sound of the voices of the swans who sang in her dream.

Until I was fifteen years of age, I was bathed daily three times in the fountain Asbadea, whose water giveth the dropsy to them that are forsworn; I was rubbed with leaves of the fleabane whereby I might be made pure. A princess of Palmyra came and sought me one evening, and offered unto me treasures that she knew were hidden in tombs. A slave of the temple of Diana slew herself for despair with the knife of the sacrifice; and the governor of Cilicia, when that he had come to an end of all his promises, cried out, before all my family, that he would put me to death. But he it was who died, three days later, slain by the Romans.

DAMIS. [To S. Anthony, nudging him with his elbow.] Said I not so! How wondrous a man!

APOLLONIUS. Throughout four years following did I keep complete silence after the manner of the Pythagoreans. The most sudden pain forced not a sigh from me; when I entered into the theatre men withdrew from me as though I were a spirit.

DAMIS. Wouldest thou have done this, thou?

APOLLONIUS. When the time of my silence was accomplished, I, I alone, took it upon me to instruct the priests who had lost the knowledge of their forefathers, and I gave forth this prayer: "O Gods! . . ."

S. ANTHONY. Wherefore "Gods"? The Gods? What saith he?

DAMIS. Let be, let him speak on, be silent.

APOLLONIUS. Then did I set forth to learn all worships and to question all oracles. I have held converse with the wise men of the Ganges, with the soothsayers of Chaldea, with the wizards of Babylon. I have gone up into the fourteen mountains of Olympus, I have plumbed the lakes of Scythia, I have measured the breadth of the desert.

DAMIS. All this is true. I, even I, was with him.

APOLLONIUS. At first I went from Pontus even to the sea of Hyrcania, I passed around it; and I went down unto Nineveh through the country of the Baraomates wherein is buried Bucephalus. At the gates of the town there was a statue of a woman clad after the fashion of the strange nations. A man drew nigh unto me.

DAMIS. It was I, good master, it was I! At once I loved thee. Thou wert sweeter than a maiden and more beautiful than a god.

APOLLONIUS. [Not hearing him.] He desired to come with me that he might interpret for me.

DAMIS. But thou didst answer and say that thou hadst understanding of all tongues, and that thou couldest divine all thoughts. Then did I kiss the hem of thy mantle, and I set forth behind thee to walk in thy footsteps.

APOLLONIUS. After Ctesiphon we entered upon the lands of Babylon.

DAMIS. The satrap cried aloud to see one so pale.

S. ANTHONY. The story is strange!

DAMIS. Surely it was on the morrow, master, that we met that great tigress who had eight young in her womb? Then didst thou say: "Our sojourn in the house of the king shall be for a year and eight months." Never could I understand it. . . .

APOLLONIUS. The king received me standing up, nigh unto a throne of silver, in a round hall the ceiling whereof was covered with stars; and from it hung by threads that none could see, four great birds wrought of gold, and their two wings were spread out.

S. ANTHONY. Can such things be upon earth?

DAMIS. That is a great city, that Babylon! All they that dwell therein are rich; the houses are painted blue, and they have gates of bronze and stair-

cases that go down unto the river. [He draws on the ground with his staff.]
Behold, so is the fashion of it. Moreover, there are temples and open
places, baths and conduits of water. The palaces are covered with red copper; and within! Ah! couldest thou but know them!

APOLLONIUS. On the north wall there is a tower of white marble that
beareth a second, a third, a fourth, a fifth tower, and there be yet three more
towers! These towers be sepulchres . . . the eighth is a chapel wherein is a
bed. None may enter therein save the woman chosen by the priests for the
God Bel. The King of Babylon gave it unto me for a dwelling-place.

DAMIS. As for me, none heeded me. I went about the streets alone and I
learnt the customs of the people; I saw their workshops; I beheld the great
engines that bear the water into the gardens. Yet it wearied me that I was
sundered from my master.

APOLLONIUS. At the end of a year and eight months . . .

[S. Anthony starts.]

. . . on an evening we went forth from Babylon by the way that leadeth
to the land of India. Under the light of the moon we beheld a Demon.

DAMIS. Ay, in truth! She leapt on her iron hoof. She neighed like unto
an ass; she ran among the rocks. But he called curses upon her and she
vanished.

S. ANTHONY. What shall come of this, what shall follow?

APOLLONIUS. [Continuing.] At Taxilla, Phraortes, the King of the Ganges,
showed unto us his bodyguard of black men, whose stature was five cubits in
height; in the gardens of his palace under a tent of green brocade he showed
unto us a great elephant whom his women delighted to sprinkle with sweet
perfumes. Round his tusks he had necklaces of gold, and on one of these
it was written: "The son of Jupiter hath vowed Ajax holy unto the sun."
For he was the elephant of Porus who had fled from Babylon after the death
of Alexander.

DAMIS. Ay! They had found him again in a forest.

S. ANTHONY. They speak overmuch, even as drunken men.

APOLLONIUS. Phraortes made us to sit at his table. It was covered with
great fruits laid upon wide leaves, and on it were horned antelopes.

DAMIS. It was a strange land! The lords as they drank, delighted to cast
darts beneath the feet of a child that danced. But I like not that sport; evil
might happen therefrom.

APOLLONIUS. When I was ready to depart, the king gave unto me a parasol, and said unto me: "I have upon the shores of the Indus an herd of white
camels. When thou hast no further need of them, breathe into their ears
and they will return."

We went down the banks of the river; we walked by night in the light
of the fireflies that shone in the cane. The slave sang a song to drive away
the serpents, and our camels bowed their loins as they passed beneath the
trees as it were under low doorways.

Upon a day a black child who held in his hand a wand of gold led us to
the college of the wise men. Sarchas, their head man, spake unto me of my

forefathers and of all my thoughts, of all my deeds and of all my lives. He had been the river Indus, and he recalled unto me that I had guided boats on the Nile in the days of the King Sesostris.

DAMIS. But as for me, they said nought unto me, so that I know not who I had been. [S. Anthony gazes at them with amazement.]

S. ANTHONY. Their aspect is dim as it were shadows.

APOLLONIUS. And we went on our way toward the ocean. On the shores thereof we came upon the Dog-headed Ape-folk, glutted with milk, returning from their journeying in the isle of Taprobane. With them was the Indian Venus, the black and white woman, who danced naked in the midst of the apes. Around her waist were hung timbrels of ivory and her laughter was beyond measure.

The warm waves drave white pearls before us upon the sand, the amber crackled beneath our footsteps, the bones of whales whitened in the clefts of the cliffs, and long nests of green weed hanging to their ribs swung in the wind.

Continually the earth shrank, at the last it was less than the breadth of a sandal. We stood still, we cast drops of sea-water towards the sun, we turned to our right hand that we might return.

We returned through the country of silver by way of the country of the Gangarides, by the headland Comaria, through the country of the Sachalites, and of the Adramites, and of the Homerites; then did we cross the Cassanian Mountains, we passed over the Red Sea and the island of Topazus, we entered into Ethiopia by way of the kingdom of the Pigmies.

S. ANTHONY. [Aside.] How great is the earth!

DAMIS. And when we had entered into our own place once more, all they that we had known aforetime were dead. [S. Anthony bows his head.]

APOLLONIUS. [Resumes.] Then did men begin to speak of me in the world. The pestilence was laying waste Ephesus; I caused them to stone an aged beggar. . . .

DAMIS. And the pestilence departed!

S. ANTHONY. What! He driveth away sickness.

APOLLONIUS. At Cnidus I healed him that loved Venus.

DAMIS. Ay, a madman who had even promised to wed her. Love of women, what of it! Let it pass! But love for a statue, what folly! The Master laid his hand on the young man's heart and thereupon was his love quenched within him.

S. ANTHONY. What! He delivereth from devils?

APOLLONIUS. At Tarentum they were bearing the body of a young maid to be burnt, for she was dead.

DAMIS. The Master touched her lips and she rose up and called her mother.

S. ANTHONY. What! He raiseth the dead!

APOLLONIUS. I foretold his dominion unto Vespasianus.

S. ANTHONY. What! He divineth the future!

APOLLONIUS. Seated at table with him, at the baths at Baiae . . .

DAMIS. There was at Corinth . . .

S. ANTHONY. Forgive me, strangers, the hour is late.

DAMIS. A young man called Menippus . . .

S. ANTHONY. It is the hour of the first watch; get you gone!

APOLLONIUS. A dog entered, bearing in his mouth a severed hand. . . .

DAMIS. One night, in the outskirts of the city, he met a woman . . .

S. ANTHONY. Hear ye me not? Depart from me!

APOLLONIUS. He prowled hither and thither among the beds.

S. ANTHONY. Enough, enough!

APOLLONIUS. They would drive him away, but I . . .

DAMIS. Then Menippus went unto her house; they loved one another.

APOLLONIUS. And beating upon the pavement with his tail, he laid that hand on the knees of Flavius.

DAMIS. But in the morning, during the lessons in the school, Menippus was pale . . .

S. ANTHONY. [Leaping up.] Yet again! Nay, let them continue since there is not . . .

DAMIS. The Master said unto him: "O fair young man, thou dost cherish a serpent; a serpent doth cherish thee! When shall be the espousals?" And we went unto the wedding, every one of us . . .

S. ANTHONY. I do wrong, of a surety I do wrong to hearken unto all this.

DAMIS. Even at the entrance to the hall serving-men busied themselves, doors opened; yet heard we neither the sound of footsteps, nor the sound of doors. The Master sat him down nigh unto Menippus. Thereupon was the bride wroth against the wise men. But the golden vessels that were upon the tables vanished, the cupbearers, the cooks, and they that bore the baskets of bread, disappeared; the roof flew away, the walls fell down, and Apollonius alone was left standing, and at his feet was the woman, weeping bitterly. For she was a demon who did glut goodly young men with love that she might devour their flesh—for nought is of greater worth for such kind of evil spirits than the blood of lovers.

APOLLONIUS. Wouldest thou know the skill . . .

S. ANTHONY. I would know nought! Get you gone!

DAMIS. What ill have we done unto thee?

S. ANTHONY. None . . . howbeit . . . nay, let them depart!

APOLLONIUS. On the night when we came unto the gates of Rome. . . .

S. ANTHONY. [Quickly.] Ay, ay! Speak to me of the city of the popes!

APOLLONIUS. [Continuing.] A drunken man approached us, singing in a sweet voice. He sang a wedding song of Nero, and he had power to slay any that should hearken heedlessly thereunto. He bore upon his back in a box of ivory a silver chord taken from the emperor's lute. I raised my shoulders. He cast mud into our faces; then did I undo my girdle and I laid it in his hands.

DAMIS. Thou wert greatly in error!

APOLLONIUS. In the night the emperor summoned me unto his house; he was playing at knucklebones with Sporus, and he leant the elbow of his left arm upon an agate table. He turned him away, and bent his pale eyebrows, and said unto me: "Wherefore dost thou not fear me?" And I made answer unto him: "Forasmuch as God who hath made thee terrible hath made me without fear."

S. ANTHONY. [Dreamily.] There is therein somewhat not to be discovered that affrighted me. [Silence.]

DAMIS. [Beginning again in a shrill voice.] Nay, all the folk of Asia can tell thee.

S. ANTHONY. [Leaping up.] Time lacketh! Tell it another day! I am sick!

DAMIS. But hearken! At Ephesus he saw men slay Domitianus who was at Rome . . .

S. ANTHONY. [Forcing a laugh.] Can this be!

DAMIS. Ay, in the theatre, in full daylight, on the fourteenth day after the calends of October, he cried out, on a sudden: "Cæsar is being slain!" and he said further from time to time: "He rolleth about on the ground; see how he doth struggle! He raiseth himself; he striveth to fly; the doors are shut! Lo! It is finished! Behold him dead!" And verily, on that day, Titus Flavius Domitianus was slain as thou knowest.

S. ANTHONY. [Reflecting.] Without the help of the Evil One . . . verily . . .

APOLLONIUS. He, even that Domitianus, had wished to put me to death! Damis had fled with Demetrius at my command and I remained alone in my prison. . . .

DAMIS. It was wondrous hardihood, that is sure.

APOLLONIUS. Towards the fifth hour the soldiers led me to the tribunal. Mine oration was fully prepared; I held it beneath my cloak. . . .

DAMIS. We others were on the shores, of Puteoli! We deemed thee dead; we wept, each was returning to his home, when, towards the sixth hour, on a sudden thou didst appear.

S. ANTHONY. [Aside.] Even as Jesus!

DAMIS. We trembled, but thou saidst unto us: "Touch me!"

S. ANTHONY. Nay, that cannot be! Ye lie; surely ye lie.

DAMIS. Then did we depart all together.

[Silence. Damis considers S. Anthony; Apollonius draws near to him and shouts in his ear.]

I have been down into the cave of Trophonius, the son of Apollo! I pour offerings of wine through the ears of the great jars! I know the prayers of the people of India! I have kneaded for the women of Syracuse the members of roseate honey that they bear shrieking over the mountains. I have taken the scarf of the Receivers of Contention! I have clasped the serpent of Sabasius against my heart! I have laved Cybele in the waters of the Campanian gulfs, and I have passed three moons in the caverns of Samothracia.

DAMIS. [Laughing foolishly.] He! he! he! Amid the mysteries of the Kindly Goddess!

APOLLONIUS. Wilt thou come with us, and see greater stars and new gods?

S. ANTHONY. Nay! Go your way alone!

DAMIS. Let us depart!

S. ANTHONY. Begone! Flee!

APOLLONIUS. We go to the north, to the land of the swans and the snows. On the white desert doth gallop the horned roebuck whose eyes weep for the cold; the blind horse-footed folk crush the plant of the further seas with their hooves.

DAMIS. Come! It is dawn, the cock hath crowed, the horse hath neighed, the sail is set.

S. ANTHONY. Nay, the cock hath not crowed! I hear the cricket in the sand and I see the moon that stayeth ever in her place.

APOLLONIUS. Beyond the mountains, afar off, yonder, we shall pluck the apple of the Western Isles and in the perfume thereof we shall search out the cause of love. We shall smell the sweet odour of the myrrh of roses that bringeth death unto the weak. We shall bathe in the lake of roseate oil that is in the island Junonia. Thou shalt see, asleep upon the primroses, the great lizard who waketh once in every fivescore years what time the carbuncle of his eyes is ripened and falleth. The stars tremble like the gaze in men's eyes, the water-falls sing like harps, the flowers open and their breath is as the rapture of wine; thy spirit shall wax greater in the wind, and in thine heart, as in thy face. . . .

DAMIS. Master! It is time! The wind riseth, the swallows awaken, the leaf of the myrtle hath flown away!

APOLLONIUS. Yea, let us depart.

S. ANTHONY. Nay, I remain!

APOLLONIUS. Wouldest thou that I shew thee where groweth the plant Balis that raiseth the dead?

DAMIS. Ask him to give thee the tamer of men that draweth silver and iron and brass.

APOLLONIUS. [Offering him a small round ring of copper.] Wouldest thou the wayfarer's ward? behold it! Nay, take it! Thou canst descend into the burning mountains, thou canst pass through the fire and fly in the air.

S. ANTHONY. They hurt me, they hurt me sorely!

DAMIS. Thou shalt understand the speech of all beings created, their roaring, their neighing, and their cooing.

APOLLONIUS. Yea, for I have found out the secret of Tiresias, of that I am assured.

DAMIS. Ay, and furthermore he knoweth songs that compel whomsoever thou mayest desire to come unto thee.

APOLLONIUS. I have learned from the Arabians the speech of the vultures, and I have read in the grottoes of Strompharabarnax the fashion whereby to affright the rhinoceros and to give sleep unto the crocodile.

DAMIS. When we journeyed aforetime, we heard, through the bindweed, the white unicorns that ran. They lay flat upon their bellies that he might mount upon their backs.

APOLLONIUS. Thou too shalt ride upon them. Thou shalt take hold of their ears. We will go, we will go!

S. ANTHONY. [Weeping.] Woe, woe!

APOLLONIUS. What aileth thee? Come!

S. ANTHONY. [Sobbing.] Woe, woe!

DAMIS. Draw tight thy girdle, tie up thy sandals!

S. ANTHONY. [Sobbing the more.] Woe, woe, woe, woe!

APOLLONIUS. The while we fare I will expound unto thee the meaning of statues—wherefore Zeus sitteth, but Apollo standeth on his feet—wherefore Aphrodite is black at Corinth, four square at Athens, and of the form of a cone at Paphos.

S. ANTHONY. Ah! God! Let them depart, let them depart from me!

APOLLONIUS. Knowest thou her, Aphrodite of the Heavens, who glittereth beneath her arch of stars? Have they told unto thee the mysteries of Aphrodite who foreseeth? Hast thou known the kiss of the Bearded Aphrodite, or thought upon the wrath of Astarte that rageth? Nay, fear not, I shall tear off their veils, I shall break their armour in pieces, thou shalt trample upon their temples, and we shall attain even unto Her that is Mysterious, Unchangeable, even to Her of the Masters, of the brave men, of the pure, Aphrodite that turneth away, She who driveth desire from its path and slayeth the flesh.

DAMIS. Ay, and whensoever we shall find the stone of a sepulchre, so it be large enough, we will play at the dice of Athene that is played in the night-time, in the fall of the year, under the full red moon.

APOLLONIUS. [Stamping his foot.] Why cometh he not?

DAMIS. [Also stamping his foot.] Up, away!

APOLLONIUS. [Gazing fixedly at S. Anthony.] Doubtest thou me?

DAMIS. [Threatening.] Thou dost doubt him? Call, Master, call unto the lion of Numidia, he that held within him the soul of Amasis.

S. ANTHONY. My God! My God! Shall they take me by force!

APOLLONIUS. What is thy desire? Needs but the time wherein to think upon it? . . .

S. ANTHONY. [Joining his hands.] I slip! Stay me!

APOLLONIUS. Is it Wisdom? Is it glory? Wouldest thou refresh thine eyes upon wet flower of jessamine? Wouldest thou feel thy body sink into the soft flesh of languishing women as it were into a billow of the sea?

S. ANTHONY. [Holding his head and crying aloud in pain.] Again! Again!

DAMIS. Ay, indeed! The diamonds shall flow from the mountain rent open. The roses shall flower upon this thy cross. The sirens whose hinder parts are of the shell of the pearl shall cherish thee with their hair; they shall soothe thee to sleep with their songs.

S. ANTHONY. O Holy Spirit, deliver me!

APOLLONIUS. Wouldest thou that I change me to a tree, to a leopard, to a river?

S. ANTHONY. O Holy Virgin, Mother of God, pray for me!

APOLLONIUS. Wouldest thou that I compel the moon to go backward?

S. ANTHONY. O Holy Trinity, save me!

APOLLONIUS. Wouldest thou that I show thee Jerusalem all alight for the Sabbath?

S. ANTHONY. Jesus, Jesus, help me!

APOLLONIUS. Wouldest thou that I cause Jesus to appear?

S. ANTHONY. [Bewildered.] What sayest thou?

APOLLONIUS. Here, in this place! . . . He and no other! Thou shalt see the holes in His hands and the blood of His wound. He shall cast down His crown, He shall call His Father accursed, He shall bow down before me, His back shall be bowed.

DAMIS. [In a low voice, to S. Anthony.] Say that thou wouldest, say that thou wouldest!

S. ANTHONY. [Passes his hand over his face, casts scared eyes on every side, then rests his gaze on Apollonius.] Depart, get thee hence, thou accursed one! Get thee back to hell!

APOLLONIUS. [Exasperated.] From hell do I come! I am come forth from thence that I might lead thee thither! The vats of nitre seethe, the coals flame, the steel teeth clap together, and the shadows gather close to the vent-holes to see thee pass.

S. ANTHONY. [Tearing his hair.] Me! Great God! Hell for me!

PRIDE. [Rising behind S. Anthony and laying her hand on his shoulder.] For such an holy man! Impossible!

DAMIS. [With enticing gestures.] Nay, good hermit, beloved Anthony, thou pure man, thou man of renown, thou whom none can praise to his due! Have no fear, it is but his fashion of speech, it is the manner of speech that he hath learnt of the men of the East; but he is good, he is holy, he can . . .

[Damis pauses, and S. Anthony looks at Apollonius, who begins to speak in a voice that is at once vehement and suave.]

APOLLONIUS. Yet, further away than all the worlds, beyond the heavens, above all shapes, shineth the world of thought, not to be attained, not to be entered, wholly filled of the Word. We shall set forth therefrom, we shall overpass in one leap the whole firmament, and thou shalt grasp in its infinity the Everlasting, the Being! Up, away! Give me thy hand!

[And suddenly the earth opens funnelwise and forms a great gulf. Apollonius grows and grows; blood-red clouds roll beneath his bare feet and his white tunic gleams like snow.

A circle of gold round his head quivers in the air with elastic motion. He holds out his left hand to S. Anthony and with his right hand he points to the sky; his mien is royal, inspired.]

S. ANTHONY. [Bewildered.] A tumult of desire uplifteth me unto heights that terrify me, the ground fleeth away like a wave, mine head is burst in sunder.

[He clings to the cross with all his strength.]

THE VALERIANS. Lo! Here be our knives!

THE CIRCONCELLIONS. [Reappearing.] Lo! Here be our daggers!

THE CARPOCRATIANS. Lo! Here be our flowers!

THE MONTANISTS. Lo! Here be our shirts of hair, our poisons, our crosses, our racks.

MAXIMILLA AND PRISCILLA. [Weeping.] O sweet Anthony! Dost thou hear us? Come.

THE SABAEANS. Come, pray with us in our temples of stone whose shape is the shape of stars.

THE MANICHAEANS. Nay, fly unto the feast of the Sacred Chair. Thou shalt sit in the seat of Manes. We will rub thee with benzoin, thou shalt drink boiled wine, and thou shalt understand the twain Ordinances, the twelve Vessels, the five Natures, and the eight Worlds, with the Shoulderer who beareth the Earth upon his shoulders and He that holdeth in Glory, who hath six faces; he holdeth it between his fingers that it may not waver.

THE GNOSTICS. We will open unto thee Knowledge and thou shalt ascend unto the shining Yokes who shall bear thee to the breast of the Eternal Abysm in the circle unchangeable of Fulfilment. [Other Heresies arrive.]

S. ANTHONY. [Tearing his hair.] Ha! they return!

SIMON MAGUS. [With Understanding all clad in gold.] Ay, and she returneth also! She hath suffered even as thou hast, but now is she joyful, now is she prepared to sing without ceasing! Dost thou deem her fair? Dost thou desire her? She is the Thought! Love thou her! Penitence doth brighten her life unto her, love consumeth her with fire.

S. ANTHONY. How shall I pray? On whom shall I call?

[THE FALSE PROPHETESS OF CAPPADOCIA passes at a gallop at the back of the scene, bending over the back of her tigress and shaking her torch.]

On me, on me!

THE DEADLY SINS. [All cry out.] On us, on us!

LUST. Let thy flesh rejoice!

IDLENESS. Think no more thereon!

AVARICE. Seek for money!

ENVY. God hateth thee! Hate thou God!

THE CIRCONCELLIONS. Slay thyself, slay thyself!

[The Heresies and the Sins surround S. Anthony. Maximilla and Priscilla weep; Understanding begins to sing; Apollonius, with his white staff, traces circles of fire in the air; the Gnostics open their books; the False Prophetess, on the horizon, sways upon her beast.]

S. ANTHONY. [Bewildered.] O Lord, Lord! Strengthen Thou my faith! Give unto me hope! Make me to love Thee! Increase Thy wrath twofold if it so please Thee, but have pity, have pity!

[Three white figures, the Cardinal Virtues, appear on the threshold of the chapel. S. Anthony struggles to free himself.]

I come to you! Help ye me!

THE SINS. What! Thou wouldst drive us back! We are Rapture!

THE HERESIES. What! Thou dost forsake us! Us, the daughters of the Church, the manifold nature of the Doctrine of Christ! When we die, then shall she die also!

[S. Anthony strives to win to the three Virtues. Pride comes up behind him and pushes him in the back and urges him forward. Then the Heresies draw away from him and the Sins retire. Lust, sighing, seats herself upon the pig and spreads out thereon her fine spangled gown; Sloth falls asleep; Anger gnaws her nails; Avarice stoops down and grubs in the earth; Envy holds her hand before her eyes and gazes into the distance; Greed crouches down. Pride remains standing up.]

PART II

S. ANTHONY is in the chapel, between the three Cardinal Virtues. A great laugh is heard and the Devil appears, terrible, hideous, hairy—his mouth is set with tusks as of a boar; violet flames come out of his eyes. Pride straightens her stature again, Envy hisses, Lust scratches her loins, Avarice holds out her hand, Anger howls, Greed clacks her jaws together, Sloth sighs.

THE DEVIL. Aha! I will shut you up in Hell, I will scourge you with the lusts of another world that I may renew life unto your quenched strength! Is there no more? . . .

THE SINS. [All together.] It is Pride who hath saved him! We had even now caught him!

LUST. She freezeth the hearts of men in vows of godliness!

AVARICE. She casteth my treasures to the wind.

ANGER. She hath discovered mercy!

GREED. She hath ordained fasting!

IDLENESS. Her foot striketh me . . .

ENVY. She driveth me back! I rest never for running in her shadow!

PRIDE. [Descends one step of the chapel, turns her head on her shoulder, half closes her eyelids and replies.] Have I ever beseeched thee to follow me, O Envy? Why comest thou to suck from my breast the poison that swelleth it out? That it is that reneweth thy life, avow it! Thou, Avarice, thou dost delight to rest the gaze of thine eyes upon the gold of my palaces—it is I, O Anger, who give voice to thy drums! Knowest thou not, thou fool, Greed, the visions that I give unto thee? I carve thy dishes, I feast thy followers! Mine the challenges of victual, mine the wagers of drink whereof men burst, and mine the cruelty of the guttler after his meal!

THE SINS. Hearken to her boasting! Hear how she babbleth!

PRIDE. But thou, Lust, thou shouldest cherish me! I fill the hearts of the highborn women, and thence cometh to their breasts such calm and fair movement of majesty. Mine is the rustling silk, the ringing bracelet, the creaking shoe, the shameless raiment, the wide-opened eye, and the bitter excitement that ariseth for unseemly posture. I am Daring, I urge thee unto great venturings! All despised things do dry them before my hearth . . . dost thou hear the proud neighing of whoredoms triumphant?

THE SINS. What matter! We it is who do suffer!

ENVY. Nay, Father, on me shouldest thou have pity. My nails are worn away; do thou sharpen them!

GREED. Lo, I am full even to the throat! The skin of my belly rendeth in sunder. But ever I hunger, ever am I athirst! Devise thou somewhat that shall be without all victual, nay, without the creation itself!

AVARICE. Yet have I ravaged the earth and pierced mountains, I have slaughtered beasts and hewn down forests and sold all that might be sold—the body and the soul, tears and laughter, kisses and thoughts! O could I but catch the rays of the sun and melt them into pieces of gold!

ANGER. Anoint me, O My Father, with vinegar distilled by Hatred. For I fall for faintness at the smile of Lust and the enticing of Avarice. Let me break, let me grind unto powder, let me slay! Meseemeth I have the Ocean within my breast. Wrath crasheth against wrath and I quiver as do the cliffs to the beating of the tides.

SLOTH. [Yawning.] On a soft quilt of down . . . to the breath of a soft wind . . . in a bark . . . doing nought . . . ah . . . ah! [She falls asleep.]

LUST. I would feel that I sink without ceasing into rapture, as it were into a gulf that endeth not . . . where is it, that which I seem to pursue through possession? For I see, darkly, in the heart of pleasure, as it were a dim sun the rays whereof dazzle me and the heat of it enkindleth me.

O that I had hands over all my body wherewith to fondle! O that I had lips wherewith to kiss, at the tips of my fingers!

THE DEVIL. Cry not so loud! Labour all ye together. Help me! [He points to S. Anthony.]

Bring to flower in his thought new imaginations, and then shall he know dreadful despair and rendings of covetousness and fury of weariness! Make him to pass from the languor of Sloth even into the frenzy of Anger! Let him be smitten suddenly with great hunger before the lighted tables of great feasts; let him trail, rutting, over the floor of his hut, let him compare him unto them that be happy, and let him abhor the world! Let him be exalted in repentance, let him burst in sunder for pride! Make ye him yours! Make ye him mine! Go! Call together the spirits of evil, your sons and your sons' sons, with all fevers, all visions of madness, all bitterness unbounded!

[The Devil withdraws to the back of the scene and sits him down upon the body of Sloth; he places Lust between his legs, and then unfolds, like a bat, his great greenish wings whereunder the other Sins come and shelter them.

Pride, from behind him, passes her head over his shoulder and kisses him on the forehead.]

S. ANTHONY. [Between the Virtues.] Shall they return?

HOPE. We are here! Fear nought!

FAITH. [Standing upright, straight and motionless.] Believe that which thou seest not, believe that which thou knowest not—and ask not to see that thou hopest, neither to know that thou dost worship! The unbelievers hear but the voice of the flesh and the testimony of the understanding, but the sons of Christ despise the flesh and betake them to the speech of the Word. For the Word is eternal, but the flesh shall die and the understanding shall vanish away as it were the perfume of wine that is poured out upon the ground! Hope for grace that thou mayest obtain it, keep it that it may increase, despair not that it may return unto thee!

CHARITY. [On her knees, as though she were beside a dying man.] Fast for sinners, pray for them that worship idols, scourge thyself for the unclean! Pluck out of thy soul all love of this world! For as these be lessened so shall thy soul stand higher and higher, even as the pine-trees upon the mountains, whose leaves are diminished even as they draw nearer unto the heavens!

S. ANTHONY. Speak on, speak on! Infinite peace entereth within me!

HOPE. [Lifting her great blue eyes unto heaven.] The bark was tossed upon the waters and Jesus slept. They heard in the darkness the wind crying in great wrath. "Arise, Master," they said, "drive away the winds!" The bark is thine heart which beareth Faith. Suffer her not to sleep, for the tempest was strengthened because the Lord slept. When He opened again his eyelids, it passed away.

If then thou wouldest cross from the one shore unto the other, have no heed for the lightning that dazzleth thee nor for the waves that deafen thine ears—take no thought for the oars, nor for the sail, nor for the night, nor for the storm! Is not the Lord with thee?

S. ANTHONY. [Clinging close to the Virtues.] Nearer! Nearer!

FAITH. Hosanna! Glory to God! [The Sins all at once begin to howl.]

S. ANTHONY. [Leaping up.] Save me, save me!

THE VIRTUES. Be of good Courage! O Anthony! The temptations of the Evil One shall assail always the faith of mankind in the Lord, and the sanctuaries shall be shaken together in harmony by the blasts of the tempest that shall beat upon their walls.

THE SINS. Yet at the last shall they fall to pieces, for we are eternally young even as the dawn, we are strong as the flesh, we are undying even as the Spirit.

(VARIANT: *Here is intercalated a passage suppressed by Flaubert, but which figures in the manuscript of 1856 on a page gummed on to p. 76.*)

FAITH. I shall increase my stature. I shall become valorous, a conqueror.

ANGER. I shall curse. I shall persecute. I shall burn. I shall slay.

CHARITY. I shall pour forth my blood in preaching. I shall give alms freely and consolation. I shall wash away all sorrow, from the sore of the leper even to the mocking of the unbelievers.

PRIDE. I shall fill the churches with the pomp of Assyria. I shall place therein vessels of gold and purple, and inlaid work of diamonds, and canopies of ostrich feathers—and the heritor of S. Peter shall put forth the satin of his sandals for kings to kiss.

AVARICE. I shall sell the bones of martyrs, redemption of sins, the flesh of God, and the joys of heaven.

HOPE. The sound of the church bells shall be spread abroad in the winds as it were the voices of the seraphim that sing; and all the people shall bless the Most High in the sounding speech of the priests.

LOGIC. The fury of the Devil shall drive them to madness without end; their speech shall overflow, there shall be rivers of blood.

FAITH. The sweet odour of mine incense shall purify souls, and they that be strong shall free them from all love that they may the better brighten the life unto the love celestial that shall burn them without ceasing.

LUST. Ay, and man, ever agape after my joys, shall place in his sanctuaries his Goddess that dieth not, Woman! He shall dream of her crowned with stars, smiling, fair-haired, with ruddy cheeks, her breasts swollen with milk even as Cybele of the Syrians!

LOGIC. Thus shall every man in this worship satisfy the several lusts of his own heart. The master shall love it for the submission that it doth compel, and the slave for the freedom that it promiseth, the poet for the manner of its ordering, the wise man for its godly teaching; yet others shall love it for its statecraft or for its great age; for we shall breathe into it with our breath and enkindle it with our heat seeing that we are young eternally.

(End of Variant.)

THE DEVIL. Yea! Let us enter! Let us drive them forth!

A CHILD'S VOICE. Mother, mother, await me!

[Science runs up; a child, white-haired, and frail of feet.]

SCIENCE. [To Pride.] Ah, didst thou know how sick am I, what confusion there is within mine head! O my mother, to what end be these many writings that I spell out? Now and then the wind quencheth my torch, and then am I alone, weeping in the darkness.

THE SINS. What aileth him? What is his need?

AVARICE. Wilt thou come with me?

SCIENCE. Nay, I have polished thy diamonds, I have beaten out thy money, I have woven thy fine cloth.

GREED. Wilt thou come with me?

SCIENCE. Nay, I know how to make the vine grow and after what manner men hunt beasts.

ENVY. Wilt thou come with me?

SCIENCE. Nay, I have no hate.

ANGER. Wilt thou come with me?

SCIENCE. Nay, nought can irk me to wrath.

SLOTH. Rest thee!

SCIENCE. Nay . . . even as the stars on which she doth gaze my thought goeth forth ever of herself, she accomplisheth her journey that none may withstand, and together we pass in great courses about the heavens.

LUST. Wilt thou come with me?

SCIENCE. Nay! I have persecuted thee with curious zeal, I have seen the paint upon thy face sweat for thy strivings wherewith thou didst strive to get thee pleasure. Thou, O Lust, thou goest about in freedom, thou art beautiful, thou liftest up thine head. At all cross-roads of the soul is thy song heard; and thou dost pass at the end of a thought, even as an harlot passeth at the end of a street. But thou sayest nought of the sores that eat away their heart, nor of the weariness without measure that drippeth from love as from a sore. Get thee hence, begone! I am weary of thy face.

Rather do I love the weed on the flank of the cliffs, than thine hair unknotted! Rather do I love the light of the moon lengthening in the tides, than thy distraught gaze that drowneth itself in fondness. Rather do I love marble, or colours, or insects or pebbles! Rather would I have my loneliness than thine house, and my despair than thy sorrows.

PRIDE. Comfort thee, my child! Thou shalt grow greater in stature! I will give thee to drink of good bitter wine, thou shalt make thy bed upon herbs of the field.

[S. Anthony is still on his knees between the three Cardinal Virtues; they spread out their white robes in front of him to shelter him, but]

THE DEVIL. [Takes Science by the hand and points to Faith inside the chapel.] Behold her! Thou shalt utterly make an end of her!

SCIENCE. [Kicking against the door.] Open unto me! The hour hath come!

THE SINS. [Scratching the wall with their nails.] Ha! The sky is shaken! All things shall fall to pieces!

SCIENCE. I shall tell unto thee the beginnings of things! I shall display the certitude thereof before thee! Thou shalt see. . . .

FAITH. No matter! Say on!

S. ANTHONY. Our Father, which art in heaven. . . . [The Sins howl, he turns away from them.]

Ah me! What should I do?

FAITH. Pray to the Son!

SCIENCE. Yet hath Origen forbidden that!

FAITH. Make supplication unto the angels!

PRIDE. But they can have no part, as thou hast, in the virtue of Jesus Christ, seeing that they are without the body! They have not suffered, merit is not in them; they would envy thee did they know of thee.

CHARITY. Think upon the martyrs!

SCIENCE. But all worship, all love, all wickedness of whatsoever kind, these have had their martyrs, even as thy God.

S. ANTHONY. Ah me! I would fain go and pray upon their tombs!

GREED. Ay, forsooth, by night, when the little lamps shrivel in the fog in the midst of the dishes of meat and the cups that smoke . . . the faithful hold feast for the salvation of the dead, and they return thence in the morning, they stagger to and fro in the long grass.

S. ANTHONY. [Pulling the Virtues by their robes.] Answer! Speak unto them! Be swift in doing!

FAITH. Doctrine. . . .

LOGIC. [Interrupting her.] There is nought doth stablish it!

CHARITY. The loving-kindness of the Lord. . . . [Envy bursts out laugh¬ ing.]

HOPE. The joys of Heaven. . . .

LOGIC. Nay, which Heaven? Is it the garden of Moses, or Jerusalem the city of light, or the unclean heaven of Epiphanes? Shalt thou go into the stars of Manes, into the Blessed Fields of the idolators, or into the dim heaven of fire of the wise men?

Shalt thou take with thee into the mysterious firmament thy mortal body, raised up again? Yet, saith Paul of Tarsus, flesh and blood do not enter therein!

[S. Anthony can no longer hear the voices of the Virtues whose lips continue to quiver in rapid and monotonous movement, like the leaves of a tree shaken. He listens intently and stands gaping.]

LOGIC. Wherefore tempted He Judas when He gave the bag into his trust!

ENVY. Himself He yielded not, for an angel bore Him up in His Agony.

LOGIC. He was no whit clean of sin forasmuch as He was born of a woman.

SCIENCE. He was of the seed of Rahab the harlot, and Bathsheba the adulteress, and Tamar who sinned with her brother.

LOGIC. Wherefore came He not into the house of Lazarus? Wherefore rejected He His mother?

Wherefore had He need of baptism? Wherefore feared He to die?

S. ANTHONY. [To the Virtues.] Ah me! Ye grow pale!

ALL TOGETHER. Aha! Thou shalt sing! Thou shalt dance! Thou shalt laugh! [He runs, bewildered, seeking to flee.]

PRIDE. Enough hast thou prayed, Anthony! Thou hast grace!

S. ANTHONY. What? . . . Yet are the Temptations still there? [The Devil makes a swift sign to the Sins.]

PRIDE. They are there no more! Behold! [The Sins have disappeared.]

S. ANTHONY. [Looking round.] Yea, it is true.

[Pride strikes Faith in the face with the serpent she holds in her bosom, and the Virtues disappear without the hermit perceiving it.]

PRIDE. [Resumes.] Come forth from thy chapel! Come forth! Breathe the air!

S. ANTHONY. [He is now outside.] How soft is the night! How pure is the air! How the stars glitter!

[He walks up and down, his arms swinging loose. Pride stalks behind him, in his shadow.]

How can other men see to their salvation that have wives and trades and all the troubles of this life? As for me, thanks be to Heaven, nought troubleth me. In the morning I make my prayer—that is the beginning; then I give food unto my pig—that maketh me merry; then do I sweep mine hut clean, I take up my baskets; at last cometh the hour of prayer. . . . [The Devil laughs in the background.]

A while since I was much tormented, yea, I was evilly tormented. . . . Nay, I will not let those wicked thoughts return! I know now the manner of their onset. [His foot strikes against something; he picks it up.] Ha! A

THE TEMPTATION OF SAINT ANTHONY

silver goblet! and therein is a piece of gold. . . . What? . . . another, and yet another! Ah! Wonder! [The goblet fills with gold pieces.] Lo! The colour of it! It changeth! . . . It is emerald! Lo! It becometh wholly clear and full of light . . . it is a diamond! It burneth me! Ah!

[Rubies, turquoises, onyxes, pearls and topazes pour over the edge of the goblet. S. Anthony looses his hands from it; it stays in the air, the stem lengthens, and the cup of it opens out above like a great lotus flower, whence streams continually a cascade of precious stones.]

Nay! I will not! [He kicks the goblet; the vision disappears.]

When shall I be at rest? What a great sinner am I! I can have no thought but I lose my soul! Hither, hither, pangs of the flesh! [He leaps to his scourge.]

THE PIG. [Waking up.] What a dream!

I was on the shores of a lake. I entered therein, for I was athirst, and the wave thereof changed suddenly into water wherein dishes had been washed. Then a warm wind, as it were a vapour of the cooking pots, drave toward my mouth broken bits of victual that floated afar off, hither and thither. The more I ate thereof, the more I craved to eat, and I went forward continually, making with my body a furrow in the clear broth. I swam therein, distraught, I said unto myself: "Hasten!" The rottenness of all the world was spread out round about me to satisfy the desire of my belly. In the darkness I saw dimly clots of black blood, plashes of oil, blue entrails, the droppings of all beasts, with the vomits of feasts and the green drip that sweateth from sores. It thickened beneath me; my four paws sank therein; a rain of retching that fell fine as needles, pricked mine eyes, but ever I swallowed, for it was good. The lake boiled ever more and more, it pressed upon my ribs, it was unbounded, it burned me, it choked me; I would flee, but I could not move; I closed my mouth, but needs must I open it again; then did other things of themselves fling themselves therein, all bubbled in my belly, all lapped against mine ears. I howled, my throat rattled, I ate . . . pah, pah! I would fain break mine head against the stones that I may rid me of my thought!

S. ANTHONY. [Scourging himself.] Ah! No matter! Be not a coward! Ah! There, sinner, there! Suffer! Weep! Cry aloud! Yet again cry aloud! What? I shall count even to five score, even to a thousand! [He pauses.]

Nay, thou shalt not triumph over me, thou weakness of the flesh! . . . Bleed, bleed! [He recommences.]

Stay! . . . I feel nought now! . . . Doubtless the pricks catch in my vesture.

[He undoes his robe, which falls as far as his girdle. He resumes his scourging, the blows ring.]

Aha! On the breast! On the back! On the arms! On the loins! On the face! I crave for scourging, it calmeth me. Stronger! . . . Woe! Woe! . . . yet do I now desire to laugh. Ha, ha, ha! It is as though hands fondled me over all my body . . . tear we it! Ah me! My sinews break! What then?

[He stops.]

It may be the ravishment doth lessen the pangs of the flesh; I will crush it out therefrom; I will have no mercy upon it, nay, nay!
[He lashes himself in frenzy. The Devil, standing behind him, has taken his arm and is urging it in furious movement.]
In despite of myself mine arm continueth! Who urgeth me? What torment! What rapture! I can no more, my being melteth . . . I die.
[He swoons away and he thinks he sees: a street with flowering plane-trees; to the left hand, in the angle, a little house whose half-open door gives sight of a court bordered by Doric columns that support the dwelling-rooms of the first storey; between the columns can be distinguished other doors covered with blue lacquer and adorned with inlay of copper.
In the middle of the courtyard, on her knees, a woman, clad in a yellow tunic, is filling baskets and boxes. Standing upright near her, her back against a column and watching her at her task, is another woman, all in white; her garment is fastened on her shoulders with a golden brooch, and it hangs thence in great straight folds, and the toes of her bare feet, shod in openworked sandals, peer out beyond it. Two wide fair tresses, plaited in symmetrical diamond plaits, spread out over her ears; they meet and are attached behind to a garland of fine pearls, whence falls in tiny curls all the rest of her hair.]
THE COURTESAN. Hasten, Lampito! I must depart ere even the mariners be awake!
[The kneeling woman sobs; the other continues:] Hast thou put the ointment of Delos into the leaden boxes, and my sandals of Patara into the satchel scented with the powder of iris?
LAMPITO. Yea, Mistress! and here is the loosestrife for thine hair, here be the flies' feet for thine eyebrows and the roots of bear's breech for thy face.
THE COURTESAN. Hide in the bottom thereof, beneath my robes from Sybaris, the pine-wood tablets that constrain my waist, forget not the stone of the wild ass that the wizard sold unto me, nor the firestone of Egypt that preventeth childbirth.
LAMPITO. Ah! Mistress, shall I then see thee no more? [She weeps. S. Anthony sees himself—sees another S. Anthony—in the street, before the Courtesan's house.]
THE COURTESAN. Furthermore put in all that I have of spikenard, of oil of roses, of saffron—and especially of almond oil; for they tell me that it is bad in that country. Forasmuch as he loveth me since that day when he was aware at his awakening that his beard smelled sweet for that he had slept with his head upon my breast, surely I must see to it that my body give forth soft odours.
LAMPITO. He hath great riches, Mistress, this king of Pergamos?
THE COURTESAN. Ay, Lampito, he is rich! and I would not beg of my lovers of aforetime when I am old, nor be consenting unto mariners. In five years, in ten years, I shall have much gold, O Lampito! I shall return,—and even if I cannot build a portico at Sicyone as did Lamia, nor, as did Cleine the flute player, people the Peloponnesus with the brazen statues of

me, yet—this at least is my hope—I shall have the wherewithal to feed my little Syracusan hound with the cakes of Carthage. I shall get me an household after the manner of the Persians. I shall have peacocks in my courtyard and robes of purple from Hermione broidered with sprays of golden ivy—and they shall say: "Lo! It is Demonassa the Corinthian who returneth to dwell among us! Happy is he whom she doth love!" For it is ever the rich woman, O Lampito, who is desired!

LAMPITO. Mistress, the young men of Athens will die of weariness. [S. Anthony advances towards the door.]

THE COURTESAN. Who is it walketh in the street, Lampito?

LAMPITO. Doubtless it is the wind blowing in the plane-trees, my mistress.

THE COURTESAN. I fear the Archons; did they know that I would depart, they would stay me.

LAMPITO. But three mules await thee at the Golden Cross-roads, and with them a sure guide who knoweth the mountain passes.

THE FALSE S. ANTHONY. [In the street.] Shall I enter? Shall I refrain?

LAMPITO. Ah, me! The feasts will be sad! None could raise the striped skirt as thou couldest, in equal measure, in the Dorian bibasis, none could dance the martypsa in more wondrous wise! When thou turnedst around about the couches, thy body flung back, thy right arm stretched out, clapping the black castanets in thy hands, the wind of thy scarf stirred the hair upon the foreheads of the guests who bowed them forward between the torches that they might see thy dance as it passed. [The False S. Anthony stops.]

THE COURTESAN. Who is it sigheth without, Lampito?

LAMPITO. Nay, it is no one, my mistress! Doubtless it is the turtles that coo upon the terrace.

THE FALSE S. ANTHONY. Should I enter?

LAMPITO. Thou didst drink the wine of Mendes in goblets from Carchedon. Thou didst seat thee upon the knees of the great men, and each one of them, holding thy waist, desired thee to say some word. The wise men were heated, they discoursed of Beauty; the painters waved their arms, they marvelled at the fashion of thy face; the poets grew pale, they shivered under their vesture.

Surely folk of a strange land shall not praise thee, when thou dost stretch thy body forward, even as a swimmer, over the harp of Egypt with the forty golden chords, nor when the hollow lute murmureth under the ivory bow, and thy mouth whose speech is soft is opened for the songs of the Sweet Singers. O thou Demonassa, whose eyebrows are curved even as the bow of Apollo, and whose face is beautiful as the quiet sea, no longer shalt thou know the long choirs of the feast of the Law-giver pass upon the road to Eleusis, nor the theatre of Bacchus, shrill with the voices of the players, nor the harbour where the folk walk in the evening.

THE COURTESAN. Lampito, one knocketh upon the door!

LAMPITO. Nay, Mistress, it is the screen beateth against the wall.

THE FALSE S. ANTHONY. [Holding the knocker.] My knees tremble, I shall not dare.

THE COURTESAN. [Walking up and down under the colonnades, her head bowed, her arms hanging loose.] Alas, alas! I must depart! . . . Farewell to the long discourse in their halls with the beloved makers of statues, farewell to the sound of the iron chisels that rang on the marble of Paros. The Master, bare-armed, kneaded the brown clay. From the stool whereon I stood before him, I could see his great brow knit with disquiet. On my body he sought for the shape that he had imagined, and he was sore amazed, forasmuch as he found it on a sudden to be yet more wondrous than the shape within his thought; as for me, I laughed to see the despair of his craft for the form of my knee-pan and the dimples in my back. [The False S. Anthony pushes open the door.]

LAMPITO. [Throwing herself upon Demonassa.] Mistress, Mistress! It is that stranger who had bade me say nought thereof . . . [All disappear.]

S. ANTHONY. [Rises up again.] Where was I? . . . In a street in Athens? . . . yet have I never been there! . . . No matter! I am persuaded that all things yonder must be so ordered.

Whence cometh it that I still think thereon? . . . this is evil! Yet wherefore? . . . the least of my desires is so fenced about with stumbling-blocks that I can pass to and fro therein at mine ease without any fear of peril. Even had I let my desires have their will of me or ever I came into the wilderness, now would the dream of them not torment me . . . perchance. I should know the kisses that slay the soul . . . the joy of accursed love . . . the fierceness of pleasure . . . [He strikes his forehead.]

Again! Again! Whither runneth my thought? At the last I do no more possess myself, so dispersed and widespread is mine own self. [He folds his arms and sighs.]

Yet aforetime I was calm, I dwelt in the simplicity of my belief, and every morn when I awoke it was as though my soul flowered forth beneath the eye of God, as it were a meadow spread with dew steaming to the sun. Yea! Aforetime, in the beginning. . . . I had but departed from mine house.

THE PIG. I have remembrance of a farmyard, between four walls, with a pool of mire, a great and rich dungheap and a trough of new wood ever full of bran. I slept in the shadow, my snout resting upon red udders and I had ever in my throat the taste of the milk.

S. ANTHONY. Who dwelleth now there in my father's house? Ah me! How bitterly wept my mother when I departed! Hath she ever thought of me? She must be very aged . . . very aged.

[He half closes his eyes and looks towards the horizon and sees afar off in the midst of the sands some little huts of grey mud under a grove of palm-trees whose boughs sway. Dogs trail themselves over the deserted sills, a herd of buffaloes passes; he can even make out, in the palisades of dry reeds, hens pecking wheat under the bellies of the asses. But an aged woman who is spinning with a distaff comes out of her house and looks about her anxiously. She is bent double, wrinkled, lean, covered with rags; from time to time, to wipe her red eyelids, she takes her long hair in both hands—her hair that hangs over her shoulders, whiter and more tangled than the flax of her distaff; she murmurs:]

THE AGED WOMAN. The Publicans have taken away mine all! I am sick. ı . . I am about to die . . . where is he?

S. ANTHONY. Here am I, my mother! It is I, it is I! I return unto thee!

[He runs forward with outstretched arms, but strikes against the rock and covers his face with blood from the impact. He looks round him. The lamp is burning, the pig is dozing, the fragments of baskets, lying on the ground, are lifted by the wind. He weeps.]

Ah me! I am wounded . . . I suffer! . . . yet have I never harmed any man! Whence cometh all this? wherefore is it?   [Silence. He resumes:] It were well that I fasten my thoughts upon somewhat that cannot change, and that I suffer not my thoughts to stray; but whereon shall I fasten them? . . . I will even assay to read that ancient book of the Scriptures that Paul the Solitary gave unto me when he was dying!

[He goes into his hut and brings forth a book, then sits down on a bench, turns the leaves over at random, then reads:]

"And Judah was comforted, and went up unto his sheepshearers." Verily that healeth me . . . mine understanding is clear again!

"He and his friend, Hirah the Adullamite, the shepherd of his flocks." . . . [A bleating is heard on the horizon.]

It is as though I were there . . . meseemeth even that afar off. . . .

[A fiery glow spreads like dust in the atmosphere; the lands are lifted, and the sand disappears slowly beneath the grass.]

"And it was told to Tamar, saying, Behold thy father-in-law goeth up to Timnath to shear his sheep." . . .

[Great mountains outline their blue scalloped peaks against a violet sky. There are tents on the hills and flocks of black sheep: one can hear the cry of the shepherds; and the bells tinkle. S. Anthony, as he continues reading, sees facing him two paths that cross one another. A woman comes up and sits down by the way-side. Her eyeballs gleam in the rift of her white veil that passes several times about her face, raising the tips of her ears and keeping her big gold earrings clear of her head. The breeze presses her summer robing against her body, and the garment is shaken behind her and claps in the air like a flag. A shepherd comes forward, clad in a yellow cloak that is fastened round his forehead by a brass circlet. He carries a stick with a crook to it, and he walks with dignity in his goatskin sandals. He approaches her—they are face to face—they speak in a low voice; the man draws from off his finger a silver signet, and from his head the brass circlet, and lays down his staff; the woman puts the signet ring on her finger and the circlet on her arm; she takes the staff and says:]

At once! There! . . .

THE SHEPHERD. Nay, the goat's dung will spoil thy fine robe.

[They go further off, and the shepherd speaks again.] Surely there is some forgotten cistern somewhere at hand. . . .

THE WOMAN. Thou art foolish as a child, thou shepherd with the long beard!

THE SHEPHERD. [Laughing.] Thou art a merry maid! I would fain see thy face.

THE WOMAN. [She looks frightened.] Nay, nay! [She crouches down, her yellow robe is caught by the fringe in the thorns; the sun becomes so strong and so luminous that they vanish in a dazzling light. The rocks crack, the grass bursts into flame, and the whole valley smokes as though it were covered with craters. Great clouds glide over the sky, like huge purple veils borne away by the wind.]

S. ANTHONY. [Gasping, lets fall the Bible.] Ah me! I am athirst! My flesh burneth!

[All disappears, and in the slanting light of the moon is seen a clear lake that loses itself beneath tree-trunks. The thick roots standing out of the water are covered with moss. The higher branches above bow them to a dome; and here and there pierces a greenish ray of daylight that sparkles upon the leaves, shivers at the tips of the blades of grass, glitters against the pebbles, and casts lengthening ribbons of changing light over the wet sand. Hanging white vapours rend apart slowly; the dew trickles down the bark of the trees; one great willow-tree stretches across everything, from one side to the other, with one spray that falls back.]

Ah, how pleasant is it! It raineth! I hear the drops . . . and my breast is opened to the sweet smells of the green things . . . even as, aforetime in my youth, when I ran upon the mountains, chasing the lightfooted stags . . . [He falls into a reverie] and the voice of the hounds came unto me with the sound of the torrents and the murmur of the leaves.

[Two coupled greyhounds push their noses through the branches, pulling the while on their leash that is held on the finger of a young woman clad in a short-skirted robe. She walks quickly and looks behind her. A little quiver is beating against her back. The freshness of the morning has flushed to rose her oval face crowned with brown damp tresses. She throws down her arrows and her bow on the lawn, then quiets her hounds and ties them up to a privet-bush, then, standing on one foot only, she begins to undo the latchet of her Cretan shoe.]

Waters of fire run beneath my flesh—longing to live getteth hold on me. All my being roareth! I am an-hungered, I thirst!

[S. Anthony moves forward. Other women run up. They take off their vesture and hang it to the branches of the trees. They shiver, they enter the water, feeling it with their feet, throwing it into their faces. They laugh —S. Anthony laughs. They bend down—he bends down.]

Aha! rejoice, praise be unto mirth! I dabble, I drink, I am happy, I need but a well-served table! . . .

[Then appears, beneath a black sky, a vast hall, lit with golden candlesticks.

Plinths of porphyry, supporting columns that are half lost in the shadow, so high are they, form long lines, one following the other, outside the tables that lengthen out even to the horizon where appear, in a luminous mist, enormous structures, pyramids, cupolae, stairways, flights of steps—arcades with colonnades and obelisks upon domes. Between the silver-footed bronze couches and the long pitchers whence streams forth black wine, choirs of musicians crowned with violets pluck at great harps and sing in vibrant voices; at the far end, above the rest, alone, crowned with the tiara, and robed in scarlet, the King Nebuchadnezzar eats and drinks. Behind him a colossal statue, fashioned in his image, stifles nations in its arms; on the head of it is a diadem of hollow stones that hold lamps and cast blue rays of light all round it.

At the four corners of his table are four priests in white mantles and pointed bonnets, holding censers the smoke of whose incense they swing about him. On the ground below him crawl the captive kings, footless and handless; he throws them food; yet lower down stand his brethren, their eyes bandaged, for they are blind, every one of them.

Slaves run about with dishes, women pass round the tables and pour out for the guests to drink, the baskets creak for the weight of the loaves, a dromedary comes and goes, laden with pierced wine-skins whence flows vervain to freshen the pavement. The knives glimmer, the flowers drop their petals, the pyramids of fruit collapse, the candles burn.

Laughing beast-tamers lead in lions who growl. Dancing girls, their hair held in nets, turn on their hands, spitting fire through their nostrils. Negro mountebanks juggle, naked children pelt one another with snowballs that smash as they fall against the shining silver vessels. The cymbals clash, the king drinks. He wipes the perfumes from his face with his arm. He eats out of the sacred vessels. He rolls his eyes.

So great is the multitude that the sound of it is as the sea! A cloud floats over the feast, so countless are the meats and so countless the breath of men! Now and again a flake flies from off the great torches, snatched away by the wind, and crosses the hall like a shooting-star.

All of a sudden appears a man clad in goat-skins. The king falls from his throne, the columns and their capitals are overthrown like trees, the dishes clash together like waves of gold, all rise to their feet, and no more can be seen but the backs of those that flee.

S. Anthony finds himself once more in front of his hut. It is broad daylight.]

What! . . . The sun is shining! Yet a moment past I was in deep night! Yet this is indeed mine own hut, and this is mine own self of a surety. [He touches himself.] This is my body! These be mine hands! My heart beateth; and the pig is yet here . . . he lyeth on the sand, and the froth is at his mouth. Nay, nay! Bethinks we! I am alone! No one hath come hither, of that am I sure!

[But he sees facing him three riders mounted on wild asses, clad in green robes, holding lilies in their hands; they all three resemble one another in countenance. They do not move—neither do the wild asses; these lower their long ears, and stretch forth their necks, they draw back their lips and show their gums.

S. Anthony turns round; he sees yet three other riders, similar to these, on similar asses, and in the same posture. He draws back. Then the wild asses, all at the same time, go one pace forward and rub their muzzles against him, trying to bite his vesture.

There is a sound of tomtoms and little bells, and a great clamour of voices crying out, "Hither, hither . . . this is the place."

Banners appear between the clefts of the mountain, and heads of camels with red silken halters, and mules laden with baggage, and women, covered with yellow veils, riding astride on piebald horses. The panting beasts lie down. The slaves rush to the bales and untie the knots of the cords with their teeth. They unroll motley carpets, they spread glittering things upon the ground.

Arrives a white elephant, caparisoned in a golden net, shaking the tuft of ostrich feathers bound to his frontal. On his back, amidst blue woollen cushions, her legs crossed, her eyelids half closed, her head swaying, is a woman so splendidly attired that she sends forth rays on all sides of her; behind her, on the crupper, standing on one foot, is a negro, red-booted and with coral bracelets; he holds in his hand a great round leaf with which he fans her, grinning the while.

The crowd fall on their faces, the elephant bends his knees, and the Queen of Sheba, letting herself slide adown his shoulder, descends on to the carpets and advances towards S. Anthony.

Her gown is of gold brocade, divided at regular intervals by furbelows of pearls, of jet, and of sapphires; her waist is held in by its strait bodice that is adorned with applied designs in colour representing the twelve signs of the Zodiac. She has very high-heeled pattens, the one of which is black, sown with silver stars and a crescent moon, while the other, which is white, is covered with tiny drops of gold with a sun in the middle.

Her large sleeves, ornate with emeralds and birds' feathers, show naked her little round arms adorned at the wrists with ebony bracelets, and her hands, loaded with rings, end in nails so pointed that the tips of her fingers look almost like needles. A chain of flat gold, passing under her chin and up her cheeks, winds in spirals round her high head-dress powdered with blue powder, then, falling again, grazes her shoulders and passes to her bosom, fastened thereupon to a little diamond scorpion whose tongue protrudes between her breasts. Two big white pearls pull down her ears. The edges of her eyelids are painted with black. She has a brown patch on her left cheek-bone; she opens her mouth when she breathes, as though her bodice constrained her.

As she walks, she shakes a green parasol, ivory-handled, hung round with vermilion bells; twelve frizzled little nigger boys bear the long train of her beautiful gown, and an ape holds the end of it; he lifts it up from time to time to peep thereunder.]

THE QUEEN OF SHEBA. Ah, fair hermit, fair hermit! My heart faileth me!

S. ANTHONY. [Drawing back.] Begone! Thou art a vision! I know it! Get thee behind me!

THE QUEEN OF SHEBA. For my impatient stamping mine heels have grown hard, and I have broken one of my nails. I sent forth shepherds who stood upon the mountains and held their hands before their eyes. I sent forth hunters who cried thy name aloud in the woods, I sent forth spies who went over all highways and asked of every one that passed by: "Hast thou seen him?" At last, at even, I came down from my tower; nay, rather, mine handmaids bore me away in their arms, for I swooned daily when the Dog-star rose.

S. ANTHONY. [To himself.] In vain do I close mine eyelids, yet do I see her ever! . . .

THE QUEEN OF SHEBA. They brought back the life to me by burning herbs, and they put into my mouth, with an iron spoon, an Indian sweetmeat that hath this virtue that it maketh kings happy; so much thereof did I swallow that the itch of it is yet in my throat, deep down. I passed my nights with my face turned to the wall, and I wept! My tears, after many days, made two small holes in the pavement, as it were pools of sea-water in the rocks. For I love thee . . . yea, I love thee greatly! [She takes hold of his beard.]

Laugh, fair hermit, laugh! I am very merry, thou shalt see it! I play upon the lute. I dance like unto a bee. I know many many tales to tell, the one more pleasant than the other.

How shalt thou know how long a way we have come! The hooves of the camels are worn; behold the wild asses of my green riders! they are dead for weariness!

[S. Anthony looks, and indeed the asses are stretched on the ground motionless.]

Since three long moons have they run at unchanged speed, holding a pebble in their teeth wherewith to cut the wind, their tails ever stretched straight, their hams ever folded, galloping without ceasing! Never shall man find again their likes! They were mine from my mother's father, the great King Saharil, the son of Iakhschab, the son of Iaarab, the son of Kastan. Ah, did they yet live, we would harness them unto a litter that we might return swiftly unto mine house. But . . . how? . . . whereon thinkest thou? [She looks carefully at him.] Ah! When thou art wedded unto me, I will clothe thee, I will perfume thee with sweet odours, I will pluck out the hairs of thy body. '

[S. Anthony stands motionless, stiffer than a stake, pale as a dead man, his eyes wide open.]

Thou art sad of countenance! Wherefore then? Is it for leaving thine hut? Yet have I left all for thee—even unto the King Solomon, though he hath much wisdom, and twenty thousand chariots of war, and a long beard! I have brought thee my wedding gifts. Choose thou therefrom!

[She walks through the ranks of slaves and merchandise.]

Here is balm of Gennesareth, and incense from the Cape Gardefan; here is gum and cinnamon, and silfy which is good to put into sauces. Therein yonder are embroidered cloths of Asshur, and ivory from the Ganges, and purple of Elisa; in this box of snow is a wine-skin of the wine of Chalibon that is for the kings of Assyria alone; they drink it pure in the horn of an unicorn. Here be necklaces, clasps, nets, parasols; here is powder of gold of Bashan, and tin from Tartessus, blue wood from Pandion, white furs from Issedonia, carbuncles from the isle of Palaesimond, and toothpicks made of the hairs of the tachas—he is lost, he dwelleth beneath the earth. These cushions are from Emath and these fringes of mantles from Palmyra. Upon this carpet, of Babylon, there is . . . but come thou hither! Nay, come!

[She pulls S. Anthony by the sleeve. He resists. She continues:]

Yonder fine woof that crackleth in the fingers with the crackle of sparks of fire, is the wondrous yellow cloth that is brought by the merchants of Bactria. They need forty and three interpreters for their journey. I will have robes made thereof for thee and thou shalt put them on in mine house.

Push the hasps of the sycamore casket and give me the ivory box that is on the garrot of my elephant.

[Her servants draw from a box something round covered with a skin, and they bring her a little casket covered with chased work.]

Wouldest thou the buckler of Djian-ben-Djian who builded the Pyramids? Lo! Here it is! It is fashioned of seven skins of dragons, set the one over the other, jointed by screws of diamond, tanned in the gall of sons that slew their fathers. On the one side it sheweth forth all the wars that were since weapons of war were made known, and on the other are all the wars that shall be, even unto the end of the world. The thunderbolt leapeth up from off it as it were a ball of cork. If thou art brave, thou shalt put it upon thine arm and wear it when thou goest forth to the chase. Ah! Didst thou but know what I have in my little box! Turn it over! Assay to open it! None may compass that. Kiss me and I will tell thee.

[She takes S. Anthony's cheeks between her two hands; he pushes her back with outstretched arms.]

It was upon a night wherein the King Solomon lost his wit for desire of me. In the end we made a barter. He rose and went out stealthily . . . .

[She turns a pirouette.]

Ha! Fair hermit! Thou shalt not know it! Thou shalt not know!

[She shakes her parasol and all its little bells ring.]

Ay, many more things have I! I have treasures shut up in galleries where men are lost as in a wood. I have summer palaces woven in trellis of reeds, and winter palaces built of black marble. In the midst of lakes, great as seas, I have islands round as pieces of silver, wholly covered with the shell of the pearl, whose shores give forth music to the beating of the warm tides that roll toward the sand. The slaves of my kitchen take birds in my cages and catch fish in my rivers. I have gravers who sit continually graving mine image upon hard stones, I have smelters who pant for breath and cast statues of me, I have perfumers who mingle the sap of plants with vinegar and who beat out pastes, I have sewing women who cut vesture for me, and jewellers who work jewel work for me, I have tire-women who seek new tirings for my hair, and careful painters, who pour upon my wainscoting boiling gums that they cool with fans. The women of my following are sufficient for a king's household, and my eunuchs are an army. I have armed hosts, I have peoples! I have in mine antechamber a bodyguard of dwarfs who bear upon their backs horns of ivory.   [S. Anthony sighs.]

I have gazelles harnessed, I have double yokes of elephants, and coupled camels by hundreds, I have mares whose manes are so long that their hooves are caught therein when they gallop; furthermore, I have herds of oxen whose horns are so great that men hew down the woods before them when they are at pasture. I have giraffes that walk in my gardens, that stretch forth their heads upon the edge of my roof what time I take the air after that I have supped.

Seated in a shell drawn by dolphins, I pass through the caverns. I listen to the fall of the water from the stalactites. I go into the land of diamonds where the magicians who are my friends leave the fairest for my choice: then I go up again on the earth and I enter again into mine own house.

[She pouts her lips and utters a shrill whistle, and a great bird descends from the sky and settles upon the top of her head-dress and scatters the blue powder therefrom. His orange-coloured plumage looks as though it were made of metal scales. His little head surmounted with a silver tuft has a human face. He has four wings, he has vulture's claws, he has an immense peacock's tail which he spreads out in a round behind him. He takes the Queen's parasol in his beak, then totters a little before he attains his balance, then bristles all his feathers and remains motionless.]

I thank thee, fair Simorg-Anka! Thou who hast taught me where my lover was hid. Thanks be unto thee, messenger of mine heart!

He flieth like unto desire. He goeth the round of the world in his journey. In the evening he returneth and standeth at the foot of my couch; he telleth unto me all that he hath seen; he telleth of the seas that passed under him, the fish, and the ships, the great barren deserts, whereon he hath looked down from high heaven; he telleth all the harvests that bowed them in the fields and the plants that grew upon the walls of deserted cities.

[She passes her arm languidly round S. Anthony's neck.]

Ah! Didst thou but wish it! Didst thou wish . . . I have a pavilion upon an headland in the middle of a passage between two seas. It is wainscoted with plates of glass, the floor thereof is of the scales of tortoises, and it is open unto the four winds of heaven.

From on high I see my fleets return and the folk climbing the hill with their burdens upon their shoulders. We should sleep upon coverlets softer than clouds, we should drink cool drink in cups of the rind of fruits, and we should look upon the sun through windows of emerald! Come!

[The Simorg-Anka makes the glittering eyes of his tail turn like wheels, and the Queen of Sheba sighs.]

Ah me! I die! I die! [S. Anthony bows his head.]

Ah! Thou dost spurn me! . . . Farewell!

[She moves away weeping. The procession sets forth; S. Anthony looks at her; she stops.]

Art thou indeed resolved? So beautiful a woman! That hath a tuft of hair between her breasts!

[She laughs. The ape that holds the end of her robe lifts it with out-stretched arms and leaps up and down.]

Thou wilt repent, fair hermit! Thou wilt groan, thou wilt be weary. But I mock thereat! Aha! Aha! Ho! Ho!

[She goes away, her face in her hands, hopping. The slaves pass in the line before S. Anthony, the horses, the dromedaries, the elephant, the women of the Queen's following, the mules who have been reloaded, the little negro boys, the ape, the green riders holding in their hands their lilies, broken, and the Queen of Sheba departs, uttering a species of con-vulsive hiccup that is like a sob or maybe a cackle. But her trailing robe that lengthens out behind her as she advances, arrives like a tide even to S. Anthony's sandals. He puts his foot upon it; all disappears.]

S. ANTHONY. What have I done? Wretched man that I am! [He laments.]

Ah me! How shall I free me from the vision that continually persecuteth me? The pebbles of the wilderness, the bitter water that I drink, the hair-cloth that I wear, all these do change for my damnation into painted pave-ments, into floods of wine, into mantles of purple. Through my desire I do roll me in the whoredoms of the Chief cities, and repentance escapeth from my strivings as it were an handful of sand that slippeth between the fingers, close I mine hand never so tightly. This above all things doth anger me, that this my countless enemy fleeth ever! Where shall he be found?

[Rage seizes him.]

I will plunge deep into awful imaginations. I will mortify myself and compel my thoughts to fasten on sadness, seeing that repentance sufficeth not; I will search out suffering with my mind.

Yet would I love better suffering of the body, were it even beyond bearing! Yea, sooner would I wrestle with savage beasts, and behold my flesh fly apart as it were a red fruit at the edge of a sword! Ay, better would I love that! That would I welcome!

[Suddenly he perceived the interior of a tower. It is pierced by an em-brasure that cuts out a narrow square of blue sky far up in the darkness of the wall; through this embrasure flows a thin stream of sand, noiselessly, ceaselessly, so that little by little it fills the tower.

On the ground are grey masses of strange shape, vague as ruined statues. There is as it were a trembling movement throughout them, and at length S. Anthony discerns that they are men, all seated on the ground, their two arms resting on their knees, their fists under their armpits; in their right hands they hold knives; their attitude is savage and despairing. They raise their heads slowly. Their locks and the hair of their beards are white with dust, their eyeballs are yellow, their cheek-bones are sharp, their nostrils are edged with black, like those of men about to die. They come, one after the other, dragging themselves along, they strike all at the same spot against the stones of the wall, then they let fall again their great lean arms that are like dried-up vine-stocks.

But a rat passes swiftly through their midst. They fling themselves upon it with their knives; S. Anthony can distinguish no more, so furious becomes the medley. He sees them again, all huddled in a circle before a mutilated corpse from which they tear great strips with their hands. Pearly red drops sweat upon the wall. Their eyes roll terribly, their teeth clash together like the steel of sickles that meet, and S. Anthony hears them mutter: "Our fathers have eaten of the sour grapes and the teeth of the children are set on edge." But the sand that falls through the embrasure heaps up around them, and rises even to their shoulders: they repeat, "Our fathers have eaten of the sour grapes and the teeth of the children are set on edge." The sand rises to their lips, to their eyes, to their foreheads. Only the tops of their heads appear. Then all is covered up and not a sound more is heard.]

Horror! [He takes his head in both hands.] Oh! My head, my head! What shall I do that I may tear from out thereof that which filleth it? How shall I know whether in very truth I have seen these things that I have seen?

Were they indeed things . . . there would be union therein, and reason for their being . . . nay, nay! I deceive myself! . . . but I do indeed see them! They are yonder before me! I touch them! Nay, but it cannot be, it cannot be!

Meseemeth that what is without entereth into me, nay, rather, my thought goeth out like the lightning from a cloud and of itself putteth upon it a body, even here, before mine eyes! Peradventure, thus did God, in thought, devise the creation? Is it not more real than some one of these visions that dazzle mine eyes? But wherefore be they visions? Know I even what is a vision? Whereof is truth of things? Where doth the truth begin, and where doth vision end? A tide within a tide, clouds in the night-time, the wind in the wind; and after these, as it were, uncertain currents that whirl, that drive me, changing shapes without end, that rise, that fall, that are lost.

Ha! I can discern nought; but meseemeth two great beasts are here? The one crawleth, the other hovereth . . . O God! They draw nigh unto me!

[Athwart the twilight appears the Sphinx. He stretches out his paws, he slowly shakes the fillets that are upon his brow, and he crouches flat upon his belly. Leaping, flying, spitting fire through his nostrils, beating his wings with his dragon's tail, the Chimera, green-eyed, circles and bays. The ringlets of his tresses, cast to one side, mingle with the hairs on his loins; on the other side they hang down even upon the sand and sway to the swing of his whole body.]

THE SPHINX. [Motionless, looking at the Chimera.] Hither, Chimera, stay thee!

THE CHIMERA. Nay! never!

THE SPHINX. Run not so swiftly, fly not so high, bay not so loud!

THE CHIMERA. Call no more upon me! Call me no more! Forasmuch as thou art ever dumb, never dost thou move.

THE SPHINX. Nay, cease thou from casting flame into my face, from howling into my ears! Thou shalt never melt the stone of me, thou shalt not open my lips.

THE CHIMERA. Neither shalt thou seize hold of me, thou terrible Sphinx, who dost flash thy great eye, everlasting, unto the land's end.

THE SPHINX. Thou art too mad that thou shouldest abide with me.

THE CHIMERA. And thou art too heavy that thou shouldest follow me.

THE SPHINX. This long time have I seen thy twain unfolded wings glide in the tempest at the edge of the wilderness.

THE CHIMERA. This long time have I galloped over the sand and seen thine austere countenance darkening in the sun.

THE SPHINX. In the night-time, when I pass through the corridors of the labyrinth, when I hear the wind roaring under the galleries where passeth the moon, I hear the sound of thy frail feet upon the ringing pavement. Whither goest thou that thou dost flee so swiftly? . . . I, even I, remain at the foot of the stairway, I gaze at the stars in the basons of porphyry.

THE CHIMERA. Air! Air! Fire! Fire! I run upon the waves, I hover upon the mountains, I bay in the gulfs. With my trailing tail I sweep the shores of the sea. When I did lay me down upon the earth, my belly dug out valleys, and the hills have rounded their shape according to the mould of my shoulders. But thou, thou dost ever crouch, thou dost growl like unto the storm, ever again I find thee unmoved, or, it may be, scribing letters upon the sand with thy claw.

THE SPHINX. Ay, I keep my secret. I ponder. I reckon in numbers. The ocean swayeth yet in his great bed; the jackal whineth near the sepulchres; the ears of corn bow them ever to the same wind. I see the dust awhirl and the sun shining, I hear the breathing of the wind.

THE CHIMERA. I am light of heart, I am cheerful. I discover unto men dazzling visions, paradise in the clouds, happiness afar off. I pour endless madness into their souls, plans of blessedness, thoughts of the days to come, dreams of glory, sworn oaths withal of love, and righteous resolves.

I have builded strange buildings whose adornments I have graven with the nail of my claw. I it was who did hang bells upon the tomb of Porsenna. I, even I, discovered idols four-armed, worship without shame, proud tirings of the hair.

I urge the mariners unto journeys of great venture; in the mist they see the islands with green pastures, and domes and naked women that dance; they smile for all the ravishments that do sing within their soul, in the midst of the great billows that close in upon the ship that is foundered.

[S. Anthony walks to and fro between the two great beasts whose jowls graze his shoulders.]

THE SPHINX. O Phantasy, phantasy! Bear me away on thy wings that I may be freed of my sadness!

THE CHIMERA. O Unknown, Unknown! My desire is to thine eyes! As a rutting hyena, so do I go about thee. I beseech gendering of thee, the need of it eateth me up.

Open thy jaws! Lift up thy feet! Get thee upon my back!

THE SPHINX. Since that my feet have been flat upon the earth they can no more be raised. The lichen hath grown upon my mouth as it were a sore. For very pondering I have no word more to say.

THE CHIMERA. Thou liest, thou hypocrite! I have seen thine hidden manhood! Wherefore callest thou ever upon me, yet ever deniest me?

THE SPHINX. Nay, it is thou, untamed Waywardness, that dost pass and turn as it were a whirlwind.

THE CHIMERA. Shalt thou blame me? . . . How? . . . Leave me!

[He bays:] Houaho! Houaho!

THE SPHINX. Thou movest, thou dost escape me!

[He growls:] Heoum, eum!

THE CHIMERA. Shall we make trial? . . . thou doest crush me! Houaho, Houaho!

[The Chimera bays, the Sphinx growls, monstrous butterflies hum, lizards advance, bats flit, frogs leap, caterpillars crawl, great spiders crawl about.]

THE PIG. Pity on me! These fearful beasts will devour me raw!

S. ANTHONY. I am a-cold! Terror unbounded entereth into me! Methinks I see as it were wandering shapes who search for substance, or, maybe, beings created that dissolve into thoughts! They are as the gaze of an eye that passeth, as limbs unshapen that quiver, mortal appearances more transparent than bubbles of air.

THE MOUTHLESS FOLK. Breathe not too lustily! Raindrops crush us, false sounds blind us, darkness teareth us asunder. We are made of wind, of perfume, of rays of light, we are a little more than dreams, we are not wholly beings.

THE HALF-FOLK. We have but one eye, one cheek, one nostril, one hand, one leg, the half of a body, the half of an heart; we dwell wholly at our ease in our houses that are but half a house, with our half-wives and our halves of children.

THE SHADE-FOOTED FOLK. We are bound to the earth by our locks that are longer than the bindweed. We lie in the shadow of our feet that are wide as parasols, and we look athwart these upon the light of day, and our veins that intertwine one with another, and our roseate blood that goeth around in its course.

THE BLEMMYES. We have no heads and our shoulders are the broader thereby; there is no ox nor rhinoceros nor elephant who may bear what we bear.

The dim likeness of a face and the similitude of the parts thereof are printed upon our breasts; that is all! Our stomach is a thought, our humours are an imagination. The God who is our God floateth in peace in the innermost chyles.

We walk straight upon our way, we pass through all sloughs, we go warily by all gulfs; of all people we toil the most; we are the happiest, the most righteous.

THE PIGMIES. We little mannikins do swarm upon the world even as the lice upon the hump of a dromedary. Men burn us, they drown us, they crush us, yet ever we appear again with fuller life, and in greater number, terrible for the multitude of us.

THE DOG-HEADED FOLK. [An hairy people who live in the woods in disordered wise.] We climb into the trees that we may suck the eggs of birds, we pluck the nestlings, and we put their nests as it were a bonnet upon our heads. Woe unto the virgin who goeth alone unto the fountain!

Up and on, my fellows! Let us gnash our white teeth, shake we the boughs!

S. ANTHONY. Who is this doth breathe in my face this odour of sap whereat my heart fainteth?   [He sees.]

THE SADHUZAG. [A great black stag with the head of a bull, bearing between his ears a bush of white horns.]

My three score and twelve antlers are hollow even as flutes. I bow them and I straighten them . . . behold!

[He swings his horns backwards and forwards.]

When I turn me toward the south wind, a sound goeth forth from them that draweth unto me all beasts ravished. The serpents twine about my legs, the wasps cling to my nostrils, the parrots and the doves and the ibis perch upon my branches . . . listen!

[He throws back his horns, and a wondrous music unspeakable goes out from them.]

S. ANTHONY. What sounds are these! My heart is loosened! It trembleth! This music shall surely bear my heart away with it!

THE SADHUZAG. But when I turn me to the north, and bend my horns, that are more tufted than a battalion of spears, there goeth out therefrom a terrible voice, and the forests tremble; the lotus bursteth into flower, the waterfalls turn them back unto their sources, the earth doth shake for fear, and the blades of grass bristle, even as the hair on the head of a fearful man . . . hearken!

[He bows his antlers forward, and from them goes forth a music of fear.]

S. ANTHONY. Ah me! I am dissolved, and all that is in mine head is torn therefrom and doth whirl round even as the leaves of a tree in a great wind!

THE UNICORN. [Caracoling before him.] Gallop! Gallop! I have hooves of ivory, and teeth of steel, my head is the colour of purple and my body is white as snow, the horn in my forehead is white at the base and black in the middle and red at the end of it.

I travel from Chaldaea into the wilderness of Tartary, upon the banks of the Ganges and in Mesopotamia. I outrun the ostriches; I run so swiftly that I draw the wind with me. I rub my back against the palm-trees. I roll among the cane trees. With one leap I leap over rivers, and when I pass through Persepolis, it is my sport to break with mine horn the faces of the kings that are graven upon the mountain.

THE GRIFFIN. [A lion with an eagle's beak, white-winged; his body is black and his neck blue.] I, even I, do know the caverns where the old kings lie asleep! They are seated upon their thrones, they are crowned with tiaras and robed in red mantles; a chain that cometh out of the wall doth hold their heads straight, and their sceptres of emerald are laid upon their knees. Near unto them in basons of porphyry the women that they have loved float, white-robed, upon black water. Their treasures are stored in the halls, in stacks whose shape is that of a diamond, in heaps and in pyramids. There be bars longer than the masts of ships, there be cages filled with diamonds, there be suns fashioned of carbuncles.

I stand on the hoary hills, my hinder parts are against the door of the cavern, my claws are lifted up high; with my flaming eyes I spy out them that would come. It is a pale land, full of precipices, without life, a land ravaged. The black sky is spread over the valley wherein the bones of the wayfarers crumble into dust. . . . I lead thee thither, O Anthony, and the doors shall open of themselves; thou shalt smell the hot steam of the mines, thou shalt go down into the passages under the earth.

S. ANTHONY. Nay, nay! It is as though the earth did crush me! I stifle. . . .

[He lifts his forehead towards heaven.]

THE PHŒNIX. [Hovering, pauses; he has great wings of gold, rays go forth from his eyes.] I cross the firmaments, I raze the beaches where I peck at the stars as I pass; I hop on the tips of my claws upon the Milky Way as it were an hen that hoppeth amid grains of oats.

When I would sleep, I lie me down in the moon, I bend my body unto the curved shape of her. At other times I take her in my beak, and with mighty strokes of my wings I draw her through the Heavens. Then it is that she runneth so swiftly, she goeth down into the valleys, she leapeth over the brooks, she skippeth above the woods, even as a kid that wandereth in the great blue plain.

But when the flame of the suns can no longer warm my blood for that it hath grown thin, I go into the land of Arabia to seek fresh myrrh whereof I build me a nest for my burial. Then do I close my wings and make me ready to die.

The rain of the equinox that falleth upon mine ashes doth mingle them with the perfume that is still warm. A worm cometh forth, wings grow upon him, he taketh flight; he is the Phœnix, the son, raised again to life, from the father. New stars flower forth, a younger sun blazeth into light, and the idle worlds begin again to turn them.

[The Phœnix flies about in flaming circles; S. Anthony, dazzled, lowers his eyes towards the earth, and other animals appear, horned beasts, deep-bellied monsters.]

THE PIG. I am sick! Ah! How I suffer! They torment me! Woe, woe, woe, woe is me! [He runs hither and thither.] I am burned, choked, strangled! I die in all wise! My tail is pulled, my belly is pinched, my back is flayed, an asp biteth my genitals.

S. ANTHONY. Woe is me for my pig!

THE BASILISK. [A gigantic serpent, violet-hued, with three-lobed crest, advances, erect to heaven.] Beware! Thou wilt fall into my jaws! I am He that devoureth all things, I am the son of the burning mountains, I have been suckled on lava and fed upon sulphur! The rocks whereon I alight do burst, the trees that my coils do enfold are enkindled into flame, ice melteth at my look; when I pass through the burial fields, the bones of the dead leap in their graves, as it were chestnuts within an oven. I have drunk of the dew of the pastures, of the sap of plants, of the blood of beasts. I drink fire, fire draweth me unto him! I would swallow thy marrow, I would suck thine heart dry. I have two teeth, the one above, the other below, thou shalt feel the bite of them!

[The serpents hiss, the wild beasts bark, jaws clash, there is rain of drops of blood.]

THE MANTICHORA. [A lion, the colour of cinnabar, with a human face; he has three rows of red teeth, a scorpion's tail, and green eyes.]

I run after men. I seize them by the reins, and I beat their heads against the mountains that their brains may gush forth. I sweat pestilence. I spit hail. I it is who devour armies when they adventure into the wilderness. My nails are twisted into augurs, my teeth are shaped like saws, and my tail, that I raise and let fall and turn round, bristleth with darts that I fling to the right, to the left, in front, behind . . . Lo! Lo!

[The Mantichora flings the quills from his tail in successive streaks. S. Anthony, motionless in the midst of the animals, stands listening to all those voices and gazing upon all those shapes.]

THE DOWNLOOKER. [A black buffalo with a pig's head that droops to the ground and is joined to his shoulders by a lean long neck, flabby as an empty gut. His belly touches the earth at every point, and his feet disappear beneath the enormous mane of hard hairs that covers his face.]

Thus do I ever stay, gross, melancholy, fierce, ever I feel the heat of the earth under my belly.

So heavy is my head that I cannot bear it up, I roll it about me slowly; I open my jaw, and I tear up with my tongue poisonous herbs that are watered with my breath. Once I did even devour mine own feet, nor was I aware of it.

No man hath ever seen mine eyes, O Anthony; nay, they that have seen them are dead. Did I lift my swollen red eyelids, at once thou wouldst die.

S. ANTHONY. Ah! Yonder beast! . . .

Were I then to desire to look upon those eyes! Verily, his fierce witlessness draweth me thereunto, I tremble! I am drawn on I know not how toward depths full of fear, nor can I resist!

[He sees advancing sea-urchins, dolphins, fishes that walk upright upon their beards, great oysters yawning, cuttle-fish spouting forth black liquid, whales blowing water through their blow-holes, horns of ammonites unrolling like cables, and sea-grey four-footed beasts that sway damp seaweed upon their heads. Green phosphorescence glistens about their fins, at the edge of their gills, on the crest of their backs, encircling round valves, clinging to the moustaches of the seals, or trailing along the ground, like long lines of emeralds that cross one another.]

THE BEASTS OF THE SEA. [Breathing noisily.] The sand of the way hath fouled our scales and we open our mouths as it were dogs out of breath.

We will take thee, O Anthony, thou shalt come with us upon beds of wrack, through plains of coral that quiver to the ordered movement of deep billows. Thou knowest not our great waters. Many peoples dwell in the countries of the ocean. Some shelter them from the tempests. Others swim in the open sea, in the transparency of the cold waves, breathing through their trunks the water of the tides that ebb, or bearing upon their shoulders the burden of the sources of the sea. There be plants, wholly round, like unto carven suns that shelter sleeping animals. Their limbs grow with the rocks. The dim blue shell-fish doth quiver throughout its slothful body even as a flood of azure.

No sound hear we save the unceasing murmur of the great waters, and above our heads we watch the passing of the keels of the ships as it were black stars gliding in silence.

S. ANTHONY. Ah, me! I can no longer discern. . . .

[And as S. Anthony considers the beasts, yet more fearful and monstrous creatures arrive; the Tragelaphus, half-stag and half-bull; the Phalmant, blood-coloured, who bursts his belly by the might of his howling; the great weasel Pastinaca, who kills trees by his stink; the Senad, three-headed, who tears his young with his tongue; the Myrmecoleo, lion in front and ant behind, whose genitals are reversed; the serpent Aksar, whose length is sixty cubits, he who frightened Moses; the dog Cepus whose teats distil blue colour; the Porphyrus whose saliva gives death in transports of lasciviousness; the Presteros, whose touch kills the understanding; the Mirag, a horned hare who dwells in the islands of the sea.

On a sudden arrive raging whirlwinds full of wondrous forms. There are heads of alligators upon feet of roe-deer, horses' necks that end in vipers, frogs hairy as bears, owls with serpents' tails, swine with tigers' jowls, goats with the croup of a donkey, chameleons huge as hippopotami, four-footed hens, and calves with two heads, the one whereof weeps while the other bellows, quadruple fœtera that hold to one another by the naval and dance round like tops, clusters of bees unthreading like rosaries, aloes all covered with roseate postules, winged paunches that hover like gnats, bodies of women that have in place of faces open lotus-flowers, gigantic carcasses whose white joints creak shrilly; and vegetables whose sap beneath their rind throbs like blood, minerals whose facets gaze as it were eyes, polypi catching hold with their arms, contracting their sheaths, opening their pores, swelling out, increasing, advancing.

And those that have passed by return, those that are not yet come arrive. They fall from the sky, they come out of the earth, they slip down the rocks. The Dog-headed folk bark, the Shade-footed people lie down, the

Blemmyes toil, the Pigmies squabble, the Mouthless Men sob, the Unicorn neighs, the Mantichora roars, the Griffin paws the ground, the Basilisk hisses, the Phœnix soars, the Sadhuzag gives forth sounds, the Downlooker sighs, the Chimera cries aloud, the Sphinx growls—the beasts of the sea begin to wave their fins, the reptiles breathe forth their venom, the frogs hop, the gnats hum; teeth clack, wings vibrate, breasts swell, claws lengthen out, flesh flaps. Some are bringing forth, others are mating, or devouring one another in one mouthful; heaped up, pressed together, stifling for the numbers of them, multiplying at contact, they climb the one upon the other. They rise in pyramids forming a complex mound of diverse bodies, each of which stirs with its own movement, while the whole oscillates, rustles, and glows through the air that is streaked with hail, snow, rain, lightning, wherein pass whirls of sand, spouts of wind, clouds of smoke, and it is lit at once by the beams of the moon, and the rays of the sun, and greenish twilight.]

S. Anthony. The blood of my veins heateth so mightily that it will burst them. My soul overfloweth within me. I would rush forth and flee afar without this place. For I too am a beast, life swarmeth within my belly. I long to fly in the air, to swim in the water, to run in the woods. Ah! How happy should I be, had I those stout lives under their hides that none may assail! How freely would I breathe, had I those wide-spreading wings!

I would fain bay, I would bellow, I would howl! I would live in a cavern and breathe forth smoke, I would bear a trunk, I would twist my body,—and divide me throughout, be in all things, go forth in odours, come to my fulness like the plants, be shaken like sound, shine like light, be blotted beneath shapes, enter into all atoms, move about within substance, be substance myself that I might know the thoughts thereof. . . .

The Devil. [Swooping upon S. Anthony, catches him by the loins with his horns and bears him away with him, crying out.] Thou shalt know it! I will teach it unto thee!

The Pig. [Reared up on his hind paws, watches S. Anthony disappear into space.] Ah! Wherefore have I not wings even as the pig of Clazomenae!

PART III

[In space.]

S. Anthony. [Clinging to the horns of the Devil.] Whither go I?
The Devil. [Crying out.] Higher, Higher!
S. Anthony. The tops of the trees are lost to sight. The hills sink! I strangle . . . the wind, coming in great blasts, beateth my face.
The Devil. Be of good courage! Leave not hold of me!
S. Anthony. I float, lost in cold without end.
[The Devil still soars in wild wise; S. Anthony, fainting, holds his seat between his horns.]

THE DEVIL. Now, open thine eyes!

S. ANTHONY. Ah, how broad is it! How far is it! I hear the murmur of the worlds. The stars fall without noise, like snowflakes.

THE DEVIL. Seest thou down yonder a luminous substance whence come forth suns?

S. ANTHONY. Ay, and the fragments that are loosed therefrom are turned about and about!

THE DEVIL. So, without number and without end, do the souls stream forth unceasingly from the great soul. Further away, yonder golden dust that is spread abroad is but made of portions of quenched stars whose vanishing cometh to conclusion.

S. ANTHONY. Can the suns then be worn out?

THE DEVIL. Ay, the suns, but not the light that is in them! The shape perisheth, but the substance is eternal. When man dissolveth, when in one stroke that assembly of the moment is dispersed, then do all things whereof it was made depart in freedom, and worlds are ordained without ceasing . . . hast thou not discerned voices in the shaking of the reeds? The dogs that howl, do they not speak to thee of thy dead friends! [Ever they rise.]

S. ANTHONY. How do we rise! What great space is this!

THE DEVIL. Ay, thou knewest not that it was so great! Yet when thou didst move thine arm, didst thou know how thou didst move it? And when thy foot went forward, didst thou know wherefore it was? The dung of thy pig, powdering to dust in the sun, and the green beetles that did hum around it, sufficed, as though it were God, to torment thy thought, inasmuch as that which is infinitely small is no whit more easy of understanding than that which is infinitely great. But beyond the knowledge of men is there neither small nor great, for that which hath no bounds is beyond measure, eternity hath no period, God cannot be apportioned.

If the least jot or tittle of substance doth reveal unto thee as vast an horizon as the whole of all things, know that this is because there existeth in the one as in the other a gulf that none can bridge that maketh them one. Thus there are not two infinites, nor two Gods, nor two unities. He is, and beside Him is nought else!

S. ANTHONY. How shall this be? God is then in all places? Then He is in the separation of them that ponder, in the passion of them that suffer, in the doing of them that do great deeds? In all this He aideth? He is all this? . . . that part of me whereinto I never had entrance, that then was God? Nay, let us rise, higher, yet higher, even unto the end of all things!

[The firmament widens, the stars meet one another.]

THE DEVIL. Dost thou see the uncounted fires of heaven, the constellations, the stars that fall and the stars that live for tens of thousands of ages, and the stars of one day? Each one of them doth turn, each one of them doth shine, and thereof is the movement the same and the light the same! The blood of man beateth in his heart and swelleth out the veins of his feet. The breath of God goeth among the worlds and the happenings of the worlds, even as the drops of thy blood, are wholly alike the one unto the other, even as they are parts of the same whole and are themselves made or yet other parts, and so shall it continue and so shall it ever be. The breath that passeth even now through thy nostrils is the manifold conclusion of a thousand worlds created that have passed away and are gone. The thought that cometh into thee hath been led unto thee, in wanderings that are greater than is the distance from thine eyes, even unto the last of these stars. For whatsoever each man hath thought ever since men were, that hath given of itself thereto, and all substance and all spirit and all that hath appeared, all that is, finite and infinite, shaping and thought, these are bound together and confounded and do beget one another.

Are there not things unmoving that are as animals, souls that grow like the plants of the field, statues that dream, lands that are as though they pondered? . . . A mystical measure driveth all the atoms shaken together, unto the dance unending—bodies, throughout their life and their death, do but seek to enter again into the dust whence they came; the soul whose desire is unbounded hath but this hope that it may return unto God from whom it came.

S. ANTHONY. For this then is it that I have so often longed for death and sought to remember if I had not dwelt in other worlds.

THE DEVIL. Yet is not substance on the one side and spirit on the other; for then would there be an infinity of substance and an infinity of spirit, which is two infinities that would thereby be bounded, wherefore there would be no more infinity. There is not one atom that is greater than another, else are there no atoms. But forasmuch as substance containeth the manner of all things and all things are in God, where then is the difference that is seen in the parts of this whole, between the body and the soul, between the substance and the spirit . . . between good and evil?

[The wings of the Devil increase; his horns lengthen.]

S. ANTHONY. We go, we go! The breath of the height draweth me up! I see the planets below me! . . . There is no more! . . . Is this the void?

THE DEVIL. Nay, for nothing is not! [They rise ever.]

S. ANTHONY. [Fainting.] Shall I journey without ceasing? Where then is the goal?

THE DEVIL. In thyself! For how far soever thou dost return into the causes of things, and from whence soever thou dost draw the beginnings thereof, yet must it ever be that thou come to the end thereof, even to a former cause, to a more ancient ordering, to a God uncreated. But shouldest thou sever Him from the creation that thereby thou mightest the better make known that creation, dost thou make Him the better known? Nay, now is He the less understood without the creation than was the creation before He was.

The music of a lute is not the air that is stirred, nor is it the trembling of the strings nor is it the sound of the notes; from all these it cometh and it causeth all these. Nor shalt thou sever the music of the lute from the strings thereof, nor from its notes, more easily than thou shalt separate the creator from the created or the finite from the infinite, or the nature from the substance. For the music is by virtue of the ordering that is in it . . . therefore is it not free. God is by reason of His own self without whom He cannot be, and thence is He not free.

S. ANTHONY. Is He not free, the Almighty? He who is the Master?

THE DEVIL [Chuckling.] Could He bring Himself to nought? . . . Can He cause that other than Himself be God, or can He become other than God?

S. ANTHONY. Yet . . . He governeth. He doth punish. He doth reward.

THE DEVIL. This doeth He in due ordering, but of His own will hath He not made that ordering, for it is by reason of that ordering that He is. For by this alone that they are, all things bring forth other things, and these latter are known unto men as the following thereof; this deed doth give birth unto that deed whence followeth yet another deed, and thence yet another, even unto five score, nor canst thou stay any one of them.

Man who doth commit evil receiveth the chastening thereof in due time; but how knowest thou that he will not be rewarded in time to come for that he hath been punished aforetime? God is no more free that He may leave evil unpunished, than thou art free to have thought that He must punish it. Thy soul containeth God inasmuch as thy soul thinketh on God. How thinketh thy soul? Even through God! Yet the infinite cannot be otherwise than in itself. In life God liveth; in thought, of Himself, He thinketh. Forasmuch as thou art, He is in thee, so soon as thou hast understanding of Him. Thou art in Him, He is thee, thou art He—and there is but One.

S. ANTHONY. There is but One! There is but One! Then am I a part thereof! I, even I, am a part of God! My body is of the substance of all substance! My spirit is of the essence of all spirit—my soul is wholly soul! Immortality, boundlessness, all this I have, this I am! I know that I am Substance, I am Thought!

[The Devil stays, floating motionless in the air. The breath of his breast that shook S. Anthony in uneven gasps is lulled. He loosens his hands. S. Anthony clings, alone, of his own hold, to his horns.]

Now I fear no more! I am at rest. I am immense even as the infinite that enfoldeth me.

THE DEVIL. It is in this infinite that all things move! When thou didst hear but now the sound of the worlds, it was not those worlds that turned them, but rather was it in thyself that this music was. When thou wast affrighted for the gulf, thine own self did make that gulf through the lying vision of thy spirit whereby thou didst imagine measured distance in that which hath no bounds, thou didst think to see degrees in that which hath not measure. Even this brightness wherein thou didst rejoice, who can say unto thee that it is?

[The Devil's gaze hollows and spins open as it were a whirlpool. S. Anthony, lost, leans towards him and begins to descend, from stage to stage, upon the antlers of his horns.]

Who saith unto thee that they are? Canst thou see with eyes other than thine eyes, and if they are deceived, if thy soul be the judge of all things, and that soul be a lie, where will be the surety of that which was judged? What wilt thou be? What will be? Throughout the sleep of life man, even as a slothful god, thinketh darkly that he dreameth. But if it be that the awakening never come? If all this be but a mockery? How if there be but nought? Aha! thou knowest not that nothingness can be? But if it be that that which cannot be be the truth, is there any truth? Thou canst discover nought, and even couldst thou discover all, never is aught known save it be by reason of the world whereof it is and of the understanding that doth receive it. If then that world itself is not, if that understanding is not! Aha! Aha!

S. ANTHONY. [Hanging in the air, floats in front of the Devil, touching him, forehead to forehead.] But thou art . . . I touch thee!

THE DEVIL. [Opening his jowl.] Ay! I go thither. I go!

[The Devil opens his arms and S. Anthony stretches out his. But as he does so, his hand touches his robe and strikes against his rosary. He utters a cry and falls.

He finds himself in front of his hut, stretched out flat, on his back, motionless.

It is night and the two eyeballs of the pig gleam in the shadow; little by little S. Anthony returns to life; he raises himself, he begins feeling the earth round him, he looks about him.]

S. ANTHONY. What is it . . . what?

[He falls back, yawning, and looks at the ruins of the chapel, vaguely, his eyes wide open.]

Ha! My pig! I had thought him dead! . . . Wherefore? I know not! . . . My heart beateth no more! Meseemeth I am as these stones, or as an empty cistern fenced about with brambles . . . and at the bottom thereof is a great black stain.

Whence come I? Where was I?

Were I to search, were I to weary myself. But I cannot! It is beyond my strength! [He weeps.]

I understand nought of all this!

[The outline of the Devil reappears.]

Were I to pray? But I have already prayed so much. Rather should I labour . . . then must I light the lamp again! Nay, nay! Ah me! How weary am I! I would do some deed, I know not what. I would go somewhither, and I know not whither! I know not what I would! I know not what I think! I have not even strength to desire to wish!

[A thick fog falls; the bristles of the pig quiver.]

What sadness! How cold is the night! I feel as it were damp shrouds weighing upon my soul! I have death in my belly.

[He goes and sits him down upon the bench and huddles up, his arms folded, his eyes closed; then, throwing back his head, he beats it against the wall in strong regular blows; he counts them.]

One, two, three . . . one, two . . . one, two!

[He stops; the pig gets up and goes and lies down in another place.]
Whence cometh it that I do that I do, that I am that I am? I could have been other than I am; had I been born another man, then had I had another life, and I had known nought of mine own life! Were I a tree, I should bear fruit. I should be clothed with leaves, birds would perch upon me, I should be green!

Wherefore is not the pig I? Wherefore am I not the pig? Ah me! How do I suffer! I abhor mine own self! I would strangle myself could I do so!

THE PIG. I, too, am utterly weary! Rather would I be cleft into hams and hung by the houghs to the hooks of the fleshers!

[The pig flings himself down upon his belly and buries his groin in the sand. S. Anthony tears his hair, turns round, totters, stammers, and falls on the threshold of his hut.

Death appears (the pig runs away and hides). Her great shroud held by a knot on the top of her yellow skull falls to her heels and in front discovers the innermost parts of her skeleton; her cheekbones glow, her bones clatter; in her left hand she bears a long whip whose lash trails on the ground. She is seated on a black horse, lean, great of belly, and spotted here and there where his coat is torn in patches. His worn hoofs curve back like moon-crescents; his mane, full of dry leaves, waves, and in his wide nostrils is the awful sound of the wind diving deep into caverns. When Death dismounts, he wanders away to graze among the ruins of the chapel; he stumbles among the stones and breaks them here and there. Death drops her chin on her left shoulder and shoots out the black ray of her eyeless orbits; she stretches forth her long lean hand to S. Anthony, who shudders.]

DEATH. Come! I, even I, am the consoler!

[S. Anthony half rises and stretches both arms towards Death, when suddenly appears Lust behind her, wearing a crown of roses on her head. He sits down again.]

LUST. Wherefore die, O Anthony?

DEATH. [Resuming.] Nay! Die! The world is loathly! Must thou not needs rise every morning, must thou not eat, drink, come, and go? Each one of these poor happenings is added to those that follow upon it even as thread is added to thread, and life from the one end thereof even to the other is but the endless woof of all these miseries!

S. ANTHONY. Ay, so is it! Better were it, peradventure . . .

LUST. Nay, nay!

[She takes off her crown and passes it softly under his nostrils.]

The world is fair! There be flowers whose stature is greater than thine. There be lands where the incense doth smoke toward the sun, where the voice of the turtle is heard deep in the woods, where wings beat in the blue firmament. In the summer nights the long waves of hot seas unroll their fires in the white foam, and the sky is starred with gold even as the robe of a king's daughter. Hast thou swayed upon the great weeds? Hast thou gone down into the emerald mines? Hath thy body been anointed with cool ointments? Hast thou slept upon swansdown? . . . Taste thou of this, of the life magnifical that is blessed in all his days even as the wheat hath flour in every grain of his ear. Breathe the breath of the winds, sit thee down under the citron trees; lie upon the moss, bathe in the fountains; drink wine, eat flesh; have thy desire of women; hold Nature through Nature to thee with every lust of thy being, and roll thee, even as a lover, upon her broad bosom.

[S. Anthony sighs; she continues:]
Never hast thou known in thy flesh as it were the pride of a god roaring; nor hast thou known the infinite whelm thee in the ravishment of a kiss.

THE PIG. [Howling suddenly.] I desire women mad with rutting! I long for fat middens, for mire up to mine ears! I am weary. I will flee away. I will run swiftly over the dry leaves, with the wild boars and the bears!

S. ANTHONY. Ah me! My heart melteth for the imagination of such blessedness.

DEATH. Taste of them, and thou shalt see the terror of my countenance at the bottom of the empty cup, nor shall it depart from thee.

Is not thy soul filled with fumes of retching that rise even as the smoke of a burning mountain? The wind rolleth them away and they are no more. Nor shall thy despairing abide. The sun on his way drieth the tears upon thy face. Thy determinations, thy covetings, thy godliness, thy weariness, all these shall be unravelled against the ground even as the hem of my winding sheet. Therewith I cover all mankind! Therewith do I hinder all their movements! My dry bones do crack in their arms as they hold their love, and the last end of their joy is that they desire to die thereof.

[But Lust leans her smiling face upon the shoulder of Death, and the thread of her necklace is broken thereon, and the big pearls are torn off and they slip down, one by one, into the folds of her shroud. Lust says:]

LUST. What matter! I make the flowers to grow upon the tombs; all things are whirled about within my love even as the motes of dust in the sunlight!

[S. Anthony quivers; she draws nearer to him and touches him upon the shoulder lightly.]
Seest thou yonder little pathway in the sand? It shall lead thee even to the gates of the cities that are full of women. I will give thee the fairest of them, even a virgin—thou shalt corrupt her and she shall worship thee even as a god, in the amazement of her conquered flesh. Haste thee! Make speed! Lo! Her raiment is cast aside, she is stretched out among the scarlet cushions, she lifteth up her naked arms; she would embrace thee to her heart.

DEATH. Look thou more closely, to the foot of the hill, see yonder great spurge? Break the boughs of it and taste thy fingers! Then shalt thou be stretched out to thy full length . . . thou shalt know nothing more . . . thou shalt no more be anything!

S. ANTHONY. [Motionless, pallid, his teeth chattering.] Which shall I follow?

I have as it were a need to spew forth my life . . . yet do I pant for desire unconstrained. Thine heat, O Lust, that cometh forth from thy bosom enflameth my cheek; and thy breath, O Death, chilleth the hairs of my head.

[Death and Lust pace up and down in front of S. Anthony in ordered movement like chanters in a church; this is their psalm:]

LUST. My mighty voice it is that maketh the murmur of great cities; the beating of my heart is but the throbbing of mankind.

DEATH. The unending chain of all things maketh the whirlwind of nothingness and all the sound of the world is but the clapping together of my teeth.

LUST. I make madness to stand at the edge of unclean things. I give joy unto the biting of the teeth in the flesh, an enticement even in the midst of loathing.

DEATH. The tears that I have drawn from the eyes of men would fill oceans, the great works that I have thrown down would make an heap higher than all worlds.

LUST. The harlot, covered with jewels of gold, fair with the desire of all men, singeth lovewords, softly and low of voice, beneath her smoking lamp.

DEATH. The pale worms in the night of the tomb fasten them on the faces of the dead, as it were a swarm of bees that devour a fig.

LUST. Ay, and there be dead women whose arms hang loosely, their eyes are not fully closed, their black locks wind over their pale flesh: their nakedness is utterly discovered so that a man should say that it surpasseth and is deeper than all nakedness.

S. ANTHONY. Out upon you! Ye are both horrible in mine eyes!

LUST. [Crying out.] For me men slay one another, men betray and kill one another. I, even I, do overwhelm life. I make the lions to roar and the flies to buzz; I make the eagles to fly and the apes to leap; the beds of men crack beneath their kisses, metals seethe, and the stars tremble! . . . Come, come! The sap of me shall flow within thy soul as it were a river of delight.

DEATH. [Her voice is now a caress.] Nay, I am kindly. I have unbound all slavery. I have ended all sadness! Doth my sepulchre affright thee? Nay, but it shall be dissolved even as thy bones! . . . dost thou fear my dark loneliness? Thou shalt be among the company of all things that rot away!

S. ANTHONY. Cease, cease! Thine every word, as it were the stroke of a catapult, breaketh my pride even to the dust. The nothingness of all that life was, overwhelmeth me!

DEATH. I tremble beneath the earth and I swallow up the cities. I lay me down upon the waters and I overthrow the ships; the breath of my winding sheet in the heavens maketh the stars to fall, and I walk behind all glory as it were a shepherd who watcheth his sheep at the pasture. Come hither! Thou knowest me! Thou art filled of me! Without thee is nothingness, in the depth of thee is nothingness! Yet deeper goeth nothingness: it doth whirl even to endlessness! The coffin devoureth, the dust is scattered, and I, even I, shall take away the last grain that is over.

LUST. No stumbling-block is there, no will that I shall not break; seeing that action sufficeth not unto desire, I overflow into dreams. The man of God, deep in the cloister, seeth shapes of naked women pass about the pillars in the light of the moon; they stretch forth their arms unto him. The virgin in the hall sigheth for my faintness, the mariner sigheth upon the sea. I have hypocrisy that none may withstand and wrath that conquereth all things. I ravish purity. I enflame rapture; even in love crowned I dig gulfs wherein other love turneth about and about.

DEATH. [Approaching S. Anthony, lifts her arm haughtily, and speaks in her turn.] High on the cross He heard the clamour of the raging multitude that sank to rest afar off in the bye-ways. His forehead was bleeding, blood flowed from His side, a black raven pecked at His cheek, at the tears from His hollow eyes, and His locks shaken by the tempest scourged His face as it were a handful of thongs . . . then . . . [She breaks into laughter.] Even as I slay the young of the gazelle and the babes of women, so did I slay the Son of God!   [S. Anthony bursts into sobs.]

LUST. [Crying out suddenly.] Yet was nought lacking unto the first-born! The streams flowed around him to quench his thirst. The trees when he passed bowed them before his mouth. He breathed the unstained air of the world into his breast and he beheld God face to face; he hath lost all, his will was to lose all, for the savour of a kiss! [S. Anthony raises his head again.]

DEATH. [Resumes.] But thou art stronger than God! He cannot constrain thee to live—the Power who ruleth the worlds must bend presently before this thy will to be free.

S. ANTHONY. [Bursting into a fit of wild laughter.] Yea, yea! What joy would that be!

LUST. Thou canst compel Him to create a soul. He must needs obey this the fancy of thy flesh, and thou canst strike thy root deep into nature! Thy children's children shall follow thee! Within thee thou bearest hundreds of years full of works!

S. ANTHONY. Nay! Enough, enough!

LUST. Nay, look upon my face and know it! Come! It is I! Thou didst call upon me through the covetings of mystical love; thou didst breathe my breath in the hot wind of the night-time; thou didst seek mine eyes in the stars; thou didst touch my dim shape when thou didst stretch forth thine arms in the empty air.

DEATH. Nay, remember all the bitterness of thy life! Yet didst thou desire me in thine appetite for God, thou didst cherish my tenderness in the torments of thy penitence! Come, come! I am rest, nothingness, the One Alone!

LUST. Come, come! I am the truth, the joy, the movement without end, the very self of life!

[Death yawns, and Lust smiles; the one clacks her teeth, the other kilts her gown.]

S. ANTHONY. [Draws back suddenly, raises his eyes, and cries out:] Nay, but if ye do both lie? If there be another life, O Death, and yet more pains behind thee? Or shall I find in thy joys, O Lust, yet another darker void, a wider despair?

Upon the faces of dying men have I seen as it were a smile of life everlasting, and such sadness have I beheld on the lips of the living, that I know not which of ye twain is the more death-like or the better . . . Nay, nay!

[He remains motionless, closing his eyes with his hands and stopping his ears. Death and Lust bow their heads.]

THE DEVIL. [Pinches his lip, then strikes his forehead and leaps upon S. Anthony and drags him back to the back of the scene, crying out:] Hold! Look!

[Then is heard a great clamour; on the horizon is seen a confusion of shapes passing, more intangible than smoke; then comes stones, skins of beasts, fragments of metal, and pieces of wood; then a great tufted tree walking upright upon his roots; around his roughened trunk is a golden bracelet; to his boughs are hung rosaries and shells and medals. The folk, their foreheads pressed to the ground, trail along on their knees and fling kisses to him with their hands.

Death lifts her arm and strikes the great tree with her whip; he disappears.

Then pass IDOLS upon gliding sledges, idols black, white, green, violet, fashioned of wood, of silver, of copper, of stone, of marble, of straw, and of clay, of slate, and of the scales of fishes. They have big eyes and big nostrils, banners are planted in their bellies, their arms trail, their monstrous phalli rise even above their heads. The juices of meat flow through their beards, they sweat the oil of the sacrifice, and from their half-opened lips escape clouds of incense.

They stammer as though they would speak:

Ba—Ba—Ba—Bah.

DEATH. [Striking them.] Give place!

[Then arrive at one time the five idols that were before the Flood: Sawa whose face is that of a young woman, Yaguth with the face of a hare, Yank with the face of a horse, Nasr with the face of an eagle, Waad with the face of a man; they stream with sea-water and wrack-weed that has grown on their heads like hair. Death cracks her whip and they fall to the ground.

Then follows the great idol of Serandib all covered with carbuncles. In the holes of her eyes are swallows' nests; then the idol of Soumenat, four hundred hands-breadths in height, all fashioned of iron; she clung aforetime to walls of loadstone. Her exceeding great stature oversets her, she cracks and breaks of herself.

After her is a negro idol under a leafage of gold, smiling stupidly. She stands on her left leg in the posture of a man dancing, on her neck she wears a necklace of red flowers, and she blows ever the same note into a hollow reed. Then comes the blue idol of Bactria, encrusted in shell of pearl. . . .]

Swifter, swifter!

[Follows the idol of Tartary, a statue of a man in green agate; in his silver hand he holds seven featherless arrows.]

Hasten, hasten!

[Arrive the three hundred and sixty idols of the Arabians, that answer to the days of the year, increasing and dwindling in stature as they go.]

Pass on, pass on!

[Then comes the idol of the children of Ganges wrought of yellow leather, squatting on her legs, her head shaven, her finger upraised. The blows of Death tear her to pieces and the tow flies from out her limbs on all sides.

Shaking in his hands the long reins of gold that restrain his sixty-three white-maned horses, seated upon a throne of crystal beneath a pavilion of pearls whose fringes are of sapphire, the Ganges arrives, bearing all his gods in an ivory chariot. He has the head of a bull and the horns of a ram, and his clear-coloured robe is hidden under flowers of the fig tree. The fringes of the pavilion sway against one another, the manes of the horses toss, and the immense two-wheeled car rocks, now to one side, now to the other.

It is full; the gods encumber it: gods with many heads, with many arms, with many feet, gleaming with aureoles; they seem torpid, in eternal abstraction. Serpents twine about their bodies, and pass between their thighs, then, rising and bending, bow them above their heads as it were cradles of many colours. They are seated on cows, on tigers, on parrots, on gazelles, on thrones built in three stages. Their elephants' trunks sway like censers, their eyes glitter like stars, their teeth whirr like sword-blades.

They bear in their hands wheels of fire that spin round, on their breasts are triangles, round their necks are death's-heads, upon their shoulders are green palm-boughs. They pluck at harps and chant hymns, they spit flames and breathe flowers. Plants fall from their nostrils, jets of water spurt from their heads.

Goddesses, crowned with tiaras, give suck to gods who wail at their breasts that are round as worlds; others suck the nails of their toes and enwrap themselves in clear veils that reflect on their surface the confused shape of the creations.

Death cracks her whip; the Ganges lets fall the reins; the gods turn pale; they clutch one another, they gnaw their arms, their sapphires break in pieces, their lotus-flowers wither. A goddess who bore three eggs in her apron breaks them upon the ground.

They that had many heads cleave them with their swords; they that were ringed with serpents strangle themselves in their coils; they that drank out of cups cast them over their shoulders. They weep, they hide their faces in the carpets of their seats.]

S. ANTHONY. [Steps forward, panting.] Wherefore is this? Wherefore?

THE GODS OF THE GANGES. Thou Ganges of the wide banks, whither goest thou that thou drawest us in thy flood as it were blades of grass?

The elephant hath trembled upon his knees, the tortoise hath drawn in her limbs, the serpent hath loosed the tip of his tail that he held in his jaws.

Get thee back to thy source! Beyond the abode of the sun, farther than the moon, behind the sea of milk, we would drink again the drunkenness of our life everlasting, to the sound of the lutes, in the arms of our beloved.

But ever thou flowest, ever thou flowest, thou Ganges of the wide banks!

A GOD. [All covered with eyes, black, mounted on an elephant that has three trunks.] Who hath made the sacrifice of the horse one hundred times that he should rob me of my dominion? Where are ye, my twin Twilights, ye who did trot upon asses? Where art thou, Fire, thou that ridest upon the blue ram with red horns? Where art thou, Dawn, of the vermilion brow; thou who didst draw back to thee the dark cloud of night, even as a dancer who goeth forward and draweth back her robe upon her knee?

I shone from on high. I lit the fields of slaughter. I quenched all pallor. But now it is finished! This great soul is without breadth and shall die as it were a gazelle that hath outrun its strength.

A GODDESS. [Standing upon a silver globe, coifed with flowers whence go forth rays, and clad in a scarf whereon are animals painted. A diamond necklace passes three times round her neck and over her wrists and is fastened to her heels. Milk spouts from her breasts that are encircled with gold circlets.]

From meadow to meadow, from world to world, from heaven to heaven have I fled. Yet am I the wealth of souls, the sap of trees, the colour of the lotus, the warm wave, the ripe corn in the ear, I am the goddess of slow smiles; I yawn in the jaws of the cow, I bathe me in the dew.

Ah me! I have plucked too many flowers; my head is bewildered. [Her veil flies off and she runs after it.] S. Anthony had put out his arm to seize it, but there appears:

A GOD. [Wholly blue, with the head of a boar, with rings in his ears, holding in his four hands a lotus, a conch, an orb, and a sceptre.] I have raised up the drowned mountain from under the flood, I have borne the world upon my tortoise back.

With my tusks have I ripped open the giant. I have become a lion. I have become a dwarf. I have been a priest, a warrior, a tiller of the earth. With the share of a plough I have slain a monster who had a thousand arms, I have done many hard and wondrous deeds! The creations passed away, but I remained, and even as the ocean that receiveth all rivers nor is she ever the greater, so did I drink in the centuries.

What now? . . . all things reel . . . where am I? Who am I? Must I bear my serpent's head?

[A serpent's head grows upon him.]

Nay! Rather the tail of the fish that did beat the waves!

[A fish's tail grows on him.]

Shall I put on the face of the solitary?

                                        [He changes into a solitary.]
Nay, nay! It is the horse's mane that lacketh!

                                        [A horse's mane grows on him.]
I will neigh! I will raise my hoof! Nay! The lion!   .

                                        [He becomes a lion.]
My tusks!   [Tusks spring in his mouth.]
All my shapes do turn them about in confusion and escape, as though I
should spew forth the lives that travail in my stomach. Ages arrive. I
shiver as one in a fever.

[S. Anthony opens his mouth to speak. But there comes:]

A God. [Greater than all these others, magnifical, clad in glittering robes,
riding upon a swan; he has four faces with bearded chins; and in his hands
he holds a necklace whereon globes are threaded.] I am earth, I am water,
I am fire, I am air, I am knowledge, I am understanding, I am creation, dis-
solution, cause, effect; I am the invocation of books, the strength of the
strong, the purity of the pure, the holiness of the saint!

                                        [He pauses, out of breath.]
I am the Good, the Excellent, the Most High, the sacrifice and the sweet
odour of the burnt offering, the priest and the victim, the Protector, the
Comforter, the Creator! . . . [He takes breath again.]
I am the rain that doeth good, the dung of the cow, the thread of the
necklace, the refuge, the friend, the place where things must be; I am the
seed that faileth not, everlasting, ever renewed! Coming forth at the
ending of the golden egg, even as the fruit of the womb from its
covering. . . .
[He vanishes before he has time to finish his phrase.]

A Black God. [Who has one eye in his forehead, a lotus at his neck, and
a triangle under his feet. He is sad of mien.] If thou dost multiply shapes
of themselves, dost thou bring forth Being thereby? Were I to dig the
pits of the Pagada for ever, were I to raise the stairs of the tower continually, what should it profit me? All that I have suffered, is it of none
avail? My many pangs of death, the toils of my lives, so much sweat, so
many battles, so many victories! . . .
Ah! Thou nurse of mine who didst fear aforetime when thou sawedst
in my mouth the shapes of the universe shining like unto rows of teeth,
thou knowest not that at this hour my mouth is silent; the jaws thereof
send from the one to the other the void that they do bite!
In the midst of the forest the man of God who gazeth upon the sun
prayeth with his whole soul! He hath withdrawn him from the world, he
is withdrawn from himself, he freeth him altogether.
His thought beareth him whither he will, he seeth so far as his wish is,
he heareth all sounds, he taketh all shapes, but . . . were he peradventure
to render not one thereof? . . . were he to strip him of all? Ay, by the
might of his austere penitence, were he to end. . . .

                                        [In the manner of one affrighted.]

Oh!

[His car disappears, its axle clacking as that of a worn-out carriage.]

S. ANTHONY. [In melancholy.] No more! . . . howbeit they were Gods!

[But here be others who come forward, covered with long-haired skins. They blow between their fingers, their noses are blue.]

THE GODS OF THE NORTH. The sun fleeth! He runneth as though he were afraid, he closeth him as it were the wearied eye of an aged spinning woman.

We are a-cold, our bear-skins are heavy with snow, the toes of our feet pass through the holes in our shoon. Of old we sat in our great halls where the logs flamed, nigh unto long tables heaped with quarters of meat and knives with carven handles.

It was good; we drank draughts of beer, we spake unto one another of our fights of old time. The horn cups clashed their golden circlets the one against the other, and our shouts rose, as it were iron hammers that a man should throw against the roof. The roof, even the wide roof, was grooved with the wood of lances! The hanging sword-blades gave light unto us during the night-time, and our bucklers were spread upon the walls from the rafters even unto the floor.

We ate of the liver of the whale in plates of copper that had been beaten out by giants. We played at ball with rocks; we hearkened unto the songs of the captive sorcerers who wept as they leant upon their stone harps, and only at dawn, when, on a sudden, the wind blew in the heated hall, did we betake us unto our beds.

Yet we must needs depart! Then did we weep, and then were our hearts swollen even as the sea when the tide beateth at the full.

On the waste land where the ravens peck, we found the apples whereof the Gods ate when they felt the hand of age heavy upon them; they were black with rot, they crushed in the rain. Deep in the forest, nigh unto the everlasting Beech, saw we the four Harts that turn about it and eat of its leaves. The bark of it was gnawed, and the beasts chewed the cud, glutted; they stood upright upon their feet, they pawed the earth with their hoofs. At the edge of the sea-shore, where the white blocks of ice are broken in pieces, we came upon the ship that is builded of the nails of the bodies of dead men; and lo! it was empty; then did the black cock crow, he that abode below the earth in the halls of the Dead.

We are a-weary, we are a-cold, we stagger upon the ice. The wolf that runneth behind us shall eat up the moon. No longer have we the wide meadows wherein we stayed us for breathing-space in the battle. No longer have we the ships, gold-plated, even the long blue ships, whose prow cut the hills of ice when we sought upon the Ocean for the hidden Spirits who belled in the tempest. No longer have we the pointed skates whereon we fared around the poles, bearing with outstretched arms the whole firmament that turned even as we turned.

[They vanish in a whirl of snow. Anthony feels little sympathy for the Gods of the North; they are too brutal, too narrow-minded.]

THE DEVIL. Ay! All their thought was to drink even as men that live freely! Here is one of more righteous life; he cometh from Persia!

[S. Anthony sees an old man approaching, with slow steps, his eyes shut; his body is wrapped in much drapery, his white beard falls below his waist. In the air above his head floats a small figure which resembles him, but its lower parts are lost in thick plumage.]

THE OLD MAN. [Opens his eyes; the little figure stretches out its wings.] At last are the twelve thousand years accomplished! The day hath come, the great day! I thank thee, thou Ferver, thou First Soul, who livest for ever, for that thou didst let fall into mine understanding the wondrous rays of thine emerald eyes! Shalt thou not increase thy stature? And then shall we bathe together in the depths of the Word? [He gives ear, he gazes.] What is this? No more do I hear the falling of the black rain! The bodies that have been brought again to life do not rise from their graves!

[He calls.]
[Silence.]

Kaimors! Meschia! Meschiane!
My three sons have not come!

THE DEVIL. Nay!

ZOROASTER. [Starting.] Ah! It is thou, Ahrimanes!

THE DEVIL. Ay, it is I! The tempest hath blown upon thy fire, O Zoroaster! Thy wise men, uncoifed, warm their bare feet thereat, and spit in the cinders.

[Death lashes out at Ferver with her whip; he flies headlong, crying out like a wounded quail.]

ZOROASTER. [Wanders away, with bowed head, and short steps, muttering.] Yet was it goodly! I had divided God into two separate parts; on one side was the Good, on the other the Evil.

THE DEVIL. Enough! Begone!

ZOROASTER. I had encircled life in an order of priesthood; all was in place, order upon order.

THE DEVIL. It is finished! Get thee back to thy cave!

ZOROASTER. I had taught the manner of tilth, the number of the pieces of the tamarind, the shape of saucers.

DEATH. Pass away, pass away!

ZOROASTER. There were prayers for the uprising and for the lying down and for the hours when sleep was not.

[Death breathes into his back, and his vesture swells out like the sail of a boat and urges him forward. He continues:]

Lead forward the dog that he may look upon the dying! Ye must rejoice when ye behold an hedgehog. In this wise is it lawful to quench a light that thou shalt make a wind with thine hand. Three times shalt thou rinse the raiment of the dead. With the left arm alone shalt thou hold the branches of the pomegranate tree. . . .

[His voice dies away in a vague stuttering of stupidity. The sound of lowing is heard; a bull appears—a black bull, with double number of hairs on his tail; on his brow is a white triangle, and the mark of an eagle is on his back. His purple housing is torn, and he limps of his left thigh.]

APIS. Where are my priests, shod with reed-bark, they that did use to brush the hairs of my body, singing the while sacred words to a slow measure!

S. ANTHONY. [Laughing.] What folly!

THE DEVIL. Nay! It is a god who weepeth! Give thou thine ear!

APIS. From the land of Libya I saw the Sphinx fleeing; he galloped even as a jackal. The crocodiles have let fall to the bottom of the lakes the ear-pendants that they held in their mouths. The shoulders of the hawk-headed gods are whitened with the droppings of birds, and the blue sky goeth alone under the painted doorways of the empty temples.

Whither shall I go? I have browsed upon the land of Egypt even to the last blade of grass. I drag myself along the banks of the river, more and more do I suffer for the wound that I had of Cambyses.

The daughters of the Pharaohs gave themselves unto burial in caskets that were carven in mine image, and Serapis opened not save to receive my body. But when a ray of the sun had given his seed unto the heifer, men ran and took me in my pasture. I was led in procession, the castanets rang in the cornfields and the timbrels rattled on the boats; from the desert and from the river banks, from the plains and from the mountains, the people of the land of Egypt ran toward me and bowed them down before me. I was Osiris! I was God! I was the Master Worker before their eyes, the Soul made flesh, the Great All, visible unto men, peaceful, beautiful!

[He pauses, and snuffs the air.]

What now! I see red men who bring coals, who bear knives; they fold back the sleeves of their garments!

THE DEVIL. They shall slay thee, fair Epaphus; they shall devour thee; they shall tan thine hide; they shall beat slaves with thy dried ham-strings.

[Apis departs, limping, and lowing mournfully.]

S. ANTHONY. [Looking at the Devil.] Well? What now?

[The Devil is silent; but then come three couples of gods, the one following the other, presently, like the figures on a temple frieze. Uranus and Terra, Saturn and Rhea, Zeus and Hera.

S. Anthony, amazed, says:]

Yet more!

THE DEVIL. Ay! ever more!

URANUS. [Crowned with waning stars, draws Terra by the hand, drops of blood fall from his limbs.]

Let us flee! I know not what hath broken the thread that bound the lives of men unto the movements of the stars. Saturn hath torn me and the face of God appeareth no more in the countenance of the sun.

TERRA. [White-haired, following Uranus.] I had forests of mystery, I had oceans that none might measure, I had mountains that no man might attain. In the black waters dwelt dangerous beasts, and the breath of the marshes upon my face moved as it were a dark veil.

I was terrible with power, men were drunk with my perfumes, my colours dazzled their eyes, I was huge! Ah! how fair was I when I rose from the bed of Chaos; my locks were wholly disordered!

Then did men grow pale for the sound of the abysses that were mine, for the voices of the beasts, for the eclipses of the moon. They rolled them upon my flowers, they clomb in among the leaves of my trees, they gathered white pearls and curved sea-shells upon the shore. I was Nature and I was God. I was the beginning and the ending, for Him was I Without End; His Heaven could not exceed the height of my mountains.

He hath grown greater, O Uranus! And even as thou didst aforetime with the Cyclopes, my sons, whom thou didst imprison within my bowels, even so man now holloweth out my stones that he may place his dreams therein and mark increase in his despair.

SATURN. [Savage of mien, bare-armed, his head half covered with his mantle, holding his curved harp in his hand.]

In my day the eyes of man were quiet even as the eyes of oxen.

His laughter was full and his sleep was heavy.

Against the wall of clay, under the thatched roof of boughs, the flesh of the pig smoked slowly before the clear fire of dry leaves, plucked when the cranes entered into the land. The pot seethed, it was full of mallow and asphodel. The helpless babe grew up by his mother's side. Free from wayfaring and without desire, the lone households abode in peace in the depths of the land; the tiller of the soil knew not that there were seas, the fisherman knew not of the plains; he who worshipped knew no other gods.

But when the pointed burdock flowered and the grasshopper opened his wings in the yellow corn, then did men draw out the cakes of cheese from the storehouse; they drank dark wine, they sat them down under the ash-trees. Their hearts beat the stronger for the heat of the Dogstar, the threshold of their huts gave forth the smell of the goat, their maids winked their eyes as they passed by the bushes.

Never shall those days return; then was the life of man bound down wholly unto the soil, it was even as the shadow of a sundial, nor was it turned away from its course about the fixed centre thereof!

I had cast down Uranus from his throne; wherefore then came Zeus? . . .

RHEA. I, even I, did deceive thee, thou God who devourest all things!

I was eaten up with sorrow for that I did continually bring forth, yet were my children given unto destruction that would not be satisfied. Yea! I laughed when I saw thee swallow the stone that was swaddled beneath its wrappings! Yet thou knewest nothing! Thou didst devour it all!

[Death cracks her whip.]

SATURN. [Wraps himself in his cloak.] Let us return unto Erebus, let us return, O mine aged wife! The season of the delights of slaves is past, nor shall my cords of wool be undone any more.

ZEUS THE OLYMPIAN. [Holding in his hands an empty goblet. Before him stalks his eagle, torpid; the underside of its wings is red as though it were eaten of vermin; with its beak it picks up from the ground the feathers that fall from its body. Zeus looks into the bottom of his goblet.]

No more! Not even a drop!

[He leans it upon the nail of his finger, then sighs—a long sigh—then speaks again:]

When the ambrosia faileth, then do the immortals depart.

Father of Gods, of kings, and of men, I ruled the firmament. I was lord of understanding and of the dominions of men. At the bending of mine eyebrows the sky trembled. I hurled the lightning, I gathered together the clouds!

I sat upon a throne of gold in the midst of all the gods, on the summit of Olympus; I opened mine eyes and I looked upon all things. I watched the Hours in their courses, daughters of equal stature who, through Pleasure and through Pain, are made long or short for the sons of men; Apollo passed in his chariot, his curled locks shook in the wind of the stars; the Rivers leant them upon their elbows and poured forth the waters from their urns; Hephæstus beat out his metals, Ceres reaped her corn; Poseidon, troubled, did girdle the echoing Earth with his blue mantle.

The clouds rose upwards and bore the sweet smell of the burnt offerings even unto my nostrils. With the chant of the hymns arose the smoke in the leaves of the laurels and the breast of the high priest swelled to the measure of the song, and gave forth in its fulness the solemn chant of the people of the Hellenes. The hot sun shone upon the frontals of my white temples whose pillars are as a forest, and the breath of God was about them even as it were a wind from Olympus. The tribes were scattered round about me, yet they were a people. All the nations of kings knew me for their forefather, and the lords of the houses were even as I am, at their hearth. I was worshipped under all names, from the Beetle even to the Thunderer! I had known many shapes, I had had many loves. I was a bull, I was a swan, I was a shower of gold. I had visited nature, and she drew me into the soul of her; she set to it that she should become Godhead, yet should not I cease from being God. . . . O Pheidias, so beautiful didst thou fashion me that they that died ere they had beheld me, accounted themselves accursed. That thou mightest make me, thou didst take wondrous material, gold and cedar and ivory and ebony, precious stones that were lost in the beauty thereof even as the parts of some one nature are lost in the splendour of one whole. Through my bosom breathed the breath of Life; I held Victory upon mine hand, Thought was in mine eyes, and from the two sides of my head fell my locks as it were the free flowers of this the world made perfect. So great was I that the top of mine head touched the rafters of the roof. . . . Ah! thou son of Charmides, never could mankind excel thee, of a surety! Within the blue barrier of Panœus, hast thou closed in for ever and ever mankind's greatest deed, and now is it for the gods to descend thereunto. I see gods who are pale for satisfying the sorrow of weary nations. They come from lands of sickness, they are covered with rags, they weep bitterly. I am not as they are, that I should dwell under cold skies, amid strange speech, in temples where are no images. I am bound by the feet unto the ancient land, there shall I be dried up nor shall I go out therefrom. Nay, I was not moved what time the Emperor Caius would take me. Within my pedestal the builders heard the sound of great laughter for the labouring with which they laboured.

Yet shall I not wholly go down into Tartarus; somewhat of me shall remain upon earth. Those into whom Thought entereth, they that understand the Ordinance and cherish Greatness, from whatsoever God they come, these shall ever be the sons of Zeus.

HERA. [Her crown on her head, wearing golden boots with curved tips, covered with a veil sown with silver stars, bearing a pomegranate in one hand and in the other a sceptre surmounted by a cuckoo.] Whither goest thou? Stay thy feet! What aileth thee? Another love forsooth? Thou fool who dost lose thy strength nor knowest that mortals are swollen with pride when they find every morning upon their pillows hairs from off the head of Zeus!

Yet was our life sweet in the constrained balance of our strife and our love. It was diverse and magnifical, it stood unchanging even as the earth with his moving oceans and his unmoved plains. Return, thou son of Saturn, return! We will lie down upon Ida, we will hide us within the clouds in the bosom of the roseate air, and with my white arms I will surround thy neck, I will smile upon thee; I will pass my fingers through the curls of thy beard and I will rejoice thine heart, thou Father of the gods. Have I lost my dark locks or my great eyes or my golden shoon? Is it not for thy pleasure that I renew my maidenhood yearly in the fountain Canathus? Am I no more beautiful? Peradventure he thinketh me aged?

What! No sound! I go, I come, I run about Olympus. All are asleep. Even Echo seemeth to be dead.

[She cries out.]

Yea, yea! . . . my garlands of starflowers fall to pieces at the feet of mine images. The hand of the Maenad hath torn my robe in pieces, the hundred oxen of Argos have lost their wreaths, my priestess, forgetful, doth glut her with cooked fish even as a fishwife of the harbours. O Holiness of Modesty, behold it is an Harlot with painted cheeks that toucheth mine altars!

ATHENE. [She has her great helmet flanked with the Sphinx, and her ægis of the golden scales; she is draped in a peplos that falls even to her feet. She advances holding her head in her hands.] I stagger! Yet have I not danced, I have not loved, nor am I drunk with wine. When the Muses sang, when Dionysus was drunken, when Aphrodite gave herself over unto love with all the gods, I the worker, I the ordainer, I alone stood to my task; I considered laws, I prepared victory, I pondered upon herbs and lands and the souls of men; I went about in all places visiting the mighty men, I was The Foreseeing, the Light Unconquered, the Power even of great Zeus himself.

From what shore bloweth this wind that troubleth my head? In what magician's bath hath my body been bathed? Are they the juices of Medea or the ointments of Circe the wanton? My heart faileth, I am about to die.

ARES. [Very pale.] I fear, even as a slave that fleeth. I hide me in the deep valleys. That I might run the better, I have undone my breastplate, I have drawn off my greaves, I have cast away my sword, I have let fall my spear.

[He looks at his hands.]

Have I no more blood in my veins, that mine hands be so pale? Ah! how I used to swell out my cheeks to the brazen trumpets! How I drave my thighs together upon the ribs of my warhorses, whose hindquarters were mighty! The red plumes twisted and shone in the sunlight; the kings held up their heads on high, they went forth from their tents, and the two hosts ringed them round that they might look upon them. I bethink me of Thero my nurse, of Bellona my companion, of my Salians who danced with heavy steps and smote upon their bucklers; greater is my sorrow than upon that night in my youth when Diomedes wounded me when I gat me up into Olympus that I might make plaint unto Zeus.

CERES. [Seated in a chariot driven by two swans' wings that beat the air; the chariot stops, and the torch that the goddess holds in her hand goes out.] Ay! Stay thy course! Forasmuch as Poseidon hath ceased to pursue me, forasmuch as I have passed around the whole earth. Go no further! Stay!

[She takes from under her a napkin of cloth of gold and wipes her eyes therewith.]

Alas! Alas! Never more shall I see Persephone in all her glory at play amid the green shoots! She hath gone down unto the house of Pluto, nor shall she come out again therefrom.

Ye daughters of the Athenians, that wear golden grasshoppers in your hair, ye that swaddle your babes in the robe worn in the Mysteries, ye who lie upon wild savory and eat garlic that shall drive away the vapour of your sweet odours—no more shall ye go forth of an evening, in the time of the harvest, by the Sacred Gate, in your ranks, with your heads bowed and your feet bare, behind the Chariot that draweth the Basket, no more shall ye hear the lewd words of them that await you upon the bridge of the Cephisus.

POSEIDON. [Encased, as at Elis, in three robes, the one over the other. He all but falls at every step, he leans upon his trident.] What now? I cannot stretch my body out upon the shores nor may I run in the plains. They have constrained my ribs with banks, and my dolphins, even to the last one among them, are rotted away in the depths of the waters. Aforetime I entered upon the land. I made the earth to tremble, I was He that roareth, the Lord of floods, and men called upon Good Fortune whensoever they did sacrifice unto me. Monsters crowned with vipers barked without ceasing upon my sharp-pointed rocks. None could pass through the straits, all suffered shipwreck when they went round the islands.

Happy was the man who could one day draw up his galley upon the beach, stripped of her armament; then should he see once more his aged father and his mother and hang up the rudder of his wanderings to dry before the hearth of his home!

DEATH. Pass on, pass on!

HERCULES. [Streaming with sweat, panting. He lays down his club and wipes his face with his lion's skin; the jowl of it hangs over his shoulder.] Ah!

[He stays a moment before he can speak, so breathless is he.]

Men say I have accomplished twelve toils! Rather have I accomplished an hundred, an hundred thousand, maybe! First of all I did strangle two great serpents that twined them around my cradle. I tamed the Bull of Crete, the Centaurs, the Ape-folk, and the Amazons. I slew Busiris, I strangled the Lion of Nemea, I cut off the heads of the Hydra. I slew Theodomus and Lacynus, Lycus the King of the Thebans, Euripides the King of Cos, Neleus the King of Pisa, Eurytus the King of Oechalia. I brake the horn of Achelous that was a great river. I slew Geryon who had three bodies, and Cacus the son of Hephæstus.

Is this the full tale? Nay! I smote down the vulture of Prometheus, I bound Cerberus with a chain, I cleansed the stables of Augeas. I sundered the mountains of Calpe and of Abyla, I did but take hold of the tops of them even as one who draweth apart the splinters of a log with his two hands.

I have wandered in many lands. I have been in the land of India, I have gone about Gaul. I have passed over the wilderness where men thirst.

I freed the nations that were in slavery, I peopled the countries where no men dwelt; my strength waxed greater with the tale of mine years; I slew my friends when I did but sport with them, I brake benches when I sat me down thereon, I destroyed temples when I passed under their porches.

Within me was continual raging that overflowed in great bubbles, even as the new wine that maketh the bungs of the vats to leap.

I cried aloud, I ran, I rooted up trees, I troubled the rivers, the froth hissed at the corners of my lips, my stomach was sick within me, I wrestled in the loneliness, I called out aloud, if haply any·should hear.

My strength doth choke me! It is my blood that constraineth me! I need warm baths, I desire frozen water to drink. I wish to sit upon cushions, to sleep in the daytime, to shave my beard. The Queen shall lie down upon my lionskin, I shall put her robe upon me, I shall spin with her distaff, I shall assort her wool; my hands shall be white even as those of a woman. I languish . . . give me . . . give me . . .

DEATH. Pass on, pass on!

[Arrives a great black catafalque on rollers, girt with torches from top to bottom. The daïs of it is starred with silver scales and supported by four pillars of the ordinance of Solomon round which is twined a golden vine; it shelters a bed of honour which is covered with a purple covering; upon the three-cornered bed-head stand palettes loaded with perfumes burning in vessels of painted pottery. On the bed can be seen the body of a man, in wax, lying flat, as a corpse. Round the bed are alternated in rows little silver filigree baskets and oval-shaped alabaster urns; in the baskets are lettuce plants, and in the urns is a rose-coloured pomade.

Women follow the catafalque, disquiet of aspect; their unknotted hair falls the length of their bodies, as it were a veil: with their left hands they gather on to their bosoms the folds of their trailing robes and in their right hands they hold great bunches, of flowers or crystal phials filled with oil. They draw near to the catafalque, and they say:]

THE WOMEN. He is fair! He is fair! Awake! Enough hast thou slept! Lift up thine head, get thee upon thy feet!

[They sit down upon the ground, in a ring.]

Ah! He is dead! He will not open his eyes! No more will he put his hands on his hips and raise his right foot in the air and turn him round on his left heel. Weep ye! Mourn and cry aloud!

[They utter great cries, then on a sudden are silent. The crackle of the torches can be heard, and the drops that the wind tears off them fall on to the waxen corpse and melt his eyes. The women rise to their feet.]

What shall we do? Shall we stroke him with our fingers? . . . let us beat the palms of his hands! . . . So . . . So . . . breathe of our flowers! These be narcissus and wind flower that we have plucked in thy gardens. Return to life! Thou makest us afraid! Lo, how stiff is he already!

Behold, his eyes flow at their edges! His knees are twisted, and the paint of his face is poured out on to the purple coverlet. Speak! We are thine! What is thy need? Wilt thou drink wine? Wouldest thou lie in our beds? Is it thy wish to eat of the cakes of honey that we bake in the ovens? They are shaped as little birds, for thy greater merriment.

Let us touch his belly? Let us kiss him over the heart! Ha! dost thou feel our fingers heavy with rings, passing over thy body, our lips that seek thy mouth, our hair that doth brush thy thighs? Thou god languishing, deaf to our prayers!

[S. Anthony hides his face with his sleeve. The Devil pulls his arm sharply and pushes him closer to them.]

See, see how his limbs as we take hold of them remain in our hands! He is no more! He sneezeth not at the smoke of the dried herbs, he sigheth not for love in the midst of the sweet odours! . . . he is dead! . . . he is dead! . . .

S. ANTHONY. [Bending forward towards the women.] Who is this?

THE DEVIL. [Slowly.] These are the daughters of Tyre who mourn for Adonis.

[They flay their faces with their nails; they begin to cut off their hair, which they lay, the one after the other, upon the bed, and all those long locks tangled together look like serpents, fair and dark, crawling over that roseate waxen corpse that is now no more than a shapeless mass. The women kneel down and sob.]

S. ANTHONY. [Holding his head in his hands.] What is this! . . . nay! . . . but I remember! Ah! once aforetime . . . on such a night, around a corpse that lay thus . . . the myrrh smoked upon the hill, near unto the open sepulchre; the sound of weeping brake forth under the black veils that were bowed over it; women wept and their tears fell upon his naked feet, like drops of water upon white marble. . . .

[He sinks to the ground.]

THE DEVIL. [Laughing.] Up, up! Here come others! Behold!

[The catafalque of Adonis has disappeared.

The sound is heard of castanets and cymbals; men clad in motley robes and followed by a crowd of peasants lead forward an ass on whose head is a plume of boughs; his tail is adorned with ribbons, his hoofs are painted, he has a frontal of plates of gold, he has shells on his ears, on his back is a casket covered with a corded cloth; it lies between two baskets, the one of which receives the offerings of the crowd as the ass moves on; eggs, grapes, soft cheeses, hares whose ears protrude, plucked fowls, pears in quantity, copper money—the other is half full, and contains rose leaves that the leaders of the ass throw before them as they walk. They have laced boots, plaited hair, great cloaks, and ear-pendants, and their cheeks are covered with paint. They wear crowns of olive branches fastened together in the middle of their foreheads by medallions whereon are tiny figures: each medallion is set between two smaller medallions. On their bare breasts they wear yet another larger medallion. In their belts are bodkins and daggers, and they brandish whips with yellow ebony handles and triple thongs, to which are tied small sheep's bones. First of all the men take the cloth off the casket, that is covered underneath with black felt; the crowd draws apart from them, the ass stops. One of the men kilts up his gown and begins to dance round and round, playing the castanets the while; another kneels down before the casket and beats a timbrel; the eldest of the band commences in nasal tones.]

THE HIGH PRIEST. Behold the Kindly Goddess! The Idæan of the mountains! The Mighty Mother of Syria! Approach, ye worthies! She is seated between twain lions, upon her head she beareth a crown of towers, much good bringeth she to all who look upon her.

We, even we, do lead her throughout the land, beneath the fires of the sun, through the winter rains, under fair skies and under foul skies. She climbeth the passes, she glideth over the lawns, she crosseth the brooks. Ofttimes for lack of lodging we sleep under the open sky, nor is our table well spread every day. There be robbers that dwell in the woods, the wild beasts roar dreadfully in their caverns, there be roads that none can pass, for the many precipices! Behold her, behold her!

[They take off the woollen covering and reveal a casket of sycamore wood encrusted with little pebbles.]

She is taller than the cedars, she soareth in the blue firmament; she is more immense than the wind, she encompasseth the world. Her breath goeth out through the nostrils of panthers, through the leaves of plants, through the sweat of bodies. Her tears are of silver, they water the fields; her smile is the light, it is the milk of her breast that hath whitened the moon. She maketh the fountains to flow, she causeth the beard to sprout, she cracketh the bark of the fir trees that sway in the wind. Give unto her, for she abhorreth the miserly!

[The lid of the casket is raised and reveals under a housing of red silk a little image of Cybele all a-sparkle with spangles, in a chariot of wine-coloured stone drawn by two lions with frizzly manes; their paws are uplifted. The peasants push one another to see the better, the dancing man whirls ever round and round, he who beats his timbrel beats the harder; the High Priest continues:]

Her temple is builded upon the gulf wherein the waters of the Flood were hurled when it was ended. It hath gates of gold and a ceiling of gold, canopies of gold and statues of gold. There is Apollo; Hermes is there, and the Deliveress, Atlas, Helen, Hecuba, Paris, Achilles, and Alexander. In her court walk eagles and lions, horses and doves. To her great tree that burneth men hang coats and caskets; and for her is raised the mighty phallus, whose height is one hundred and twenty cubits, whereon men climb with cords, as it were, up the trunk of a palm-tree when they go up it to pluck the dates thereof.

[They give themselves mighty blows with their whips on their backs, in measured cadence.]

Smite upon the timbrel! Clash the cymbals! Blow into the flutes that have great holes!

She loveth the black pepper that ye seek in the wilderness. She loveth the flower of the almond tree, she loveth the pomegranate and the green figs, she loveth red lips and wanton looks, sweet sap and salt tears! . . . Blood! For thee! For thee!

Mother of the mountains, we praise thee!

[They carve their arms with daggers, their backs ring like hollow boxes. The music redoubles, the crowd grows. Then men in women's clothes and women in men's clothes pursue one another, uttering great clamour that loses itself on the horizon in the quiver of the lyres and the rustle of the kisses. Their diaphanous robes cling to their bodies. Therefrom drips roseate blood, and soon, over all that multitude of shifting tints, wavering, far-distant, appears a new god who bears between his thighs an almond-tree loaded with fruit. The veils on their heads fly off, the incense whirls, the steel rings. Eunuch priests enwrap the women in their lace-covered dalmatics.

But other gods arrive, beyond numbering, infinite. They pass like followings of dry leaves before an autumn wind, so swiftly that none can see them, and they weep, all, so loud that none can hear what they say. Death reties a knot in the lash of her whip. S. Anthony, bewildered, wishes to fly, but the Devil restrains him and resumes:]

THE DEVIL. Yonder is Atys of Phrygia. He casteth away his stone axe, he goeth to weep in the woods for his lost manhood. Here is that Derceto of Babylon who hath the hinderparts of a fish. Yonder is the ancient Oannes, there is the Deliveress covered in her veils, here is Moloch who spitteth fire through his nostrils, whose belly is filled with men, and he howleth even as a burning forest.

DEATH. [Laughing.] Aha! Behold! So hot is he in his flames that he himself melteth.

THE DEVIL. Look thou! Here be the Maidens Avengers to whom men sacrificed sucking-pigs!

THE PIG. Horror!

THE DEVIL. Yonder is the Saviour of Cities, from Elis! There be the Pure Ones of Pallantium! Yonder is Hephæstus, the Lord of smiths! Here cometh the kindly god Hermes with his hat for the rain and his shoon for the wayfaring.

DEATH. [Striking them.] Journey on! Journey on!

THE DEVIL. Here cometh the great Artemis, black, anointed with myrrh; her elbows are pressed against her body, her hands are opened, her feet are joined together, lions are upon her shoulders and harts about her womb, on her flanks are bees, she hath a necklace of marigolds, she hath a buckler of griffins and three ranks of breasts that shake with a great noise. But the skin of her body eateth her up beneath the bandages that constrain her.

[Death laughs.]

THE DEVIL. Behold the Forager of the Patraeans, and the Chantress of Orchomenos, the Firebearer of the mount Crathis, Stymphalia who hath the thighs of a bird, Eurynome the daughter of Ocean; and here be all others called Artemis, the Midwife, the Huntress, the Healer, the Lightbearer, the Mistress of harbours who is coifed with crayfish.

S. ANTHONY. What is that to me? Wherefore stayest thou me here to gape at the sight of them?

THE DEVIL. [Continuing.] She who hath white scabs on her face is Rubigo, the goddess of the itch; hard by her is Angeronia who freeth from disquiet, and the foul Perfica who discovered the staff of lust. Here is Æsculapius, the son of the Sun, drawn by his mules; his elbow is upon the rim of his chariot and his chin resteth within his left hand. It is as though he pondered deeply.

DEATH. [Striking him.] Make thyself to live, thou that diest not!

THE DEVIL. The wide-mouthed Fauns follow old Pan of the shepherds who striketh his hands together in the midst of his flock. They grin, they are hairy, their foreheads are covered with red spots even as the lime-trees in the springtime. Lo! Yonder is Priapus and the Lord of Landmarks, the goddess Epona, and Acca Laurentia, and Anna of the years that pass.

S. ANTHONY. Enough, enough! Leave me! My head is bewildered in the whirl of all these gods that pass!

THE DEVIL. Behold one who watcheth over children when they walk abroad, another who giveth fever, another who maketh men pale, another who giveth fear. These do shape the babe within the womb, those turn it round, others draw it forth, others watch over the cooking-pots, others cause the door hinges to creak, others drive the waves on to the shore.

S. ANTHONY. [Slowly.] What a multitude!

THE DEVIL. Ay, a multitude; and thou hast not seen all. And there be yet others, of whom not so much as the very dust of them can be any more found.

Yet shall they appear again upon a day, even as the dead that rise again, and man, pitiless man, shall judge them; the great and the lowly, they that were austere and they that were merry, they that had heads of beasts and they that had·wings; they shall stand every one of them before him in long ranks, pale and silent even as a conquered host. Then shall the negro grind his teeth and draw nigh unto his idol; he shall thrust his fist under the jaw thereof and shall spit in its face.

The children of Javan shall overturn their white statues with the tips of their toes in scorn, and they that dwell in the North, whose eyes are red with the snow, shall see their dim gods of mist and sorrow melt in the sunlight. Their bracelets and their crowns, their dried-up urns and their rusted blades shall be cast into the winds; the hollow of their breasts shall ring to the touch of the finger, and the dwellers in Olympus shall crumble to dust in the thunder of the laughter of the vengeance of the sons of men. For they gave nought, they were hard as the stones of their temples, and more brutish than the beeves of their sacrifice.

S. ANTHONY. Infinite sadness is upon me! [He weeps.]
How many prayers have men made unto them! How many burnt offerings have smoked for them! Yet they were strong, nor did any doubt arise touching their majesty.

Where are ye now, ye poor souls athirst with hopes that never were satisfied? [He bursts into sobbing.]
What are these sounds? . . . who singeth thus? [He listens.]
It doth crackle and buzz and twitter, and yet is there somewhat more . . . it seemeth slow; it is unrolled, then returneth it again!

APOLLO. [His cloak thrown back over his left arm, he plays upon a huge lute that is held by a strap that passes around his neck.] I sing to the lute . . .
[He coughs.]
I sing to the lute. . . . I sing of the ordering of the world. [He coughs.]
To the law of measure, to substance, to all that liveth.

[A string breaks and lashes his face. He tightens a pin and it breaks. He touches another and makes a mistake, he goes from one string to another; they all break with a crack and bring confusion.]

DEATH. So long hast thou been naked, so hast thou fared over all Greece, that thou canst no more, thou canst but spit, thou must die. Thou wert forsooth the purifier, the sweet singer of songs, the founder of cities? Was it not so? Now is there no song to sing, there is no city to found. The cities are all built, the fold are aged. The Prophetess is lost, nor shall she be found again.

The strong men that rubbed them with oil, the young men that ran races, the drivers who cried aloud, they stood up in their chariots of ivory, the wise men who held converse under the boughs of the rose-laurels,—
[She strikes him.]

Follow thou them! Begone! Fair god of the world of shapeliness that should
have no end!

[Apollo slings his lute over his back and departs. Comes Bacchus, drawn
by panthers. He is coifed with myrtle, and he looks at himself, smiling, in a
crystal mirror. Around him are the Sileni in red woollen cloaks, the Satyrs
covered with goatskins, the Maenads with their leopard skins on their
shoulders; they sing, they drink, they dance, they blow on flutes, they
throw on to the ground flat timbrels that spin and drone.

The Bacchantes, dishevelled, hold black masks in their hands; to the
sound of the music they swing the bunches of grapes that droop over their
foreheads, they devour the necklaces of dried figs that hang round their
necks, they clash their bucklers together, they strike themselves with ivy-
wreathed staves, they cast fierce glances about them from under eyebrows
black and velvety as a caterpillar's back.

The Satyrs clasp them tight in their arms; from on high they pour out
the wine from their urns and smear the laughing faces of the drunken
Maenads.]

THE BACCHANTS AND THE BACCHANTES. Beat down the vine poles! Trample
the grape in the wine presses with your heels! Thou fair god who wearest
the golden baldrick, drink thou long draughts in thy bottomless bowl!
Evoé! Bacchus! Evoé!

Thou hast conquered India, Thracia, and Lydia. The hosts fled when
Mimallon raged and shouted upon the mountains. The people awoke and
crowded around thee. The eyes of the Bacchantes shone among the leaves.
Evoé! Bacchus! Evoé!

Thou father of masques and of wine, the gods of old time stopped their
ears at the wondrous offence of thy disordered measure. Thine is the new
song, and thine are the measures that follow in ceaseless ordinance! Thine is
the laughter of the harvesters of the vintage, thine are the hidden springs
and the torchlit feasts, thine is the fox who goeth stealthily into the vines
that he may eat the green grapes.

The joy of thee passeth from people to people! Thou deliverest the slave,
thou art holy, thou art God, Evoé!

[Death lashes out with her whip; all disappears; then:]

THE MUSES. [Garbed in black mantles, their heads bowed.] Somewhat
that is no more lived in the air when the folk were young. Their breasts
were four-square and their speech fell, even as their dress, in great straight
folds, fringed with gold. In the lessons of the wise teachers as in the play of
the jugglers or the ordinance of the state, in the statues, in the plenishing of
the house, in the trappings of horses, in the tiring of hair, in all things was
fulness of beauty that uplifted life. The men of subtle thought did teach the
fair women; the sculptors found mountains of marble awaiting them.

S. ANTHONY. [Sighs.] Ah! It was fair! It was lovely! It was beautiful!
I know it!

THE MUSES. Weep for the great theatres and the naked dancers! Thou,
Thalia, thou goddess of the domed brow, where is thy brazen club, where

is thy laugh that rolled upon the multitudes even as the wind of the South upon the tides that flow among the islands? Thou, grave Melpomene, thou hast lost thy quires! Forgotten is the high boot, forgotten are the trailing cloaks, forgotten is the chant that passed in gusts through the terrors of tragedy, and the strait saying that did freeze the skin! Thou, slender Terpsichore, whose daughters are the Sirens, hast thou no memory of thy measured steps that men likened unto the dancing of the stars, the while the master of the instruments did beat out the measure with his iron sole! These great raptures be ended! Now come the fighters, the hunchbacks, the jesters!

Clio hath been ravished, she hath been the servant of them that confound the governance of the city, she that was the Priestess of the great feasts groweth fat on the meats of the multitude; men have made books nor do they take thought for the speech thereof! For those whose lives are nought need frail buildings, for the service of slaves must be strait garb. The merchants and the base fellows and the harlots have bought all Beauty with the gold of their commerce; the halls of the cunning artificers are filled with all the whoredoms of the understanding, they are opened unto the multitude, they bow them to their desire; they make pleasant sport for the common folk.

Thou Shapen Beauty of ancient days, thou whose leaves were young alway, thou who didst draw in thy sap from the innermost parts of the earth, and sway thy pointed peak in the blue heaven; thy bark was rough, and thy boughs were many, and the shade of thee was spread out afar; thou didst stay the thirst of the chosen peoples with ruddy fruit that the mighty plucked. Now have the cockchafers dropped down upon thy leaves as it were a cloud; men have cleft thee in pieces, they have sawed thee into planks, they have ground thee to powder; and the asses browse upon the remnant of thy verdure.

[The Muses depart and Aphrodite arrives; she is wholly naked; she glances from side to side, disquieted. She utters a cry of terror as she perceives Lust.]

APHRODITE. Have mercy! Begone! Leave me! Thy kisses have turned my fairest colours pale! Aforetime was I free, I was pure, the seas shook for love at the touch of my heels! I bathed and none could grasp me! I swam in the blue firmament wherein my girdle, for which the west winds strove, shone, wide and magnifical, even as the rainbow fallen from Olympus. I was Beauty! I was Shapeliness! I trembled above the world asleep; Substance was dried up at the sight of mine eyes, of itself it strengthened into just shapes. The craftsman in his anguish called upon me at his task, the young man summoned me in the hour of his desire; women spake my name in the dream of their motherhood. Thou, thou, foul craving, thou hast brought dishonour upon me!

DEATH. Pass on, fair Aphrodite! Thou shalt find purity in mine arms!

[The sound is heard of one sobbing.]

EROS. [Appears, blear-eyed, lean, puny, gasping, wretched. His fillet is too loose, it has fallen over his face; he weeps noisily, he digs his fist into his eye.]

Is it my fault? [He weeps.]
Aforetime all the world did cherish me. [Again he weeps.]
My torch is quenched!

I have lost mine arrows; once was I cradled in green gardens. My finger was upon my lips, I smiled, my locks were curled, ever I moved in loveliness. I was wreathed with roses, I was garlanded in riddles and cunning speech. I made sport unto myself in Olympus with the ensigns of the gods. I was the enchantment of life, the lord of souls, trouble everlasting.

I shiver for hunger, for cold, for weariness, and for sorrow. Now are all hearts won by Mammon. When I knock at the doors of men, they make pretence to be deaf! Some have I seen who looked upon me with a fierce eye, who betook them again to their work.

DEATH. Away with thee! begone! The world is weary of thy name! Thou hast set its teeth on edge with the honey of thy fondness!
[She kicks him.]

THE GODS OF THE HEARTH. [Covered with worn-out skins of dogs, squatting, their knees against their chins, like old mangy apes.] We . . .

DEATH. [Striking them.] Pass on, pass on!

THE GODS OF THE HEARTH. The house is open, the keys are lost, the host hath betrayed his faith! No more are men-servants submiss, children do no more honour their parents, no more are fathers feared, no longer are there great families! . . . In the ashes the cricket mourneth for the dead remembrance, for the worship of the home!

[Death wipes her brow with the skirt of her shroud; S. Anthony stands motionless with his eyes fixed on the horizon; yonder comes the dwarf-god Crepitus, rolling in mid air, bluish, lightfloating.]

CREPITUS. [In a fluty voice.] I too was honoured aforetime. Men poured forth wine before me. I was a god.

The Athenian hailed me as an herald of good fortune; the godly Roman cursed me and clenched his fists; the priest of Egypt abstained from eating of beans, he trembled at my voice, he grew pale at the smell of me. When the vinegar of the soldiers flowed over the untrimmed beards, while men feasted on acorns and shallots and raw onions, while the torn goat's flesh seethed in the sour butter of the shepherds, then no man gave heed to his neighbour, none were constrained. The solid food gave strength of sound unto the stomach—in the sunlight of the fields men eased them slowly.

So went I without offence, even as the other needs of daily life, even as Mena who tormenteth the virgins, or gentle Rumina who watched over the breast of the nurse that is swollen with blue veins. I was merry, I called forth laughter! The guests lay at ease by reason of me and breathed forth their merriment through the openings of their bodies.

I have known days of pride! The good Aristophanes sent me forth in the Masque, the emperor Claudius made me sit at his table. In the folds of the dress of the nobles I went about in majesty. The vessels of gold sounded

beneath me, even as dulcimers, and when the bowels of the master, filled
with lampreys, with truffles, and with pasties, disgorged them noisily, the
watchful world learnt that Cæsar had dined.

But now men are red with shame for me. They strive to hide me. Only
among the common folk am I known; men cry aloud at my name!

[Crepitus vanishes with a moan.]

[Silence. A clap of thunder! The Devil trembles. S. Anthony falls, face
downwards, to the earth.]

A VOICE. I was the Lord of hosts! I was the Lord, the Lord God!

I was terrible as the jaws of a lion, I was mightier than the torrents. I was
higher than the mountains. I appeared in the clouds with a wrathful countenance.

I lead the fathers of the people who went in search of wives who should
bear seed unto them. I governed the steps of the swift dromedaries, I appointed the meeting-places at the edge of the well whereon was the shadow
of a yellow palm-tree.

I let loose the rain as it were through taps of silver, I sundered the seas
with my feet, I clapped the cedars together with mine hands; upon the
hills I unfolded the tents of Jacob, I led my people in their flight across
the sands.

I, even I, burnt Sodom. I, even I, drowned the whole earth in the flood.
I swallowed up Pharaoh with his princes the sons of kings, with their
chariots of war and their drivers.

I was a jealous god, I hated the other gods, I abhorred the other peoples,
and my chosen people I chastened with pitiless wrath. I brayed the unclean
to powder as in a mortar, I cast down the proud; my desolation went forth
to the right and to the left even as a camel that is let loose in a field of corn.

I chose out the simple to deliver Israel. Angels with wings of flame spake
unto them in the bushes; then did the shepherds cast down their staves,
they went forth to war. The women anointed themselves with spikenard
and cinnamon and myrrh; they put on fine raiment, and shoon with high
heels, they went, full of good courage and brave of heart; they sought out
the captains, they cut off their heads. Then did my glory ring forth above
the sound of the cymbals. In the roll of the thunder it spake aloud upon the
mountains; the wind as it passed ravished the prophets; they rolled them
naked in the dry valleys; they lay flat upon their bellies that they might
hearken unto the voice of the sea; they rose up suddenly and called upon
my name.

They came by night into the halls of kings, upon the carpet of the
throne they shook the dust from off their cloaks; they called down my
vengeance; they spake of Babylon and the stripes of slavery. The lions were
mild before them, the flames of the furnace drew aside from their bodies,
the wizards howled aloud in their anger and cut themselves with knives.

I graved my law upon tables of stone; I bound my people therewith as it
were the belt of a wayfarer that constraineth his body. They were my
people—I was their God! The earth was mine, all men were mine, their

thoughts and their works, their tools of the field and their houses. Mine ark lay in a threefold sanctuary behind the veils of purple and the lighted candle-sticks. One whole tribe did serve before me, they swung the censers; they builded me a ceiling of beams of cedar-wood—the high priest was robed in robes whose colour was as the colour of an hyacinth, he wore on his breast precious stones set in ordered rows.

Evil! Evil! The Holy of Holies is opened. The veil is rent, the ark is lost, the savour of the sacrifice hath gone out into all the winds through the rifts in the walls. In the sepulchres of Israel the vulture of Libya sheltereth her brood. My temple is destroyed, my people are scattered. They have strangled the priests with the cords of their vesture; the strong men have perished by the sword, the women are led captive; the vessels are molten, every one of them.

This is that God of Nazareth who hath passed through Judæa. Even as a whirlwind in the autumn, so hath he drawn away my servants. His apostles have churches, and his mother, also his family, and all his friends; I, even I, have not one temple! There is no prayer for me alone! Not a stone that beareth my name graven thereon! Nor is Jordan of the muddy waters more sorrowful and desolate than I am.

[The Voice passes away.]

I was the Lord of hosts! The Lord! The Lord God!

[Death yawns. S. Anthony is stretched upon the ground, unmoving. Lust leans her back against the door of the hut, her right knee is drawn up on to her left knee; she unravels the hem of her gown, and the threads of it, swayed by the wind, flutter about the pig, fall upon his eyelids, and tickle his nostrils.]

THE DEVIL. [Stretches out his claw and lays it upon S. Anthony and cries:] They have passed away!

LOGIC. Verily, and in truth, forasmuch as they . . .

[S. Anthony opens his eyes once more.]

Forasmuch as they have passed away, thy god also . . .

S. ANTHONY. [Rises to his feet, seizes a pebble and hurls it at Logic.] Nay! Never! Thou art death unto the soul! Get thee behind me!

[He kneels down.]

Pity, O my God! Pardon me! Love me! . . . It is Thy grace that maketh men pure, Thy love that maketh them good. Have pity on me, have pity!

THE DEVIL. There is no pity! Compassion shall not descend upon a sinner such as thou art.

S. ANTHONY. [Praying.] O Jesus, thou Son of God, Who art God even as the Father, God even as the Holy Spirit! . . . Ye are One!

THE DEVIL. I am many! My name is Legion!

S. ANTHONY. Thou didst send Thy Son . . .

THE DEVIL. Another shall come!

S. ANTHONY. To stablish Thy church!

THE DEVIL. He shall overturn it!

[The Devil, placing himself behind S. Anthony, shouts in his ear so loudly that S. Anthony on his knees bends like a reed, now falling on to his wrists, now raising himself again, yet ever continuing his prayer; the Devil says the while:]

He shall be born in Babylon, likewise of a virgin, one made holy unto the Lord, but who shall have committed fornication with her father. He shall cause himself to be circumcised among the Hebrews; he shall build up again the Temple. He shall convert first of all proconsuls, then princes and kings— the Emperor of Taprobane, the Queen of Scythia, and three popes, the one after the other. He shall send his messengers over all ways and his prophets unto all nations, and his armed men against all cities.

He shall be fair to look upon; women shall be driven to madness because of him.

He shall fill the multitudes with food; men shall fall asleep at the gates; their stomachs shall be filled even to their teeth. He shall satisfy the lust of the lustful, the greed of the covetous, the desire of the eye, the jealous belly. He shall raise up the mighty and shall put down the humble; he shall slay the faithful with the sword, he shall smite them to earth with clubs, he shall grind them to powder with pestles, and he shall burn every sanctuary as it were an henroost that is full of vermin.

The mules of his slaves shall lie upon litter of laurels, they shall eat up the flour of the poor in the cradle of Christ Jesus. He shall establish gladiators upon the hill of Calvary, and in the place of the Holy Sepulchre shall he set up a brothel of black women who shall wear rings in their noses and shall cry aloud words of horror.

He shall walk upon the sea, he shall fly in the air, and he shall descend beneath the earth as it were a fish that plungeth. He shall raise up tempests, he shall still the waves of the sea. He shall make the dead trees to blossom and he shall wither up the trees that are in flower. Diamonds shall flow over his sandals and sweet odours shall come forth from his breath. Wheresoever he shall bear his hands there shall flow drops of blood, and he shall make answer, "I am Messias."

S. ANTHONY. [Praying.] O Dove of the Holy Spirit, cause the coolness of the winds of heaven to pass over my face. Let my tears flow and bear away my soul into the outpouring of love without end.

THE DEVIL. He shall summon the soothsayers from all lands; he shall speak all tongues; he shall understand all writings. It shall be as though the whole world were mad, and men shall say unto one another: "What shall this be? What is this that cometh to pass?" And when he shall have preached over all the earth for the space of two years and one hundred and eighty and three days; when he shall have persecuted the faithful so that they turn them away from their faith or testify unto it in death; when he shall have overthrown the Holy Places and opened all dungeons, and slain all the priests, and gathered unto him the multitudes; when he shall possess kingdoms and treasures and armed hosts, then shall the Heavens send down at one time the prophet Elias and the prophet Enoch; and he shall slay Elias and he shall slay Enoch; their skulls shall be scratched with the points of spears; they shall be boxes for paints and caskets for sweet odours.

S. ANTHONY. I hear the voice of the evil one that howleth round about me; but in thy strength, O Lord Almighty, will I laugh his wrath to scorn. I will sing thy praises during the terror of temptation. Lo, I am even as one that falleth into the sea, who giveth great strokes with his loins that he may get him again into his boat. Take me unto thee, O Lord; receive me; show unto me thy pity and loving-kindness.

THE DEVIL. Then shall the dream of evil blossom as a flower of the darkness, greater than the sun. Then shall there be raptures of pride so bitter and so long, and delights of lust so furious, and so overwhelming a pestilence of nothing, that the angels shall rend their wings and the holy men shall curse their holiness, the martyrs shall repent them of their torment, and the chosen of God shall gather around Jesus and shall scoff at Him in their wrath. He shall be forsaken in His heaven; hell shall overflow her borders and shall be poured forth over all the earth.

[S. Anthony continues his prayer. Pride bows her head and withdraws her into her mantle. Anger stands motionless. Envy closes her eyes. All the daughters of the Evil One are in consternation. But the Devil opens his great green wing, and whirling it rapidly round and round like a sling he rubs it against the lips of the seven Sins, who rush helter-skelter round S. Anthony, howling horribly.]

LUST. Wouldest thou virgins white as the moon? Or lovest thou better women whose colour is as amber, whose mocking is haughty, who shall twine even as vipers in the coils of wantonness that findeth ever a new thing? It is more fierce than hatred, it is earnest as prayer. Thou shalt feel against thy flanks the cold of their golden bracelets, and thy flesh shall leap beneath their kisses, thy soul shall melt in their eyeballs, all thy being shall be dissolved in the vapours of raging madness.

ANGER. Hither! Hither! Thou shalt disgorge thy soul of the fury that doth stifle her; thou knowest not the delights of murder, the rapture that cometh upon thee when thou dost lift up the knife, the joy that eateth thee up when it falleth again and driveth deep.

GREED. Thou shalt have at once and for thyself alone spiced red flesh, steaming more than a cloud; thou shalt have thick frozen drink. Thou shalt eat of fruits whose colour quivereth, that seem to be alive even as the beasts. Thou shalt eat thereof and thou shalt drink thereof continually and without ceasing, even until thou dost slaver and burst in sunder.

AVARICE. Wouldest thou heaps of gold, palaces, peoples, and ships with purple sails, wouldest thou baths of jasper? Thou shalt roll thyself upon mounds of silver piled up as it were cut clover, and at the clash of the metal thou shalt hear in thy heart the sound of all corruption and all dominion.

S. ANTHONY. Nay, nay. I love better the rattle of my rosary, the wood of my crucifix, and the hard earth of my cell floor.

ENVY. All that thou couldest not attain unto, that will I abase for thy satisfying. Thou shalt see the wise men confounded, and the great brought low, and the rich made poor; the fair scornful women after whom thou hast lusted shall weep beneath the lantern of a brothel amidst shipmen and carters who shall spit in their faces.

SLOTH. Bury thyself close in sleep, plunge thee in the blessedness of sloth-fulness! Thy thought, even as a vulture that hath lost his breath, shall shorten and ever shorten her flight that she may alight upon the earth. Thou shalt taste of the stillness of nothing in the delight of living, and thou shalt come to be as it were a trembling, like unto a plant made man.

SCIENCE. [Triumphing.] I will discover unto thee the place where suns shall appear, I will shew unto thee the cavern on the shores of the sea where rotteth the body of Cleopatra. I will raise up again the ages and I will open the earth before thine eyes; thou shalt understand Nature and Thought, good and evil, and thine unbounded love shall enfold all the manifold creation even as the firmament. A thirst for the truth, more faithful than is the hope of Heaven, shall compel thee toward God, and thou shalt feel Him grow in the outspreading of thine understanding like as the firmament that shall be widened even as thy thought is unfolded day by day.

PRIDE. Thou must be unto thyself as though thou wast the centre of the world; thou shalt be pure and thou shalt be strong, wholly untroubled and great of understanding even as the Lord Himself. Up! Lift up thine head! Stand face to face with God! Spurn all things! There is no triumph whereof the worth is as the joy of making mockery thereof; nay, this doth surpass even the highest mountain-tops, even this that thou shouldest spurn them for that they are too low. Tend thou this fierce pleasure for thyself, scratch upon thy sore, worship thine own self.

S. ANTHONY. I will abase myself, O Lord, I will bow my forehead and my pride in the dust. I would stand continually before Thee even as a ram upon the altar, as the kine of a smoking burnt offering.

[Then the Devil waves aside all the Sins with his hand, and advances, stooping, towards S. Anthony.]

Ay! drive them back! They are aged, and thou needest them no more to compel thee to me. Seest thou not what desire after evil maketh men to pant in the chase after me, since the beginning of the world? But we meet—now, even now, I hold them in my arms. The breath of my mouth is the air of their thoughts, and I who damned them through the body now damn them through the understanding. A new madness compelleth mankind into the abysm, for they are glutted. Dost thou hear the principalities and powers? They rot, they crack in the darkness even as palaces that fall to the ground? The Gods are dead and Babel is again uplifted. Evil doth triumph at the last; and in the vastness that he hath conquered, he proclaimeth by the voices of all things his great and awful hosannah for that he hath been made God. Wouldest thou that he enter within thee? Wouldest thou feast thee upon his infinite beauty? Wouldest thou become the Devil?

S. ANTHONY. [Praying.] Pity! Pity! Blessed be Thy name, blessed be Thy works, and blessed be Thine anger! I seek not to understand Thee, I seek only to love Thee; I desire not to live, I would not die. O Holy Virgin! O Christ Jesus! O Holy Spirit! Pity! Be pitiful unto me!

[Then the sky is rent open and clouds gathering greatly upon themselves reveal the sun who appears in the midst of them—an immense sun, gold-coloured, with great slanting rays that pass between the swellings of the clouds like the ropes of a pavilion half opened. The sun strikes full on S. Anthony's face. The Devil bows his head; the Sins, livid and all a-sweat, rattle in the throat from exhaustion.]

THE PIG. [Rejoicing.] Ah! the good sun! Such fear had I in the night!

THE DEVIL. [In a strong voice.] The hour hath struck! We must go hence!

[Death mounts her steed once more; the Sins have disappeared.]

S. ANTHONY. [Raises his arms to heaven; the tears flow from his eyes; he cries out:] I thank Thee, I give thanks unto Thee, O Lord!

THE DEVIL. [Turns in one bound and says to him:] What matter! Seeing that the sins are in thine heart, and that desolation rolleth about within thine head! Draw thy shirt of hair close about thee, fast, tear thyself in pieces, humble thee. Search thou for sayings of highest holiness, seek out the bitterest penitence, and then shalt thou feel vapours of wantonness that flow within thy wounded flesh. Thine empty stomach shall call for the great feasts, and the words of thy prayer shall be changed in thy mouth even unto cries of despair. The satisfaction of thy godliness shall swell thee with pride, the weariness of thy merit shall summon up envy unto thee! When lust after all things hath left thee, then shall come the covetings of the spirit, and thou shalt beat with thine head upon the stones of the altar, thou shalt kiss thy cross, but the flame of thine heart shall not warm the metal of it! Thou shalt search for a knife; I shall return, I shall return!

S. ANTHONY. [Praying.] As it may please Thee, O Lord!

[The Devil goes away, laughing.]

S. ANTHONY. Make me to love Thee!

THE DEVIL. Ha, ha, ha!

S. ANTHONY. Jesus, sweet Jesus!

THE DEVIL. Ha, ha, ha!

S. ANTHONY. Have pity upon me, have pity upon me!

THE DEVIL. Ha, ha, ha!

S. ANTHONY. Jesus, Jesus!

THE DEVIL. Ha, ha, ha!

[The Devil's laugh repeats in the distance; S. Anthony continues his prayer.]